P9-EDA-739

THE WALKING DEAD

BOOK SEVEN

a continuing story of survival horror.

created by Robert Kirkman

image comics presents

The Walking Dead
book seven

ROBERT KIRKMAN
creator, writer

CHARLIE ADLARD
penciler, inker, cover

CLIFF RATHBURN
gray tones

RUS WOOTON
letterer

SINA GRACE
editor

Original series covers by
CHARLIE ADLARD & CLIFF RATHBURN

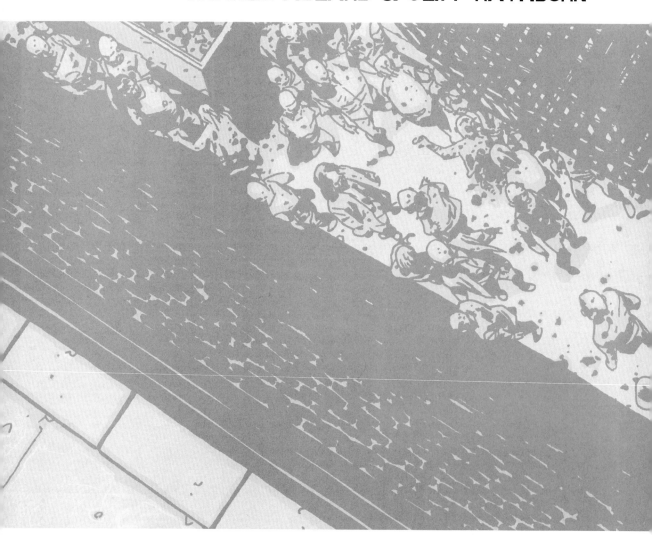

Robert Kirkman
chief executive officer

J.J. Didde
president

www.skybound.com

Robert Kirkman
chief operating officer

Erik Larsen
chief financial officer

Todd McFarlane
president

Marc Silvestri
chief executive officer

Jim Valentino
vice-president

www.imagecomics.com

Sina Grace
editorial director

Shawn Kirkham
director of business development

Tim Daniel
digital content manager

Eric Stephenson
publisher

Todd Martinez
sales & licensing coordinator

Sarah deLaine
pr & marketing coordinator

Branwyn Bigglestone
accounts manager

Emily Miller
administrative assistant

Jamie Parreno
marketing assistant

Chad Manion
assistant to mr. grace

Sydney Pennington
assistant to mr. kirkham

Megan Pope
at susan blond inc.
public relations

Kevin Yuen
digital rights coordinator

Tyler Shainline
production manager

Drew Gill
art director

Jonathan Chan
senior production artist

Monica Garcia
production artist

Vincent Kukua
production artist

Jana Cook
production artist

Chapter Thirteen:
Too Far Gone

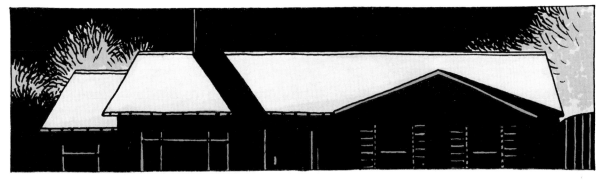

GET IT TOGETHER, ABRAHAM.

YOU'VE BEEN OUT THERE BEFORE...

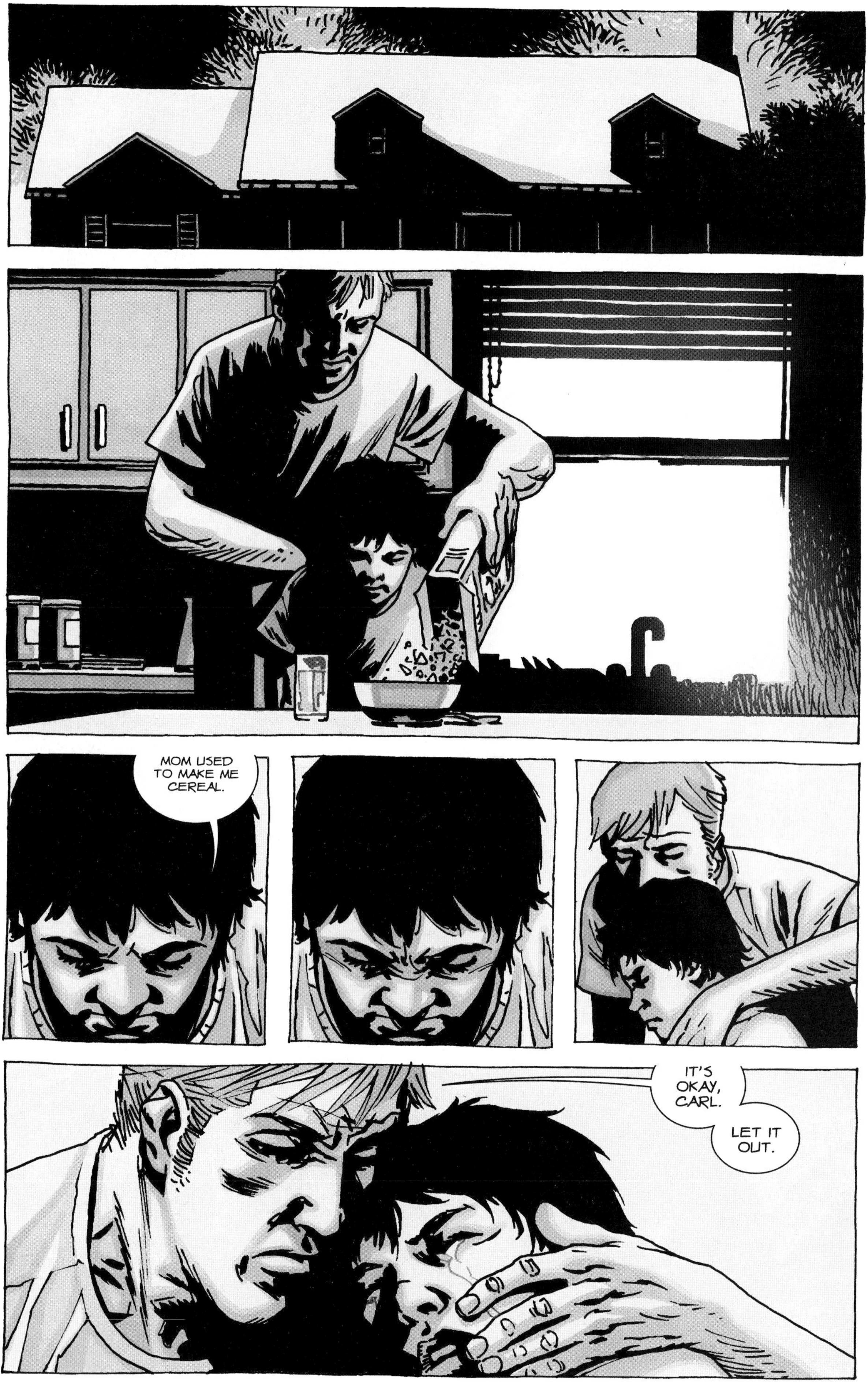
MOM USED TO MAKE ME CEREAL.
IT'S OKAY, CARL.
LET IT OUT.

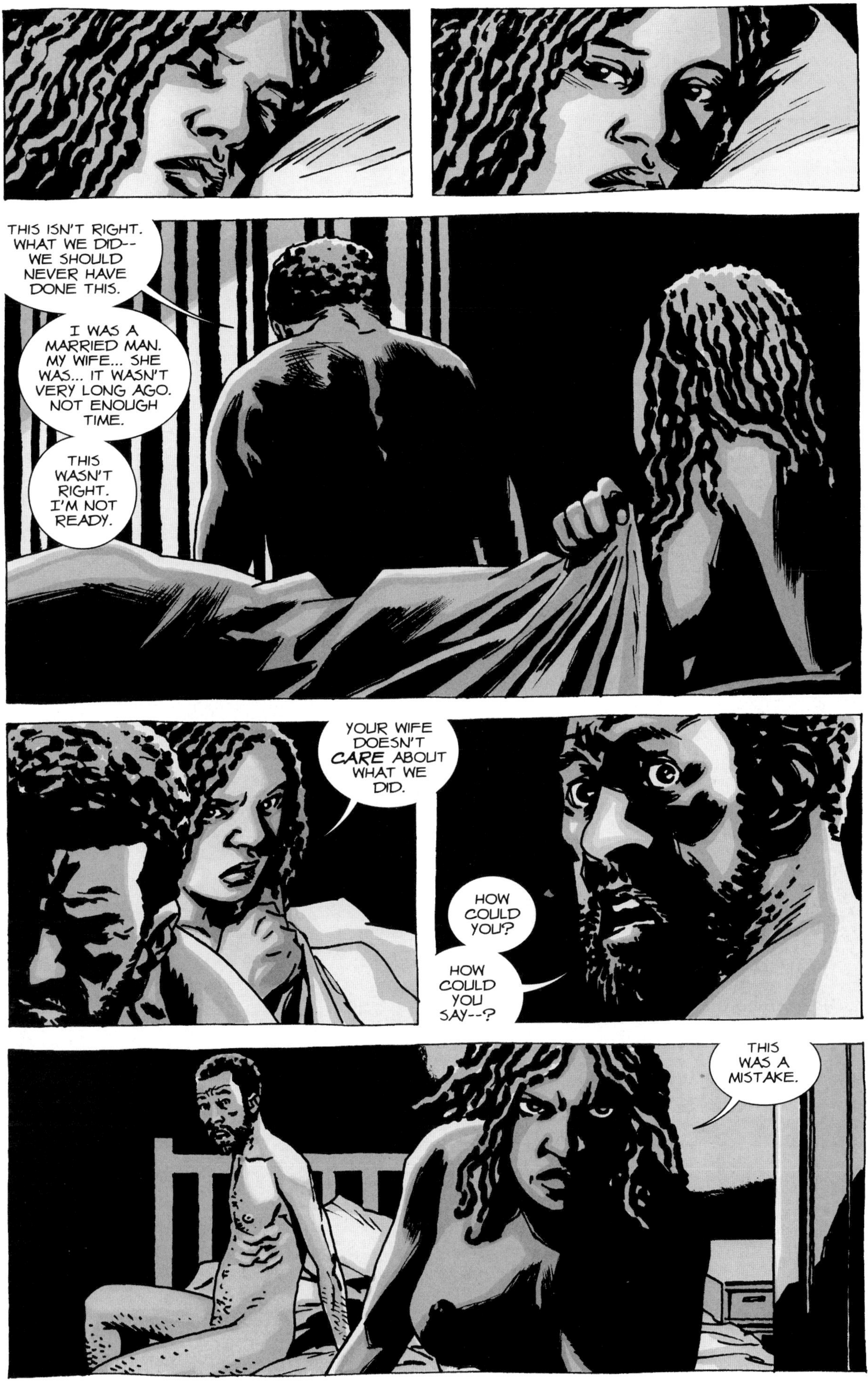
THIS ISN'T RIGHT. WHAT WE DID-- WE SHOULD NEVER HAVE DONE THIS.
I WAS A MARRIED MAN. MY WIFE... SHE WAS... IT WASN'T VERY LONG AGO. NOT ENOUGH TIME.
THIS WASN'T RIGHT. I'M NOT READY.
YOUR WIFE DOESN'T CARE ABOUT WHAT WE DID.
HOW COULD YOU?
HOW COULD YOU SAY--?
THIS WAS A MISTAKE.

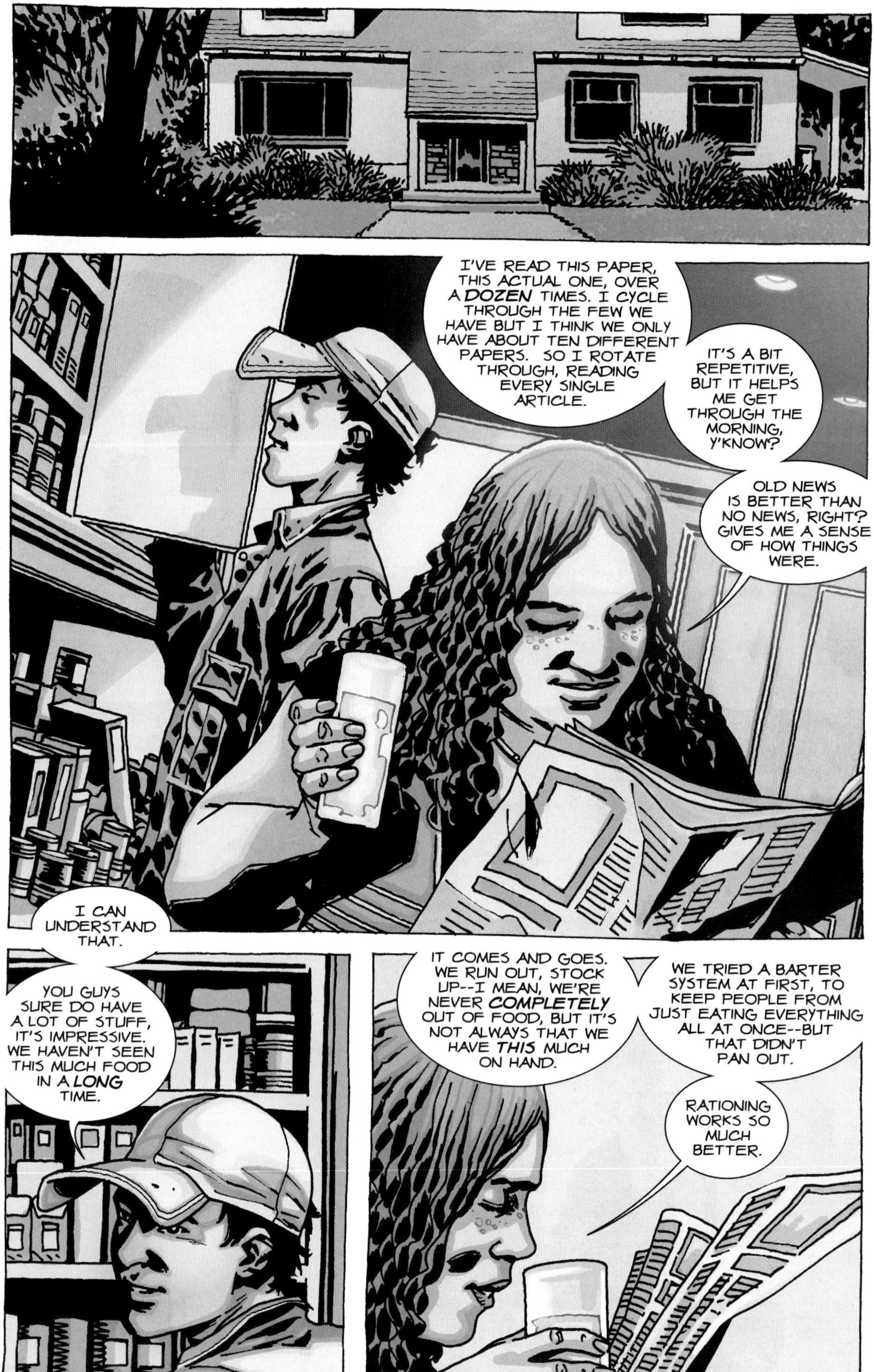
I'VE READ THIS PAPER, THIS ACTUAL ONE, OVER A DOZEN TIMES. I CYCLE THROUGH THE FEW WE HAVE BUT I THINK WE ONLY HAVE ABOUT TEN DIFFERENT PAPERS. SO I ROTATE THROUGH, READING EVERY SINGLE ARTICLE.
IT'S A BIT REPETITIVE, BUT IT HELPS ME GET THROUGH THE MORNING, Y'KNOW?
OLD NEWS IS BETTER THAN NO NEWS, RIGHT? GIVES ME A SENSE OF HOW THINGS WERE.
I CAN UNDERSTAND THAT.
YOU GUYS SURE DO HAVE A LOT OF STUFF, IT'S IMPRESSIVE. WE HAVEN'T SEEN THIS MUCH FOOD IN A LONG TIME.
IT COMES AND GOES. WE RUN OUT, STOCK UP--I MEAN, WE'RE NEVER COMPLETELY OUT OF FOOD, BUT IT'S NOT ALWAYS THAT WE HAVE THIS MUCH ON HAND.
WE TRIED A BARTER SYSTEM AT FIRST, TO KEEP PEOPLE FROM JUST EATING EVERYTHING ALL AT ONCE--BUT THAT DIDN'T PAN OUT.
RATIONING WORKS SO MUCH BETTER.

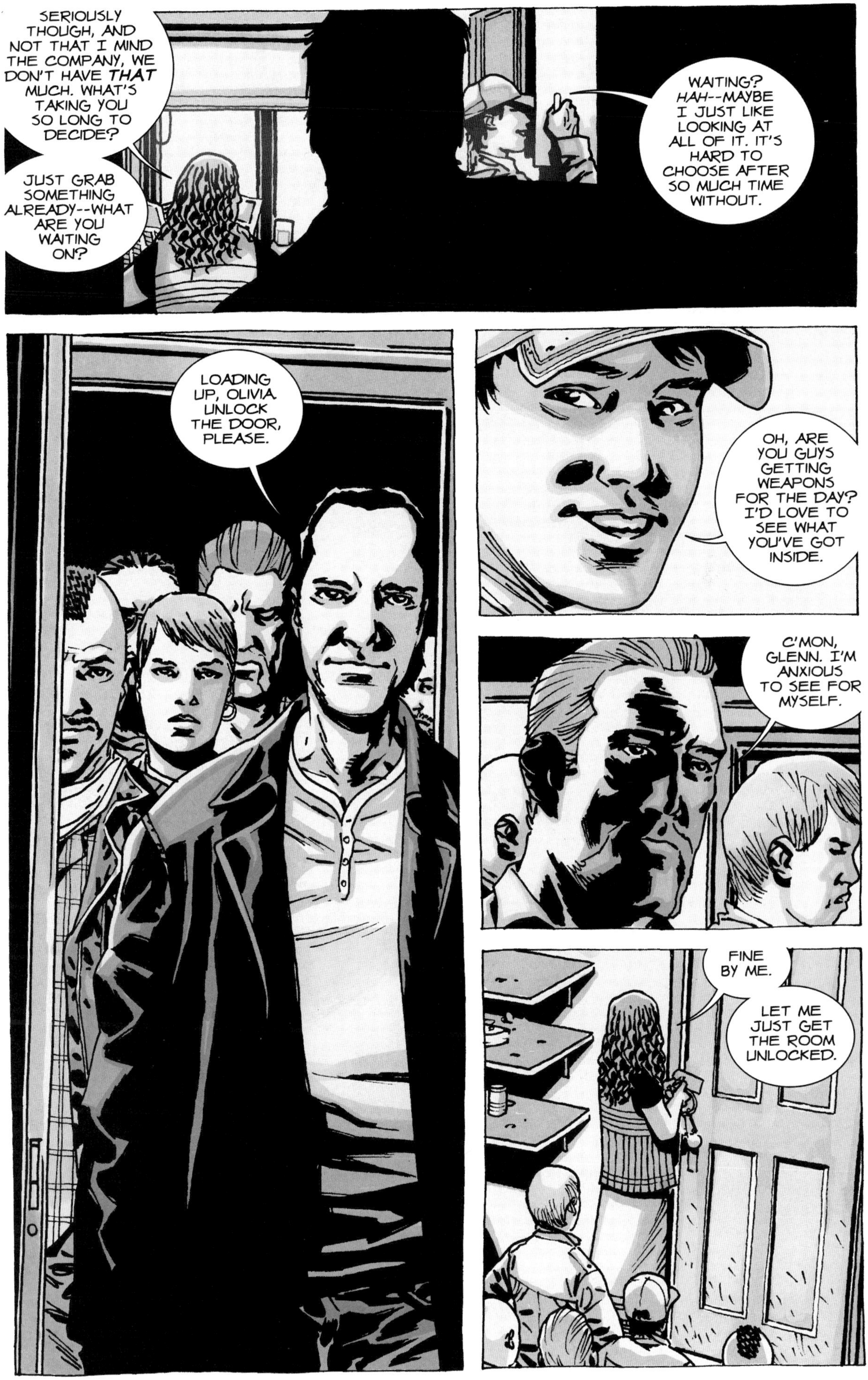
SERIOUSLY THOUGH, AND NOT THAT I MIND THE COMPANY, WE DON'T HAVE *THAT* MUCH. WHAT'S TAKING YOU SO LONG TO DECIDE?
JUST GRAB SOMETHING ALREADY--WHAT ARE YOU WAITING ON?
WAITING? *HAH*--MAYBE I JUST LIKE LOOKING AT ALL OF IT. IT'S HARD TO CHOOSE AFTER SO MUCH TIME WITHOUT.
LOADING UP, OLIVIA. UNLOCK THE DOOR, PLEASE.
OH, ARE YOU GUYS GETTING WEAPONS FOR THE DAY? I'D LOVE TO SEE WHAT YOU'VE GOT INSIDE.
C'MON, GLENN. I'M ANXIOUS TO SEE FOR MYSELF.
FINE BY ME.
LET ME JUST GET THE ROOM UNLOCKED.

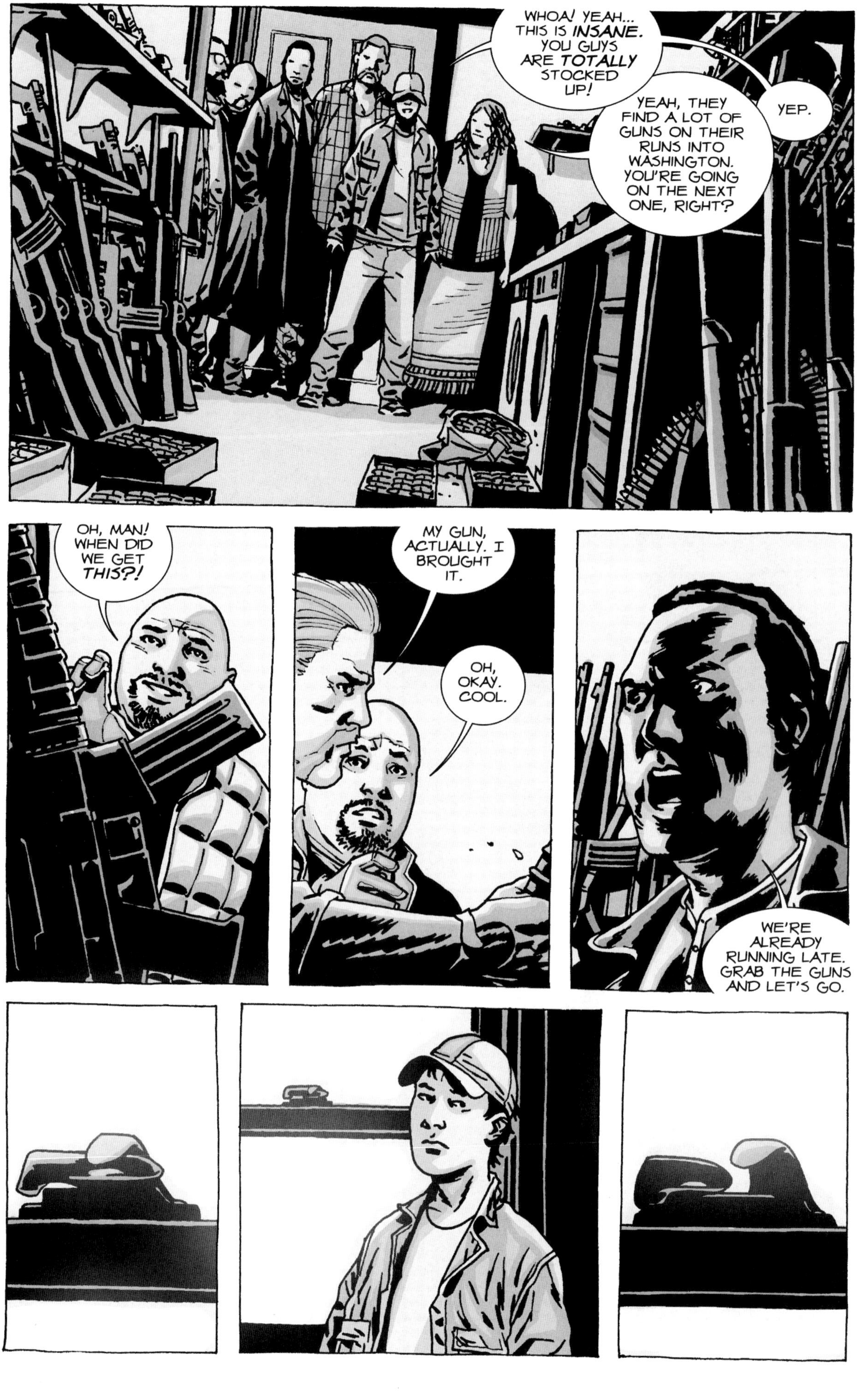
WHOA! YEAH... THIS IS INSANE. YOU GUYS ARE TOTALLY STOCKED UP!
YEP.
YEAH, THEY FIND A LOT OF GUNS ON THEIR RUNS INTO WASHINGTON. YOU'RE GOING ON THE NEXT ONE, RIGHT?
OH, MAN! WHEN DID WE GET THIS?!
MY GUN, ACTUALLY. I BROUGHT IT.
OH, OKAY. COOL.
WE'RE ALREADY RUNNING LATE. GRAB THE GUNS AND LET'S GO.

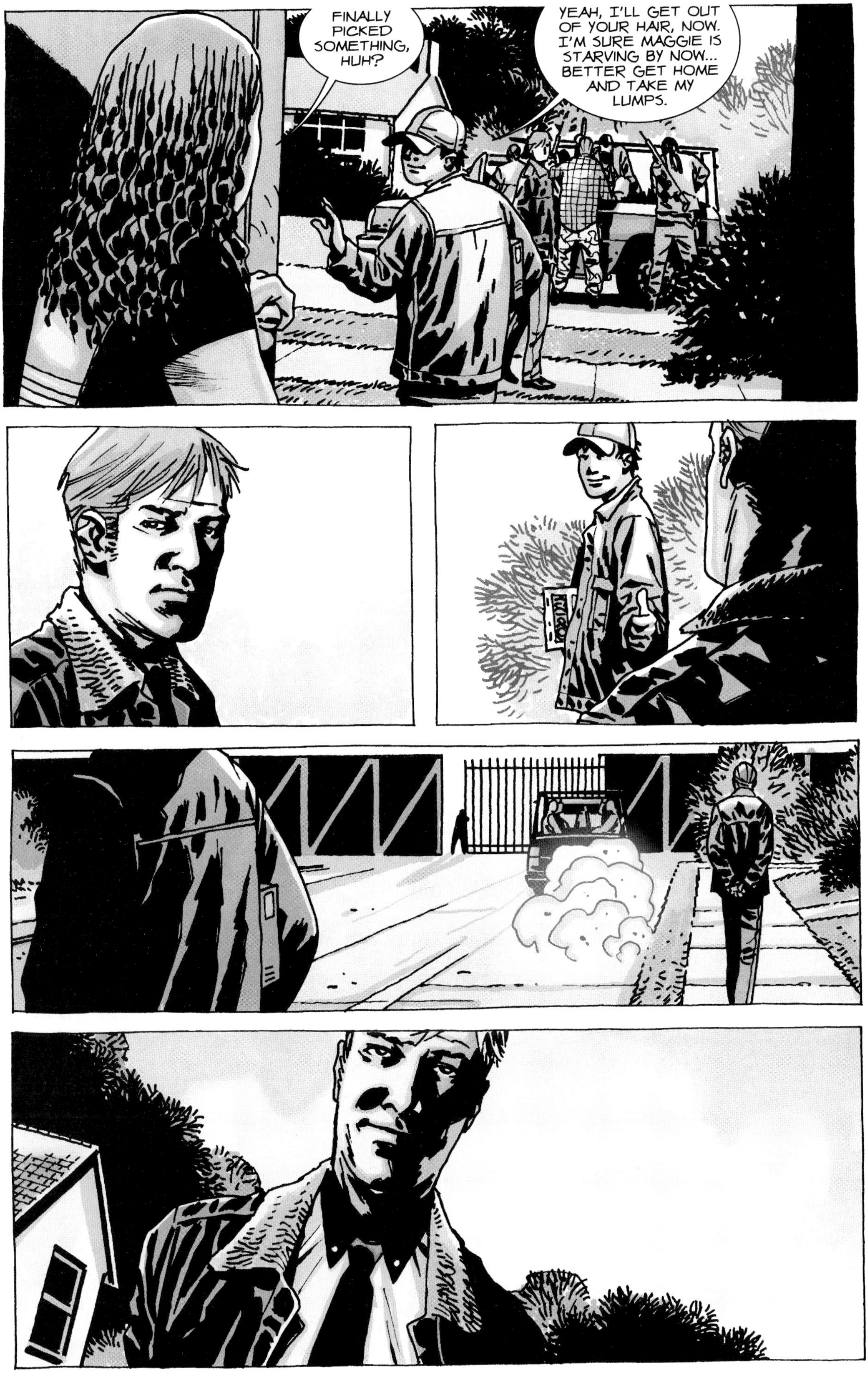
FINALLY PICKED SOMETHING, HUH?
YEAH, I'LL GET OUT OF YOUR HAIR, NOW. I'M SURE MAGGIE IS STARVING BY NOW... BETTER GET HOME AND TAKE MY LUMPS.

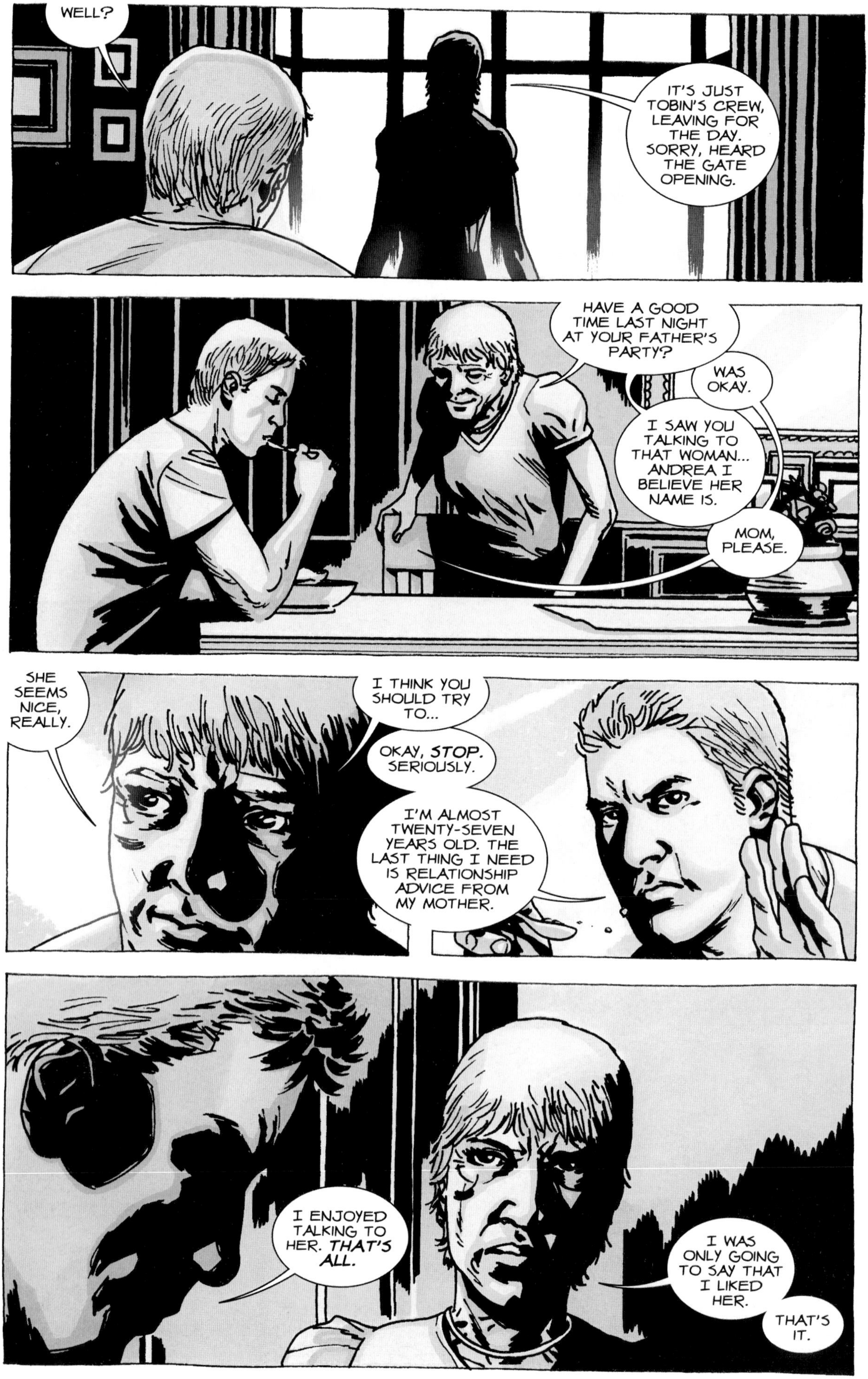
WELL?
IT'S JUST TOBIN'S CREW, LEAVING FOR THE DAY. SORRY, HEARD THE GATE OPENING.
HAVE A GOOD TIME LAST NIGHT AT YOUR FATHER'S PARTY?
WAS OKAY.
I SAW YOU TALKING TO THAT WOMAN... ANDREA I BELIEVE HER NAME IS.
MOM, PLEASE.
SHE SEEMS NICE, REALLY.
I THINK YOU SHOULD TRY TO...
OKAY, STOP. SERIOUSLY.
I'M ALMOST TWENTY-SEVEN YEARS OLD. THE LAST THING I NEED IS RELATIONSHIP ADVICE FROM MY MOTHER.
I ENJOYED TALKING TO HER. THAT'S ALL.
I WAS ONLY GOING TO SAY THAT I LIKED HER.
THAT'S IT.

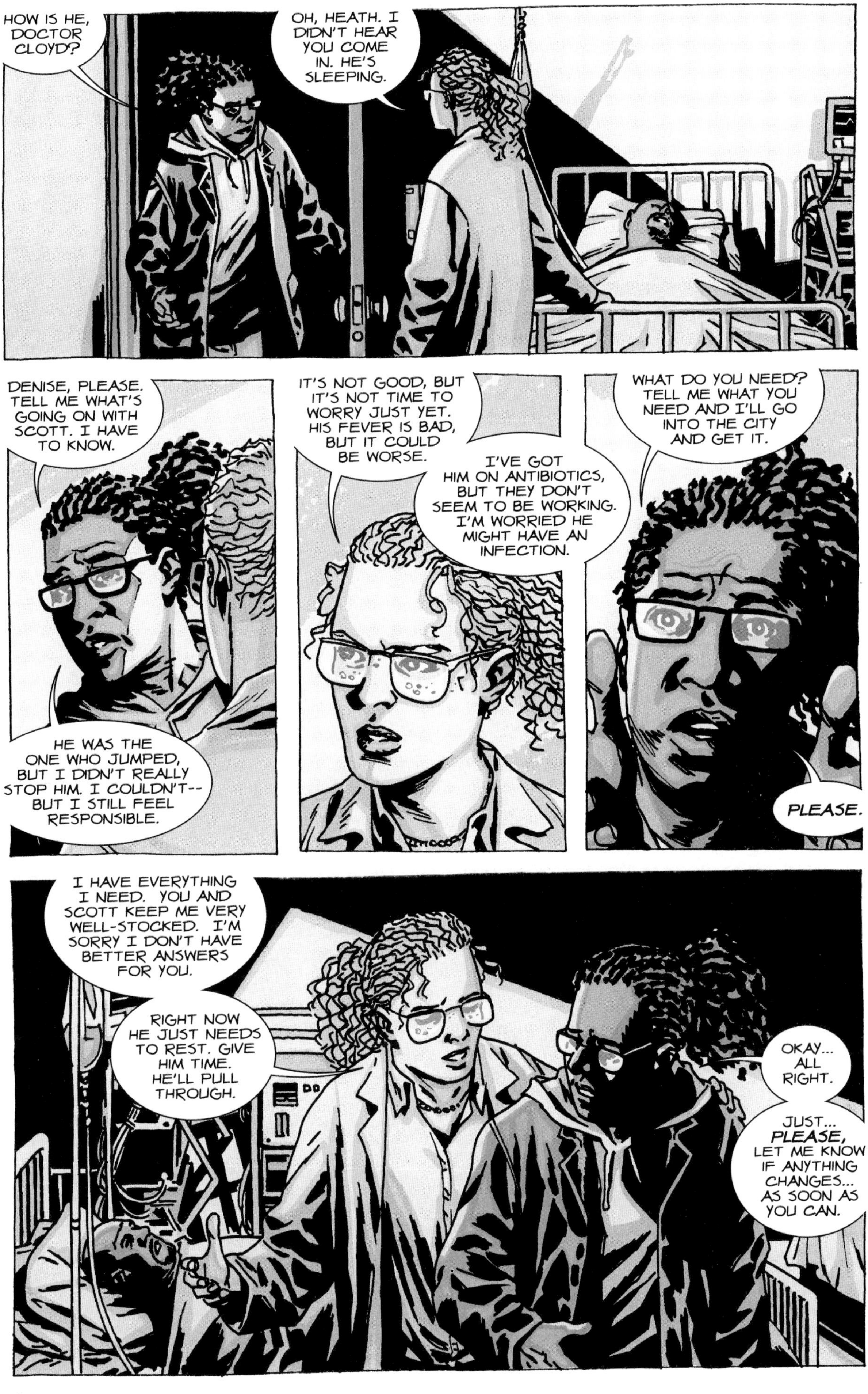
HOW IS HE, DOCTOR CLOYD?
OH, HEATH. I DIDN'T HEAR YOU COME IN. HE'S SLEEPING.
DENISE, PLEASE. TELL ME WHAT'S GOING ON WITH SCOTT. I HAVE TO KNOW.
HE WAS THE ONE WHO JUMPED, BUT I DIDN'T REALLY STOP HIM. I COULDN'T-- BUT I STILL FEEL RESPONSIBLE.
IT'S NOT GOOD, BUT IT'S NOT TIME TO WORRY JUST YET. HIS FEVER IS BAD, BUT IT COULD BE WORSE.
I'VE GOT HIM ON ANTIBIOTICS, BUT THEY DON'T SEEM TO BE WORKING. I'M WORRIED HE MIGHT HAVE AN INFECTION.
WHAT DO YOU NEED? TELL ME WHAT YOU NEED AND I'LL GO INTO THE CITY AND GET IT.
PLEASE.
I HAVE EVERYTHING I NEED. YOU AND SCOTT KEEP ME VERY WELL-STOCKED. I'M SORRY I DON'T HAVE BETTER ANSWERS FOR YOU.
RIGHT NOW HE JUST NEEDS TO REST. GIVE HIM TIME. HE'LL PULL THROUGH.
OKAY... ALL RIGHT.
JUST... *PLEASE,* LET ME KNOW IF ANYTHING CHANGES... AS SOON AS YOU CAN.

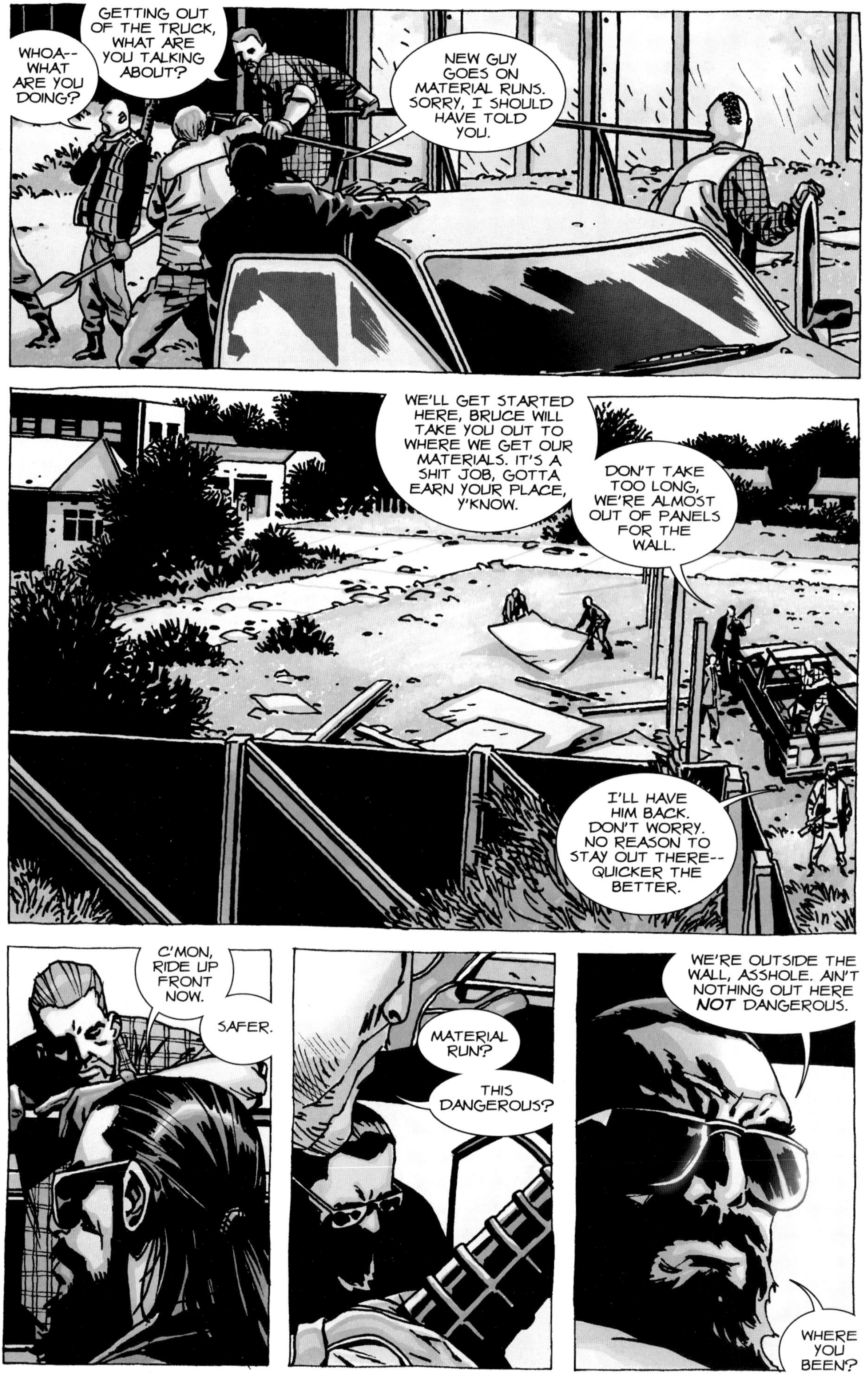
WHOA-- WHAT ARE YOU DOING?
GETTING OUT OF THE TRUCK, WHAT ARE YOU TALKING ABOUT?
NEW GUY GOES ON MATERIAL RUNS. SORRY, I SHOULD HAVE TOLD YOU.
WE'LL GET STARTED HERE, BRUCE WILL TAKE YOU OUT TO WHERE WE GET OUR MATERIALS. IT'S A SHIT JOB, GOTTA EARN YOUR PLACE, Y'KNOW.
DON'T TAKE TOO LONG, WE'RE ALMOST OUT OF PANELS FOR THE WALL.
I'LL HAVE HIM BACK. DON'T WORRY. NO REASON TO STAY OUT THERE-- QUICKER THE BETTER.
C'MON, RIDE UP FRONT NOW.
SAFER.
MATERIAL RUN?
THIS DANGEROUS?
WE'RE OUTSIDE THE WALL, ASSHOLE. AIN'T NOTHING OUT HERE NOT DANGEROUS.
WHERE YOU BEEN?

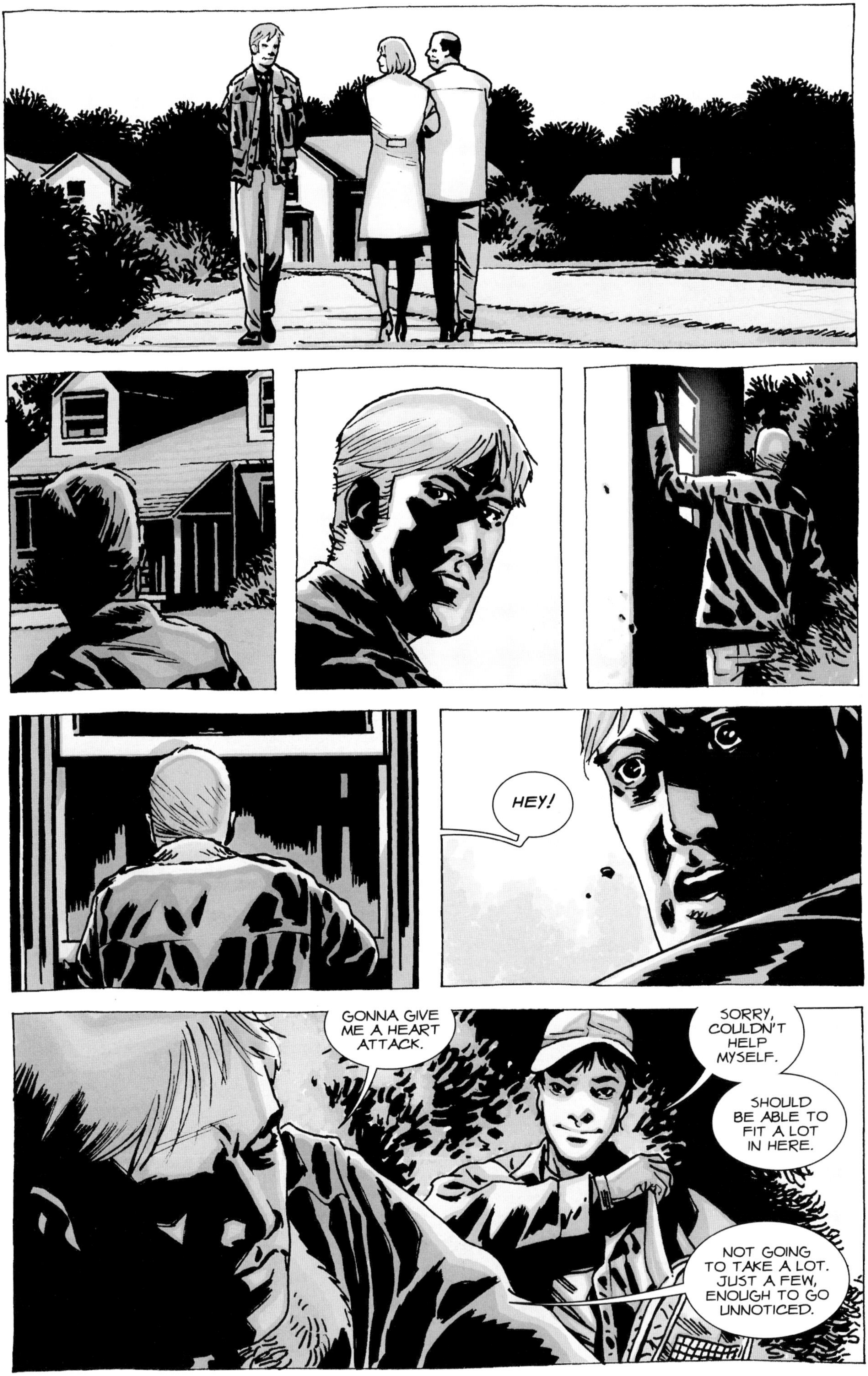
HEY!
GONNA GIVE ME A HEART ATTACK.
SORRY, COULDN'T HELP MYSELF.
SHOULD BE ABLE TO FIT A LOT IN HERE.
NOT GOING TO TAKE A LOT. JUST A FEW, ENOUGH TO GO UNNOTICED.

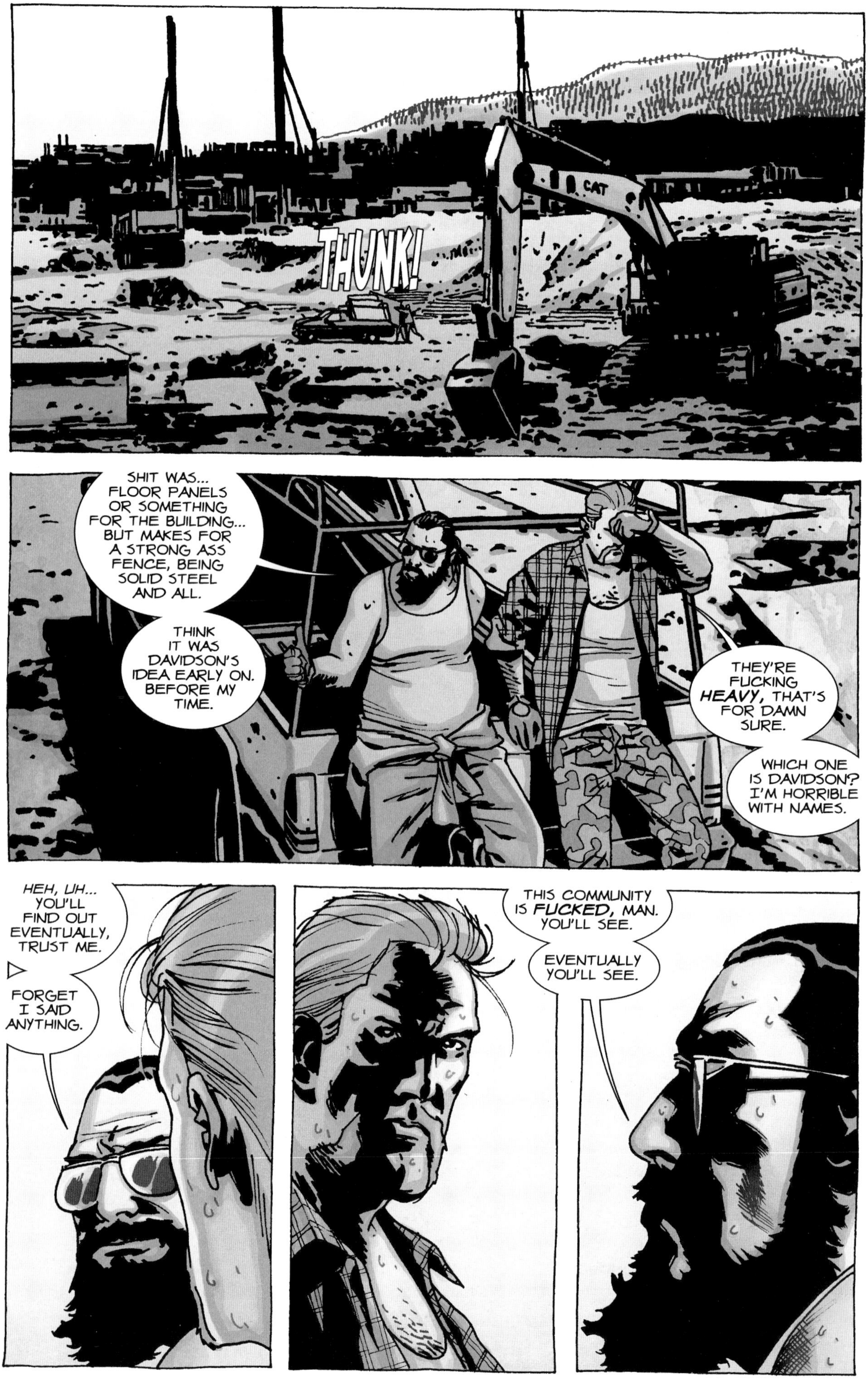
THUNK!
SHIT WAS... FLOOR PANELS OR SOMETHING FOR THE BUILDING... BUT MAKES FOR A STRONG ASS FENCE, BEING SOLID STEEL AND ALL.
THINK IT WAS DAVIDSON'S IDEA EARLY ON. BEFORE MY TIME.
THEY'RE FUCKING HEAVY, THAT'S FOR DAMN SURE.
WHICH ONE IS DAVIDSON? I'M HORRIBLE WITH NAMES.
HEH, UH... YOU'LL FIND OUT EVENTUALLY, TRUST ME.
FORGET I SAID ANYTHING.
THIS COMMUNITY IS FUCKED, MAN. YOU'LL SEE.
EVENTUALLY YOU'LL SEE.

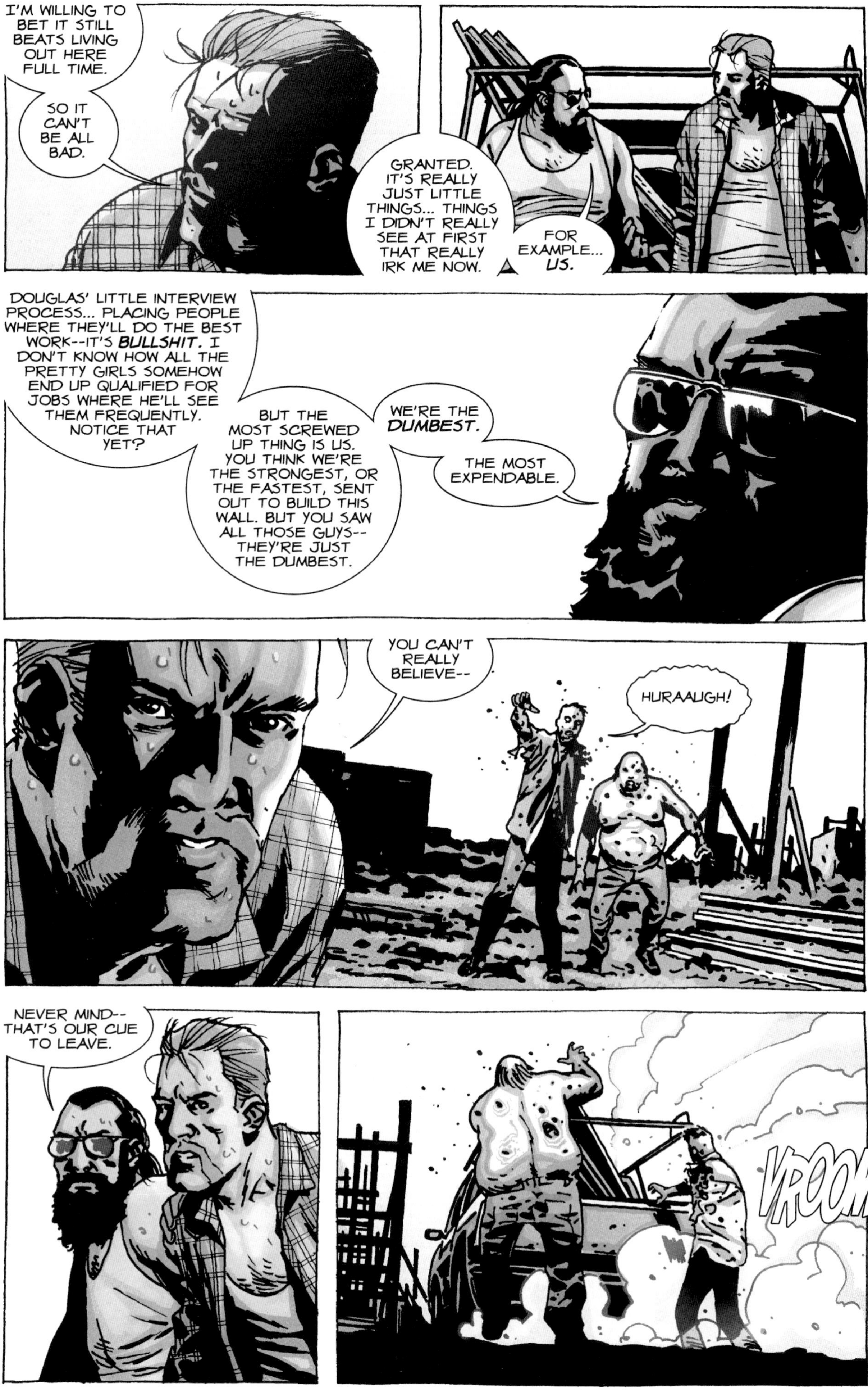
I'M WILLING TO BET IT STILL BEATS LIVING OUT HERE FULL TIME.
SO IT CAN'T BE ALL BAD.
GRANTED. IT'S REALLY JUST LITTLE THINGS... THINGS I DIDN'T REALLY SEE AT FIRST THAT REALLY IRK ME NOW.
FOR EXAMPLE... US.
DOUGLAS' LITTLE INTERVIEW PROCESS... PLACING PEOPLE WHERE THEY'LL DO THE BEST WORK--IT'S BULLSHIT. I DON'T KNOW HOW ALL THE PRETTY GIRLS SOMEHOW END UP QUALIFIED FOR JOBS WHERE HE'LL SEE THEM FREQUENTLY. NOTICE THAT YET?
BUT THE MOST SCREWED UP THING IS US. YOU THINK WE'RE THE STRONGEST, OR THE FASTEST, SENT OUT TO BUILD THIS WALL. BUT YOU SAW ALL THOSE GUYS-- THEY'RE JUST THE DUMBEST.
WE'RE THE DUMBEST.
THE MOST EXPENDABLE.
YOU CAN'T REALLY BELIEVE--
HURAAUGH!
NEVER MIND-- THAT'S OUR CUE TO LEAVE.
VROOM!

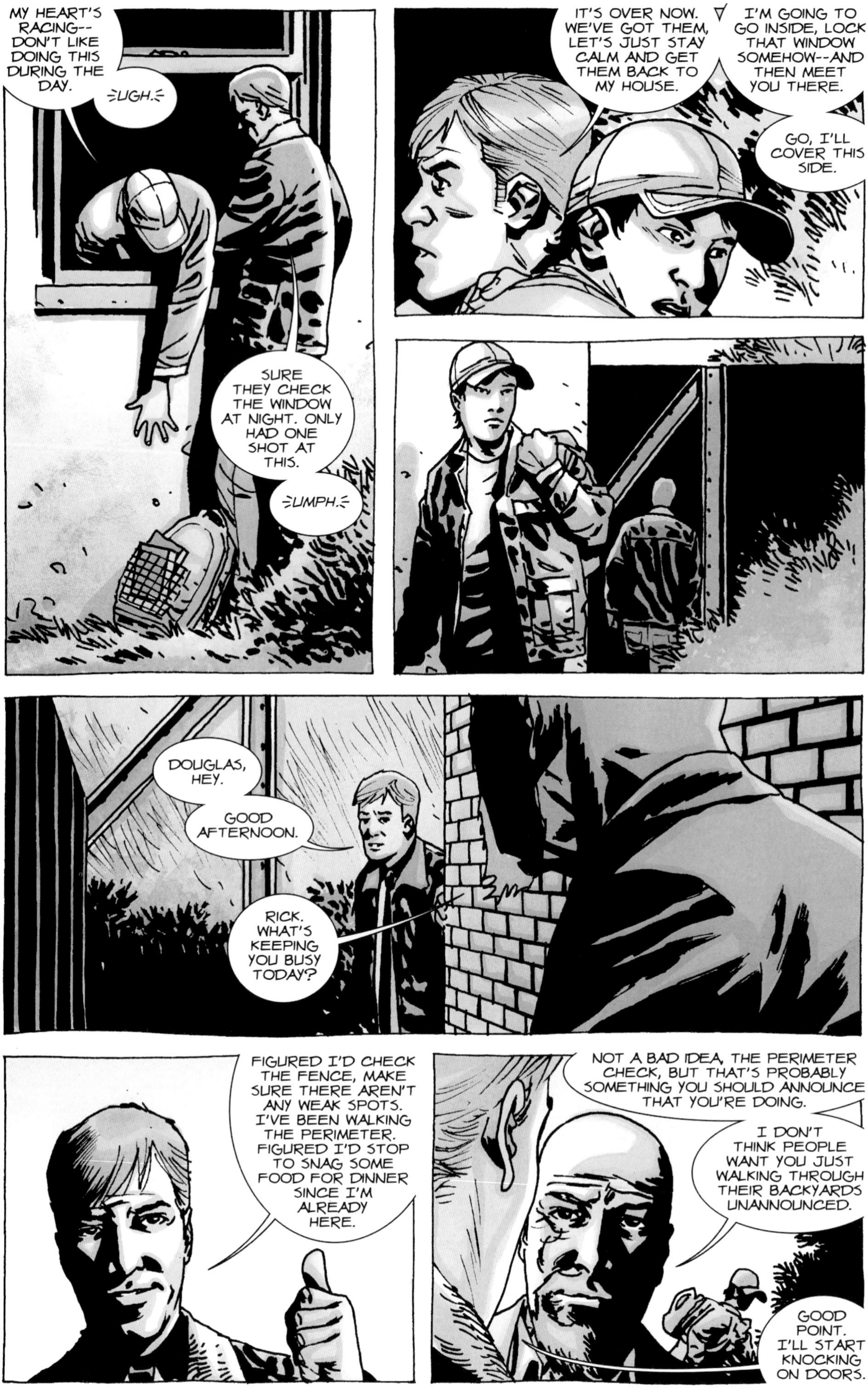
MY HEART'S RACING-- DON'T LIKE DOING THIS DURING THE DAY.
UGH.
SURE THEY CHECK THE WINDOW AT NIGHT. ONLY HAD ONE SHOT AT THIS.
UMPH.
IT'S OVER NOW. WE'VE GOT THEM, LET'S JUST STAY CALM AND GET THEM BACK TO MY HOUSE.
I'M GOING TO GO INSIDE, LOCK THAT WINDOW SOMEHOW--AND THEN MEET YOU THERE.
GO, I'LL COVER THIS SIDE.
DOUGLAS, HEY.
GOOD AFTERNOON.
RICK. WHAT'S KEEPING YOU BUSY TODAY?
FIGURED I'D CHECK THE FENCE, MAKE SURE THERE AREN'T ANY WEAK SPOTS. I'VE BEEN WALKING THE PERIMETER. FIGURED I'D STOP TO SNAG SOME FOOD FOR DINNER SINCE I'M ALREADY HERE.
NOT A BAD IDEA, THE PERIMETER CHECK, BUT THAT'S PROBABLY SOMETHING YOU SHOULD ANNOUNCE THAT YOU'RE DOING.
I DON'T THINK PEOPLE WANT YOU JUST WALKING THROUGH THEIR BACKYARDS UNANNOUNCED.
GOOD POINT. I'LL START KNOCKING ON DOORS.

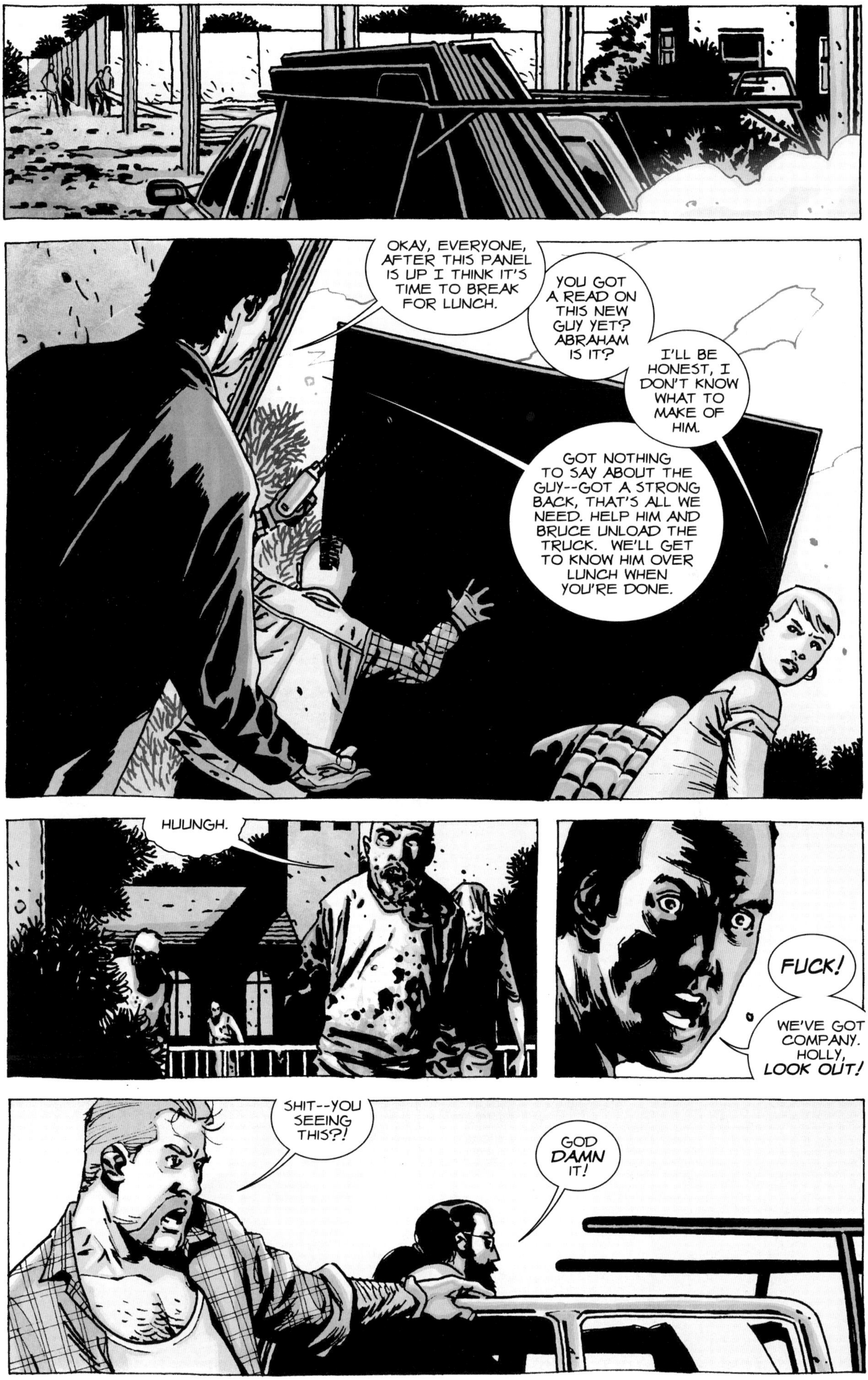
OKAY, EVERYONE, AFTER THIS PANEL IS UP I THINK IT'S TIME TO BREAK FOR LUNCH.
YOU GOT A READ ON THIS NEW GUY YET? ABRAHAM IS IT?
I'LL BE HONEST, I DON'T KNOW WHAT TO MAKE OF HIM.
GOT NOTHING TO SAY ABOUT THE GUY--GOT A STRONG BACK, THAT'S ALL WE NEED. HELP HIM AND BRUCE UNLOAD THE TRUCK. WE'LL GET TO KNOW HIM OVER LUNCH WHEN YOU'RE DONE.
HUUNGH.
FUCK!
WE'VE GOT COMPANY. HOLLY, LOOK OUT!
SHIT--YOU SEEING THIS?!
GOD DAMN IT!

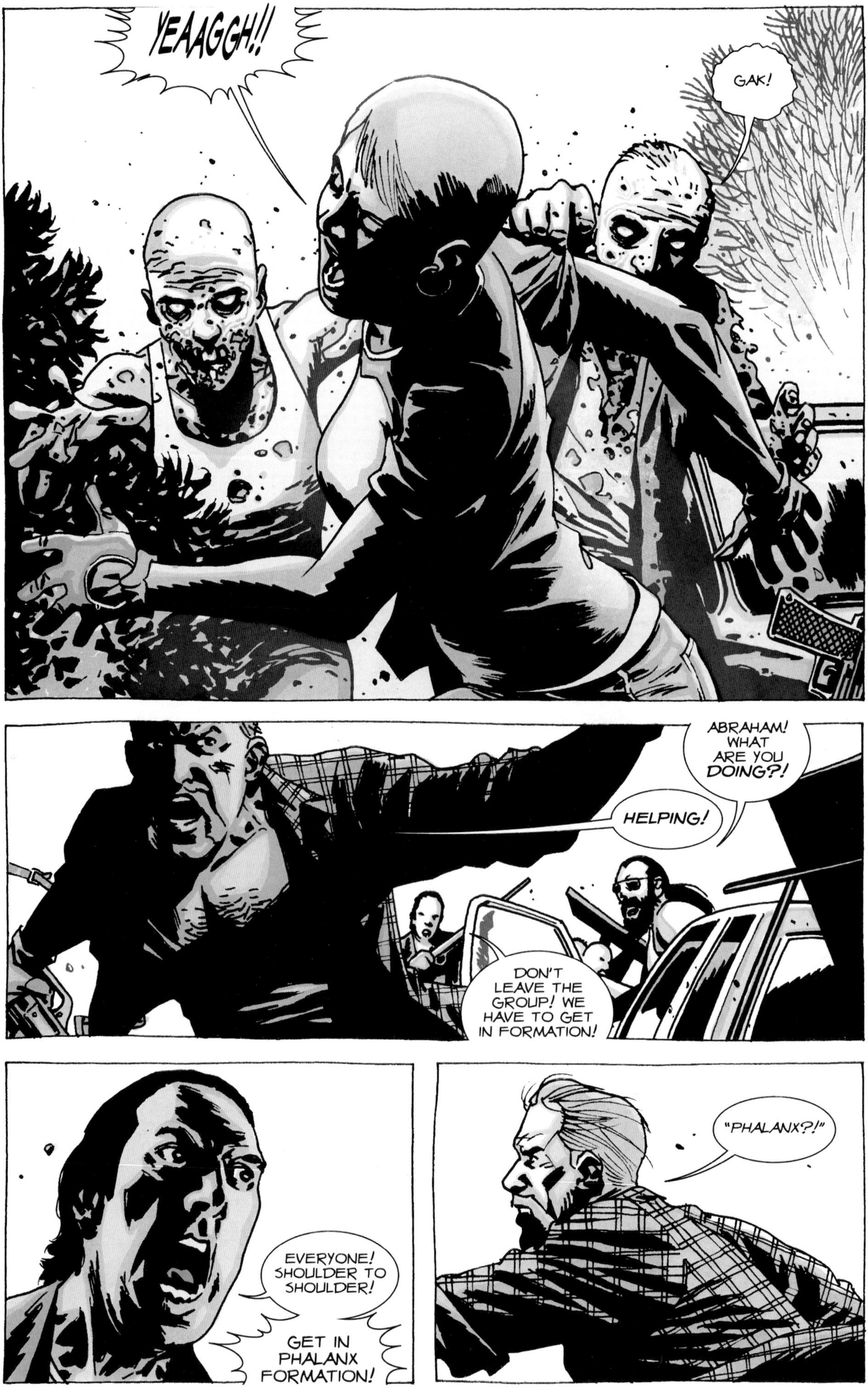
YEAAGGH!!
GAK!
ABRAHAM! WHAT ARE YOU DOING?!
HELPING!
DON'T LEAVE THE GROUP! WE HAVE TO GET IN FORMATION!
EVERYONE! SHOULDER TO SHOULDER!
GET IN PHALANX FORMATION!
"PHALANX?!"

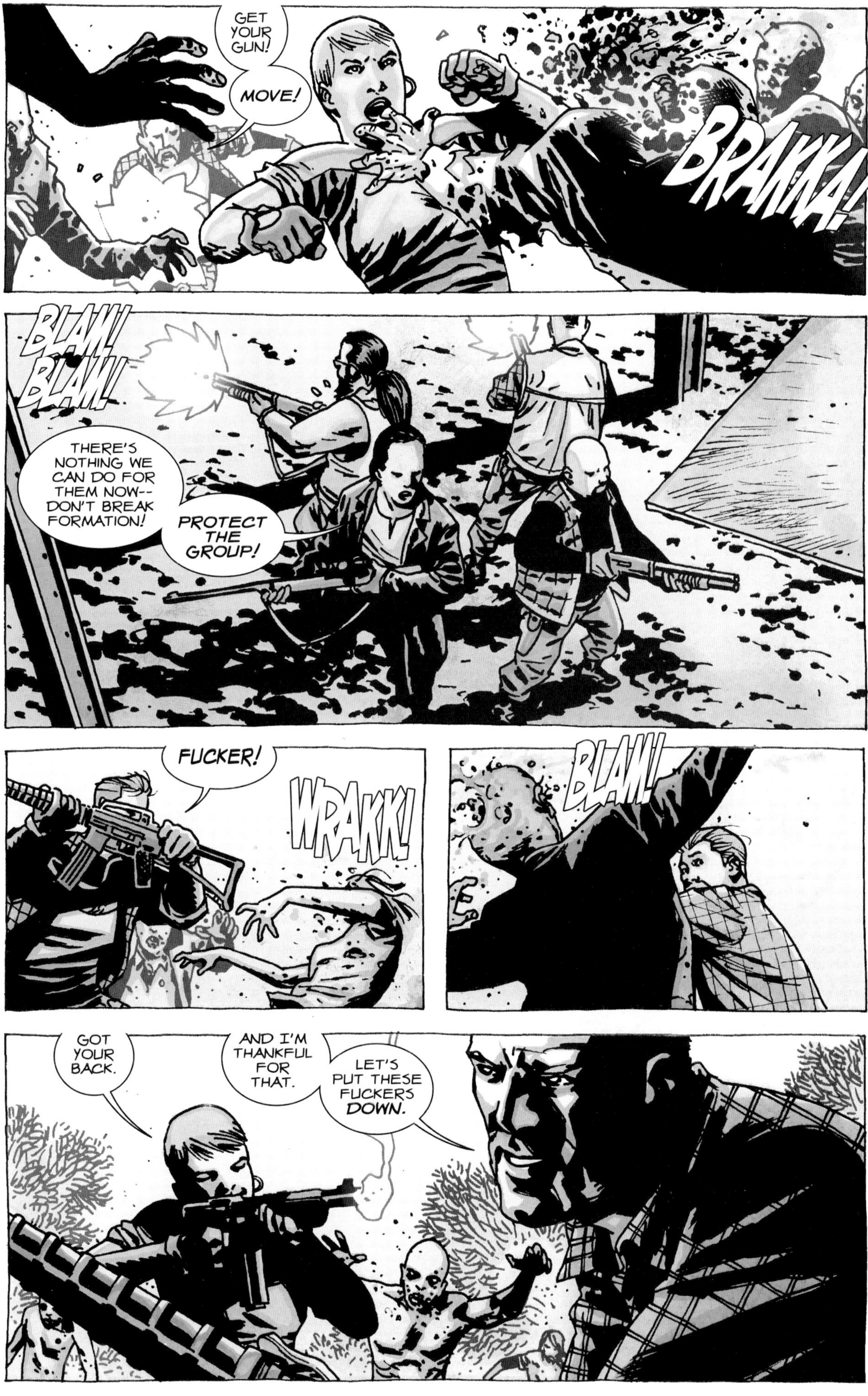
GET YOUR GUN!
MOVE!
BRAKKA!
BLAM! BLAM!
THERE'S NOTHING WE CAN DO FOR THEM NOW--DON'T BREAK FORMATION!
PROTECT THE GROUP!
FUCKER!
WRAKK!
BLAM!
GOT YOUR BACK.
AND I'M THANKFUL FOR THAT.
LET'S PUT THESE FUCKERS DOWN.

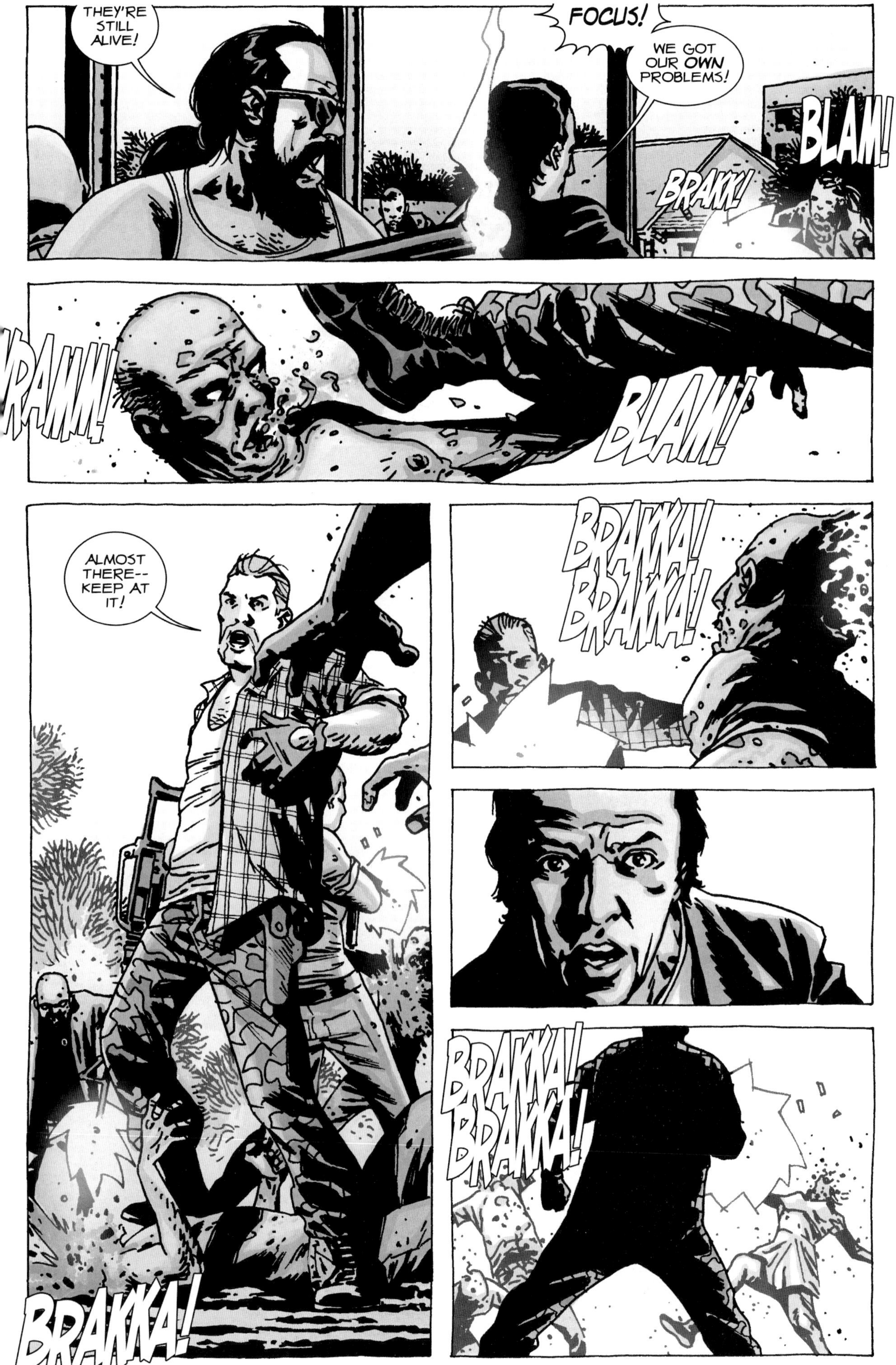
THEY'RE STILL ALIVE!
FOCUS!
WE GOT OUR OWN PROBLEMS!
BRAKK!
BLAM!
VRAMM!
BLAM!
ALMOST THERE-- KEEP AT IT!
BRAKKA!
BRAKKA! BRAKKA!
BRAKKA! BRAKKA!

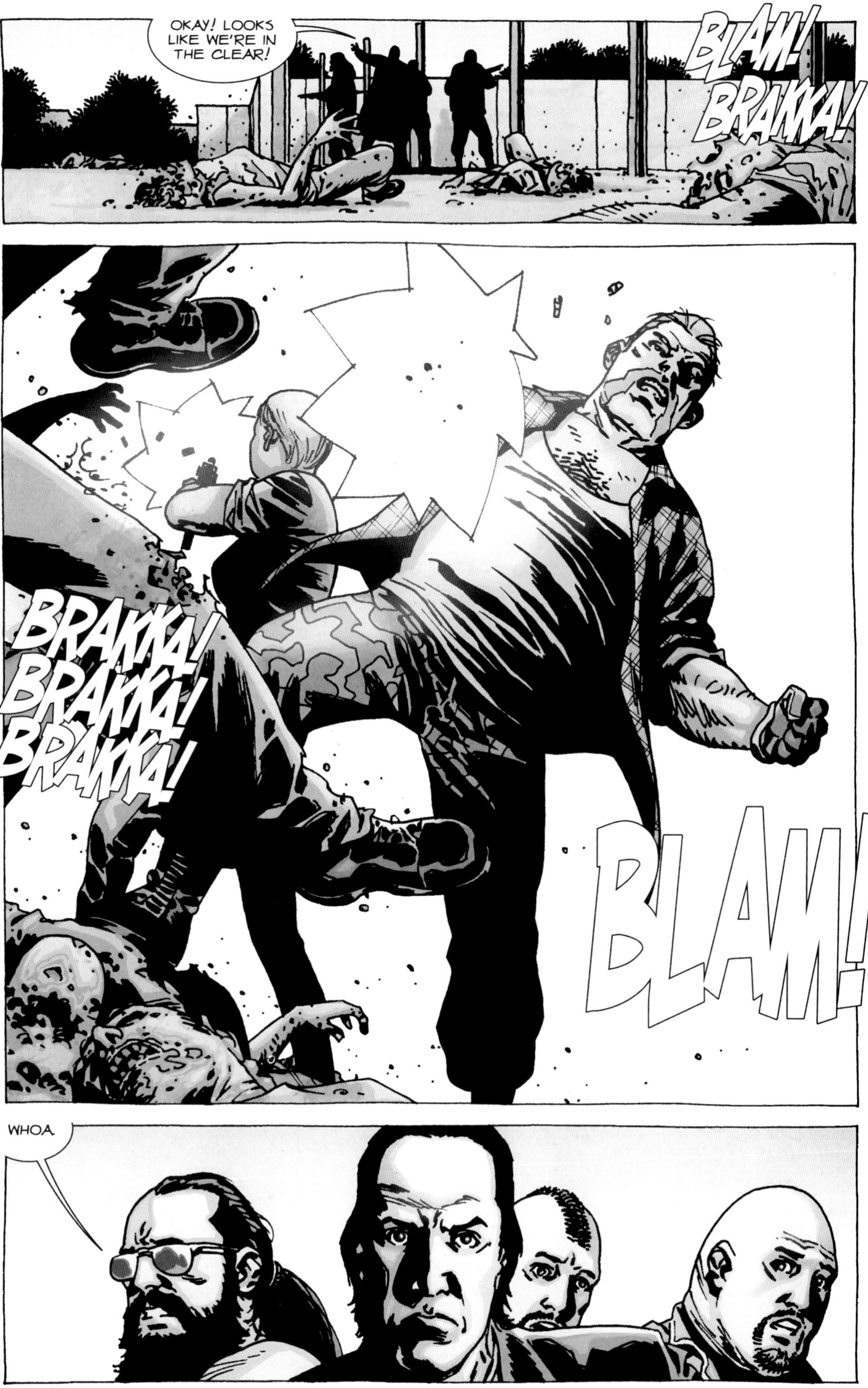
OKAY! LOOKS LIKE WE'RE IN THE CLEAR!
BLAM! BRAKKA!
BRAKKA! BRAKKA! BRAKKA!
BLAM!
WHOA.

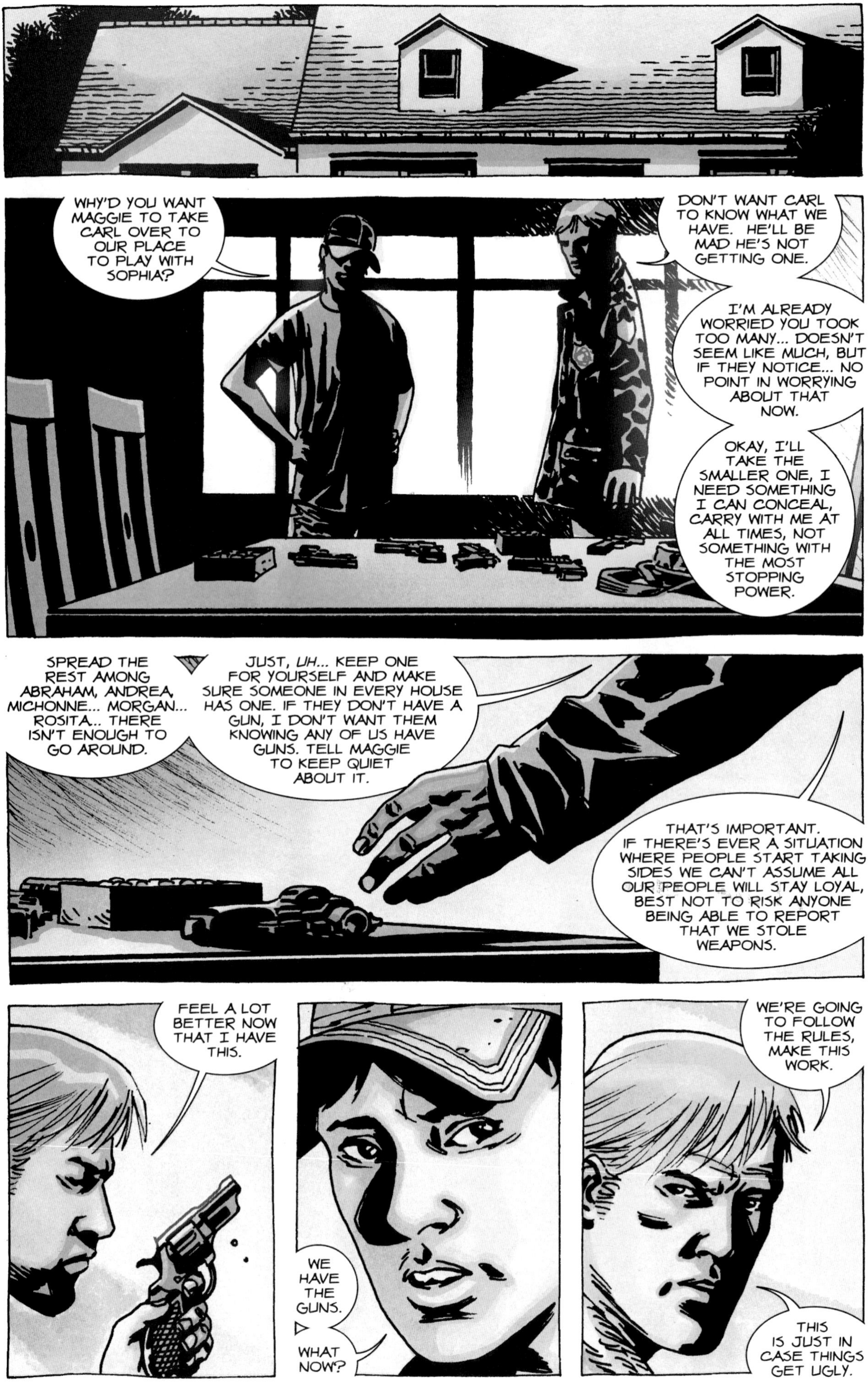
WHY'D YOU WANT MAGGIE TO TAKE CARL OVER TO OUR PLACE TO PLAY WITH SOPHIA?
DON'T WANT CARL TO KNOW WHAT WE HAVE. HE'LL BE MAD HE'S NOT GETTING ONE.
I'M ALREADY WORRIED YOU TOOK TOO MANY... DOESN'T SEEM LIKE MUCH, BUT IF THEY NOTICE... NO POINT IN WORRYING ABOUT THAT NOW.
OKAY, I'LL TAKE THE SMALLER ONE, I NEED SOMETHING I CAN CONCEAL, CARRY WITH ME AT ALL TIMES, NOT SOMETHING WITH THE MOST STOPPING POWER.
SPREAD THE REST AMONG ABRAHAM, ANDREA, MICHONNE... MORGAN... ROSITA... THERE ISN'T ENOUGH TO GO AROUND.
JUST, *UH*... KEEP ONE FOR YOURSELF AND MAKE SURE SOMEONE IN EVERY HOUSE HAS ONE. IF THEY DON'T HAVE A GUN, I DON'T WANT THEM KNOWING ANY OF US HAVE GUNS. TELL MAGGIE TO KEEP QUIET ABOUT IT.
THAT'S IMPORTANT. IF THERE'S EVER A SITUATION WHERE PEOPLE START TAKING SIDES WE CAN'T ASSUME ALL OUR PEOPLE WILL STAY LOYAL, BEST NOT TO RISK ANYONE BEING ABLE TO REPORT THAT WE STOLE WEAPONS.
FEEL A LOT BETTER NOW THAT I HAVE THIS.
WE HAVE THE GUNS.
WHAT NOW?
WE'RE GOING TO FOLLOW THE RULES, MAKE THIS WORK.
THIS IS JUST IN CASE THINGS GET UGLY.

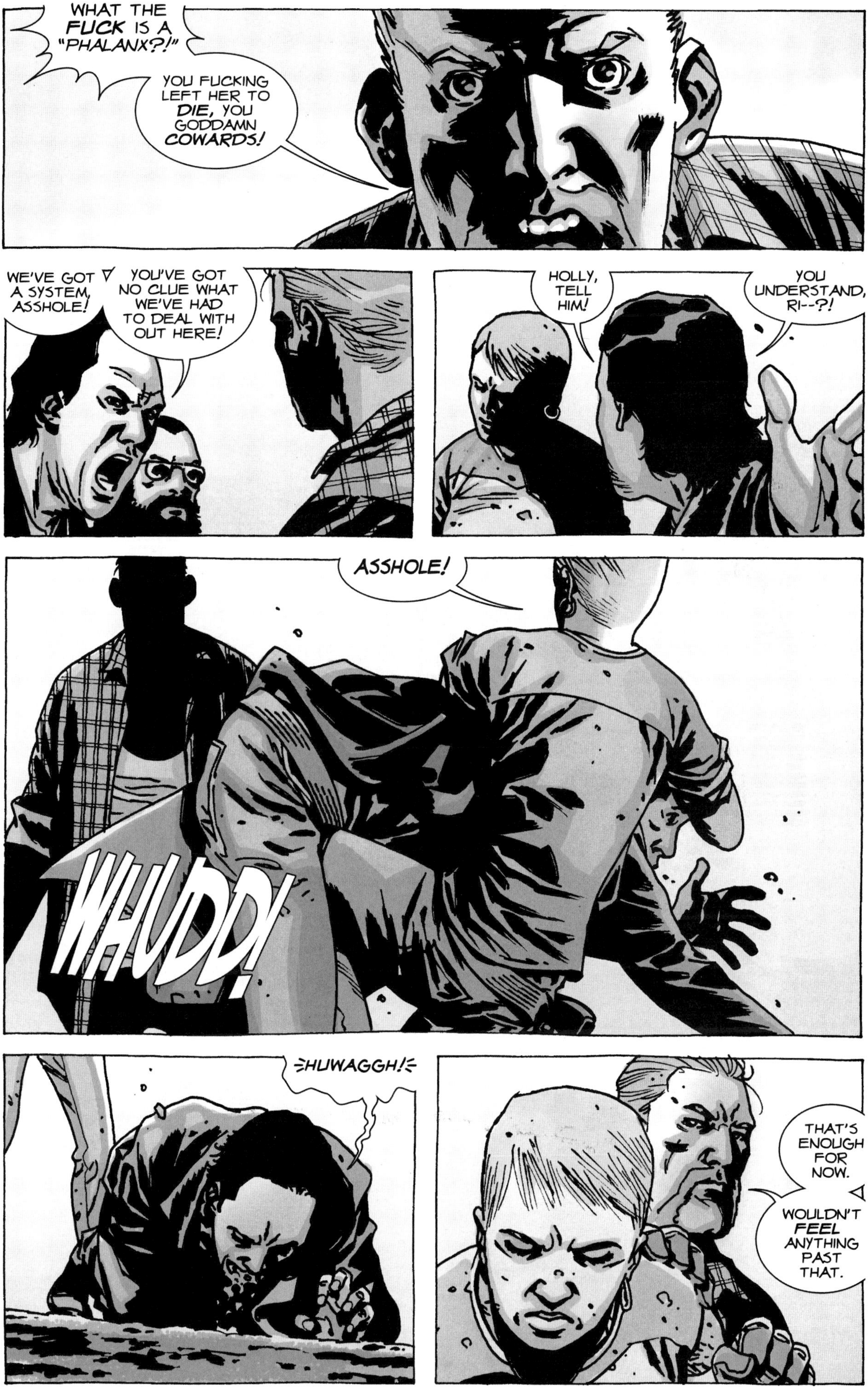
WHAT THE FUCK IS A "PHALANX?!"
YOU FUCKING LEFT HER TO DIE, YOU GODDAMN COWARDS!
WE'VE GOT A SYSTEM, ASSHOLE!
YOU'VE GOT NO CLUE WHAT WE'VE HAD TO DEAL WITH OUT HERE!
HOLLY, TELL HIM!
YOU UNDERSTAND, RI--?!
ASSHOLE!
WHUDD!
HUWAGGH!
THAT'S ENOUGH FOR NOW.
WOULDN'T FEEL ANYTHING PAST THAT.

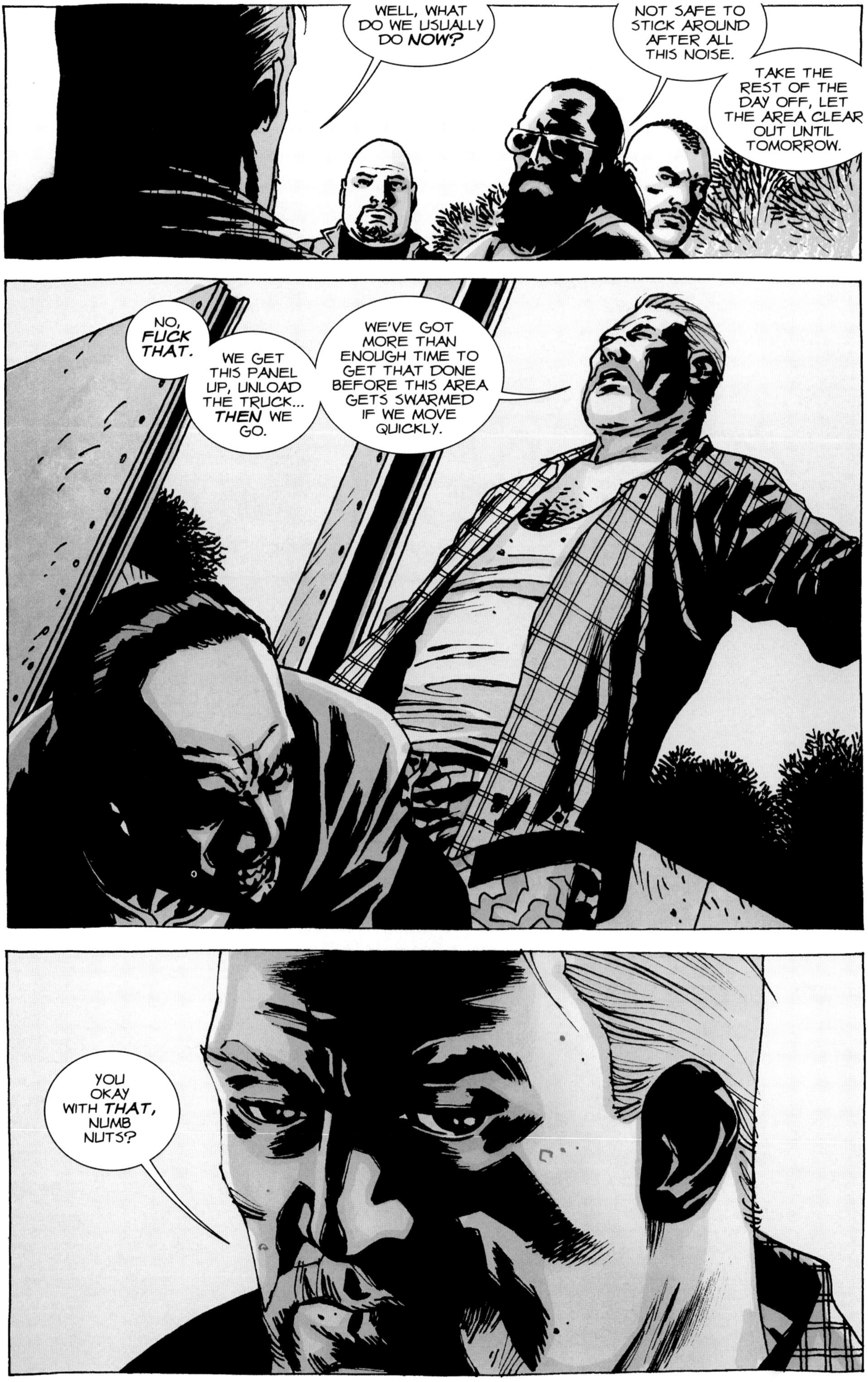
WELL, WHAT DO WE USUALLY DO NOW?
NOT SAFE TO STICK AROUND AFTER ALL THIS NOISE.
TAKE THE REST OF THE DAY OFF, LET THE AREA CLEAR OUT UNTIL TOMORROW.
NO, FUCK THAT.
WE GET THIS PANEL UP, UNLOAD THE TRUCK... THEN WE GO.
WE'VE GOT MORE THAN ENOUGH TIME TO GET THAT DONE BEFORE THIS AREA GETS SWARMED IF WE MOVE QUICKLY.
YOU OKAY WITH THAT, NUMB NUTS?

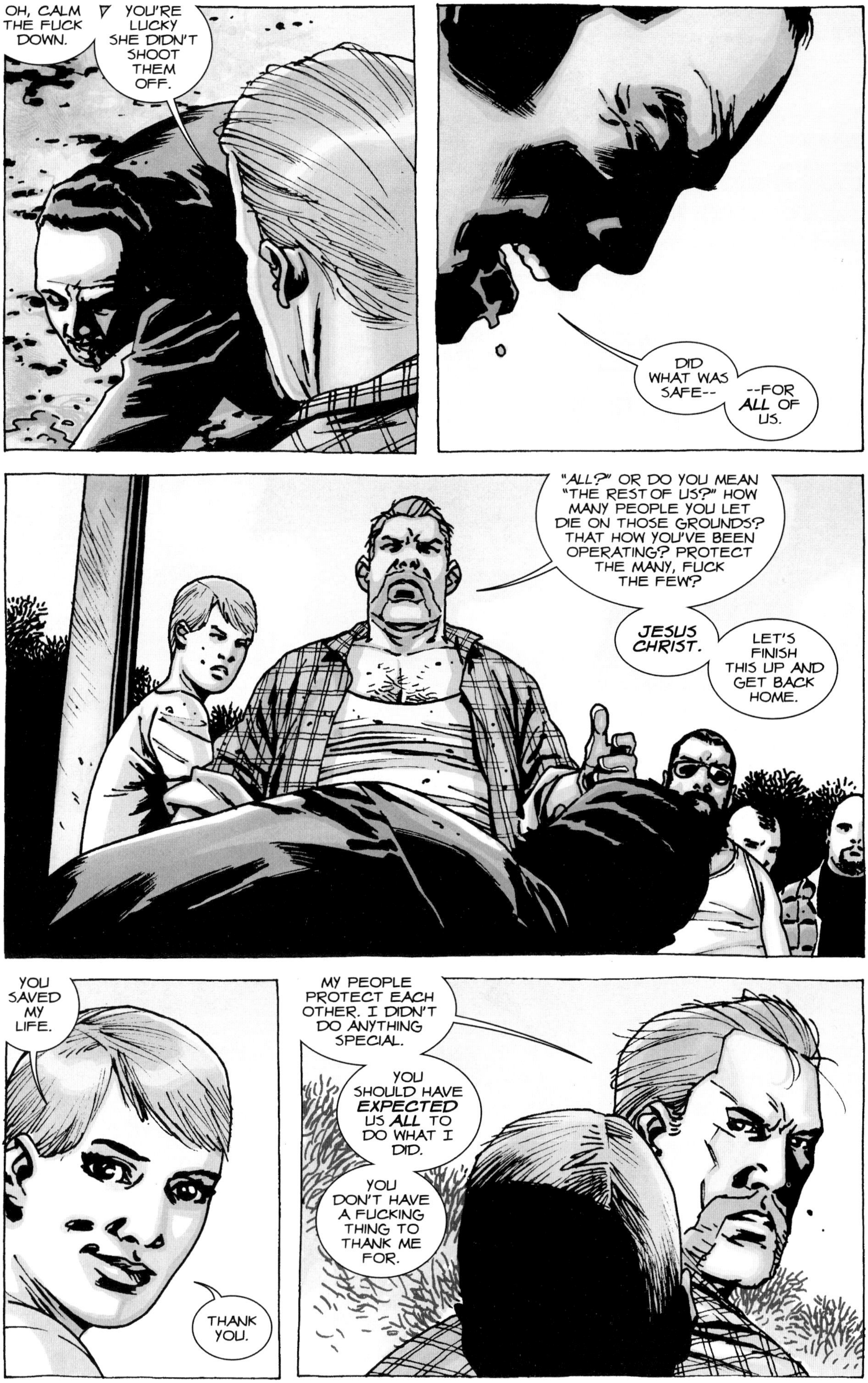
OH, CALM THE FUCK DOWN.
YOU'RE LUCKY SHE DIDN'T SHOOT THEM OFF.
DID WHAT WAS SAFE--
--FOR ALL OF US.
"ALL?" OR DO YOU MEAN "THE REST OF US?" HOW MANY PEOPLE YOU LET DIE ON THOSE GROUNDS? THAT HOW YOU'VE BEEN OPERATING? PROTECT THE MANY, FUCK THE FEW?
JESUS CHRIST.
LET'S FINISH THIS UP AND GET BACK HOME.
YOU SAVED MY LIFE.
THANK YOU.
MY PEOPLE PROTECT EACH OTHER. I DIDN'T DO ANYTHING SPECIAL.
YOU SHOULD HAVE EXPECTED US ALL TO DO WHAT I DID.
YOU DON'T HAVE A FUCKING THING TO THANK ME FOR.

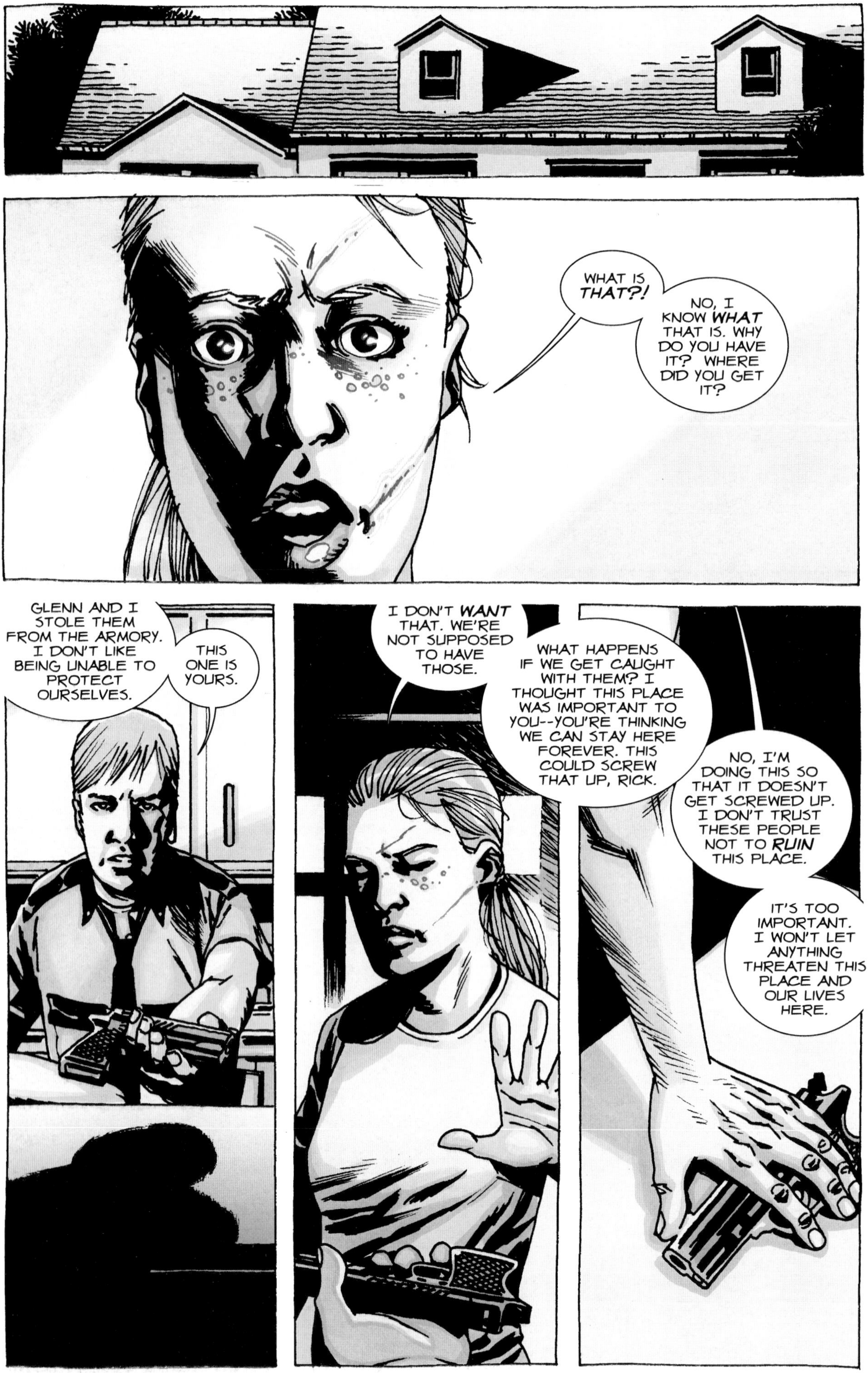
WHAT IS THAT?!
NO, I KNOW WHAT THAT IS. WHY DO YOU HAVE IT? WHERE DID YOU GET IT?
GLENN AND I STOLE THEM FROM THE ARMORY. I DON'T LIKE BEING UNABLE TO PROTECT OURSELVES.
THIS ONE IS YOURS.
I DON'T WANT THAT. WE'RE NOT SUPPOSED TO HAVE THOSE.
WHAT HAPPENS IF WE GET CAUGHT WITH THEM? I THOUGHT THIS PLACE WAS IMPORTANT TO YOU--YOU'RE THINKING WE CAN STAY HERE FOREVER. THIS COULD SCREW THAT UP, RICK.
NO, I'M DOING THIS SO THAT IT DOESN'T GET SCREWED UP. I DON'T TRUST THESE PEOPLE NOT TO RUIN THIS PLACE.
IT'S TOO IMPORTANT. I WON'T LET ANYTHING THREATEN THIS PLACE AND OUR LIVES HERE.

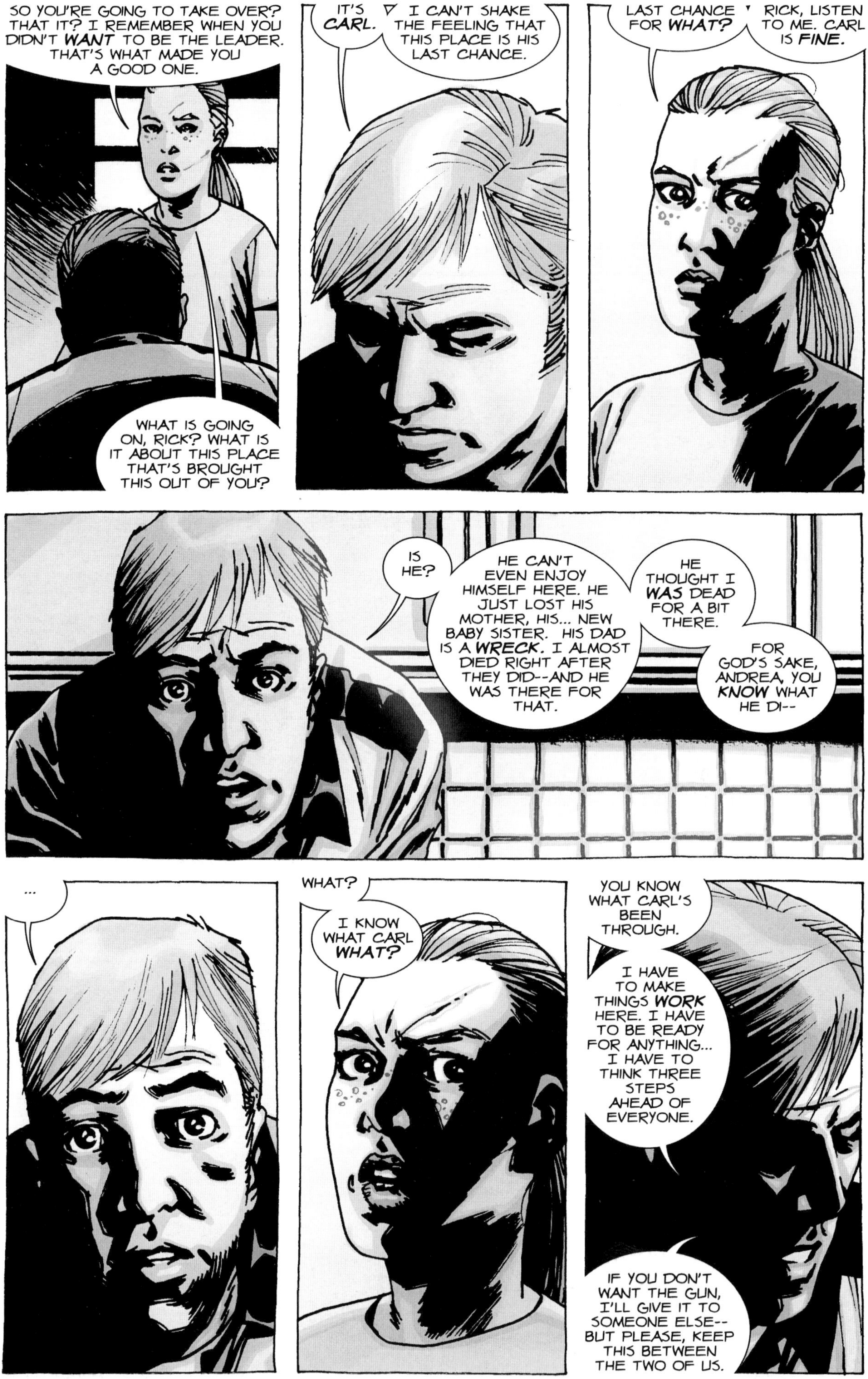

SO YOU'RE GOING TO TAKE OVER? THAT IT? I REMEMBER WHEN YOU DIDN'T WANT TO BE THE LEADER. THAT'S WHAT MADE YOU A GOOD ONE.
WHAT IS GOING ON, RICK? WHAT IS IT ABOUT THIS PLACE THAT'S BROUGHT THIS OUT OF YOU?
IT'S CARL.
I CAN'T SHAKE THE FEELING THAT THIS PLACE IS HIS LAST CHANCE.
LAST CHANCE FOR WHAT?
RICK, LISTEN TO ME. CARL IS FINE.
IS HE?
HE CAN'T EVEN ENJOY HIMSELF HERE. HE JUST LOST HIS MOTHER, HIS... NEW BABY SISTER. HIS DAD IS A WRECK. I ALMOST DIED RIGHT AFTER THEY DID--AND HE WAS THERE FOR THAT.
HE THOUGHT I WAS DEAD FOR A BIT THERE.
FOR GOD'S SAKE, ANDREA, YOU KNOW WHAT HE DI--
...
WHAT?
I KNOW WHAT CARL WHAT?
YOU KNOW WHAT CARL'S BEEN THROUGH.
I HAVE TO MAKE THINGS WORK HERE. I HAVE TO BE READY FOR ANYTHING... I HAVE TO THINK THREE STEPS AHEAD OF EVERYONE.
IF YOU DON'T WANT THE GUN, I'LL GIVE IT TO SOMEONE ELSE-- BUT PLEASE, KEEP THIS BETWEEN THE TWO OF US.

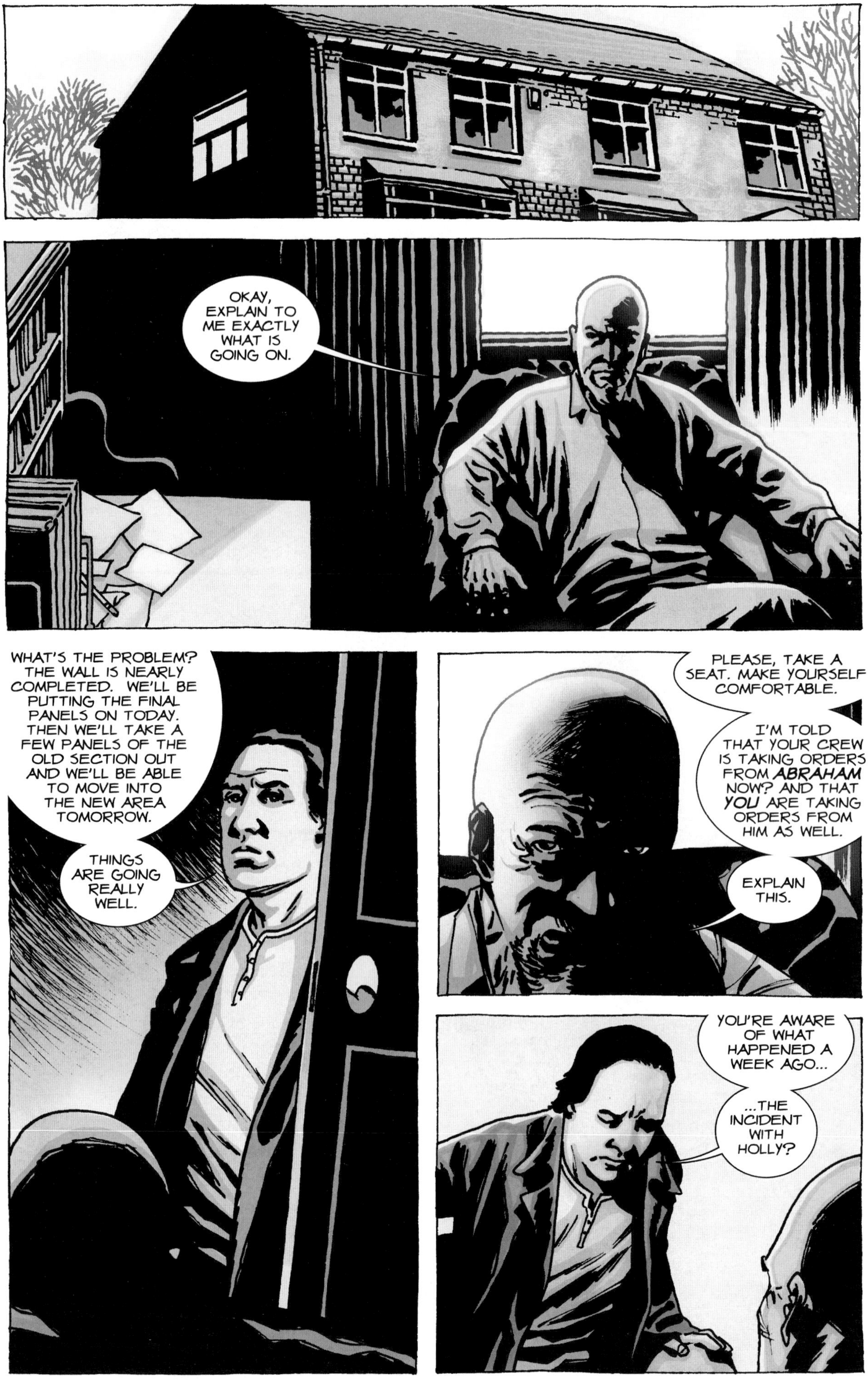
OKAY, EXPLAIN TO ME EXACTLY WHAT IS GOING ON.
WHAT'S THE PROBLEM? THE WALL IS NEARLY COMPLETED. WE'LL BE PUTTING THE FINAL PANELS ON TODAY. THEN WE'LL TAKE A FEW PANELS OF THE OLD SECTION OUT AND WE'LL BE ABLE TO MOVE INTO THE NEW AREA TOMORROW.
THINGS ARE GOING REALLY WELL.
PLEASE, TAKE A SEAT. MAKE YOURSELF COMFORTABLE.
I'M TOLD THAT YOUR CREW IS TAKING ORDERS FROM ***ABRAHAM*** NOW? AND THAT ***YOU*** ARE TAKING ORDERS FROM HIM AS WELL.
EXPLAIN THIS.
YOU'RE AWARE OF WHAT HAPPENED A WEEK AGO...
...THE INCIDENT WITH HOLLY?

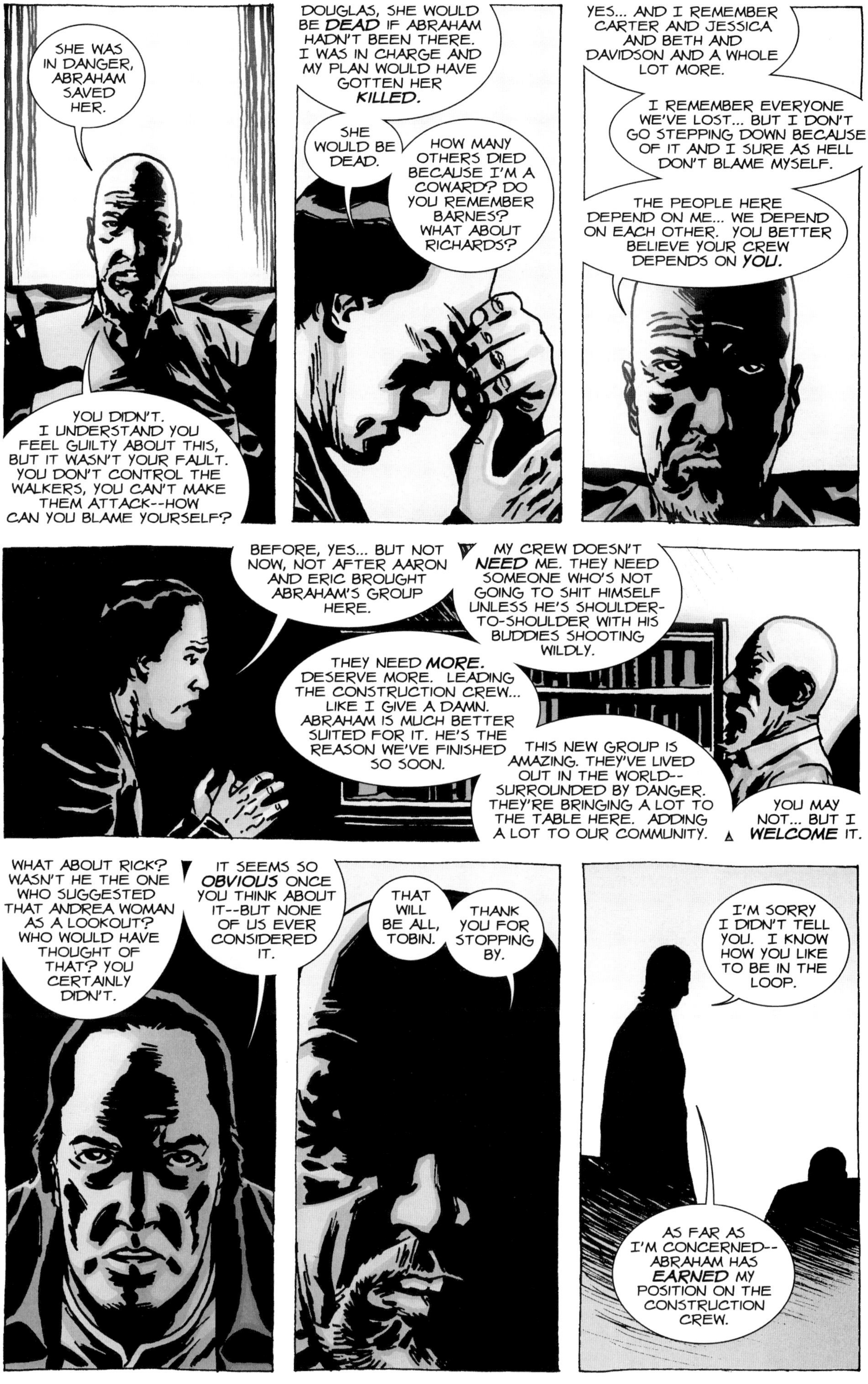
SHE WAS IN DANGER, ABRAHAM SAVED HER.
YOU DIDN'T. I UNDERSTAND YOU FEEL GUILTY ABOUT THIS, BUT IT WASN'T YOUR FAULT. YOU DON'T CONTROL THE WALKERS, YOU CAN'T MAKE THEM ATTACK--HOW CAN YOU BLAME YOURSELF?
DOUGLAS, SHE WOULD BE DEAD IF ABRAHAM HADN'T BEEN THERE. I WAS IN CHARGE AND MY PLAN WOULD HAVE GOTTEN HER KILLED.
SHE WOULD BE DEAD.
HOW MANY OTHERS DIED BECAUSE I'M A COWARD? DO YOU REMEMBER BARNES? WHAT ABOUT RICHARDS?
YES... AND I REMEMBER CARTER AND JESSICA AND BETH AND DAVIDSON AND A WHOLE LOT MORE.
I REMEMBER EVERYONE WE'VE LOST... BUT I DON'T GO STEPPING DOWN BECAUSE OF IT AND I SURE AS HELL DON'T BLAME MYSELF.
THE PEOPLE HERE DEPEND ON ME... WE DEPEND ON EACH OTHER. YOU BETTER BELIEVE YOUR CREW DEPENDS ON YOU.
BEFORE, YES... BUT NOT NOW, NOT AFTER AARON AND ERIC BROUGHT ABRAHAM'S GROUP HERE.
MY CREW DOESN'T NEED ME. THEY NEED SOMEONE WHO'S NOT GOING TO SHIT HIMSELF UNLESS HE'S SHOULDER-TO-SHOULDER WITH HIS BUDDIES SHOOTING WILDLY.
THEY NEED MORE. DESERVE MORE. LEADING THE CONSTRUCTION CREW... LIKE I GIVE A DAMN. ABRAHAM IS MUCH BETTER SUITED FOR IT. HE'S THE REASON WE'VE FINISHED SO SOON.
THIS NEW GROUP IS AMAZING. THEY'VE LIVED OUT IN THE WORLD--SURROUNDED BY DANGER. THEY'RE BRINGING A LOT TO THE TABLE HERE. ADDING A LOT TO OUR COMMUNITY.
YOU MAY NOT... BUT I WELCOME IT.
WHAT ABOUT RICK? WASN'T HE THE ONE WHO SUGGESTED THAT ANDREA WOMAN AS A LOOKOUT? WHO WOULD HAVE THOUGHT OF THAT? YOU CERTAINLY DIDN'T.
IT SEEMS SO OBVIOUS ONCE YOU THINK ABOUT IT--BUT NONE OF US EVER CONSIDERED IT.
THAT WILL BE ALL, TOBIN.
THANK YOU FOR STOPPING BY.
I'M SORRY I DIDN'T TELL YOU. I KNOW HOW YOU LIKE TO BE IN THE LOOP.
AS FAR AS I'M CONCERNED-- ABRAHAM HAS EARNED MY POSITION ON THE CONSTRUCTION CREW.

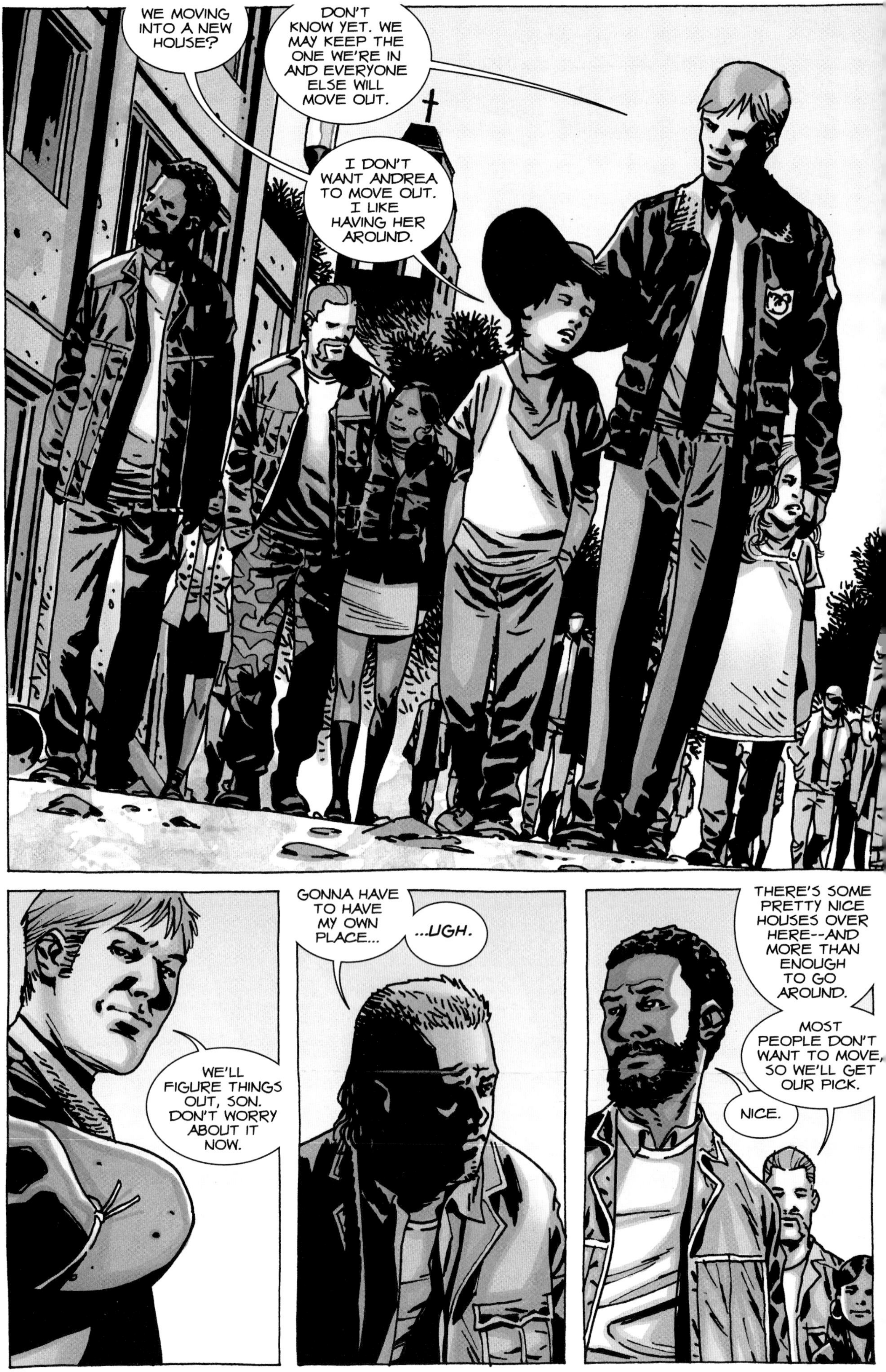

WE MOVING INTO A NEW HOUSE?
DON'T KNOW YET. WE MAY KEEP THE ONE WE'RE IN AND EVERYONE ELSE WILL MOVE OUT.
I DON'T WANT ANDREA TO MOVE OUT. I LIKE HAVING HER AROUND.
WE'LL FIGURE THINGS OUT, SON. DON'T WORRY ABOUT IT NOW.
GONNA HAVE TO HAVE MY OWN PLACE...
...UGH.
THERE'S SOME PRETTY NICE HOUSES OVER HERE--AND MORE THAN ENOUGH TO GO AROUND.
MOST PEOPLE DON'T WANT TO MOVE, SO WE'LL GET OUR PICK.
NICE.

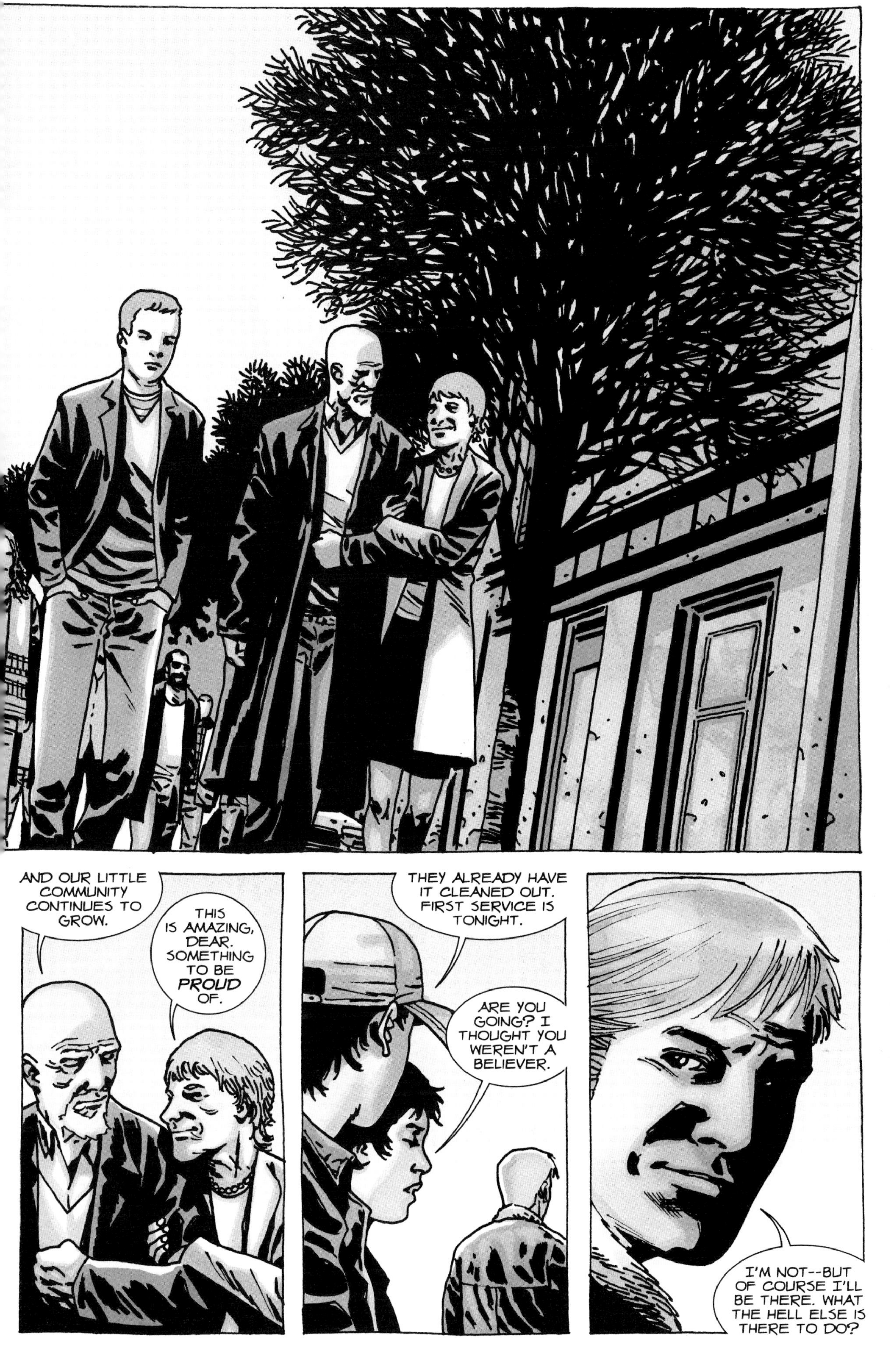
AND OUR LITTLE COMMUNITY CONTINUES TO GROW.
THIS IS AMAZING, DEAR. SOMETHING TO BE PROUD OF.
THEY ALREADY HAVE IT CLEANED OUT. FIRST SERVICE IS TONIGHT.
ARE YOU GOING? I THOUGHT YOU WEREN'T A BELIEVER.
I'M NOT--BUT OF COURSE I'LL BE THERE. WHAT THE HELL ELSE IS THERE TO DO?

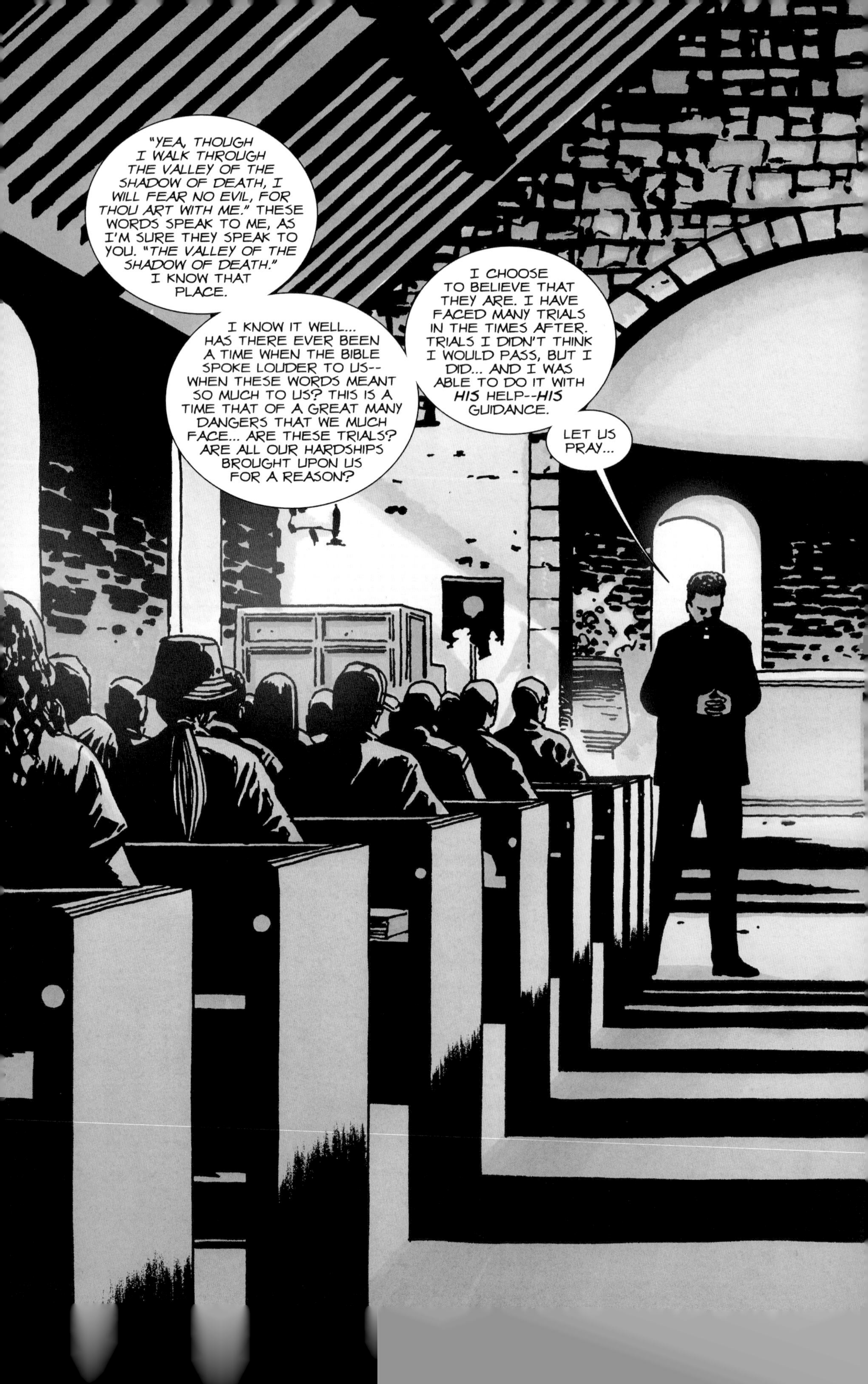
"YEA, THOUGH I WALK THROUGH THE VALLEY OF THE SHADOW OF DEATH, I WILL FEAR NO EVIL, FOR THOU ART WITH ME." THESE WORDS SPEAK TO ME, AS I'M SURE THEY SPEAK TO YOU. "THE VALLEY OF THE SHADOW OF DEATH." I KNOW THAT PLACE.
I KNOW IT WELL... HAS THERE EVER BEEN A TIME WHEN THE BIBLE SPOKE LOUDER TO US-- WHEN THESE WORDS MEANT SO MUCH TO US? THIS IS A TIME THAT OF A GREAT MANY DANGERS THAT WE MUCH FACE... ARE THESE TRIALS? ARE ALL OUR HARDSHIPS BROUGHT UPON US FOR A REASON?
I CHOOSE TO BELIEVE THAT THEY ARE. I HAVE FACED MANY TRIALS IN THE TIMES AFTER. TRIALS I DIDN'T THINK I WOULD PASS, BUT I DID... AND I WAS ABLE TO DO IT WITH HIS HELP--HIS GUIDANCE.
LET US PRAY...

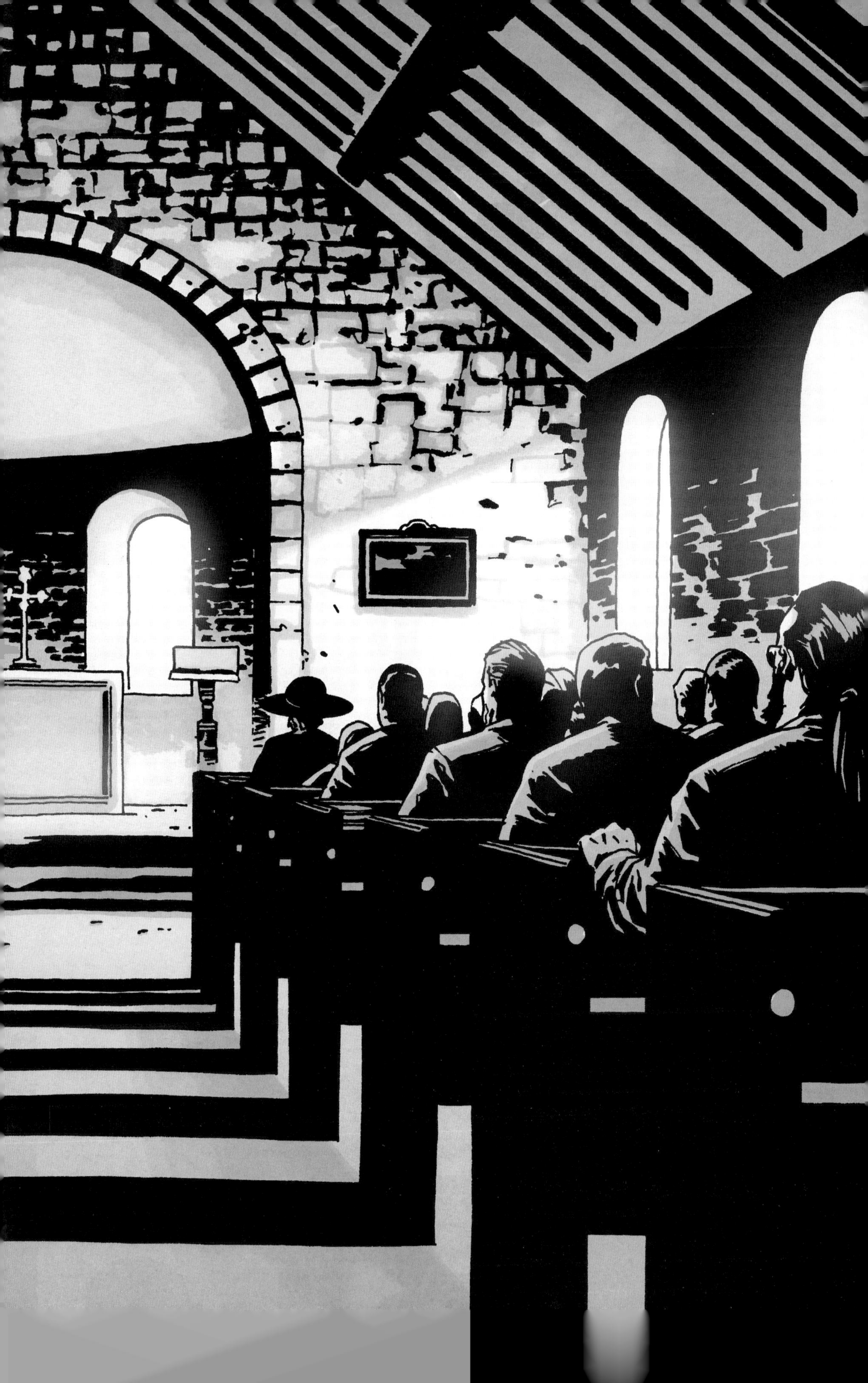

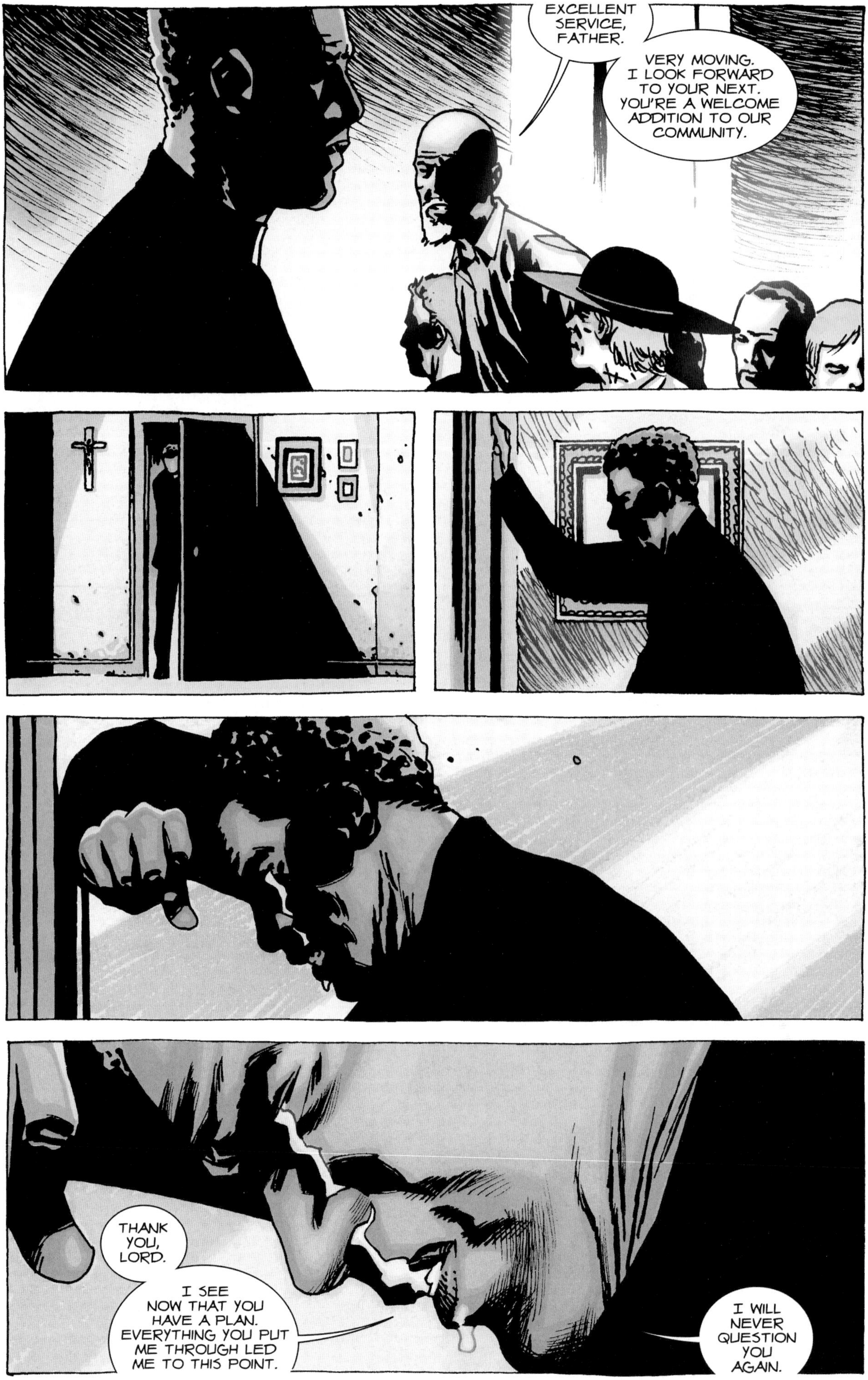
EXCELLENT SERVICE, FATHER.
VERY MOVING. I LOOK FORWARD TO YOUR NEXT. YOU'RE A WELCOME ADDITION TO OUR COMMUNITY.
THANK YOU, LORD.
I SEE NOW THAT YOU HAVE A PLAN. EVERYTHING YOU PUT ME THROUGH LED ME TO THIS POINT.
I WILL NEVER QUESTION YOU AGAIN.

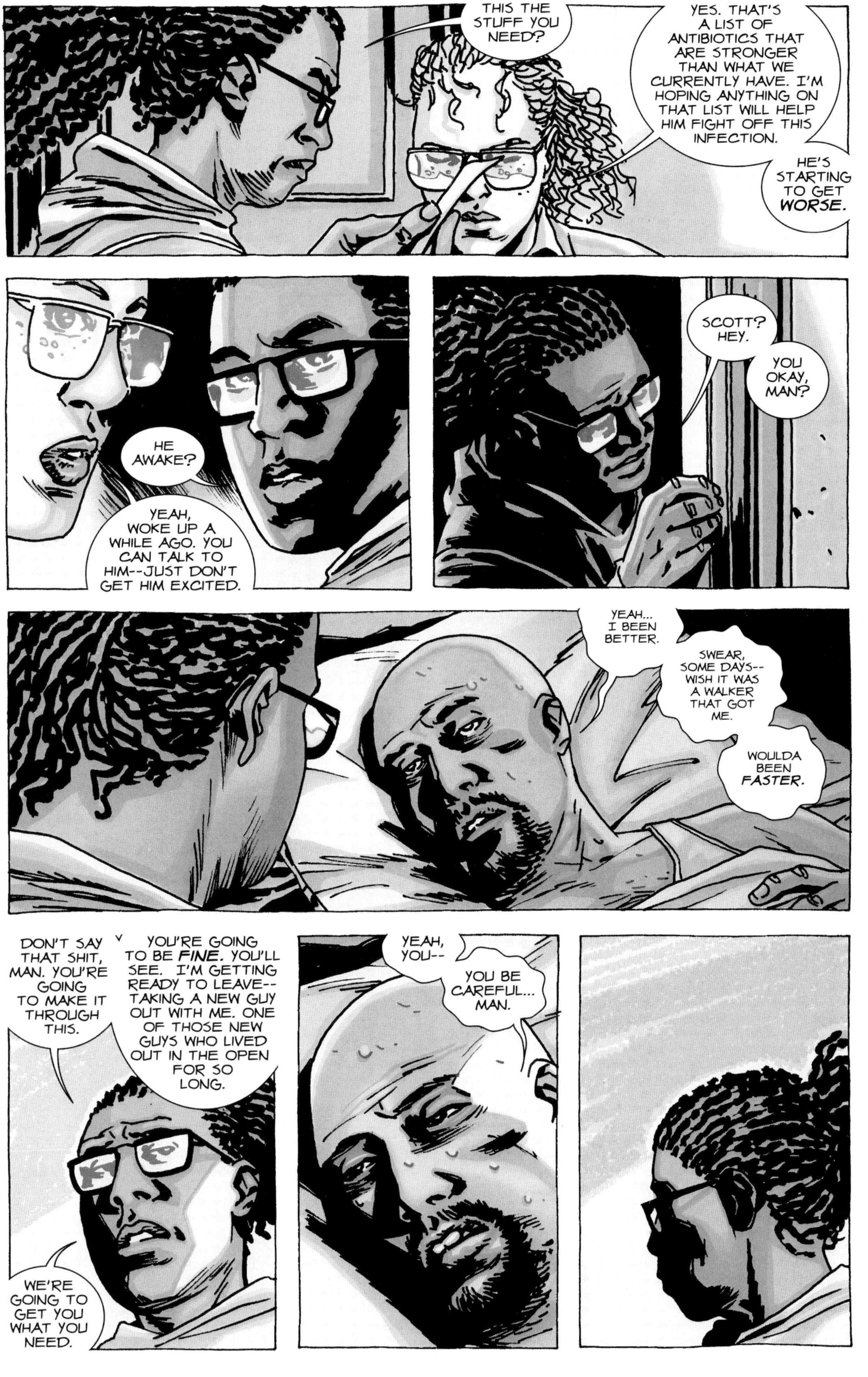
THIS THE STUFF YOU NEED?
YES. THAT'S A LIST OF ANTIBIOTICS THAT ARE STRONGER THAN WHAT WE CURRENTLY HAVE. I'M HOPING ANYTHING ON THAT LIST WILL HELP HIM FIGHT OFF THIS INFECTION.
HE'S STARTING TO GET ***WORSE.***
HE AWAKE?
YEAH, WOKE UP A WHILE AGO. YOU CAN TALK TO HIM--JUST DON'T GET HIM EXCITED.
SCOTT? HEY.
YOU OKAY, MAN?
YEAH... I BEEN BETTER.
SWEAR, SOME DAYS-- WISH IT WAS A WALKER THAT GOT ME.
WOULDA BEEN ***FASTER.***
DON'T SAY THAT SHIT, MAN. YOU'RE GOING TO MAKE IT THROUGH THIS.
YOU'RE GOING TO BE ***FINE.*** YOU'LL SEE. I'M GETTING READY TO LEAVE-- TAKING A NEW GUY OUT WITH ME. ONE OF THOSE NEW GUYS WHO LIVED OUT IN THE OPEN FOR SO LONG.
WE'RE GOING TO GET YOU WHAT YOU NEED.
YEAH, YOU--
YOU BE CAREFUL... MAN.

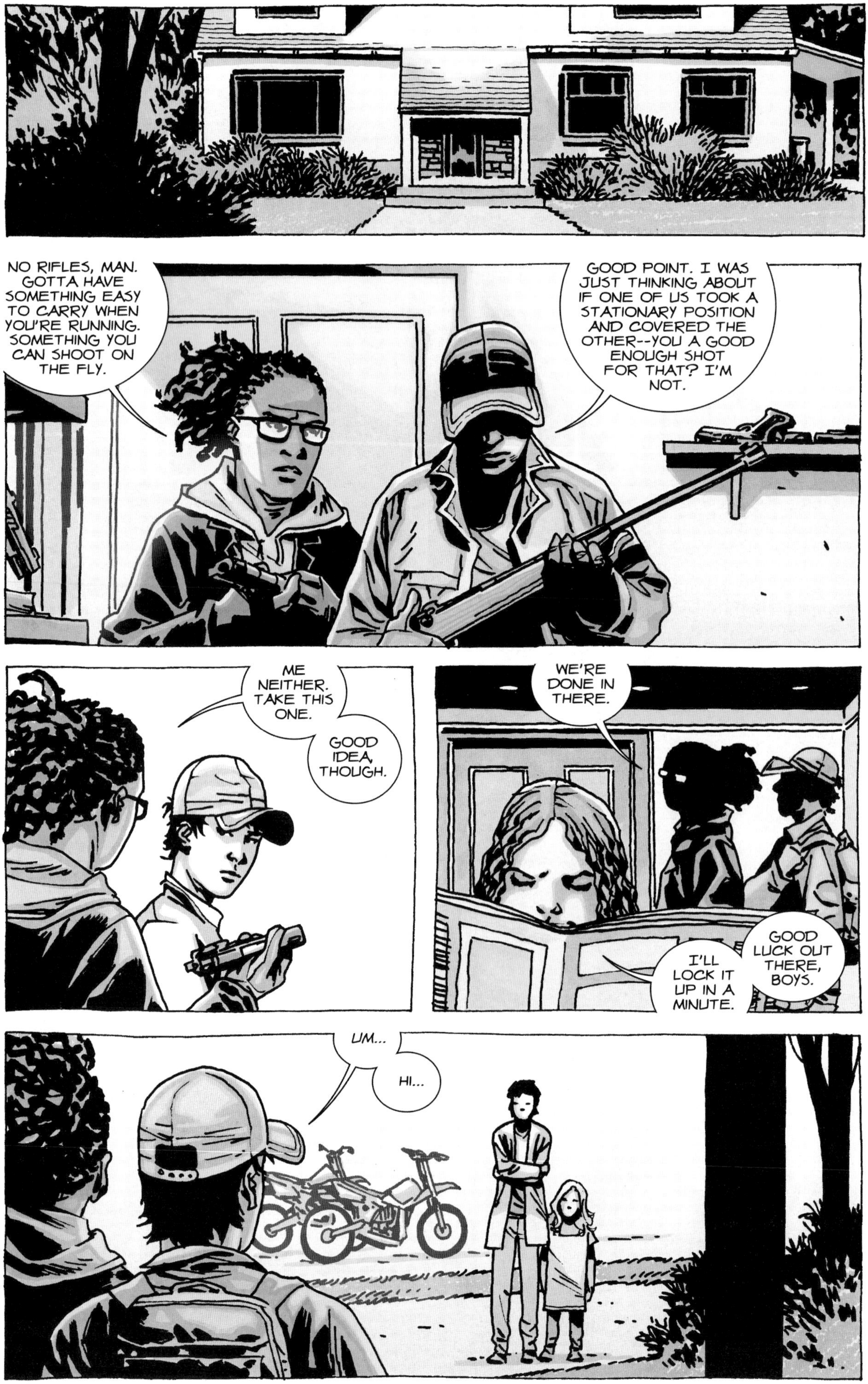
NO RIFLES, MAN. GOTTA HAVE SOMETHING EASY TO CARRY WHEN YOU'RE RUNNING. SOMETHING YOU CAN SHOOT ON THE FLY.
GOOD POINT. I WAS JUST THINKING ABOUT IF ONE OF US TOOK A STATIONARY POSITION AND COVERED THE OTHER--YOU A GOOD ENOUGH SHOT FOR THAT? I'M NOT.
ME NEITHER. TAKE THIS ONE.
GOOD IDEA, THOUGH.
WE'RE DONE IN THERE.
I'LL LOCK IT UP IN A MINUTE.
GOOD LUCK OUT THERE, BOYS.
UM...
HI...

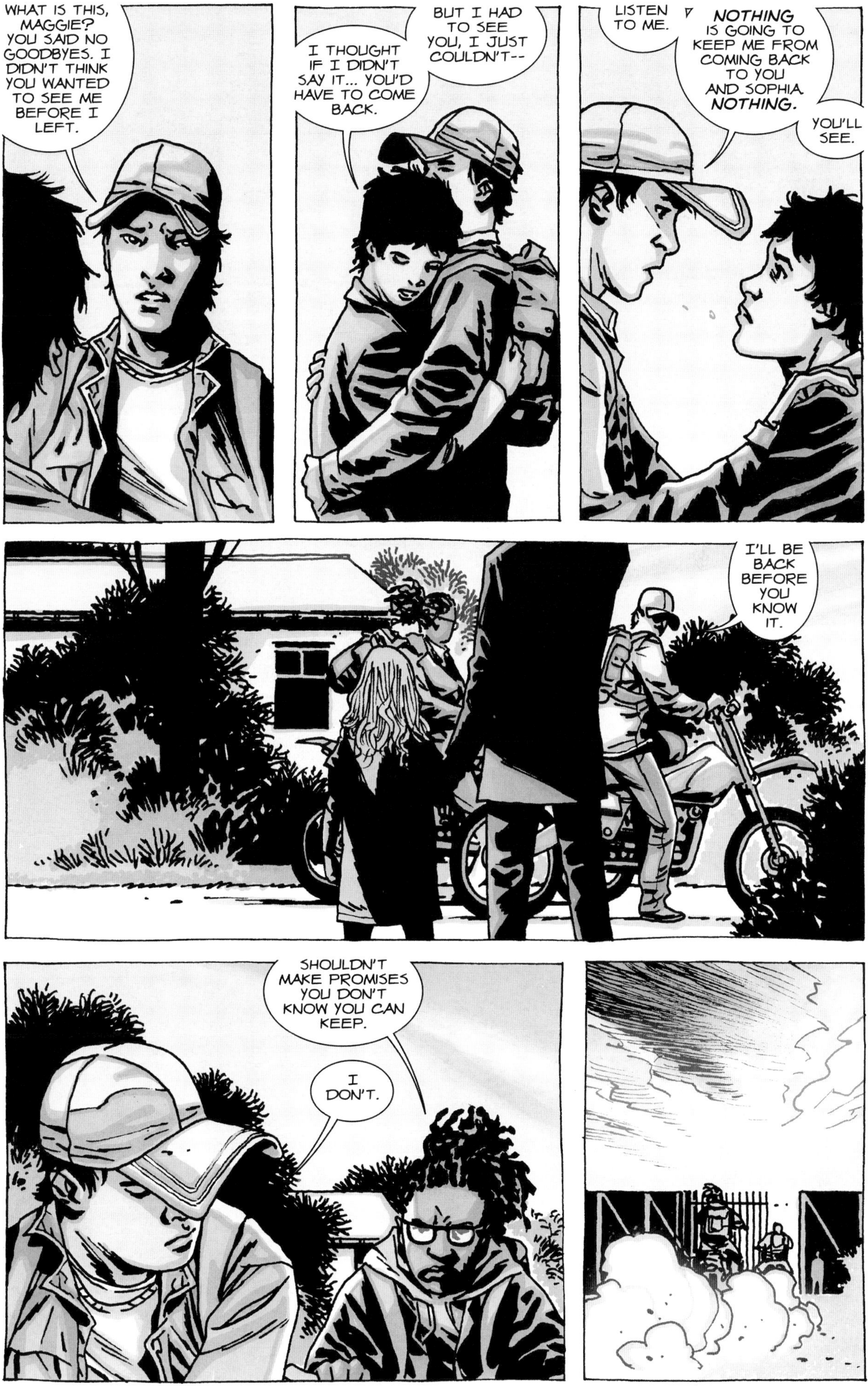
WHAT IS THIS, MAGGIE? YOU SAID NO GOODBYES. I DIDN'T THINK YOU WANTED TO SEE ME BEFORE I LEFT.
I THOUGHT IF I DIDN'T SAY IT... YOU'D HAVE TO COME BACK.
BUT I HAD TO SEE YOU, I JUST COULDN'T--
LISTEN TO ME.
NOTHING IS GOING TO KEEP ME FROM COMING BACK TO YOU AND SOPHIA. NOTHING.
YOU'LL SEE.
I'LL BE BACK BEFORE YOU KNOW IT.
SHOULDN'T MAKE PROMISES YOU DON'T KNOW YOU CAN KEEP.
I DON'T.

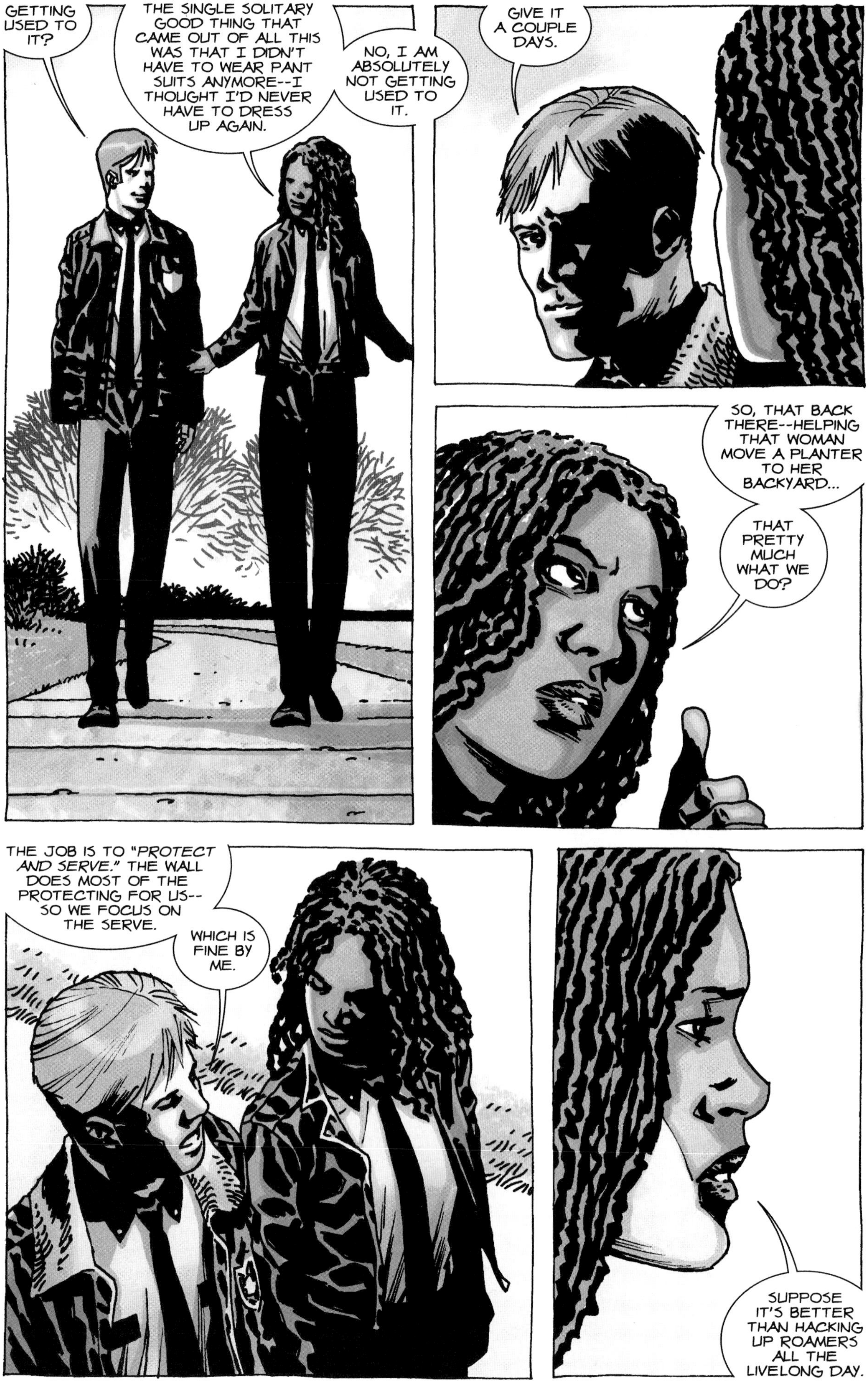
GETTING USED TO IT?
THE SINGLE SOLITARY GOOD THING THAT CAME OUT OF ALL THIS WAS THAT I DIDN'T HAVE TO WEAR PANT SUITS ANYMORE--I THOUGHT I'D NEVER HAVE TO DRESS UP AGAIN.
NO, I AM ABSOLUTELY NOT GETTING USED TO IT.
GIVE IT A COUPLE DAYS.
SO, THAT BACK THERE--HELPING THAT WOMAN MOVE A PLANTER TO HER BACKYARD...
THAT PRETTY MUCH WHAT WE DO?
THE JOB IS TO "*PROTECT AND SERVE.*" THE WALL DOES MOST OF THE PROTECTING FOR US--SO WE FOCUS ON THE SERVE.
WHICH IS FINE BY ME.
SUPPOSE IT'S BETTER THAN HACKING UP ROAMERS ALL THE LIVELONG DAY.

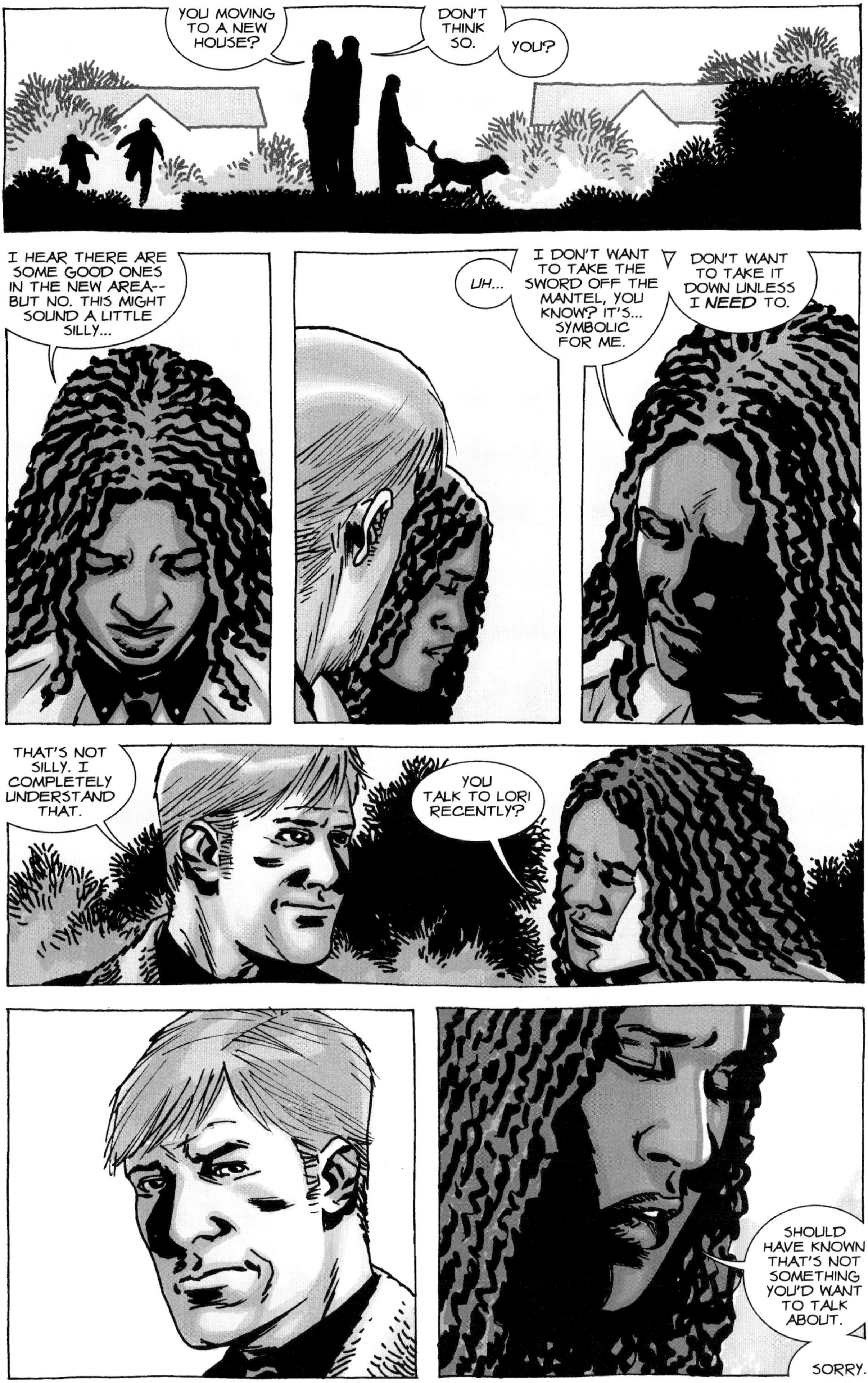
YOU MOVING TO A NEW HOUSE?
DON'T THINK SO.
YOU?
I HEAR THERE ARE SOME GOOD ONES IN THE NEW AREA-- BUT NO. THIS MIGHT SOUND A LITTLE SILLY...
UH...
I DON'T WANT TO TAKE THE SWORD OFF THE MANTEL, YOU KNOW? IT'S... SYMBOLIC FOR ME.
DON'T WANT TO TAKE IT DOWN UNLESS I NEED TO.
THAT'S NOT SILLY. I COMPLETELY UNDERSTAND THAT.
YOU TALK TO LORI RECENTLY?
SHOULD HAVE KNOWN THAT'S NOT SOMETHING YOU'D WANT TO TALK ABOUT.
SORRY.

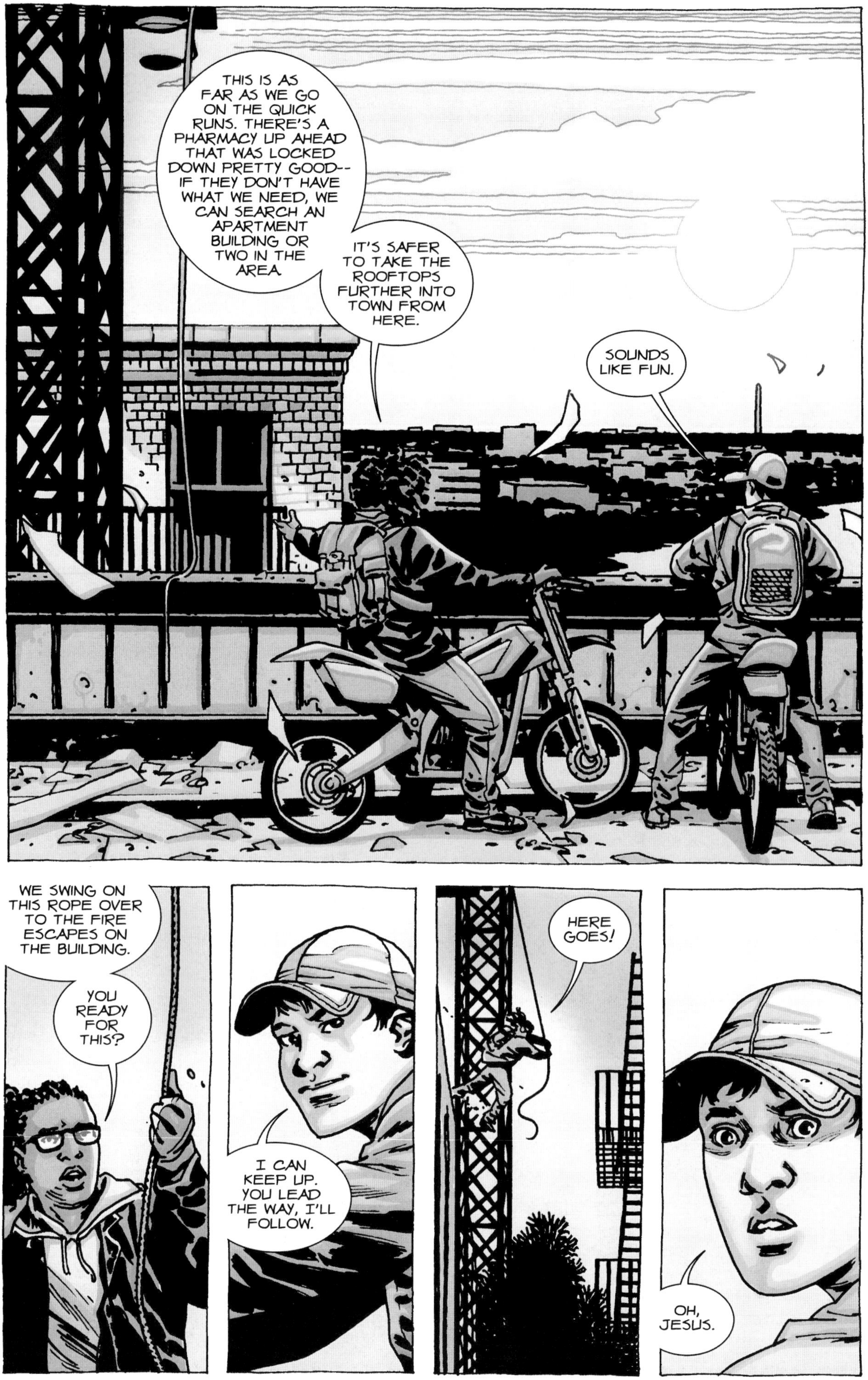
THIS IS AS FAR AS WE GO ON THE QUICK RUNS. THERE'S A PHARMACY UP AHEAD THAT WAS LOCKED DOWN PRETTY GOOD-- IF THEY DON'T HAVE WHAT WE NEED, WE CAN SEARCH AN APARTMENT BUILDING OR TWO IN THE AREA.
IT'S SAFER TO TAKE THE ROOFTOPS FURTHER INTO TOWN FROM HERE.
SOUNDS LIKE FUN.
WE SWING ON THIS ROPE OVER TO THE FIRE ESCAPES ON THE BUILDING.
YOU READY FOR THIS?
I CAN KEEP UP. YOU LEAD THE WAY, I'LL FOLLOW.
HERE GOES!
OH, JESUS.

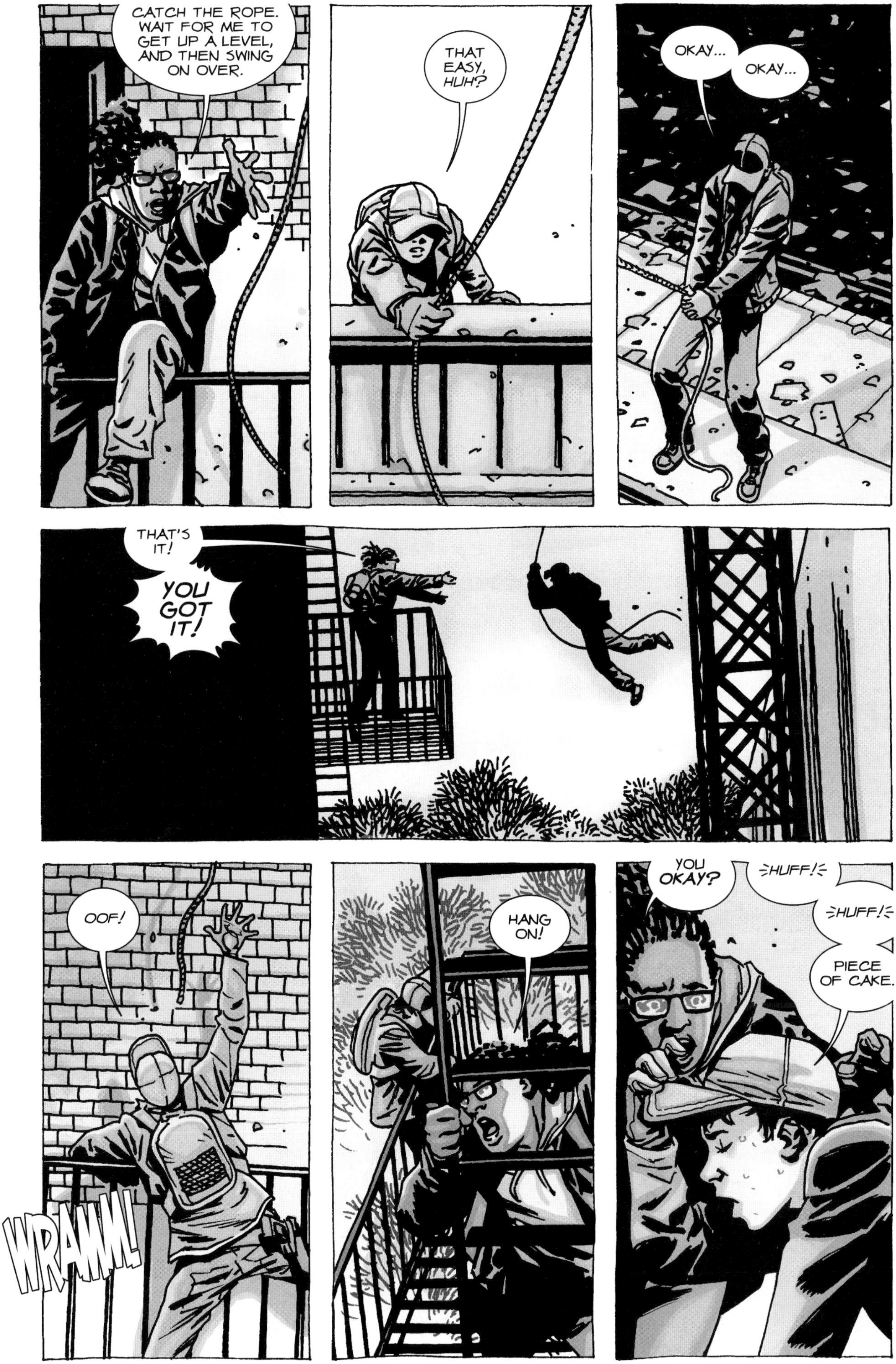
CATCH THE ROPE. WAIT FOR ME TO GET UP A LEVEL, AND THEN SWING ON OVER.
THAT EASY, HUH?
OKAY...
OKAY...
THAT'S IT!
YOU GOT IT!
OOF!
WRAMM!
HANG ON!
YOU OKAY?
HUFF!
HUFF!
PIECE OF CAKE.

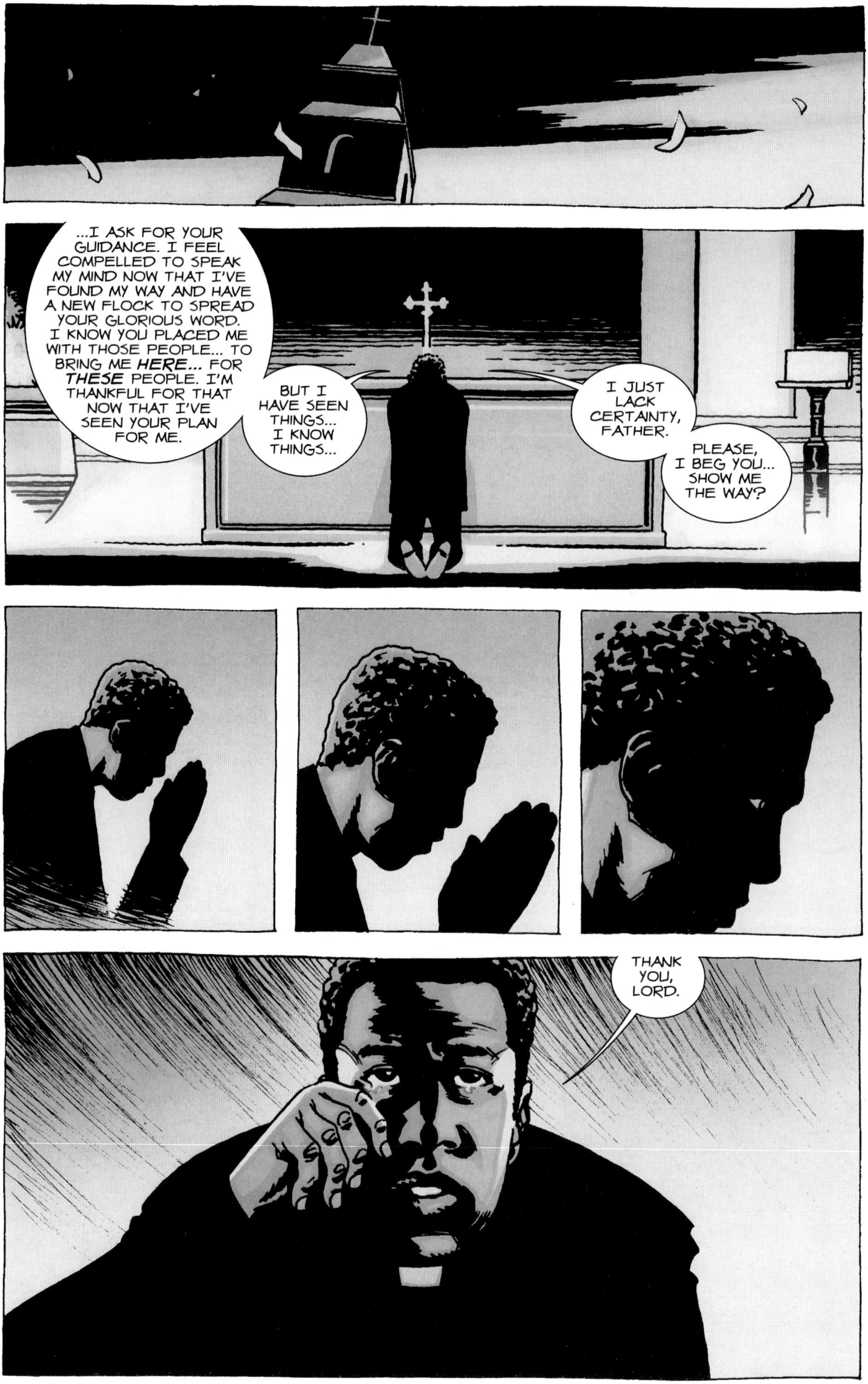

...I ASK FOR YOUR GUIDANCE. I FEEL COMPELLED TO SPEAK MY MIND NOW THAT I'VE FOUND MY WAY AND HAVE A NEW FLOCK TO SPREAD YOUR GLORIOUS WORD. I KNOW YOU PLACED ME WITH THOSE PEOPLE... TO BRING ME *HERE...* FOR *THESE* PEOPLE. I'M THANKFUL FOR THAT NOW THAT I'VE SEEN YOUR PLAN FOR ME.
BUT I HAVE SEEN THINGS... I KNOW THINGS...
I JUST LACK CERTAINTY, FATHER.
PLEASE, I BEG YOU... SHOW ME THE WAY?
THANK YOU, LORD.

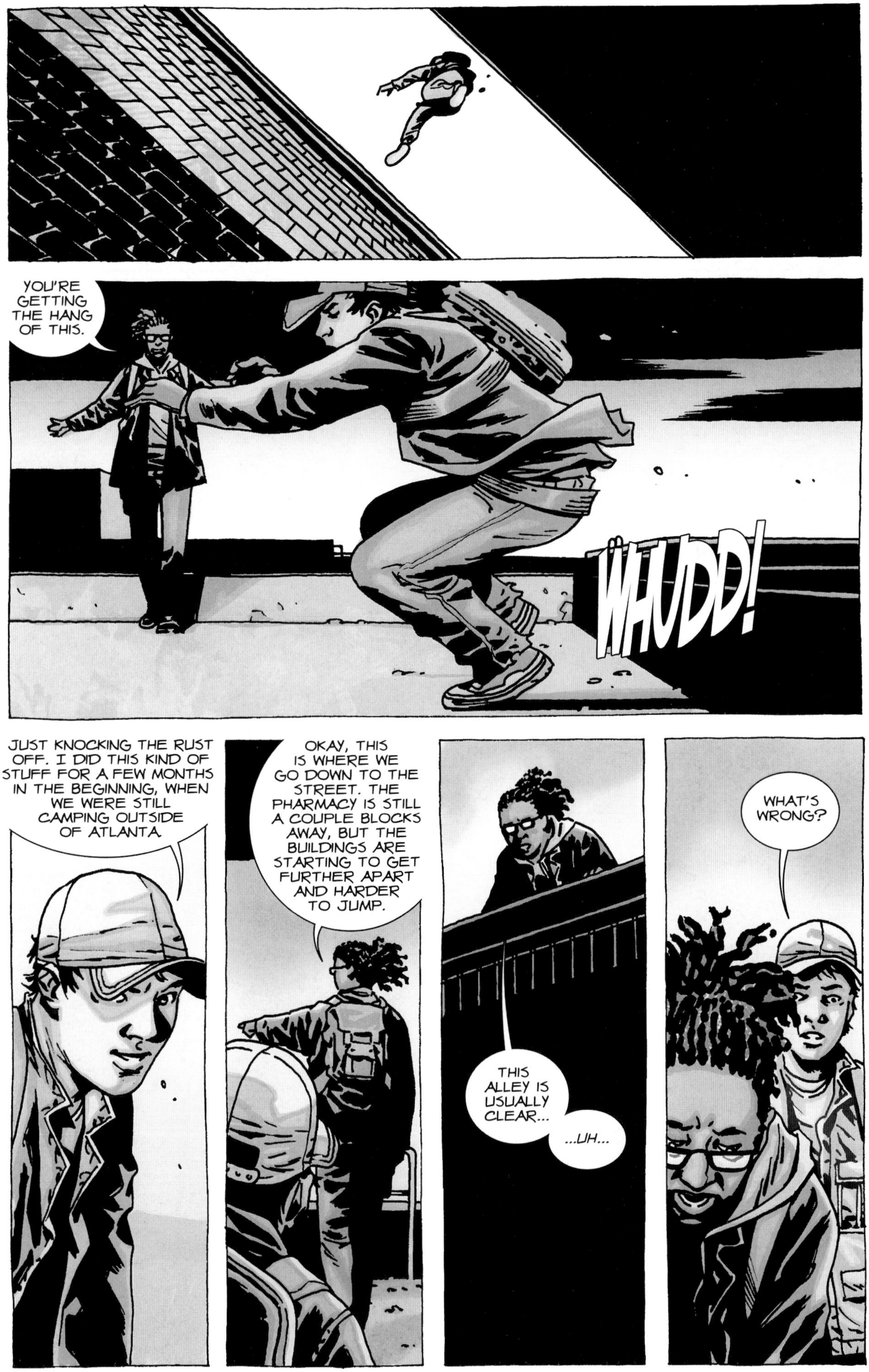
YOU'RE GETTING THE HANG OF THIS.
WHUDD!
JUST KNOCKING THE RUST OFF. I DID THIS KIND OF STUFF FOR A FEW MONTHS IN THE BEGINNING, WHEN WE WERE STILL CAMPING OUTSIDE OF ATLANTA.
OKAY, THIS IS WHERE WE GO DOWN TO THE STREET. THE PHARMACY IS STILL A COUPLE BLOCKS AWAY, BUT THE BUILDINGS ARE STARTING TO GET FURTHER APART AND HARDER TO JUMP.
THIS ALLEY IS USUALLY CLEAR...
...UH...
WHAT'S WRONG?

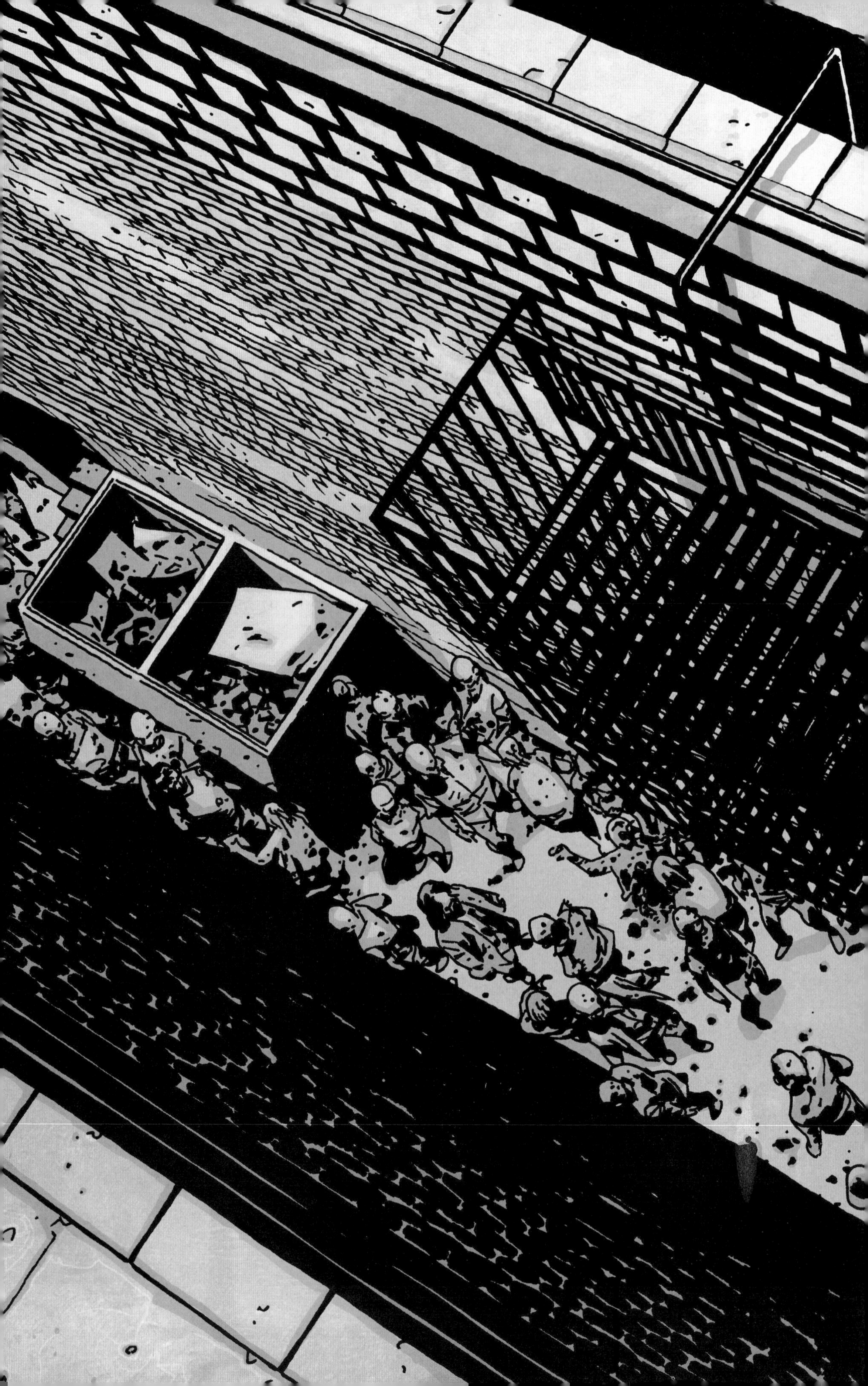

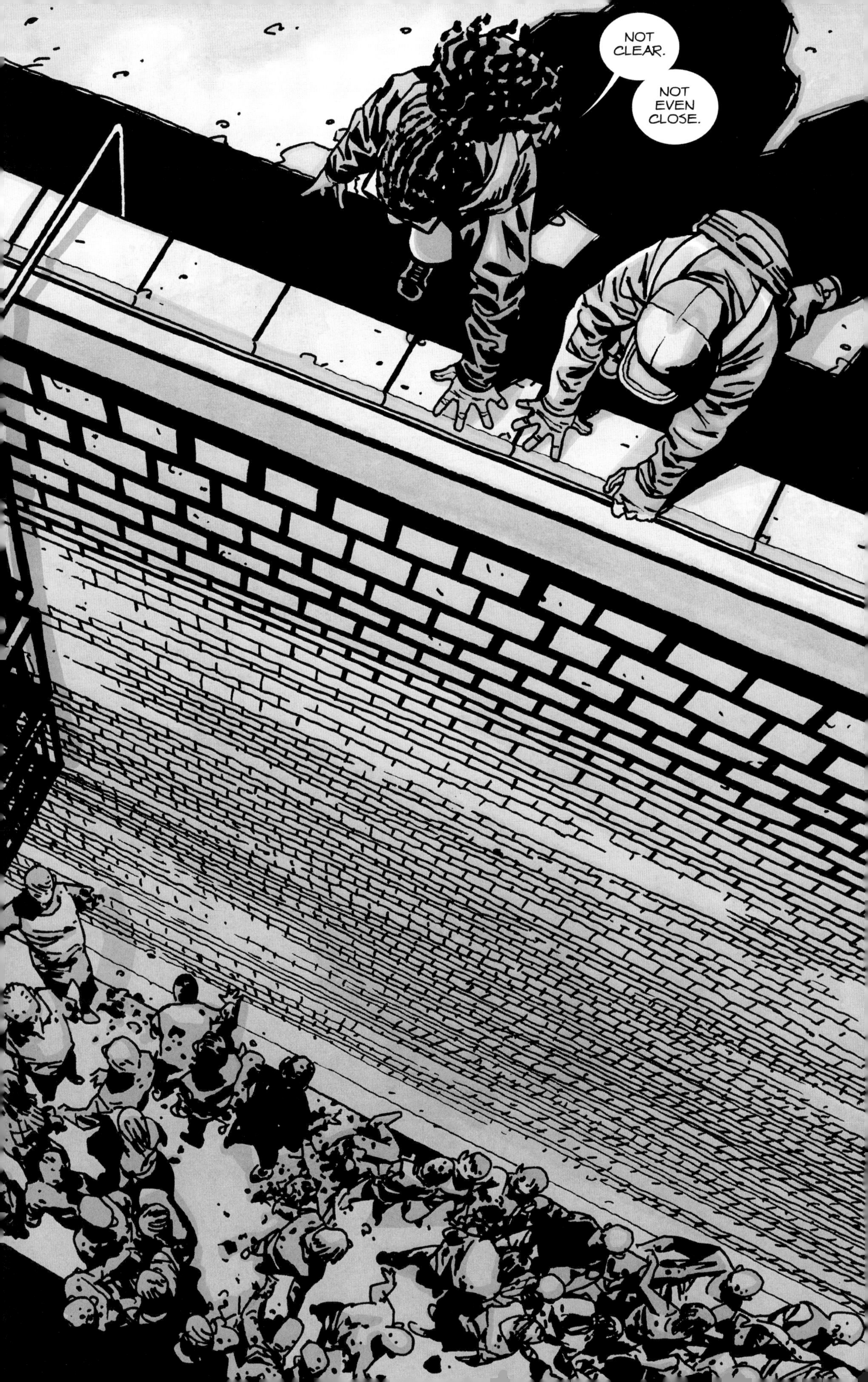
NOT CLEAR.
NOT EVEN CLOSE.

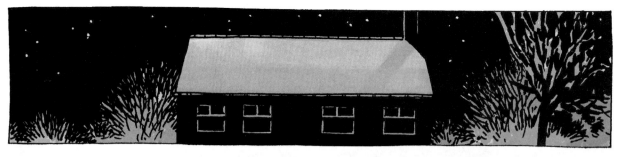

WHAT IS IT YOU WANTED TO TALK TO ME ABOUT, GABRIEL?

I'M SORRY, SIR. THIS JUST COULDN'T WAIT.

I'M SO VERY THANKFUL YOU'VE ALLOWED US TO COME LIVE HERE. THE PEOPLE HERE ARE SO KIND AND ACCEPTING.

AS HAPPY AS I AM THAT YOU LET US IN, I FEAR YOU MAY HAVE MADE A GRAVE MISTAKE IN DOING SO.

THESE PEOPLE WHO WERE WITH ME, ARE *NOT* GOOD PEOPLE. THEY'VE DONE THINGS... *HORRIBLE* THINGS...

...UNSPEAKABLE THINGS.

THEY SIMPLY DON'T *BELONG* HERE.

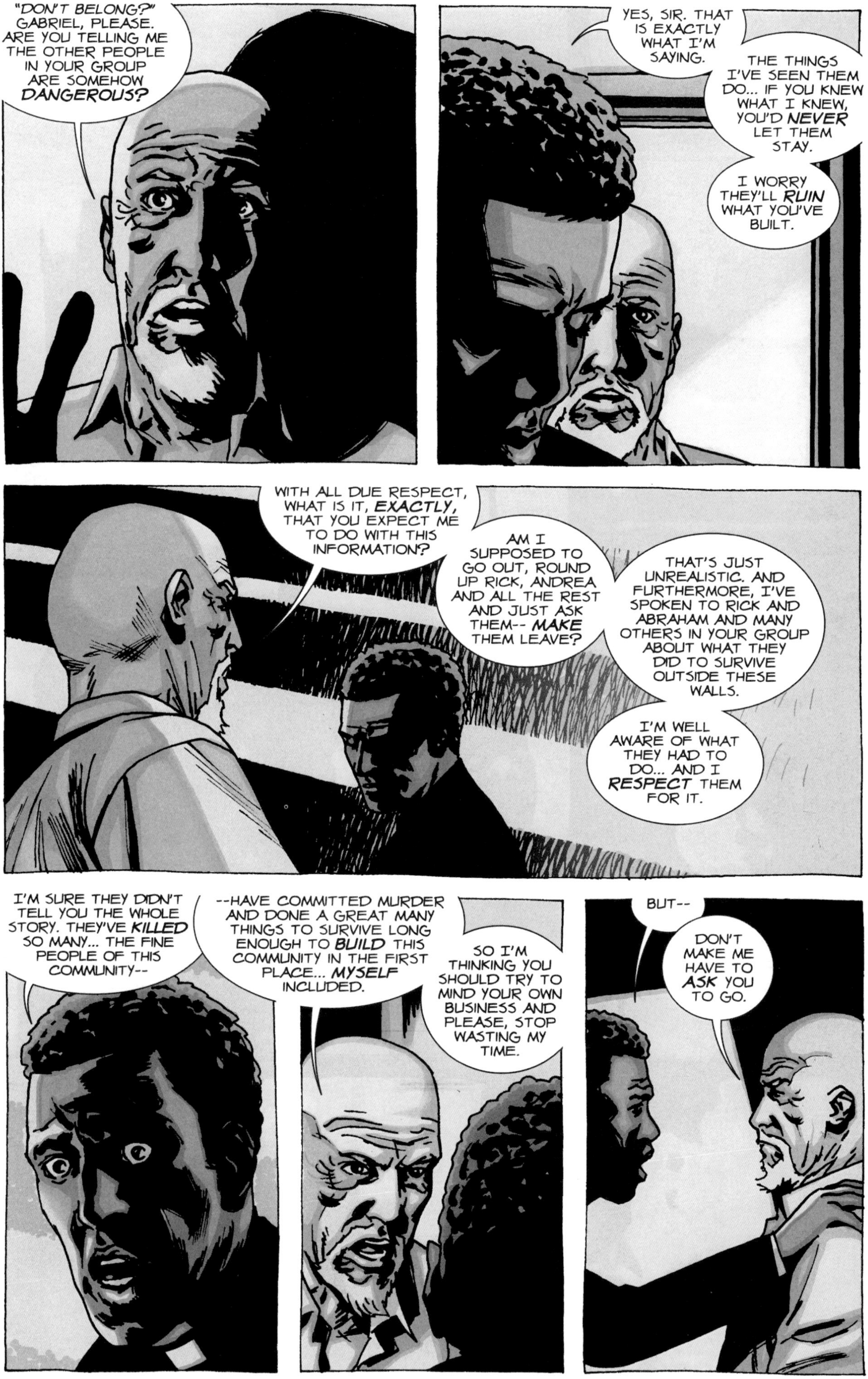
"DON'T BELONG?" GABRIEL, PLEASE. ARE YOU TELLING ME THE OTHER PEOPLE IN YOUR GROUP ARE SOMEHOW DANGEROUS?
YES, SIR. THAT IS EXACTLY WHAT I'M SAYING.
THE THINGS I'VE SEEN THEM DO... IF YOU KNEW WHAT I KNEW, YOU'D NEVER LET THEM STAY.
I WORRY THEY'LL RUIN WHAT YOU'VE BUILT.
WITH ALL DUE RESPECT, WHAT IS IT, EXACTLY, THAT YOU EXPECT ME TO DO WITH THIS INFORMATION?
AM I SUPPOSED TO GO OUT, ROUND UP RICK, ANDREA AND ALL THE REST AND JUST ASK THEM-- MAKE THEM LEAVE?
THAT'S JUST UNREALISTIC. AND FURTHERMORE, I'VE SPOKEN TO RICK AND ABRAHAM AND MANY OTHERS IN YOUR GROUP ABOUT WHAT THEY DID TO SURVIVE OUTSIDE THESE WALLS.
I'M WELL AWARE OF WHAT THEY HAD TO DO... AND I RESPECT THEM FOR IT.
I'M SURE THEY DIDN'T TELL YOU THE WHOLE STORY. THEY'VE KILLED SO MANY... THE FINE PEOPLE OF THIS COMMUNITY--
--HAVE COMMITTED MURDER AND DONE A GREAT MANY THINGS TO SURVIVE LONG ENOUGH TO BUILD THIS COMMUNITY IN THE FIRST PLACE... MYSELF INCLUDED.
SO I'M THINKING YOU SHOULD TRY TO MIND YOUR OWN BUSINESS AND PLEASE, STOP WASTING MY TIME.
BUT--
DON'T MAKE ME HAVE TO ASK YOU TO GO.

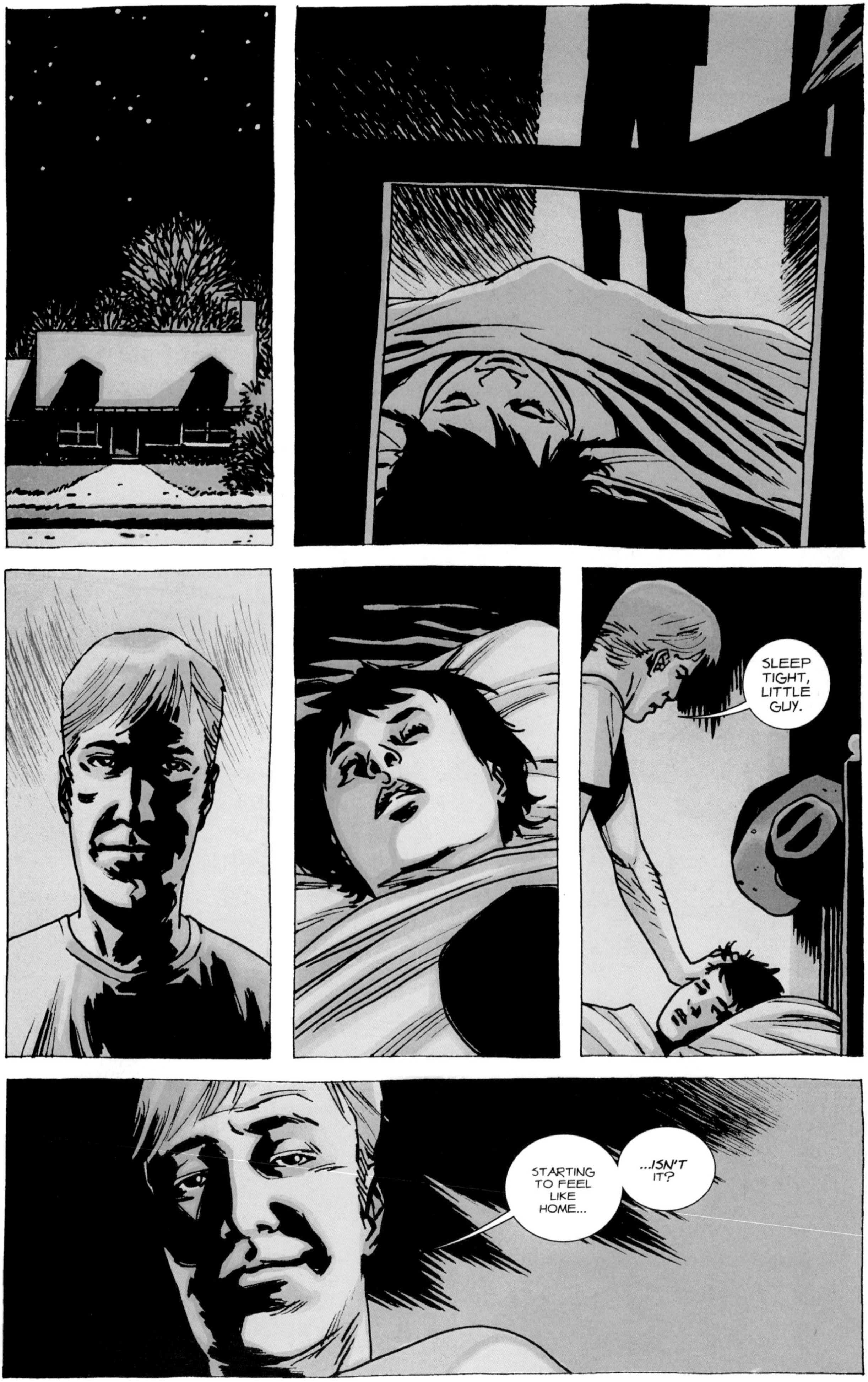
SLEEP TIGHT, LITTLE GUY.
STARTING TO FEEL LIKE HOME...
...ISN'T IT?

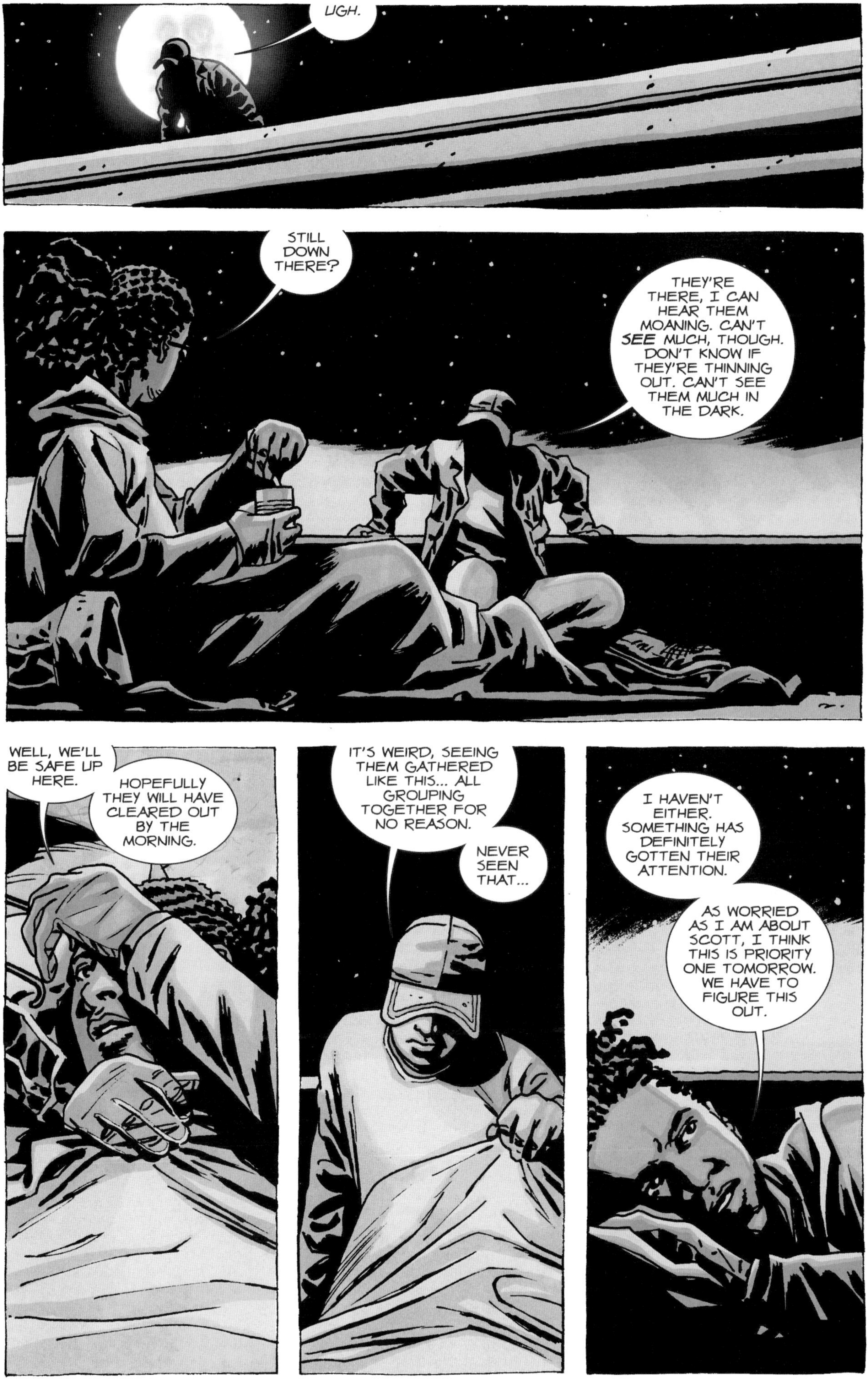
UGH.
STILL DOWN THERE?
THEY'RE THERE, I CAN HEAR THEM MOANING. CAN'T SEE MUCH, THOUGH. DON'T KNOW IF THEY'RE THINNING OUT. CAN'T SEE THEM MUCH IN THE DARK.
WELL, WE'LL BE SAFE UP HERE.
HOPEFULLY THEY WILL HAVE CLEARED OUT BY THE MORNING.
IT'S WEIRD, SEEING THEM GATHERED LIKE THIS... ALL GROUPING TOGETHER FOR NO REASON.
NEVER SEEN THAT...
I HAVEN'T EITHER. SOMETHING HAS DEFINITELY GOTTEN THEIR ATTENTION.
AS WORRIED AS I AM ABOUT SCOTT, I THINK THIS IS PRIORITY ONE TOMORROW. WE HAVE TO FIGURE THIS OUT.

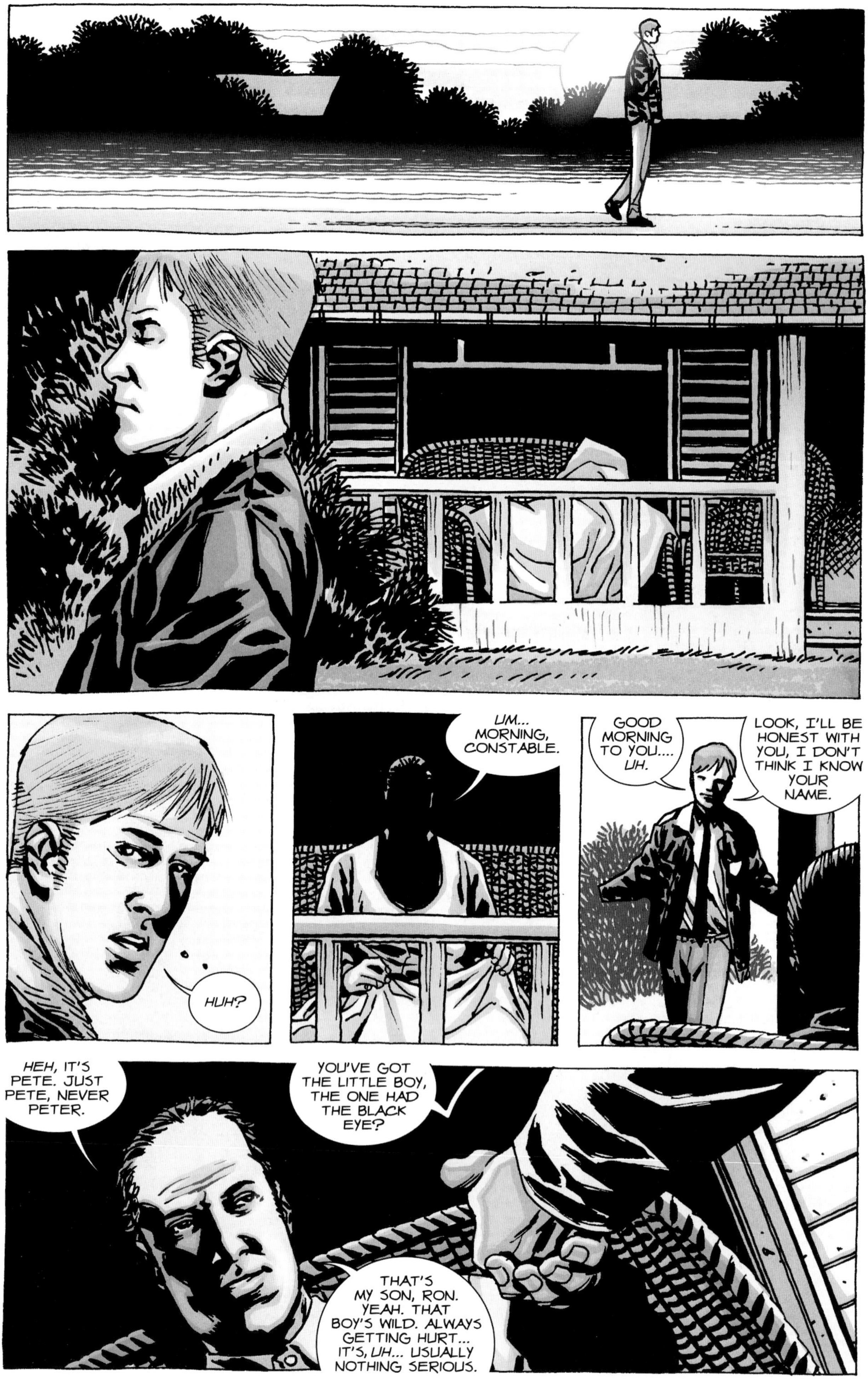
HUH?
UM... MORNING, CONSTABLE.
GOOD MORNING TO YOU.... UH.
LOOK, I'LL BE HONEST WITH YOU, I DON'T THINK I KNOW YOUR NAME.
HEH, IT'S PETE. JUST PETE, NEVER PETER.
YOU'VE GOT THE LITTLE BOY, THE ONE HAD THE BLACK EYE?
THAT'S MY SON, RON. YEAH. THAT BOY'S WILD. ALWAYS GETTING HURT... IT'S, UH... USUALLY NOTHING SERIOUS.

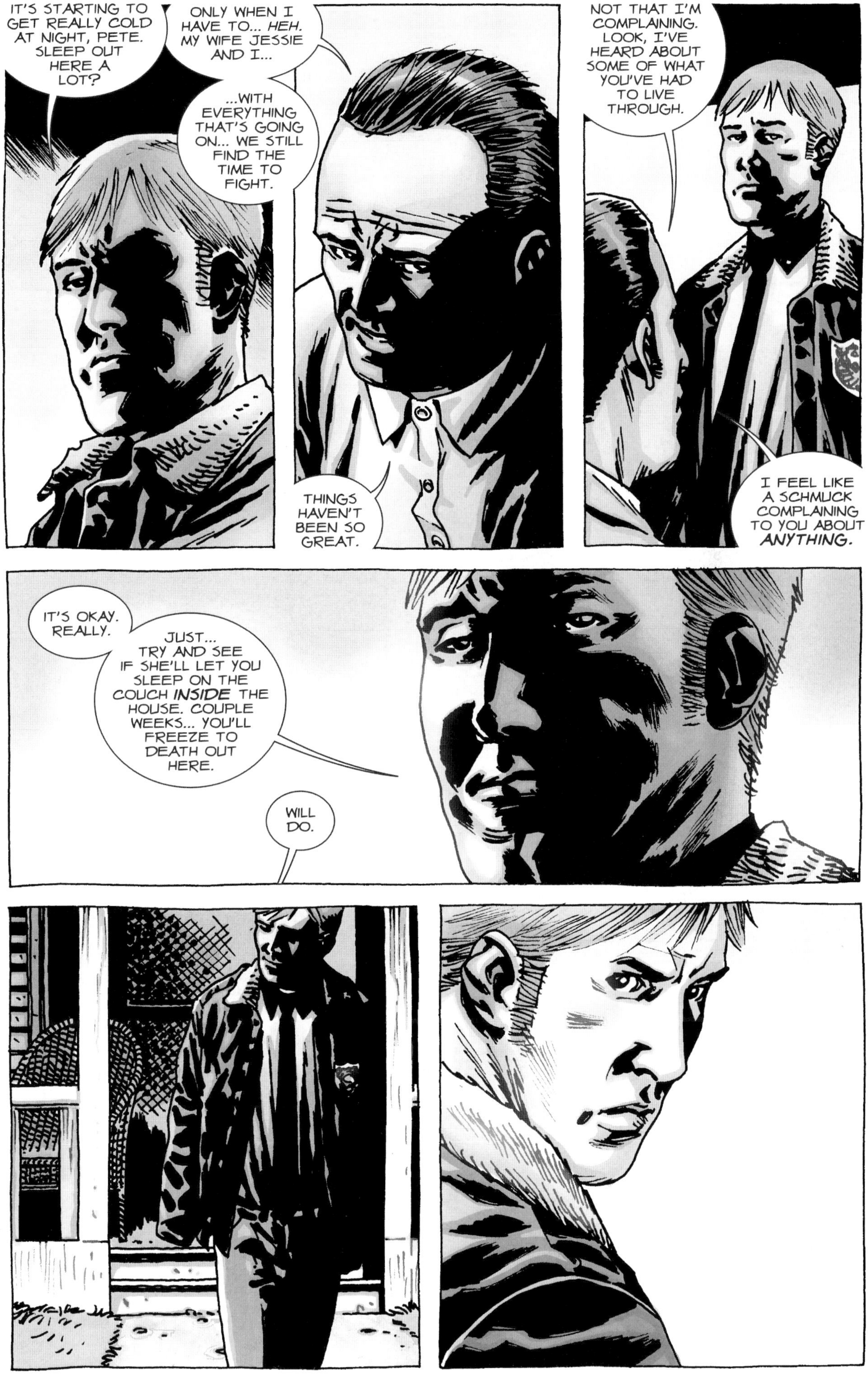
IT'S STARTING TO GET REALLY COLD AT NIGHT, PETE. SLEEP OUT HERE A LOT?
ONLY WHEN I HAVE TO... HEH. MY WIFE JESSIE AND I...
...WITH EVERYTHING THAT'S GOING ON... WE STILL FIND THE TIME TO FIGHT.
THINGS HAVEN'T BEEN SO GREAT.
NOT THAT I'M COMPLAINING. LOOK, I'VE HEARD ABOUT SOME OF WHAT YOU'VE HAD TO LIVE THROUGH.
I FEEL LIKE A SCHMUCK COMPLAINING TO YOU ABOUT ANYTHING.
IT'S OKAY. REALLY.
JUST... TRY AND SEE IF SHE'LL LET YOU SLEEP ON THE COUCH INSIDE THE HOUSE. COUPLE WEEKS... YOU'LL FREEZE TO DEATH OUT HERE.
WILL DO.

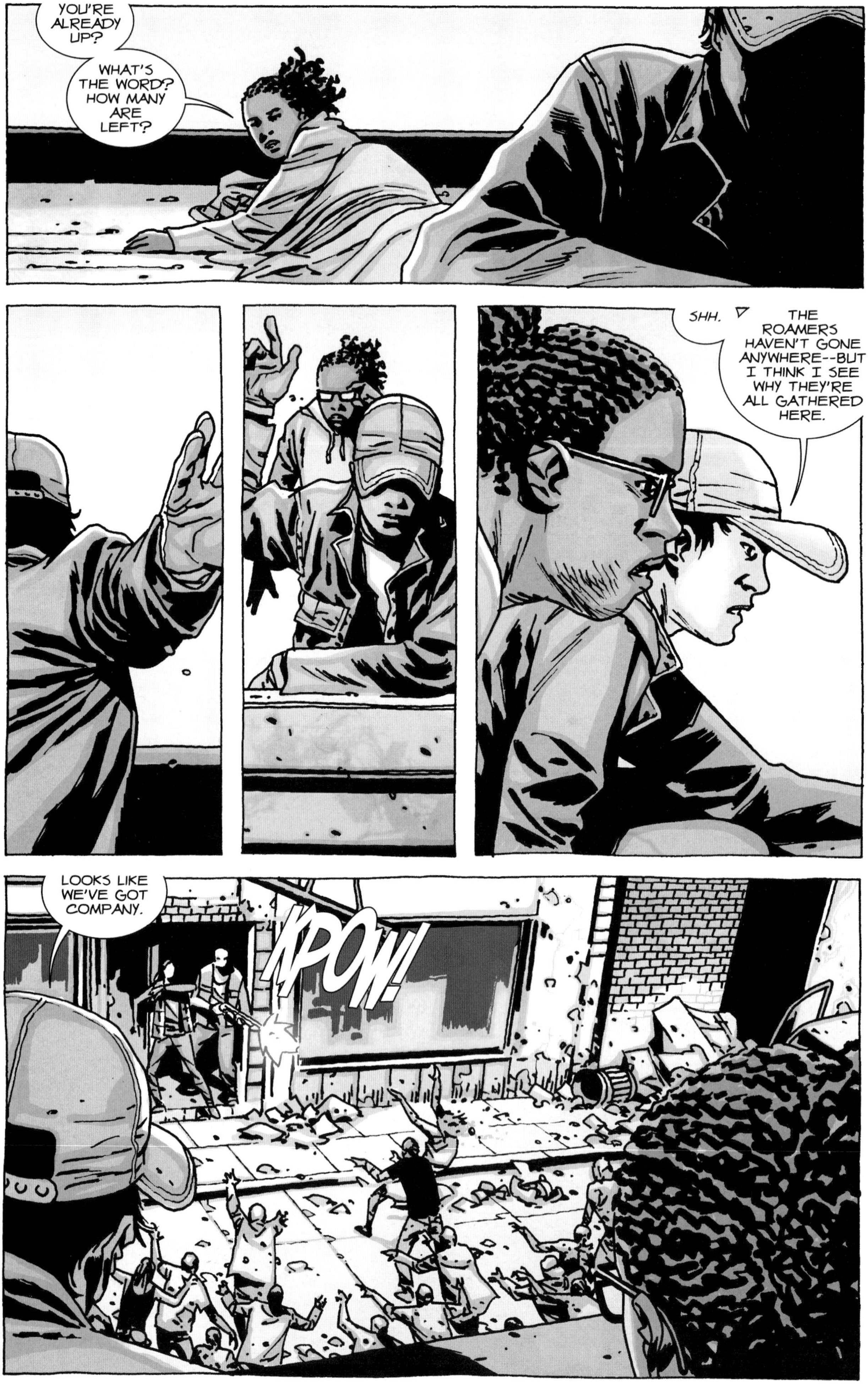
YOU'RE ALREADY UP?
WHAT'S THE WORD? HOW MANY ARE LEFT?
SHH.
THE ROAMERS HAVEN'T GONE ANYWHERE--BUT I THINK I SEE WHY THEY'RE ALL GATHERED HERE.
LOOKS LIKE WE'VE GOT COMPANY.
KPOW!

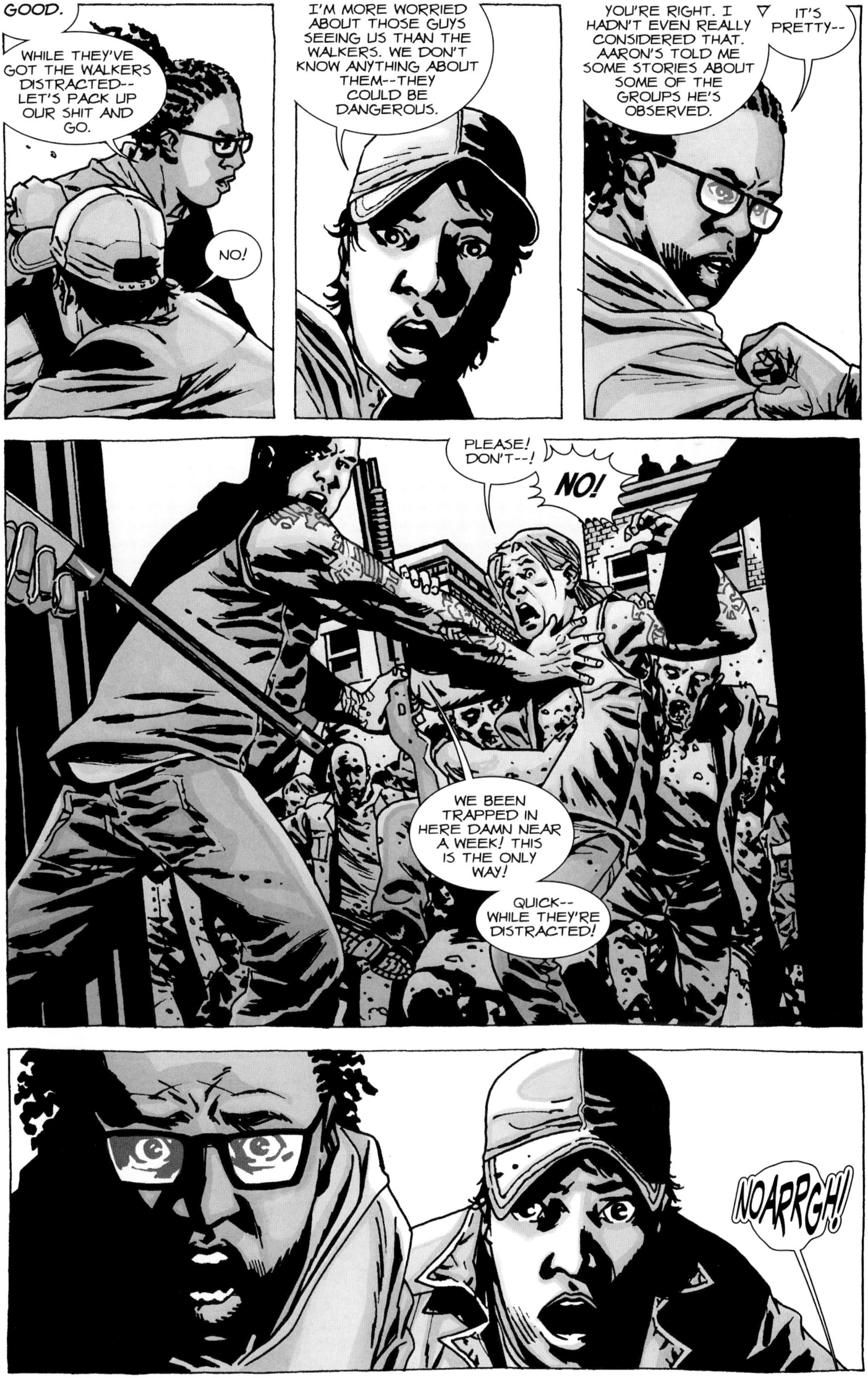
GOOD.
WHILE THEY'VE GOT THE WALKERS DISTRACTED-- LET'S PACK UP OUR SHIT AND GO.
NO!
I'M MORE WORRIED ABOUT THOSE GUYS SEEING US THAN THE WALKERS. WE DON'T KNOW ANYTHING ABOUT THEM--THEY COULD BE DANGEROUS.
YOU'RE RIGHT. I HADN'T EVEN REALLY CONSIDERED THAT. AARON'S TOLD ME SOME STORIES ABOUT SOME OF THE GROUPS HE'S OBSERVED.
IT'S PRETTY--
PLEASE! DON'T--!
NO!
WE BEEN TRAPPED IN HERE DAMN NEAR A WEEK! THIS IS THE ONLY WAY!
QUICK-- WHILE THEY'RE DISTRACTED!
NOARRGH!

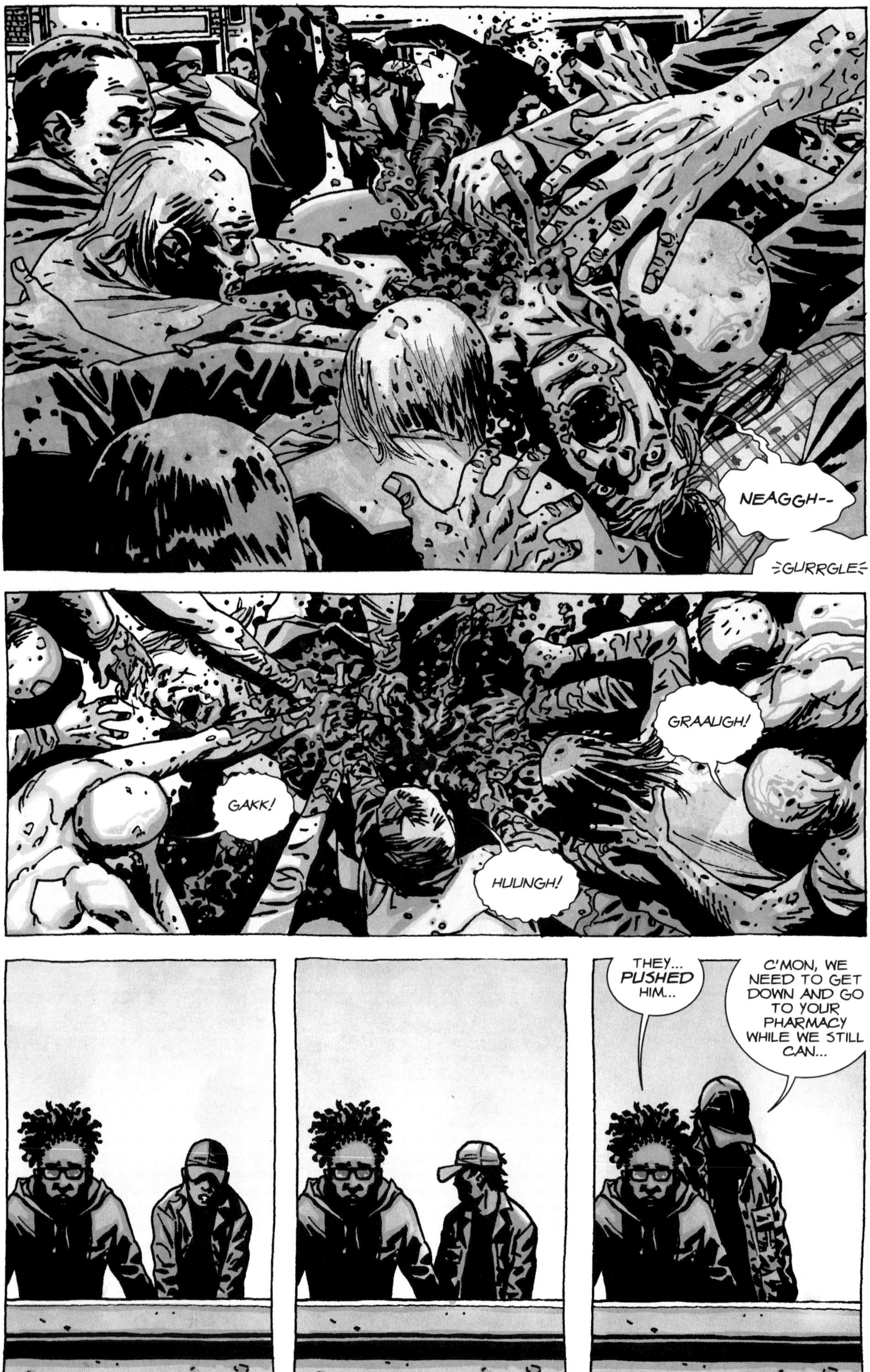
NEAGGH--
GURRGLE
GRAAUGH!
GAKK!
HUUNGH!
THEY... PUSHED HIM...
C'MON, WE NEED TO GET DOWN AND GO TO YOUR PHARMACY WHILE WE STILL CAN...

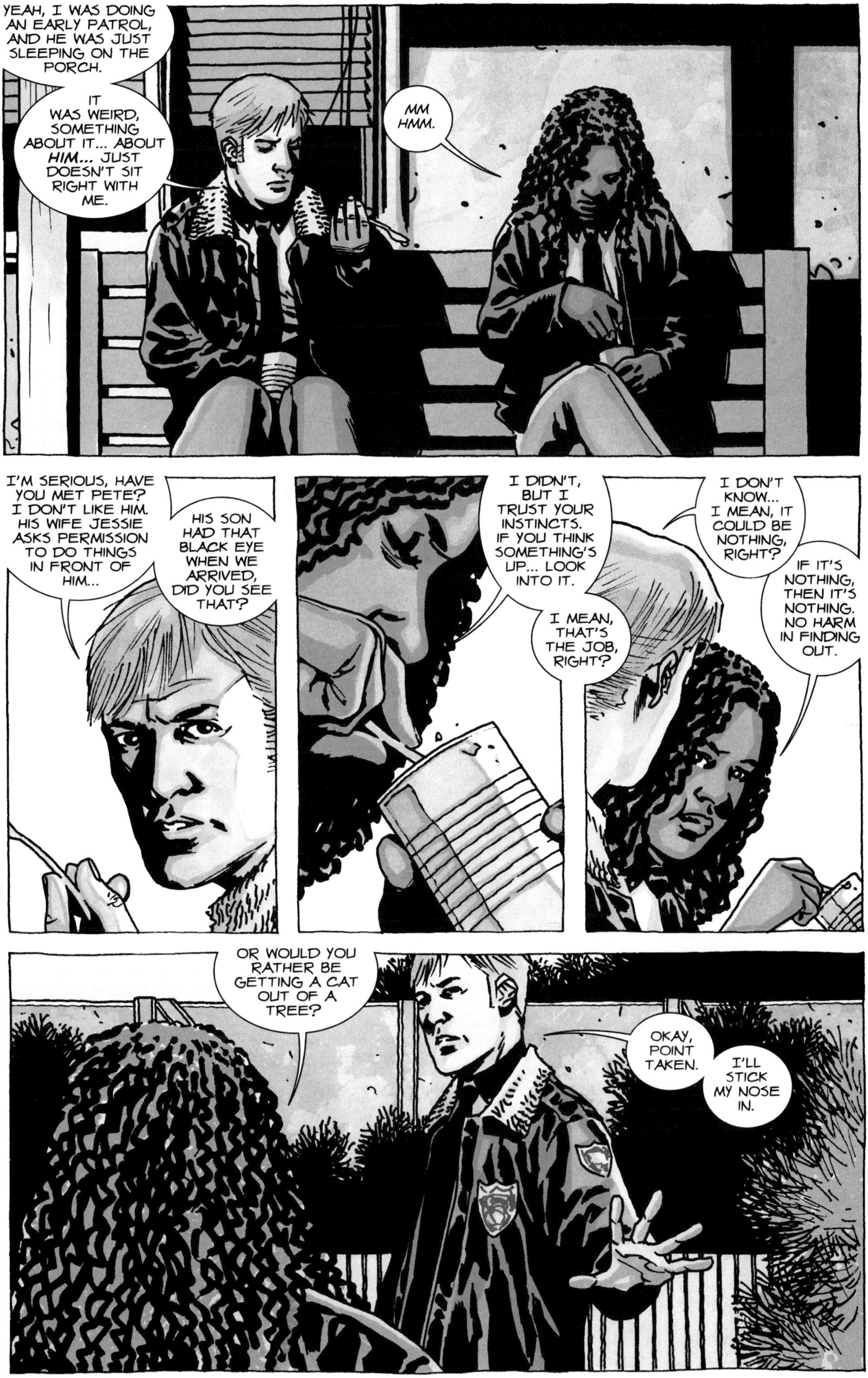

YEAH, I WAS DOING AN EARLY PATROL, AND HE WAS JUST SLEEPING ON THE PORCH.
IT WAS WEIRD, SOMETHING ABOUT IT... ABOUT *HIM...* JUST DOESN'T SIT RIGHT WITH ME.
MM HMM.
I'M SERIOUS, HAVE YOU MET PETE? I DON'T LIKE HIM. HIS WIFE JESSIE ASKS PERMISSION TO DO THINGS IN FRONT OF HIM...
HIS SON HAD THAT BLACK EYE WHEN WE ARRIVED, DID YOU SEE THAT?
I DIDN'T, BUT I TRUST YOUR INSTINCTS. IF YOU THINK SOMETHING'S UP... LOOK INTO IT.
I MEAN, THAT'S THE JOB, RIGHT?
I DON'T KNOW... I MEAN, IT COULD BE NOTHING, RIGHT?
IF IT'S NOTHING, THEN IT'S NOTHING. NO HARM IN FINDING OUT.
OR WOULD YOU RATHER BE GETTING A CAT OUT OF A TREE?
OKAY, POINT TAKEN.
I'LL STICK MY NOSE IN.

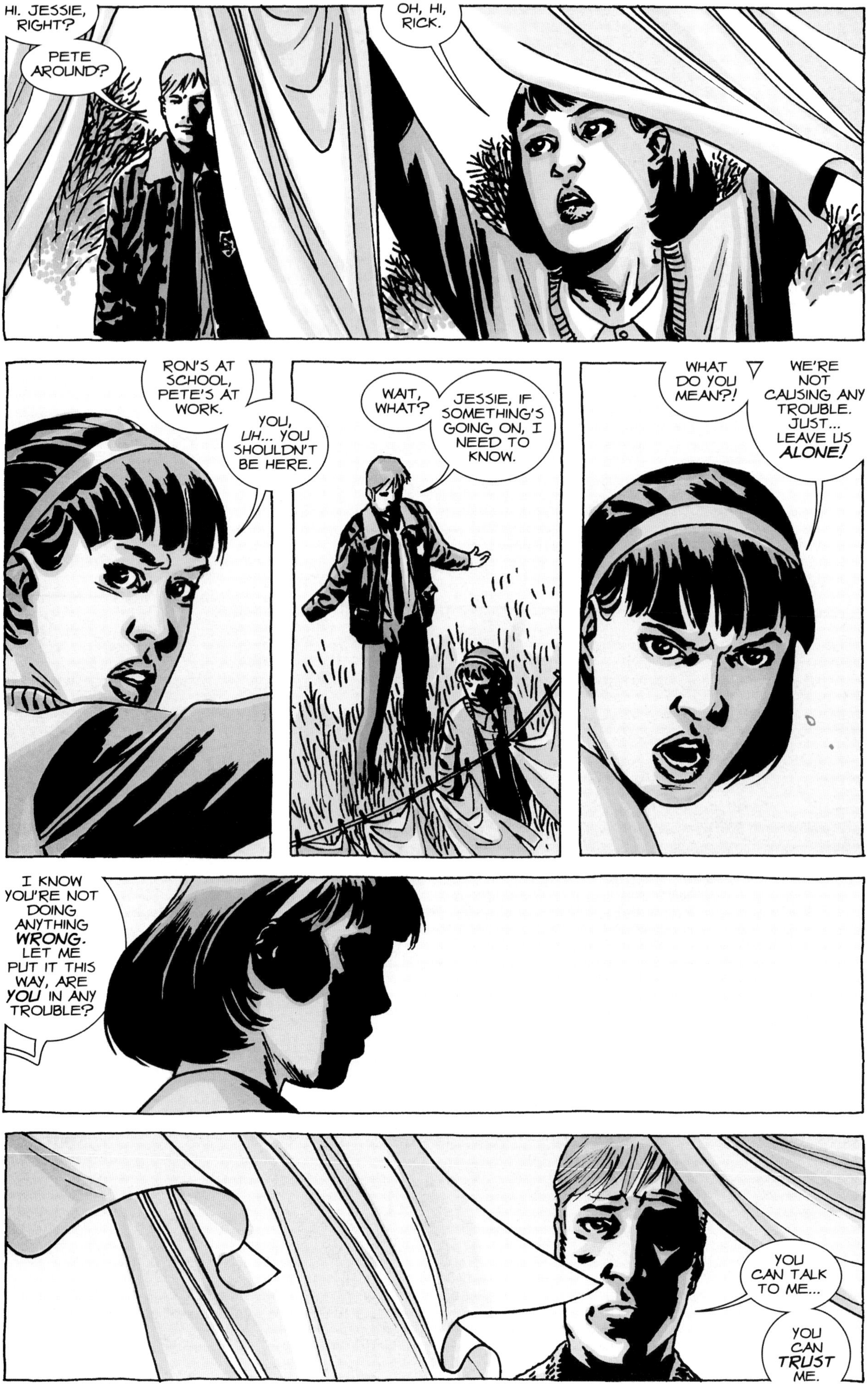
HI. JESSIE, RIGHT?
PETE AROUND?
OH, HI, RICK.
RON'S AT SCHOOL, PETE'S AT WORK.
YOU, UH... YOU SHOULDN'T BE HERE.
WAIT, WHAT?
JESSIE, IF SOMETHING'S GOING ON, I NEED TO KNOW.
WHAT DO YOU MEAN?!
WE'RE NOT CAUSING ANY TROUBLE. JUST... LEAVE US ALONE!
I KNOW YOU'RE NOT DOING ANYTHING WRONG. LET ME PUT IT THIS WAY, ARE YOU IN ANY TROUBLE?
YOU CAN TALK TO ME...
YOU CAN TRUST ME.

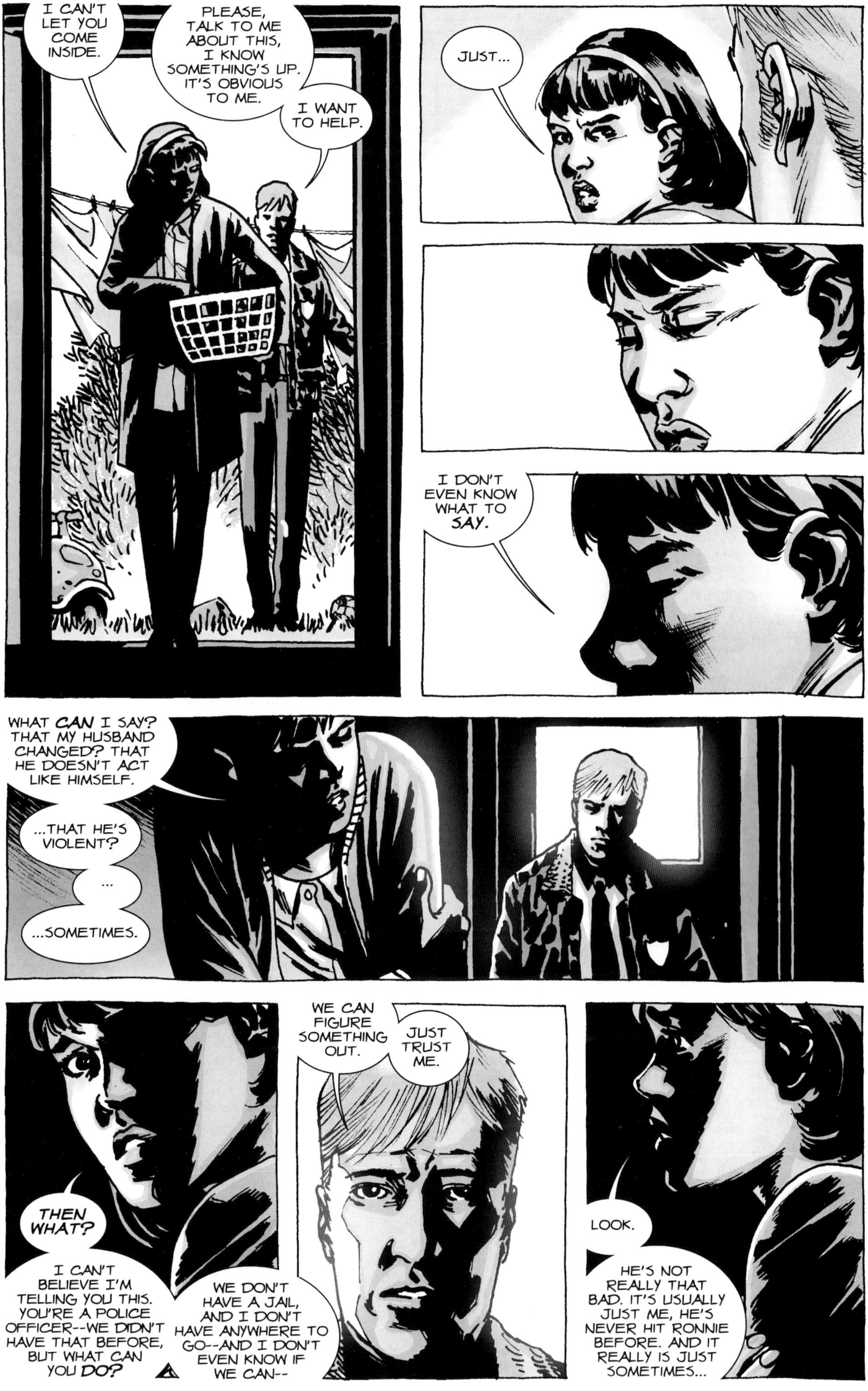
I CAN'T LET YOU COME INSIDE.
PLEASE, TALK TO ME ABOUT THIS, I KNOW SOMETHING'S UP. IT'S OBVIOUS TO ME.
I WANT TO HELP.
JUST...
I DON'T EVEN KNOW WHAT TO *SAY.*
WHAT *CAN* I SAY? THAT MY HUSBAND CHANGED? THAT HE DOESN'T ACT LIKE HIMSELF.
...THAT HE'S VIOLENT?
...
...SOMETIMES.
THEN WHAT?
I CAN'T BELIEVE I'M TELLING YOU THIS. YOU'RE A POLICE OFFICER--WE DIDN'T HAVE THAT BEFORE, BUT WHAT CAN YOU *DO?*
WE DON'T HAVE A JAIL, AND I DON'T HAVE ANYWHERE TO GO--AND I DON'T EVEN KNOW IF WE CAN--
WE CAN FIGURE SOMETHING OUT.
JUST TRUST ME.
LOOK.
HE'S NOT REALLY THAT BAD. IT'S USUALLY JUST ME, HE'S NEVER HIT RONNIE BEFORE. AND IT REALLY IS JUST SOMETIMES...

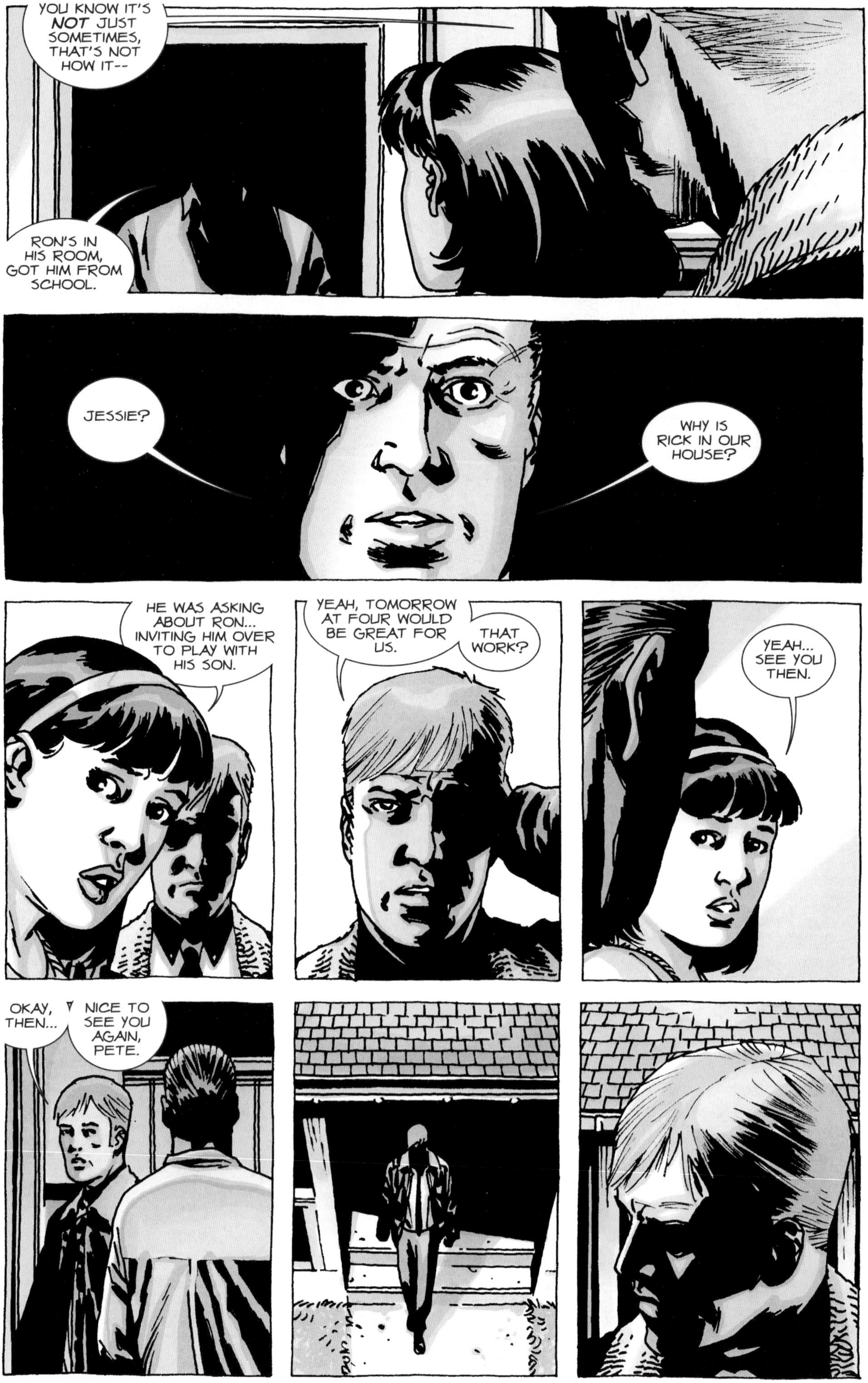
YOU KNOW IT'S NOT JUST SOMETIMES, THAT'S NOT HOW IT--
RON'S IN HIS ROOM, GOT HIM FROM SCHOOL.
JESSIE?
WHY IS RICK IN OUR HOUSE?
HE WAS ASKING ABOUT RON... INVITING HIM OVER TO PLAY WITH HIS SON.
YEAH, TOMORROW AT FOUR WOULD BE GREAT FOR US.
THAT WORK?
YEAH... SEE YOU THEN.
OKAY, THEN...
NICE TO SEE YOU AGAIN, PETE.

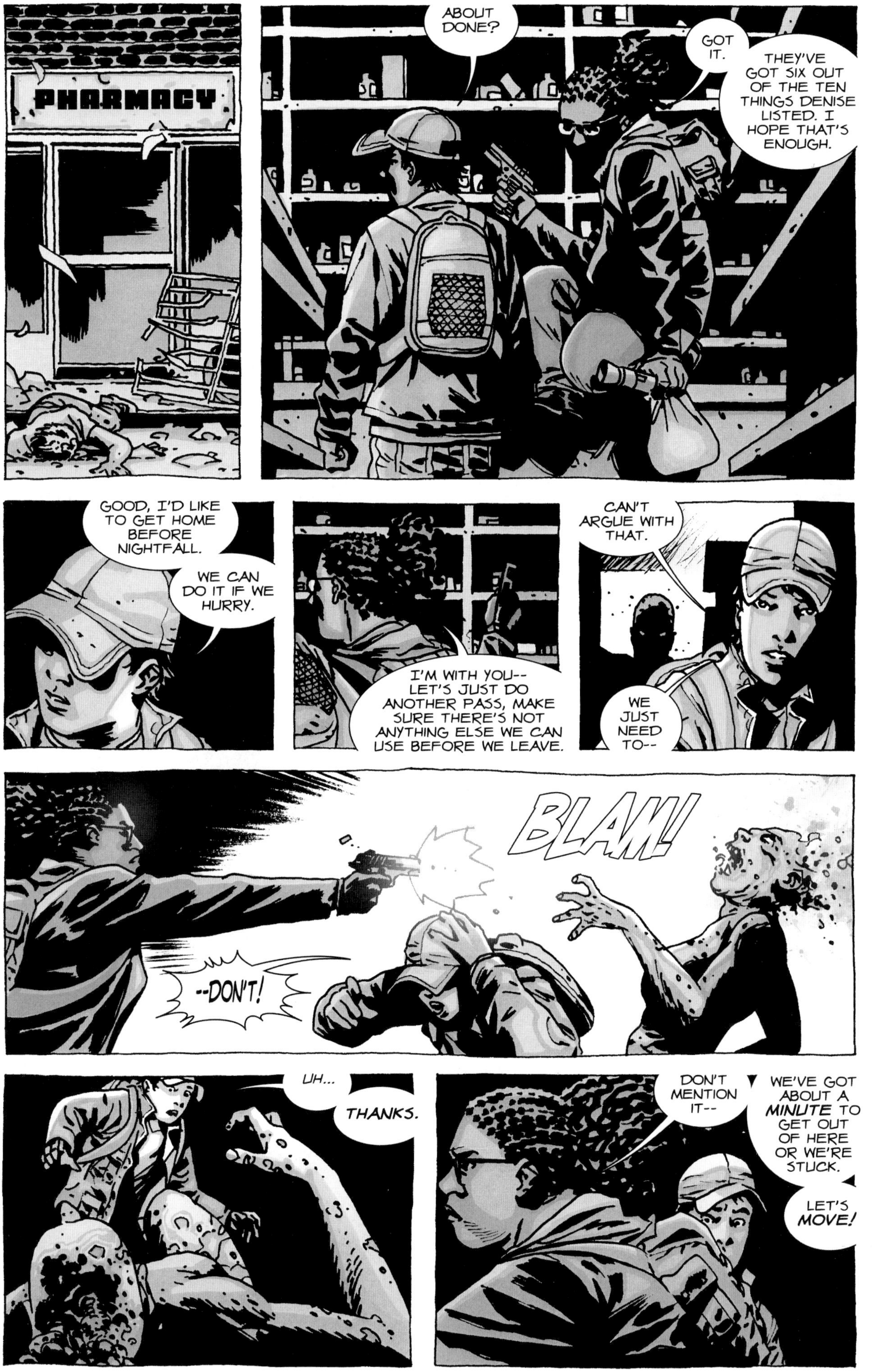
PHARMACY
ABOUT DONE?
GOT IT.
THEY'VE GOT SIX OUT OF THE TEN THINGS DENISE LISTED. I HOPE THAT'S ENOUGH.
GOOD, I'D LIKE TO GET HOME BEFORE NIGHTFALL.
WE CAN DO IT IF WE HURRY.
I'M WITH YOU-- LET'S JUST DO ANOTHER PASS, MAKE SURE THERE'S NOT ANYTHING ELSE WE CAN USE BEFORE WE LEAVE.
CAN'T ARGUE WITH THAT.
WE JUST NEED TO--
BLAM!
--DON'T!
UH...
THANKS.
DON'T MENTION IT--
WE'VE GOT ABOUT A MINUTE TO GET OUT OF HERE OR WE'RE STUCK.
LET'S MOVE!

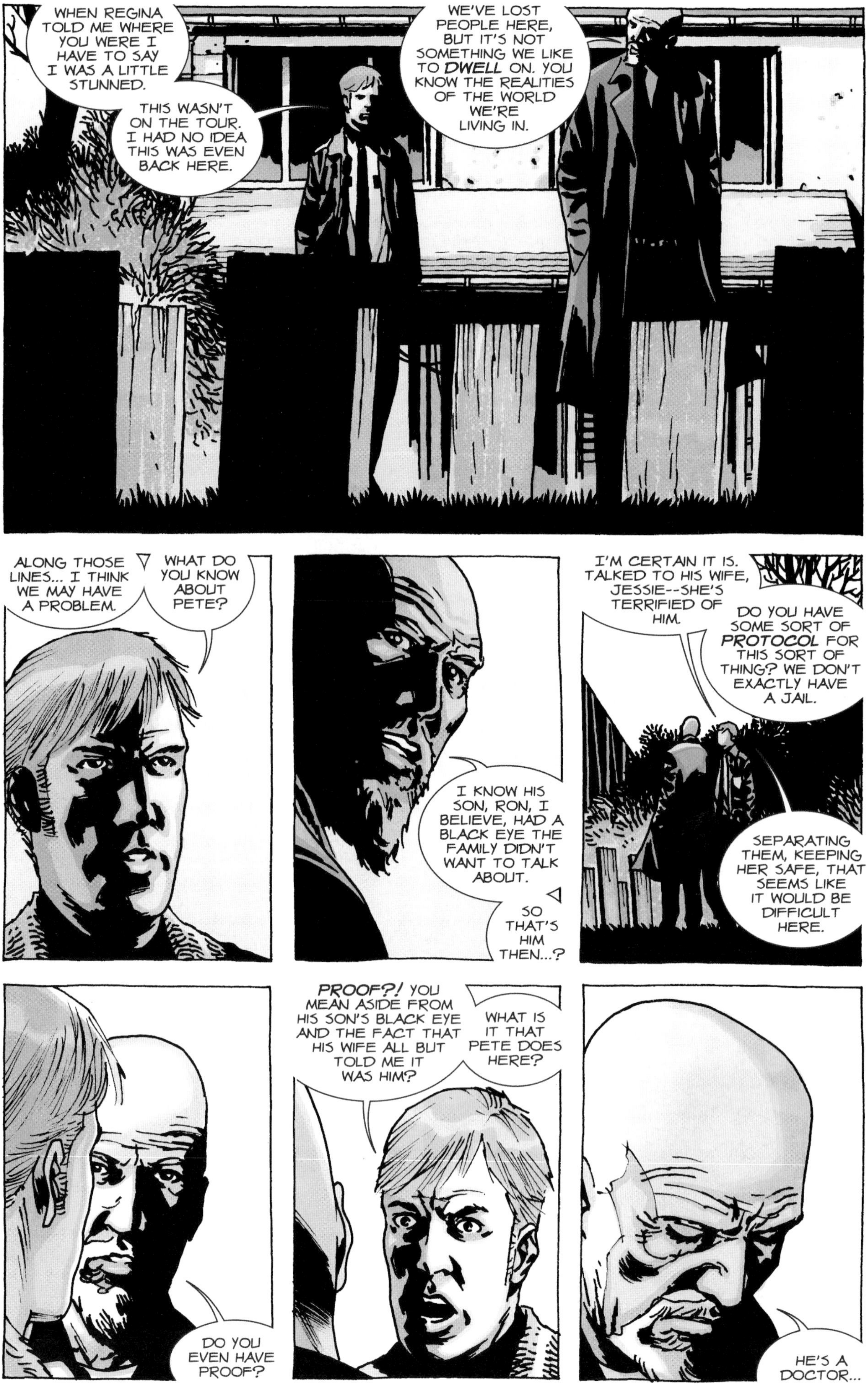

WHEN REGINA TOLD ME WHERE YOU WERE I HAVE TO SAY I WAS A LITTLE STUNNED.
THIS WASN'T ON THE TOUR. I HAD NO IDEA THIS WAS EVEN BACK HERE.
WE'VE LOST PEOPLE HERE, BUT IT'S NOT SOMETHING WE LIKE TO DWELL ON. YOU KNOW THE REALITIES OF THE WORLD WE'RE LIVING IN.
ALONG THOSE LINES... I THINK WE MAY HAVE A PROBLEM.
WHAT DO YOU KNOW ABOUT PETE?
I KNOW HIS SON, RON, I BELIEVE, HAD A BLACK EYE THE FAMILY DIDN'T WANT TO TALK ABOUT.
SO THAT'S HIM THEN...?
I'M CERTAIN IT IS. TALKED TO HIS WIFE, JESSIE--SHE'S TERRIFIED OF HIM.
DO YOU HAVE SOME SORT OF PROTOCOL FOR THIS SORT OF THING? WE DON'T EXACTLY HAVE A JAIL.
SEPARATING THEM, KEEPING HER SAFE, THAT SEEMS LIKE IT WOULD BE DIFFICULT HERE.
DO YOU EVEN HAVE PROOF?
PROOF?! YOU MEAN ASIDE FROM HIS SON'S BLACK EYE AND THE FACT THAT HIS WIFE ALL BUT TOLD ME IT WAS HIM?
WHAT IS IT THAT PETE DOES HERE?
HE'S A DOCTOR...

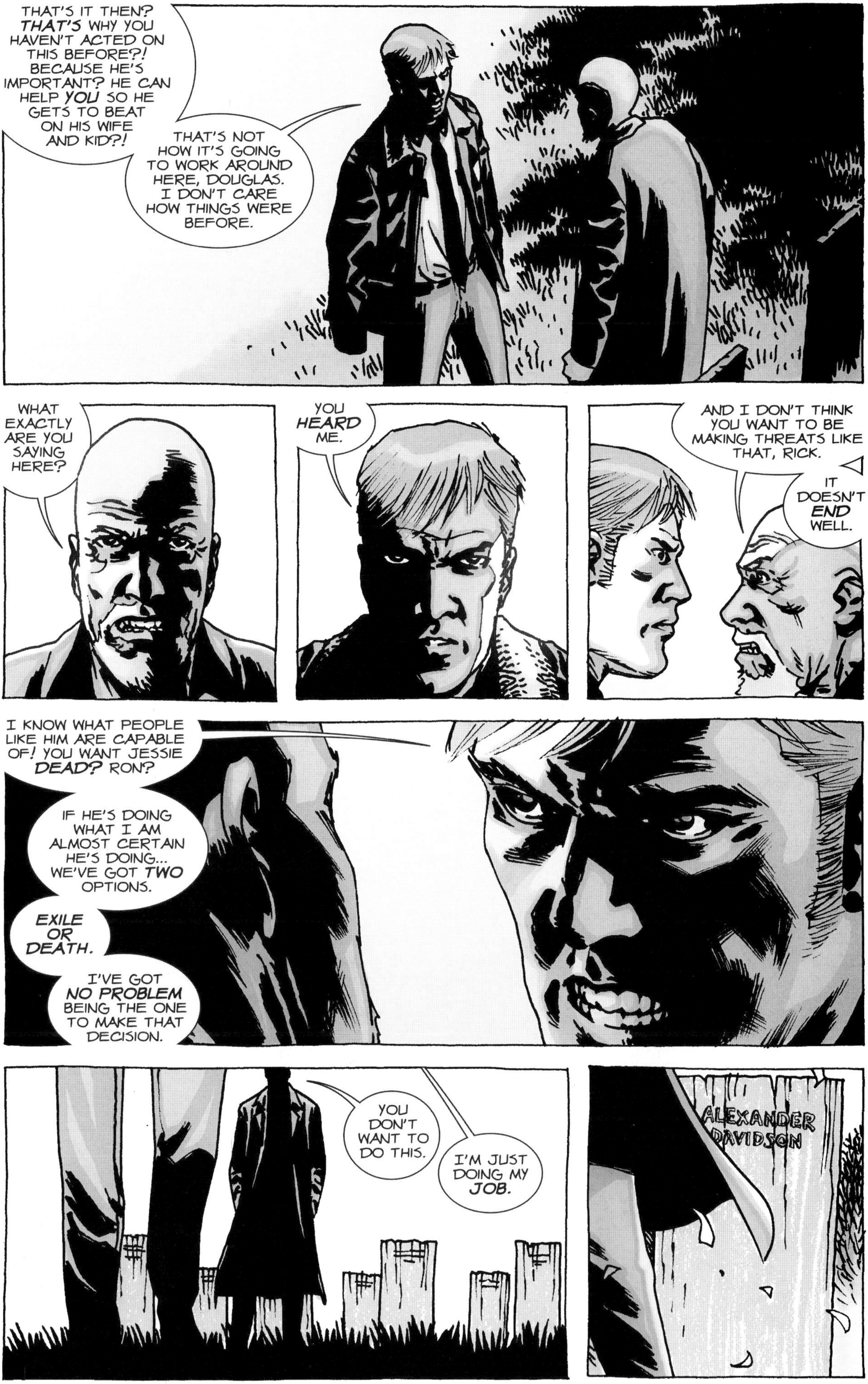

THAT'S IT THEN? THAT'S WHY YOU HAVEN'T ACTED ON THIS BEFORE?! BECAUSE HE'S IMPORTANT? HE CAN HELP YOU SO HE GETS TO BEAT ON HIS WIFE AND KID?!
THAT'S NOT HOW IT'S GOING TO WORK AROUND HERE, DOUGLAS. I DON'T CARE HOW THINGS WERE BEFORE.
WHAT EXACTLY ARE YOU SAYING HERE?
YOU HEARD ME.
AND I DON'T THINK YOU WANT TO BE MAKING THREATS LIKE THAT, RICK.
IT DOESN'T END WELL.
I KNOW WHAT PEOPLE LIKE HIM ARE CAPABLE OF! YOU WANT JESSIE DEAD? RON?
IF HE'S DOING WHAT I AM ALMOST CERTAIN HE'S DOING... WE'VE GOT TWO OPTIONS.
EXILE OR DEATH.
I'VE GOT NO PROBLEM BEING THE ONE TO MAKE THAT DECISION.
YOU DON'T WANT TO DO THIS.
I'M JUST DOING MY JOB.
ALEXANDER DAVIDSON

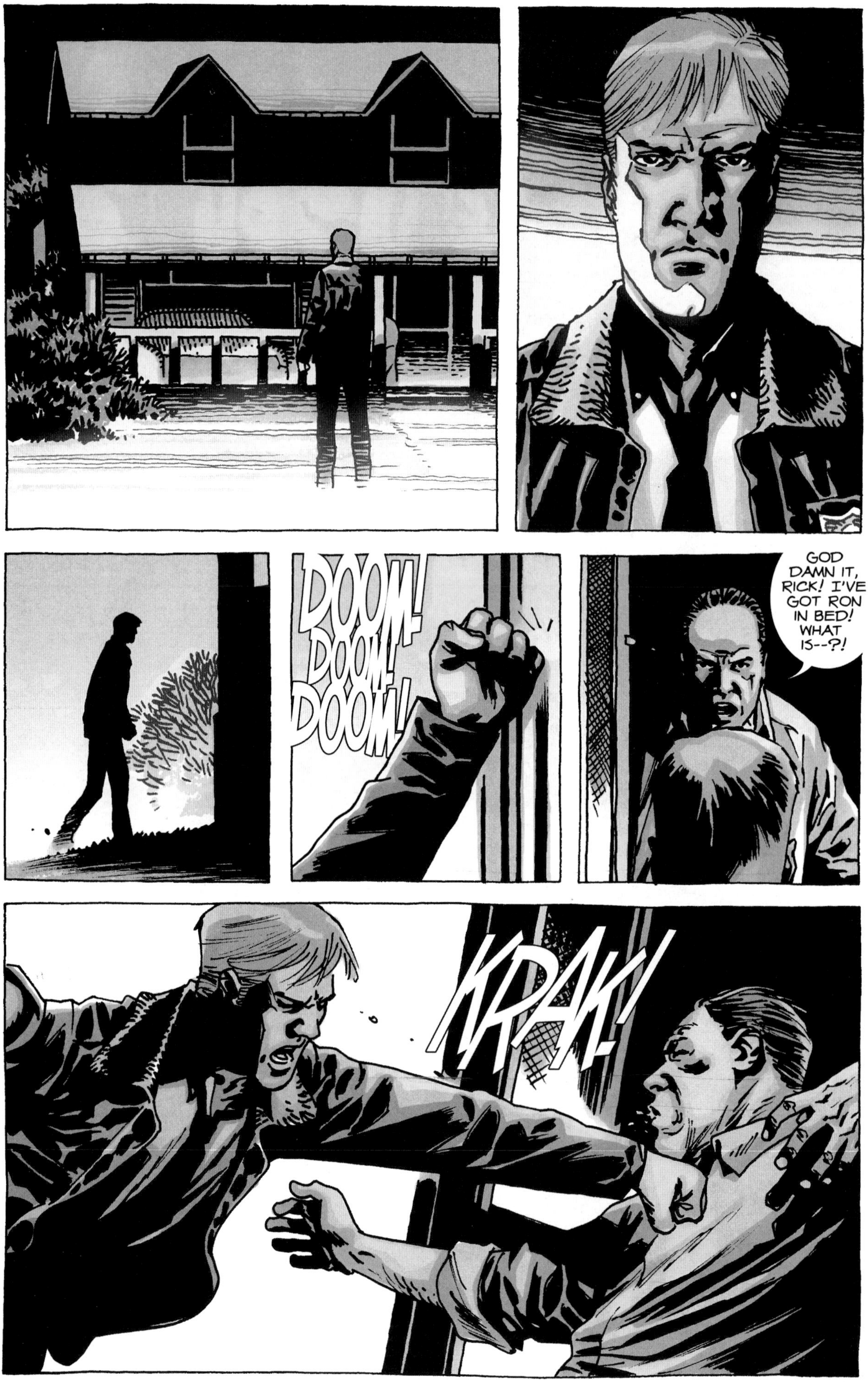
DOOM! DOOM! DOOM!
GOD DAMN IT, RICK! I'VE GOT RON IN BED! WHAT IS--?!
KRAK!

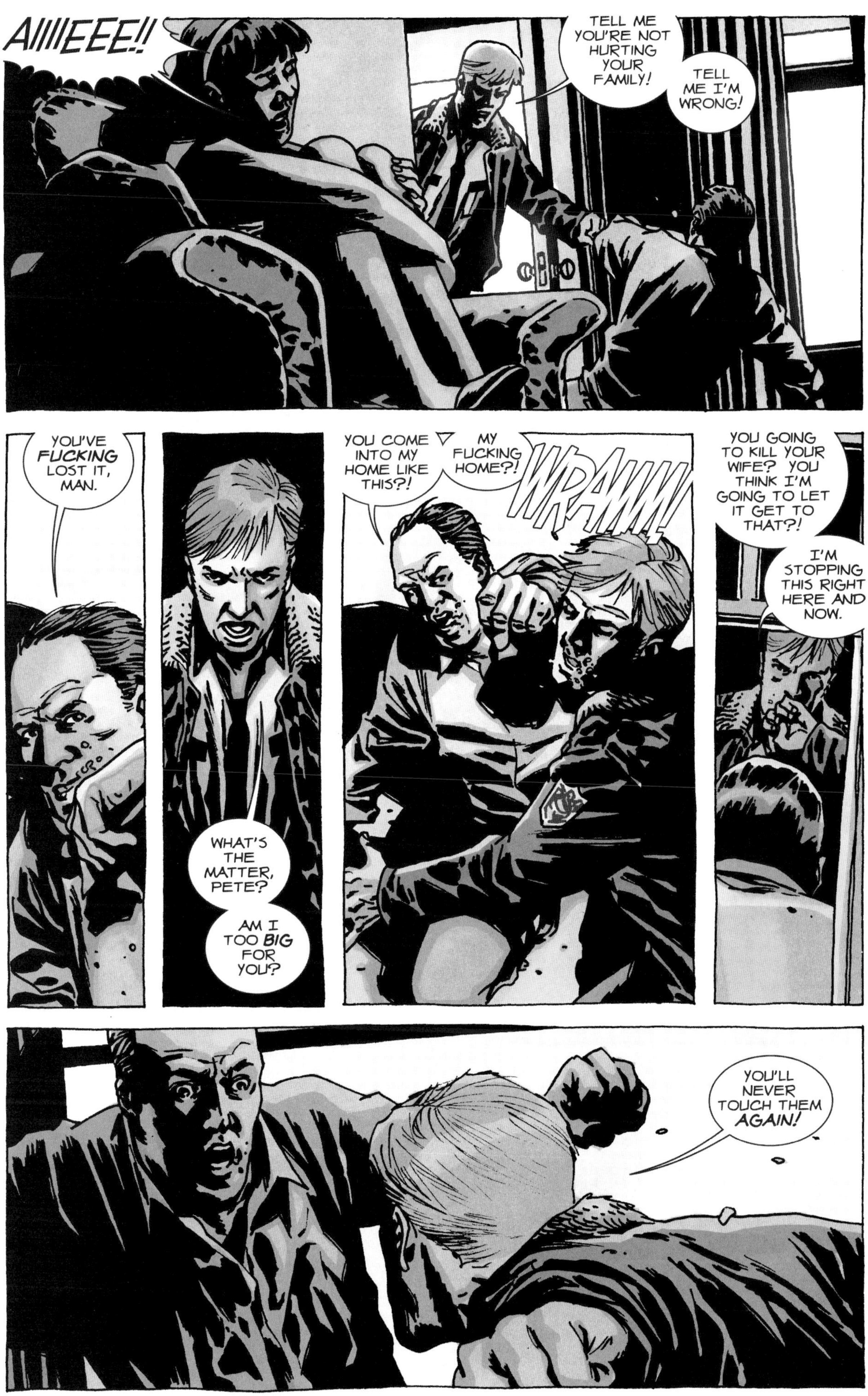
AIIIEEE!!
TELL ME YOU'RE NOT HURTING YOUR FAMILY!
TELL ME I'M WRONG!
YOU'VE FUCKING LOST IT, MAN.
WHAT'S THE MATTER, PETE?
AM I TOO BIG FOR YOU?
YOU COME INTO MY HOME LIKE THIS?!
MY FUCKING HOME?!
WRAMM!
YOU GOING TO KILL YOUR WIFE? YOU THINK I'M GOING TO LET IT GET TO THAT?!
I'M STOPPING THIS RIGHT HERE AND NOW.
YOU'LL NEVER TOUCH THEM AGAIN!

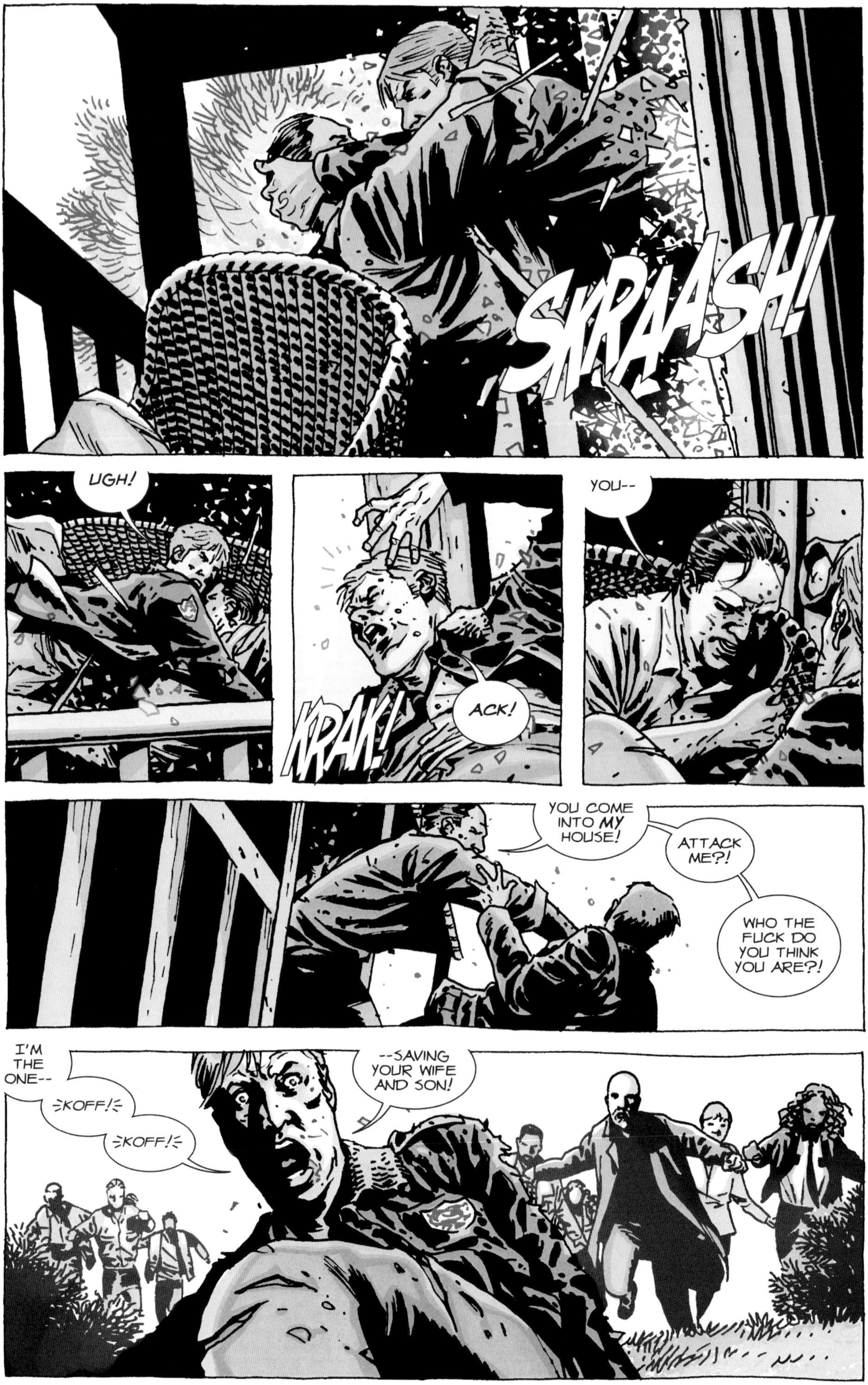
SKRAASH!
UGH!
KRAK!
ACK!
YOU--
YOU COME INTO MY HOUSE!
ATTACK ME?!
WHO THE FUCK DO YOU THINK YOU ARE?!
I'M THE ONE--
KOFF!
KOFF!
--SAVING YOUR WIFE AND SON!

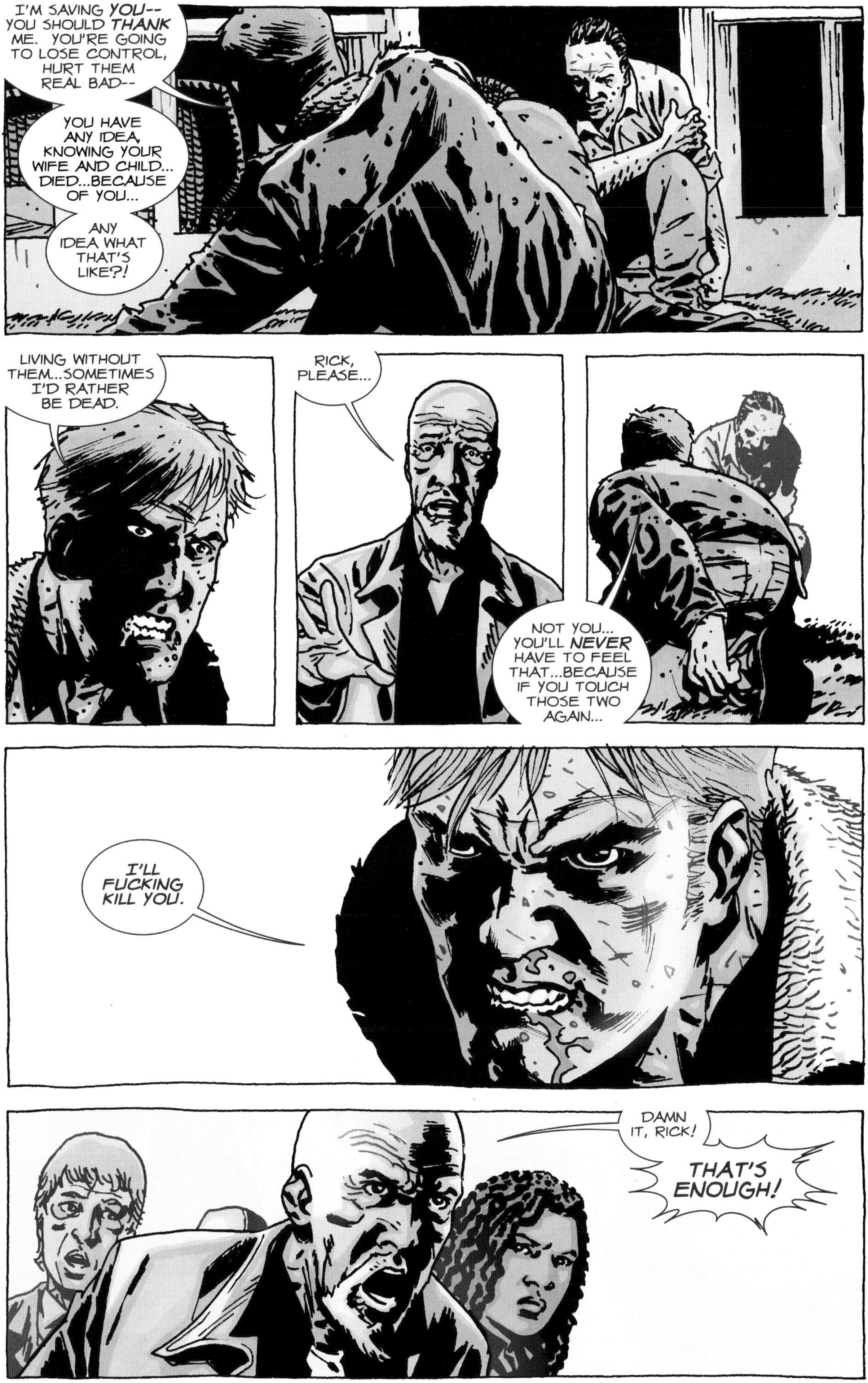

I'M SAVING YOU-- YOU SHOULD THANK ME. YOU'RE GOING TO LOSE CONTROL, HURT THEM REAL BAD--
YOU HAVE ANY IDEA, KNOWING YOUR WIFE AND CHILD... DIED...BECAUSE OF YOU...
ANY IDEA WHAT THAT'S LIKE?!
LIVING WITHOUT THEM...SOMETIMES I'D RATHER BE DEAD.
RICK, PLEASE...
NOT YOU... YOU'LL NEVER HAVE TO FEEL THAT...BECAUSE IF YOU TOUCH THOSE TWO AGAIN...
I'LL FUCKING KILL YOU.
DAMN IT, RICK!
THAT'S ENOUGH!

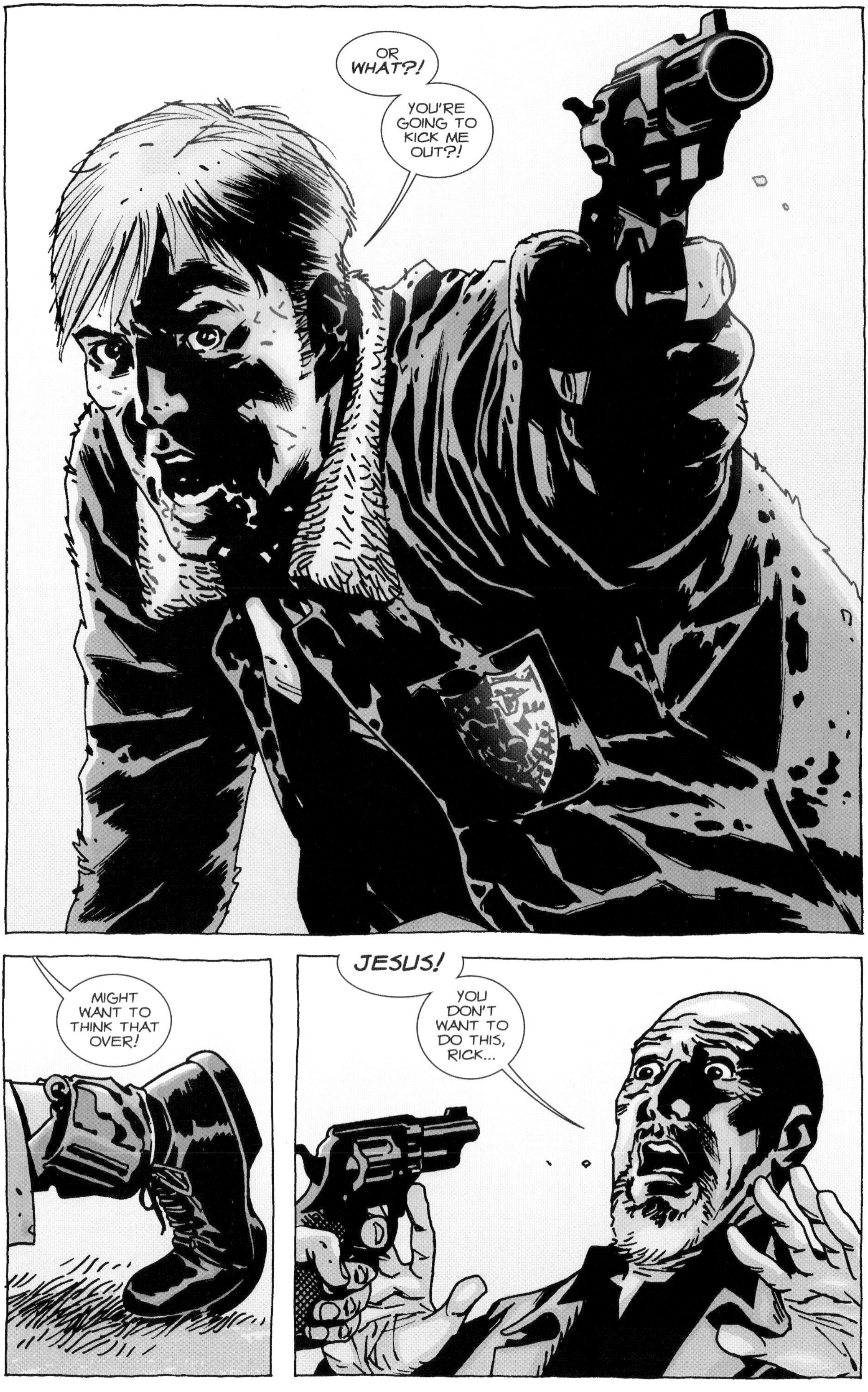
OR WHAT?!
YOU'RE GOING TO KICK ME OUT?!
MIGHT WANT TO THINK THAT OVER!
JESUS!
YOU DON'T WANT TO DO THIS, RICK...

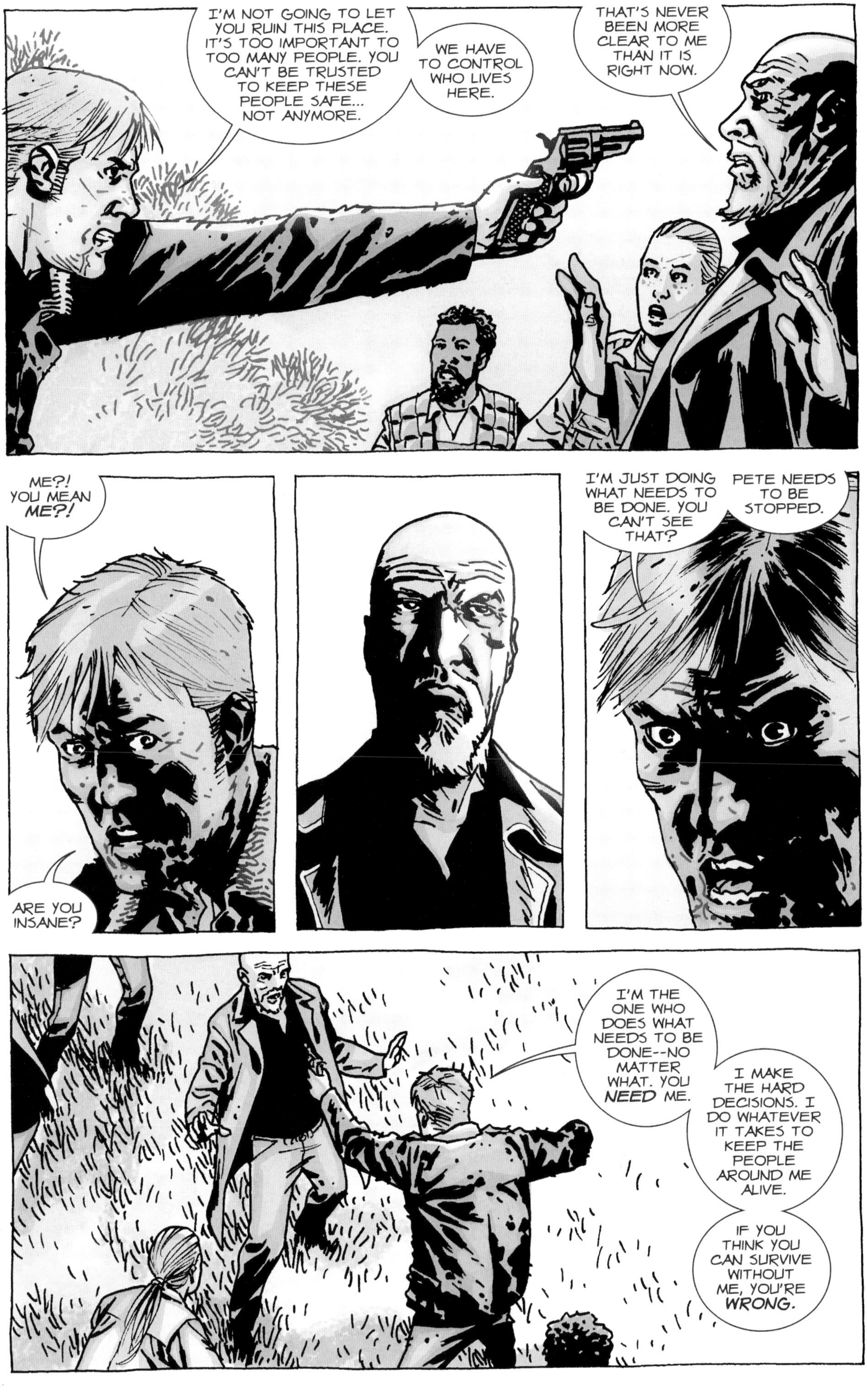
I'M NOT GOING TO LET YOU RUIN THIS PLACE. IT'S TOO IMPORTANT TO TOO MANY PEOPLE. YOU CAN'T BE TRUSTED TO KEEP THESE PEOPLE SAFE... NOT ANYMORE.
WE HAVE TO CONTROL WHO LIVES HERE.
THAT'S NEVER BEEN MORE CLEAR TO ME THAN IT IS RIGHT NOW.
ME?! YOU MEAN *ME?!*
ARE YOU INSANE?
I'M JUST DOING WHAT NEEDS TO BE DONE. YOU CAN'T SEE THAT?
PETE NEEDS TO BE STOPPED.
I'M THE ONE WHO DOES WHAT NEEDS TO BE DONE--NO MATTER WHAT. YOU ***NEED*** ME.
I MAKE THE HARD DECISIONS. I DO WHATEVER IT TAKES TO KEEP THE PEOPLE AROUND ME ALIVE.
IF YOU THINK YOU CAN SURVIVE WITHOUT ME, YOU'RE ***WRONG.***

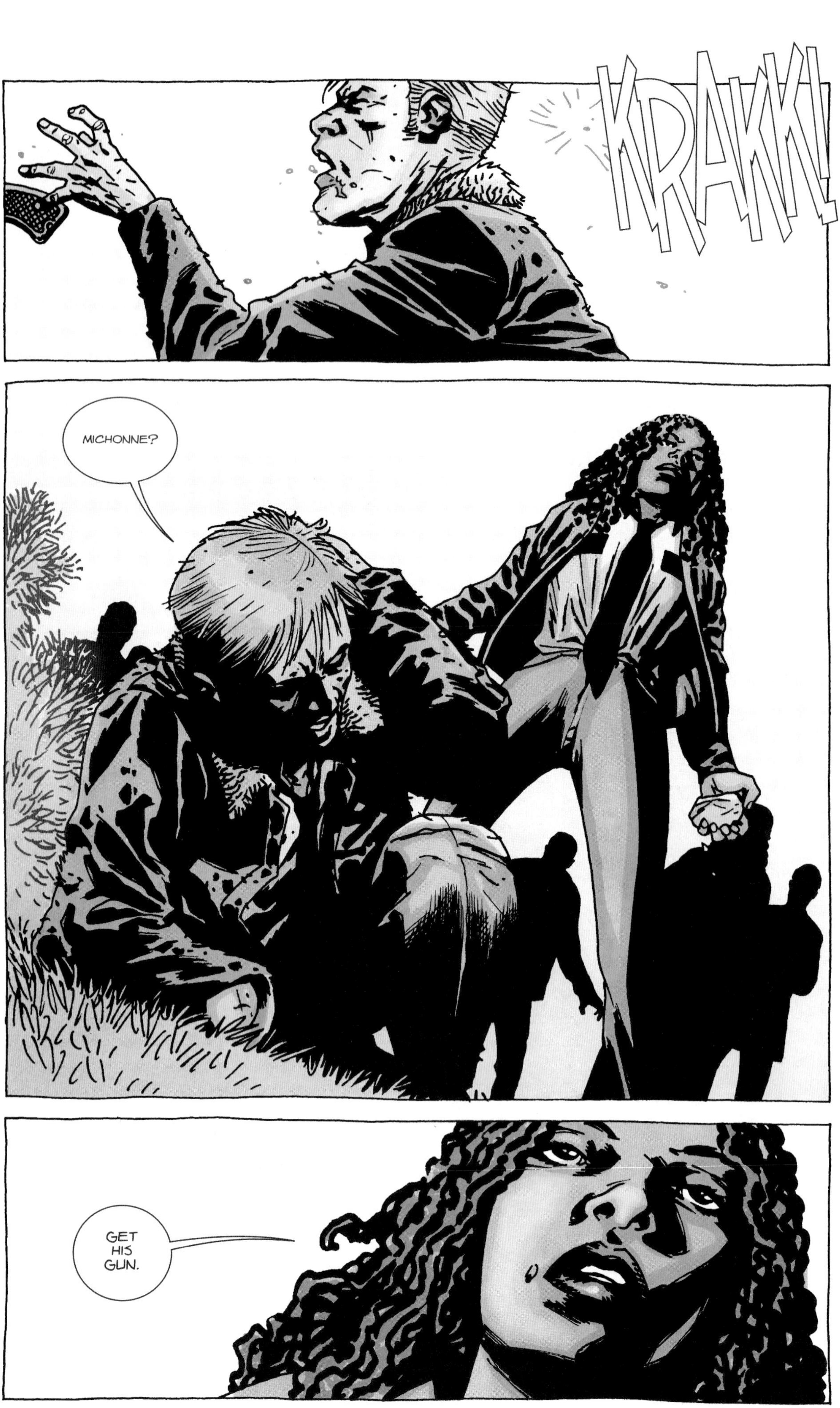
KRAKK!
MICHONNE?
GET HIS GUN.

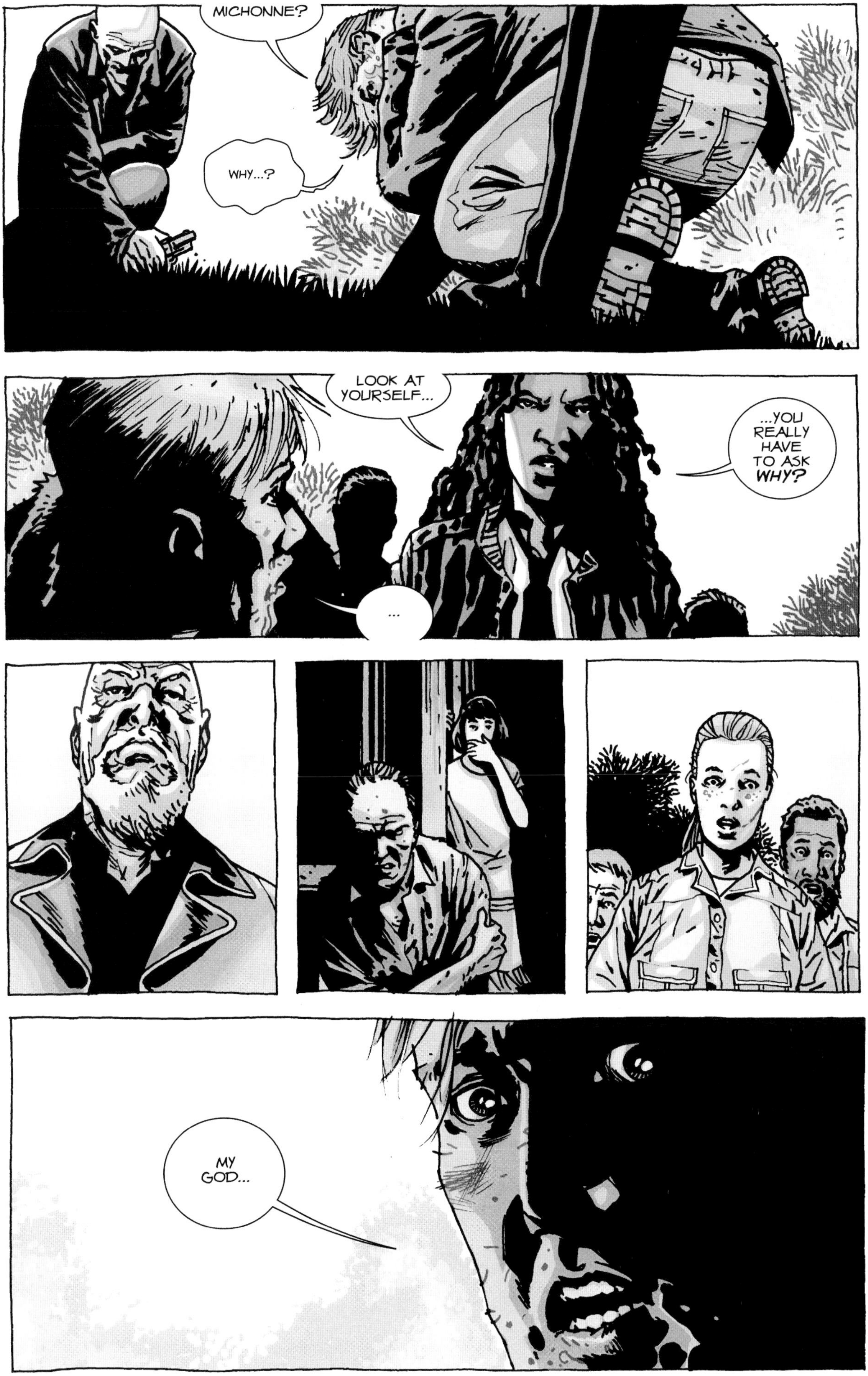
MICHONNE?
WHY...?
LOOK AT YOURSELF...
...YOU REALLY HAVE TO ASK WHY?
...
MY GOD...

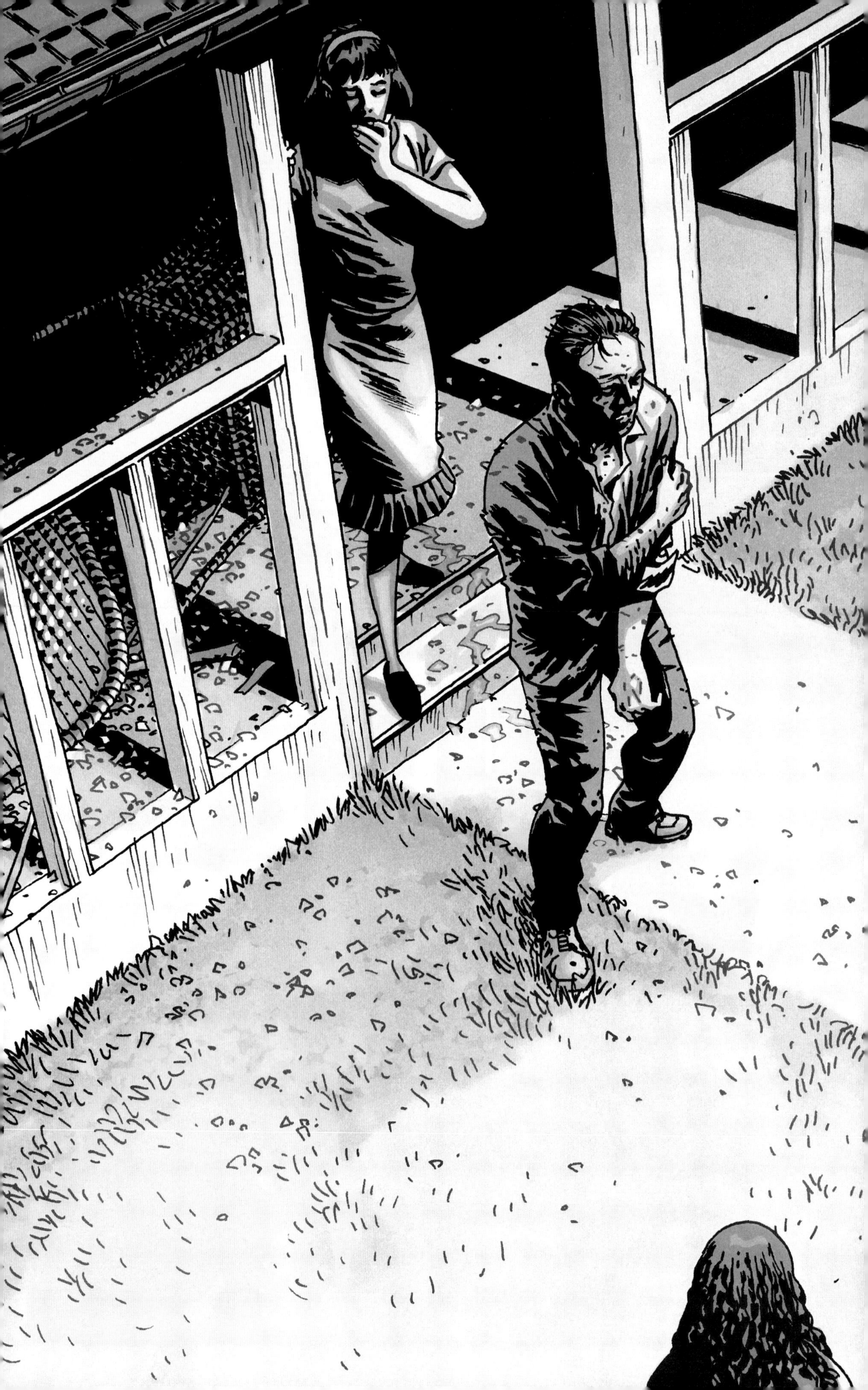

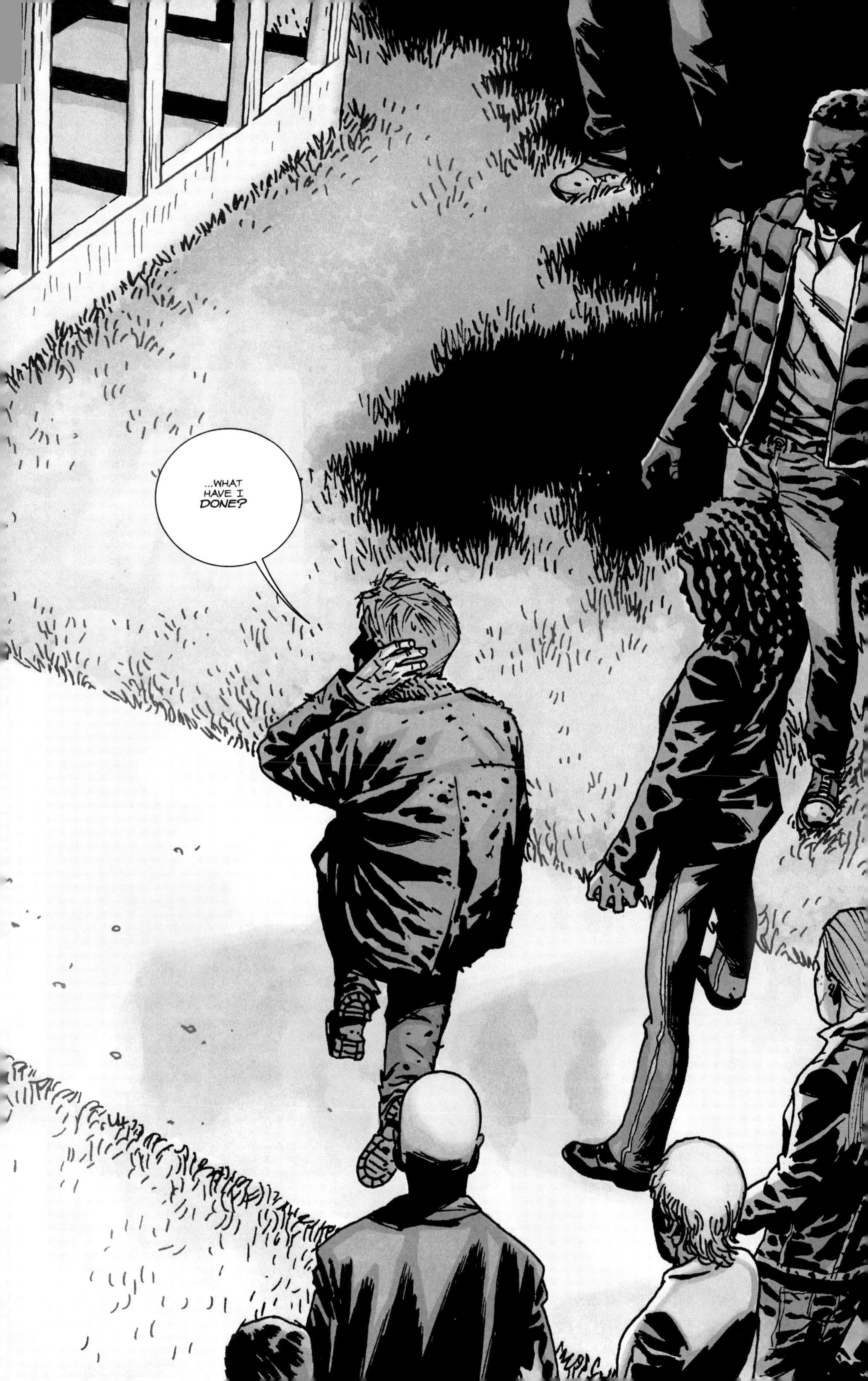
...WHAT HAVE I DONE?

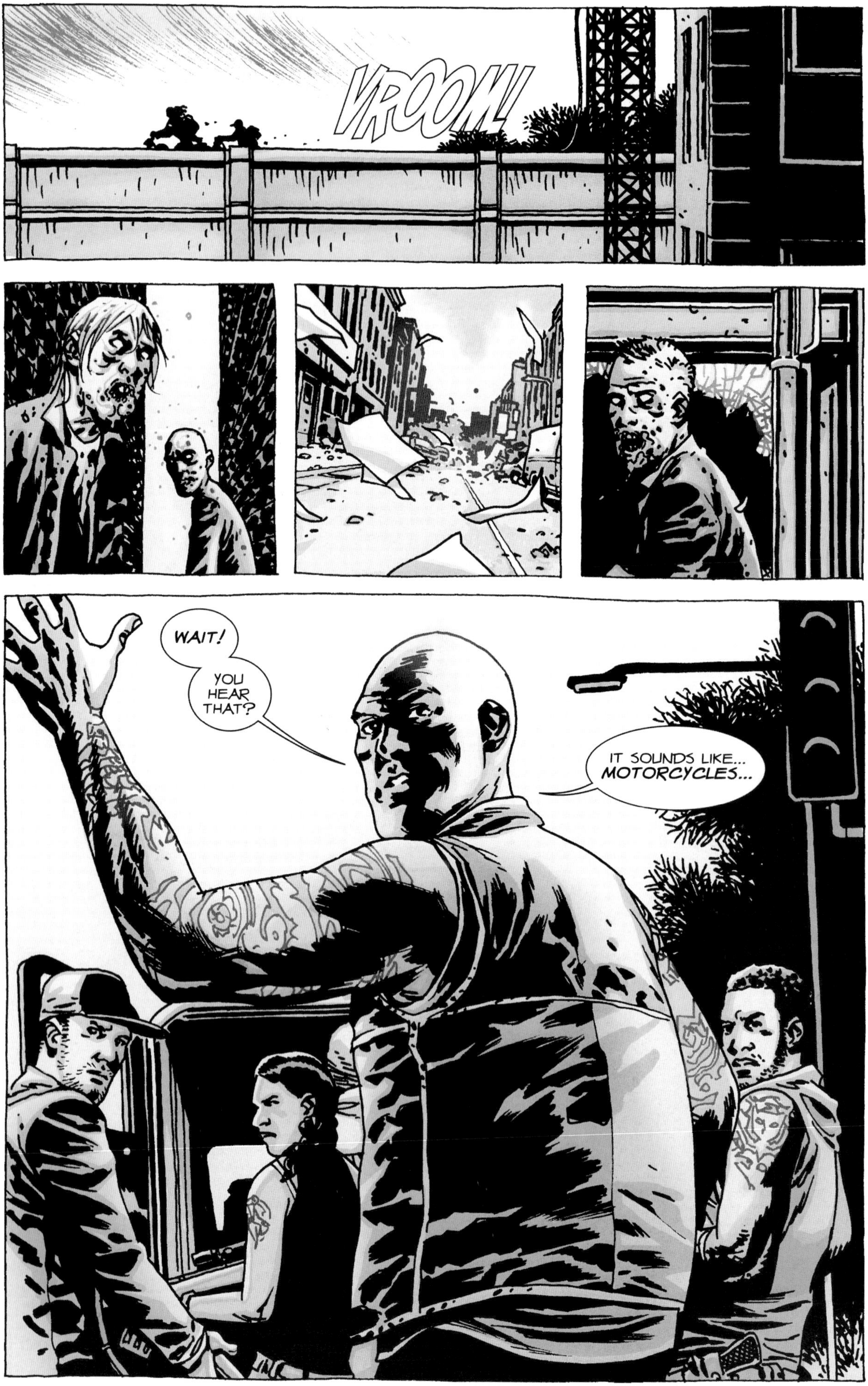
VROOM!
WAIT!
YOU HEAR THAT?
IT SOUNDS LIKE... MOTORCYCLES...

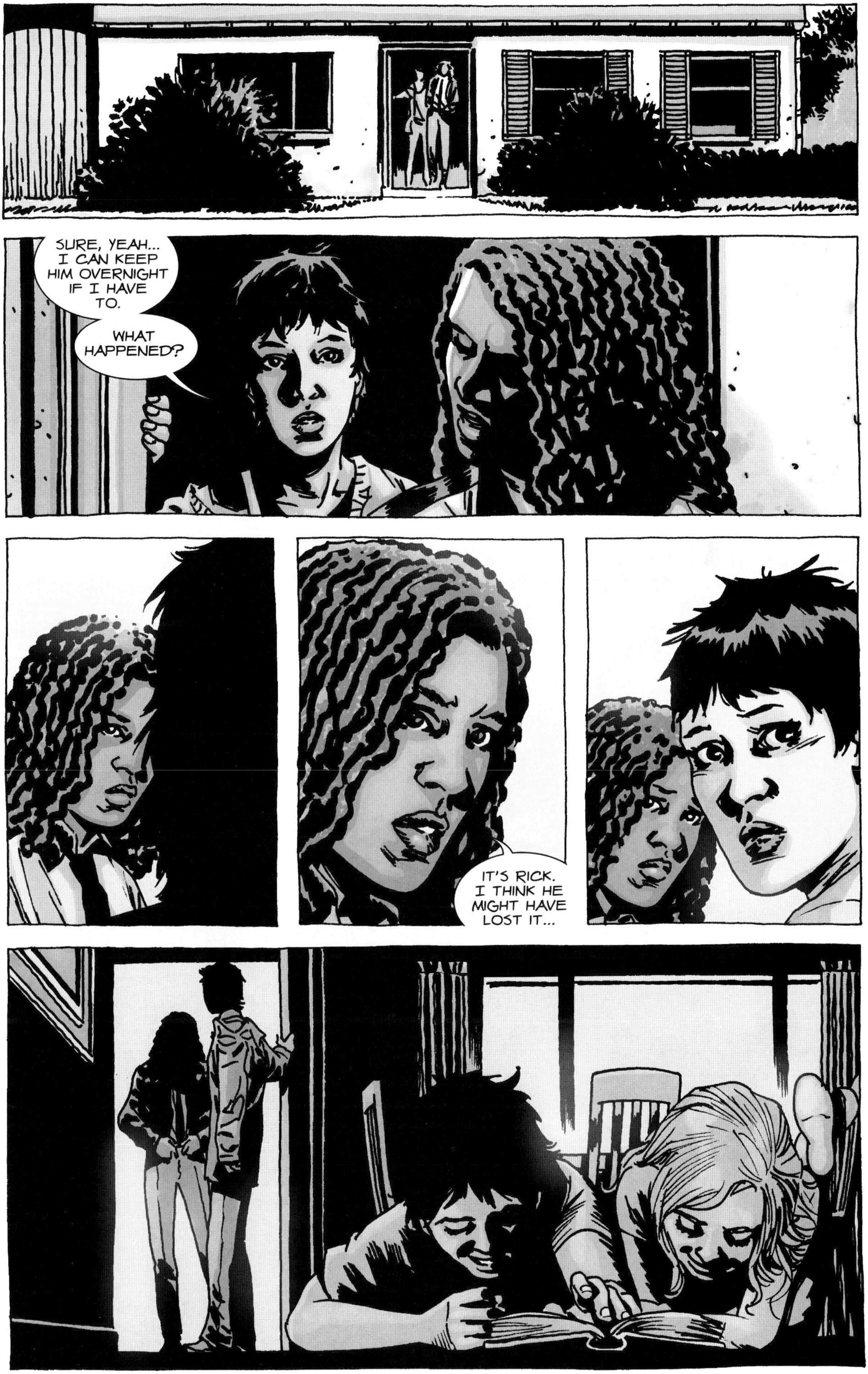
SURE, YEAH... I CAN KEEP HIM OVERNIGHT IF I HAVE TO.
WHAT HAPPENED?
IT'S RICK. I THINK HE MIGHT HAVE LOST IT...

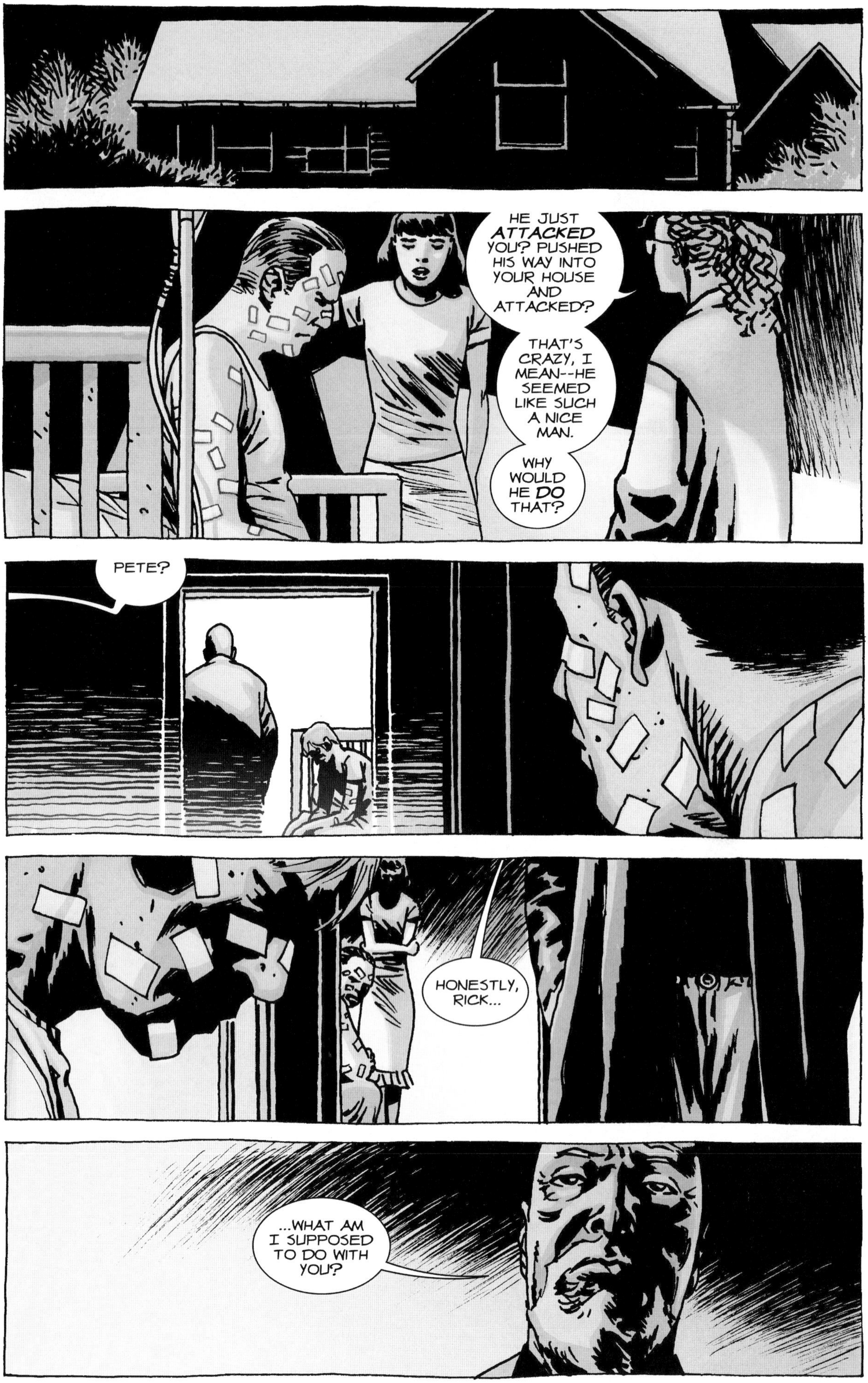
HE JUST ATTACKED YOU? PUSHED HIS WAY INTO YOUR HOUSE AND ATTACKED?
THAT'S CRAZY, I MEAN--HE SEEMED LIKE SUCH A NICE MAN.
WHY WOULD HE DO THAT?
PETE?
HONESTLY, RICK...
...WHAT AM I SUPPOSED TO DO WITH YOU?

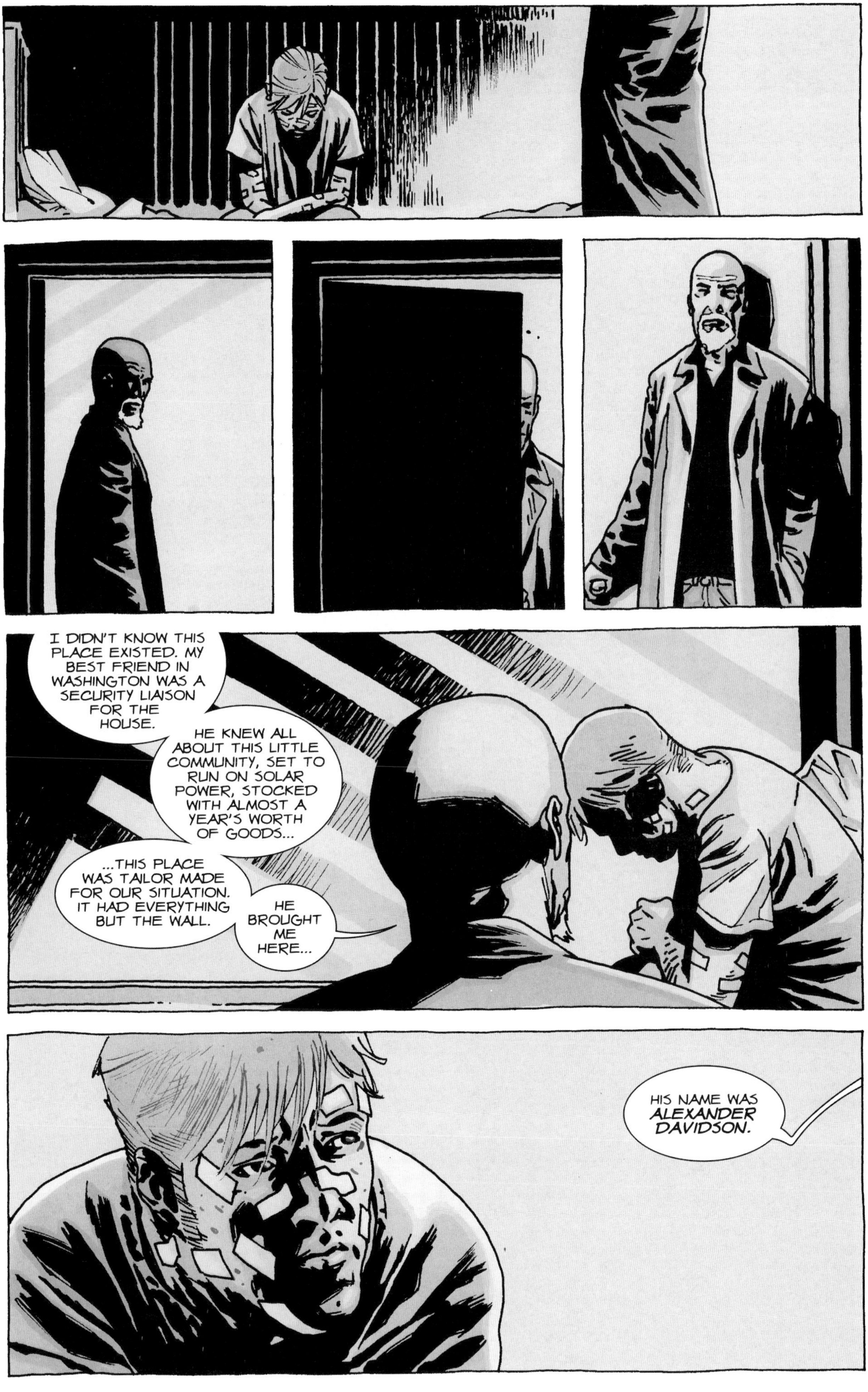

I DIDN'T KNOW THIS PLACE EXISTED. MY BEST FRIEND IN WASHINGTON WAS A SECURITY LIAISON FOR THE HOUSE.
HE KNEW ALL ABOUT THIS LITTLE COMMUNITY, SET TO RUN ON SOLAR POWER, STOCKED WITH ALMOST A YEAR'S WORTH OF GOODS...
...THIS PLACE WAS TAILOR MADE FOR OUR SITUATION. IT HAD EVERYTHING BUT THE WALL.
HE BROUGHT ME HERE...
HIS NAME WAS *ALEXANDER DAVIDSON.*

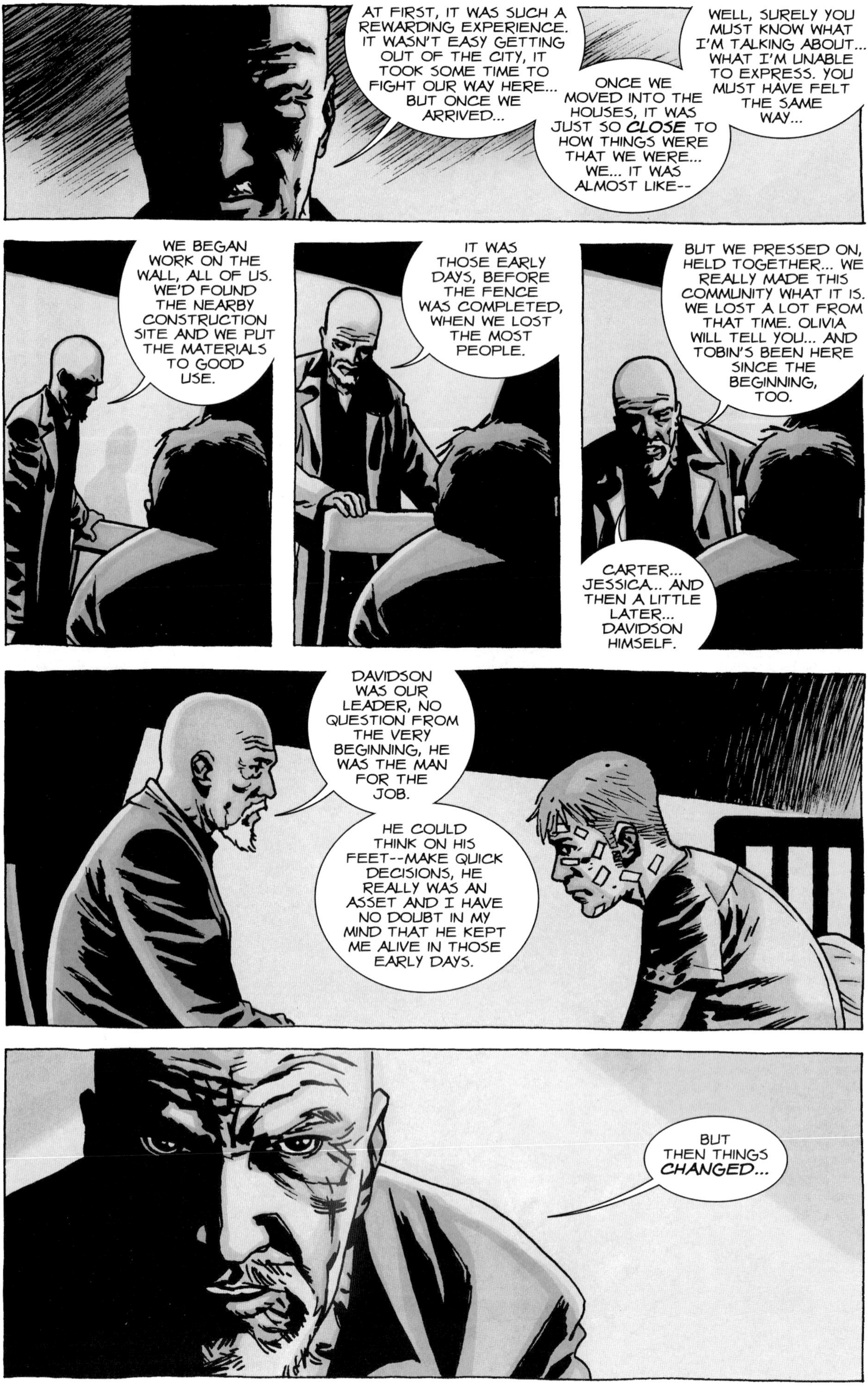
AT FIRST, IT WAS SUCH A REWARDING EXPERIENCE. IT WASN'T EASY GETTING OUT OF THE CITY, IT TOOK SOME TIME TO FIGHT OUR WAY HERE... BUT ONCE WE ARRIVED...
ONCE WE MOVED INTO THE HOUSES, IT WAS JUST SO **CLOSE** TO HOW THINGS WERE THAT WE WERE... WE... IT WAS ALMOST LIKE--
WELL, SURELY YOU MUST KNOW WHAT I'M TALKING ABOUT... WHAT I'M UNABLE TO EXPRESS. YOU MUST HAVE FELT THE SAME WAY...
WE BEGAN WORK ON THE WALL, ALL OF US. WE'D FOUND THE NEARBY CONSTRUCTION SITE AND WE PUT THE MATERIALS TO GOOD USE.
IT WAS THOSE EARLY DAYS, BEFORE THE FENCE WAS COMPLETED, WHEN WE LOST THE MOST PEOPLE.
BUT WE PRESSED ON, HELD TOGETHER... WE REALLY MADE THIS COMMUNITY WHAT IT IS. WE LOST A LOT FROM THAT TIME. OLIVIA WILL TELL YOU... AND TOBIN'S BEEN HERE SINCE THE BEGINNING, TOO.
CARTER... JESSICA... AND THEN A LITTLE LATER... DAVIDSON HIMSELF.
DAVIDSON WAS OUR LEADER, NO QUESTION FROM THE VERY BEGINNING, HE WAS THE MAN FOR THE JOB.
HE COULD THINK ON HIS FEET--MAKE QUICK DECISIONS, HE REALLY WAS AN ASSET AND I HAVE NO DOUBT IN MY MIND THAT HE KEPT ME ALIVE IN THOSE EARLY DAYS.
BUT THEN THINGS ***CHANGED...***

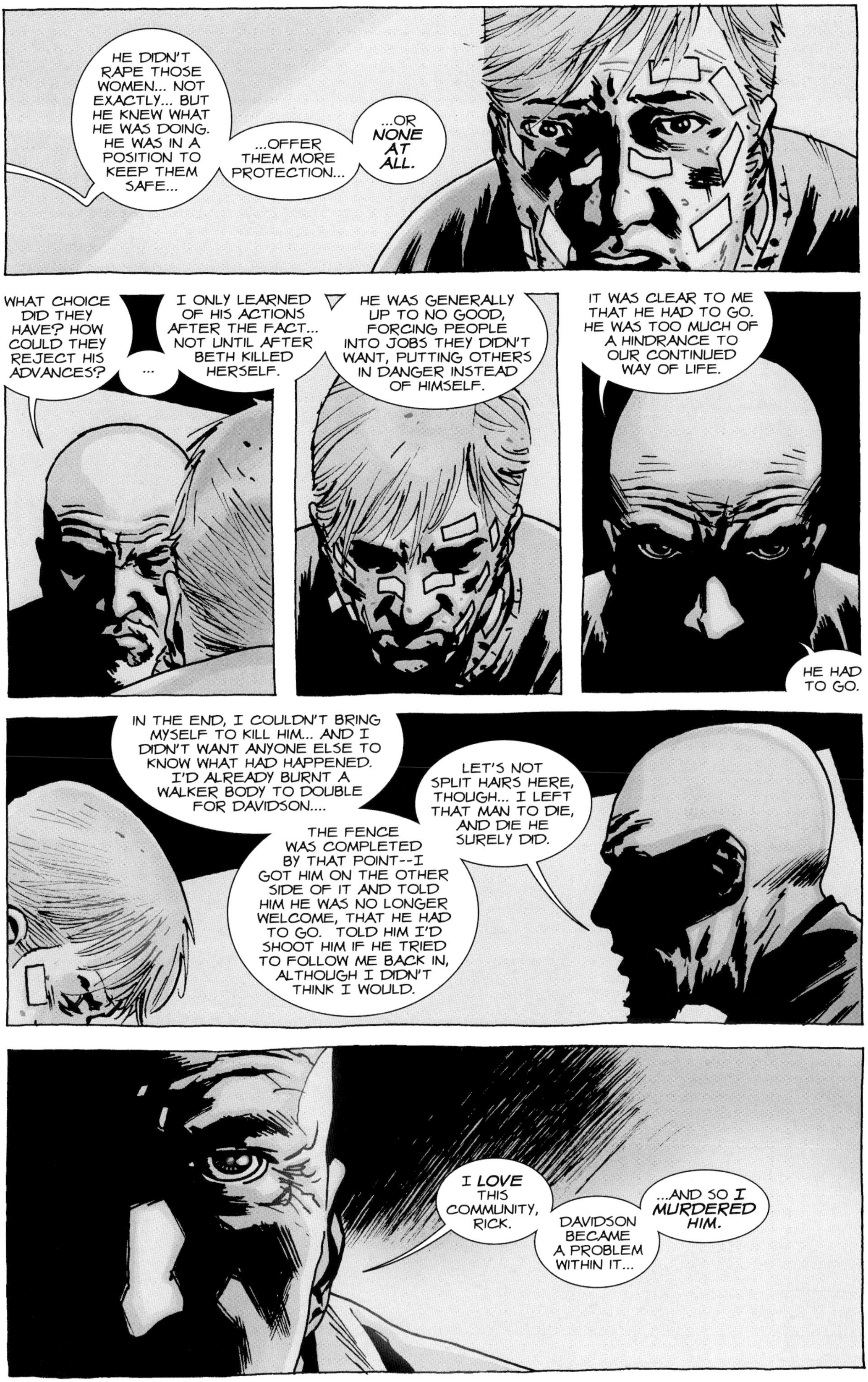
HE DIDN'T RAPE THOSE WOMEN... NOT EXACTLY... BUT HE KNEW WHAT HE WAS DOING. HE WAS IN A POSITION TO KEEP THEM SAFE...
...OFFER THEM MORE PROTECTION...
...OR NONE AT ALL.
WHAT CHOICE DID THEY HAVE? HOW COULD THEY REJECT HIS ADVANCES?
...
I ONLY LEARNED OF HIS ACTIONS AFTER THE FACT... NOT UNTIL AFTER BETH KILLED HERSELF.
HE WAS GENERALLY UP TO NO GOOD, FORCING PEOPLE INTO JOBS THEY DIDN'T WANT, PUTTING OTHERS IN DANGER INSTEAD OF HIMSELF.
IT WAS CLEAR TO ME THAT HE HAD TO GO. HE WAS TOO MUCH OF A HINDRANCE TO OUR CONTINUED WAY OF LIFE.
HE HAD TO GO.
IN THE END, I COULDN'T BRING MYSELF TO KILL HIM... AND I DIDN'T WANT ANYONE ELSE TO KNOW WHAT HAD HAPPENED. I'D ALREADY BURNT A WALKER BODY TO DOUBLE FOR DAVIDSON....
THE FENCE WAS COMPLETED BY THAT POINT--I GOT HIM ON THE OTHER SIDE OF IT AND TOLD HIM HE WAS NO LONGER WELCOME, THAT HE HAD TO GO. TOLD HIM I'D SHOOT HIM IF HE TRIED TO FOLLOW ME BACK IN, ALTHOUGH I DIDN'T THINK I WOULD.
LET'S NOT SPLIT HAIRS HERE, THOUGH... I LEFT THAT MAN TO DIE, AND DIE HE SURELY DID.
I LOVE THIS COMMUNITY, RICK.
DAVIDSON BECAME A PROBLEM WITHIN IT...
...AND SO I MURDERED HIM.

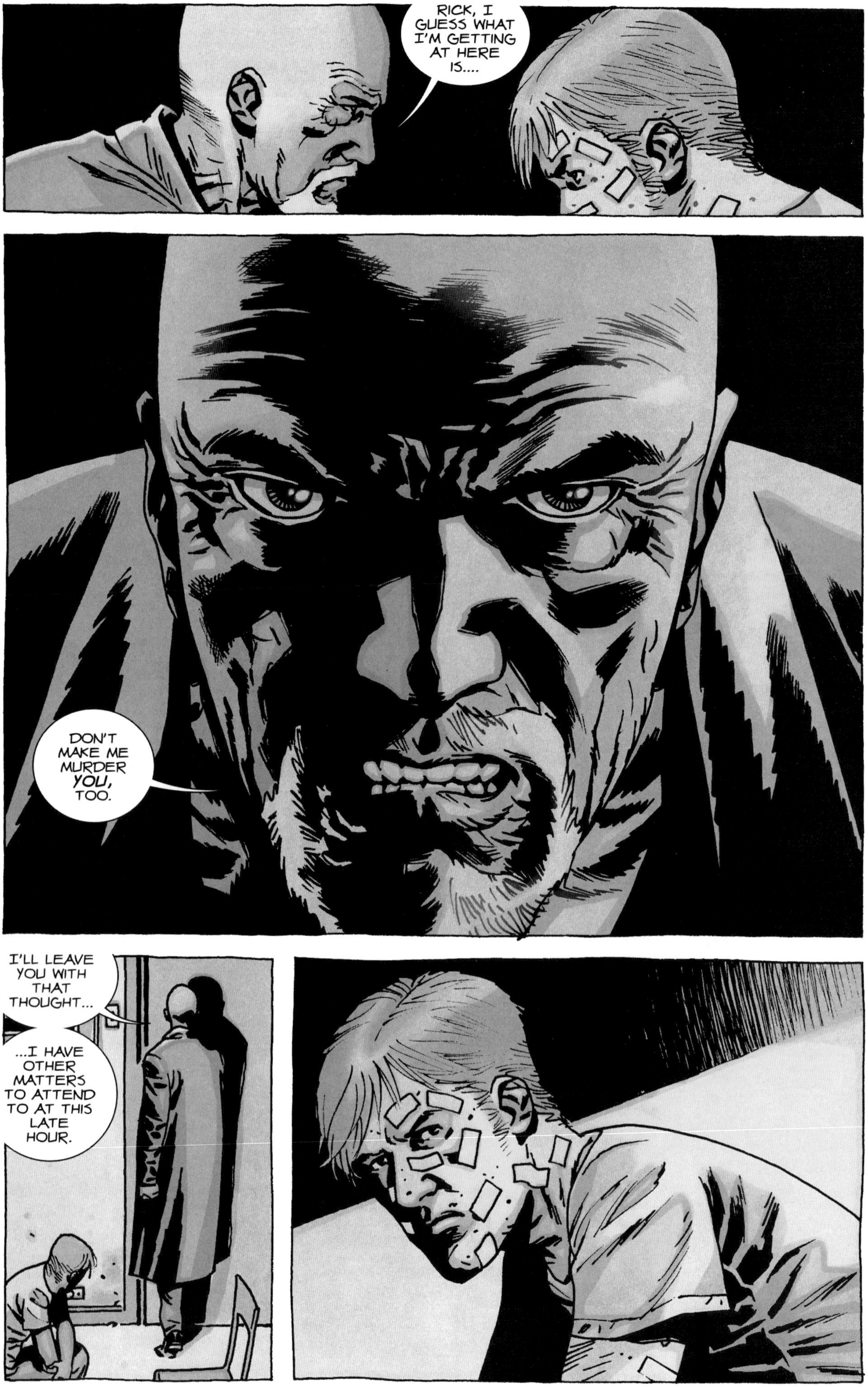
RICK, I GUESS WHAT I'M GETTING AT HERE IS....
DON'T MAKE ME MURDER YOU, TOO.
I'LL LEAVE YOU WITH THAT THOUGHT...
...I HAVE OTHER MATTERS TO ATTEND TO AT THIS LATE HOUR.

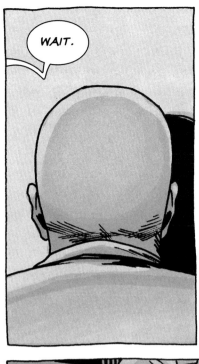

WAIT.

YES?

I NEVER WANTED TO BE A LEADER.

I DIDN'T NEED THE PRESSURE, DIDN'T *WANT* THE RESPONSIBILITY. WITH ALL THAT WAS GOING ON... I HAD OTHER THINGS ON MY MIND. MY WIFE AND SON TO PROTECT.

MY PARTNER SHANE... HE WAS THE LEADER OF OUR GROUP AT FIRST. NOT THAT WE TOOK THE TIME TO MAKE THOSE DISTINCTIONS, BUT HE WAS THE ONE EVERYONE LOOKED TO FOR ANSWERS.

IT DIDN'T REALLY MATTER TO ME UNTIL HE STARTED MAKING DECISIONS THAT WEREN'T GOOD FOR THE GROUP...

HE WANTED TO STAY ON THE OUTSKIRTS OF ATLANTA... BUT IT WAS TOO DANGEROUS. HE THOUGHT HELP WAS COMING. HE HAD HIS REASONS, BUT IT DIDN'T MAKE THINGS ANY LESS DANGEROUS.

WE BUTTED HEADS... THERE WERE A LOT OF ARGUMENTS.

THINGS EVEN GOT HEATED. HE DIDN'T LIKE THAT PEOPLE WERE STARTING TO AGREE WITH ME.

HE HELPED MY WIFE AND SON GET TO ATLANTA... I WAS IN A HOSPITAL HEALING FROM A GUNSHOT WOUND, I CAUGHT UP TO THEM LATER.

I'D DRIFTED INTO A COMA... THEY BOTH THOUGHT I WAS DEAD... THINKING ABOUT IT, WHY WOULDN'T THEY?

THEY WERE ALWAYS CLOSE... HE WAS MY BEST FRIEND, SHE WAS MY WIFE... THEY SPENT A LOT OF TIME TOGETHER BEFORE ALL THIS HAPPENED.

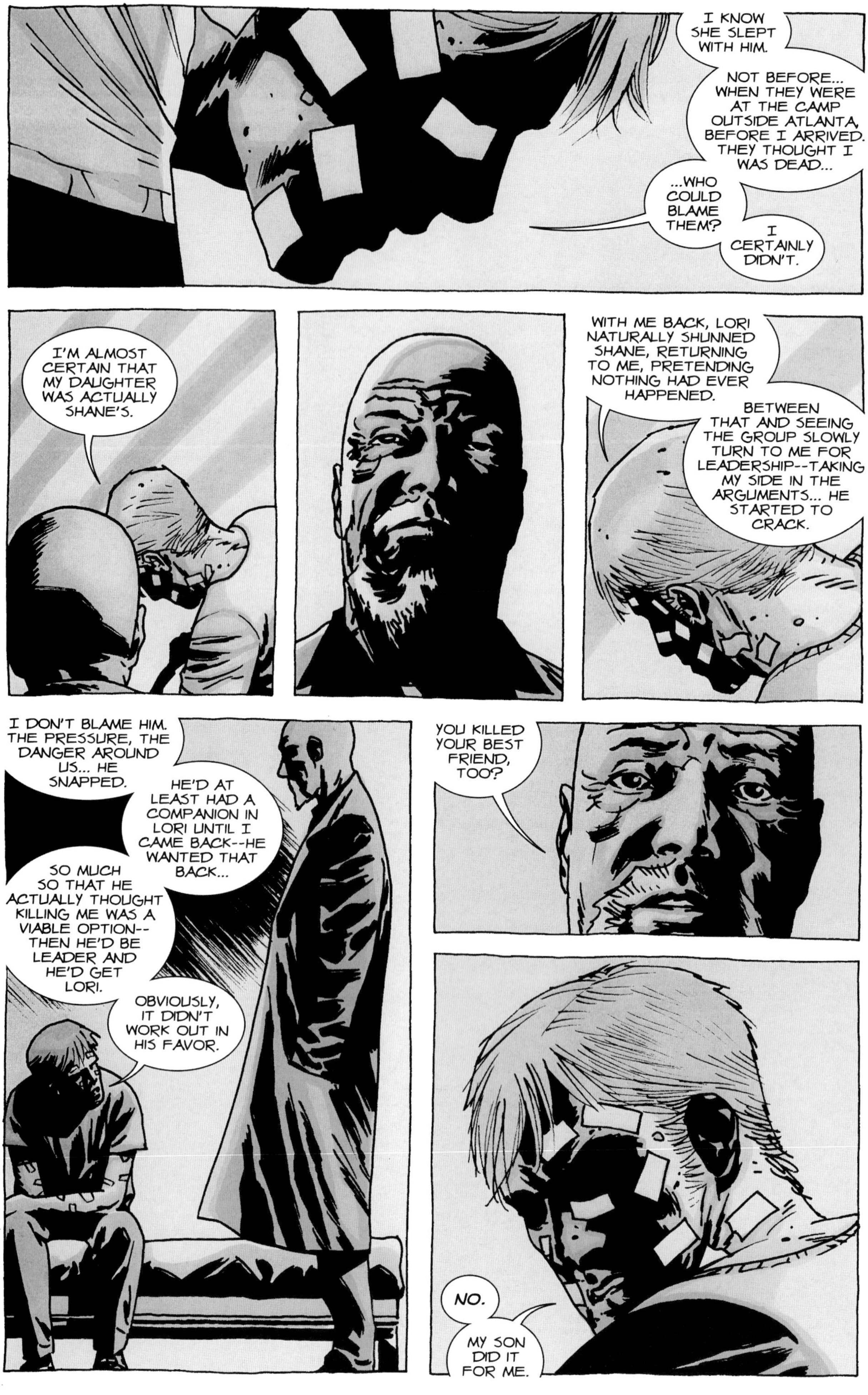
I KNOW SHE SLEPT WITH HIM.
NOT BEFORE... WHEN THEY WERE AT THE CAMP OUTSIDE ATLANTA, BEFORE I ARRIVED. THEY THOUGHT I WAS DEAD...
...WHO COULD BLAME THEM?
I CERTAINLY DIDN'T.
I'M ALMOST CERTAIN THAT MY DAUGHTER WAS ACTUALLY SHANE'S.
WITH ME BACK, LORI NATURALLY SHUNNED SHANE, RETURNING TO ME, PRETENDING NOTHING HAD EVER HAPPENED.
BETWEEN THAT AND SEEING THE GROUP SLOWLY TURN TO ME FOR LEADERSHIP--TAKING MY SIDE IN THE ARGUMENTS... HE STARTED TO CRACK.
I DON'T BLAME HIM. THE PRESSURE, THE DANGER AROUND US... HE SNAPPED.
HE'D AT LEAST HAD A COMPANION IN LORI UNTIL I CAME BACK--HE WANTED THAT BACK...
SO MUCH SO THAT HE ACTUALLY THOUGHT KILLING ME WAS A VIABLE OPTION-- THEN HE'D BE LEADER AND HE'D GET LORI.
OBVIOUSLY, IT DIDN'T WORK OUT IN HIS FAVOR.
YOU KILLED YOUR BEST FRIEND, TOO?
NO.
MY SON DID IT FOR ME.

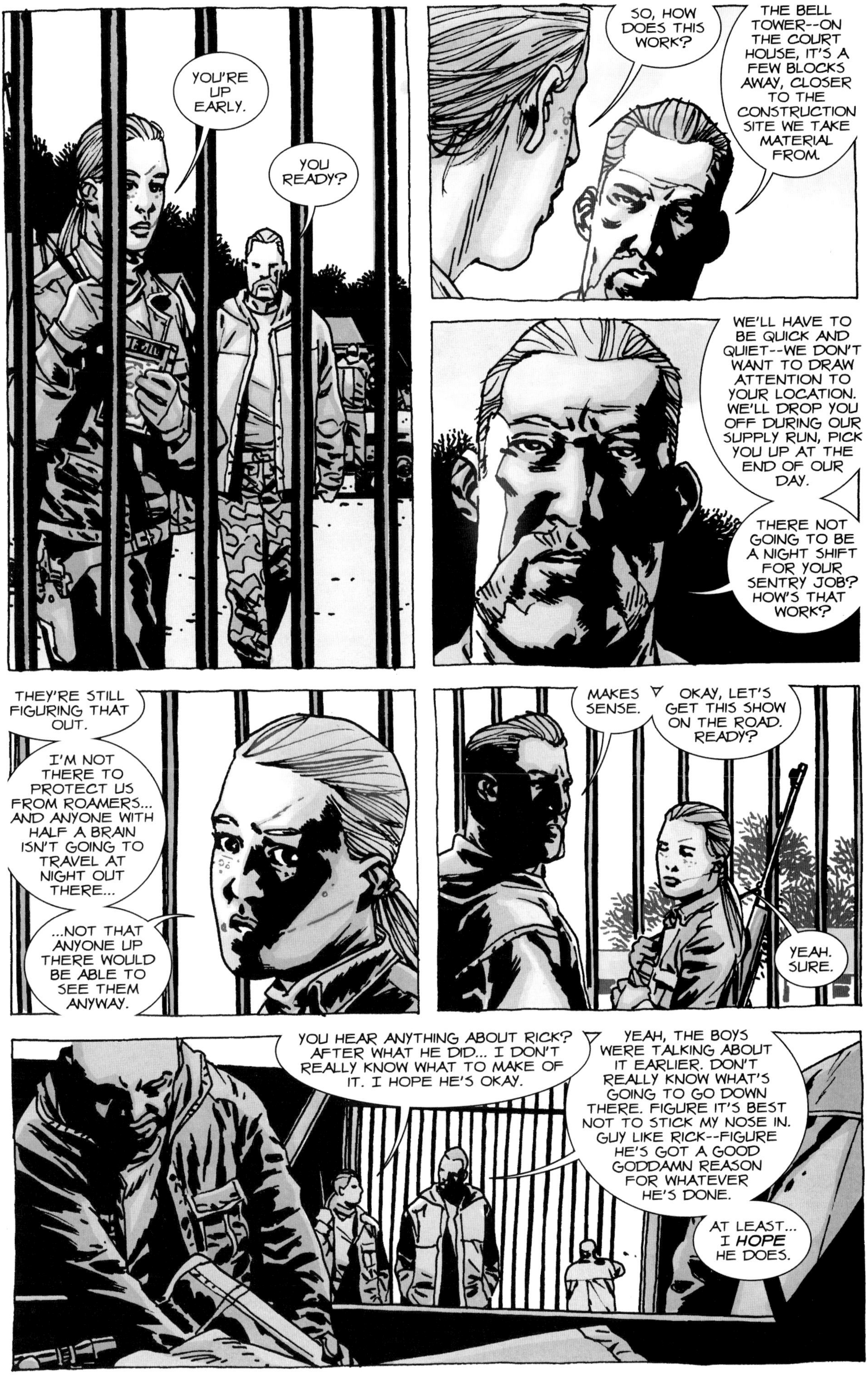

YOU'RE UP EARLY.
YOU READY?
SO, HOW DOES THIS WORK?
THE BELL TOWER--ON THE COURT HOUSE, IT'S A FEW BLOCKS AWAY, CLOSER TO THE CONSTRUCTION SITE WE TAKE MATERIAL FROM.
WE'LL HAVE TO BE QUICK AND QUIET--WE DON'T WANT TO DRAW ATTENTION TO YOUR LOCATION. WE'LL DROP YOU OFF DURING OUR SUPPLY RUN, PICK YOU UP AT THE END OF OUR DAY.
THERE NOT GOING TO BE A NIGHT SHIFT FOR YOUR SENTRY JOB? HOW'S THAT WORK?
THEY'RE STILL FIGURING THAT OUT.
I'M NOT THERE TO PROTECT US FROM ROAMERS... AND ANYONE WITH HALF A BRAIN ISN'T GOING TO TRAVEL AT NIGHT OUT THERE...
...NOT THAT ANYONE UP THERE WOULD BE ABLE TO SEE THEM ANYWAY.
MAKES SENSE.
OKAY, LET'S GET THIS SHOW ON THE ROAD. READY?
YEAH. SURE.
YOU HEAR ANYTHING ABOUT RICK? AFTER WHAT HE DID... I DON'T REALLY KNOW WHAT TO MAKE OF IT. I HOPE HE'S OKAY.
YEAH, THE BOYS WERE TALKING ABOUT IT EARLIER. DON'T REALLY KNOW WHAT'S GOING TO GO DOWN THERE. FIGURE IT'S BEST NOT TO STICK MY NOSE IN. GUY LIKE RICK--FIGURE HE'S GOT A GOOD GODDAMN REASON FOR WHATEVER HE'S DONE.
AT LEAST... I *HOPE* HE DOES.

GO AND GET YOUR SON, TALK TO HIM A LITTLE, TELL HIM WHATEVER YOU NEED TO. I DON'T WANT HIM TO WORRY ABOUT YOU.

WHEN YOU'RE DONE I'D LIKE YOU TO COME BY MY HOUSE.

WE'VE GOT ONE LAST THING TO TALK ABOUT.

OH... HEY, RICK.

TODAY WAS THE FIRST DAY? I'D FORGOTTEN.

ARE YOU OKAY?

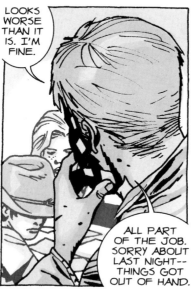

LOOKS WORSE THAN IT IS. I'M FINE.

ALL PART OF THE JOB. SORRY ABOUT LAST NIGHT-- THINGS GOT OUT OF HAND.

IT'S OKAY, HE WAS FINE. WE'RE OKAY.

REALLY, MAGGIE-- THANKS. I DON'T WANT TO BE A DISRUPTION, I JUST WANT TO TALK TO HIM.

CARL?

...

WHERE WERE YOU?

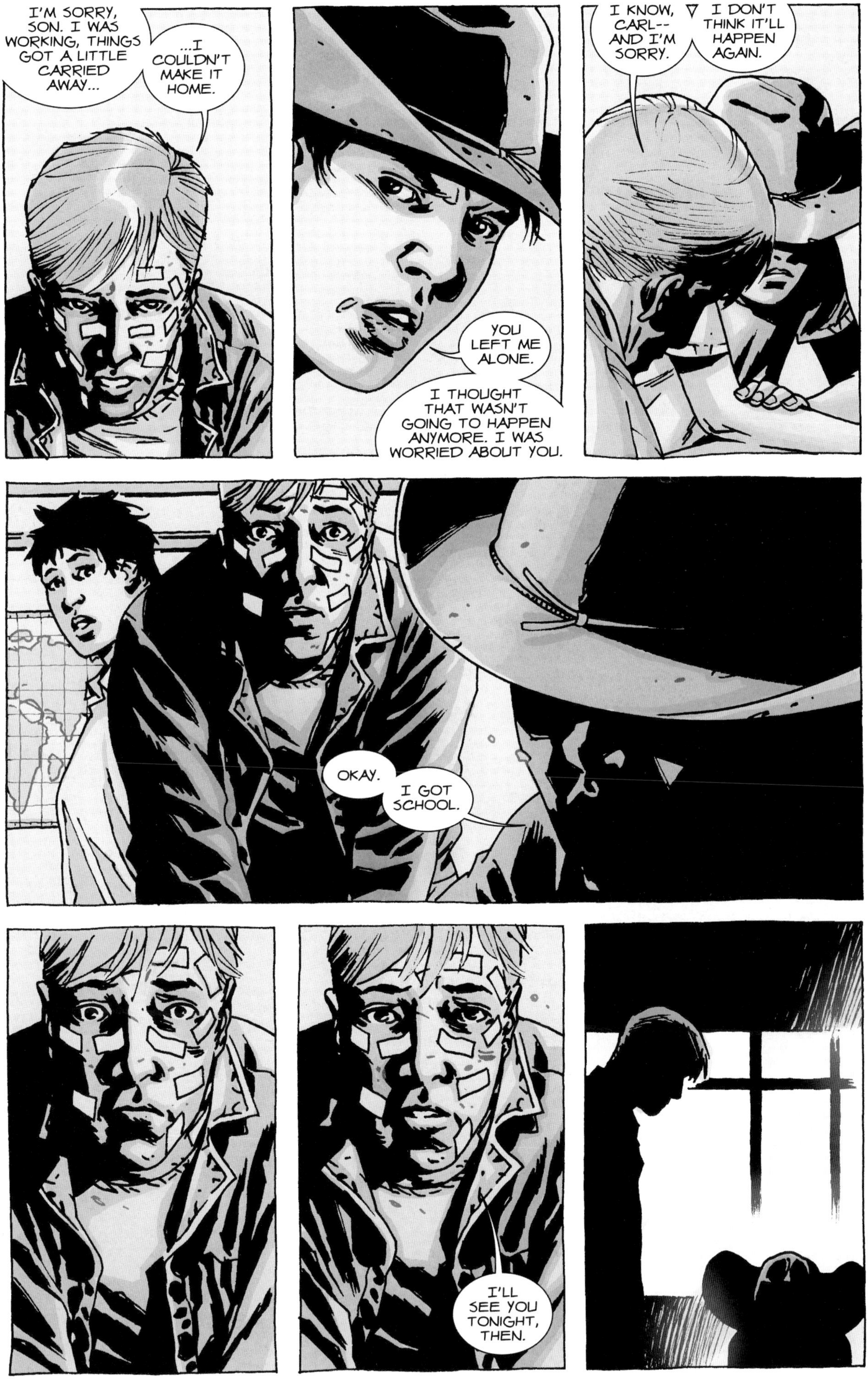
I'M SORRY, SON. I WAS WORKING, THINGS GOT A LITTLE CARRIED AWAY...
...I COULDN'T MAKE IT HOME.
YOU LEFT ME ALONE.
I THOUGHT THAT WASN'T GOING TO HAPPEN ANYMORE. I WAS WORRIED ABOUT YOU.
I KNOW, CARL-- AND I'M SORRY.
I DON'T THINK IT'LL HAPPEN AGAIN.
OKAY.
I GOT SCHOOL.
I'LL SEE YOU TONIGHT, THEN.

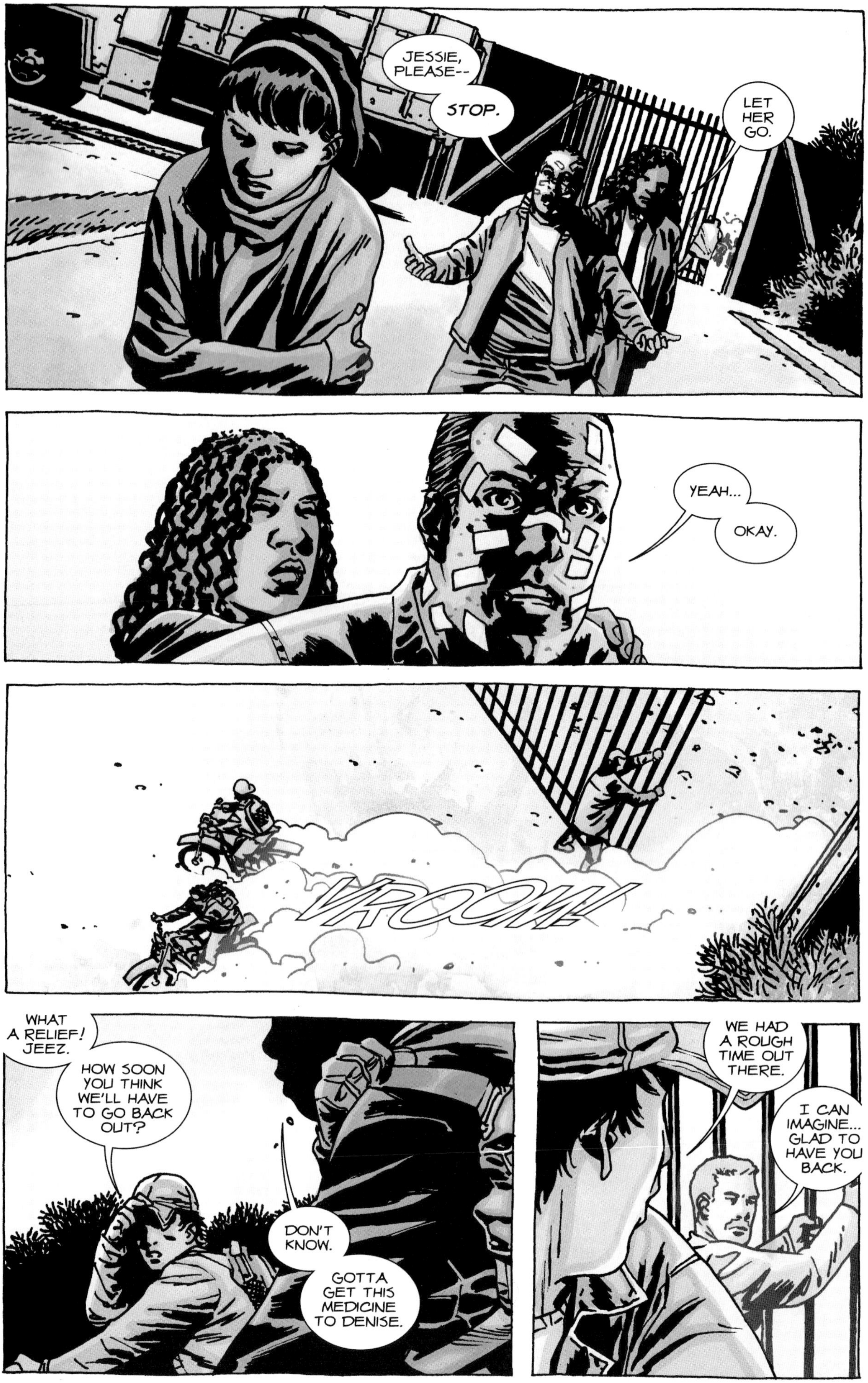
JESSIE, PLEASE--
STOP.
LET HER GO.
YEAH...
OKAY.
VROOOM!
WHAT A RELIEF! JEEZ.
HOW SOON YOU THINK WE'LL HAVE TO GO BACK OUT?
DON'T KNOW.
GOTTA GET THIS MEDICINE TO DENISE.
WE HAD A ROUGH TIME OUT THERE.
I CAN IMAGINE... GLAD TO HAVE YOU BACK.

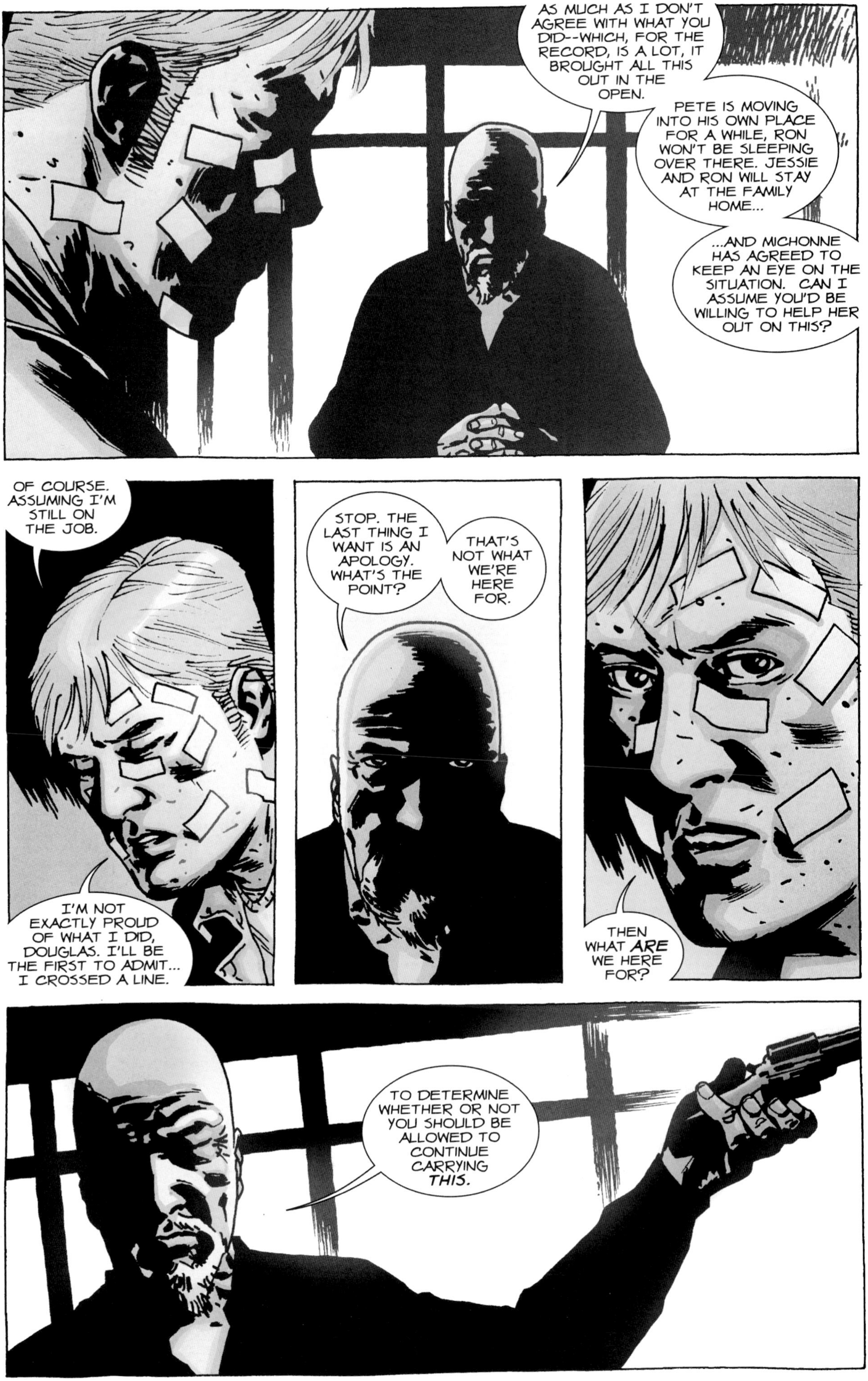
AS MUCH AS I DON'T AGREE WITH WHAT YOU DID--WHICH, FOR THE RECORD, IS A LOT, IT BROUGHT ALL THIS OUT IN THE OPEN.
PETE IS MOVING INTO HIS OWN PLACE FOR A WHILE, RON WON'T BE SLEEPING OVER THERE. JESSIE AND RON WILL STAY AT THE FAMILY HOME...
...AND MICHONNE HAS AGREED TO KEEP AN EYE ON THE SITUATION. CAN I ASSUME YOU'D BE WILLING TO HELP HER OUT ON THIS?
OF COURSE. ASSUMING I'M STILL ON THE JOB.
I'M NOT EXACTLY PROUD OF WHAT I DID, DOUGLAS. I'LL BE THE FIRST TO ADMIT... I CROSSED A LINE.
STOP. THE LAST THING I WANT IS AN APOLOGY. WHAT'S THE POINT?
THAT'S NOT WHAT WE'RE HERE FOR.
THEN WHAT *ARE* WE HERE FOR?
TO DETERMINE WHETHER OR NOT YOU SHOULD BE ALLOWED TO CONTINUE CARRYING *THIS.*

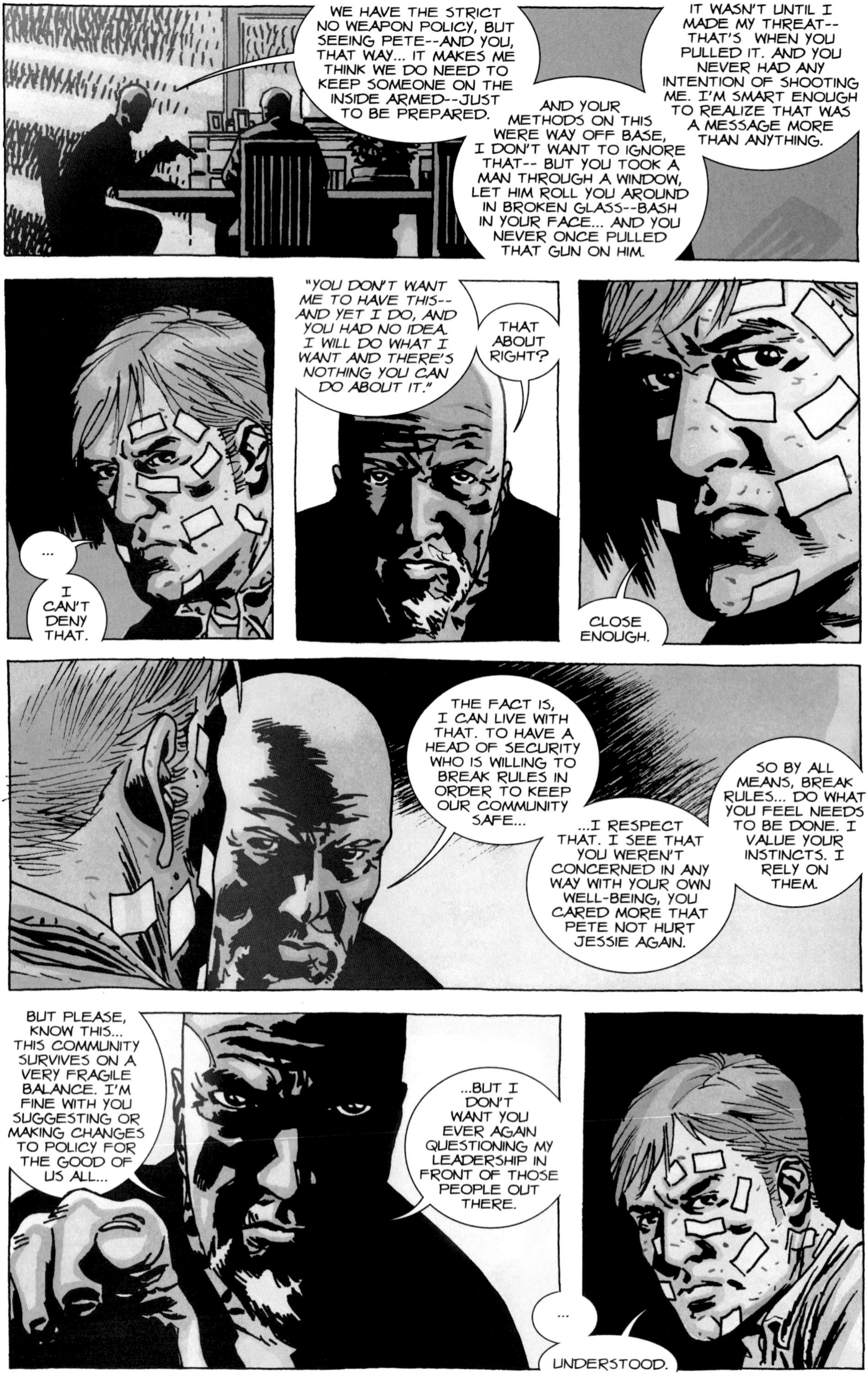
WE HAVE THE STRICT NO WEAPON POLICY, BUT SEEING PETE--AND YOU, THAT WAY... IT MAKES ME THINK WE DO NEED TO KEEP SOMEONE ON THE INSIDE ARMED--JUST TO BE PREPARED.
AND YOUR METHODS ON THIS WERE WAY OFF BASE, I DON'T WANT TO IGNORE THAT-- BUT YOU TOOK A MAN THROUGH A WINDOW, LET HIM ROLL YOU AROUND IN BROKEN GLASS--BASH IN YOUR FACE... AND YOU NEVER ONCE PULLED THAT GUN ON HIM.
IT WASN'T UNTIL I MADE MY THREAT-- THAT'S WHEN YOU PULLED IT. AND YOU NEVER HAD ANY INTENTION OF SHOOTING ME. I'M SMART ENOUGH TO REALIZE THAT WAS A MESSAGE MORE THAN ANYTHING.
...
I CAN'T DENY THAT.
"YOU DON'T WANT ME TO HAVE THIS-- AND YET I DO, AND YOU HAD NO IDEA. I WILL DO WHAT I WANT AND THERE'S NOTHING YOU CAN DO ABOUT IT."
THAT ABOUT RIGHT?
CLOSE ENOUGH.
THE FACT IS, I CAN LIVE WITH THAT. TO HAVE A HEAD OF SECURITY WHO IS WILLING TO BREAK RULES IN ORDER TO KEEP OUR COMMUNITY SAFE...
...I RESPECT THAT. I SEE THAT YOU WEREN'T CONCERNED IN ANY WAY WITH YOUR OWN WELL-BEING, YOU CARED MORE THAT PETE NOT HURT JESSIE AGAIN.
SO BY ALL MEANS, BREAK RULES... DO WHAT YOU FEEL NEEDS TO BE DONE. I VALUE YOUR INSTINCTS. I RELY ON THEM.
BUT PLEASE, KNOW THIS... THIS COMMUNITY SURVIVES ON A VERY FRAGILE BALANCE. I'M FINE WITH YOU SUGGESTING OR MAKING CHANGES TO POLICY FOR THE GOOD OF US ALL...
...BUT I DON'T WANT YOU EVER AGAIN QUESTIONING MY LEADERSHIP IN FRONT OF THOSE PEOPLE OUT THERE.
...
UNDERSTOOD.

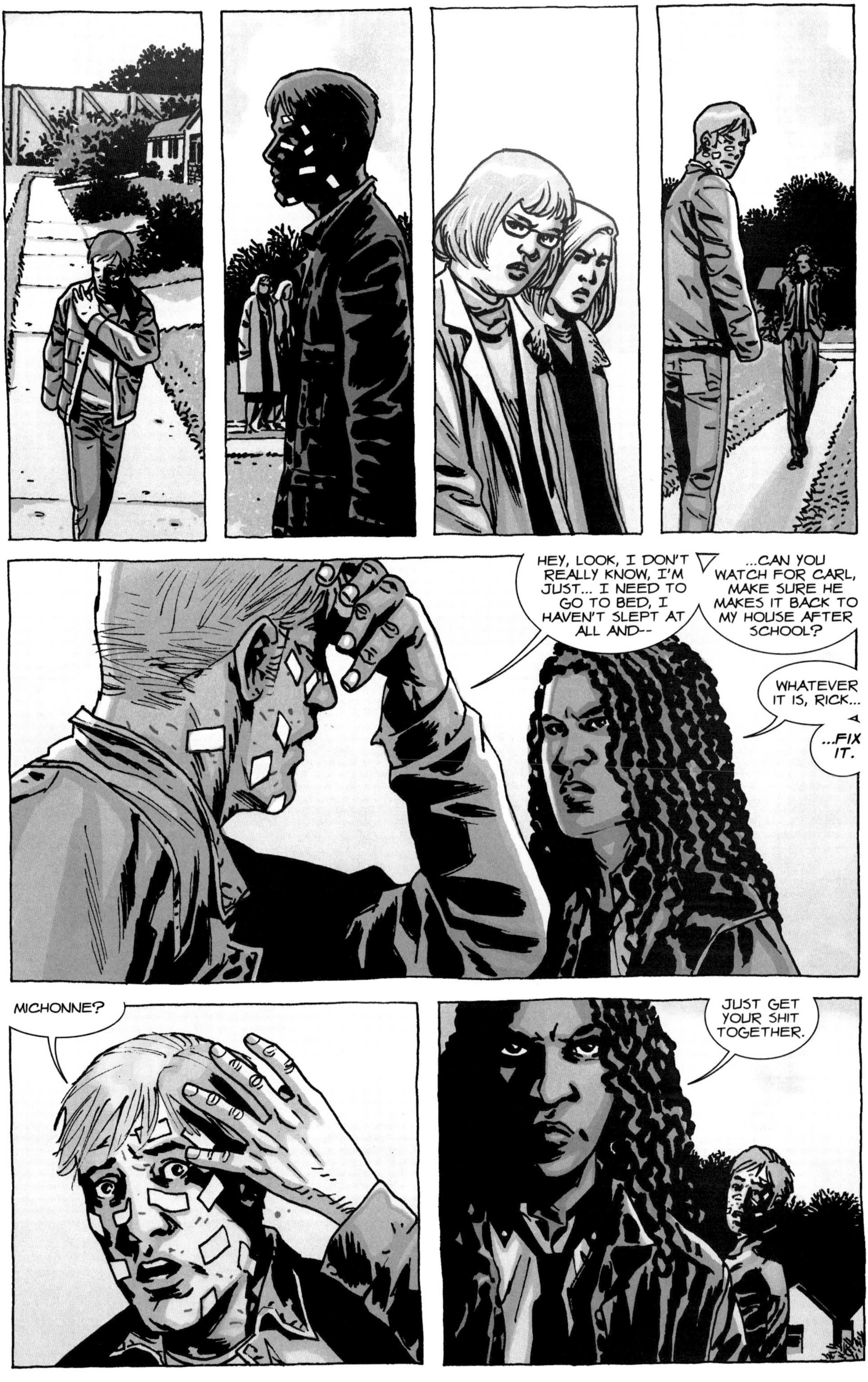
HEY, LOOK, I DON'T REALLY KNOW, I'M JUST... I NEED TO GO TO BED, I HAVEN'T SLEPT AT ALL AND--
...CAN YOU WATCH FOR CARL, MAKE SURE HE MAKES IT BACK TO MY HOUSE AFTER SCHOOL?
WHATEVER IT IS, RICK...
...FIX IT.
MICHONNE?
JUST GET YOUR SHIT TOGETHER.

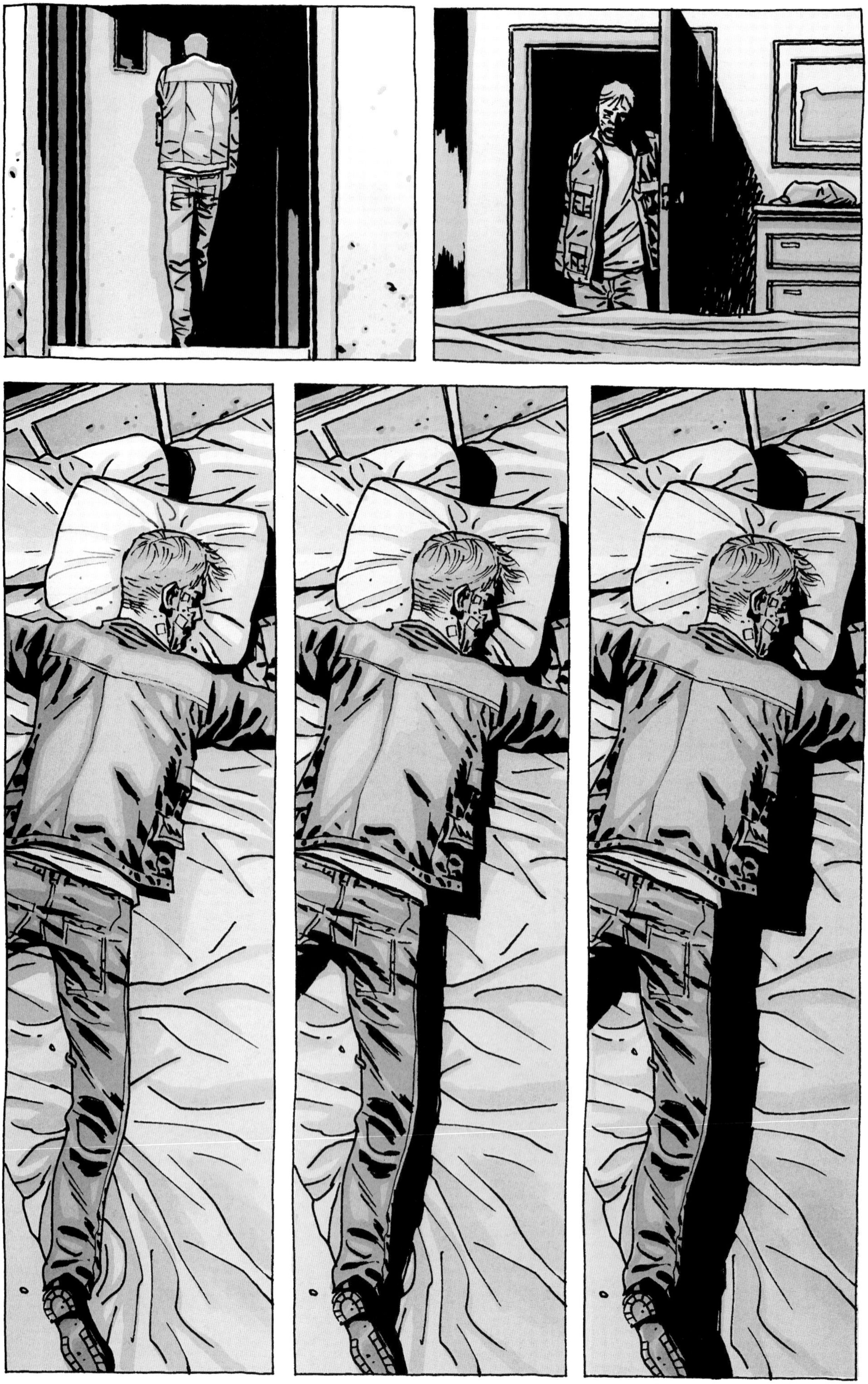

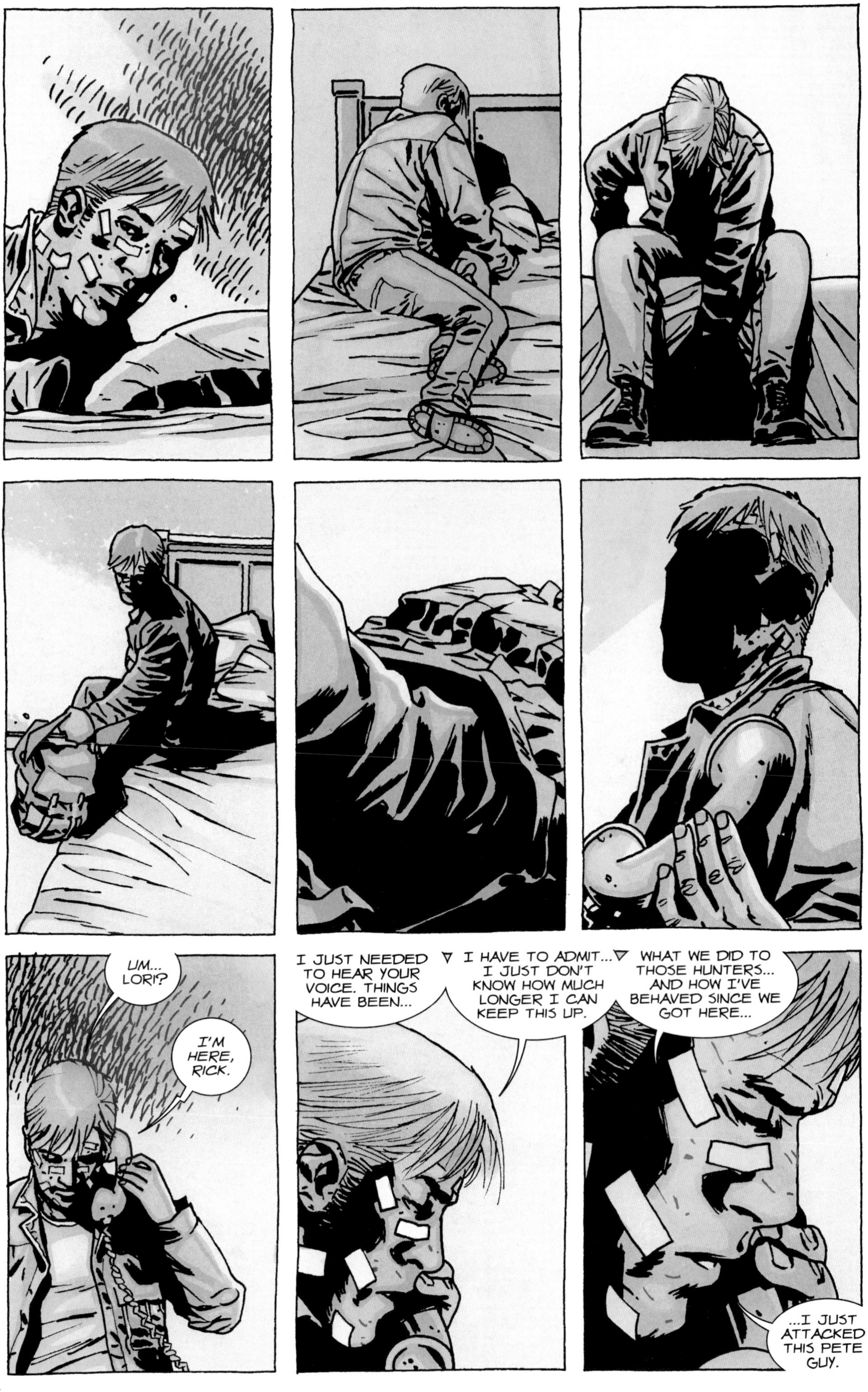
UM... LORI?
I'M HERE, RICK.
I JUST NEEDED TO HEAR YOUR VOICE. THINGS HAVE BEEN...
I HAVE TO ADMIT... I JUST DON'T KNOW HOW MUCH LONGER I CAN KEEP THIS UP.
WHAT WE DID TO THOSE HUNTERS... AND HOW I'VE BEHAVED SINCE WE GOT HERE...
...I JUST ATTACKED THIS PETE GUY.

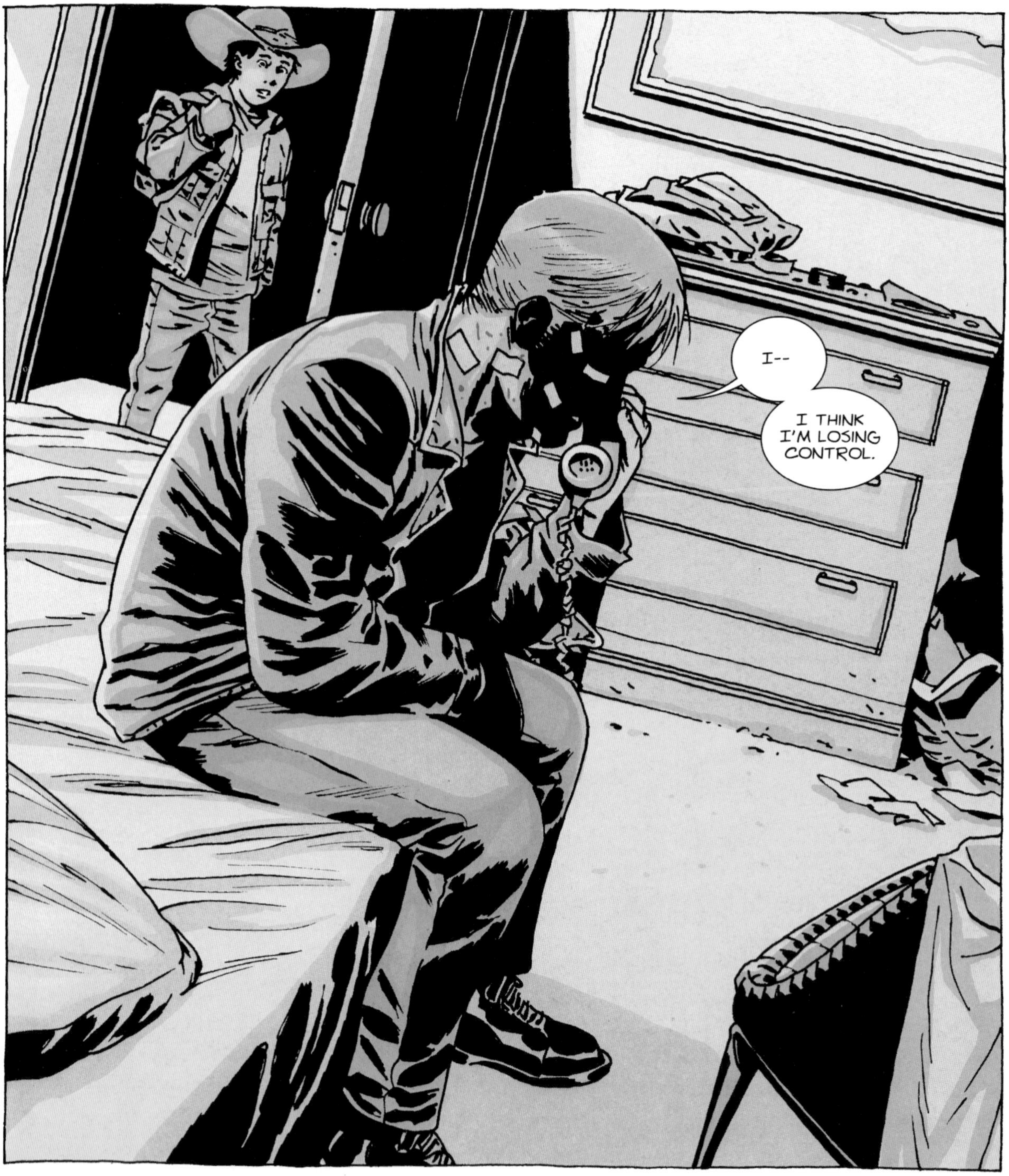
I--
I THINK I'M LOSING CONTROL.

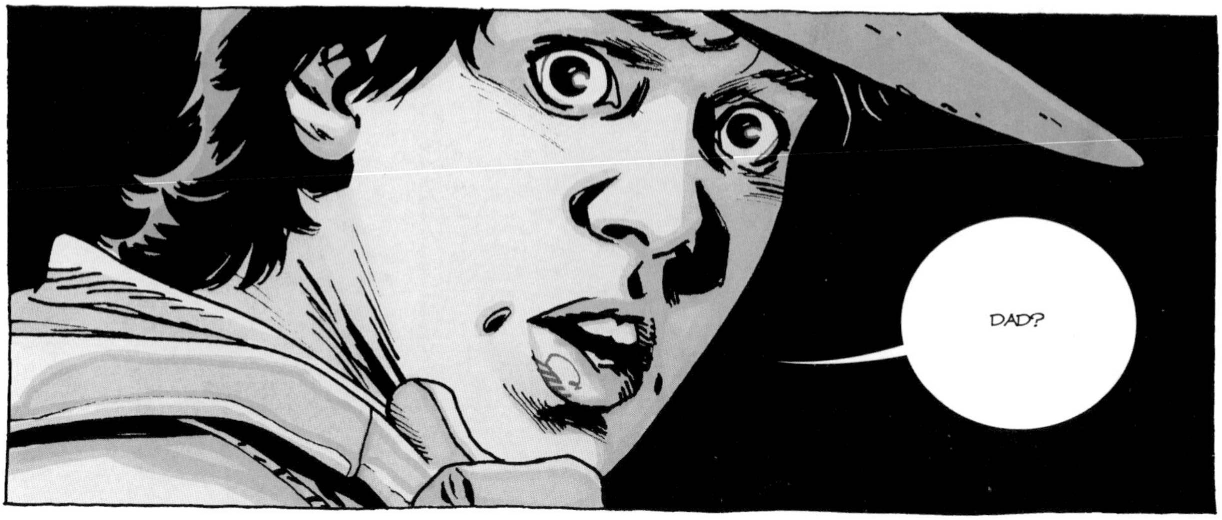
DAD?

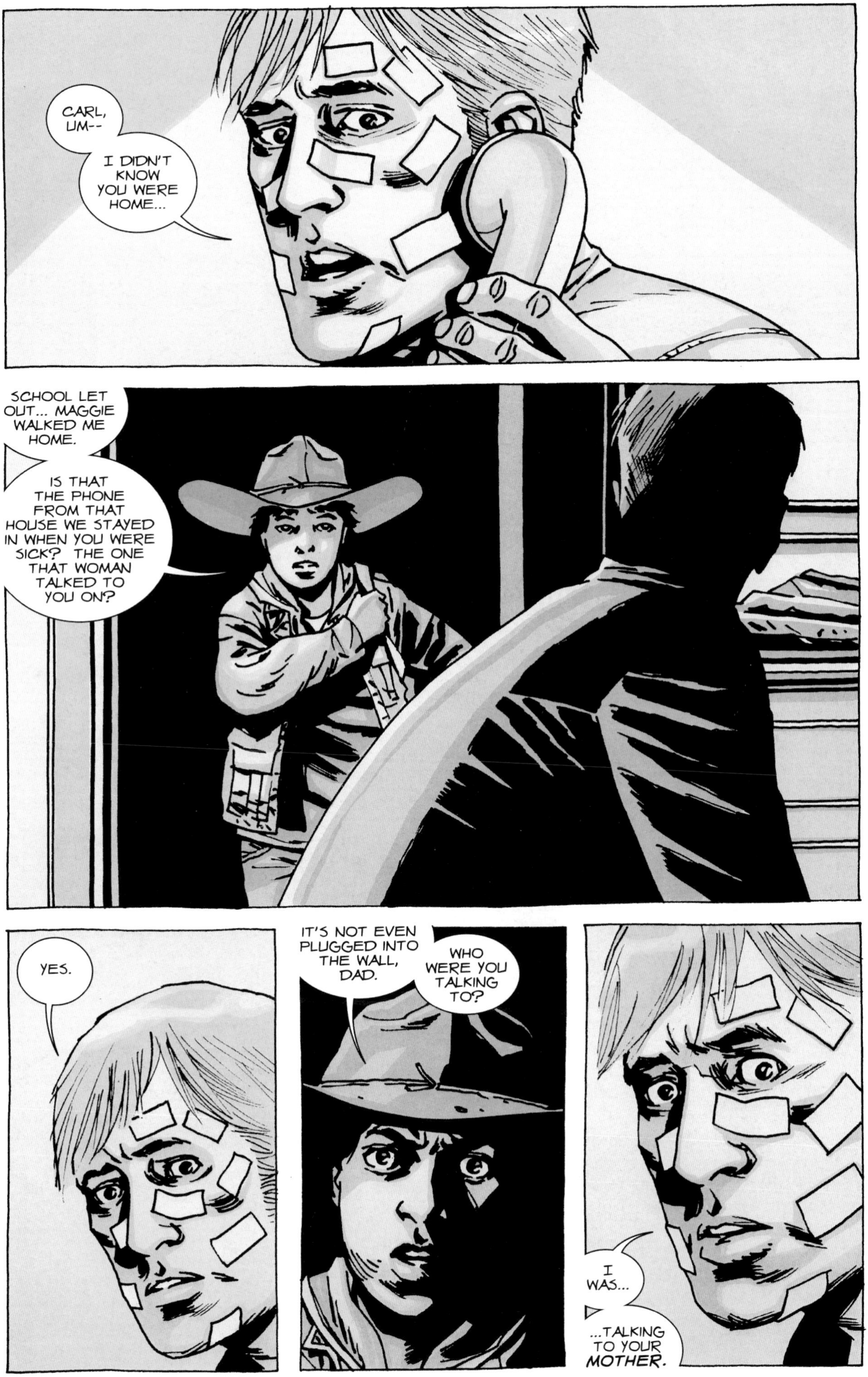
CARL, UM--
I DIDN'T KNOW YOU WERE HOME...
SCHOOL LET OUT... MAGGIE WALKED ME HOME.
IS THAT THE PHONE FROM THAT HOUSE WE STAYED IN WHEN YOU WERE SICK? THE ONE THAT WOMAN TALKED TO YOU ON?
YES.
IT'S NOT EVEN PLUGGED INTO THE WALL, DAD.
WHO WERE YOU TALKING TO?
I WAS...
...TALKING TO YOUR *MOTHER*.

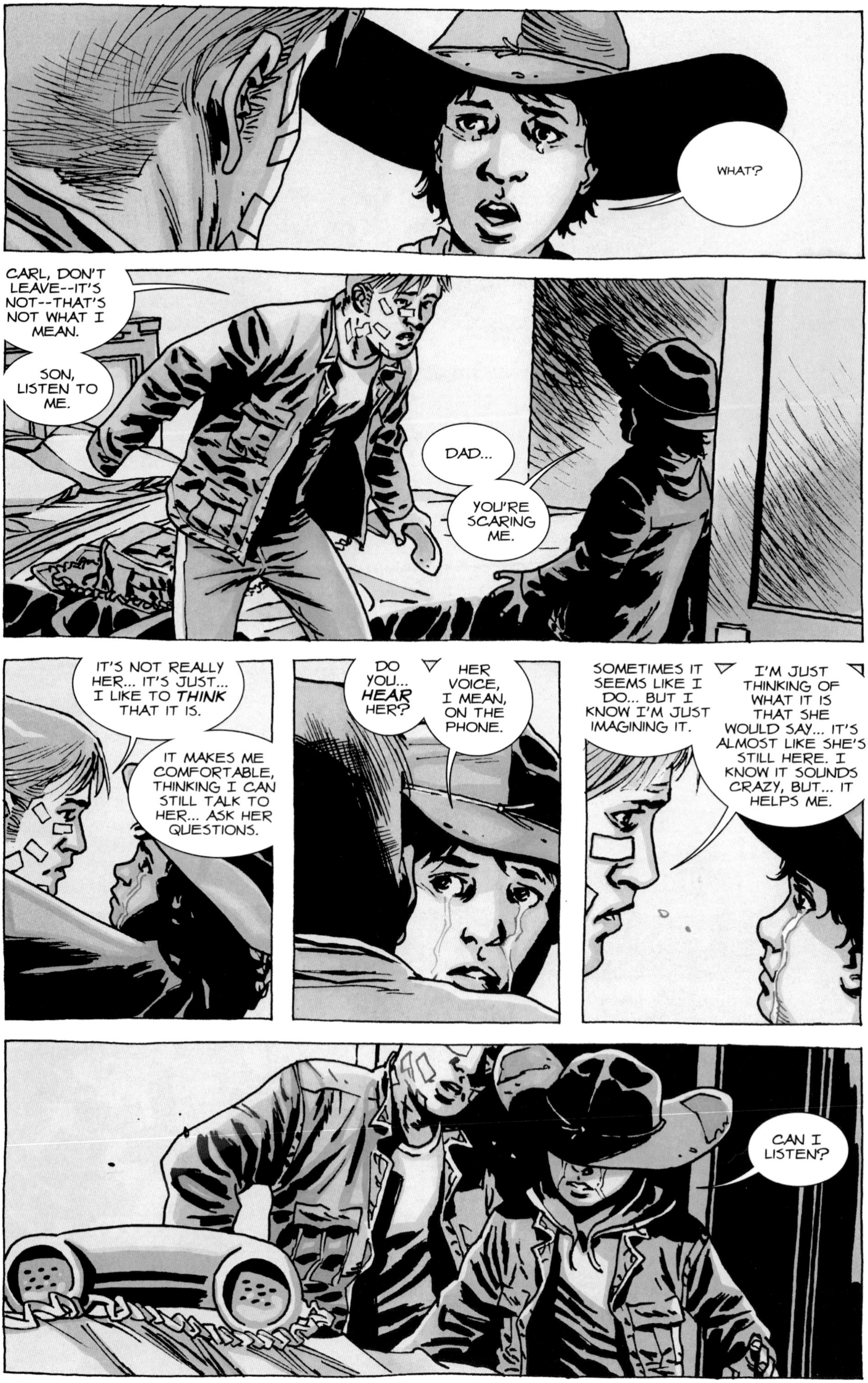
WHAT?
CARL, DON'T LEAVE--IT'S NOT--THAT'S NOT WHAT I MEAN.
SON, LISTEN TO ME.
DAD...
YOU'RE SCARING ME.
IT'S NOT REALLY HER... IT'S JUST... I LIKE TO THINK THAT IT IS.
IT MAKES ME COMFORTABLE, THINKING I CAN STILL TALK TO HER... ASK HER QUESTIONS.
DO YOU... HEAR HER?
HER VOICE, I MEAN, ON THE PHONE.
SOMETIMES IT SEEMS LIKE I DO... BUT I KNOW I'M JUST IMAGINING IT.
I'M JUST THINKING OF WHAT IT IS THAT SHE WOULD SAY... IT'S ALMOST LIKE SHE'S STILL HERE. I KNOW IT SOUNDS CRAZY, BUT... IT HELPS ME.
CAN I LISTEN?

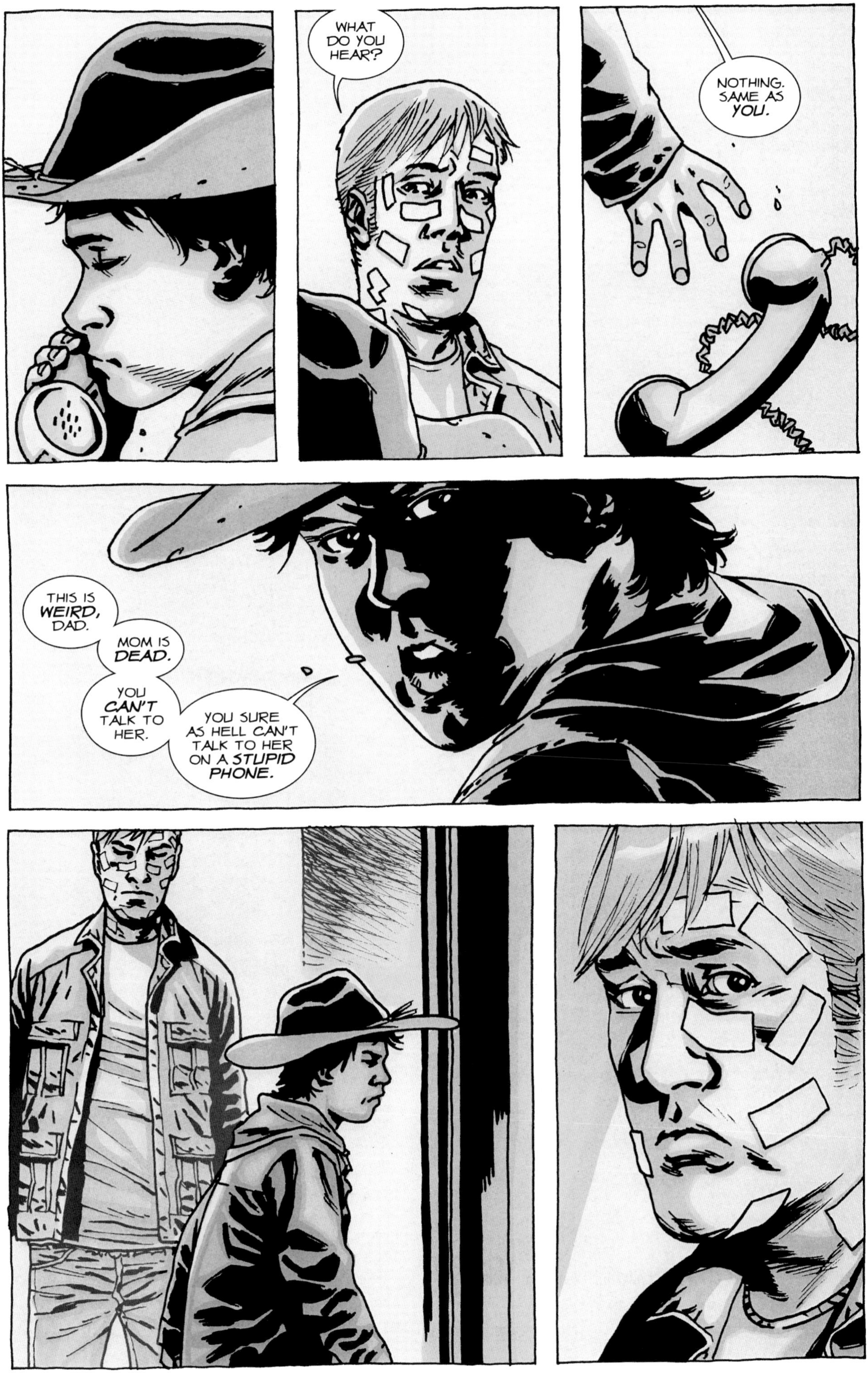
WHAT DO YOU HEAR?
NOTHING. SAME AS YOU.
THIS IS WEIRD, DAD.
MOM IS DEAD.
YOU CAN'T TALK TO HER.
YOU SURE AS HELL CAN'T TALK TO HER ON A STUPID PHONE.

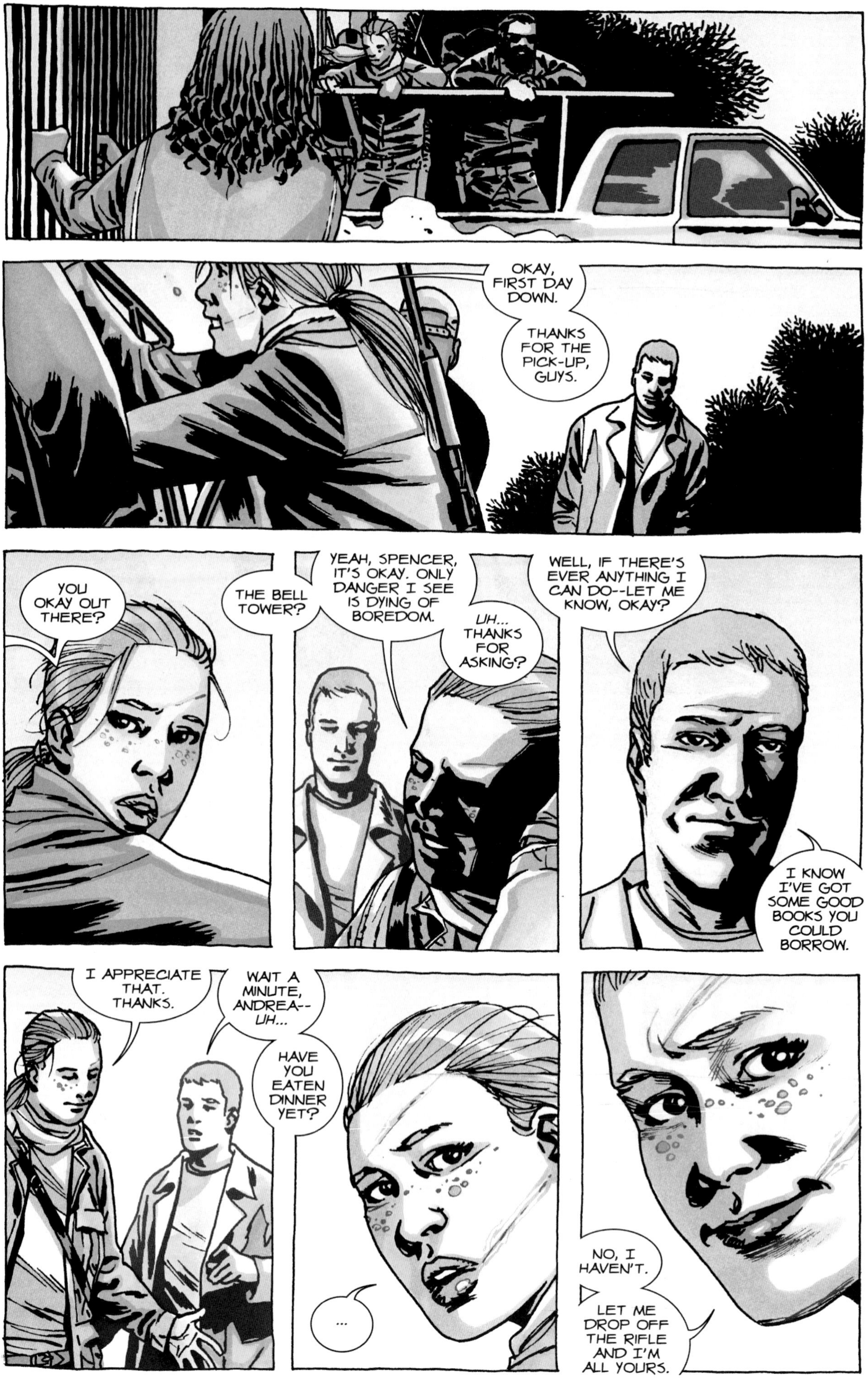
OKAY, FIRST DAY DOWN.
THANKS FOR THE PICK-UP, GUYS.
YOU OKAY OUT THERE?
THE BELL TOWER?
YEAH, SPENCER, IT'S OKAY. ONLY DANGER I SEE IS DYING OF BOREDOM.
UH... THANKS FOR ASKING?
WELL, IF THERE'S EVER ANYTHING I CAN DO--LET ME KNOW, OKAY?
I KNOW I'VE GOT SOME GOOD BOOKS YOU COULD BORROW.
I APPRECIATE THAT. THANKS.
WAIT A MINUTE, ANDREA--UH...
HAVE YOU EATEN DINNER YET?
...
NO, I HAVEN'T.
LET ME DROP OFF THE RIFLE AND I'M ALL YOURS.

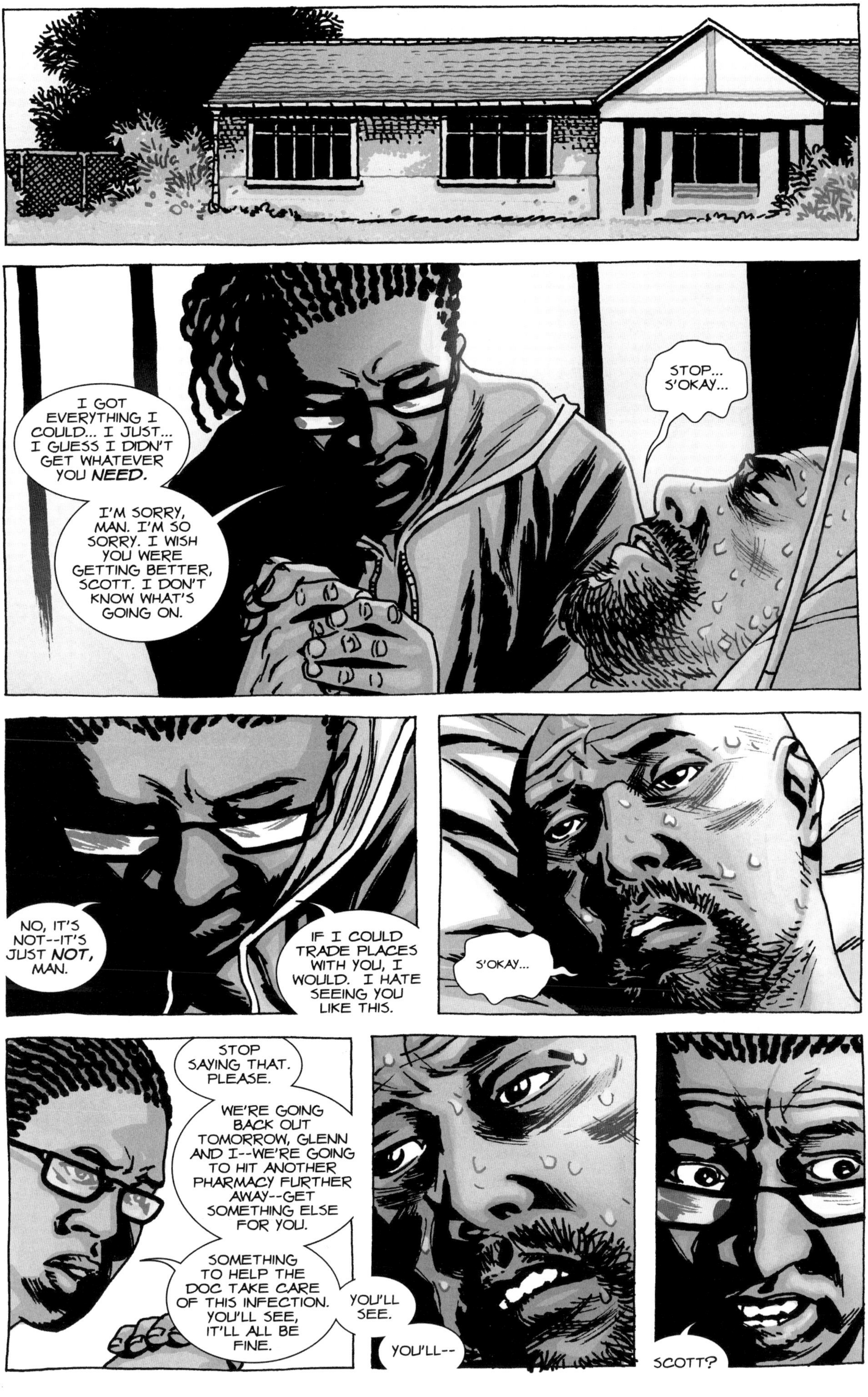
I GOT EVERYTHING I COULD... I JUST... I GUESS I DIDN'T GET WHATEVER YOU NEED.
I'M SORRY, MAN. I'M SO SORRY. I WISH YOU WERE GETTING BETTER, SCOTT. I DON'T KNOW WHAT'S GOING ON.
STOP... S'OKAY...
NO, IT'S NOT--IT'S JUST NOT, MAN.
IF I COULD TRADE PLACES WITH YOU, I WOULD. I HATE SEEING YOU LIKE THIS.
S'OKAY...
STOP SAYING THAT. PLEASE.
WE'RE GOING BACK OUT TOMORROW, GLENN AND I--WE'RE GOING TO HIT ANOTHER PHARMACY FURTHER AWAY--GET SOMETHING ELSE FOR YOU.
SOMETHING TO HELP THE DOC TAKE CARE OF THIS INFECTION. YOU'LL SEE, IT'LL ALL BE FINE.
YOU'LL SEE.
YOU'LL--
SCOTT?

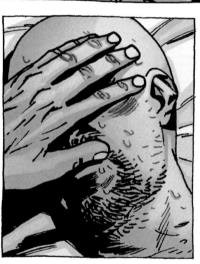

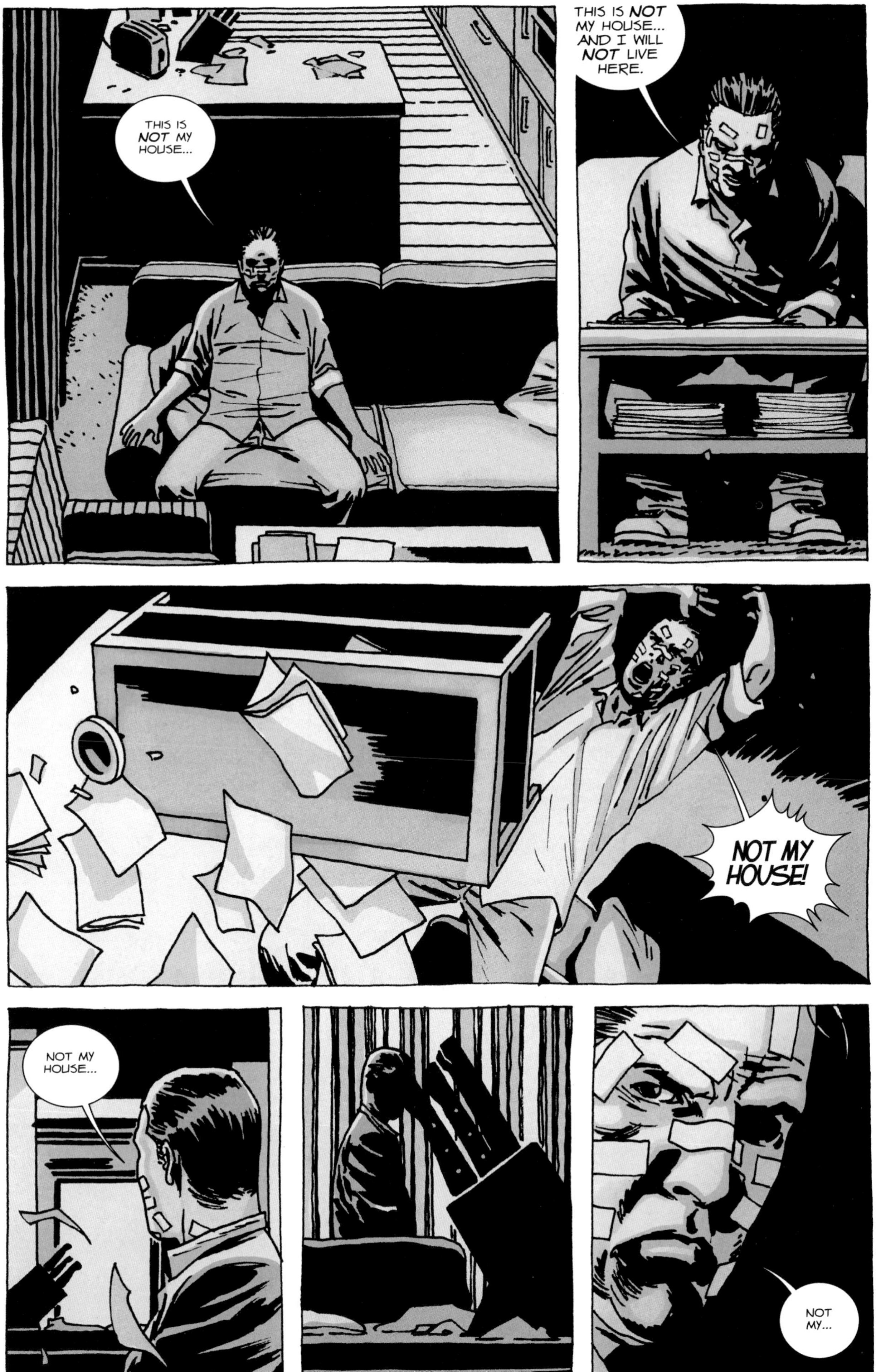
THIS IS NOT MY HOUSE...
THIS IS NOT MY HOUSE... AND I WILL NOT LIVE HERE.
NOT MY HOUSE!
NOT MY HOUSE...
NOT MY...

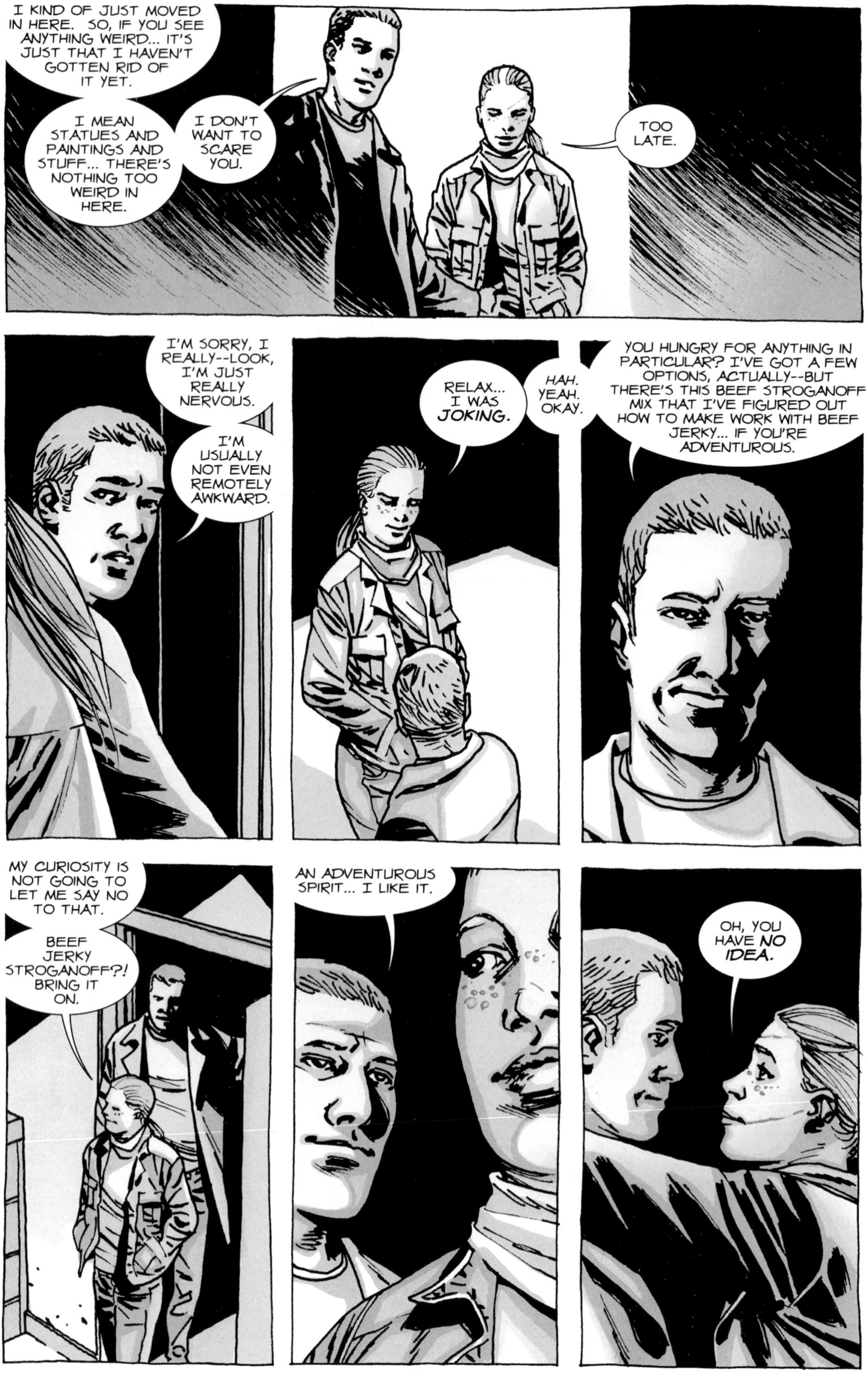
I KIND OF JUST MOVED IN HERE. SO, IF YOU SEE ANYTHING WEIRD... IT'S JUST THAT I HAVEN'T GOTTEN RID OF IT YET.
I DON'T WANT TO SCARE YOU.
I MEAN STATUES AND PAINTINGS AND STUFF... THERE'S NOTHING TOO WEIRD IN HERE.
TOO LATE.
I'M SORRY, I REALLY--LOOK, I'M JUST REALLY NERVOUS.
I'M USUALLY NOT EVEN REMOTELY AWKWARD.
RELAX... I WAS JOKING.
HAH. YEAH. OKAY.
YOU HUNGRY FOR ANYTHING IN PARTICULAR? I'VE GOT A FEW OPTIONS, ACTUALLY--BUT THERE'S THIS BEEF STROGANOFF MIX THAT I'VE FIGURED OUT HOW TO MAKE WORK WITH BEEF JERKY... IF YOU'RE ADVENTUROUS.
MY CURIOSITY IS NOT GOING TO LET ME SAY NO TO THAT.
BEEF JERKY STROGANOFF?! BRING IT ON.
AN ADVENTUROUS SPIRIT... I LIKE IT.
OH, YOU HAVE NO IDEA.

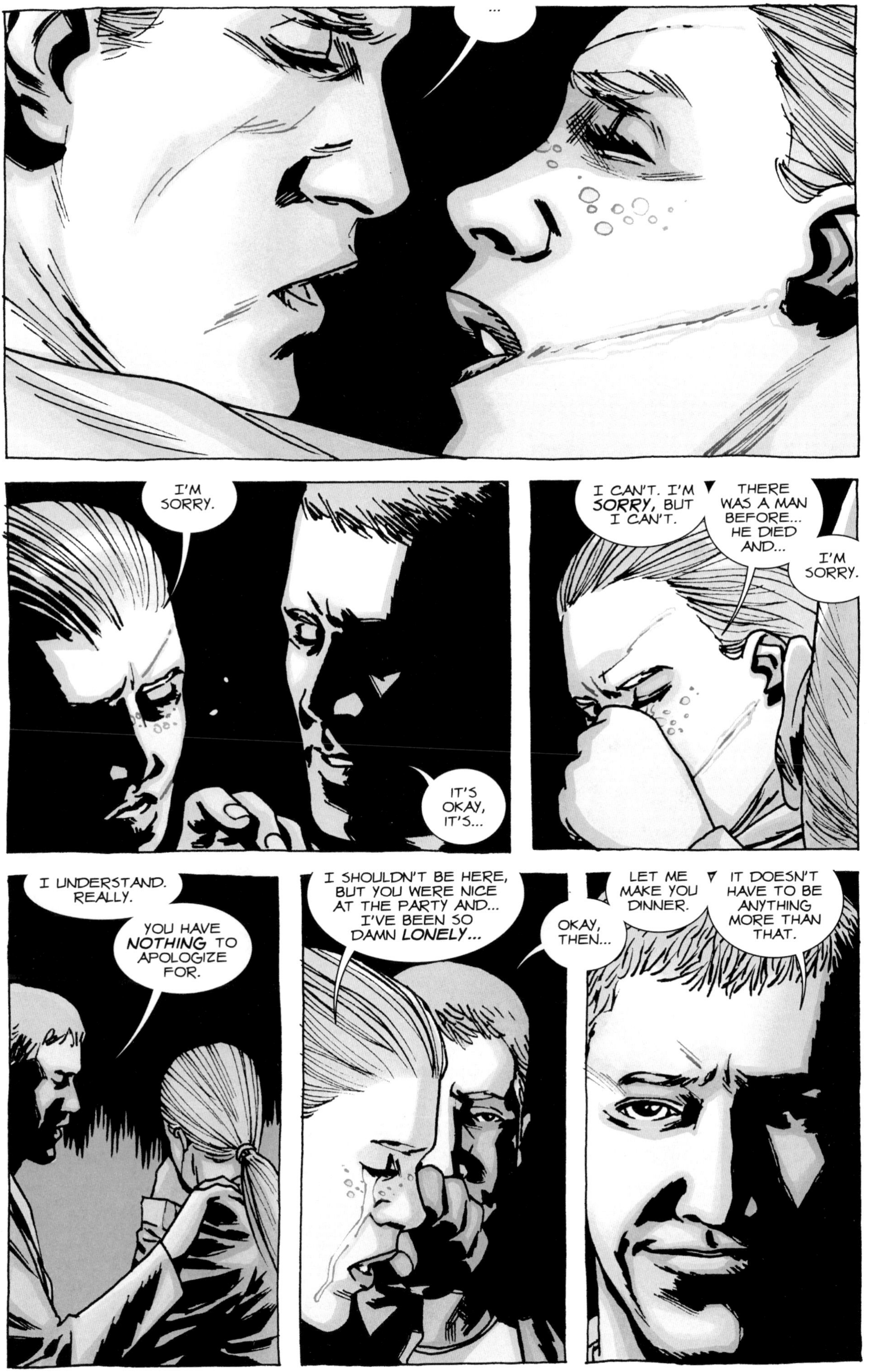
...
I'M SORRY.
IT'S OKAY, IT'S...
I CAN'T. I'M SORRY, BUT I CAN'T.
THERE WAS A MAN BEFORE... HE DIED AND...
I'M SORRY.
I UNDERSTAND. REALLY.
YOU HAVE NOTHING TO APOLOGIZE FOR.
I SHOULDN'T BE HERE, BUT YOU WERE NICE AT THE PARTY AND... I'VE BEEN SO DAMN LONELY...
OKAY, THEN...
LET ME MAKE YOU DINNER.
IT DOESN'T HAVE TO BE ANYTHING MORE THAN THAT.

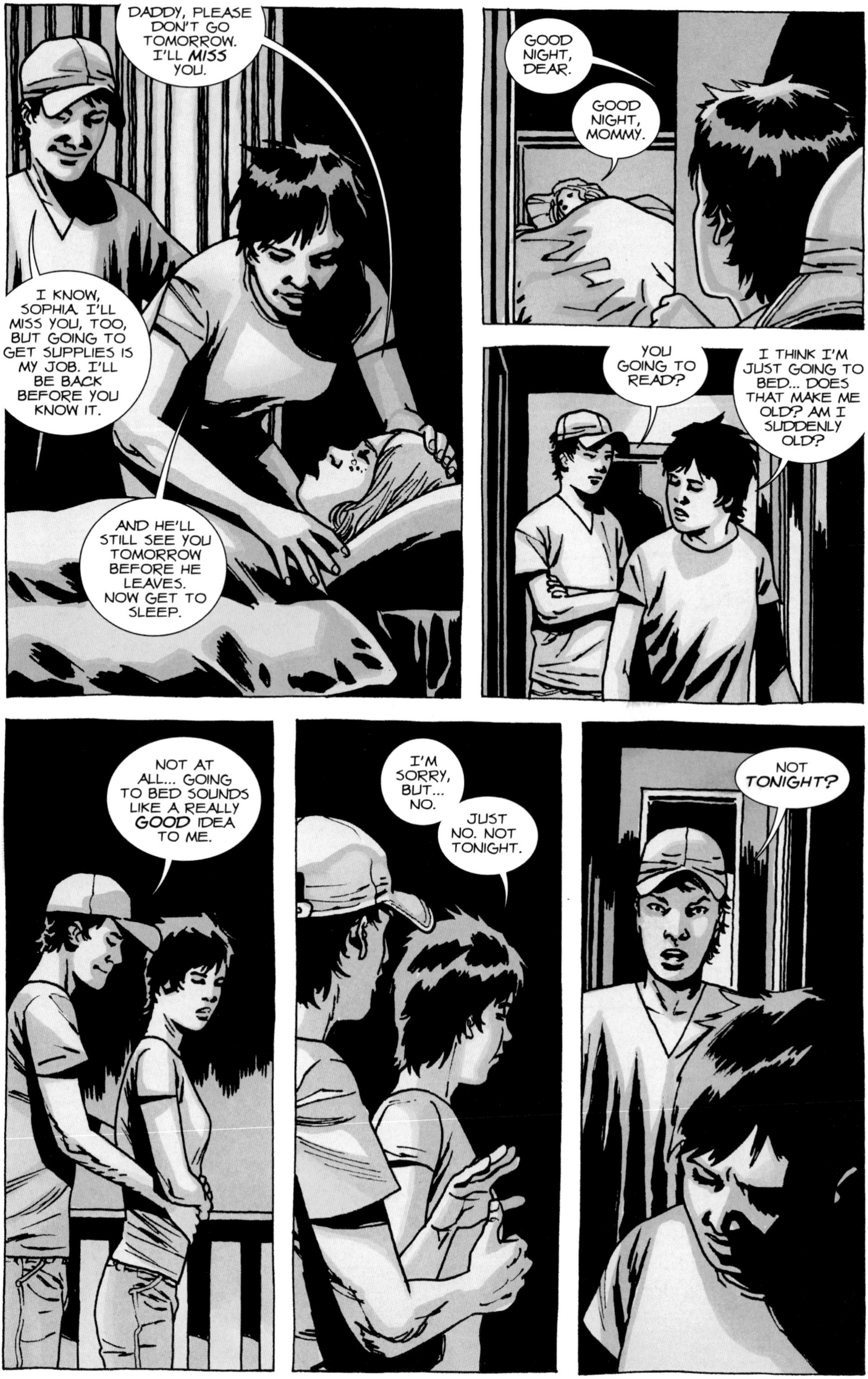
DADDY, PLEASE DON'T GO TOMORROW. I'LL MISS YOU.
I KNOW, SOPHIA. I'LL MISS YOU, TOO, BUT GOING TO GET SUPPLIES IS MY JOB. I'LL BE BACK BEFORE YOU KNOW IT.
AND HE'LL STILL SEE YOU TOMORROW BEFORE HE LEAVES. NOW GET TO SLEEP.
GOOD NIGHT, DEAR.
GOOD NIGHT, MOMMY.
YOU GOING TO READ?
I THINK I'M JUST GOING TO BED... DOES THAT MAKE ME OLD? AM I SUDDENLY OLD?
NOT AT ALL... GOING TO BED SOUNDS LIKE A REALLY GOOD IDEA TO ME.
I'M SORRY, BUT... NO.
JUST NO. NOT TONIGHT.
NOT TONIGHT?

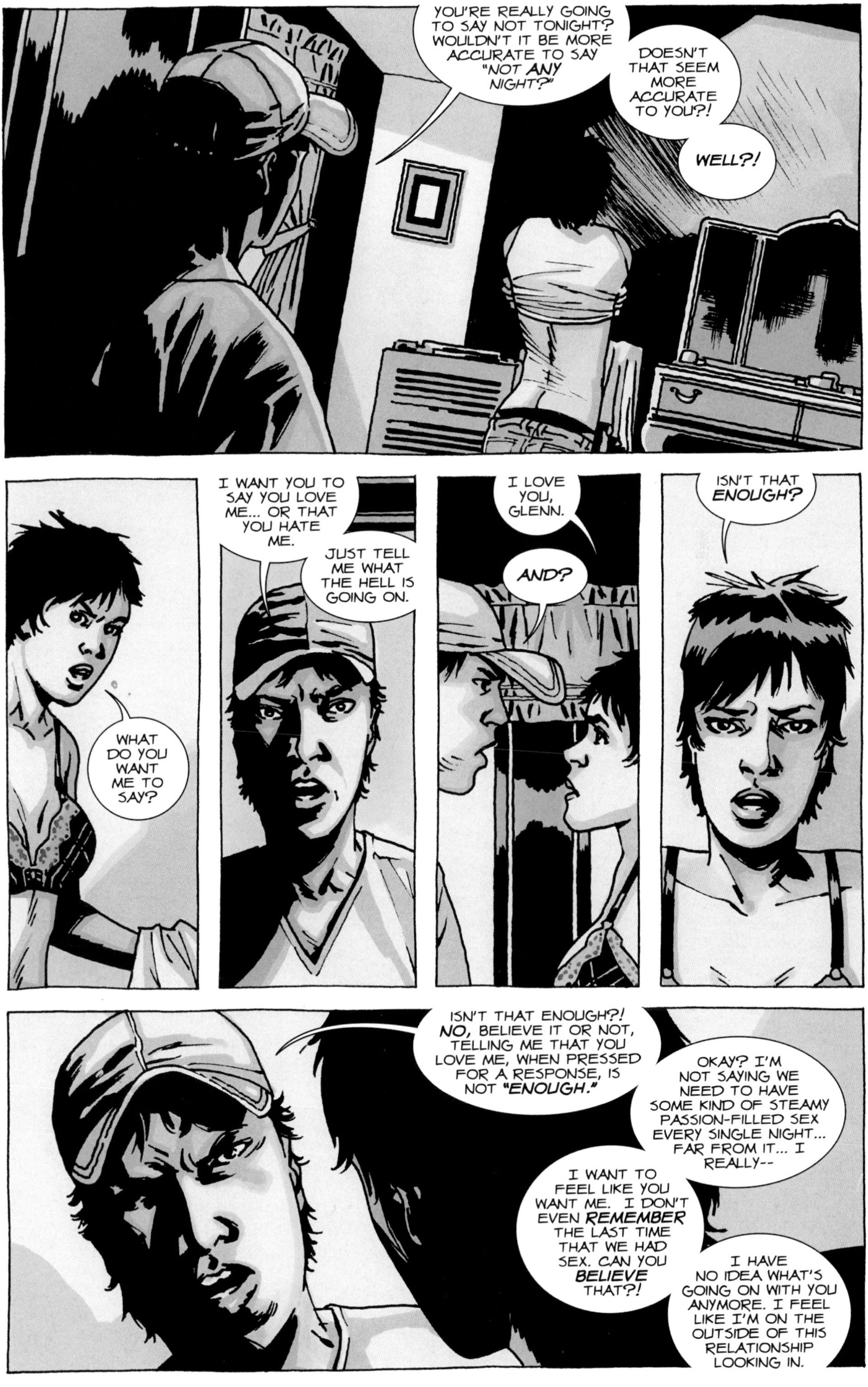

YOU'RE REALLY GOING TO SAY NOT TONIGHT? WOULDN'T IT BE MORE ACCURATE TO SAY "NOT ANY NIGHT?"
DOESN'T THAT SEEM MORE ACCURATE TO YOU?!
WELL?!
WHAT DO YOU WANT ME TO SAY?
I WANT YOU TO SAY YOU LOVE ME... OR THAT YOU HATE ME.
JUST TELL ME WHAT THE HELL IS GOING ON.
I LOVE YOU, GLENN.
AND?
ISN'T THAT ENOUGH?
ISN'T THAT ENOUGH?! NO, BELIEVE IT OR NOT, TELLING ME THAT YOU LOVE ME, WHEN PRESSED FOR A RESPONSE, IS NOT "ENOUGH."
OKAY? I'M NOT SAYING WE NEED TO HAVE SOME KIND OF STEAMY PASSION-FILLED SEX EVERY SINGLE NIGHT... FAR FROM IT... I REALLY--
I WANT TO FEEL LIKE YOU WANT ME. I DON'T EVEN REMEMBER THE LAST TIME THAT WE HAD SEX. CAN YOU BELIEVE THAT?!
I HAVE NO IDEA WHAT'S GOING ON WITH YOU ANYMORE. I FEEL LIKE I'M ON THE OUTSIDE OF THIS RELATIONSHIP LOOKING IN.

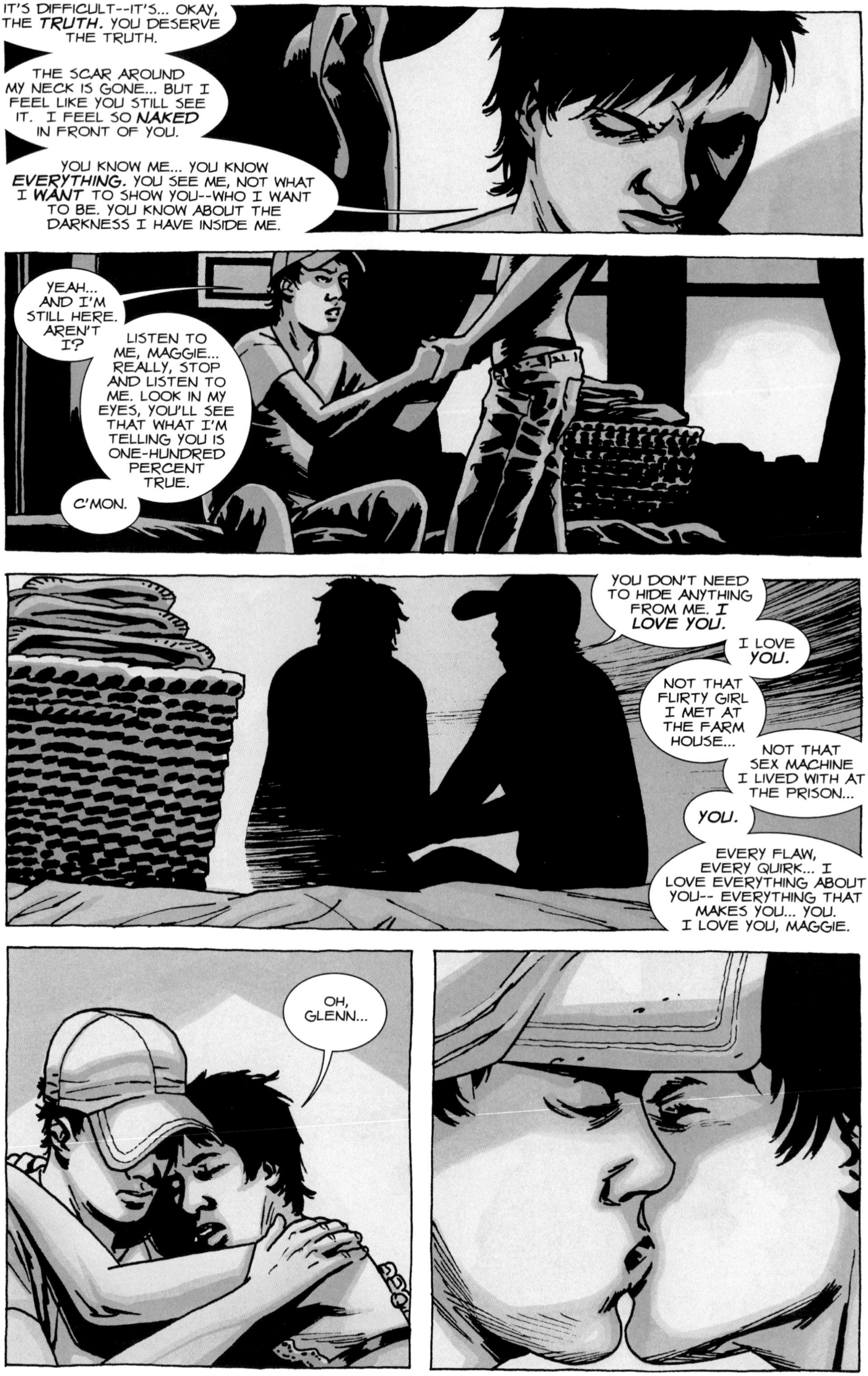
IT'S DIFFICULT--IT'S... OKAY, THE TRUTH. YOU DESERVE THE TRUTH.
THE SCAR AROUND MY NECK IS GONE... BUT I FEEL LIKE YOU STILL SEE IT. I FEEL SO NAKED IN FRONT OF YOU.
YOU KNOW ME... YOU KNOW EVERYTHING. YOU SEE ME, NOT WHAT I WANT TO SHOW YOU--WHO I WANT TO BE. YOU KNOW ABOUT THE DARKNESS I HAVE INSIDE ME.
YEAH... AND I'M STILL HERE. AREN'T I?
LISTEN TO ME, MAGGIE... REALLY, STOP AND LISTEN TO ME. LOOK IN MY EYES, YOU'LL SEE THAT WHAT I'M TELLING YOU IS ONE-HUNDRED PERCENT TRUE.
C'MON.
YOU DON'T NEED TO HIDE ANYTHING FROM ME. I LOVE YOU.
I LOVE YOU.
NOT THAT FLIRTY GIRL I MET AT THE FARM HOUSE...
NOT THAT SEX MACHINE I LIVED WITH AT THE PRISON...
YOU.
EVERY FLAW, EVERY QUIRK... I LOVE EVERYTHING ABOUT YOU-- EVERYTHING THAT MAKES YOU... YOU. I LOVE YOU, MAGGIE.
OH, GLENN...

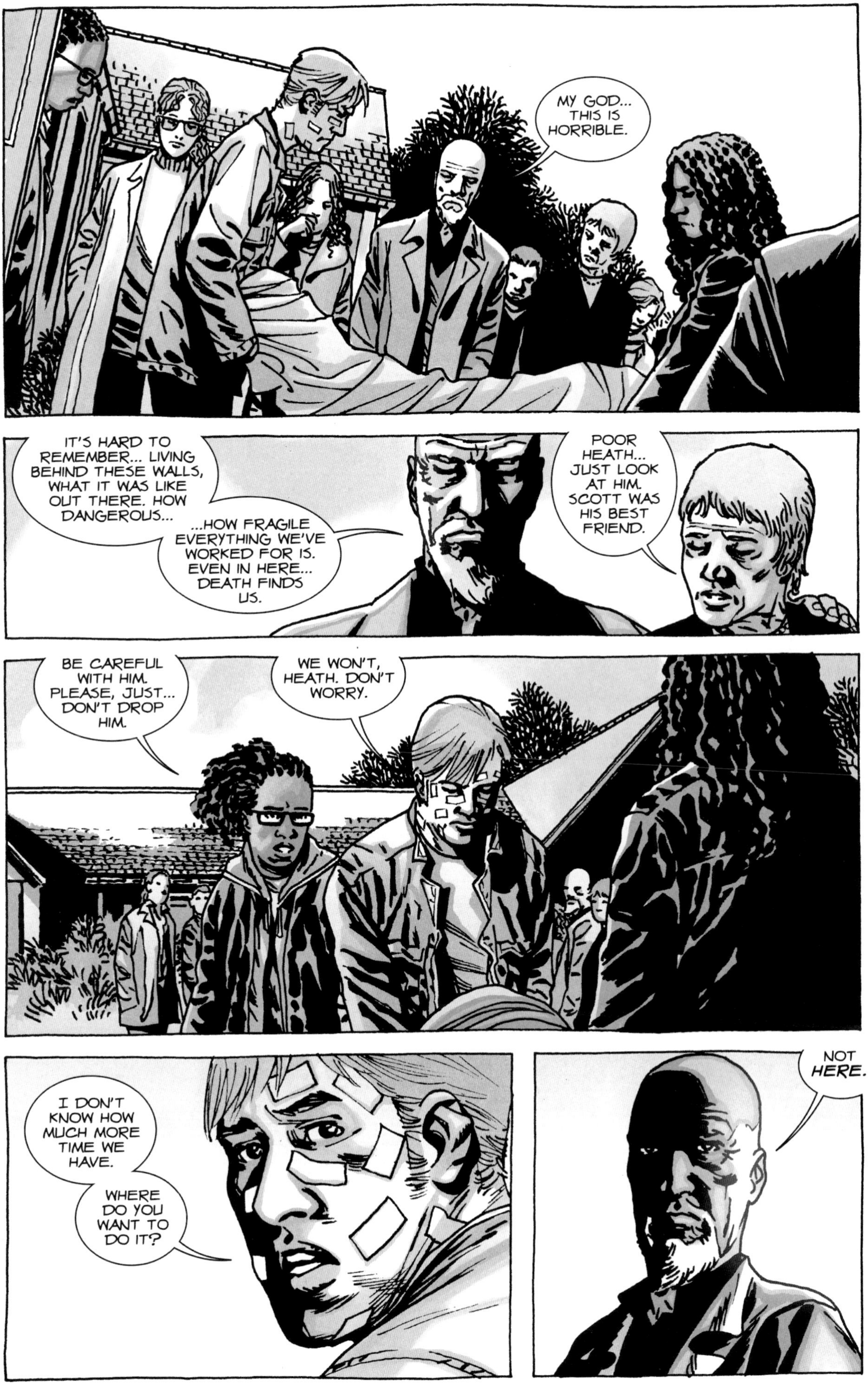
MY GOD... THIS IS HORRIBLE.
IT'S HARD TO REMEMBER... LIVING BEHIND THESE WALLS, WHAT IT WAS LIKE OUT THERE. HOW DANGEROUS...
...HOW FRAGILE EVERYTHING WE'VE WORKED FOR IS. EVEN IN HERE... DEATH FINDS US.
POOR HEATH... JUST LOOK AT HIM. SCOTT WAS HIS BEST FRIEND.
BE CAREFUL WITH HIM. PLEASE, JUST... DON'T DROP HIM.
WE WON'T, HEATH. DON'T WORRY.
I DON'T KNOW HOW MUCH MORE TIME WE HAVE.
WHERE DO YOU WANT TO DO IT?
NOT *HERE.*

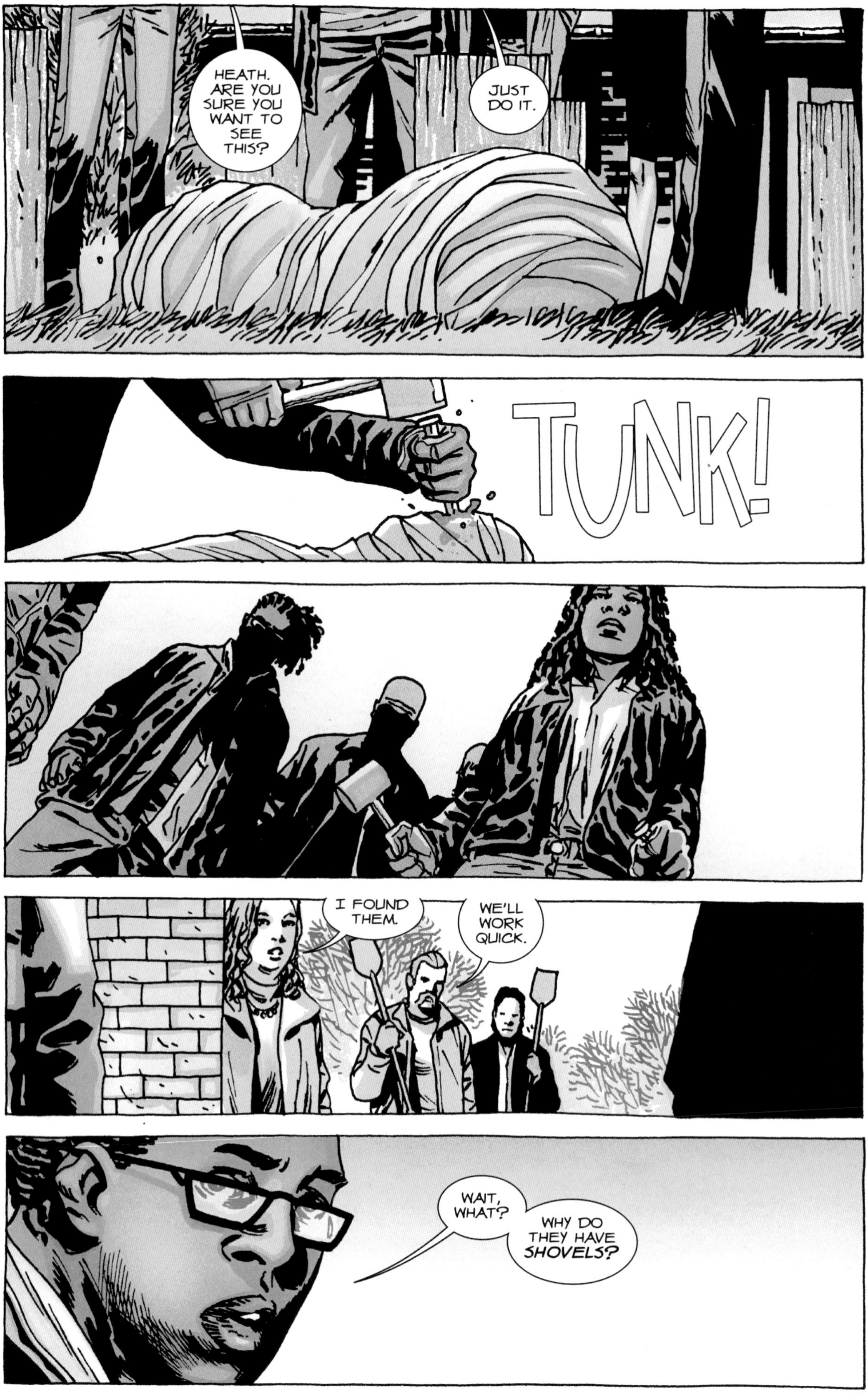
HEATH. ARE YOU SURE YOU WANT TO SEE THIS?
JUST DO IT.
TUNK!
I FOUND THEM.
WE'LL WORK QUICK.
WAIT, WHAT?
WHY DO THEY HAVE SHOVELS?

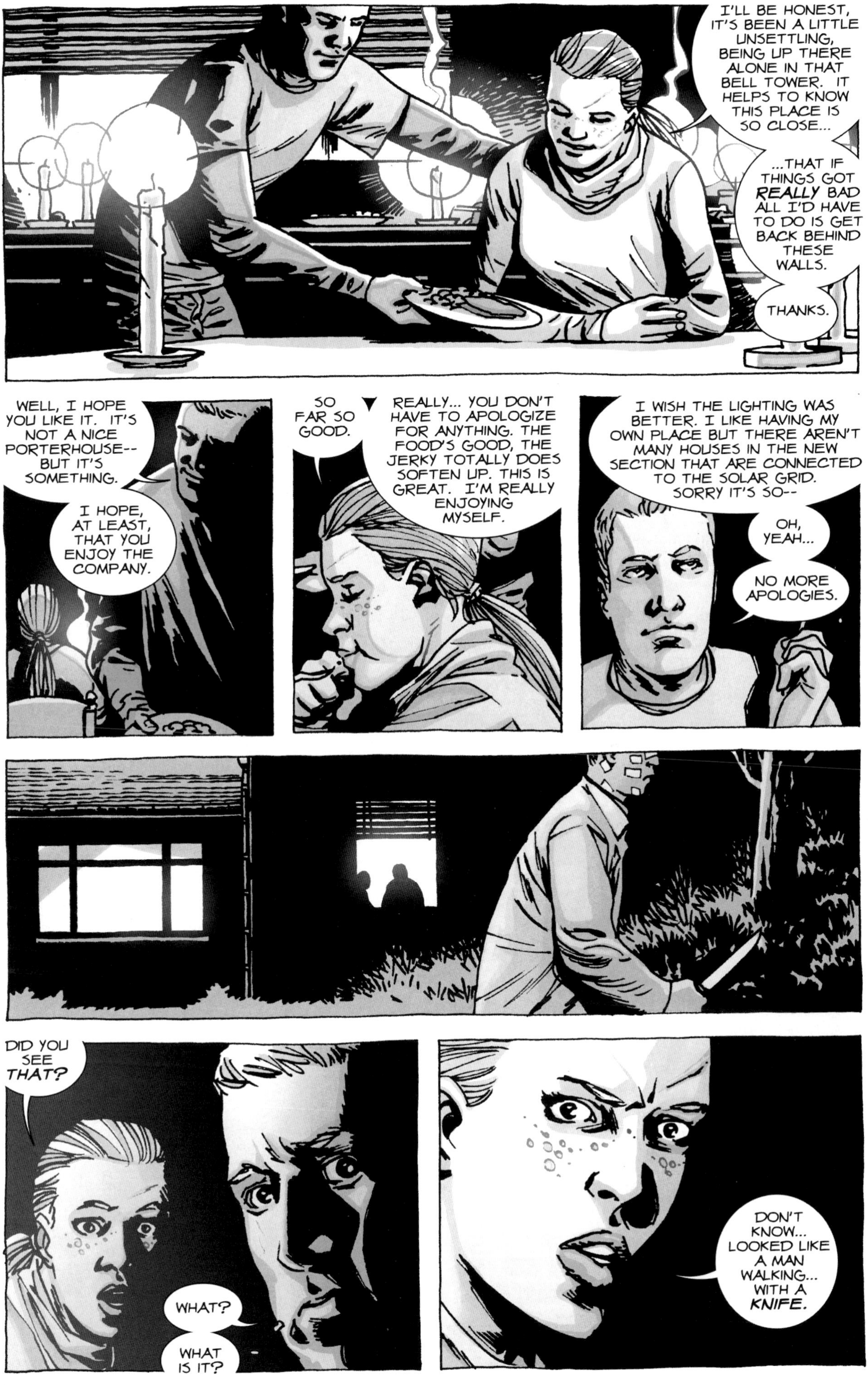
I'LL BE HONEST, IT'S BEEN A LITTLE UNSETTLING, BEING UP THERE ALONE IN THAT BELL TOWER. IT HELPS TO KNOW THIS PLACE IS SO CLOSE...
...THAT IF THINGS GOT REALLY BAD ALL I'D HAVE TO DO IS GET BACK BEHIND THESE WALLS.
THANKS.
WELL, I HOPE YOU LIKE IT. IT'S NOT A NICE PORTERHOUSE-- BUT IT'S SOMETHING.
I HOPE, AT LEAST, THAT YOU ENJOY THE COMPANY.
SO FAR SO GOOD.
REALLY... YOU DON'T HAVE TO APOLOGIZE FOR ANYTHING. THE FOOD'S GOOD, THE JERKY TOTALLY DOES SOFTEN UP. THIS IS GREAT. I'M REALLY ENJOYING MYSELF.
I WISH THE LIGHTING WAS BETTER. I LIKE HAVING MY OWN PLACE BUT THERE AREN'T MANY HOUSES IN THE NEW SECTION THAT ARE CONNECTED TO THE SOLAR GRID. SORRY IT'S SO--
OH, YEAH...
NO MORE APOLOGIES.
DID YOU SEE THAT?
WHAT?
WHAT IS IT?
DON'T KNOW... LOOKED LIKE A MAN WALKING... WITH A KNIFE.

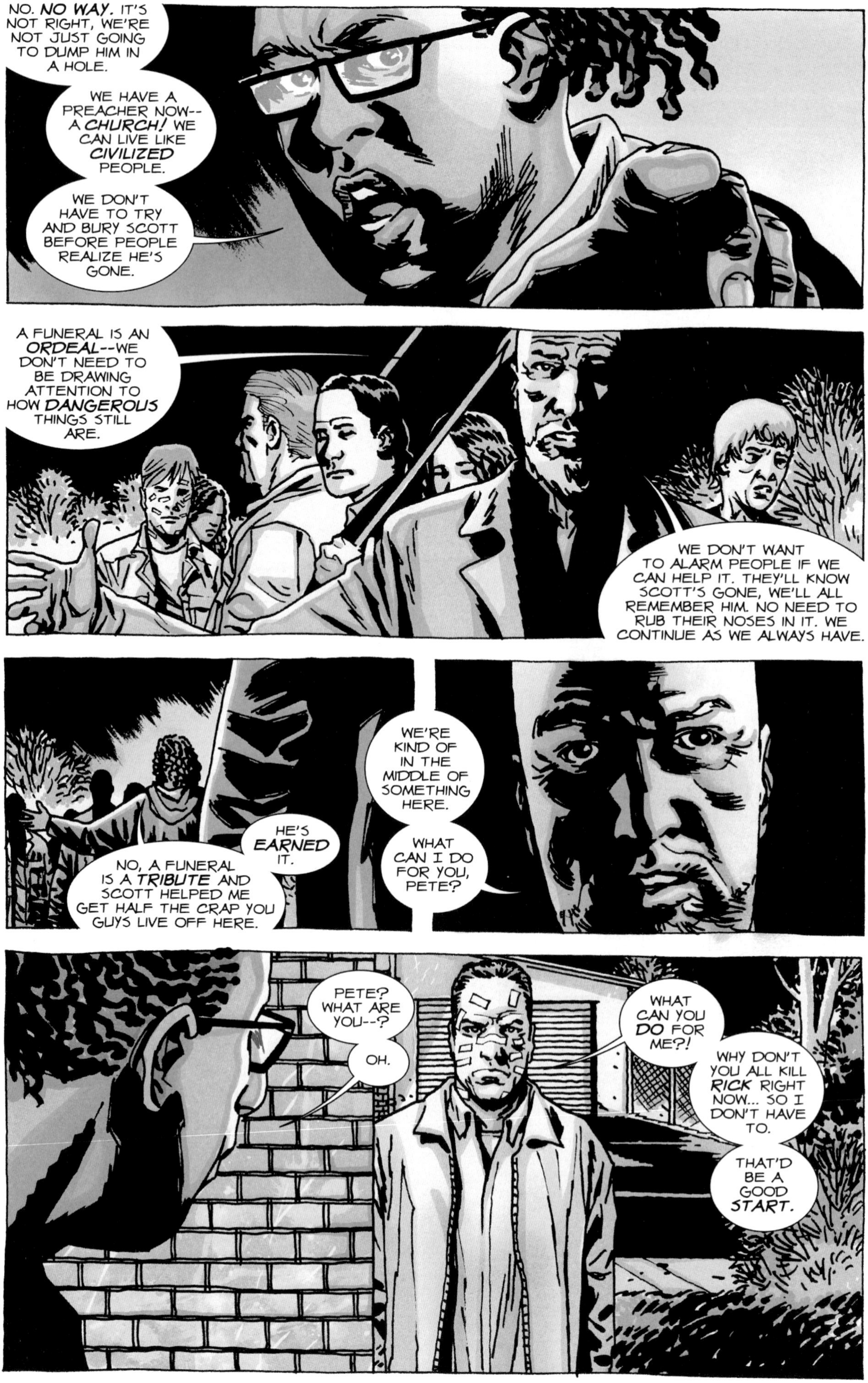

NO. NO WAY. IT'S NOT RIGHT, WE'RE NOT JUST GOING TO DUMP HIM IN A HOLE.
WE HAVE A PREACHER NOW-- A CHURCH! WE CAN LIVE LIKE CIVILIZED PEOPLE.
WE DON'T HAVE TO TRY AND BURY SCOTT BEFORE PEOPLE REALIZE HE'S GONE.
A FUNERAL IS AN ORDEAL--WE DON'T NEED TO BE DRAWING ATTENTION TO HOW DANGEROUS THINGS STILL ARE.
WE DON'T WANT TO ALARM PEOPLE IF WE CAN HELP IT. THEY'LL KNOW SCOTT'S GONE, WE'LL ALL REMEMBER HIM. NO NEED TO RUB THEIR NOSES IN IT. WE CONTINUE AS WE ALWAYS HAVE.
NO, A FUNERAL IS A TRIBUTE AND SCOTT HELPED ME GET HALF THE CRAP YOU GUYS LIVE OFF HERE.
HE'S EARNED IT.
WE'RE KIND OF IN THE MIDDLE OF SOMETHING HERE.
WHAT CAN I DO FOR YOU, PETE?
PETE? WHAT ARE YOU--?
OH.
WHAT CAN YOU DO FOR ME?!
WHY DON'T YOU ALL KILL RICK RIGHT NOW... SO I DON'T HAVE TO.
THAT'D BE A GOOD START.

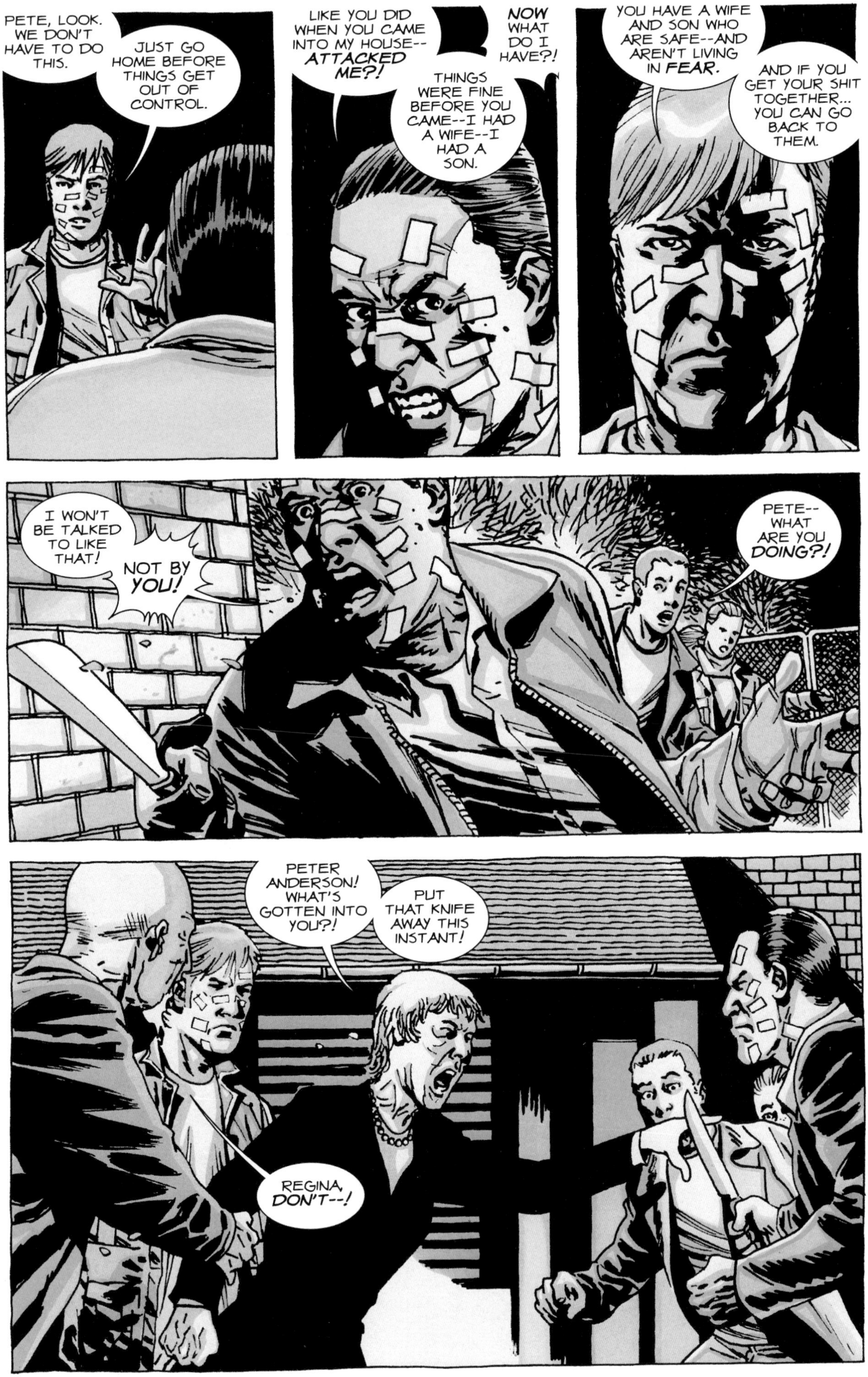
PETE, LOOK. WE DON'T HAVE TO DO THIS.
JUST GO HOME BEFORE THINGS GET OUT OF CONTROL.
LIKE YOU DID WHEN YOU CAME INTO MY HOUSE-- ATTACKED ME?!
THINGS WERE FINE BEFORE YOU CAME--I HAD A WIFE--I HAD A SON.
NOW WHAT DO I HAVE?!
YOU HAVE A WIFE AND SON WHO ARE SAFE--AND AREN'T LIVING IN FEAR.
AND IF YOU GET YOUR SHIT TOGETHER... YOU CAN GO BACK TO THEM.
I WON'T BE TALKED TO LIKE THAT!
NOT BY YOU!
PETE-- WHAT ARE YOU DOING?!
PETER ANDERSON! WHAT'S GOTTEN INTO YOU?!
PUT THAT KNIFE AWAY THIS INSTANT!
REGINA, DON'T--!

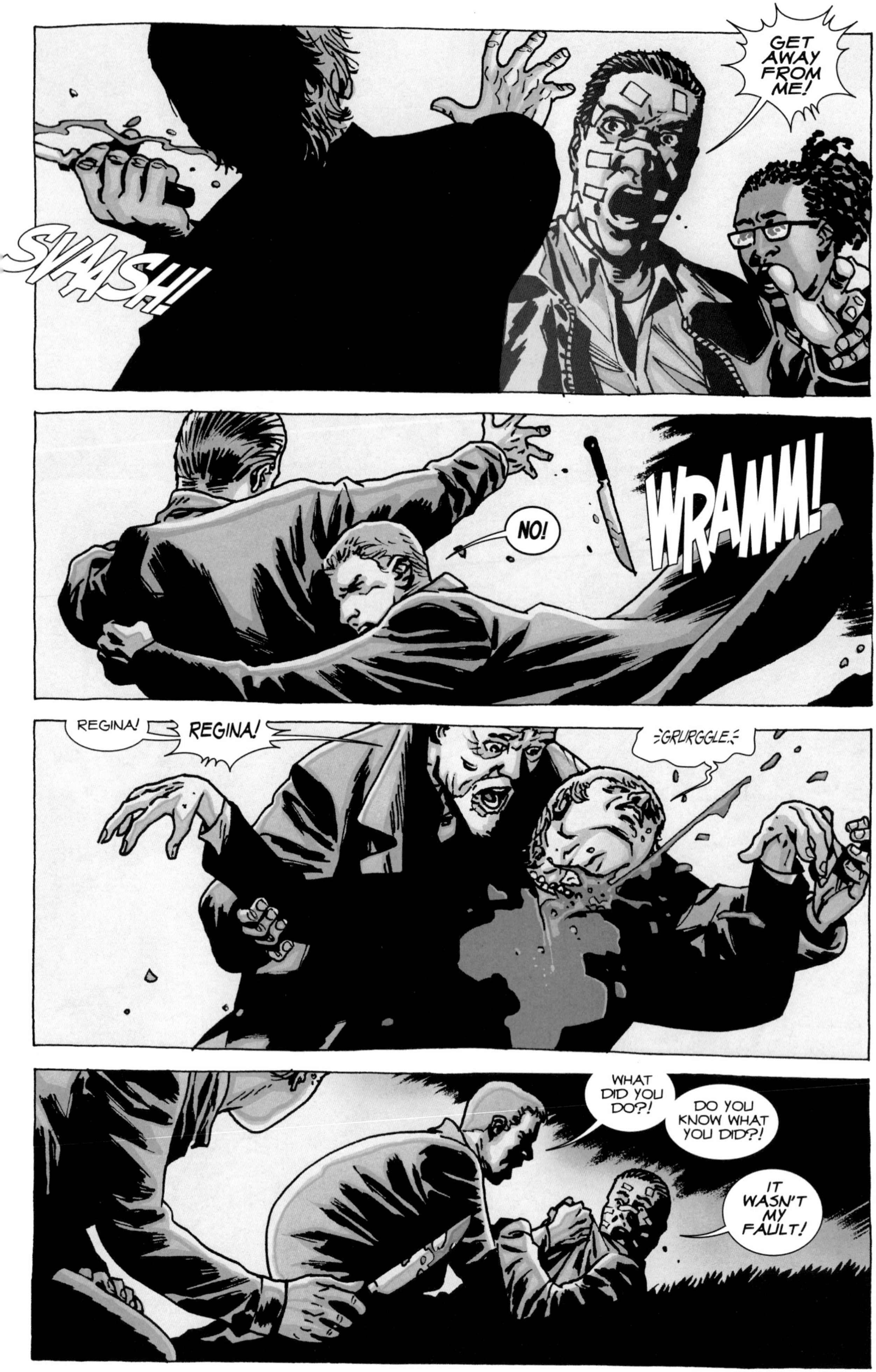
GET AWAY FROM ME!
SVAASH!
NO!
WRAMM!
REGINA!
REGINA!
GRURGGLE
WHAT DID YOU DO?!
DO YOU KNOW WHAT YOU DID?!
IT WASN'T MY FAULT!

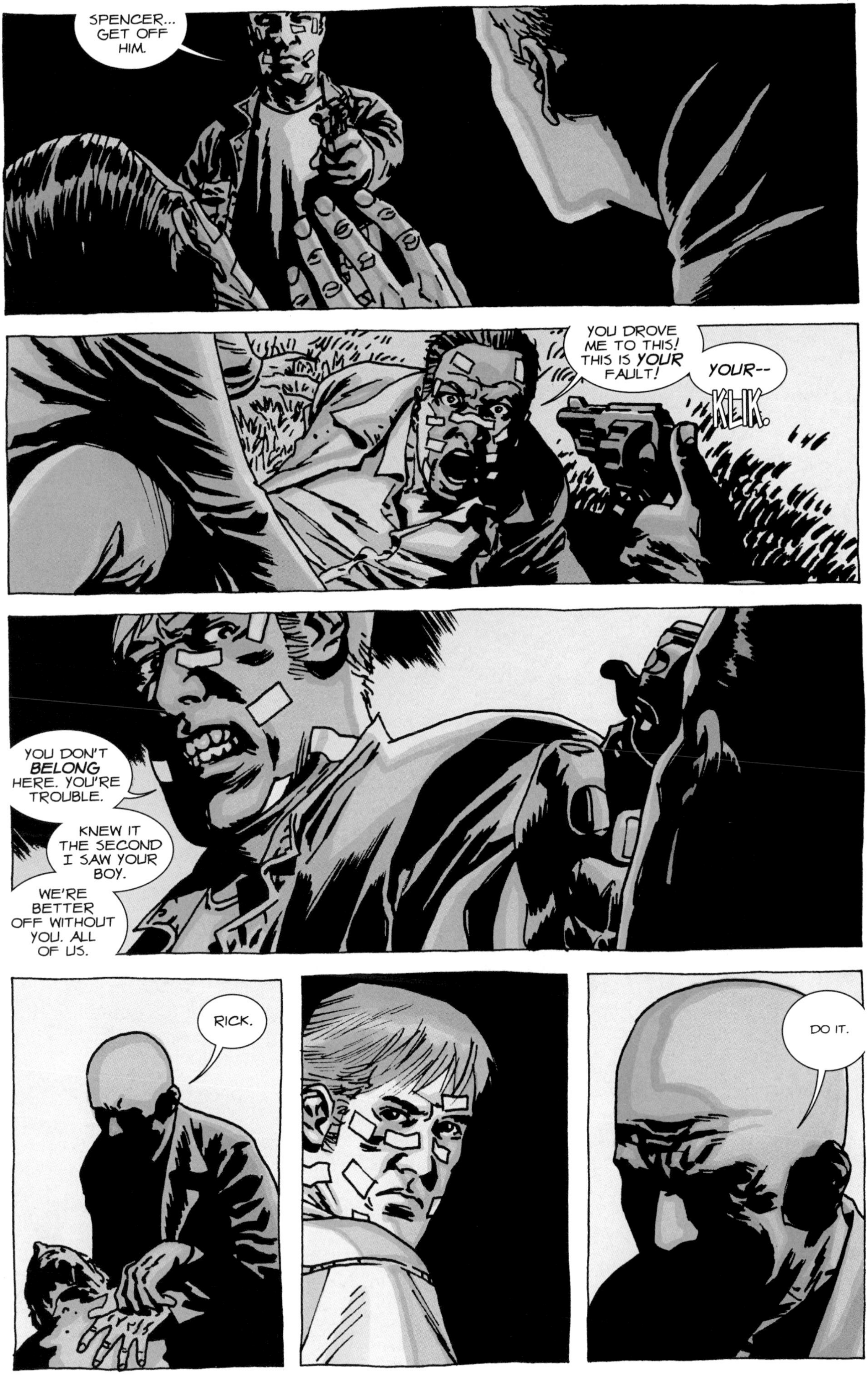
SPENCER... GET OFF HIM.
YOU DROVE ME TO THIS! THIS IS *YOUR* FAULT!
YOUR--
KLIK.
YOU DON'T *BELONG* HERE. YOU'RE TROUBLE.
KNEW IT THE SECOND I SAW YOUR BOY.
WE'RE BETTER OFF WITHOUT YOU. ALL OF US.
RICK.
DO IT.

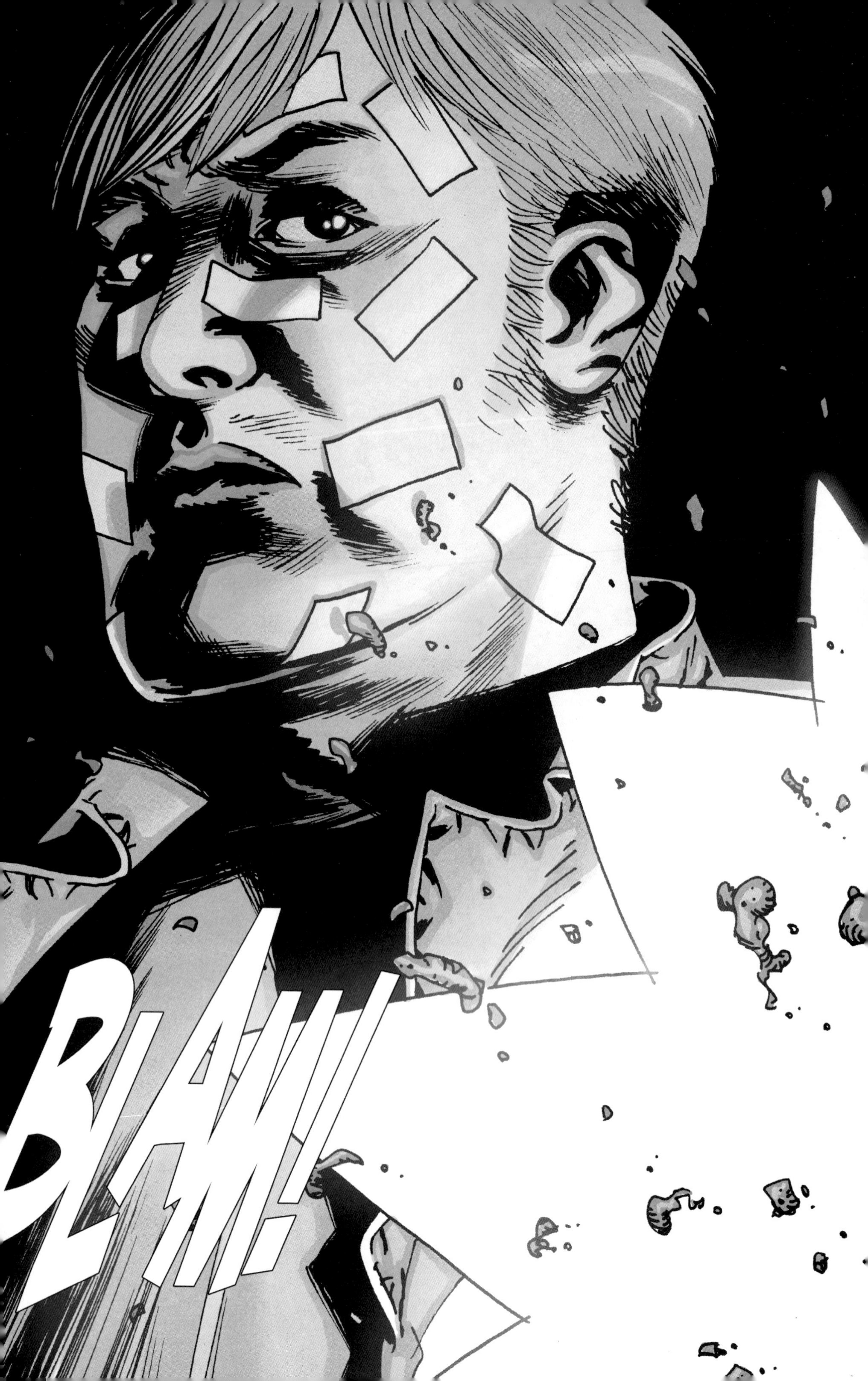
BLAM!

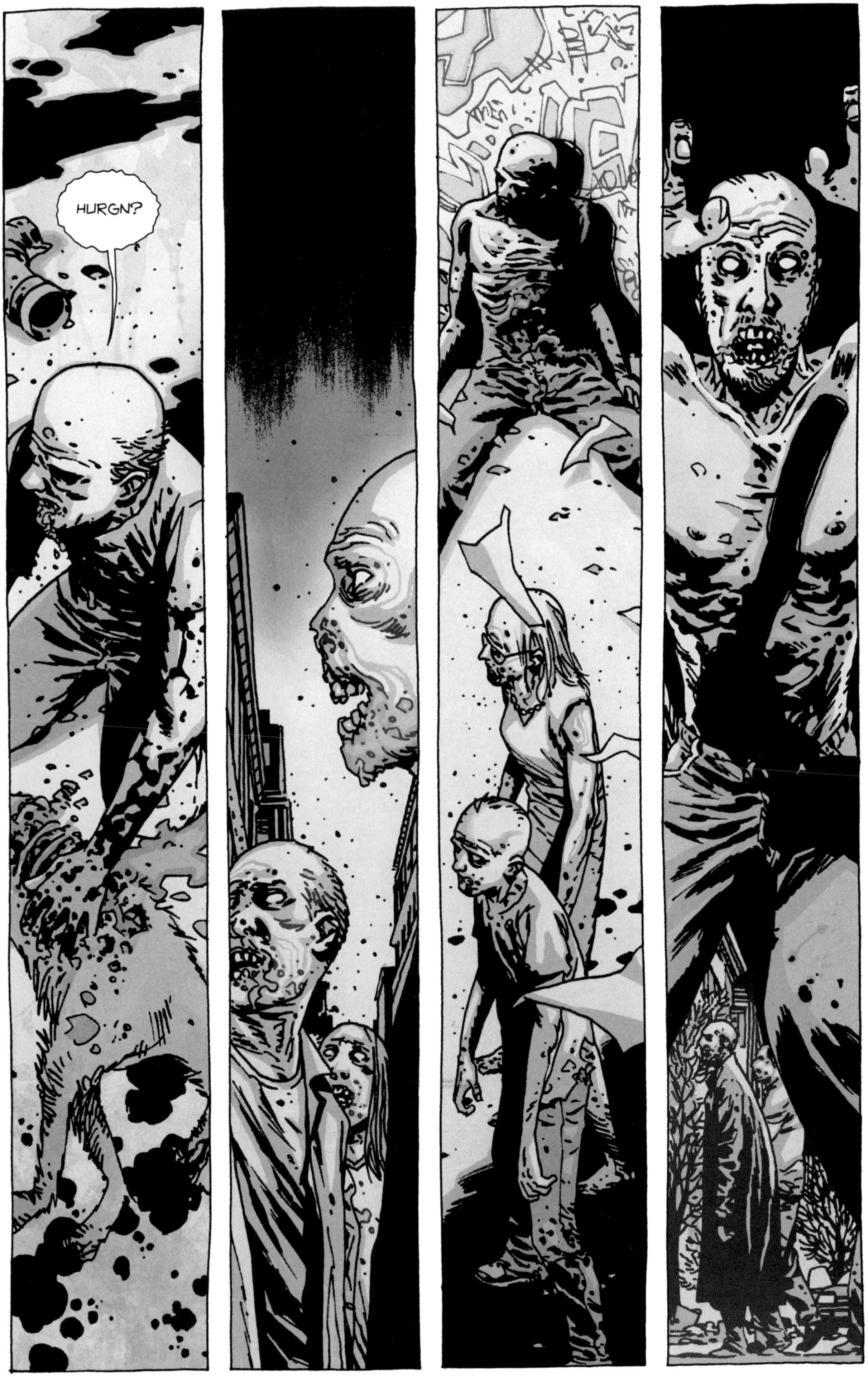
HURGN?

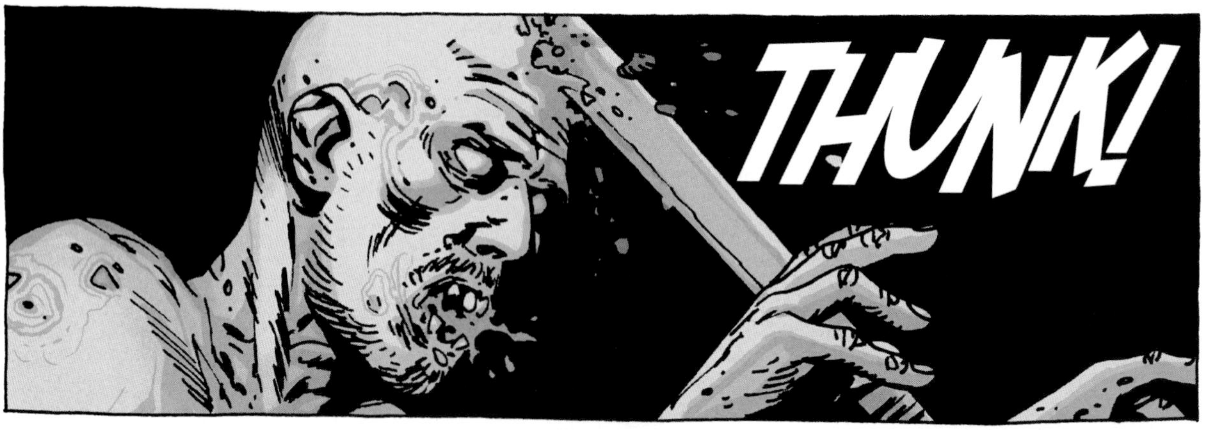
THUNK!

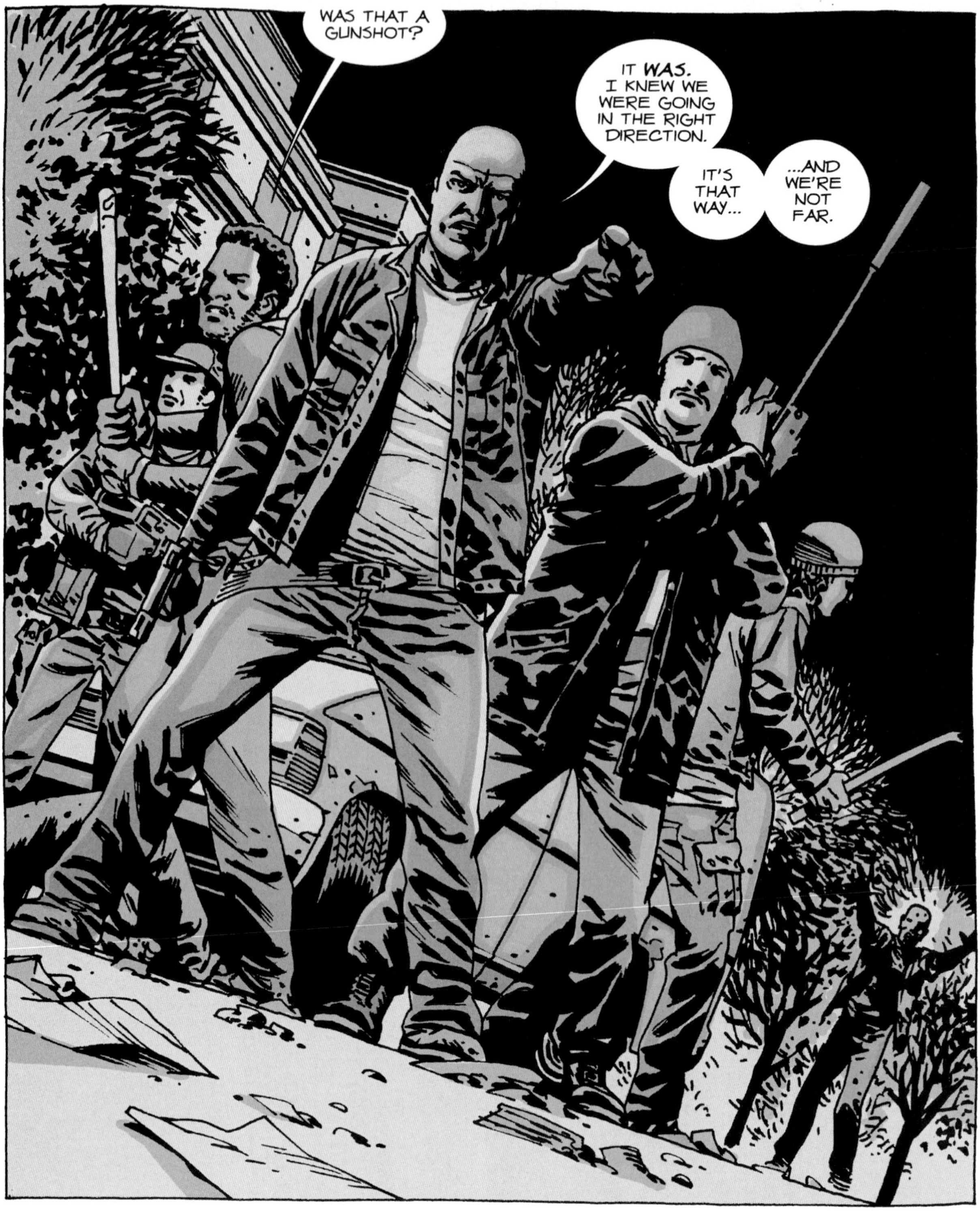
WAS THAT A GUNSHOT?
IT WAS. I KNEW WE WERE GOING IN THE RIGHT DIRECTION.
IT'S THAT WAY...
...AND WE'RE NOT FAR.

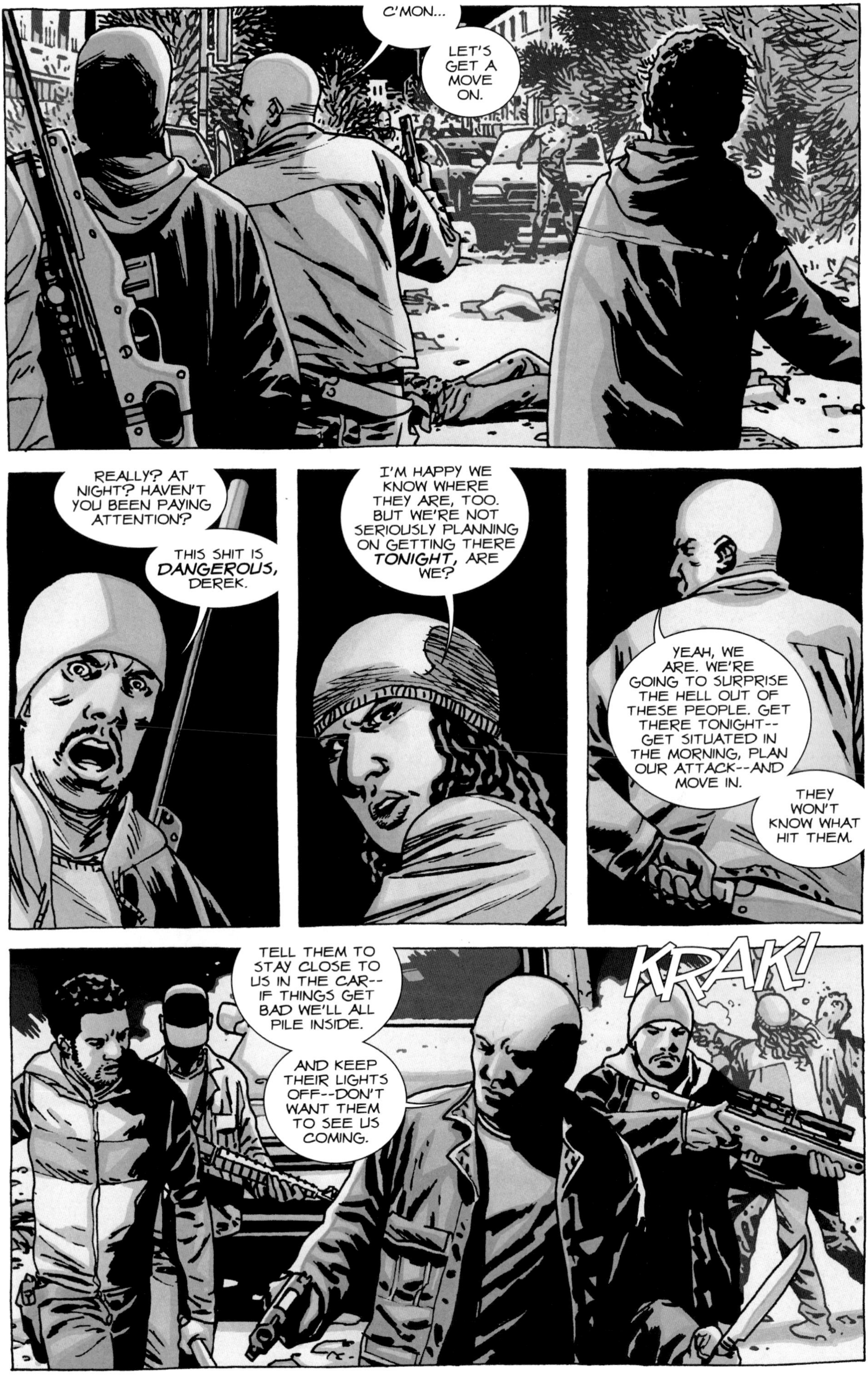
C'MON...
LET'S GET A MOVE ON.
REALLY? AT NIGHT? HAVEN'T YOU BEEN PAYING ATTENTION?
THIS SHIT IS DANGEROUS, DEREK.
I'M HAPPY WE KNOW WHERE THEY ARE, TOO. BUT WE'RE NOT SERIOUSLY PLANNING ON GETTING THERE TONIGHT, ARE WE?
YEAH, WE ARE. WE'RE GOING TO SURPRISE THE HELL OUT OF THESE PEOPLE. GET THERE TONIGHT--GET SITUATED IN THE MORNING, PLAN OUR ATTACK--AND MOVE IN.
THEY WON'T KNOW WHAT HIT THEM.
TELL THEM TO STAY CLOSE TO US IN THE CAR--IF THINGS GET BAD WE'LL ALL PILE INSIDE.
AND KEEP THEIR LIGHTS OFF--DON'T WANT THEM TO SEE US COMING.
KRAK!

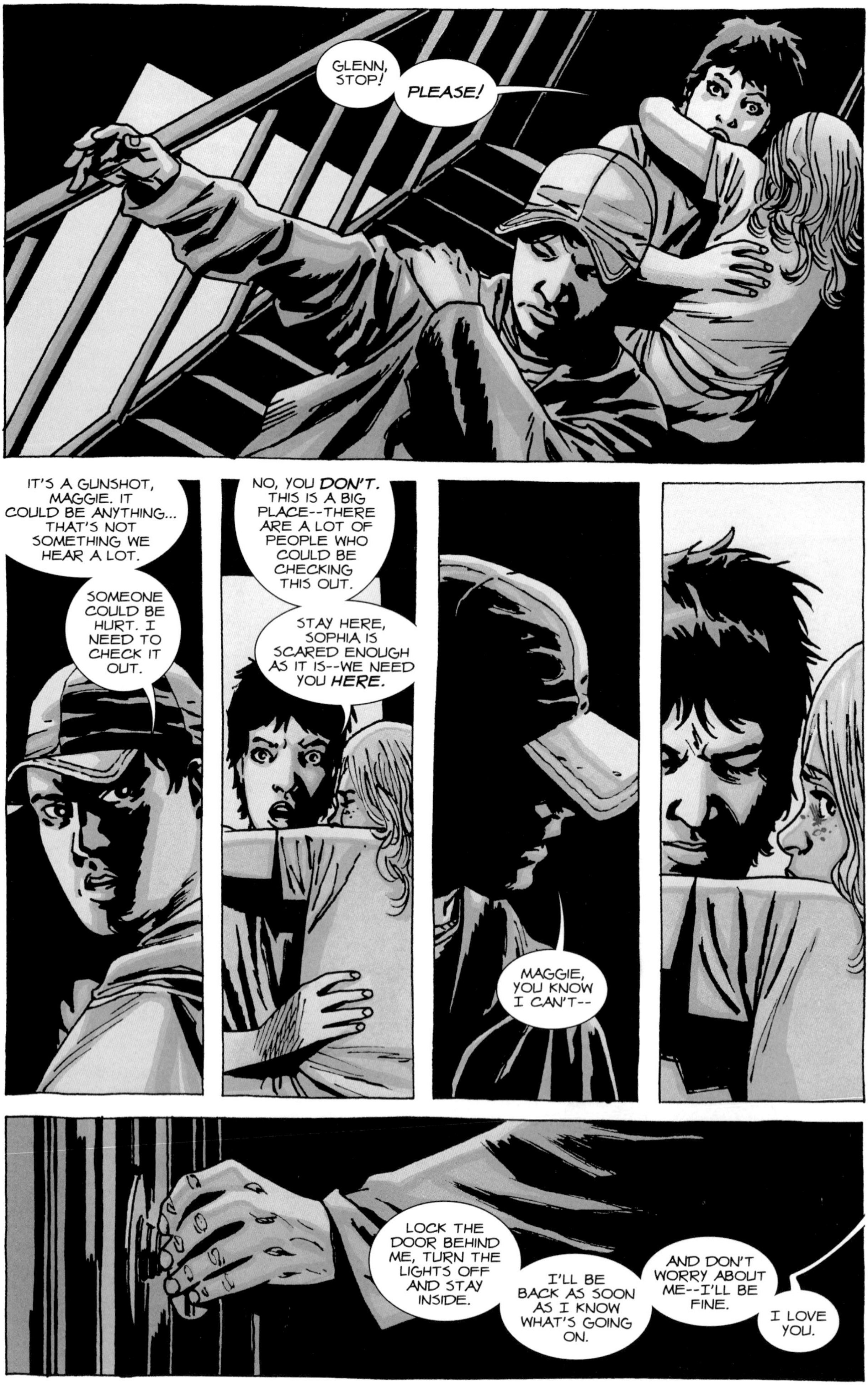
GLENN, STOP!
PLEASE!
IT'S A GUNSHOT, MAGGIE. IT COULD BE ANYTHING... THAT'S NOT SOMETHING WE HEAR A LOT.
SOMEONE COULD BE HURT. I NEED TO CHECK IT OUT.
NO, YOU DON'T. THIS IS A BIG PLACE--THERE ARE A LOT OF PEOPLE WHO COULD BE CHECKING THIS OUT.
STAY HERE, SOPHIA IS SCARED ENOUGH AS IT IS--WE NEED YOU HERE.
MAGGIE, YOU KNOW I CAN'T--
LOCK THE DOOR BEHIND ME, TURN THE LIGHTS OFF AND STAY INSIDE.
I'LL BE BACK AS SOON AS I KNOW WHAT'S GOING ON.
AND DON'T WORRY ABOUT ME--I'LL BE FINE.
I LOVE YOU.

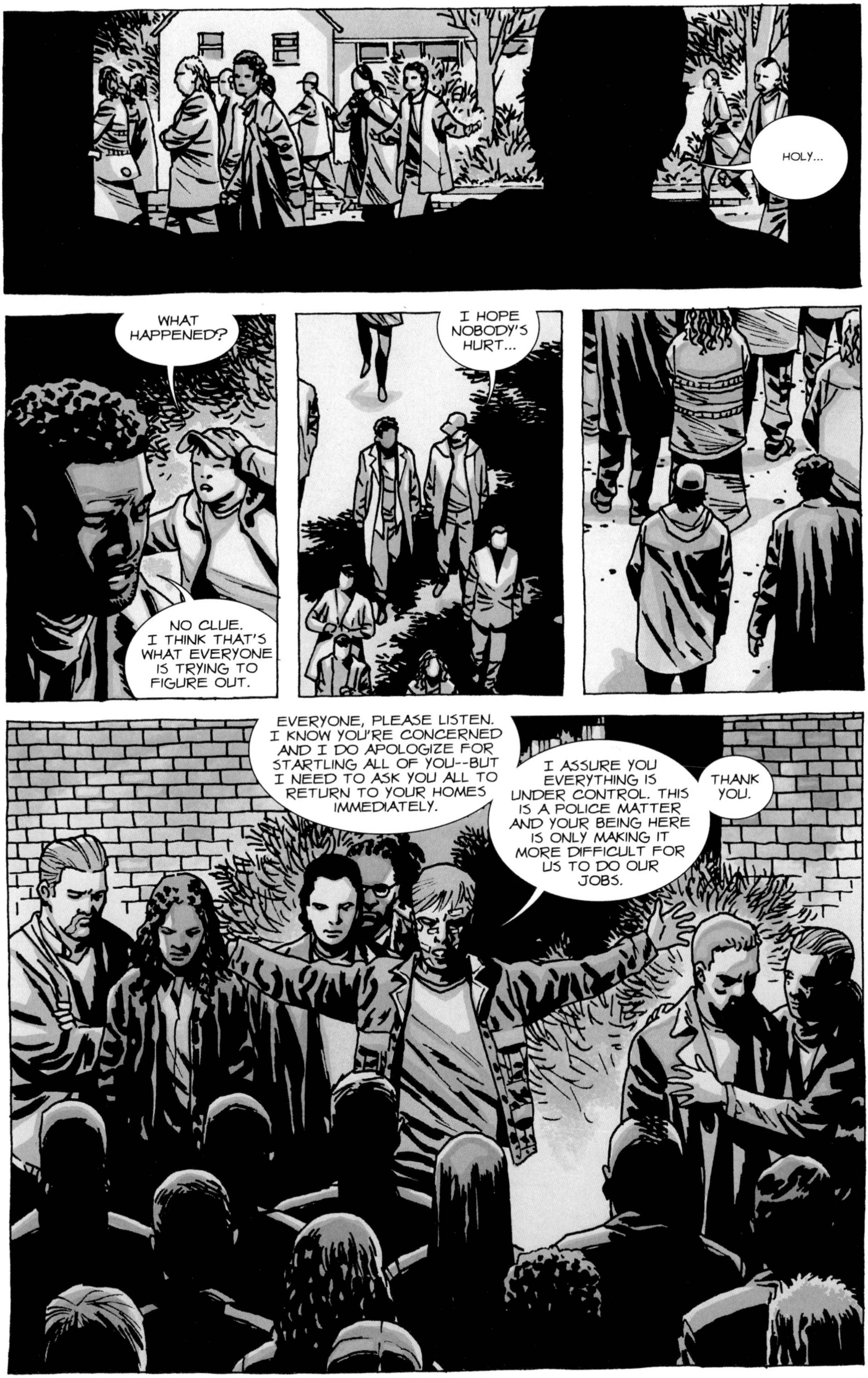
HOLY...
WHAT HAPPENED?
NO CLUE. I THINK THAT'S WHAT EVERYONE IS TRYING TO FIGURE OUT.
I HOPE NOBODY'S HURT...
EVERYONE, PLEASE LISTEN. I KNOW YOU'RE CONCERNED AND I DO APOLOGIZE FOR STARTLING ALL OF YOU--BUT I NEED TO ASK YOU ALL TO RETURN TO YOUR HOMES IMMEDIATELY.
I ASSURE YOU EVERYTHING IS UNDER CONTROL. THIS IS A POLICE MATTER AND YOUR BEING HERE IS ONLY MAKING IT MORE DIFFICULT FOR US TO DO OUR JOBS.
THANK YOU.

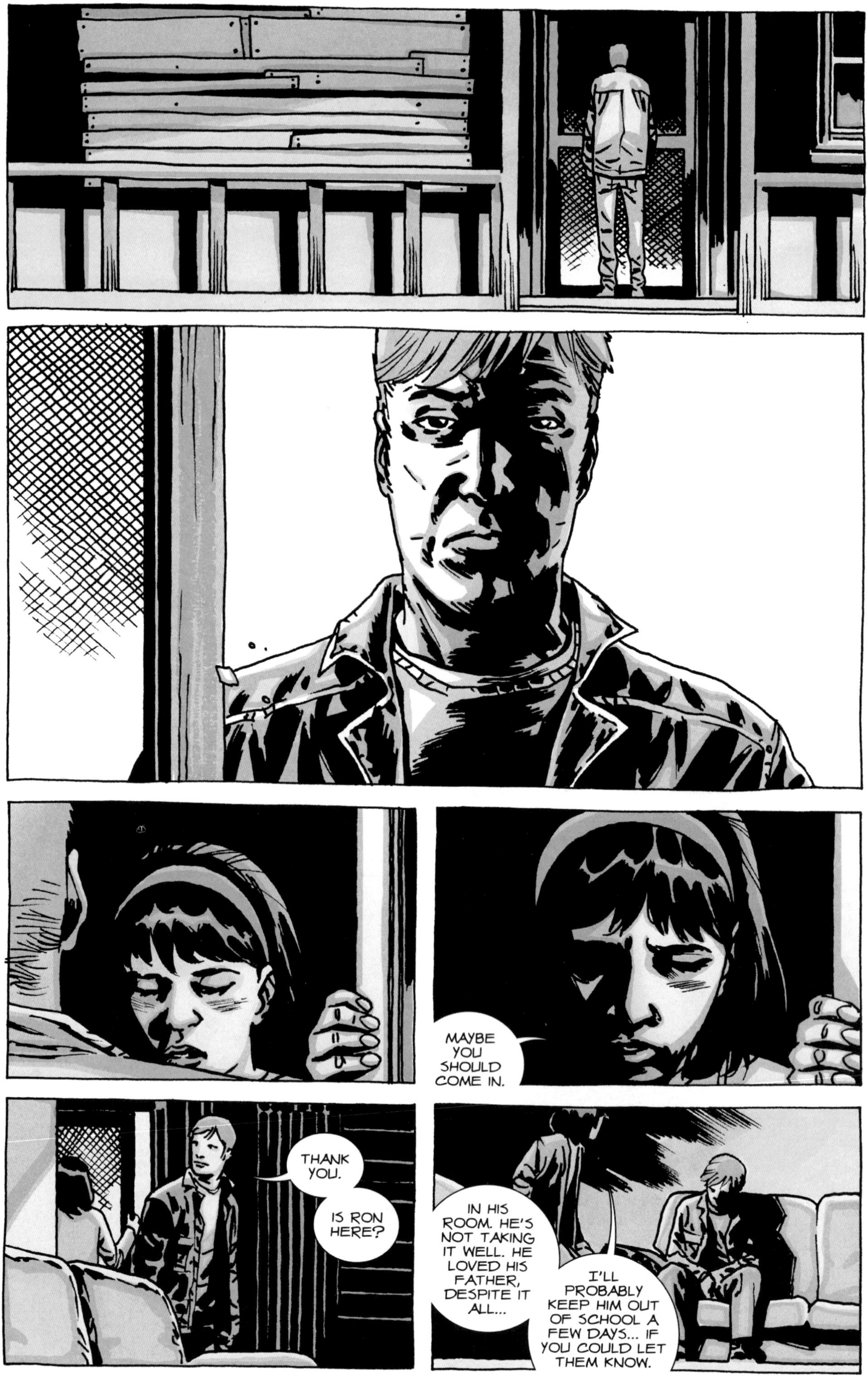
MAYBE YOU SHOULD COME IN.
THANK YOU.
IS RON HERE?
IN HIS ROOM. HE'S NOT TAKING IT WELL. HE LOVED HIS FATHER, DESPITE IT ALL...
I'LL PROBABLY KEEP HIM OUT OF SCHOOL A FEW DAYS... IF YOU COULD LET THEM KNOW.

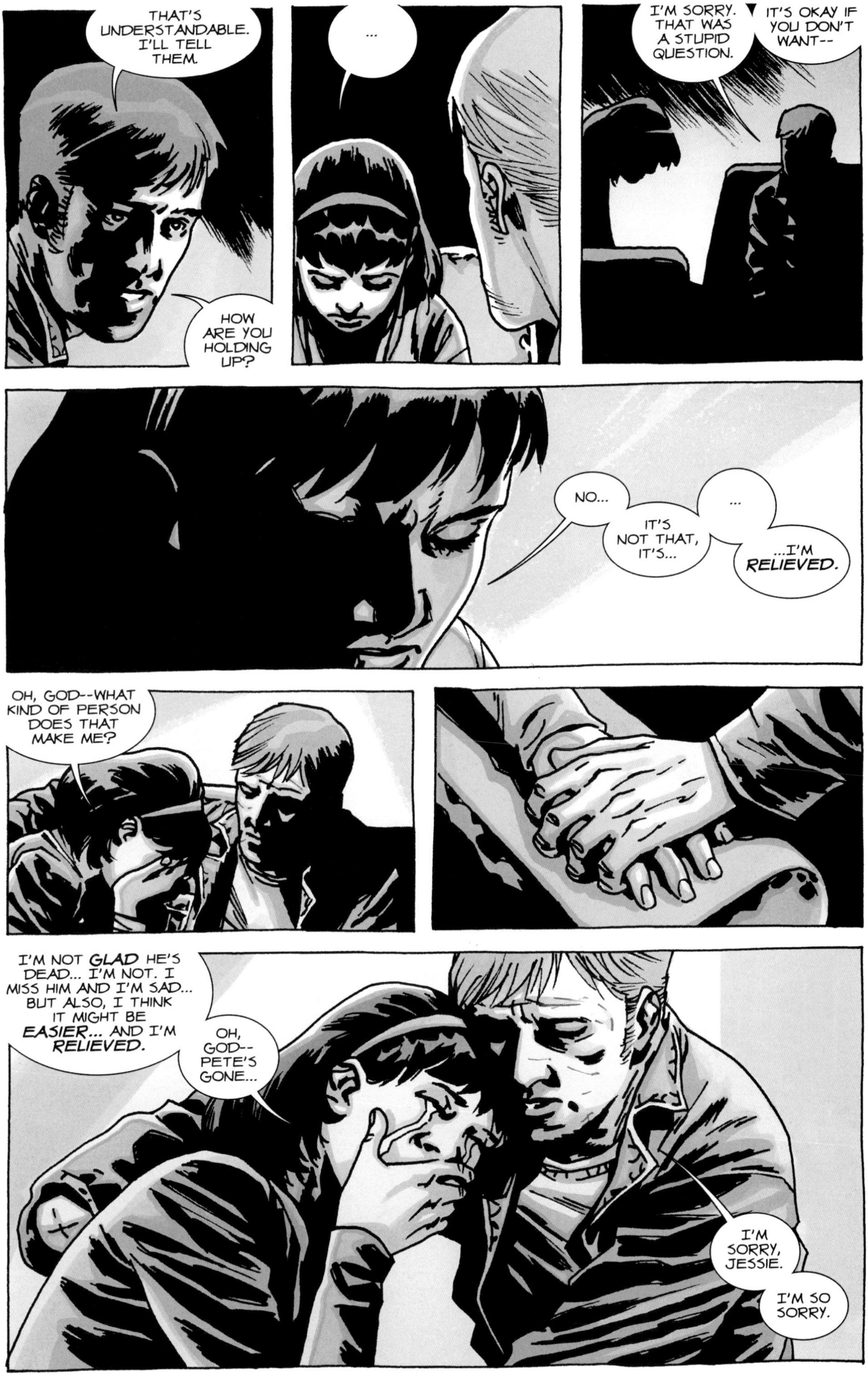
THAT'S UNDERSTANDABLE. I'LL TELL THEM.
HOW ARE YOU HOLDING UP?
...
I'M SORRY. THAT WAS A STUPID QUESTION.
IT'S OKAY IF YOU DON'T WANT--
NO...
IT'S NOT THAT, IT'S...
...
...I'M *RELIEVED.*
OH, GOD--WHAT KIND OF PERSON DOES THAT MAKE ME?
I'M NOT *GLAD* HE'S DEAD... I'M NOT. I MISS HIM AND I'M SAD... BUT ALSO, I THINK IT MIGHT BE *EASIER...* AND I'M *RELIEVED.*
OH, GOD-- PETE'S GONE...
I'M SORRY, JESSIE.
I'M SO SORRY.

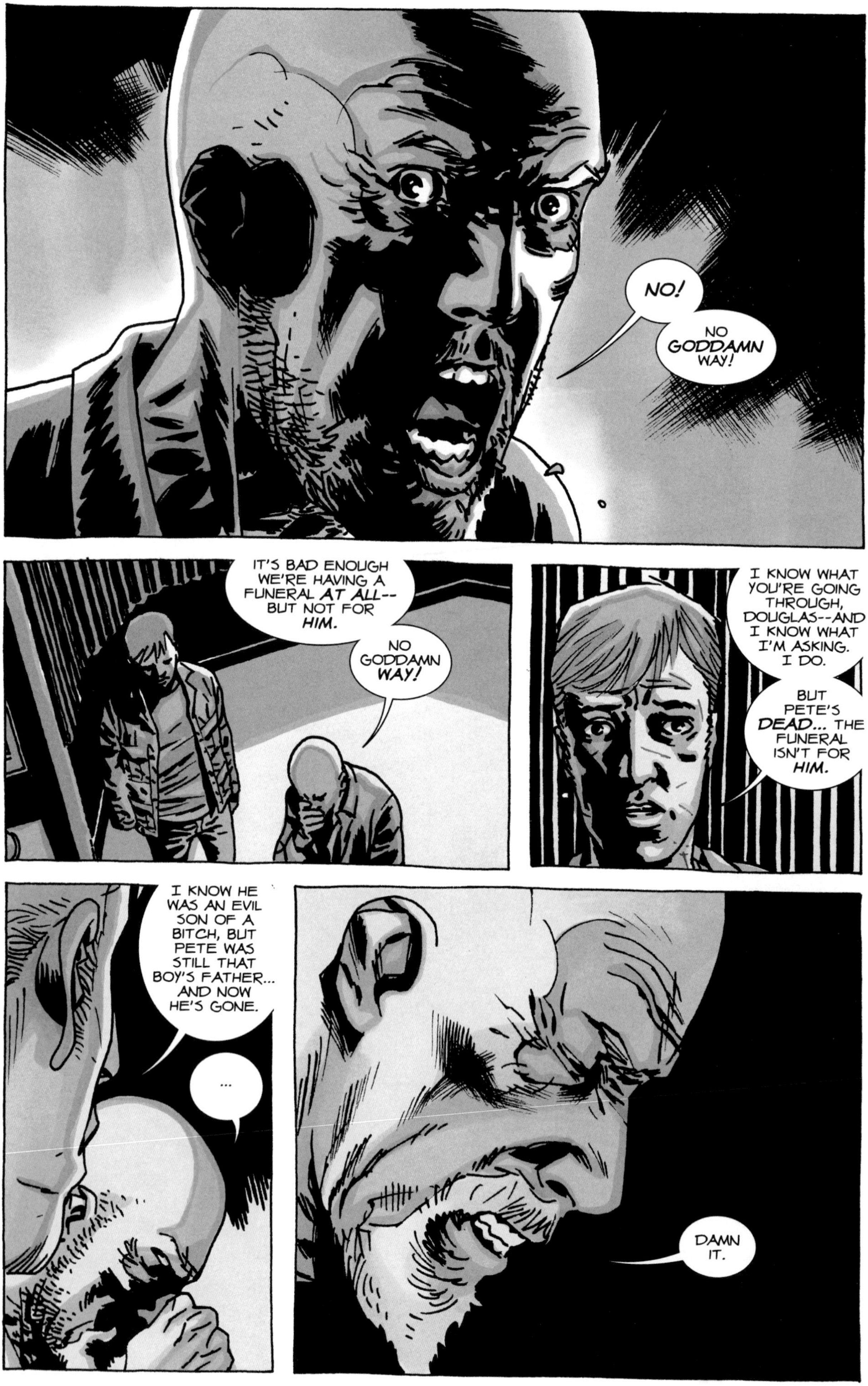
NO!
NO GODDAMN WAY!
IT'S BAD ENOUGH WE'RE HAVING A FUNERAL AT ALL-- BUT NOT FOR HIM.
NO GODDAMN WAY!
I KNOW WHAT YOU'RE GOING THROUGH, DOUGLAS--AND I KNOW WHAT I'M ASKING. I DO.
BUT PETE'S DEAD... THE FUNERAL ISN'T FOR HIM.
I KNOW HE WAS AN EVIL SON OF A BITCH, BUT PETE WAS STILL THAT BOY'S FATHER... AND NOW HE'S GONE.
...
DAMN IT.

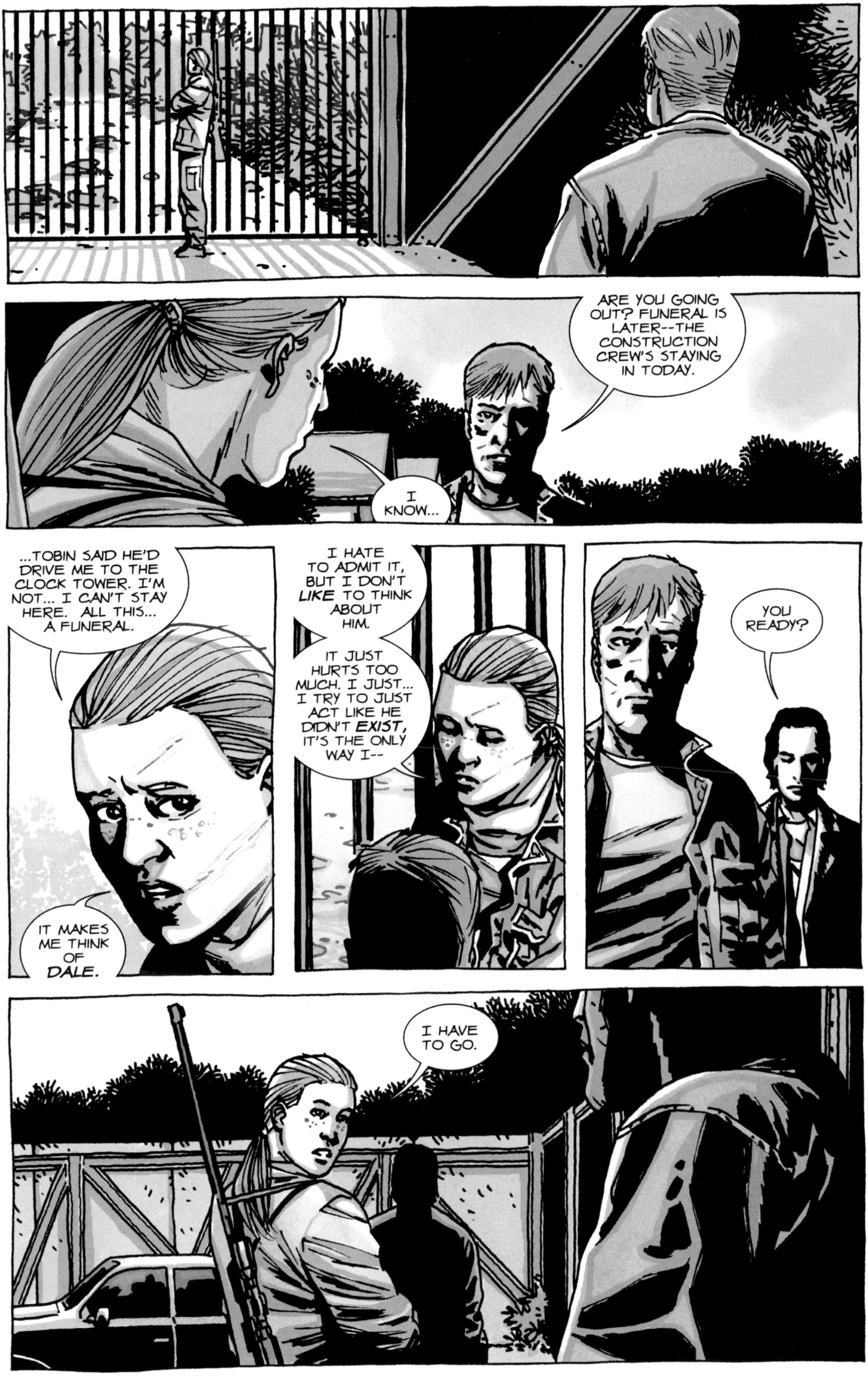
ARE YOU GOING OUT? FUNERAL IS LATER--THE CONSTRUCTION CREW'S STAYING IN TODAY.
I KNOW...
...TOBIN SAID HE'D DRIVE ME TO THE CLOCK TOWER. I'M NOT... I CAN'T STAY HERE. ALL THIS... A FUNERAL.
IT MAKES ME THINK OF DALE.
I HATE TO ADMIT IT, BUT I DON'T LIKE TO THINK ABOUT HIM.
IT JUST HURTS TOO MUCH. I JUST... I TRY TO JUST ACT LIKE HE DIDN'T EXIST, IT'S THE ONLY WAY I--
YOU READY?
I HAVE TO GO.

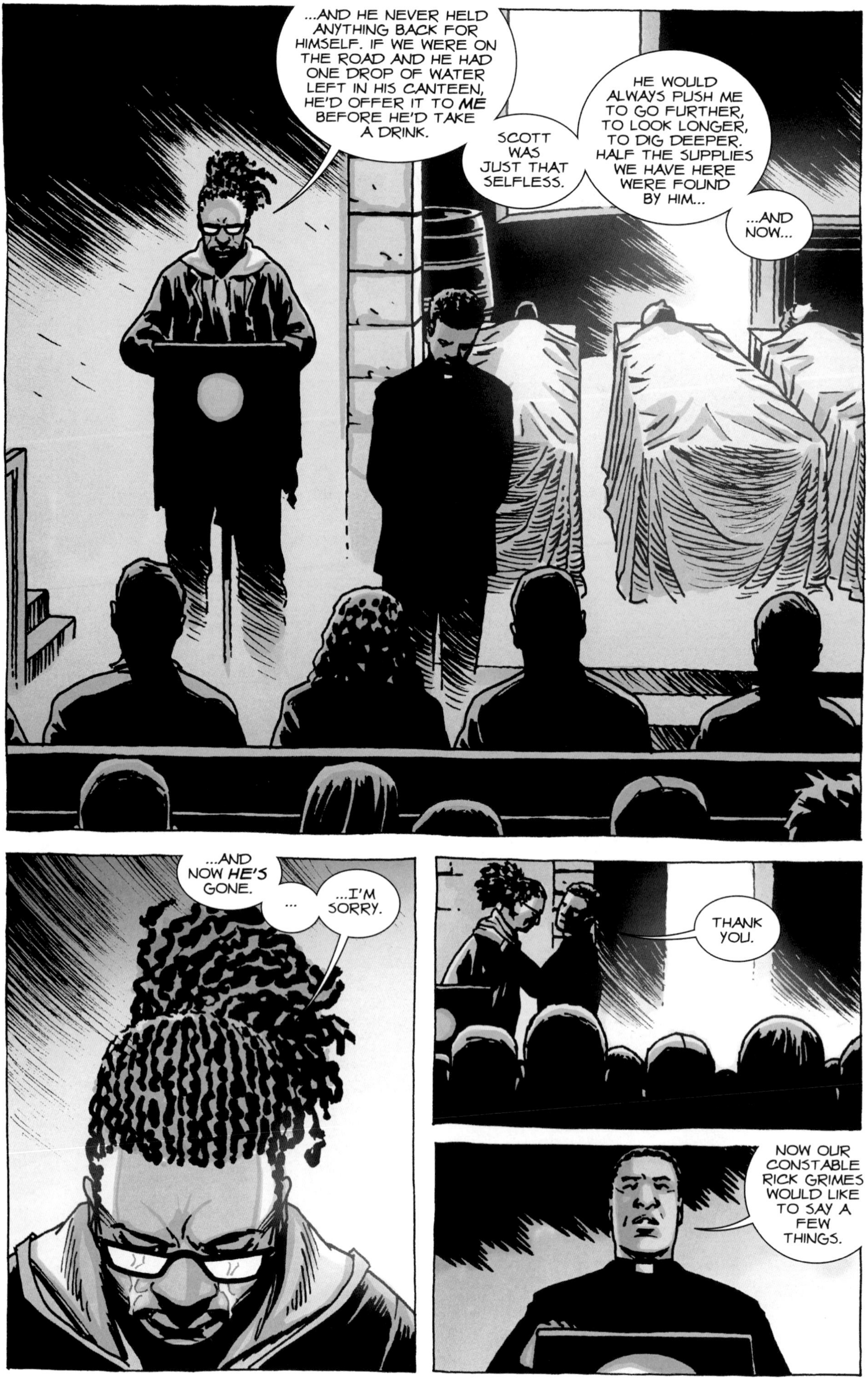
...AND HE NEVER HELD ANYTHING BACK FOR HIMSELF. IF WE WERE ON THE ROAD AND HE HAD ONE DROP OF WATER LEFT IN HIS CANTEEN, HE'D OFFER IT TO ME BEFORE HE'D TAKE A DRINK.
SCOTT WAS JUST THAT SELFLESS.
HE WOULD ALWAYS PUSH ME TO GO FURTHER, TO LOOK LONGER, TO DIG DEEPER. HALF THE SUPPLIES WE HAVE HERE WERE FOUND BY HIM...
...AND NOW...
...AND NOW HE'S GONE.
...
...I'M SORRY.
THANK YOU.
NOW OUR CONSTABLE RICK GRIMES WOULD LIKE TO SAY A FEW THINGS.

DO ANY OF US REALLY KNOW WHO WE ARE? AND EVEN IF WE DO *NOW*, DID WE KNOW BEFORE ALL THIS STARTED HAPPENING?

WITHOUT THIS ADVERSITY, THIS HARDSHIP, HOW DO WE REALLY *KNOW* WHO WE ARE, AND WHAT TRULY MATTERS TO US?

THIS IS SOMETHING I FIND MYSELF THINKING ABOUT A LOT, NOW THAT I'M LIVING HERE AND I HAVE THE LUXURY OF SPENDING TIME WITH MY THOUGHTS.

THE THINGS I'VE DONE TO SURVIVE INFORM WHO I AM AS A PERSON. I AM A MAN WHO WILL DO THINGS TO PROTECT MY FAMILY. A LOT OF THESE THINGS I'VE DONE... I'M *NOT* PROUD OF.

ARE THESE THINGS *MY FAULT?* I KNOW I WOULD NOT HAVE DONE THEM WERE THE SITUATION DIFFERENT... SO HOW AM I TO BLAME?

PETE WAS A LOVING HUSBAND AND A FATHER AND HE DID SOME BAD, UNFORGIVABLE THINGS... BUT AT THE END OF THE DAY, HOW CAN WE JUDGE HIM...

IS THAT WHO PETE REALLY WAS? OR IS THAT WHO HE WAS MADE INTO BY HIS SURROUNDINGS?

...HOW CAN *I?*

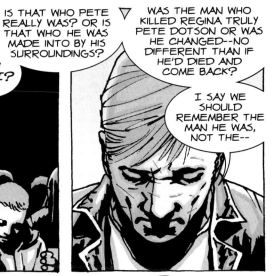

WAS THE MAN WHO KILLED REGINA TRULY PETE DOTSON OR WAS HE CHANGED--NO DIFFERENT THAN IF HE'D DIED AND COME BACK?

I SAY WE SHOULD REMEMBER THE MAN HE WAS, NOT THE--

K-POW!

ABRAHAM, GUYS, YOU'RE WITH ME. MICHONNE, GO BACK--MAKE SURE EVERYONE STAYS IN THE CHURCH, AND BE PREPARED FOR WHAT COMES NEXT IF THINGS GET BAD.

I'VE GOT NO CLUE WHAT I'M WALKING INTO. THAT *WASN'T* ANDREA. SOMEONE'S AT THE GATE AND THEY'VE GOT A GUN.

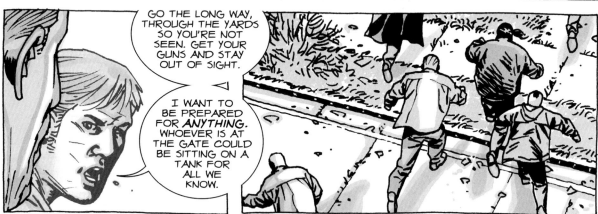

GO THE LONG WAY, THROUGH THE YARDS SO YOU'RE NOT SEEN. GET YOUR GUNS AND STAY OUT OF SIGHT.

I WANT TO BE PREPARED FOR *ANYTHING*. WHOEVER IS AT THE GATE COULD BE SITTING ON A TANK FOR ALL WE KNOW.

OKAY, STRANGER, YOU'VE GOT MY ATTENTION.

WHAT CAN I DO FOR YOU?

ISN'T THAT *OBVIOUS?*

LITTLE PIG, LITTLE PIG...

...LET ME IN.

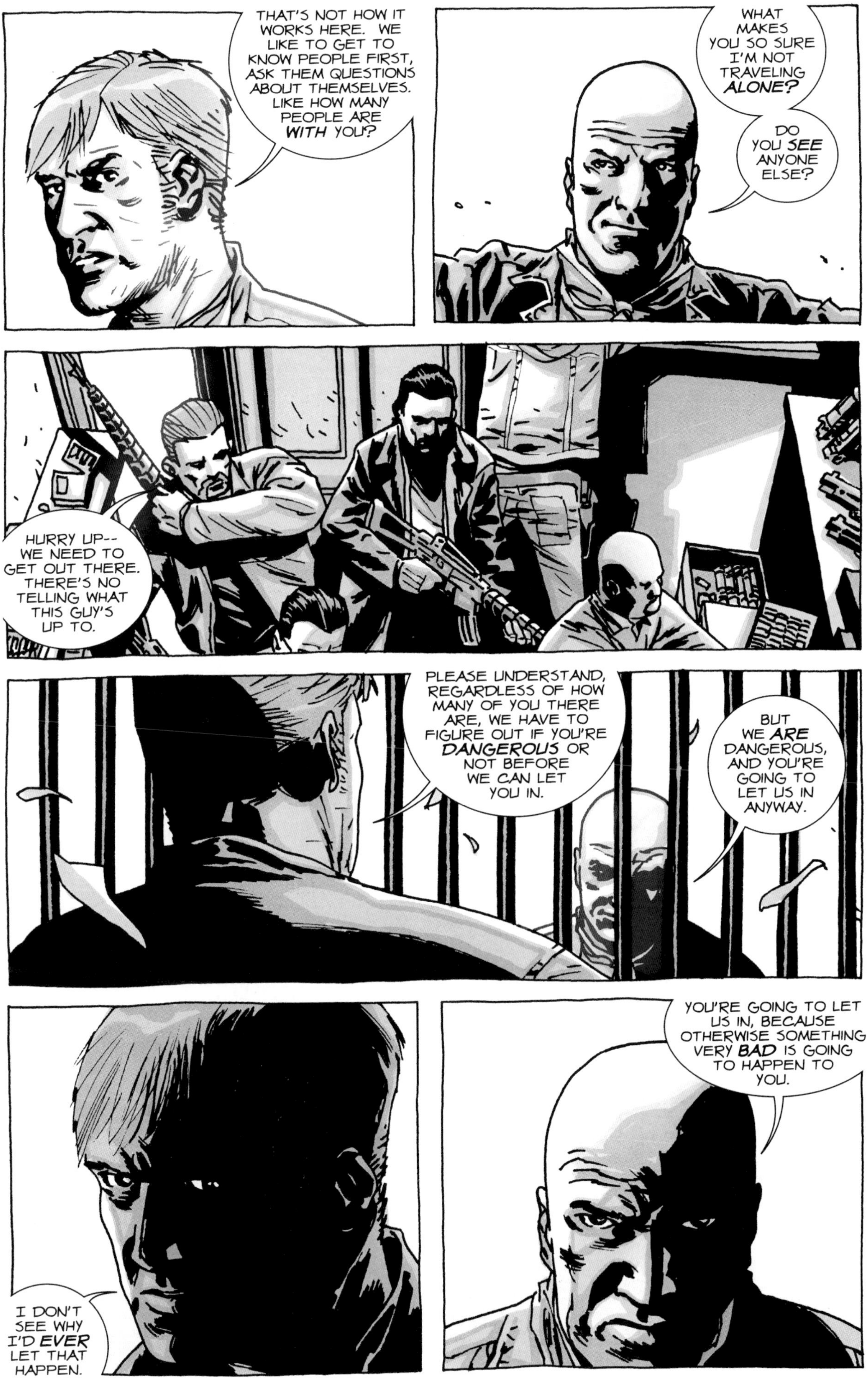

THAT'S NOT HOW IT WORKS HERE. WE LIKE TO GET TO KNOW PEOPLE FIRST, ASK THEM QUESTIONS ABOUT THEMSELVES. LIKE HOW MANY PEOPLE ARE *WITH* YOU?
WHAT MAKES YOU SO SURE I'M NOT TRAVELING *ALONE?*
DO YOU *SEE* ANYONE ELSE?
HURRY UP-- WE NEED TO GET OUT THERE. THERE'S NO TELLING WHAT THIS GUY'S UP TO.
PLEASE UNDERSTAND, REGARDLESS OF HOW MANY OF YOU THERE ARE, WE HAVE TO FIGURE OUT IF YOU'RE *DANGEROUS* OR NOT BEFORE WE CAN LET YOU IN.
BUT WE *ARE* DANGEROUS, AND YOU'RE GOING TO LET US IN ANYWAY.
I DON'T SEE WHY I'D *EVER* LET THAT HAPPEN.
YOU'RE GOING TO LET US IN, BECAUSE OTHERWISE SOMETHING VERY *BAD* IS GOING TO HAPPEN TO YOU.

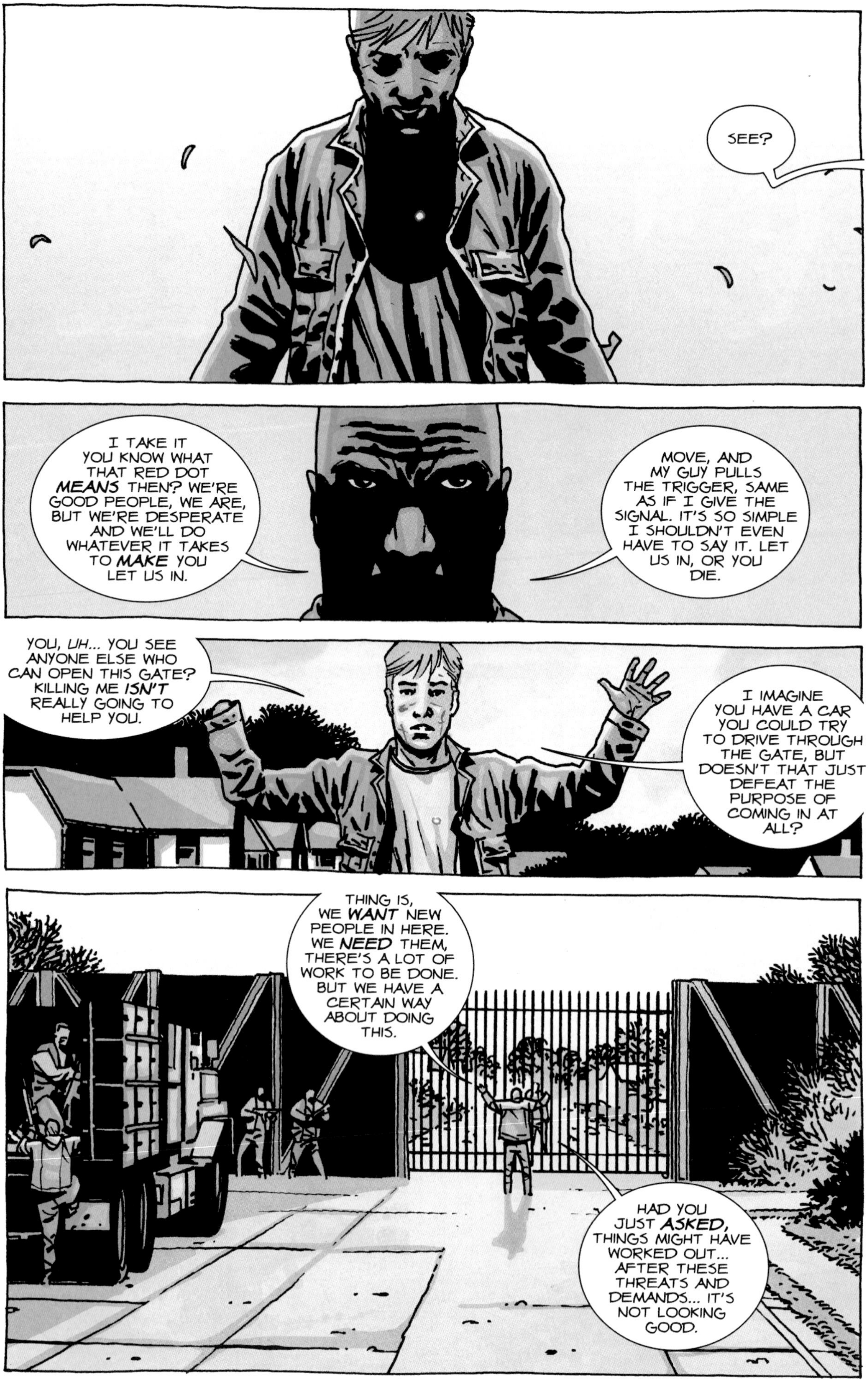
SEE?
I TAKE IT YOU KNOW WHAT THAT RED DOT MEANS THEN? WE'RE GOOD PEOPLE, WE ARE, BUT WE'RE DESPERATE AND WE'LL DO WHATEVER IT TAKES TO MAKE YOU LET US IN.
MOVE, AND MY GUY PULLS THE TRIGGER, SAME AS IF I GIVE THE SIGNAL. IT'S SO SIMPLE I SHOULDN'T EVEN HAVE TO SAY IT. LET US IN, OR YOU DIE.
YOU, UH... YOU SEE ANYONE ELSE WHO CAN OPEN THIS GATE? KILLING ME ISN'T REALLY GOING TO HELP YOU.
I IMAGINE YOU HAVE A CAR YOU COULD TRY TO DRIVE THROUGH THE GATE, BUT DOESN'T THAT JUST DEFEAT THE PURPOSE OF COMING IN AT ALL?
THING IS, WE WANT NEW PEOPLE IN HERE. WE NEED THEM, THERE'S A LOT OF WORK TO BE DONE. BUT WE HAVE A CERTAIN WAY ABOUT DOING THIS.
HAD YOU JUST ASKED, THINGS MIGHT HAVE WORKED OUT... AFTER THESE THREATS AND DEMANDS... IT'S NOT LOOKING GOOD.

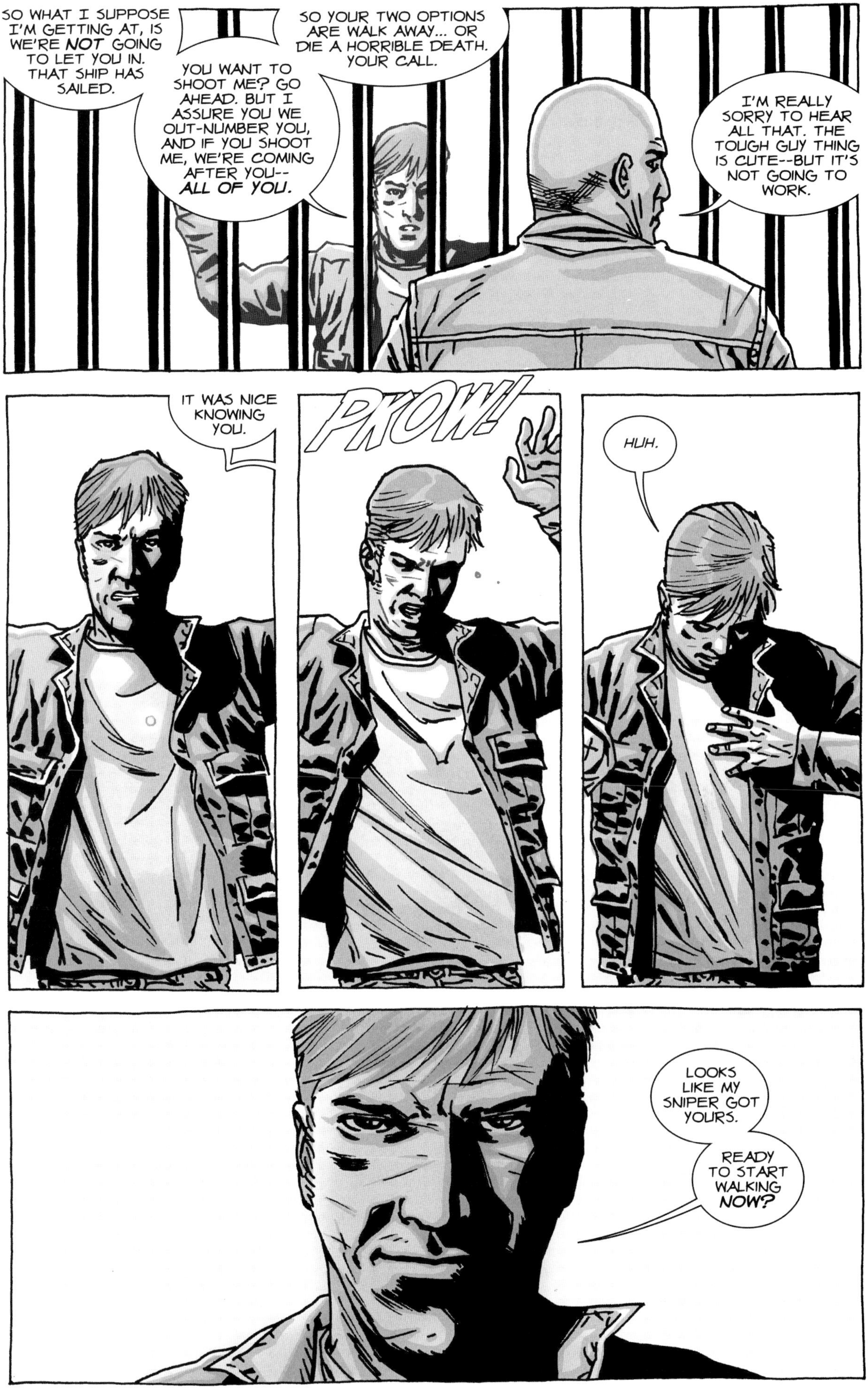
SO WHAT I SUPPOSE I'M GETTING AT, IS WE'RE NOT GOING TO LET YOU IN. THAT SHIP HAS SAILED.
YOU WANT TO SHOOT ME? GO AHEAD. BUT I ASSURE YOU WE OUT-NUMBER YOU, AND IF YOU SHOOT ME, WE'RE COMING AFTER YOU-- ALL OF YOU.
SO YOUR TWO OPTIONS ARE WALK AWAY... OR DIE A HORRIBLE DEATH. YOUR CALL.
I'M REALLY SORRY TO HEAR ALL THAT. THE TOUGH GUY THING IS CUTE--BUT IT'S NOT GOING TO WORK.
IT WAS NICE KNOWING YOU.
PKOW!
HUH.
LOOKS LIKE MY SNIPER GOT YOURS.
READY TO START WALKING NOW?

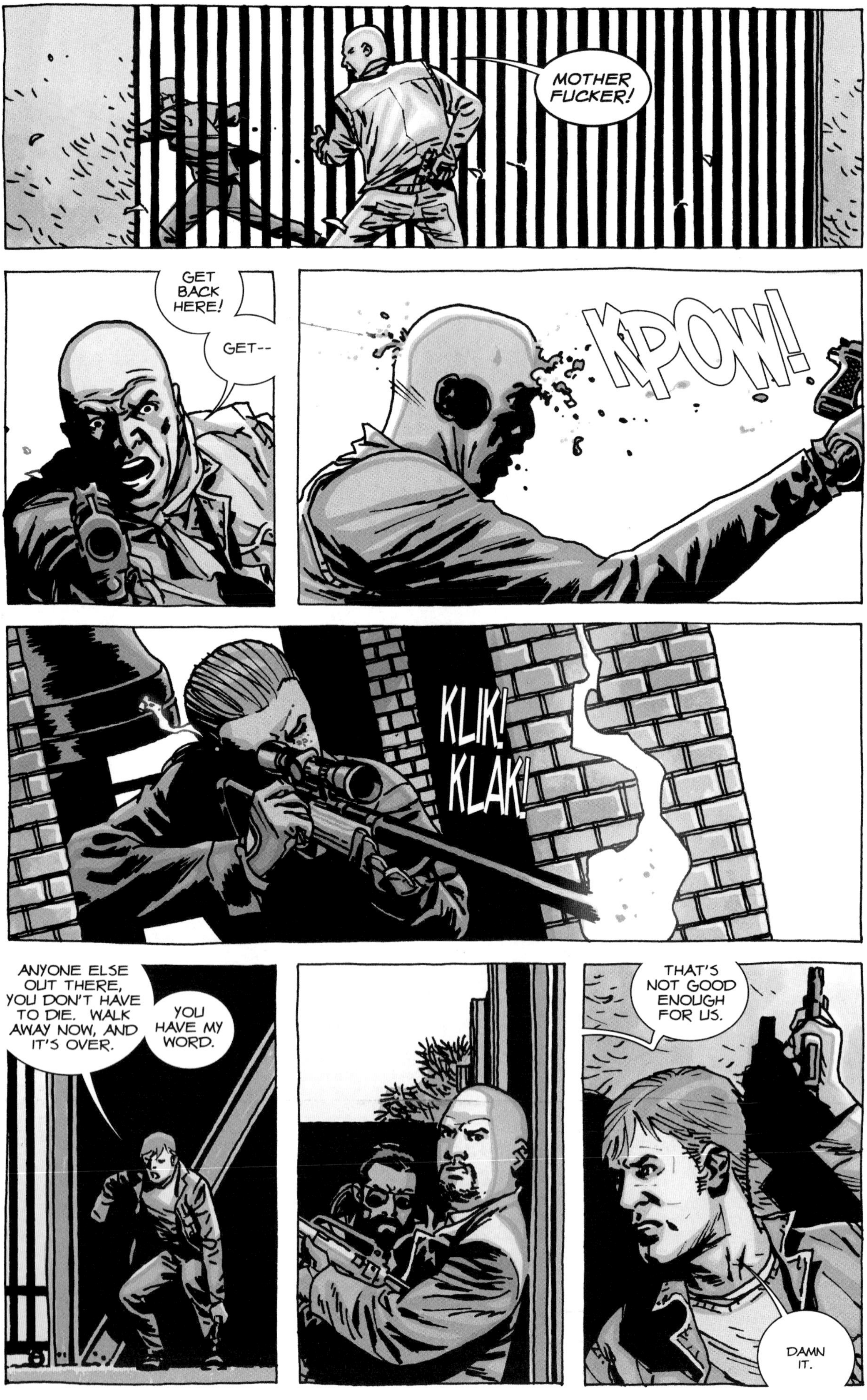
MOTHER FUCKER!
GET BACK HERE!
GET--
KPOW!
KLIK! KLAK!
ANYONE ELSE OUT THERE, YOU DON'T HAVE TO DIE. WALK AWAY NOW, AND IT'S OVER.
YOU HAVE MY WORD.
THAT'S NOT GOOD ENOUGH FOR US.
DAMN IT.

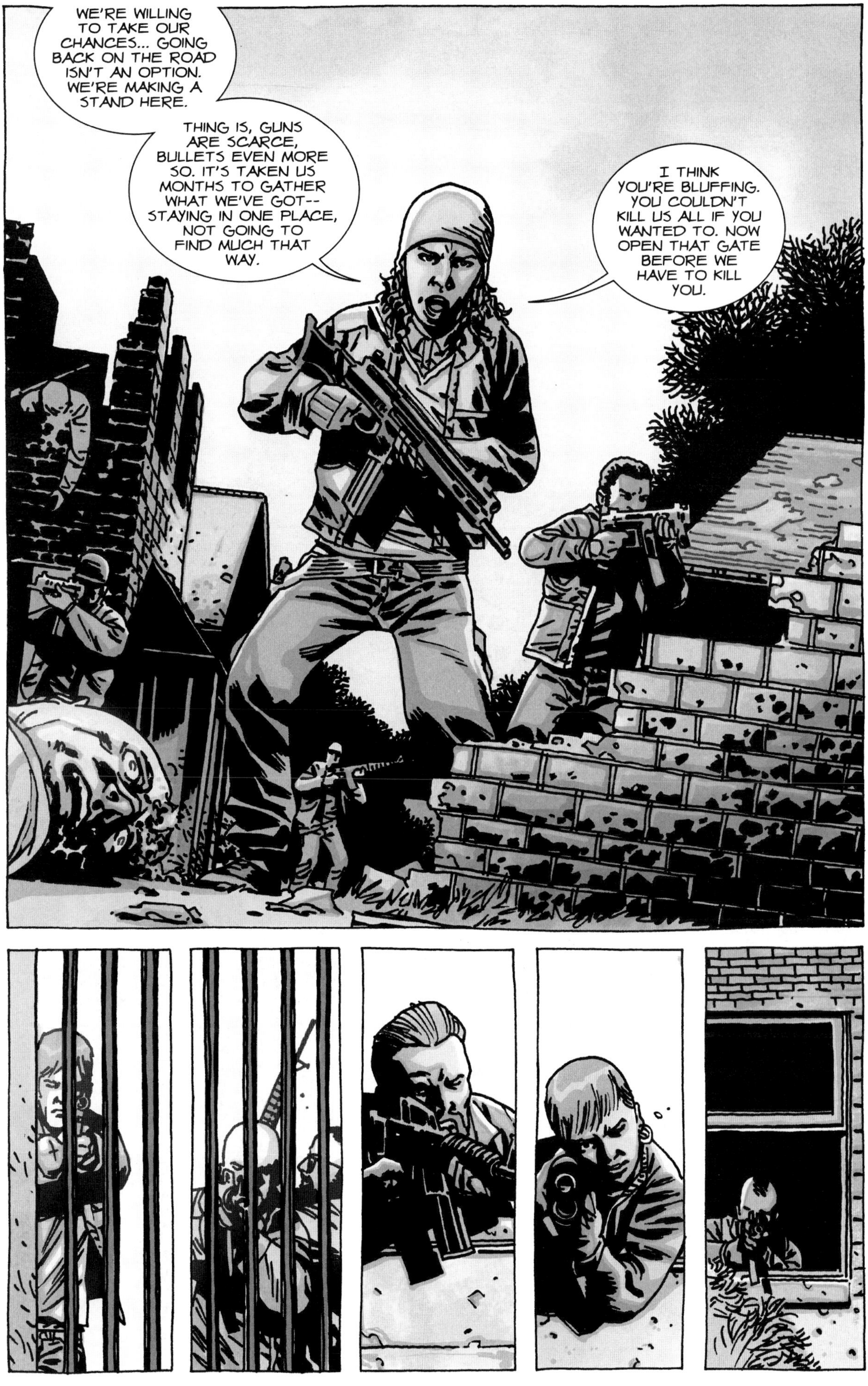
WE'RE WILLING TO TAKE OUR CHANCES... GOING BACK ON THE ROAD ISN'T AN OPTION. WE'RE MAKING A STAND HERE.
THING IS, GUNS ARE SCARCE, BULLETS EVEN MORE SO. IT'S TAKEN US MONTHS TO GATHER WHAT WE'VE GOT-- STAYING IN ONE PLACE, NOT GOING TO FIND MUCH THAT WAY.
I THINK YOU'RE BLUFFING. YOU COULDN'T KILL US ALL IF YOU WANTED TO. NOW OPEN THAT GATE BEFORE WE HAVE TO KILL YOU.

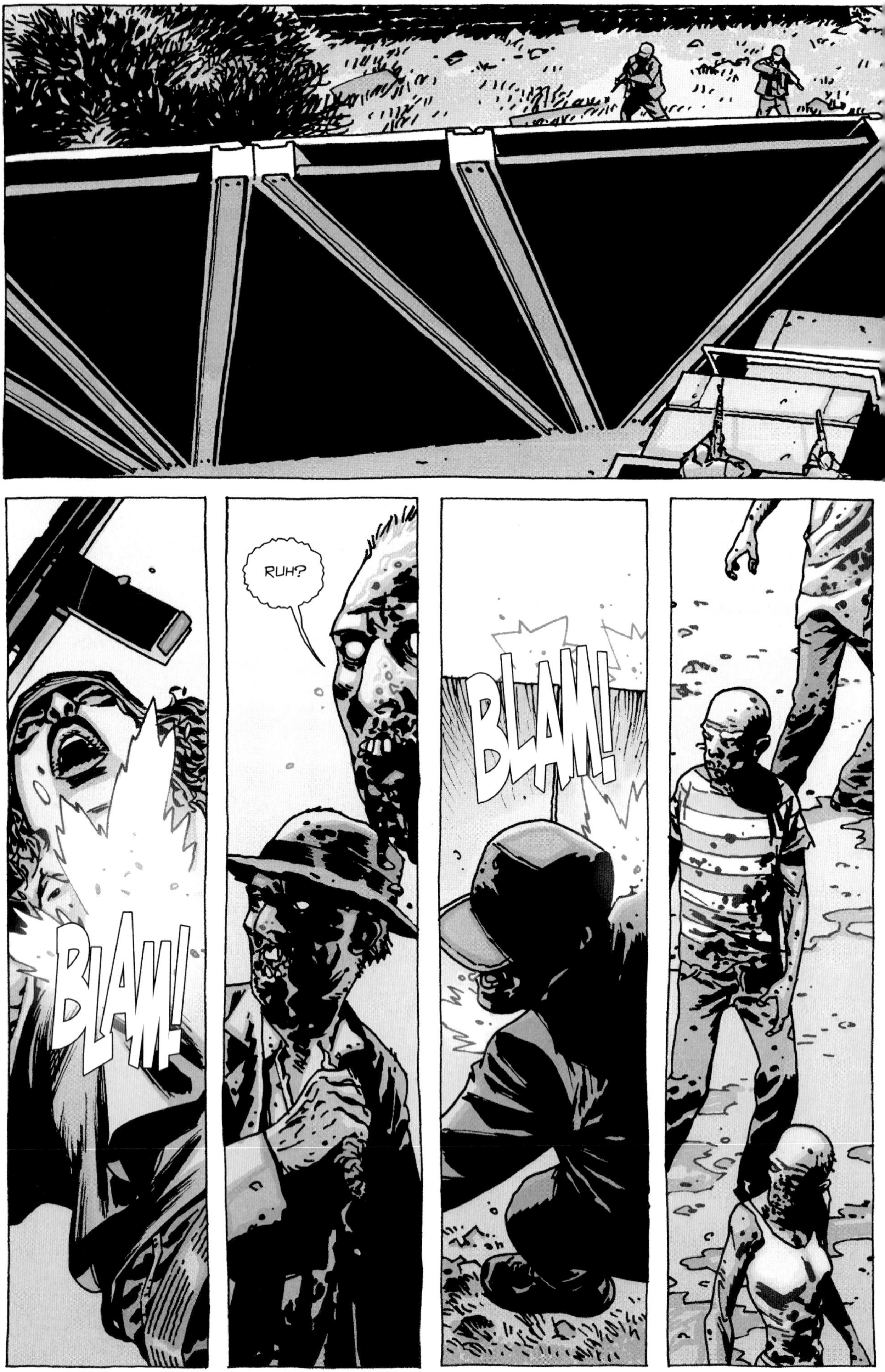
BLAM!
RUH?
BLAM!

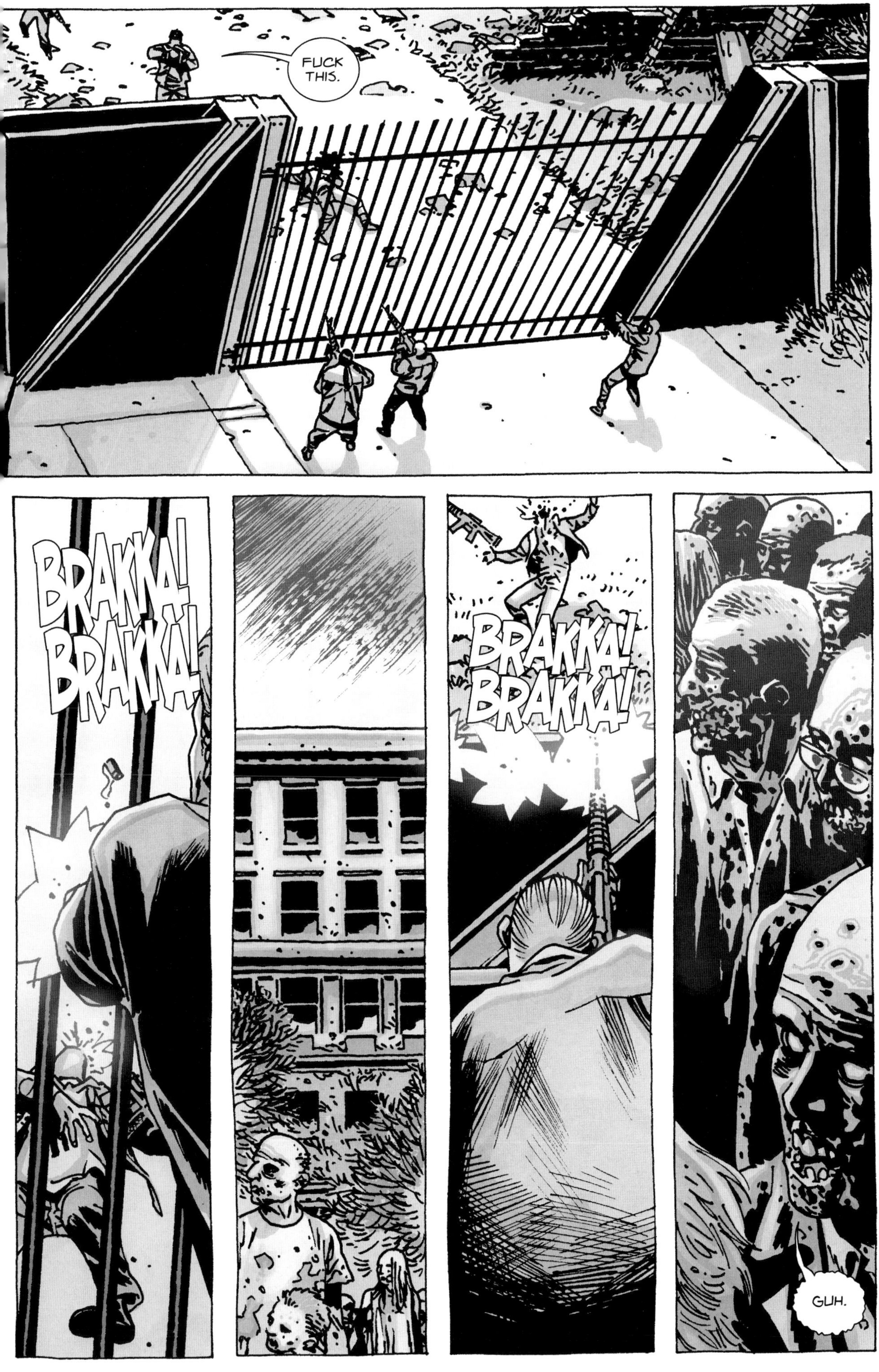
FUCK THIS.
BRAKKA! BRAKKA!
BRAKKA! BRAKKA!
GUH.

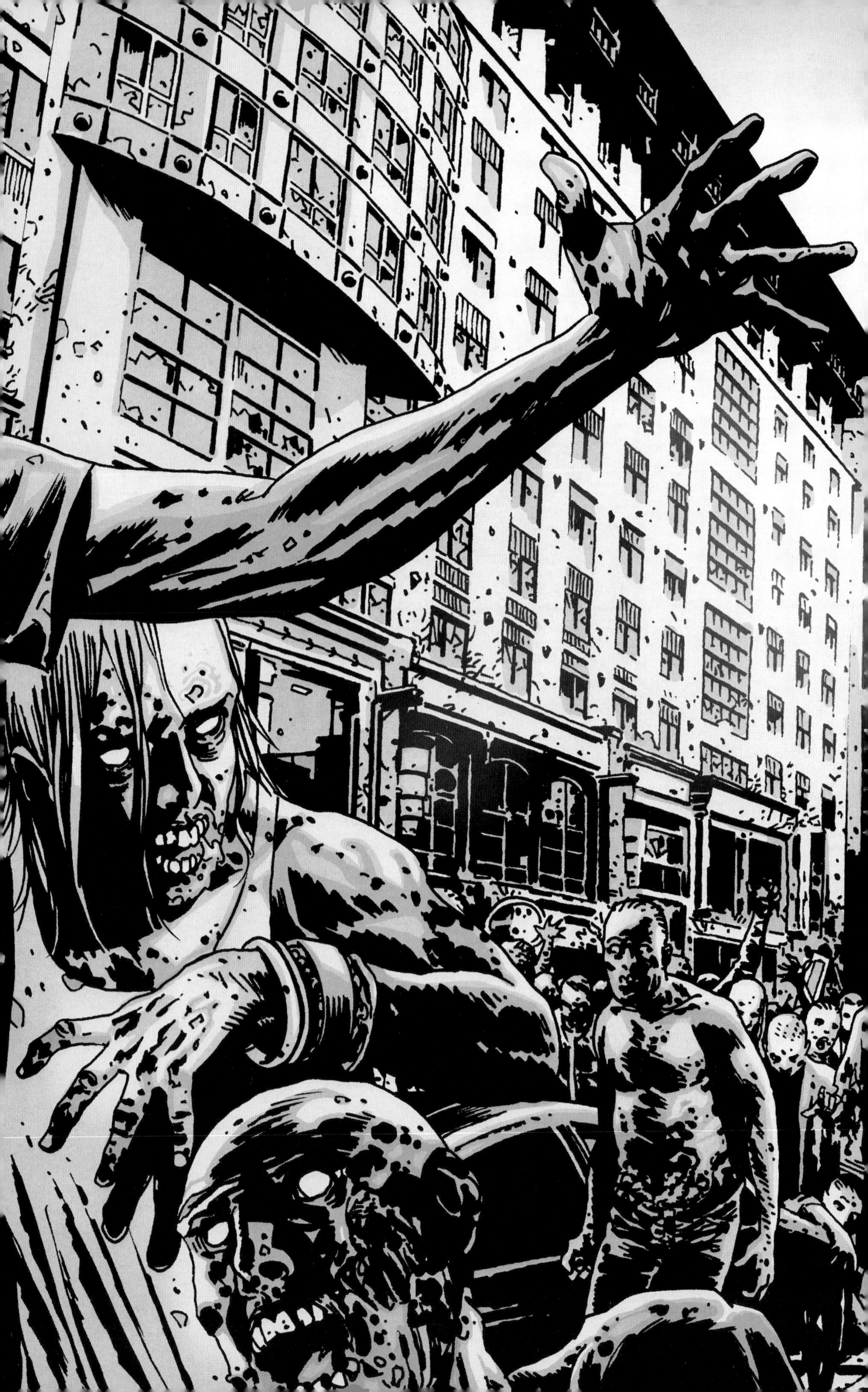

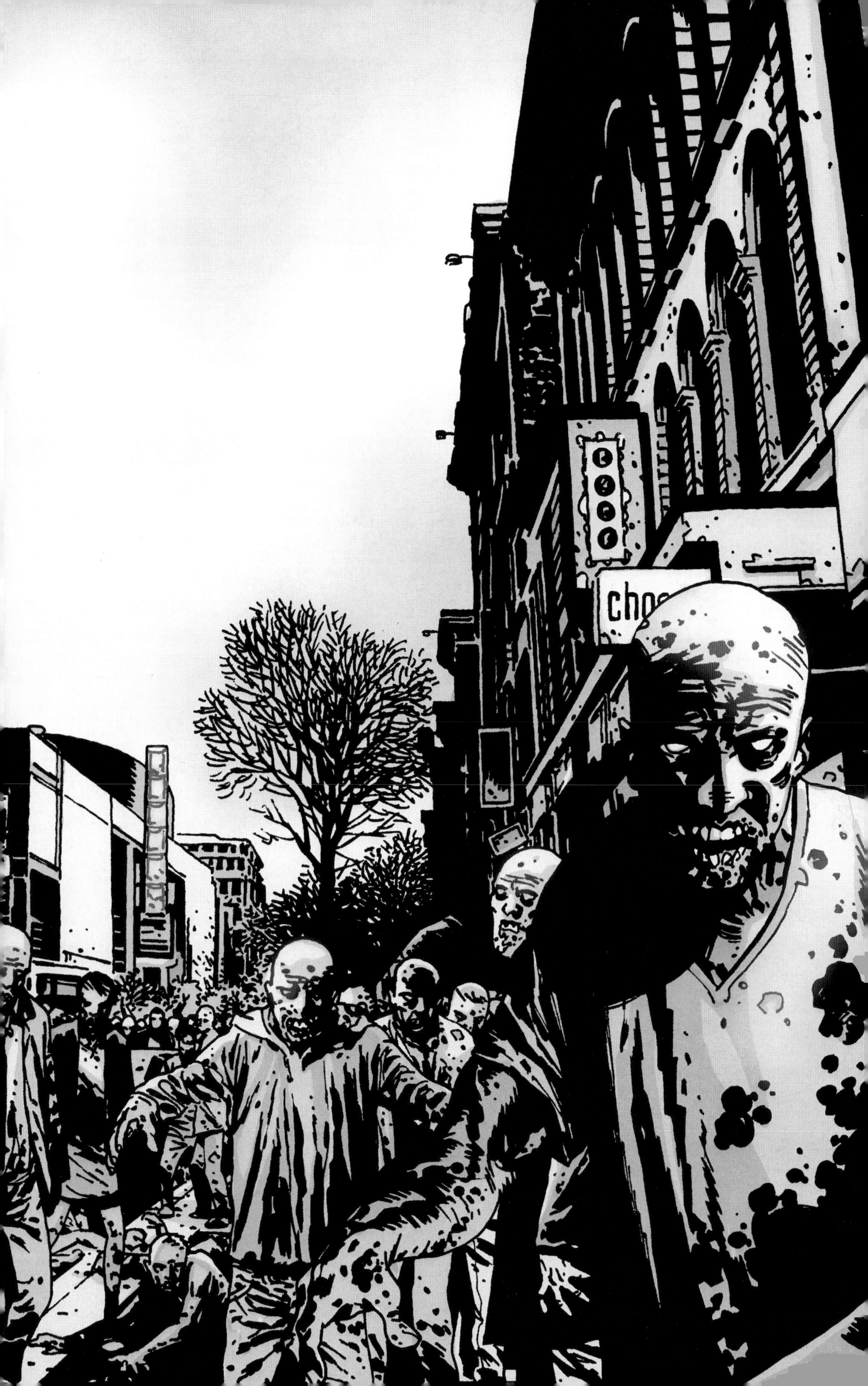

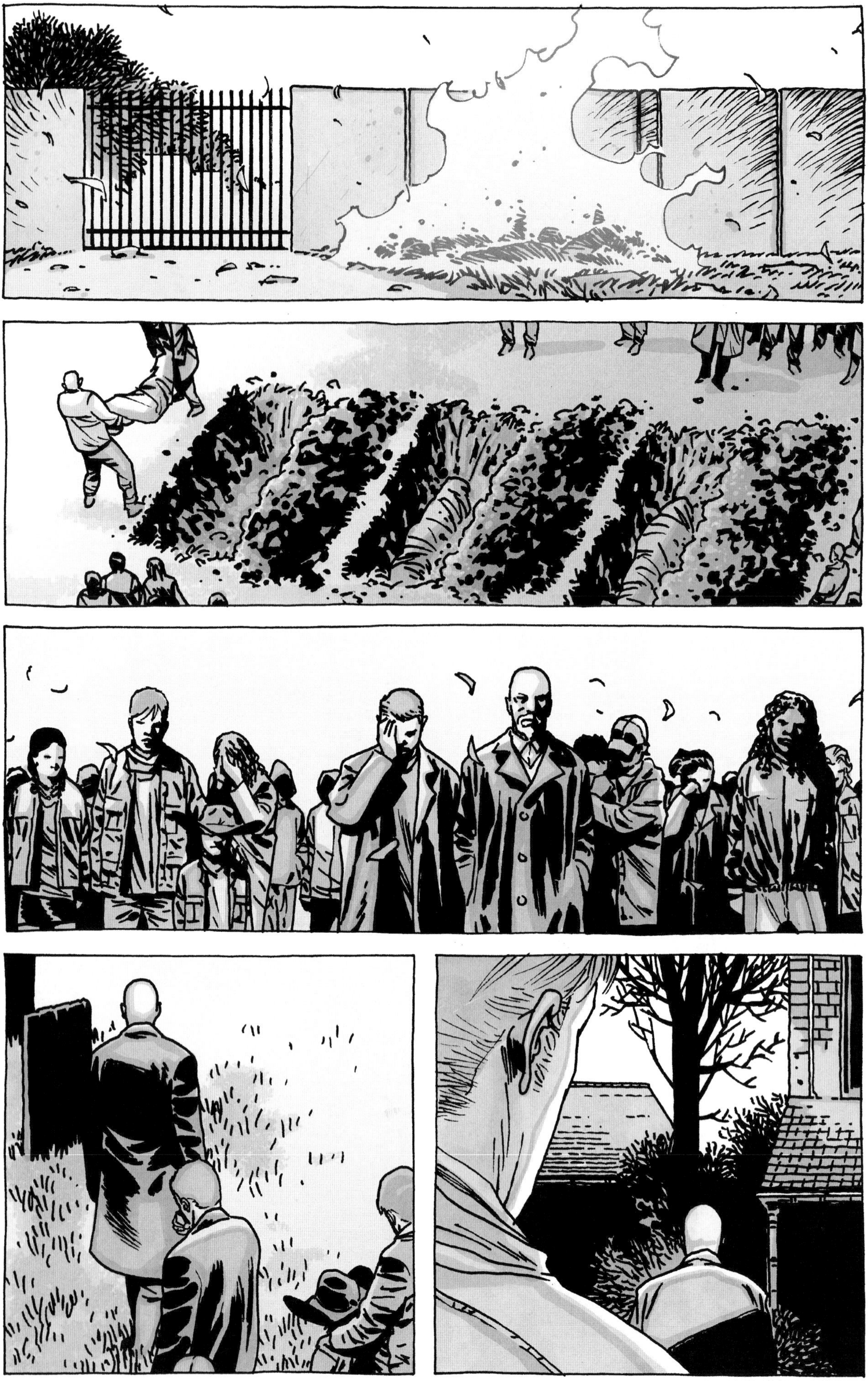

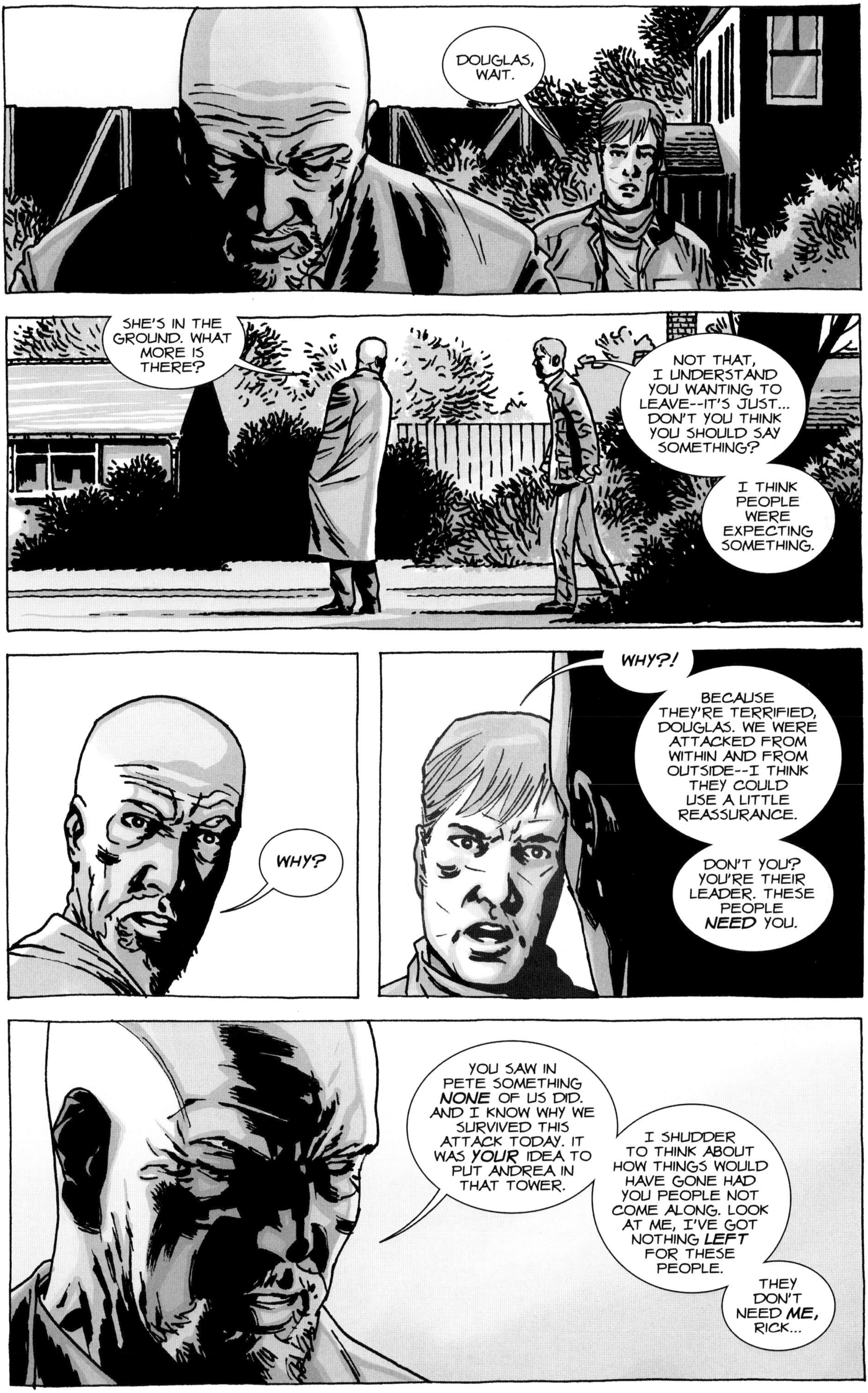
DOUGLAS, WAIT.
SHE'S IN THE GROUND. WHAT MORE IS THERE?
NOT THAT, I UNDERSTAND YOU WANTING TO LEAVE--IT'S JUST... DON'T YOU THINK YOU SHOULD SAY SOMETHING?
I THINK PEOPLE WERE EXPECTING SOMETHING.
WHY?
WHY?!
BECAUSE THEY'RE TERRIFIED, DOUGLAS. WE WERE ATTACKED FROM WITHIN AND FROM OUTSIDE--I THINK THEY COULD USE A LITTLE REASSURANCE.
DON'T YOU? YOU'RE THEIR LEADER. THESE PEOPLE NEED YOU.
YOU SAW IN PETE SOMETHING NONE OF US DID. AND I KNOW WHY WE SURVIVED THIS ATTACK TODAY. IT WAS YOUR IDEA TO PUT ANDREA IN THAT TOWER.
I SHUDDER TO THINK ABOUT HOW THINGS WOULD HAVE GONE HAD YOU PEOPLE NOT COME ALONG. LOOK AT ME, I'VE GOT NOTHING LEFT FOR THESE PEOPLE.
THEY DON'T NEED ME, RICK...

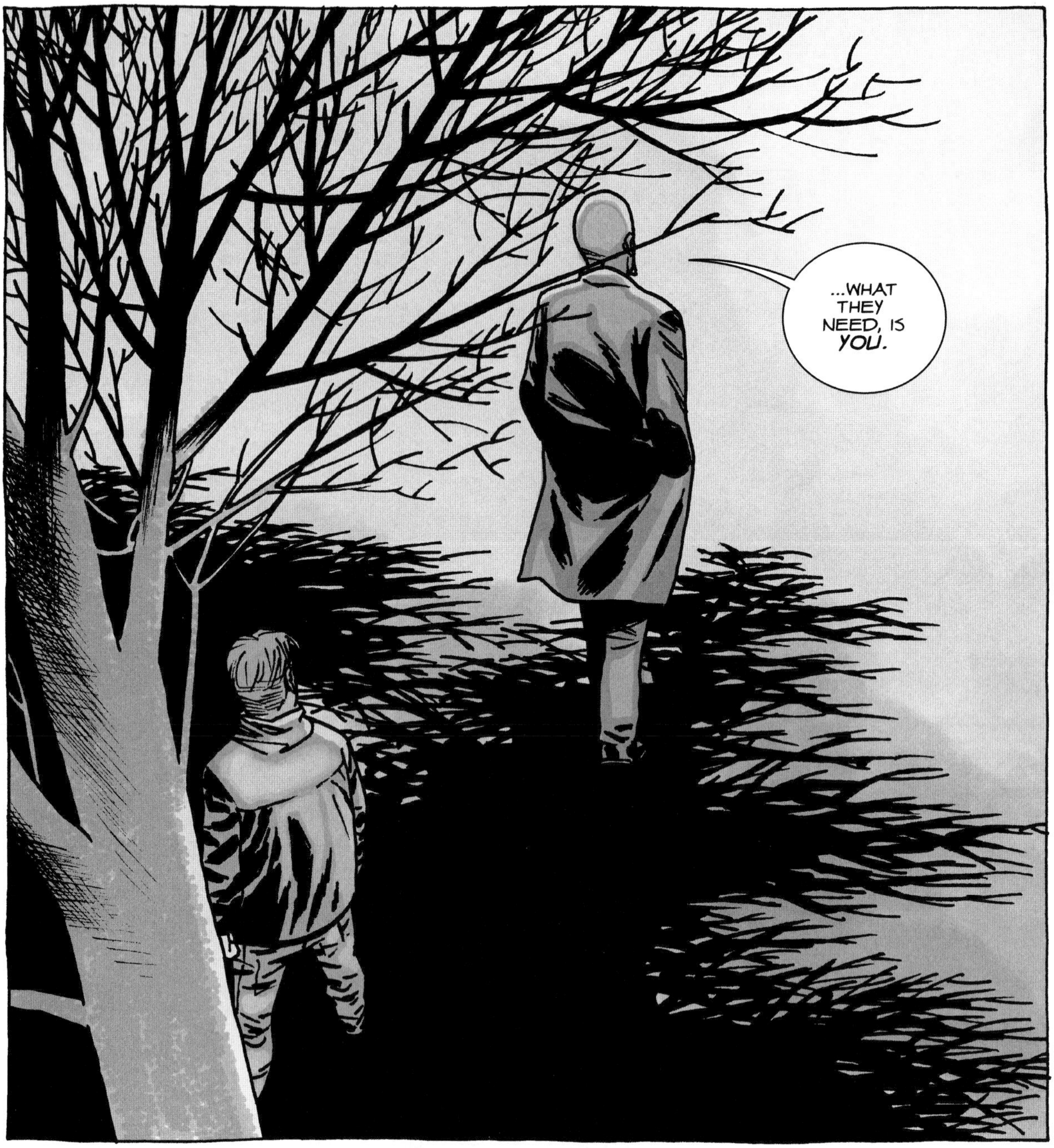
...WHAT THEY NEED, IS YOU.

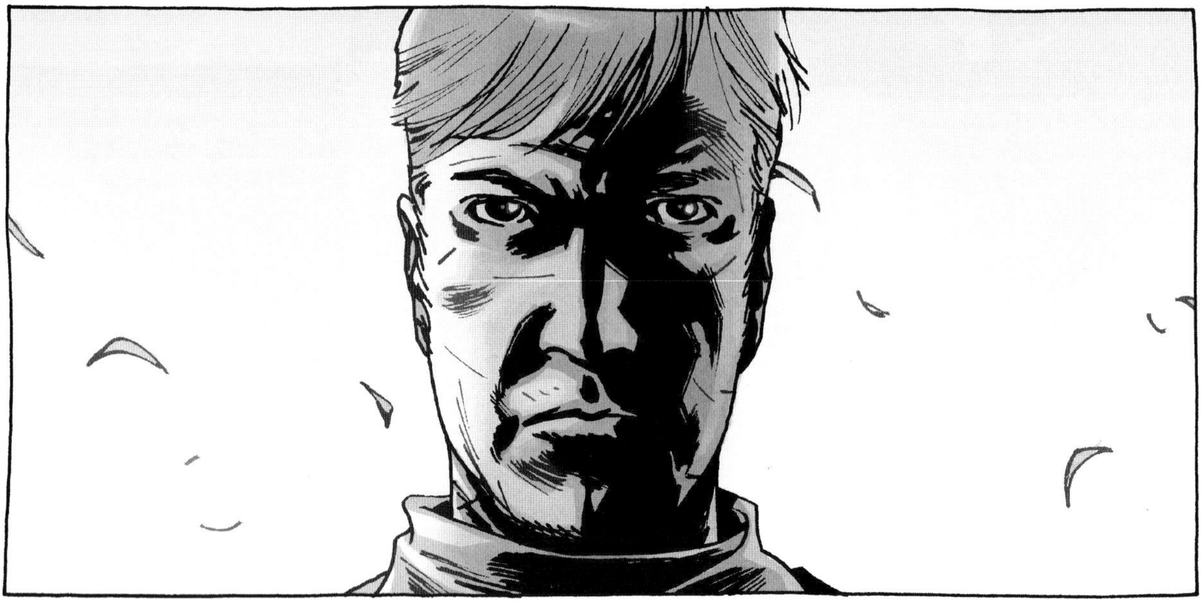

Chapter Fourteen:
No Way Out

YOU SLEEP?

BARELY. A FEW MINUTES HERE AND THERE, IT FELT LIKE.

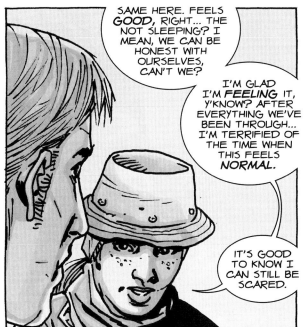

SAME HERE. FEELS *GOOD*, RIGHT... THE NOT SLEEPING? I MEAN, WE CAN BE HONEST WITH OURSELVES, CAN'T WE?

I'M GLAD I'M *FEELING* IT, Y'KNOW? AFTER EVERYTHING WE'VE BEEN THROUGH... I'M TERRIFIED OF THE TIME WHEN THIS FEELS *NORMAL*.

IT'S GOOD TO KNOW I CAN STILL BE SCARED.

NOT SO SCARED YOU COULDN'T SAVE MY LIFE.

THANK YOU FOR THAT.

I'M SURE WE'RE FAR FROM EVEN THERE. BUT IT WAS AN *AWESOME* SHOT, WASN'T IT?

I'M STILL AMAZED. HOW IS IT YOU FOUND THEIR SHOOTER--I MEAN, THAT'S SOME LUCK THERE, YOU SPOTTING THE GUY IN TIME TO, I MEAN...

...HE COULD HAVE *KILLED* ME.

HE WAS THE FIRST ONE I SAW, CLIMBING ON TOP OF THE AWNING AT THE BANK ACROSS FROM ME. I WAS ABOVE HIM.

HE'S THE REASON I NOTICED THE OTHERS AT THE GATE, POOR DUMB BASTARDS. WASN'T SURE HE WAS WITH THEM UNTIL HE PUT THE GUN ON YOU.

THAT'S WHY I DIDN'T POP HIM ON SIGHT...

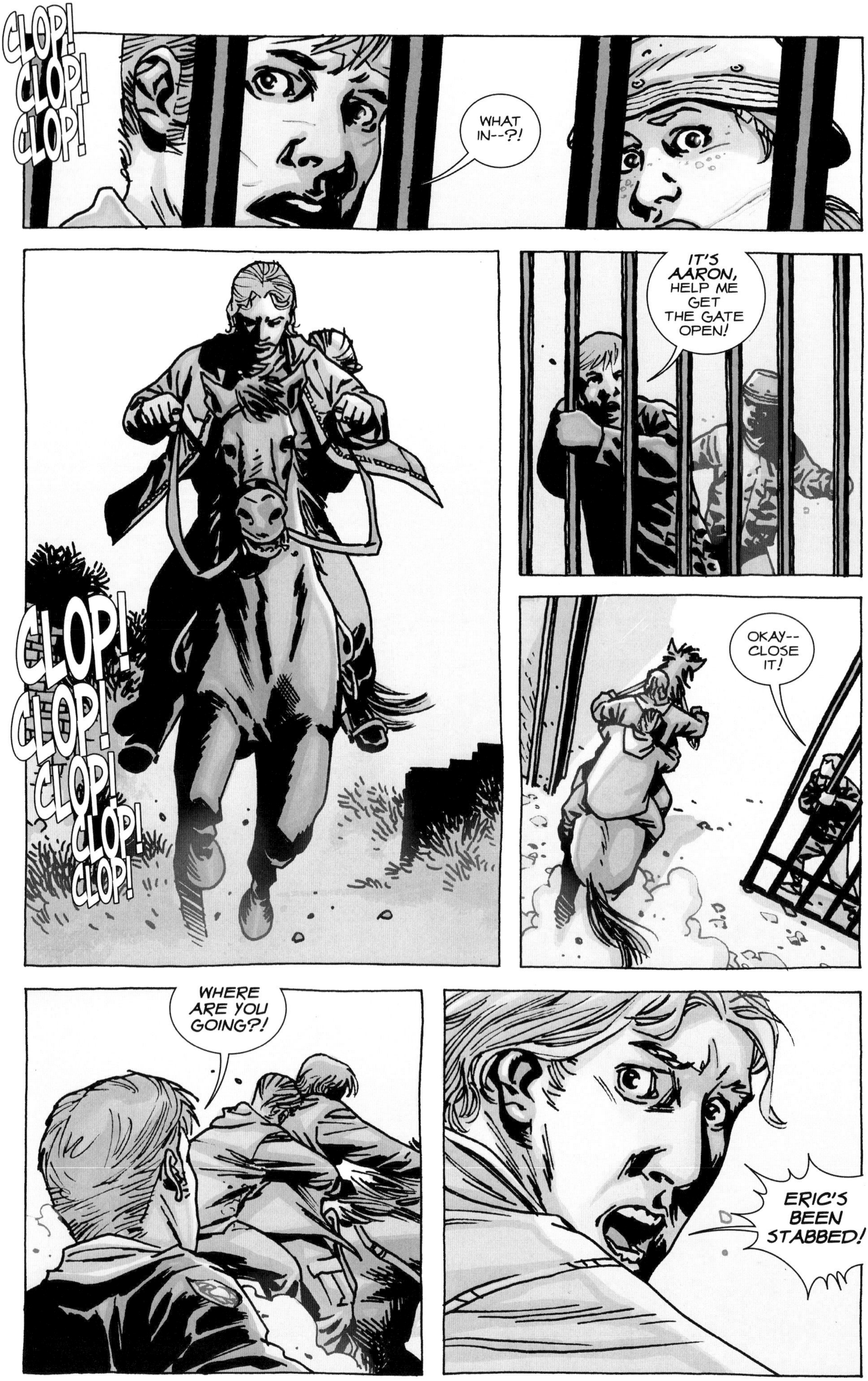
CLOP! CLOP! CLOP!
WHAT IN--?!
CLOP! CLOP! CLOP! CLOP! CLOP!
IT'S AARON, HELP ME GET THE GATE OPEN!
OKAY-- CLOSE IT!
WHERE ARE YOU GOING?!
ERIC'S BEEN STABBED!

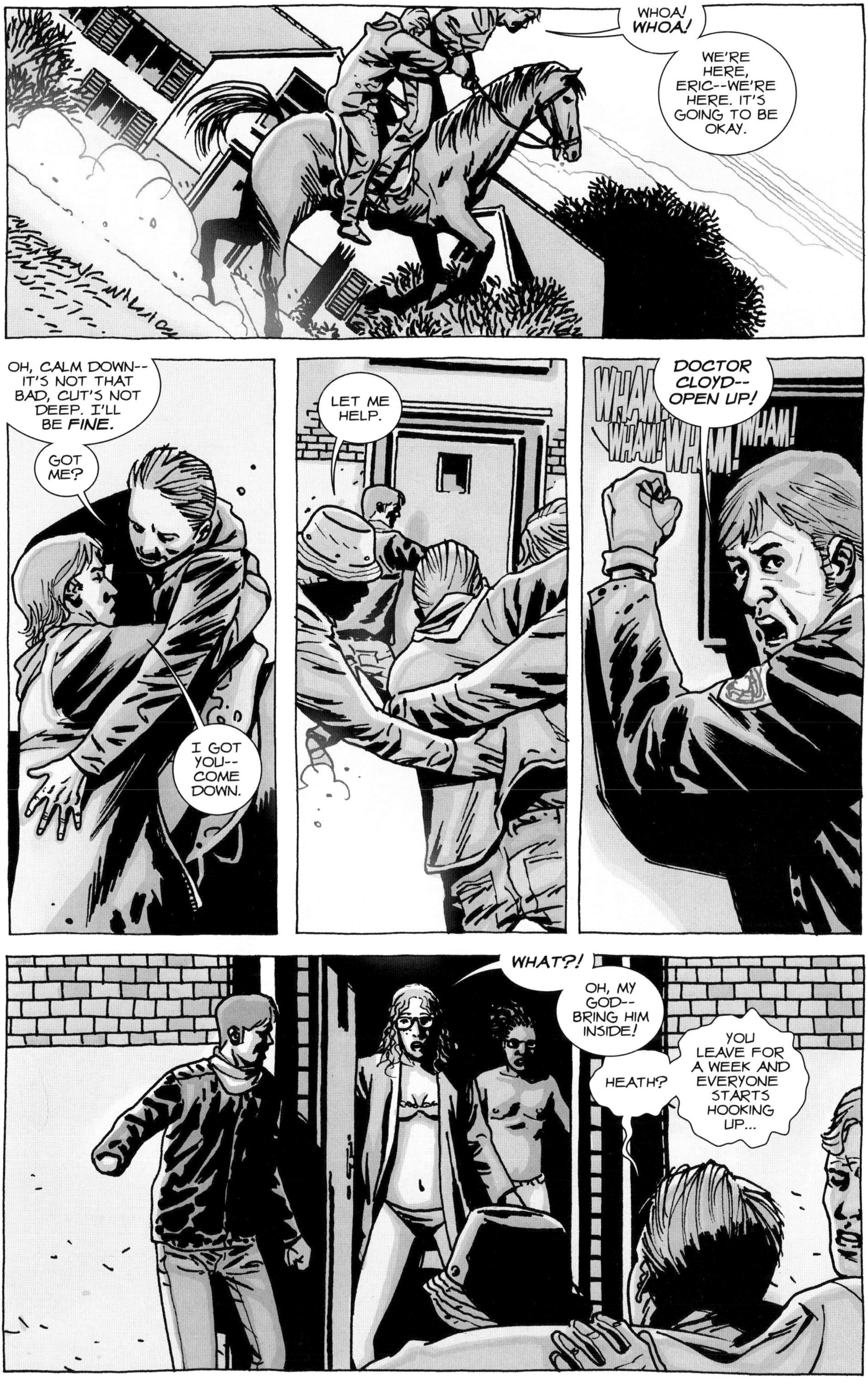
WHOA! WHOA!
WE'RE HERE, ERIC--WE'RE HERE. IT'S GOING TO BE OKAY.
OH, CALM DOWN-- IT'S NOT THAT BAD, CUT'S NOT DEEP. I'LL BE FINE.
GOT ME?
I GOT YOU-- COME DOWN.
LET ME HELP.
WHAM! WHAM! WHAM! WHAM!
DOCTOR CLOYD-- OPEN UP!
WHAT?!
OH, MY GOD-- BRING HIM INSIDE!
HEATH?
YOU LEAVE FOR A WEEK AND EVERYONE STARTS HOOKING UP...

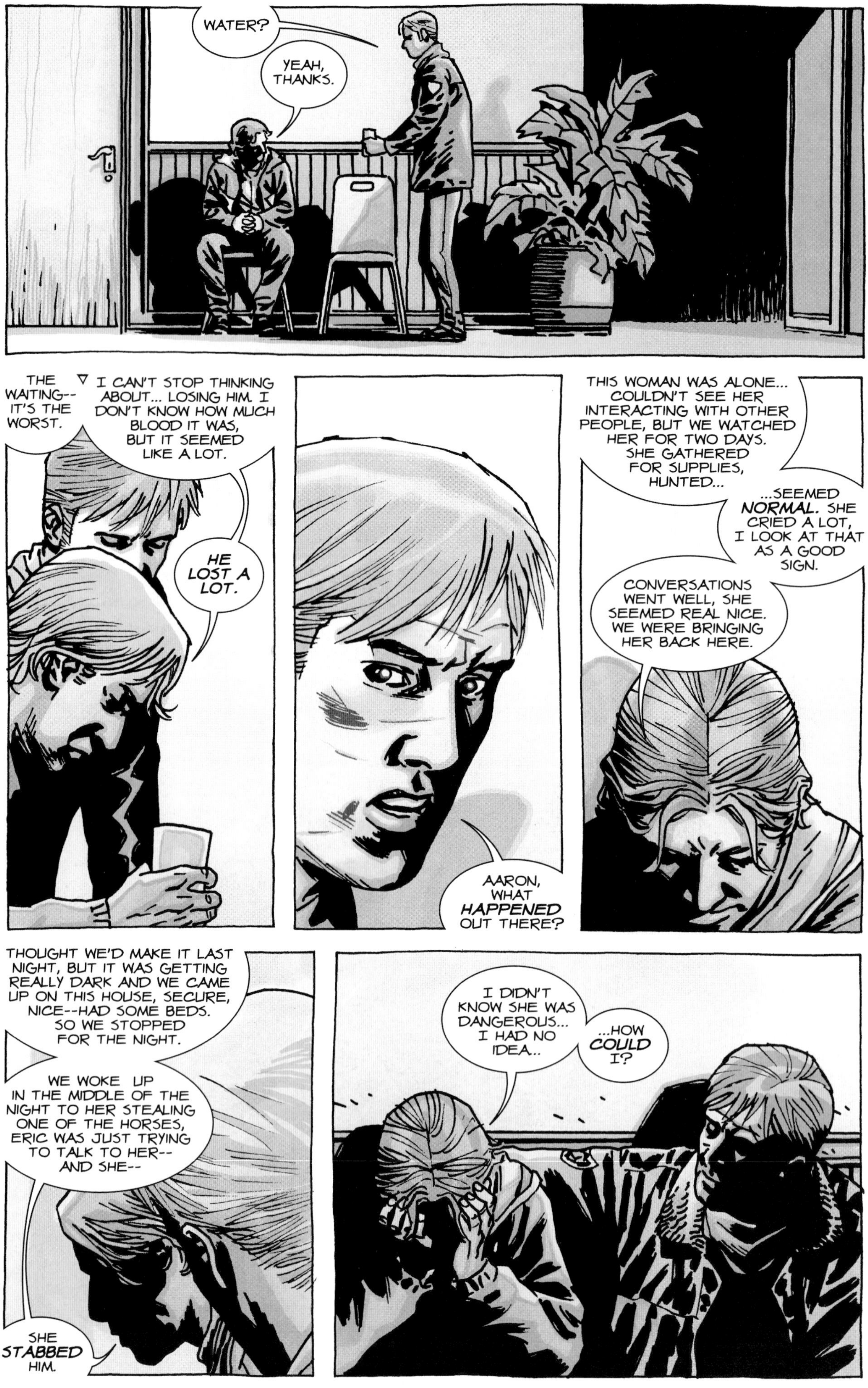
WATER?
YEAH, THANKS.
THE WAITING-- IT'S THE WORST.
I CAN'T STOP THINKING ABOUT... LOSING HIM. I DON'T KNOW HOW MUCH BLOOD IT WAS, BUT IT SEEMED LIKE A LOT.
HE LOST A LOT.
AARON, WHAT HAPPENED OUT THERE?
THIS WOMAN WAS ALONE... COULDN'T SEE HER INTERACTING WITH OTHER PEOPLE, BUT WE WATCHED HER FOR TWO DAYS. SHE GATHERED FOR SUPPLIES, HUNTED...
...SEEMED NORMAL. SHE CRIED A LOT, I LOOK AT THAT AS A GOOD SIGN.
CONVERSATIONS WENT WELL, SHE SEEMED REAL NICE. WE WERE BRINGING HER BACK HERE.
THOUGHT WE'D MAKE IT LAST NIGHT, BUT IT WAS GETTING REALLY DARK AND WE CAME UP ON THIS HOUSE, SECURE, NICE--HAD SOME BEDS. SO WE STOPPED FOR THE NIGHT.
WE WOKE UP IN THE MIDDLE OF THE NIGHT TO HER STEALING ONE OF THE HORSES, ERIC WAS JUST TRYING TO TALK TO HER-- AND SHE--
SHE STABBED HIM.
I DIDN'T KNOW SHE WAS DANGEROUS... I HAD NO IDEA...
...HOW COULD I?

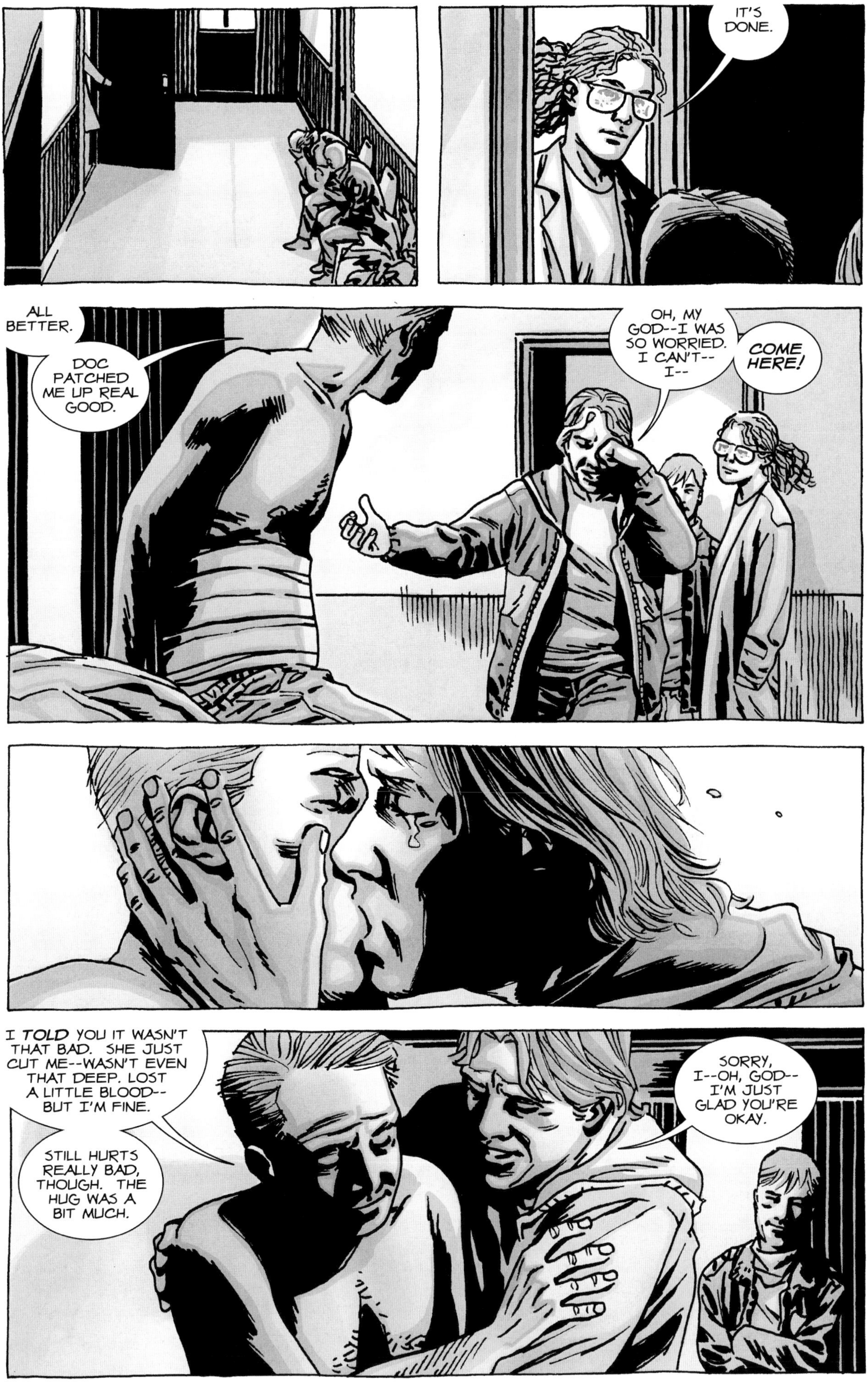
IT'S DONE.
ALL BETTER.
DOC PATCHED ME UP REAL GOOD.
OH, MY GOD--I WAS SO WORRIED. I CAN'T-- I--
COME HERE!
I TOLD YOU IT WASN'T THAT BAD. SHE JUST CUT ME--WASN'T EVEN THAT DEEP. LOST A LITTLE BLOOD-- BUT I'M FINE.
STILL HURTS REALLY BAD, THOUGH. THE HUG WAS A BIT MUCH.
SORRY, I--OH, GOD-- I'M JUST GLAD YOU'RE OKAY.

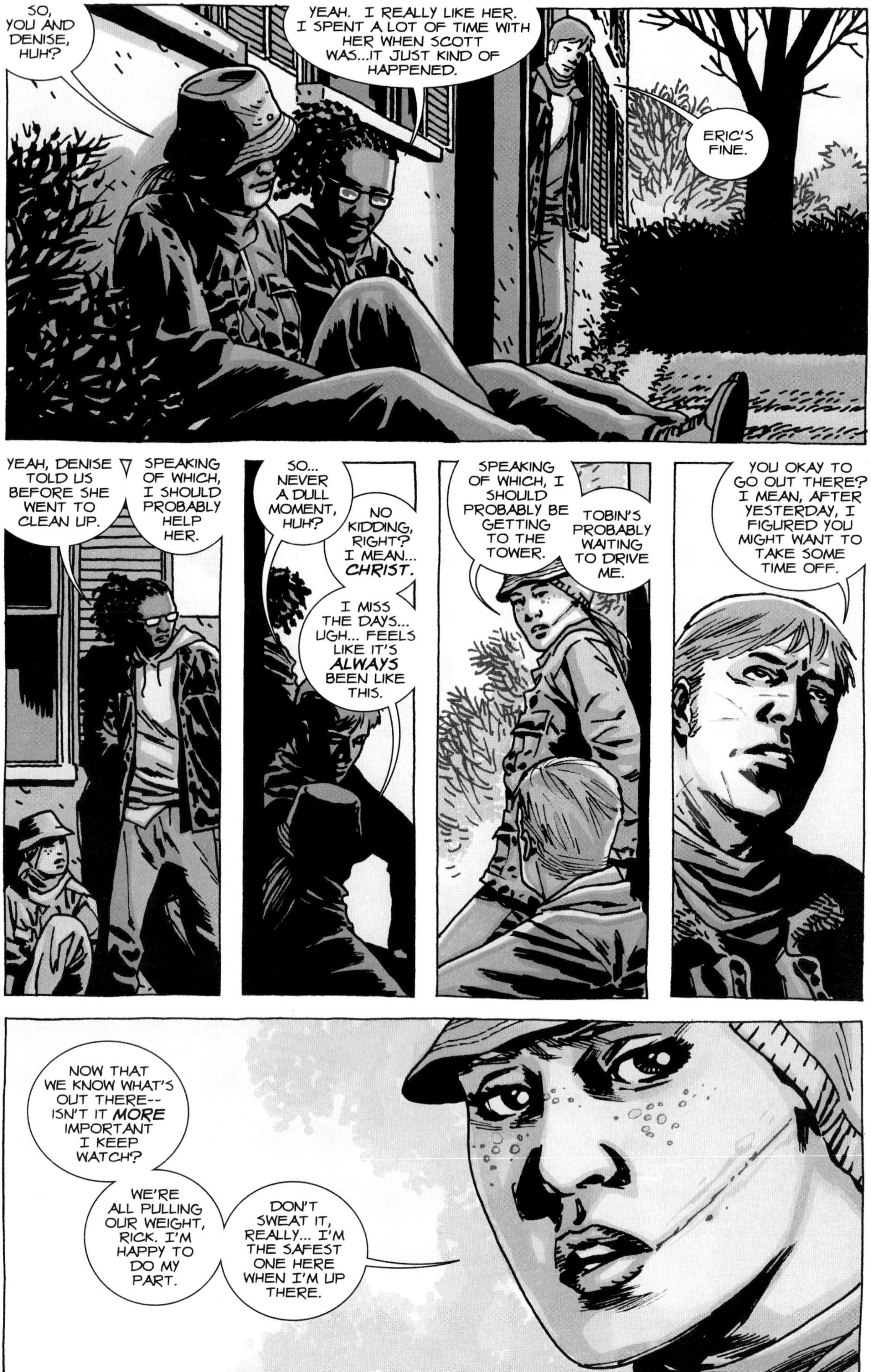
SO, YOU AND DENISE, HUH?
YEAH. I REALLY LIKE HER. I SPENT A LOT OF TIME WITH HER WHEN SCOTT WAS...IT JUST KIND OF HAPPENED.
ERIC'S FINE.
YEAH, DENISE TOLD US BEFORE SHE WENT TO CLEAN UP.
SPEAKING OF WHICH, I SHOULD PROBABLY HELP HER.
SO... NEVER A DULL MOMENT, HUH?
NO KIDDING, RIGHT? I MEAN... CHRIST.
I MISS THE DAYS... UGH... FEELS LIKE IT'S ALWAYS BEEN LIKE THIS.
SPEAKING OF WHICH, I SHOULD PROBABLY BE GETTING TO THE TOWER.
TOBIN'S PROBABLY WAITING TO DRIVE ME.
YOU OKAY TO GO OUT THERE? I MEAN, AFTER YESTERDAY, I FIGURED YOU MIGHT WANT TO TAKE SOME TIME OFF.
NOW THAT WE KNOW WHAT'S OUT THERE-- ISN'T IT MORE IMPORTANT I KEEP WATCH?
WE'RE ALL PULLING OUR WEIGHT, RICK. I'M HAPPY TO DO MY PART.
DON'T SWEAT IT, REALLY... I'M THE SAFEST ONE HERE WHEN I'M UP THERE.

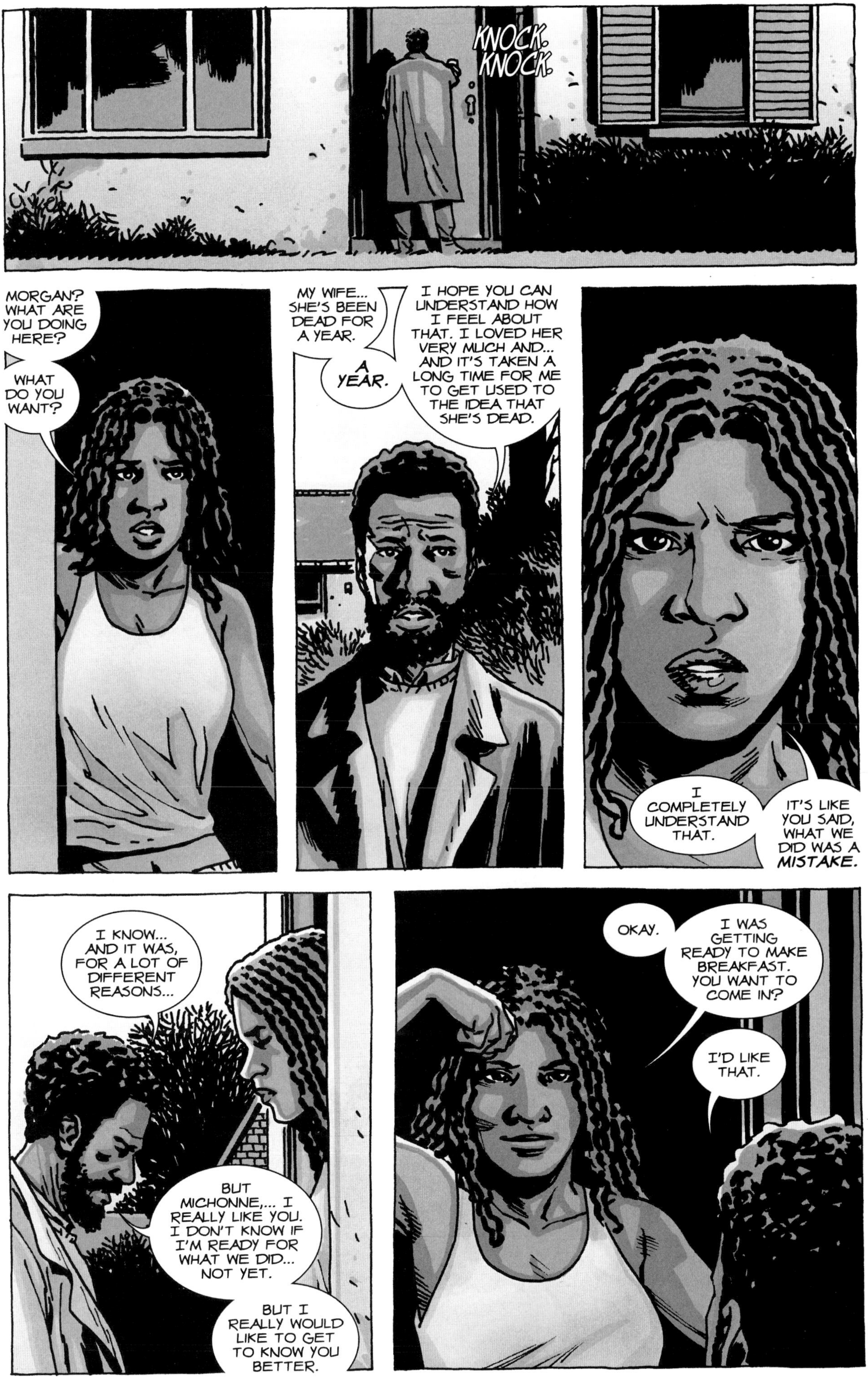
KNOCK. KNOCK.
MORGAN? WHAT ARE YOU DOING HERE?
WHAT DO YOU WANT?
MY WIFE... SHE'S BEEN DEAD FOR A YEAR.
A YEAR.
I HOPE YOU CAN UNDERSTAND HOW I FEEL ABOUT THAT. I LOVED HER VERY MUCH AND... AND IT'S TAKEN A LONG TIME FOR ME TO GET USED TO THE IDEA THAT SHE'S DEAD.
I COMPLETELY UNDERSTAND THAT.
IT'S LIKE YOU SAID, WHAT WE DID WAS A MISTAKE.
I KNOW... AND IT WAS, FOR A LOT OF DIFFERENT REASONS...
BUT MICHONNE,... I REALLY LIKE YOU. I DON'T KNOW IF I'M READY FOR WHAT WE DID... NOT YET.
BUT I REALLY WOULD LIKE TO GET TO KNOW YOU BETTER.
OKAY.
I WAS GETTING READY TO MAKE BREAKFAST. YOU WANT TO COME IN?
I'D LIKE THAT.

MORNING, SON. WHEN'D YOU GET UP?

I GOT UP WHEN YOU LEFT. I HEARD YOU CLOSING THE DOOR... WHERE'D YOU GO?

DIDN'T SLEEP WELL LAST NIGHT, WENT TO CHECK THE GATE, SEE HOW THINGS WERE ON THE OTHER SIDE OF THE FENCE.

YOU OKAY?

YEAH. WHY?

WHY? WE WERE ATTACKED YESTERDAY, I THOUGHT YOU MIGHT BE SCARED.

WELL, I'M NOT.

WHAT HAPPENED WAS A GOOD THING. NOW MAYBE EVERYONE WILL STOP PRETENDING WE'RE ALL SAFE.

CARL, I--

YEAH, DAD?

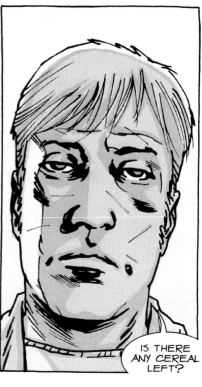

IS THERE ANY CEREAL LEFT?

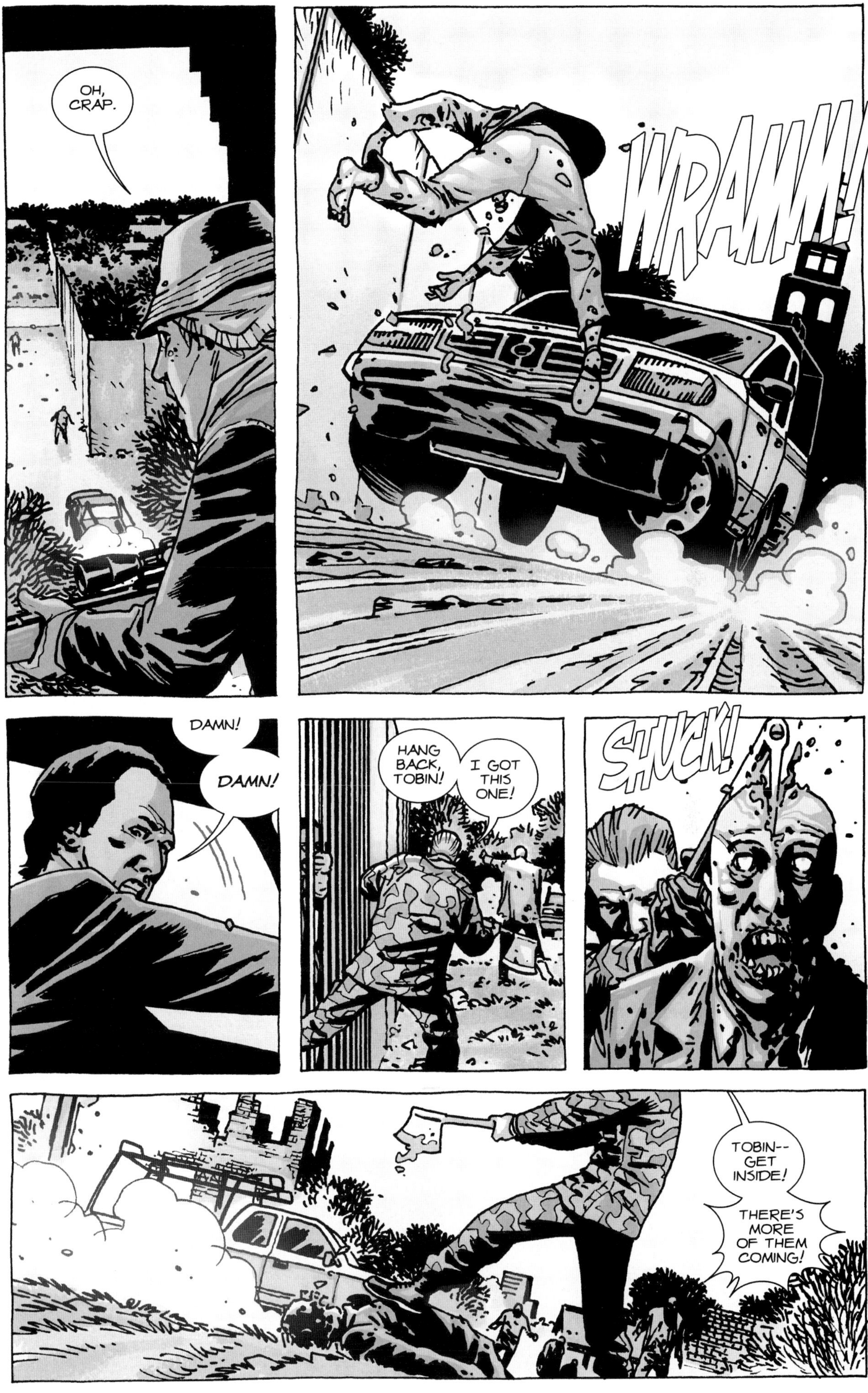
OH, CRAP.
WRAMM!
DAMN!
DAMN!
HANG BACK, TOBIN!
I GOT THIS ONE!
SHUCK!
TOBIN-- GET INSIDE!
THERE'S MORE OF THEM COMING!

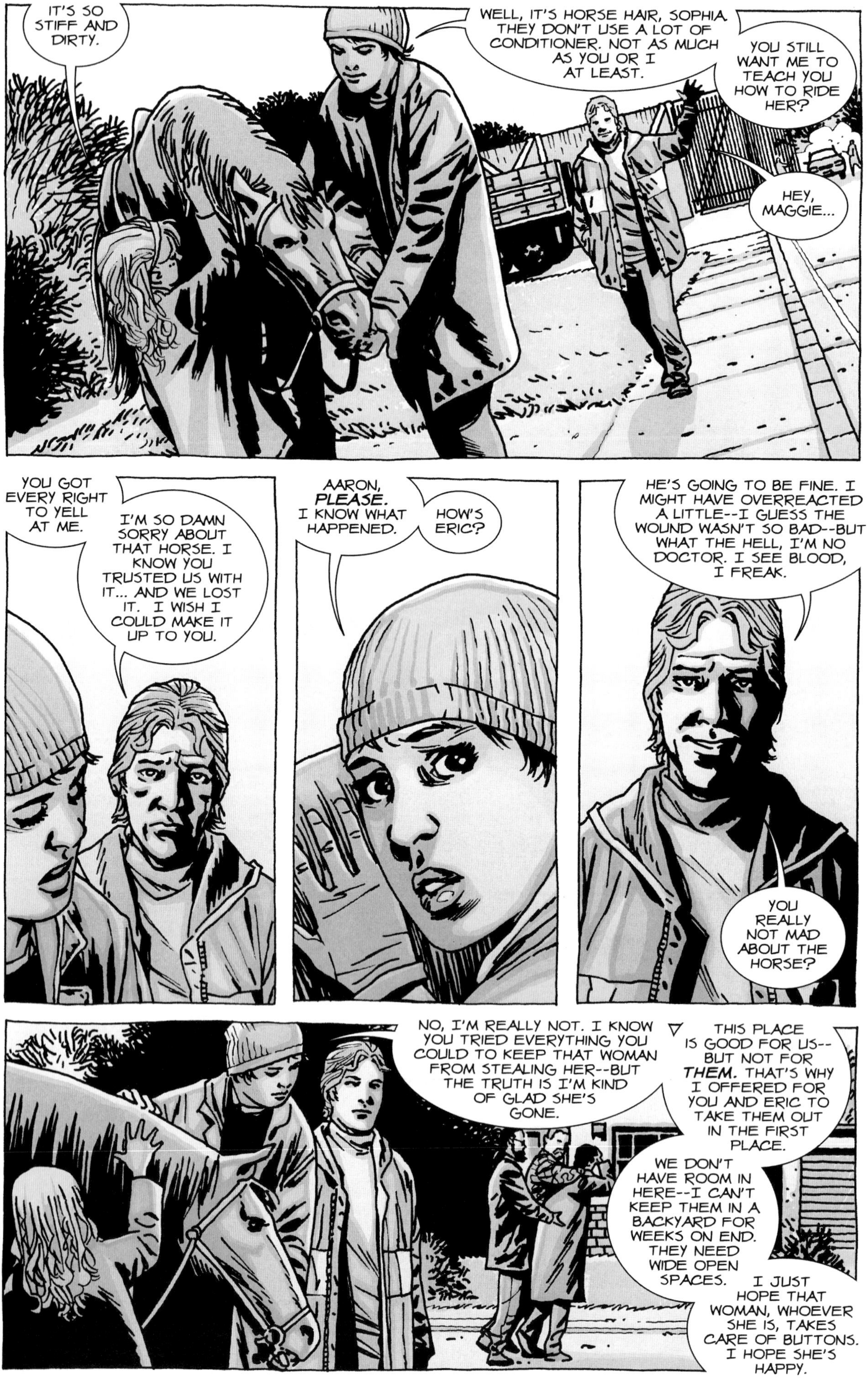
IT'S SO STIFF AND DIRTY.
WELL, IT'S HORSE HAIR, SOPHIA. THEY DON'T USE A LOT OF CONDITIONER. NOT AS MUCH AS YOU OR I AT LEAST.
YOU STILL WANT ME TO TEACH YOU HOW TO RIDE HER?
HEY, MAGGIE...
YOU GOT EVERY RIGHT TO YELL AT ME.
I'M SO DAMN SORRY ABOUT THAT HORSE. I KNOW YOU TRUSTED US WITH IT... AND WE LOST IT. I WISH I COULD MAKE IT UP TO YOU.
AARON, PLEASE. I KNOW WHAT HAPPENED.
HOW'S ERIC?
HE'S GOING TO BE FINE. I MIGHT HAVE OVERREACTED A LITTLE--I GUESS THE WOUND WASN'T SO BAD--BUT WHAT THE HELL, I'M NO DOCTOR. I SEE BLOOD, I FREAK.
YOU REALLY NOT MAD ABOUT THE HORSE?
NO, I'M REALLY NOT. I KNOW YOU TRIED EVERYTHING YOU COULD TO KEEP THAT WOMAN FROM STEALING HER--BUT THE TRUTH IS I'M KIND OF GLAD SHE'S GONE.
THIS PLACE IS GOOD FOR US--BUT NOT FOR THEM. THAT'S WHY I OFFERED FOR YOU AND ERIC TO TAKE THEM OUT IN THE FIRST PLACE.
WE DON'T HAVE ROOM IN HERE--I CAN'T KEEP THEM IN A BACKYARD FOR WEEKS ON END. THEY NEED WIDE OPEN SPACES.
I JUST HOPE THAT WOMAN, WHOEVER SHE IS, TAKES CARE OF BUTTONS. I HOPE SHE'S HAPPY.

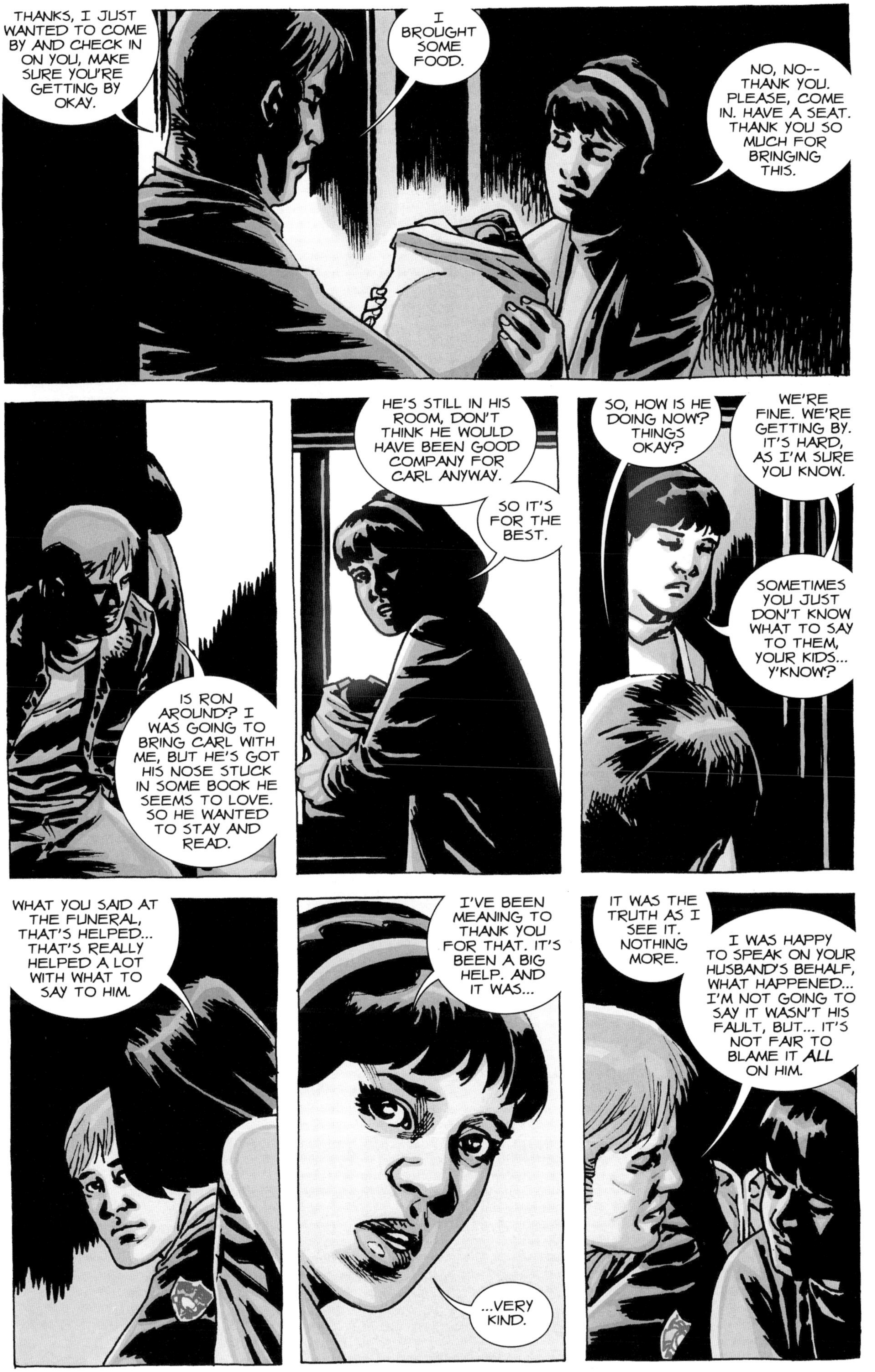
THANKS, I JUST WANTED TO COME BY AND CHECK IN ON YOU, MAKE SURE YOU'RE GETTING BY OKAY.
I BROUGHT SOME FOOD.
NO, NO-- THANK YOU. PLEASE, COME IN. HAVE A SEAT. THANK YOU SO MUCH FOR BRINGING THIS.
IS RON AROUND? I WAS GOING TO BRING CARL WITH ME, BUT HE'S GOT HIS NOSE STUCK IN SOME BOOK HE SEEMS TO LOVE. SO HE WANTED TO STAY AND READ.
HE'S STILL IN HIS ROOM, DON'T THINK HE WOULD HAVE BEEN GOOD COMPANY FOR CARL ANYWAY.
SO IT'S FOR THE BEST.
SO, HOW IS HE DOING NOW? THINGS OKAY?
WE'RE FINE. WE'RE GETTING BY. IT'S HARD, AS I'M SURE YOU KNOW.
SOMETIMES YOU JUST DON'T KNOW WHAT TO SAY TO THEM, YOUR KIDS... Y'KNOW?
WHAT YOU SAID AT THE FUNERAL, THAT'S HELPED... THAT'S REALLY HELPED A LOT WITH WHAT TO SAY TO HIM.
I'VE BEEN MEANING TO THANK YOU FOR THAT. IT'S BEEN A BIG HELP. AND IT WAS...
...VERY KIND.
IT WAS THE TRUTH AS I SEE IT. NOTHING MORE.
I WAS HAPPY TO SPEAK ON YOUR HUSBAND'S BEHALF, WHAT HAPPENED... I'M NOT GOING TO SAY IT WASN'T HIS FAULT, BUT... IT'S NOT FAIR TO BLAME IT *ALL* ON HIM.

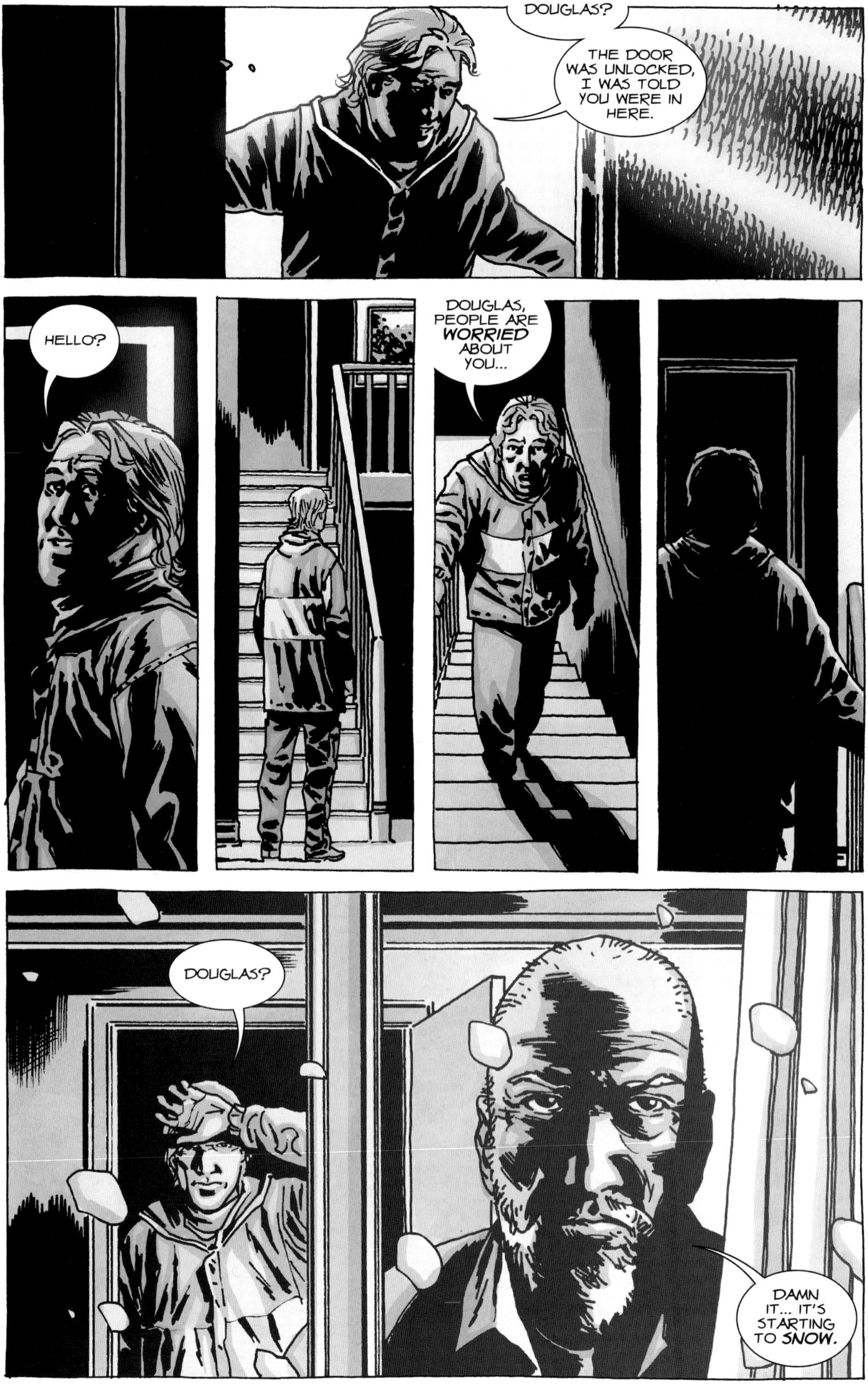
DOUGLAS?
THE DOOR WAS UNLOCKED, I WAS TOLD YOU WERE IN HERE.
HELLO?
DOUGLAS, PEOPLE ARE WORRIED ABOUT YOU...
DOUGLAS?
DAMN IT... IT'S STARTING TO SNOW.

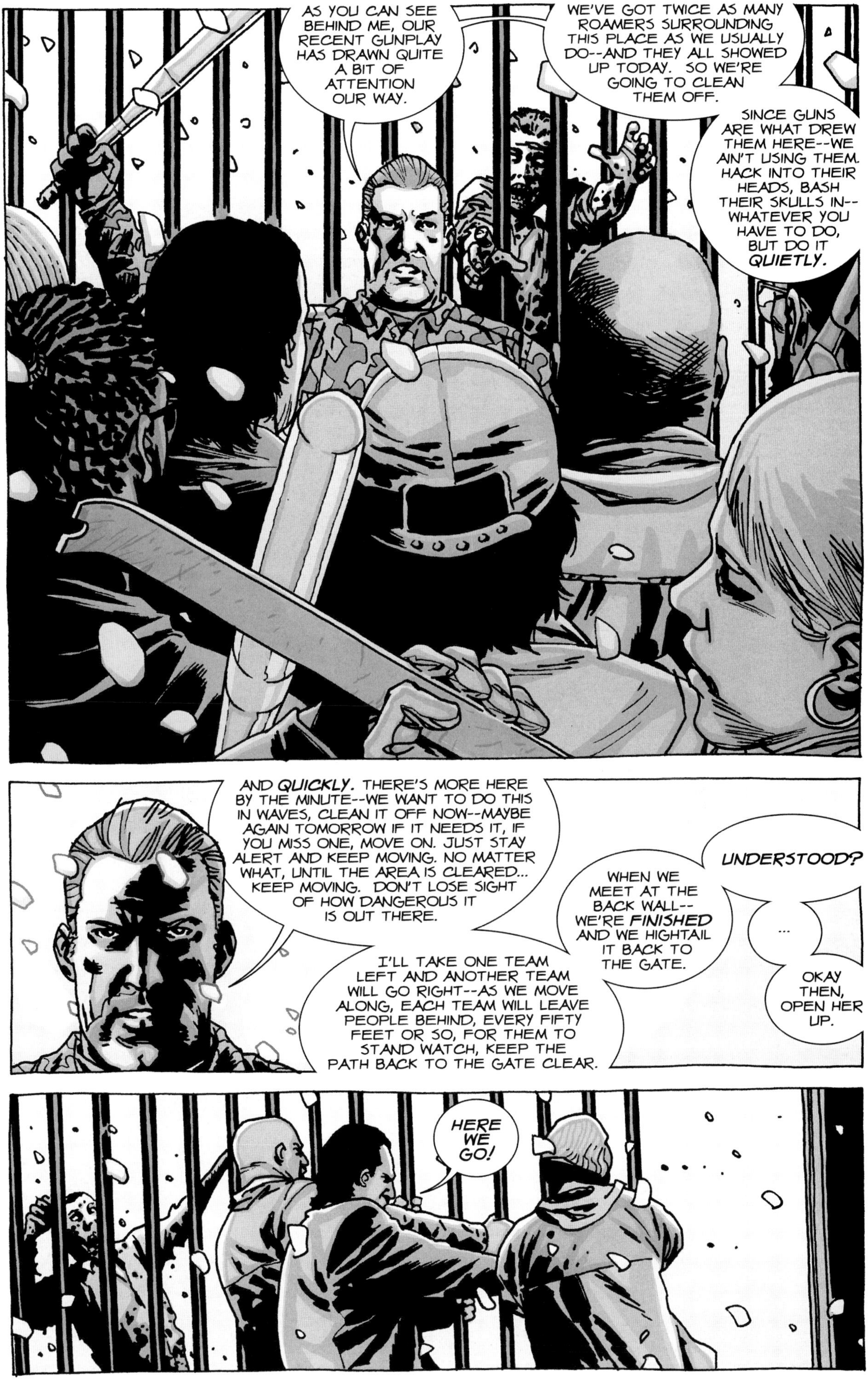
AS YOU CAN SEE BEHIND ME, OUR RECENT GUNPLAY HAS DRAWN QUITE A BIT OF ATTENTION OUR WAY.
WE'VE GOT TWICE AS MANY ROAMERS SURROUNDING THIS PLACE AS WE USUALLY DO--AND THEY ALL SHOWED UP TODAY. SO WE'RE GOING TO CLEAN THEM OFF.
SINCE GUNS ARE WHAT DREW THEM HERE--WE AIN'T USING THEM. HACK INTO THEIR HEADS, BASH THEIR SKULLS IN--WHATEVER YOU HAVE TO DO, BUT DO IT *QUIETLY.*
AND *QUICKLY.* THERE'S MORE HERE BY THE MINUTE--WE WANT TO DO THIS IN WAVES, CLEAN IT OFF NOW--MAYBE AGAIN TOMORROW IF IT NEEDS IT, IF YOU MISS ONE, MOVE ON. JUST STAY ALERT AND KEEP MOVING. NO MATTER WHAT, UNTIL THE AREA IS CLEARED... KEEP MOVING. DON'T LOSE SIGHT OF HOW DANGEROUS IT IS OUT THERE.
I'LL TAKE ONE TEAM LEFT AND ANOTHER TEAM WILL GO RIGHT--AS WE MOVE ALONG, EACH TEAM WILL LEAVE PEOPLE BEHIND, EVERY FIFTY FEET OR SO, FOR THEM TO STAND WATCH, KEEP THE PATH BACK TO THE GATE CLEAR.
WHEN WE MEET AT THE BACK WALL--WE'RE *FINISHED* AND WE HIGHTAIL IT BACK TO THE GATE.
UNDERSTOOD?
...
OKAY THEN, OPEN HER UP.
HERE WE GO!

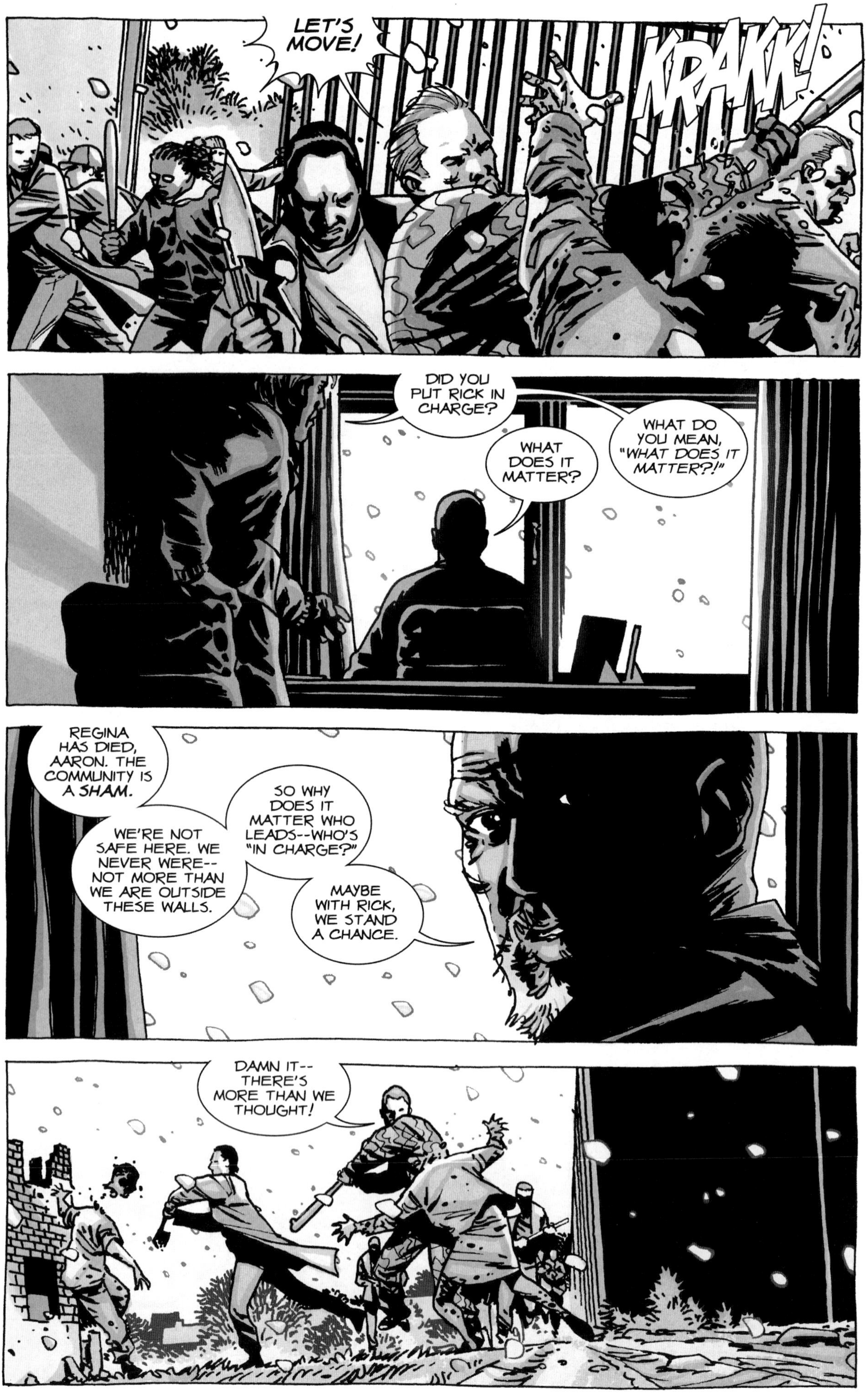
LET'S MOVE!
KRAKK!
DID YOU PUT RICK IN CHARGE?
WHAT DOES IT MATTER?
WHAT DO YOU MEAN, "WHAT DOES IT MATTER?!"
REGINA HAS DIED, AARON. THE COMMUNITY IS A SHAM.
WE'RE NOT SAFE HERE. WE NEVER WERE-- NOT MORE THAN WE ARE OUTSIDE THESE WALLS.
SO WHY DOES IT MATTER WHO LEADS--WHO'S "IN CHARGE?"
MAYBE WITH RICK, WE STAND A CHANCE.
DAMN IT-- THERE'S MORE THAN WE THOUGHT!

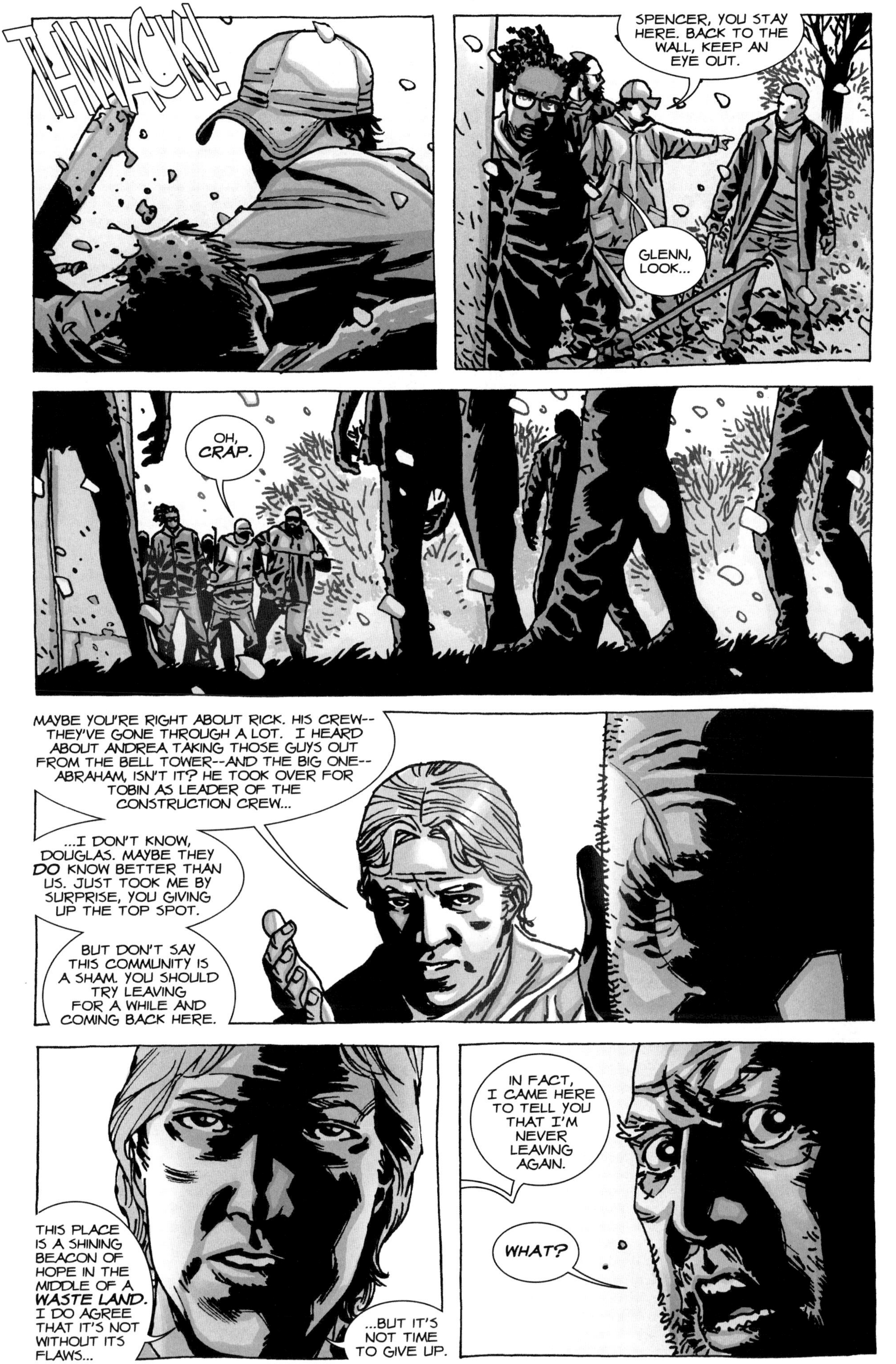
THWACK!
SPENCER, YOU STAY HERE. BACK TO THE WALL, KEEP AN EYE OUT.
GLENN, LOOK...
OH, CRAP.
MAYBE YOU'RE RIGHT ABOUT RICK. HIS CREW-- THEY'VE GONE THROUGH A LOT. I HEARD ABOUT ANDREA TAKING THOSE GUYS OUT FROM THE BELL TOWER--AND THE BIG ONE-- ABRAHAM, ISN'T IT? HE TOOK OVER FOR TOBIN AS LEADER OF THE CONSTRUCTION CREW...
...I DON'T KNOW, DOUGLAS. MAYBE THEY DO KNOW BETTER THAN US. JUST TOOK ME BY SURPRISE, YOU GIVING UP THE TOP SPOT.
BUT DON'T SAY THIS COMMUNITY IS A SHAM. YOU SHOULD TRY LEAVING FOR A WHILE AND COMING BACK HERE.
THIS PLACE IS A SHINING BEACON OF HOPE IN THE MIDDLE OF A WASTE LAND. I DO AGREE THAT IT'S NOT WITHOUT ITS FLAWS...
...BUT IT'S NOT TIME TO GIVE UP.
IN FACT, I CAME HERE TO TELL YOU THAT I'M NEVER LEAVING AGAIN.
WHAT?

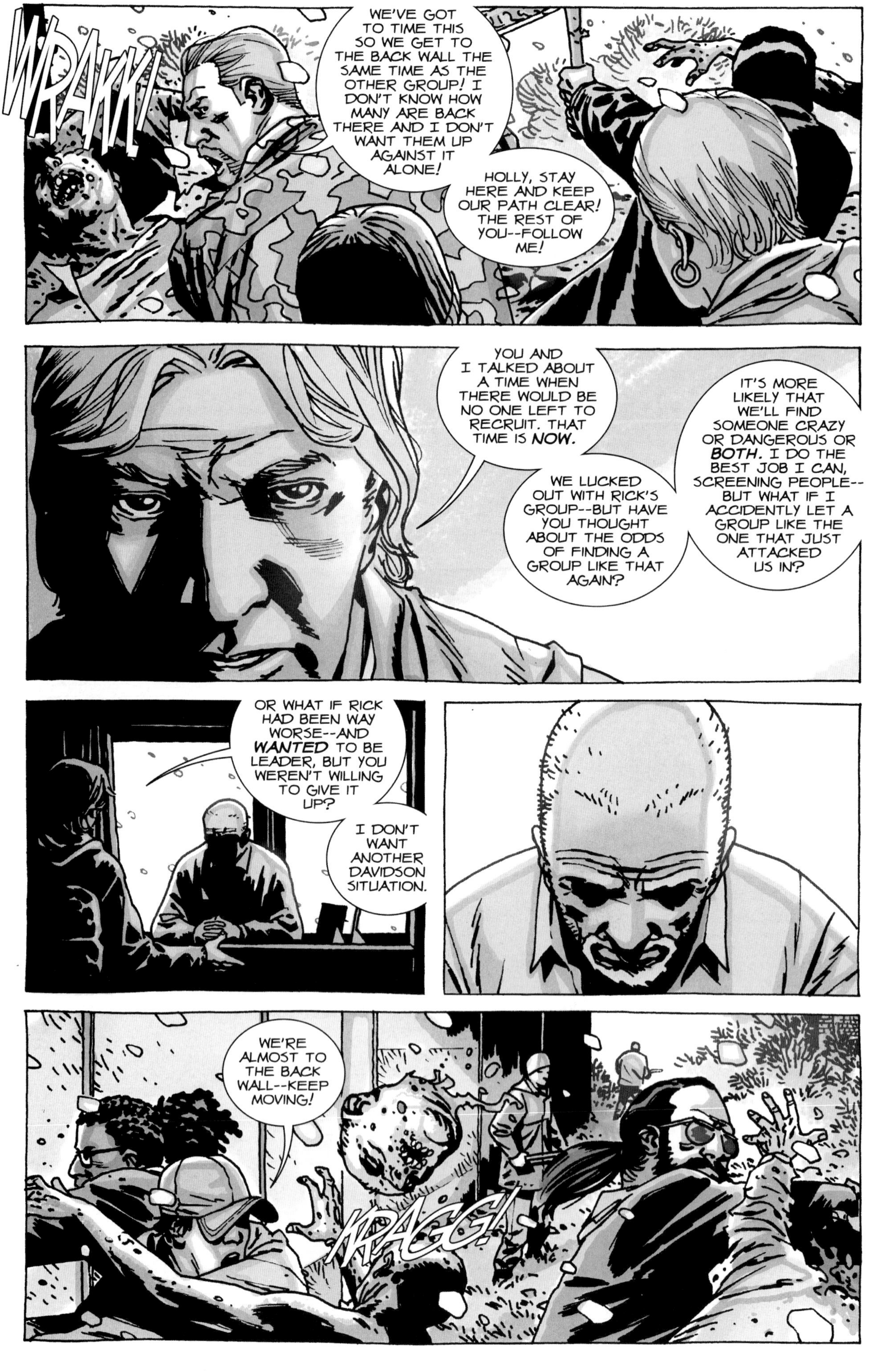
WRAKK!
WE'VE GOT TO TIME THIS SO WE GET TO THE BACK WALL THE SAME TIME AS THE OTHER GROUP! I DON'T KNOW HOW MANY ARE BACK THERE AND I DON'T WANT THEM UP AGAINST IT ALONE!
HOLLY, STAY HERE AND KEEP OUR PATH CLEAR! THE REST OF YOU--FOLLOW ME!
YOU AND I TALKED ABOUT A TIME WHEN THERE WOULD BE NO ONE LEFT TO RECRUIT. THAT TIME IS **NOW.**
WE LUCKED OUT WITH RICK'S GROUP--BUT HAVE YOU THOUGHT ABOUT THE ODDS OF FINDING A GROUP LIKE THAT AGAIN?
IT'S MORE LIKELY THAT WE'LL FIND SOMEONE CRAZY OR DANGEROUS OR **BOTH.** I DO THE BEST JOB I CAN, SCREENING PEOPLE--BUT WHAT IF I ACCIDENTLY LET A GROUP LIKE THE ONE THAT JUST ATTACKED US IN?
OR WHAT IF RICK HAD BEEN WAY WORSE--AND **WANTED** TO BE LEADER, BUT YOU WEREN'T WILLING TO GIVE IT UP?
I DON'T WANT ANOTHER DAVIDSON SITUATION.
WE'RE ALMOST TO THE BACK WALL--KEEP MOVING!
KRAGG!

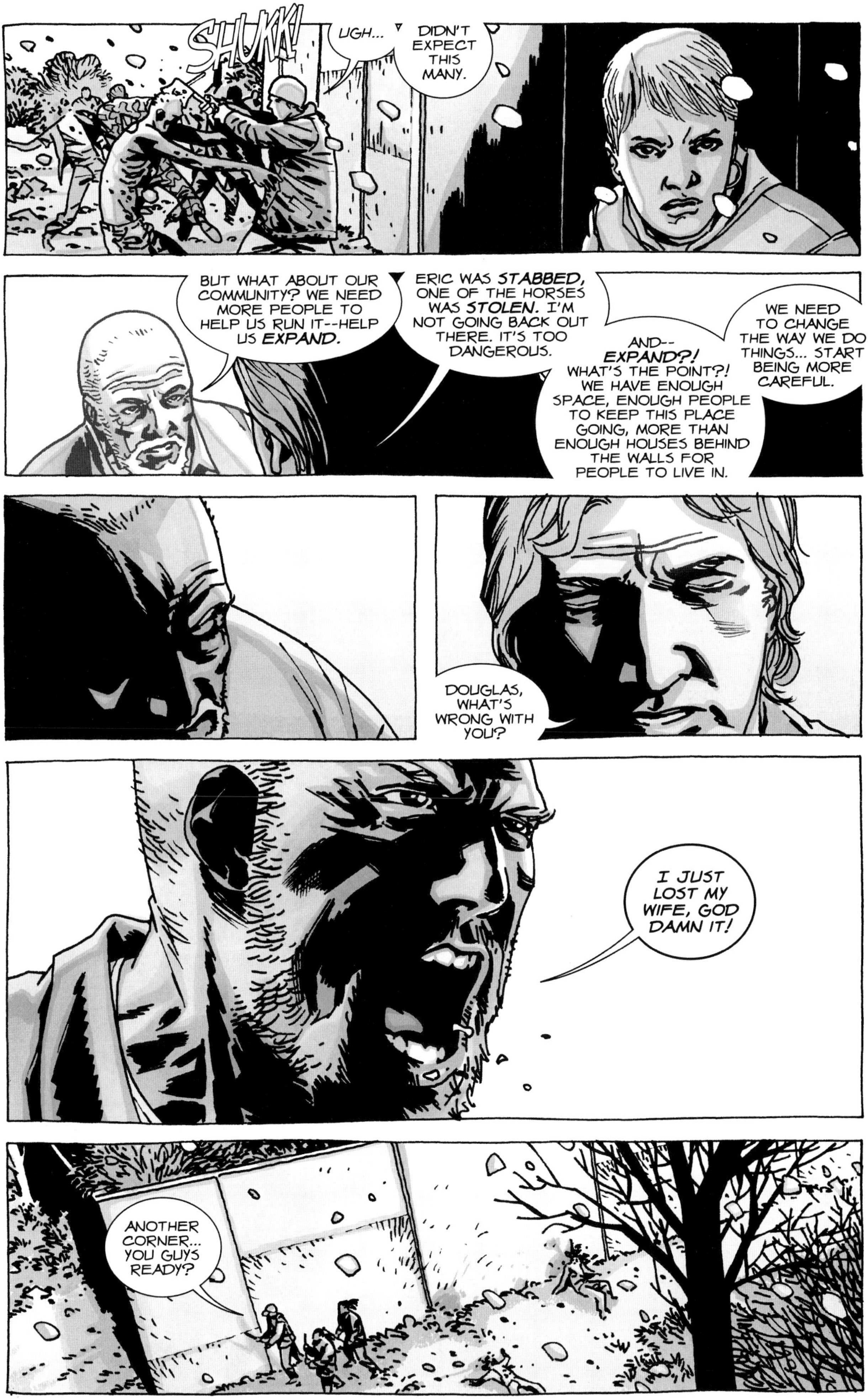
SHUKK!
UGH...
DIDN'T EXPECT THIS MANY.
BUT WHAT ABOUT OUR COMMUNITY? WE NEED MORE PEOPLE TO HELP US RUN IT--HELP US EXPAND.
ERIC WAS STABBED, ONE OF THE HORSES WAS STOLEN. I'M NOT GOING BACK OUT THERE. IT'S TOO DANGEROUS.
WE NEED TO CHANGE THE WAY WE DO THINGS... START BEING MORE CAREFUL.
AND-- EXPAND?! WHAT'S THE POINT?! WE HAVE ENOUGH SPACE, ENOUGH PEOPLE TO KEEP THIS PLACE GOING, MORE THAN ENOUGH HOUSES BEHIND THE WALLS FOR PEOPLE TO LIVE IN.
DOUGLAS, WHAT'S WRONG WITH YOU?
I JUST LOST MY WIFE, GOD DAMN IT!
ANOTHER CORNER... YOU GUYS READY?

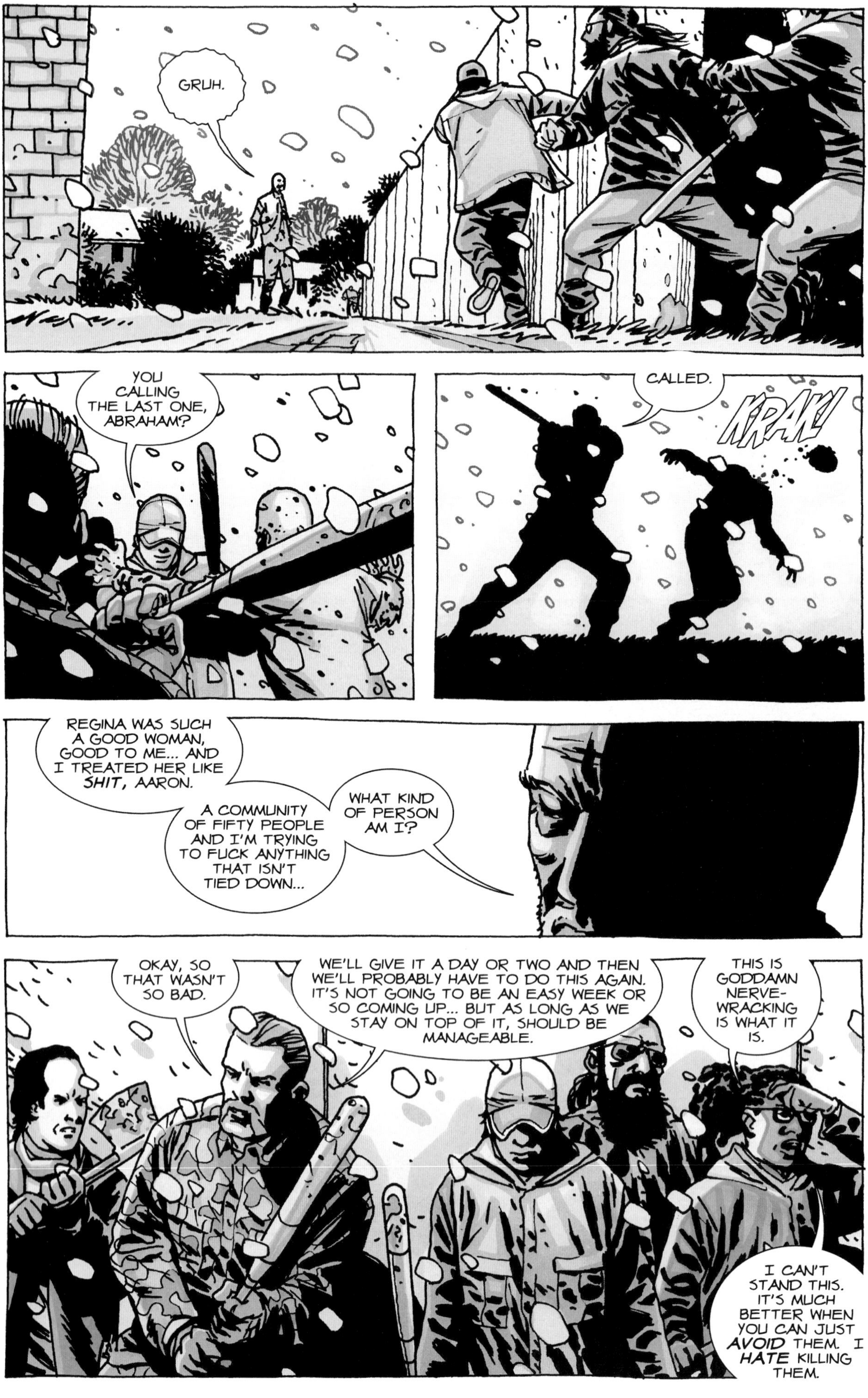
GRUH.
YOU CALLING THE LAST ONE, ABRAHAM?
CALLED.
KRAK!
REGINA WAS SUCH A GOOD WOMAN, GOOD TO ME... AND I TREATED HER LIKE SHIT, AARON.
A COMMUNITY OF FIFTY PEOPLE AND I'M TRYING TO FUCK ANYTHING THAT ISN'T TIED DOWN...
WHAT KIND OF PERSON AM I?
OKAY, SO THAT WASN'T SO BAD.
WE'LL GIVE IT A DAY OR TWO AND THEN WE'LL PROBABLY HAVE TO DO THIS AGAIN. IT'S NOT GOING TO BE AN EASY WEEK OR SO COMING UP... BUT AS LONG AS WE STAY ON TOP OF IT, SHOULD BE MANAGEABLE.
THIS IS GODDAMN NERVE-WRACKING IS WHAT IT IS.
I CAN'T STAND THIS. IT'S MUCH BETTER WHEN YOU CAN JUST AVOID THEM. I HATE KILLING THEM.

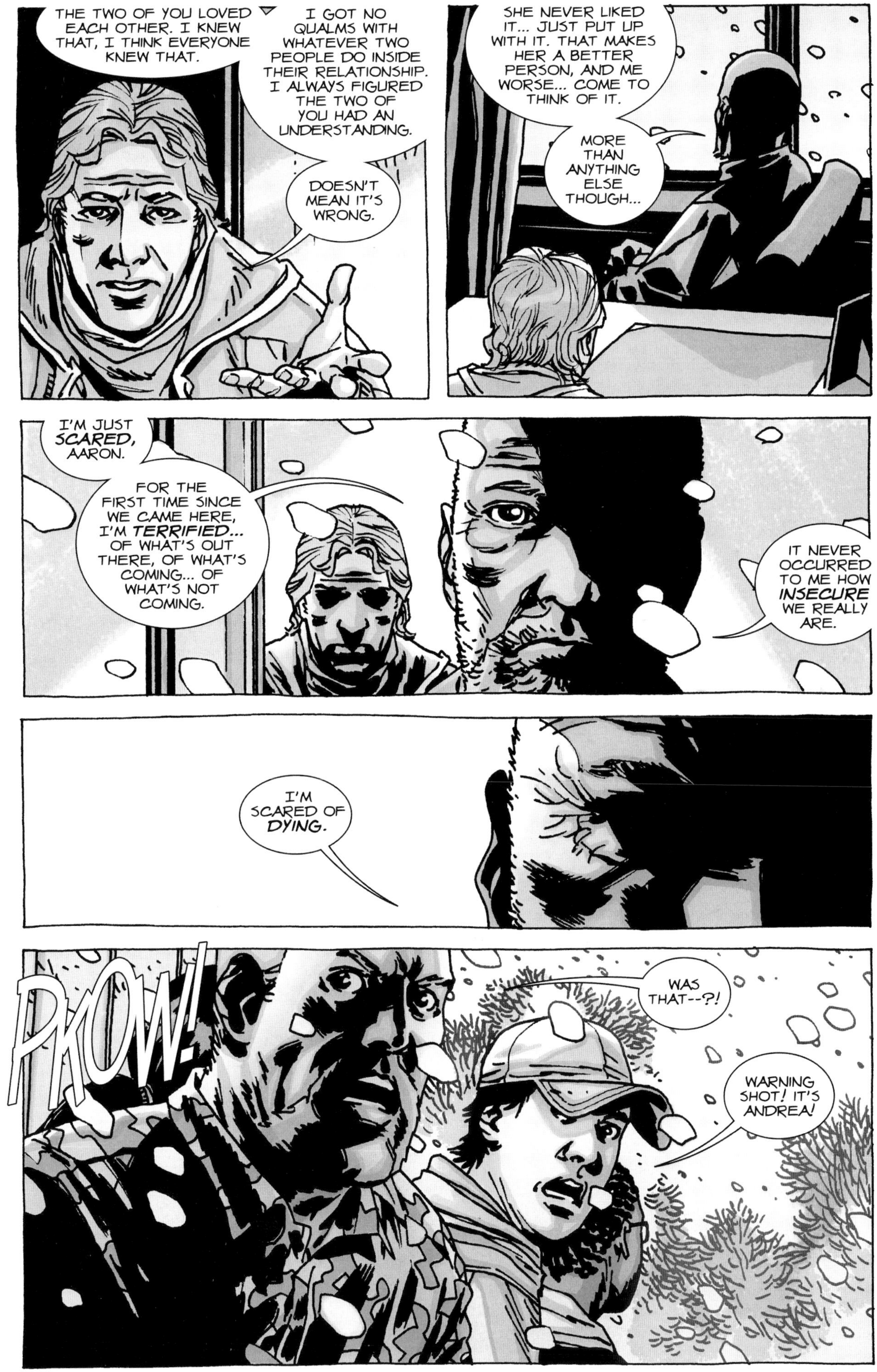
THE TWO OF YOU LOVED EACH OTHER. I KNEW THAT, I THINK EVERYONE KNEW THAT.
I GOT NO QUALMS WITH WHATEVER TWO PEOPLE DO INSIDE THEIR RELATIONSHIP. I ALWAYS FIGURED THE TWO OF YOU HAD AN UNDERSTANDING.
DOESN'T MEAN IT'S WRONG.
SHE NEVER LIKED IT... JUST PUT UP WITH IT. THAT MAKES HER A BETTER PERSON, AND ME WORSE... COME TO THINK OF IT.
MORE THAN ANYTHING ELSE THOUGH...
I'M JUST SCARED, AARON.
FOR THE FIRST TIME SINCE WE CAME HERE, I'M TERRIFIED... OF WHAT'S OUT THERE, OF WHAT'S COMING... OF WHAT'S NOT COMING.
IT NEVER OCCURRED TO ME HOW INSECURE WE REALLY ARE.
I'M SCARED OF DYING.
PKOW!
WAS THAT--?!
WARNING SHOT! IT'S ANDREA!

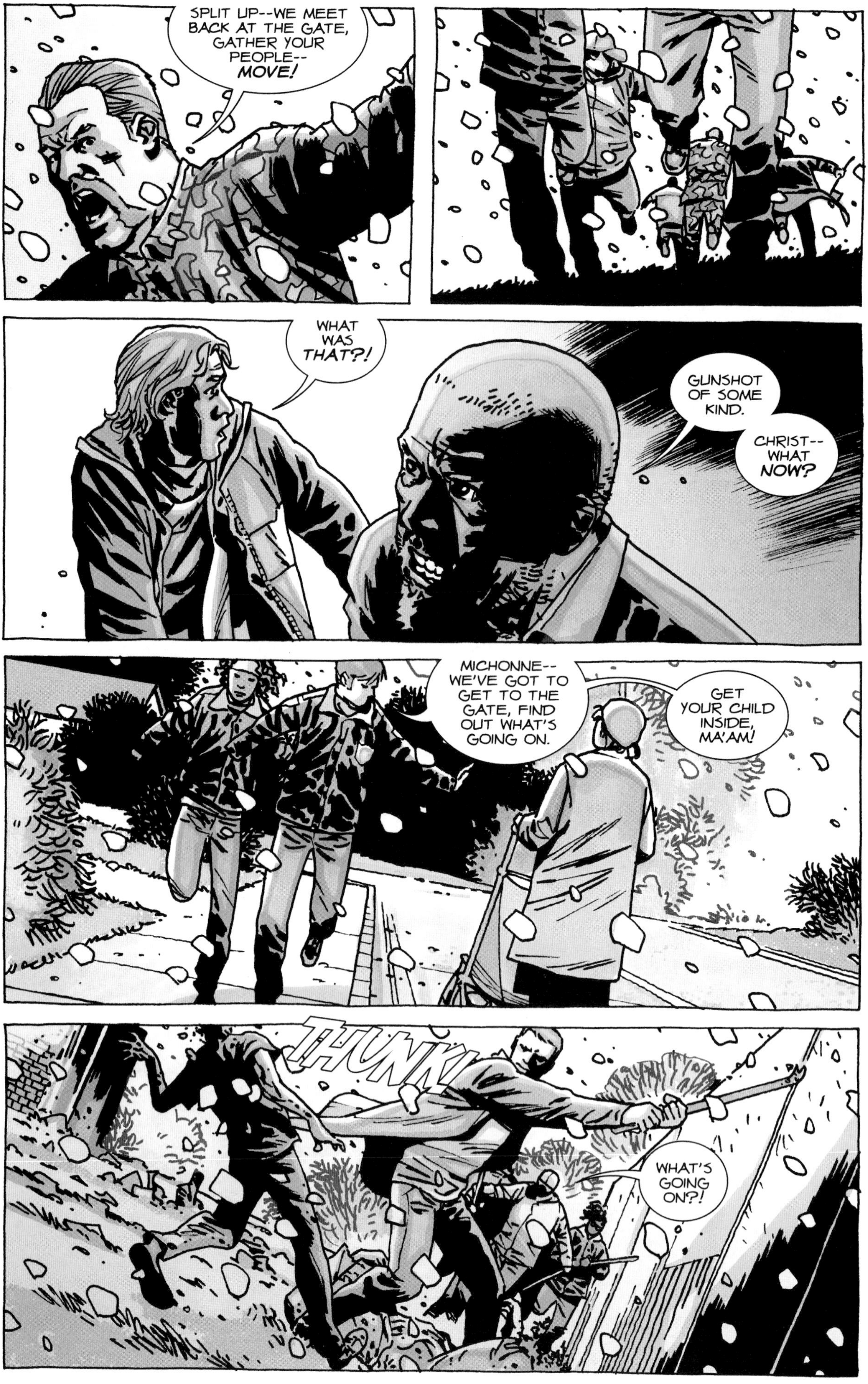
SPLIT UP--WE MEET BACK AT THE GATE, GATHER YOUR PEOPLE-- MOVE!
WHAT WAS THAT?!
GUNSHOT OF SOME KIND.
CHRIST-- WHAT NOW?
MICHONNE-- WE'VE GOT TO GET TO THE GATE, FIND OUT WHAT'S GOING ON.
GET YOUR CHILD INSIDE, MA'AM!
THUNK!
WHAT'S GOING ON?!

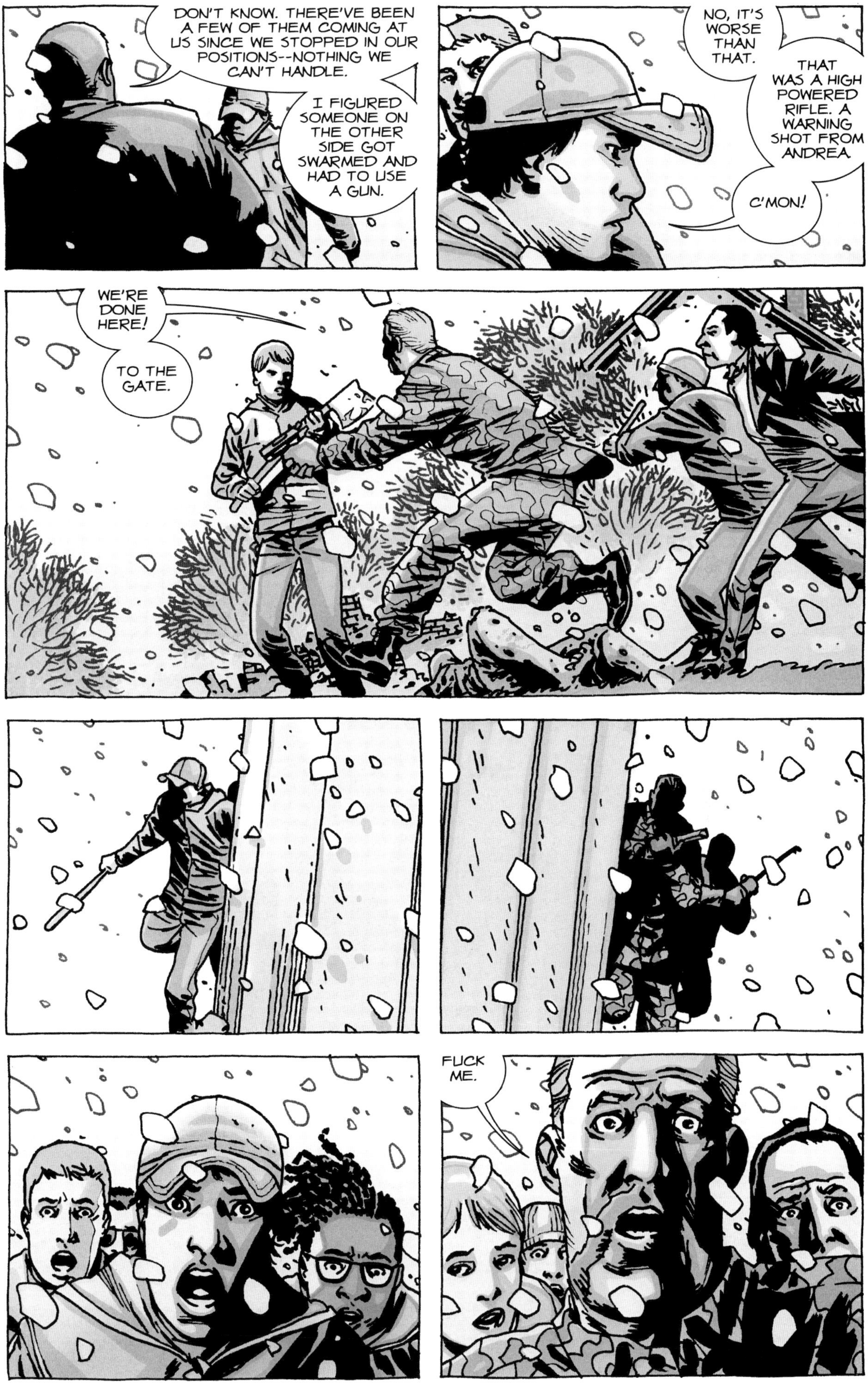
DON'T KNOW. THERE'VE BEEN A FEW OF THEM COMING AT US SINCE WE STOPPED IN OUR POSITIONS--NOTHING WE CAN'T HANDLE.
I FIGURED SOMEONE ON THE OTHER SIDE GOT SWARMED AND HAD TO USE A GUN.
NO, IT'S WORSE THAN THAT.
THAT WAS A HIGH POWERED RIFLE. A WARNING SHOT FROM ANDREA.
C'MON!
WE'RE DONE HERE!
TO THE GATE.
FUCK ME.

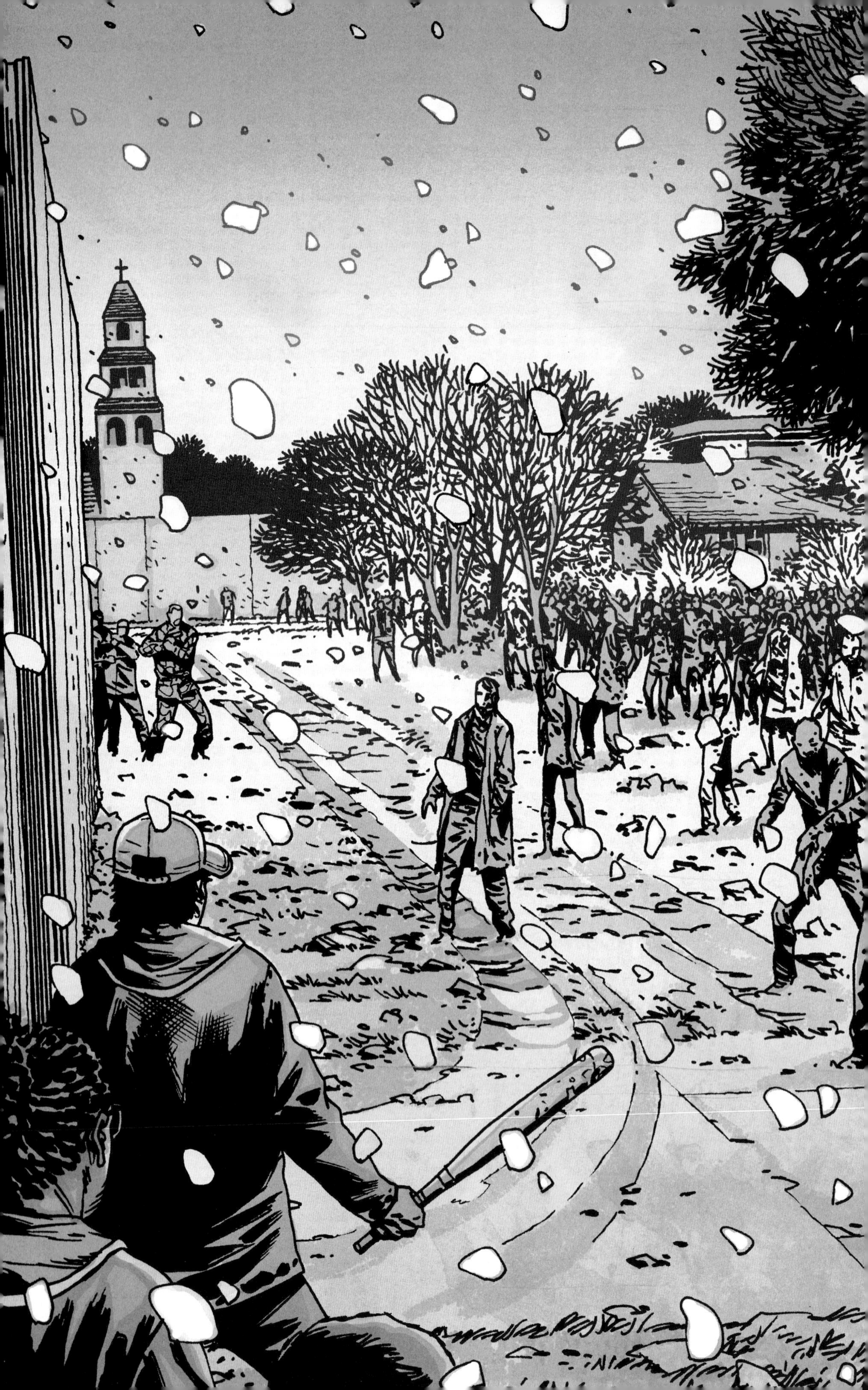

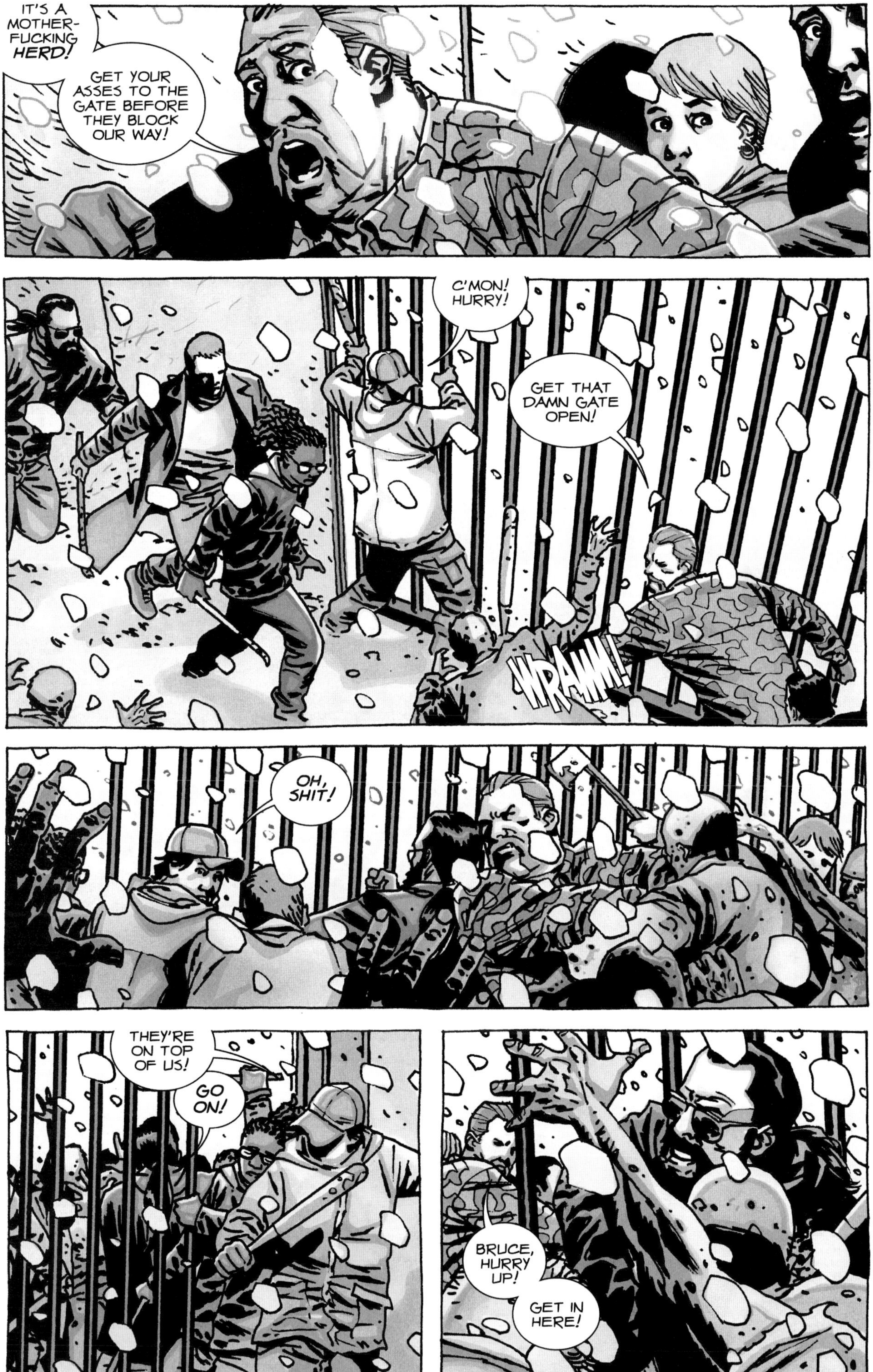
IT'S A MOTHER-FUCKING HERD!
GET YOUR ASSES TO THE GATE BEFORE THEY BLOCK OUR WAY!
C'MON! HURRY!
GET THAT DAMN GATE OPEN!
WRAMM!
OH, SHIT!
THEY'RE ON TOP OF US!
GO ON!
BRUCE, HURRY UP!
GET IN HERE!

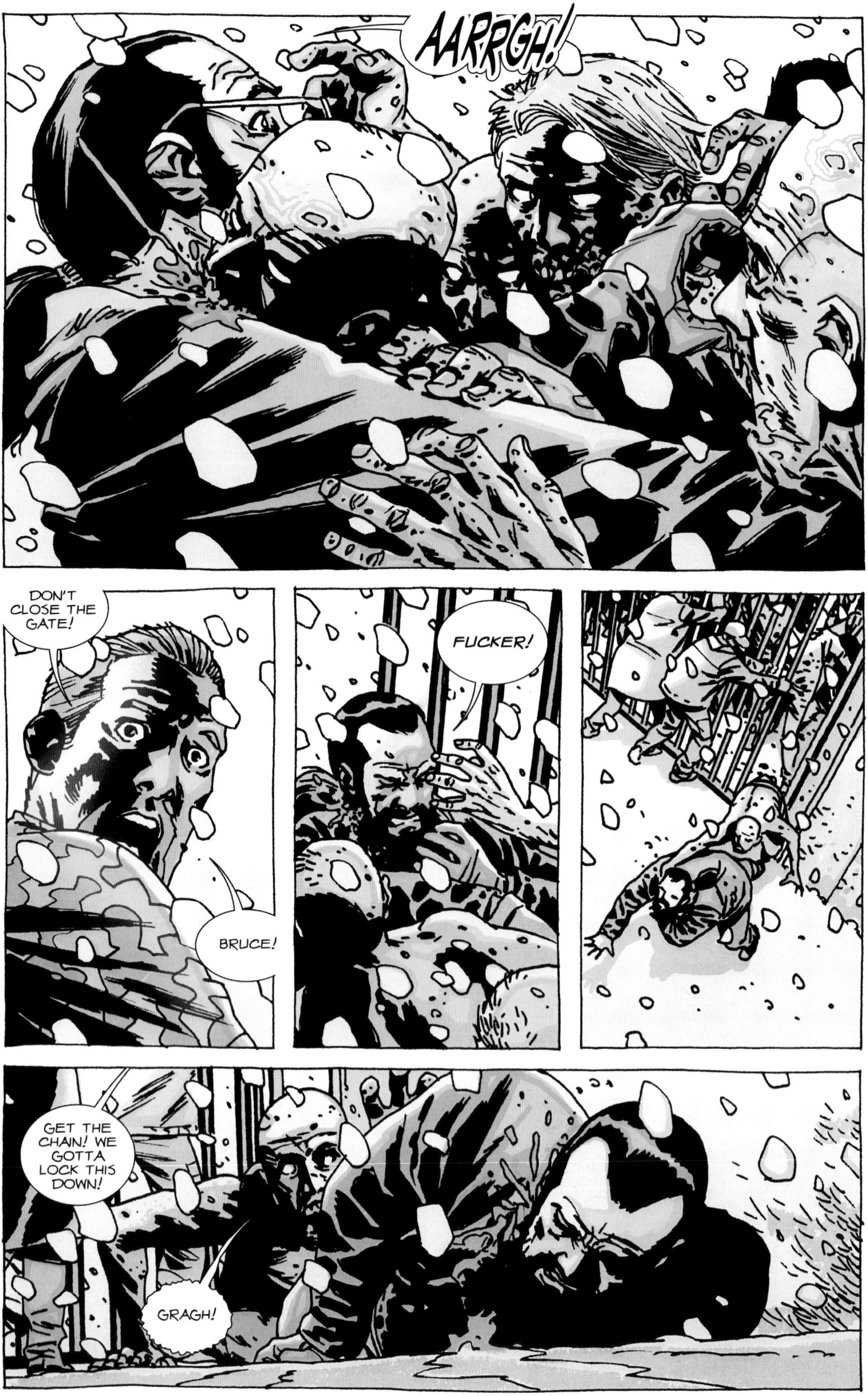
AARRGH!
DON'T CLOSE THE GATE!
BRUCE!
FUCKER!
GET THE CHAIN! WE GOTTA LOCK THIS DOWN!
GRAGH!

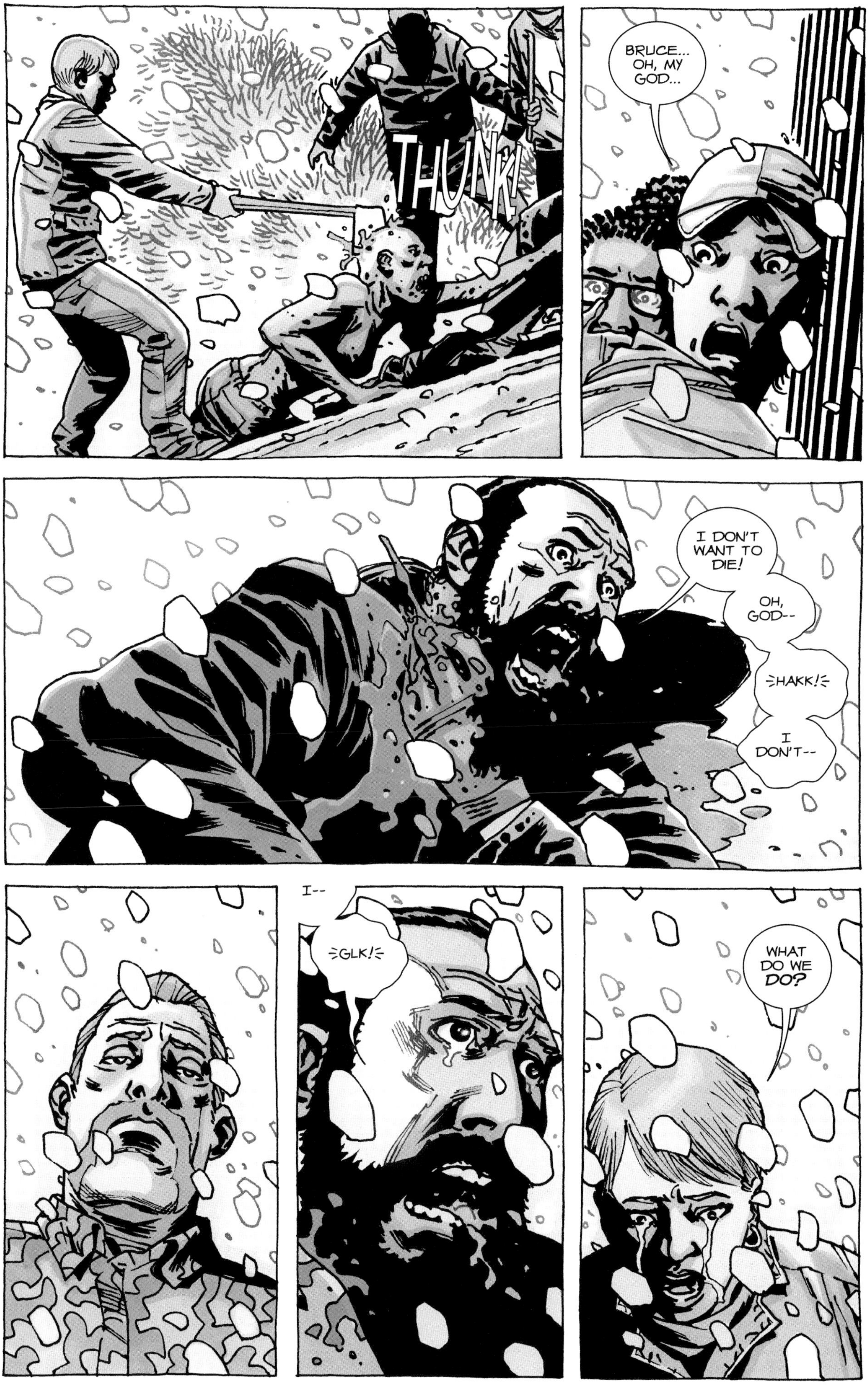
THUNK!
BRUCE... OH, MY GOD...
I DON'T WANT TO DIE!
OH, GOD--
HAKK!
I DON'T--
I--
GLK!
WHAT DO WE DO?

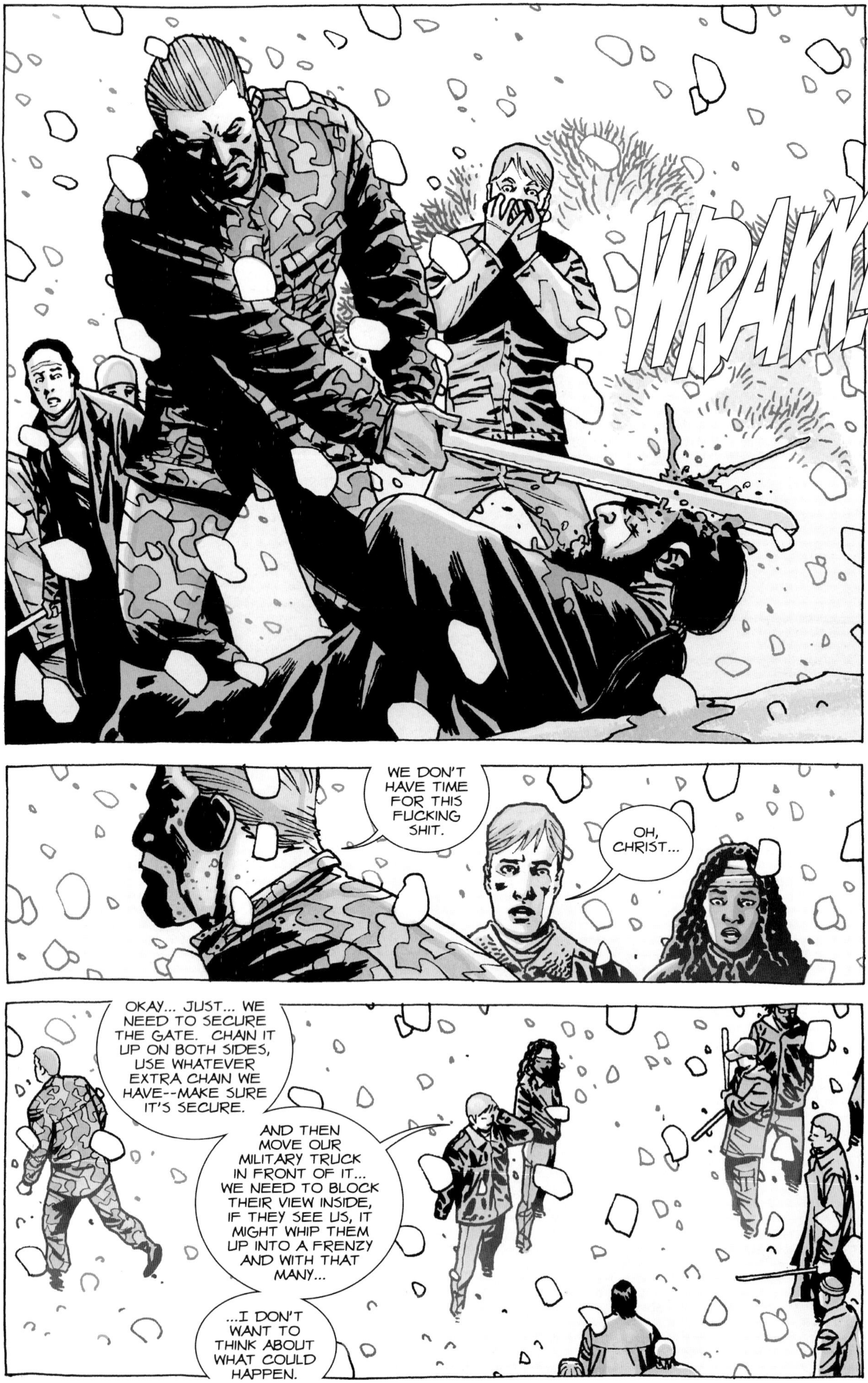
WRAKK!!
WE DON'T HAVE TIME FOR THIS FUCKING SHIT.
OH, CHRIST...
OKAY... JUST... WE NEED TO SECURE THE GATE. CHAIN IT UP ON BOTH SIDES, USE WHATEVER EXTRA CHAIN WE HAVE--MAKE SURE IT'S SECURE.
AND THEN MOVE OUR MILITARY TRUCK IN FRONT OF IT... WE NEED TO BLOCK THEIR VIEW INSIDE, IF THEY SEE US, IT MIGHT WHIP THEM UP INTO A FRENZY AND WITH THAT MANY...
...I DON'T WANT TO THINK ABOUT WHAT COULD HAPPEN.

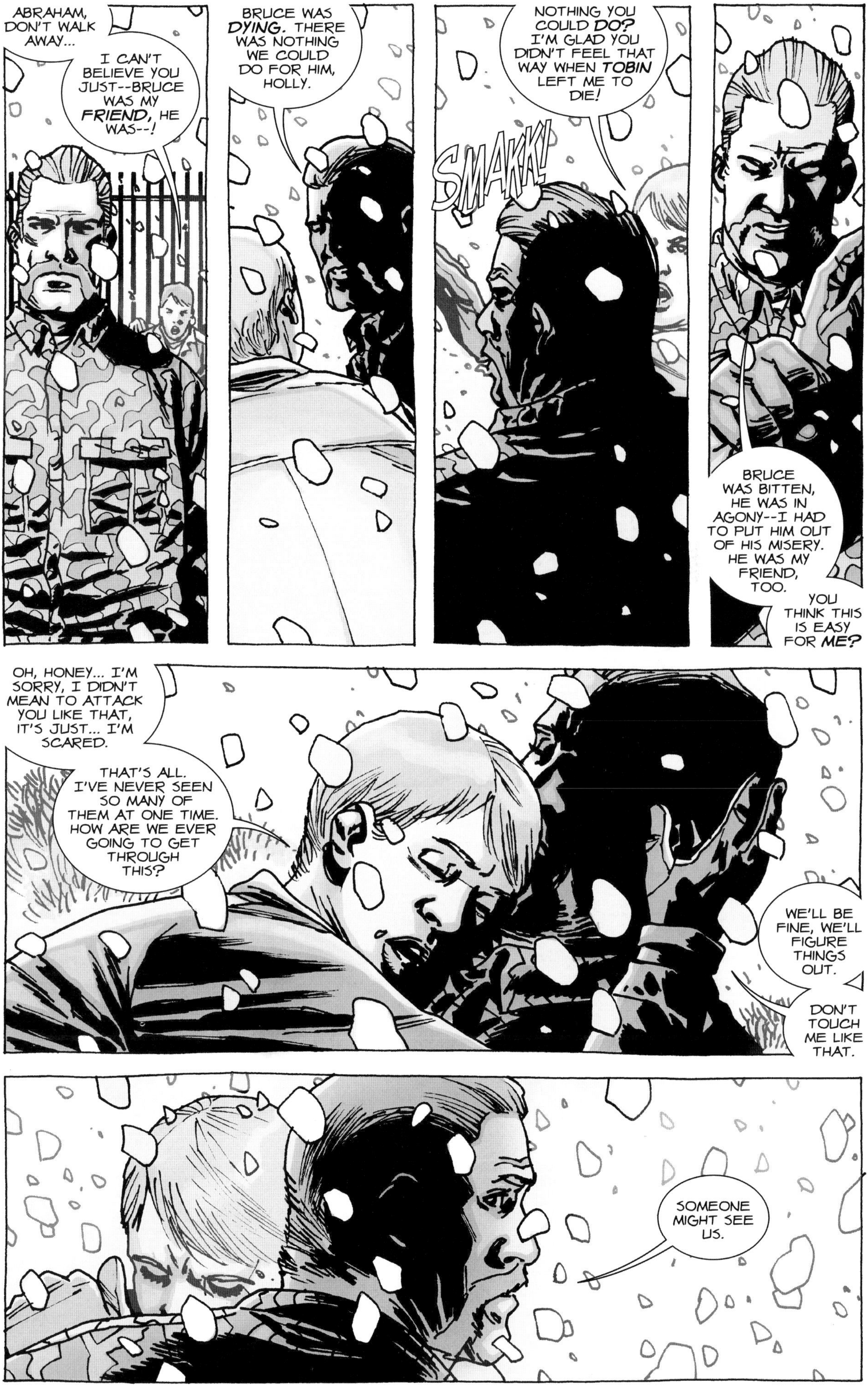

ABRAHAM, DON'T WALK AWAY...
I CAN'T BELIEVE YOU JUST--BRUCE WAS MY FRIEND, HE WAS--!
BRUCE WAS DYING. THERE WAS NOTHING WE COULD DO FOR HIM, HOLLY.
NOTHING YOU COULD DO? I'M GLAD YOU DIDN'T FEEL THAT WAY WHEN TOBIN LEFT ME TO DIE!
SMAKK!
BRUCE WAS BITTEN, HE WAS IN AGONY--I HAD TO PUT HIM OUT OF HIS MISERY. HE WAS MY FRIEND, TOO.
YOU THINK THIS IS EASY FOR ME?
OH, HONEY... I'M SORRY, I DIDN'T MEAN TO ATTACK YOU LIKE THAT, IT'S JUST... I'M SCARED.
THAT'S ALL. I'VE NEVER SEEN SO MANY OF THEM AT ONE TIME. HOW ARE WE EVER GOING TO GET THROUGH THIS?
WE'LL BE FINE, WE'LL FIGURE THINGS OUT.
DON'T TOUCH ME LIKE THAT.
SOMEONE MIGHT SEE US.

WHAT THE *HELL* ARE WE GOING TO *DO?!*

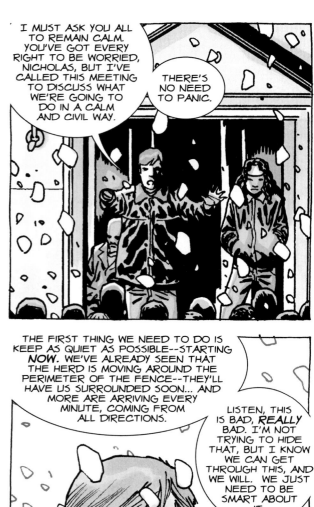

I MUST ASK YOU ALL TO REMAIN CALM. YOU'VE GOT EVERY RIGHT TO BE WORRIED, NICHOLAS, BUT I'VE CALLED THIS MEETING TO DISCUSS WHAT WE'RE GOING TO DO IN A CALM AND CIVIL WAY.

THERE'S NO NEED TO PANIC.

THE FIRST THING WE NEED TO DO IS KEEP AS QUIET AS POSSIBLE--STARTING *NOW.* WE'VE ALREADY SEEN THAT THE HERD IS MOVING AROUND THE PERIMETER OF THE FENCE--THEY'LL HAVE US SURROUNDED SOON... AND MORE ARE ARRIVING EVERY MINUTE, COMING FROM ALL DIRECTIONS.

LISTEN, THIS IS BAD, *REALLY* BAD. I'M NOT TRYING TO HIDE THAT, BUT I KNOW WE CAN GET THROUGH THIS, AND WE WILL. WE JUST NEED TO BE SMART ABOUT IT.

WHAT ABOUT *FOOD?* IF WE'RE TRAPPED HERE WE'RE NOT GOING TO BE ABLE TO GO OUT AND GATHER MORE.

WINTER IS *HERE.* WHAT DO WE DO IF WE RUN OUT?

WE'VE GOT ENOUGH FOOD TO LAST US AT LEAST A MONTH, AND IF WE START RATIONING NOW, LONGER THAN THAT. WE SHOULD BE OKAY.

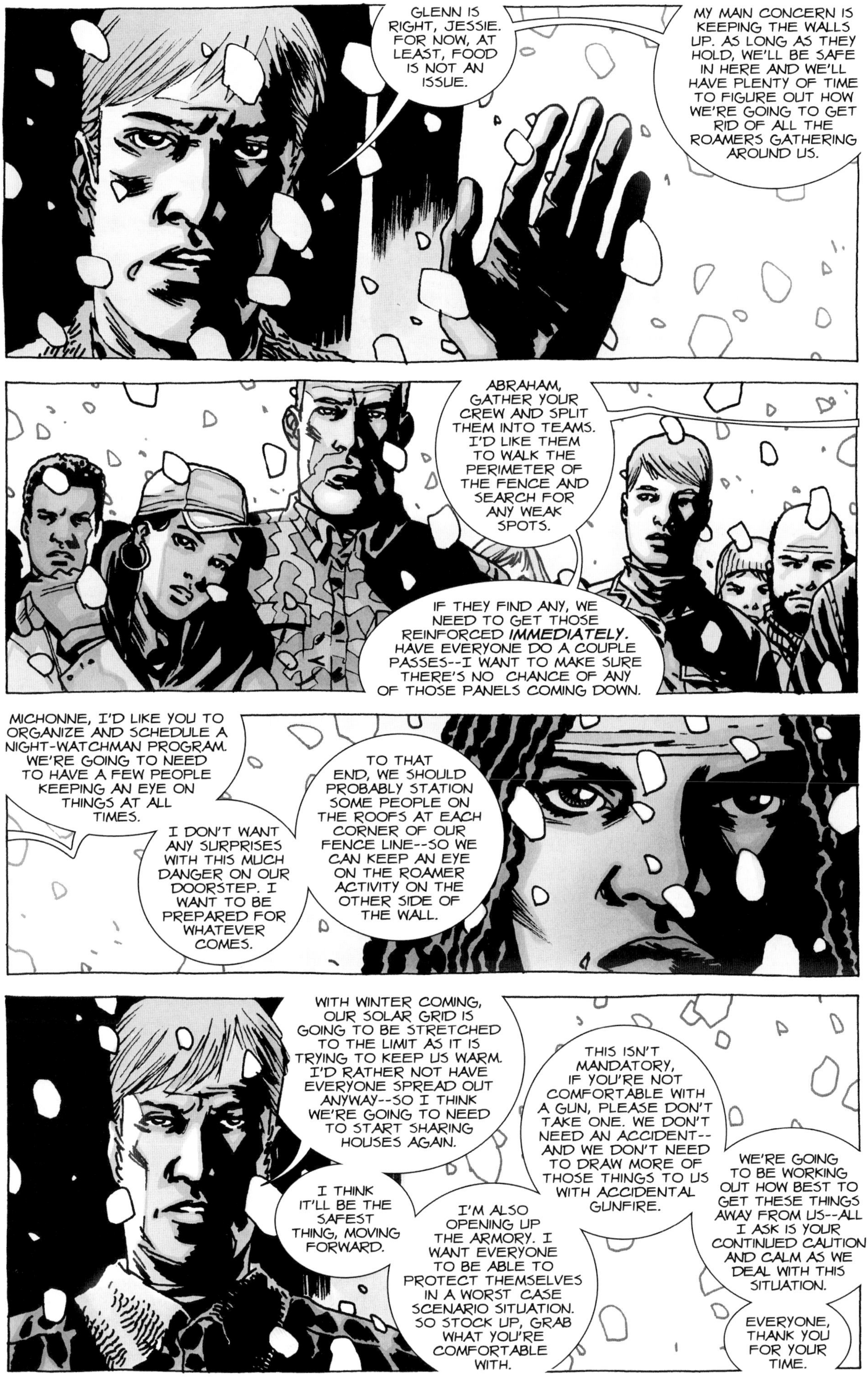

GLENN IS RIGHT, JESSIE. FOR NOW, AT LEAST, FOOD IS NOT AN ISSUE.
MY MAIN CONCERN IS KEEPING THE WALLS UP. AS LONG AS THEY HOLD, WE'LL BE SAFE IN HERE AND WE'LL HAVE PLENTY OF TIME TO FIGURE OUT HOW WE'RE GOING TO GET RID OF ALL THE ROAMERS GATHERING AROUND US.
ABRAHAM, GATHER YOUR CREW AND SPLIT THEM INTO TEAMS. I'D LIKE THEM TO WALK THE PERIMETER OF THE FENCE AND SEARCH FOR ANY WEAK SPOTS.
IF THEY FIND ANY, WE NEED TO GET THOSE REINFORCED *IMMEDIATELY.* HAVE EVERYONE DO A COUPLE PASSES--I WANT TO MAKE SURE THERE'S NO CHANCE OF ANY OF THOSE PANELS COMING DOWN.
MICHONNE, I'D LIKE YOU TO ORGANIZE AND SCHEDULE A NIGHT-WATCHMAN PROGRAM. WE'RE GOING TO NEED TO HAVE A FEW PEOPLE KEEPING AN EYE ON THINGS AT ALL TIMES.
I DON'T WANT ANY SURPRISES WITH THIS MUCH DANGER ON OUR DOORSTEP. I WANT TO BE PREPARED FOR WHATEVER COMES.
TO THAT END, WE SHOULD PROBABLY STATION SOME PEOPLE ON THE ROOFS AT EACH CORNER OF OUR FENCE LINE--SO WE CAN KEEP AN EYE ON THE ROAMER ACTIVITY ON THE OTHER SIDE OF THE WALL.
WITH WINTER COMING, OUR SOLAR GRID IS GOING TO BE STRETCHED TO THE LIMIT AS IT IS TRYING TO KEEP US WARM. I'D RATHER NOT HAVE EVERYONE SPREAD OUT ANYWAY--SO I THINK WE'RE GOING TO NEED TO START SHARING HOUSES AGAIN.
I THINK IT'LL BE THE SAFEST THING, MOVING FORWARD.
I'M ALSO OPENING UP THE ARMORY. I WANT EVERYONE TO BE ABLE TO PROTECT THEMSELVES IN A WORST CASE SCENARIO SITUATION. SO STOCK UP, GRAB WHAT YOU'RE COMFORTABLE WITH.
THIS ISN'T MANDATORY, IF YOU'RE NOT COMFORTABLE WITH A GUN, PLEASE DON'T TAKE ONE. WE DON'T NEED AN ACCIDENT--AND WE DON'T NEED TO DRAW MORE OF THOSE THINGS TO US WITH ACCIDENTAL GUNFIRE.
WE'RE GOING TO BE WORKING OUT HOW BEST TO GET THESE THINGS AWAY FROM US--ALL I ASK IS YOUR CONTINUED CAUTION AND CALM AS WE DEAL WITH THIS SITUATION.
EVERYONE, THANK YOU FOR YOUR TIME.

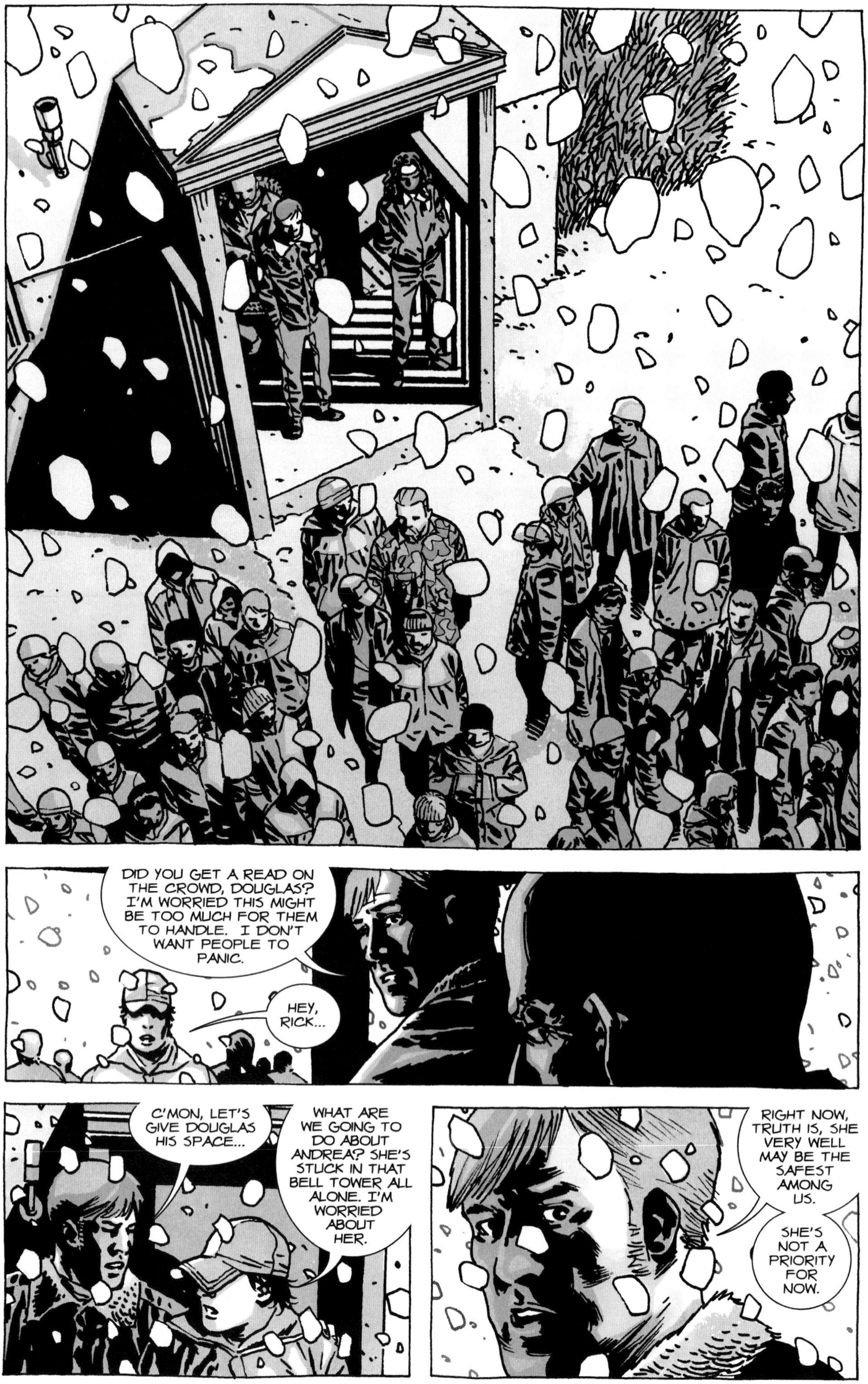
DID YOU GET A READ ON THE CROWD, DOUGLAS? I'M WORRIED THIS MIGHT BE TOO MUCH FOR THEM TO HANDLE. I DON'T WANT PEOPLE TO PANIC.
HEY, RICK...
C'MON, LET'S GIVE DOUGLAS HIS SPACE...
WHAT ARE WE GOING TO DO ABOUT ANDREA? SHE'S STUCK IN THAT BELL TOWER ALL ALONE. I'M WORRIED ABOUT HER.
RIGHT NOW, TRUTH IS, SHE VERY WELL MAY BE THE SAFEST AMONG US.
SHE'S NOT A PRIORITY FOR NOW.

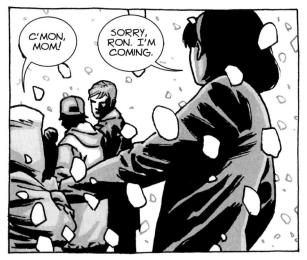

C'MON, MOM!

SORRY, RON. I'M COMING.

WELL, MORGAN. YOU READY TO TAKE A SHIFT ON MY NIGHT WATCH CREW?

WHY NOT? YOU KNOW I DON'T SLEEP VERY MUCH ANYWAY.

YOU DON'T HAVE TO WORRY ABOUT THAT ONE. ANDREA IS ONE OF *THEM.* THOSE PEOPLE DEALT WITH ALL KINDS OF CRAP LIKE THIS BEFORE THEY CAME HERE.

SHE'LL BE *FINE.*

I KNOW... I KNOW...

TRAPPED INSIDE? SO WHAT--I WAS NEVER PLANNING ON LEAVING AGAIN ANYWAY.

I HEAR YOU.

ROSITA, YOU GO ON AHEAD. HOLLY AND I ARE GOING TO GO TO THE ARMORY, MEET EVERYONE THERE TO ARM UP--AND THEN WE'RE GOING TO DO THE WALL-CHECK RICK ASKED FOR.

I'LL BE HOME A LITTLE LATE TONIGHT, I'M SURE.

I UNDERSTAND. LOVE YOU.

YOU, TOO.

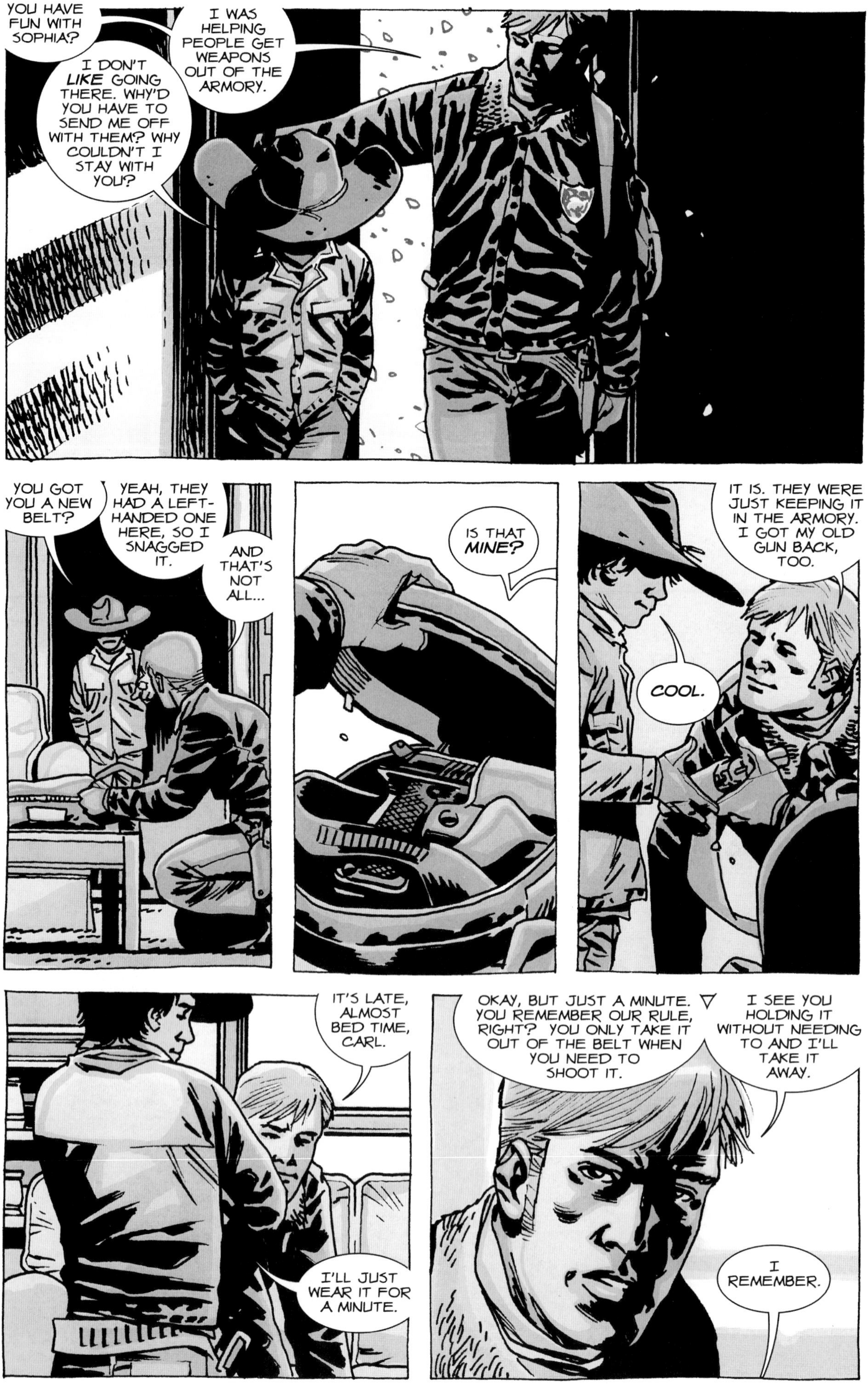
YOU HAVE FUN WITH SOPHIA?
I WAS HELPING PEOPLE GET WEAPONS OUT OF THE ARMORY.
I DON'T LIKE GOING THERE. WHY'D YOU HAVE TO SEND ME OFF WITH THEM? WHY COULDN'T I STAY WITH YOU?
YOU GOT YOU A NEW BELT?
YEAH, THEY HAD A LEFT-HANDED ONE HERE, SO I SNAGGED IT.
AND THAT'S NOT ALL...
IS THAT MINE?
IT IS. THEY WERE JUST KEEPING IT IN THE ARMORY. I GOT MY OLD GUN BACK, TOO.
COOL.
IT'S LATE, ALMOST BED TIME, CARL.
I'LL JUST WEAR IT FOR A MINUTE.
OKAY, BUT JUST A MINUTE. YOU REMEMBER OUR RULE, RIGHT? YOU ONLY TAKE IT OUT OF THE BELT WHEN YOU NEED TO SHOOT IT.
I SEE YOU HOLDING IT WITHOUT NEEDING TO AND I'LL TAKE IT AWAY.
I REMEMBER.

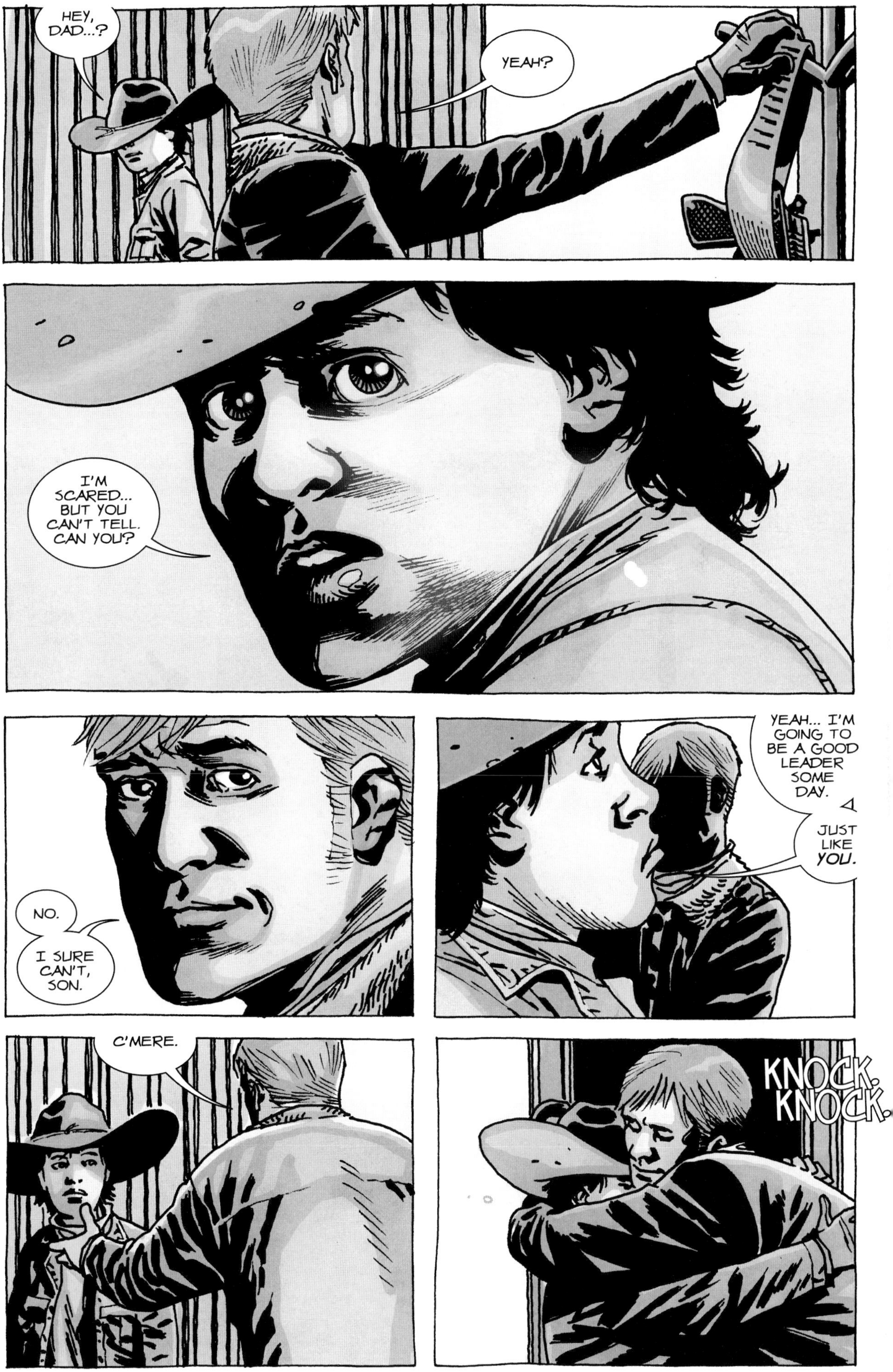
HEY, DAD...?
YEAH?
I'M SCARED... BUT YOU CAN'T TELL. CAN YOU?
NO.
I SURE CAN'T, SON.
YEAH... I'M GOING TO BE A GOOD LEADER SOME DAY.
JUST LIKE *YOU.*
C'MERE.
KNOCK. KNOCK.

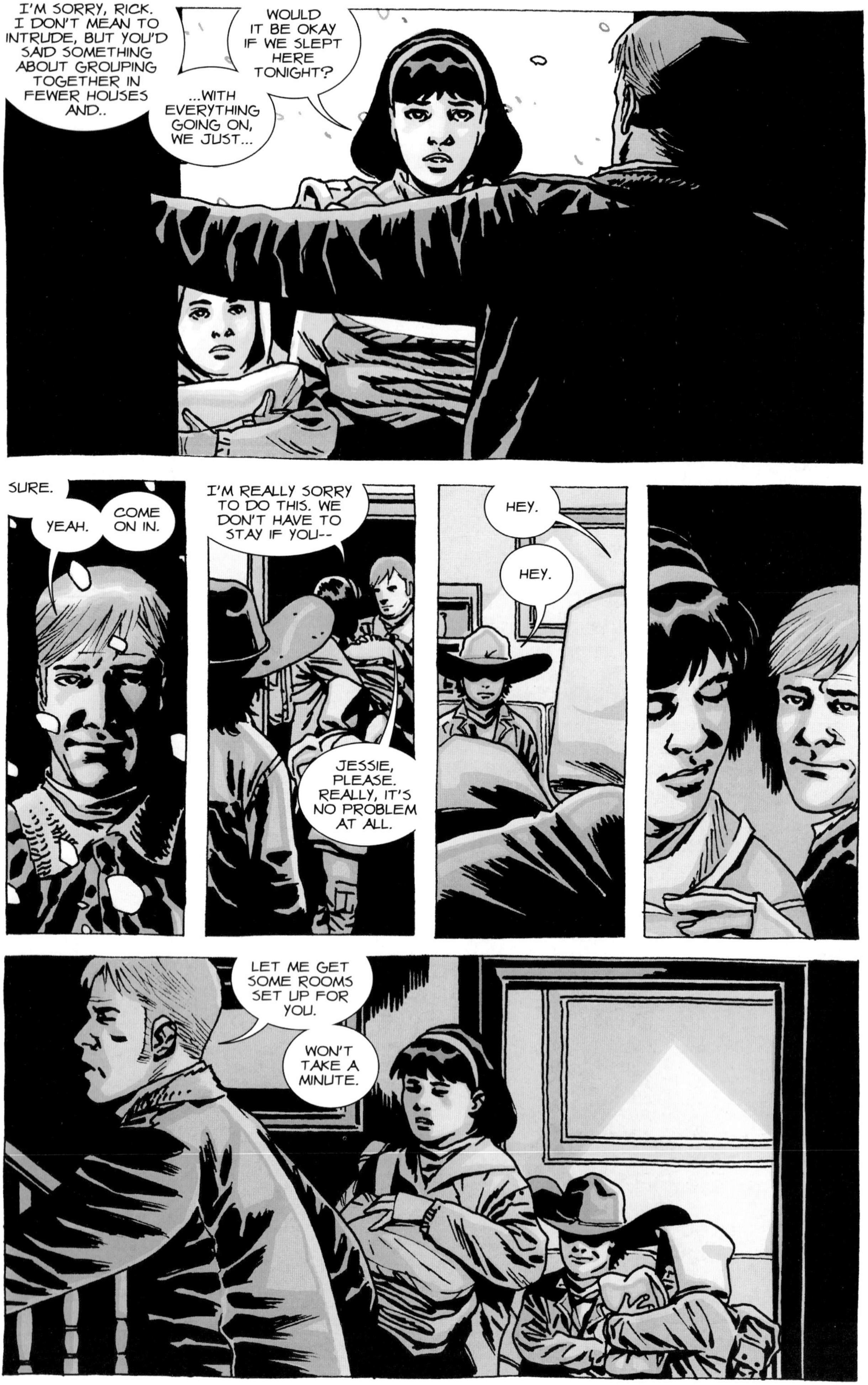
I'M SORRY, RICK. I DON'T MEAN TO INTRUDE, BUT YOU'D SAID SOMETHING ABOUT GROUPING TOGETHER IN FEWER HOUSES AND..
...WITH EVERYTHING GOING ON, WE JUST...
WOULD IT BE OKAY IF WE SLEPT HERE TONIGHT?
SURE.
YEAH.
COME ON IN.
I'M REALLY SORRY TO DO THIS. WE DON'T HAVE TO STAY IF YOU--
JESSIE, PLEASE. REALLY, IT'S NO PROBLEM AT ALL.
HEY.
HEY.
LET ME GET SOME ROOMS SET UP FOR YOU.
WON'T TAKE A MINUTE.

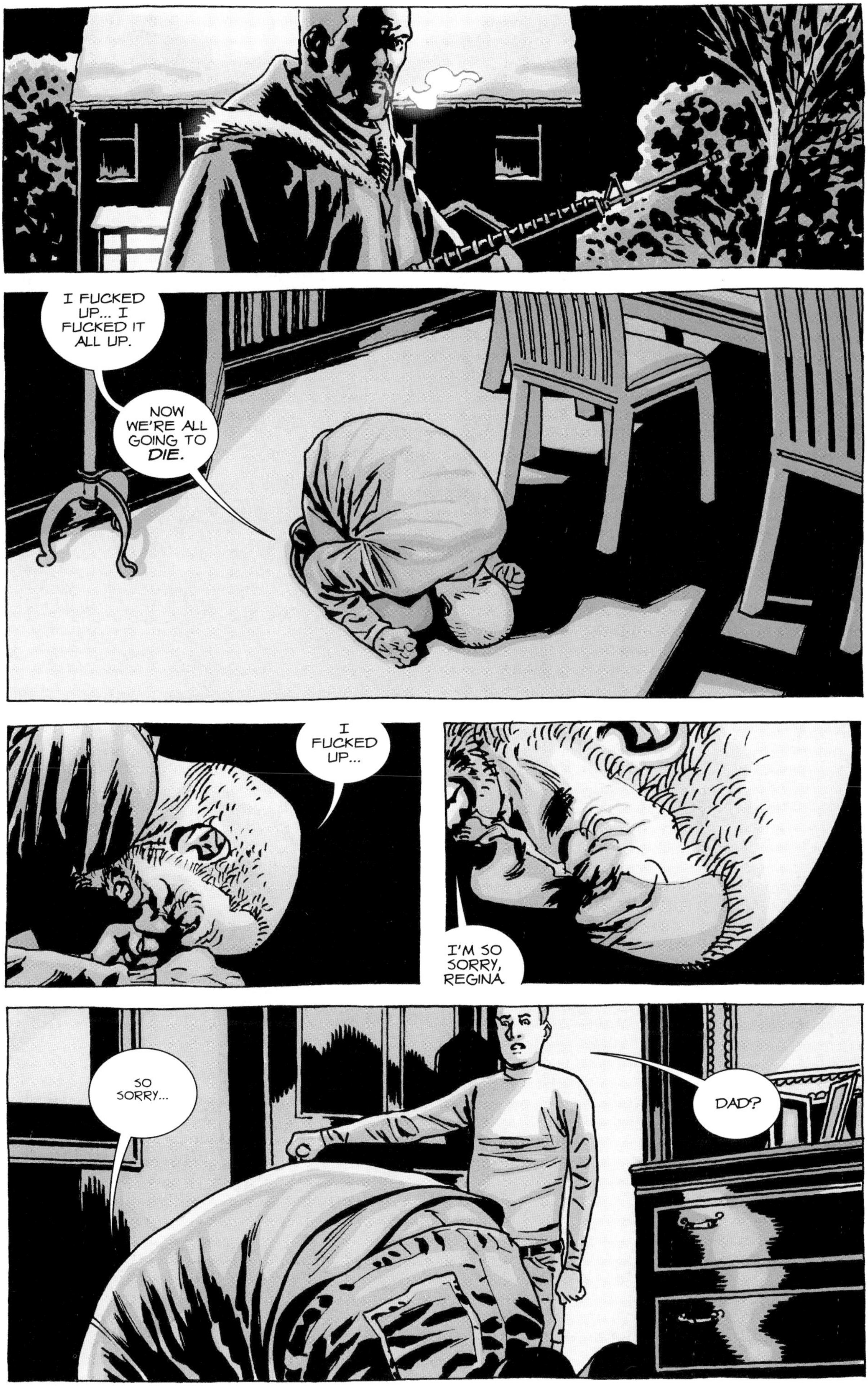

I FUCKED UP... I FUCKED IT ALL UP.
NOW WE'RE ALL GOING TO DIE.
I FUCKED UP...
I'M SO SORRY, REGINA.
SO SORRY...
DAD?

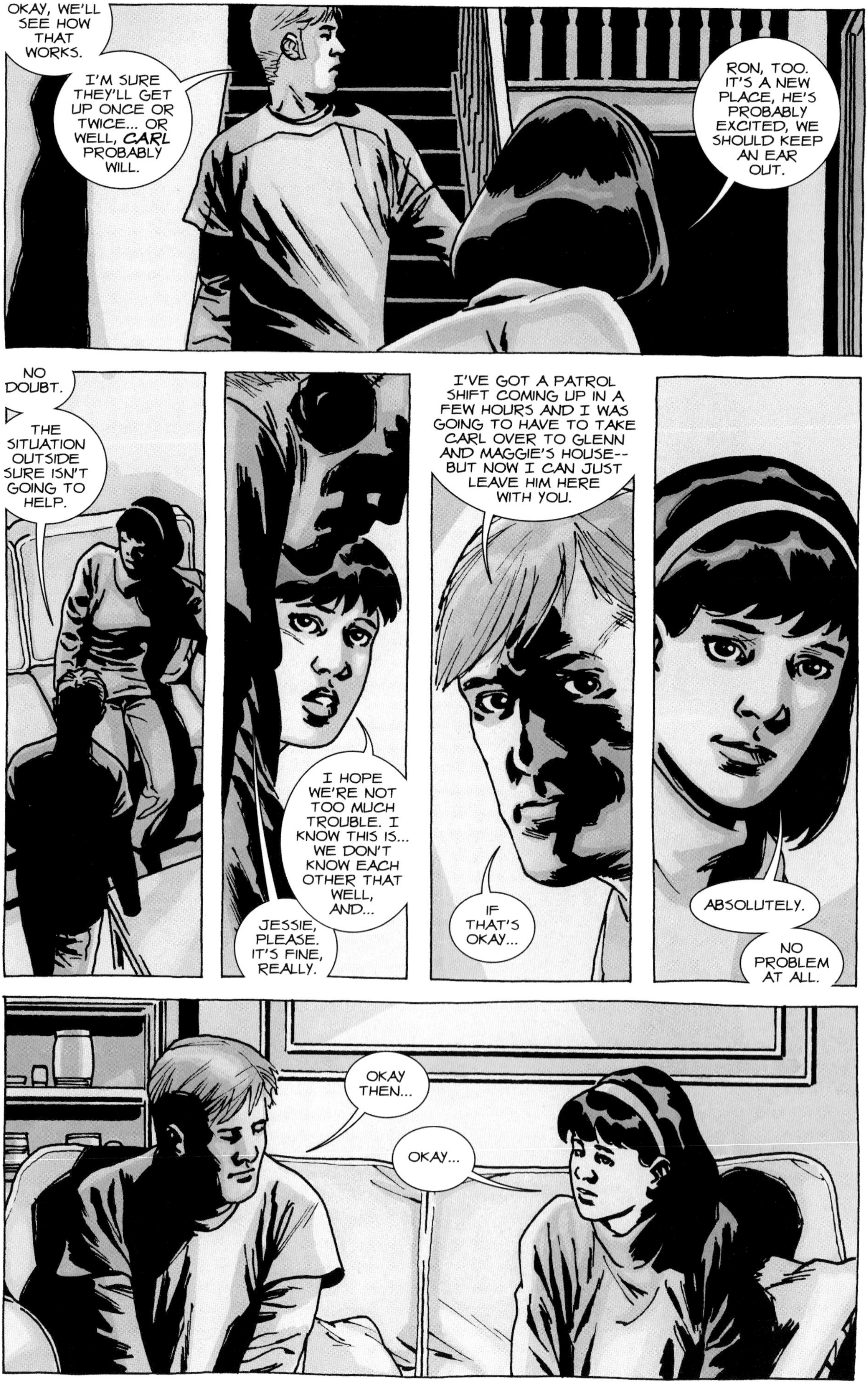
OKAY, WE'LL SEE HOW THAT WORKS.
I'M SURE THEY'LL GET UP ONCE OR TWICE... OR WELL, CARL PROBABLY WILL.
RON, TOO. IT'S A NEW PLACE, HE'S PROBABLY EXCITED, WE SHOULD KEEP AN EAR OUT.
NO DOUBT.
THE SITUATION OUTSIDE SURE ISN'T GOING TO HELP.
I HOPE WE'RE NOT TOO MUCH TROUBLE. I KNOW THIS IS... WE DON'T KNOW EACH OTHER THAT WELL, AND...
JESSIE, PLEASE. IT'S FINE, REALLY.
I'VE GOT A PATROL SHIFT COMING UP IN A FEW HOURS AND I WAS GOING TO HAVE TO TAKE CARL OVER TO GLENN AND MAGGIE'S HOUSE-- BUT NOW I CAN JUST LEAVE HIM HERE WITH YOU.
IF THAT'S OKAY...
ABSOLUTELY.
NO PROBLEM AT ALL.
OKAY THEN...
OKAY...

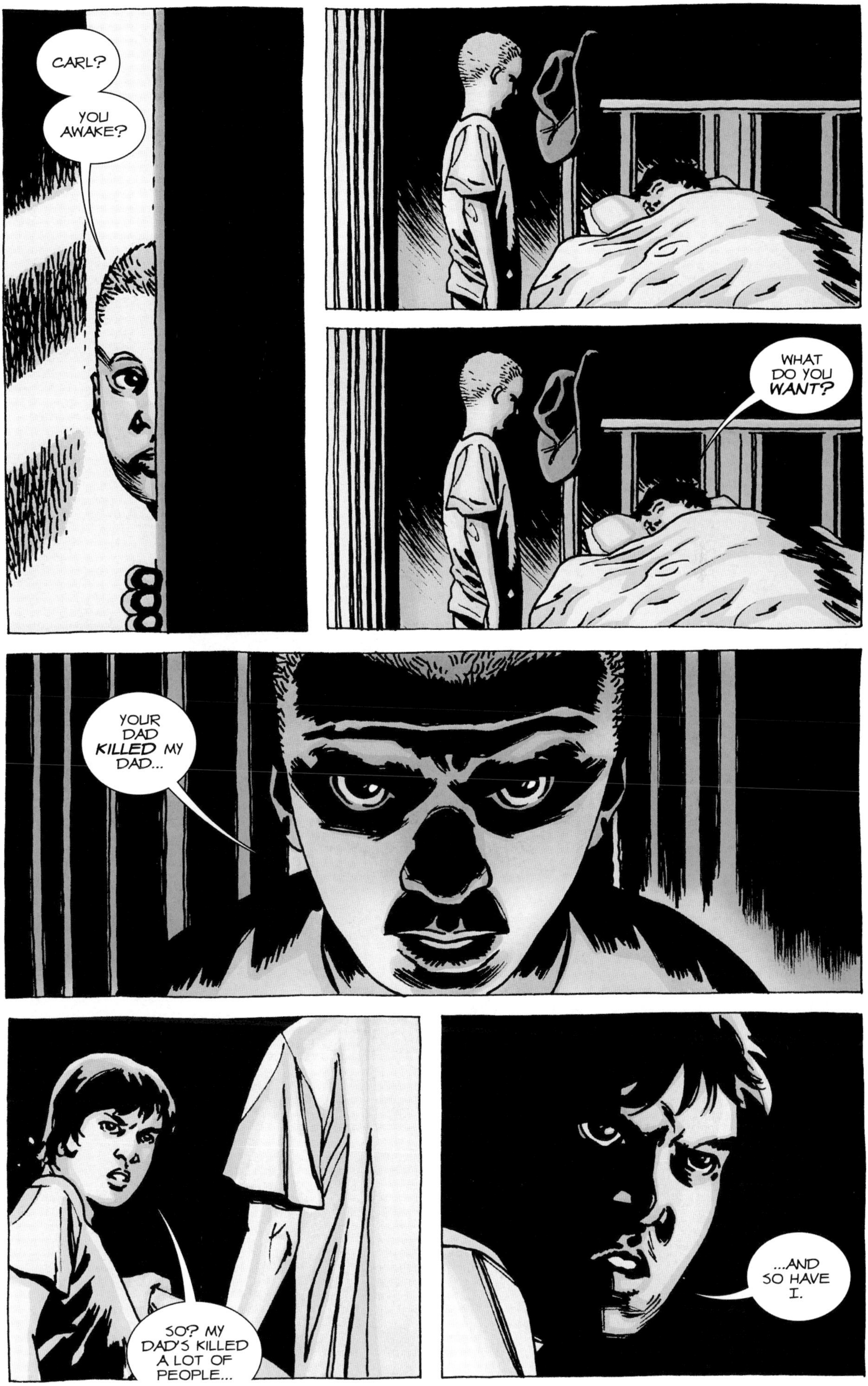
CARL?
YOU AWAKE?
WHAT DO YOU *WANT?*
YOUR DAD *KILLED* MY DAD...
SO? MY DAD'S KILLED A LOT OF PEOPLE...
...AND SO HAVE I.

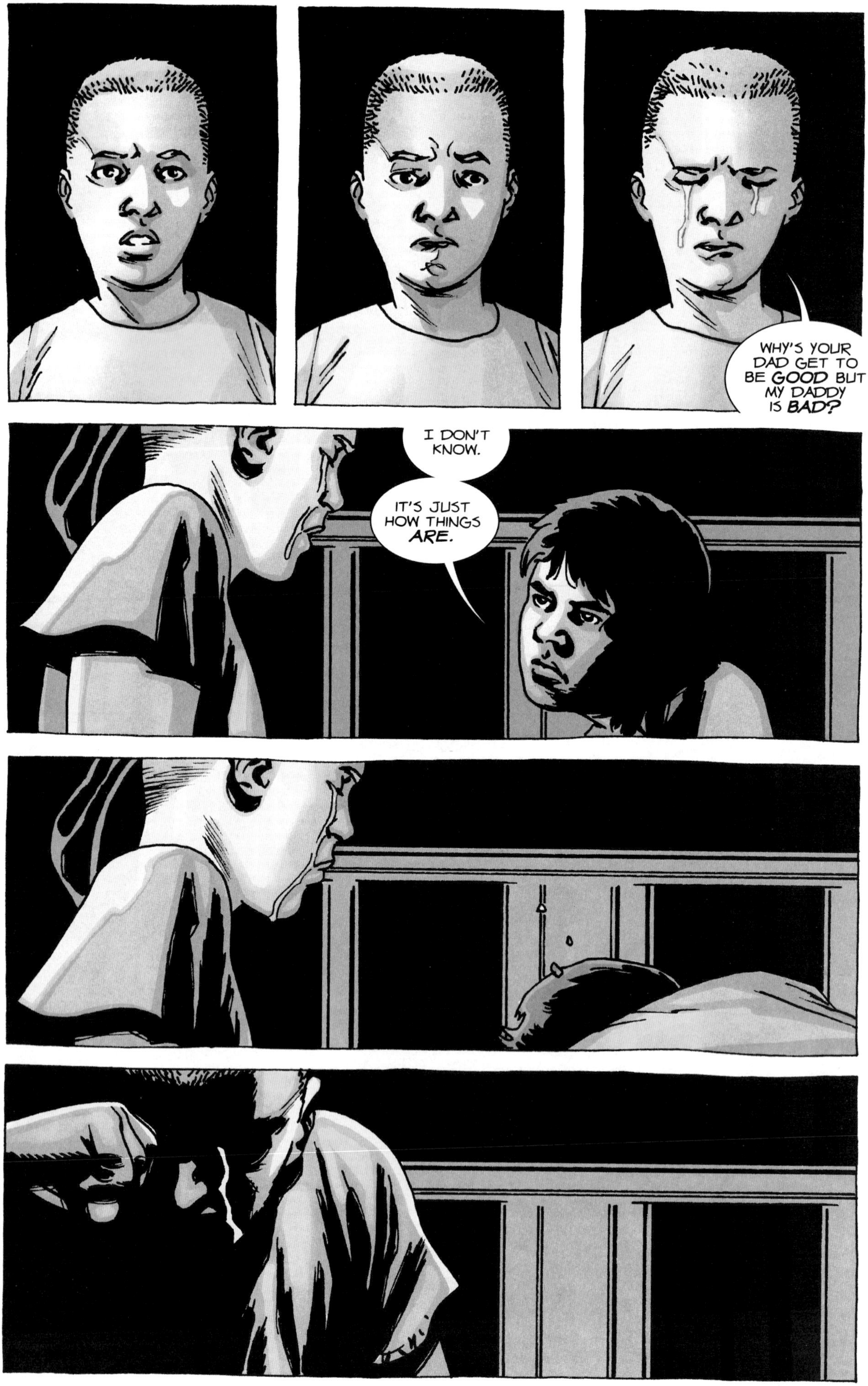
WHY'S YOUR DAD GET TO BE GOOD BUT MY DADDY IS BAD?
I DON'T KNOW.
IT'S JUST HOW THINGS ARE.

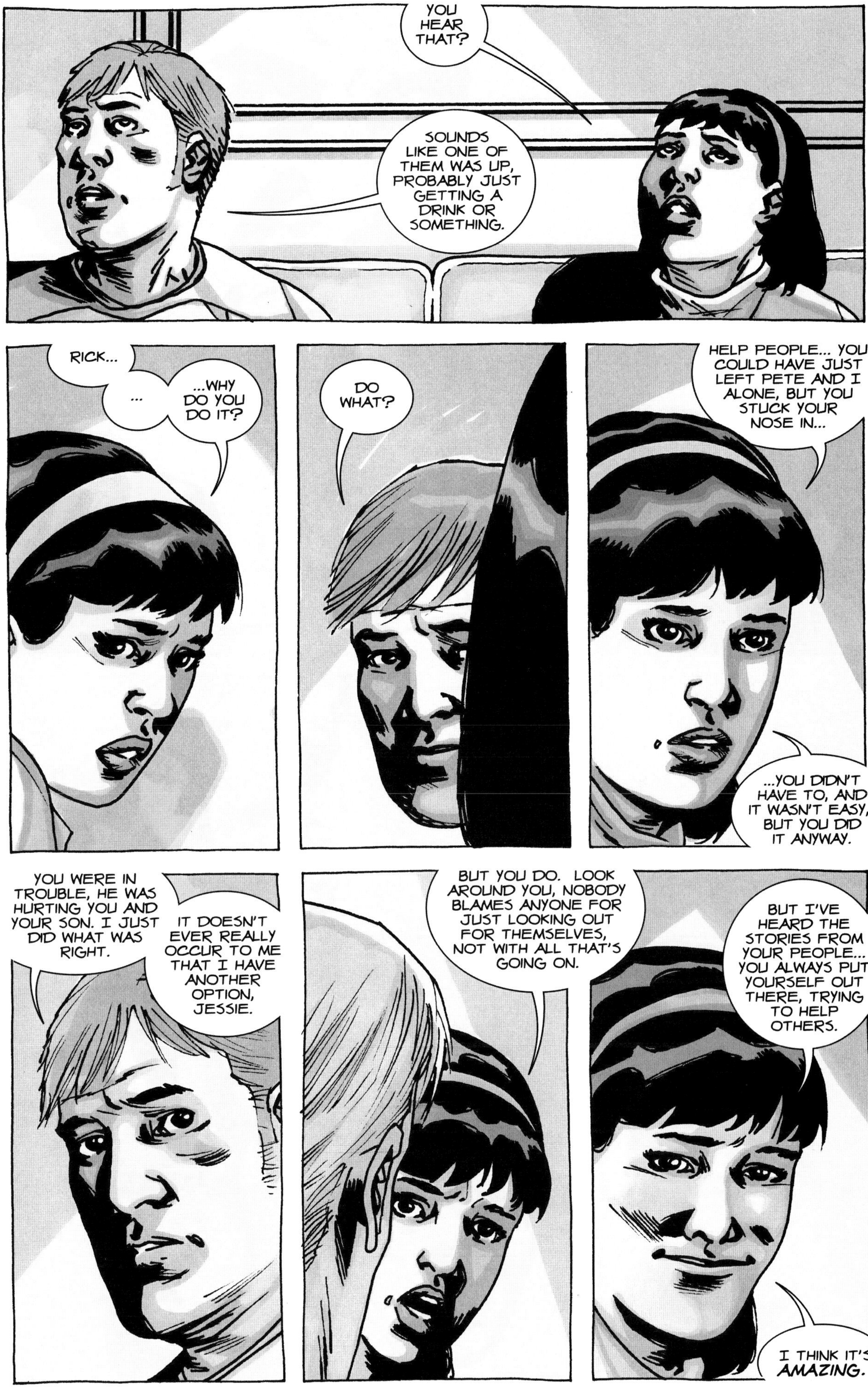
YOU HEAR THAT?
SOUNDS LIKE ONE OF THEM WAS UP, PROBABLY JUST GETTING A DRINK OR SOMETHING.
RICK...
...
...WHY DO YOU DO IT?
DO WHAT?
HELP PEOPLE... YOU COULD HAVE JUST LEFT PETE AND I ALONE, BUT YOU STUCK YOUR NOSE IN...
...YOU DIDN'T HAVE TO, AND IT WASN'T EASY, BUT YOU DID IT ANYWAY.
YOU WERE IN TROUBLE, HE WAS HURTING YOU AND YOUR SON. I JUST DID WHAT WAS RIGHT.
IT DOESN'T EVER REALLY OCCUR TO ME THAT I HAVE ANOTHER OPTION, JESSIE.
BUT YOU DO. LOOK AROUND YOU, NOBODY BLAMES ANYONE FOR JUST LOOKING OUT FOR THEMSELVES, NOT WITH ALL THAT'S GOING ON.
BUT I'VE HEARD THE STORIES FROM YOUR PEOPLE... YOU ALWAYS PUT YOURSELF OUT THERE, TRYING TO HELP OTHERS.
I THINK IT'S *AMAZING.*

IT'S *NOT*.

EVERYTHING I'VE DONE, FOR THE GOOD OF MY GROUP... HAS ALWAYS MOSTLY BEEN DONE TO PROTECT MY FAMILY.

THAT'S WHAT'S IMPORTANT TO ME.

PETE WAS DANGEROUS, HE WAS HURTING YOU... BUT IF HE'S DOING THAT, WHERE DOES IT END? EVENTUALLY THAT GETS OUT TO OTHER PEOPLE... PUTS THEM IN DANGER.

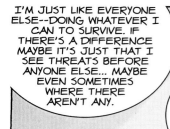

I'M JUST LIKE EVERYONE ELSE--DOING WHATEVER I CAN TO SURVIVE. IF THERE'S A DIFFERENCE MAYBE IT'S JUST THAT I SEE THREATS BEFORE ANYONE ELSE... MAYBE EVEN SOMETIMES WHERE THERE AREN'T ANY.

I DON'T KNOW...

SO I'M NO BETTER THAN THOSE WHO DIDN'T DO A THING.

BUT DON'T GET ME WRONG, AND I'M GLAD I HELPED YOU... BUT I WAS DOING IT TO KEEP MY SON SAFE.

YOU CAN ARGUE ALL YOU WANT, BUT I JUST DON'T SEE IT THAT WAY.

YOU'RE *SPECIAL*.

WELL, THANK YOU. REALLY.

I KIND OF... I SHOULD BE GETTING TO BED. I'VE GOT THAT PATROL COMING UP.

YEAH, SURE.

SORRY TO KEEP YOU UP.

GOOD NIGHT.

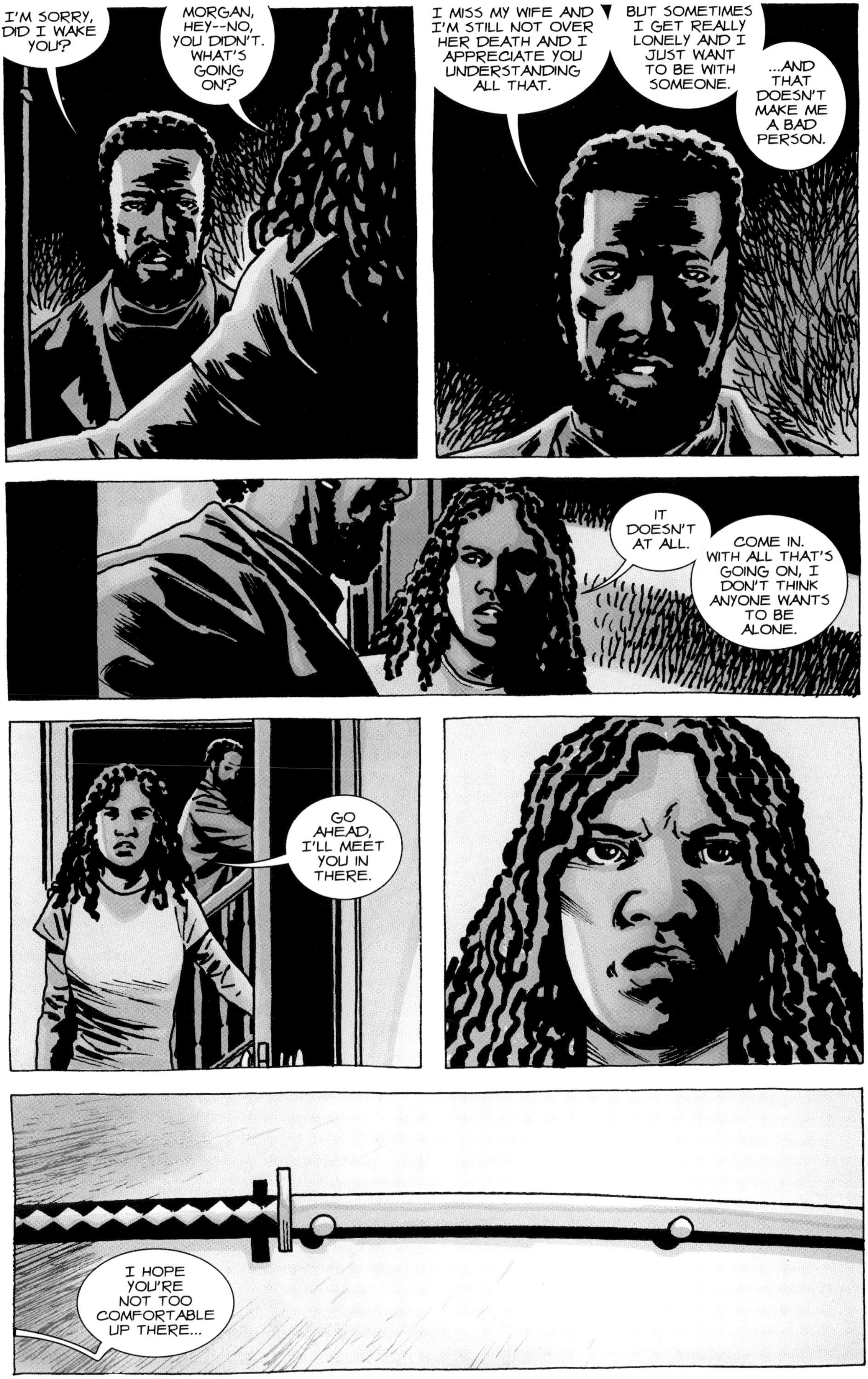
I'M SORRY, DID I WAKE YOU?
MORGAN, HEY--NO, YOU DIDN'T. WHAT'S GOING ON?
I MISS MY WIFE AND I'M STILL NOT OVER HER DEATH AND I APPRECIATE YOU UNDERSTANDING ALL THAT.
BUT SOMETIMES I GET REALLY LONELY AND I JUST WANT TO BE WITH SOMEONE.
...AND THAT DOESN'T MAKE ME A BAD PERSON.
IT DOESN'T AT ALL.
COME IN. WITH ALL THAT'S GOING ON, I DON'T THINK ANYONE WANTS TO BE ALONE.
GO AHEAD, I'LL MEET YOU IN THERE.
I HOPE YOU'RE NOT TOO COMFORTABLE UP THERE...

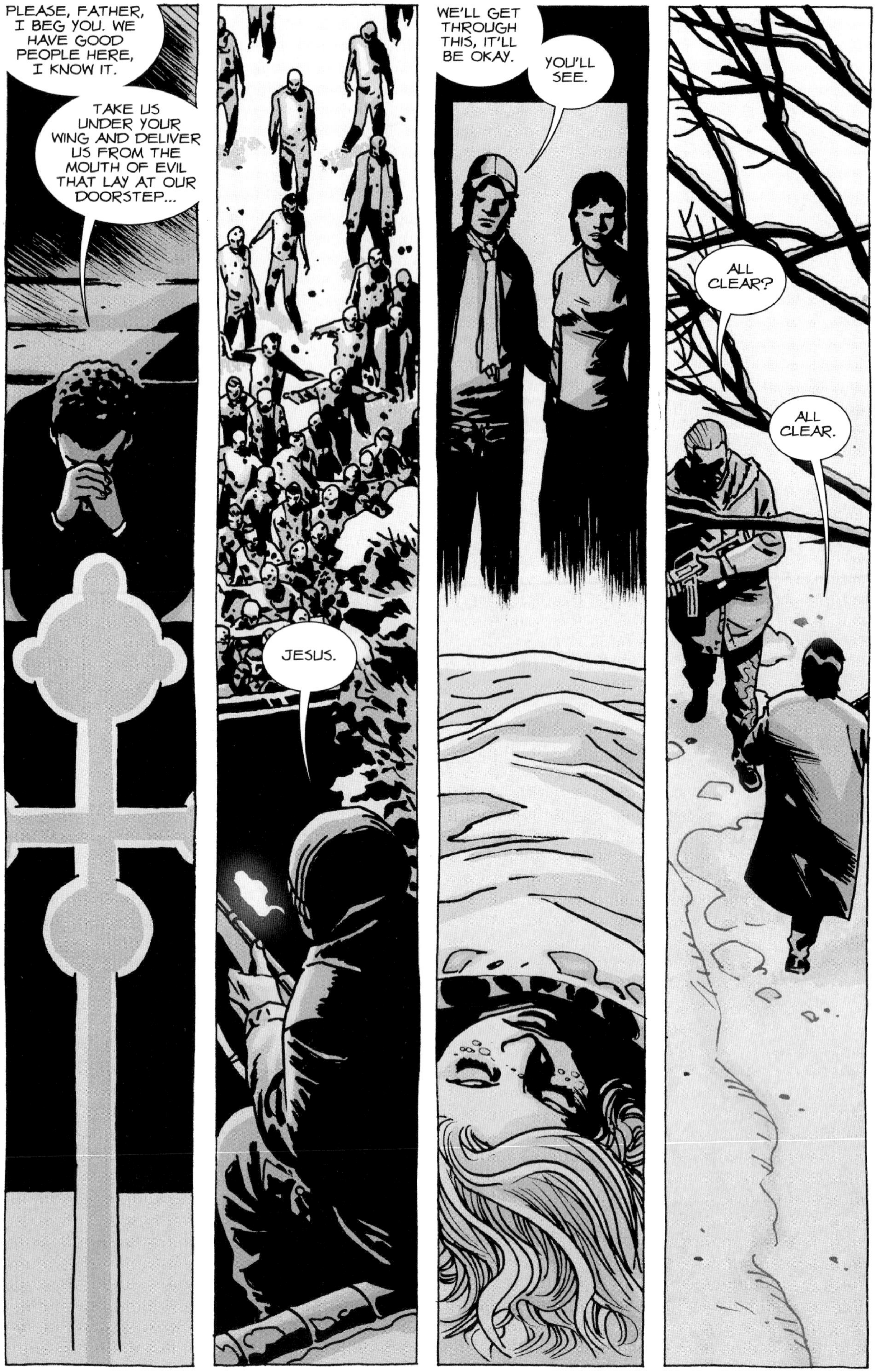
PLEASE, FATHER, I BEG YOU. WE HAVE GOOD PEOPLE HERE, I KNOW IT.
TAKE US UNDER YOUR WING AND DELIVER US FROM THE MOUTH OF EVIL THAT LAY AT OUR DOORSTEP...
JESUS.
WE'LL GET THROUGH THIS, IT'LL BE OKAY.
YOU'LL SEE.
ALL CLEAR?
ALL CLEAR.

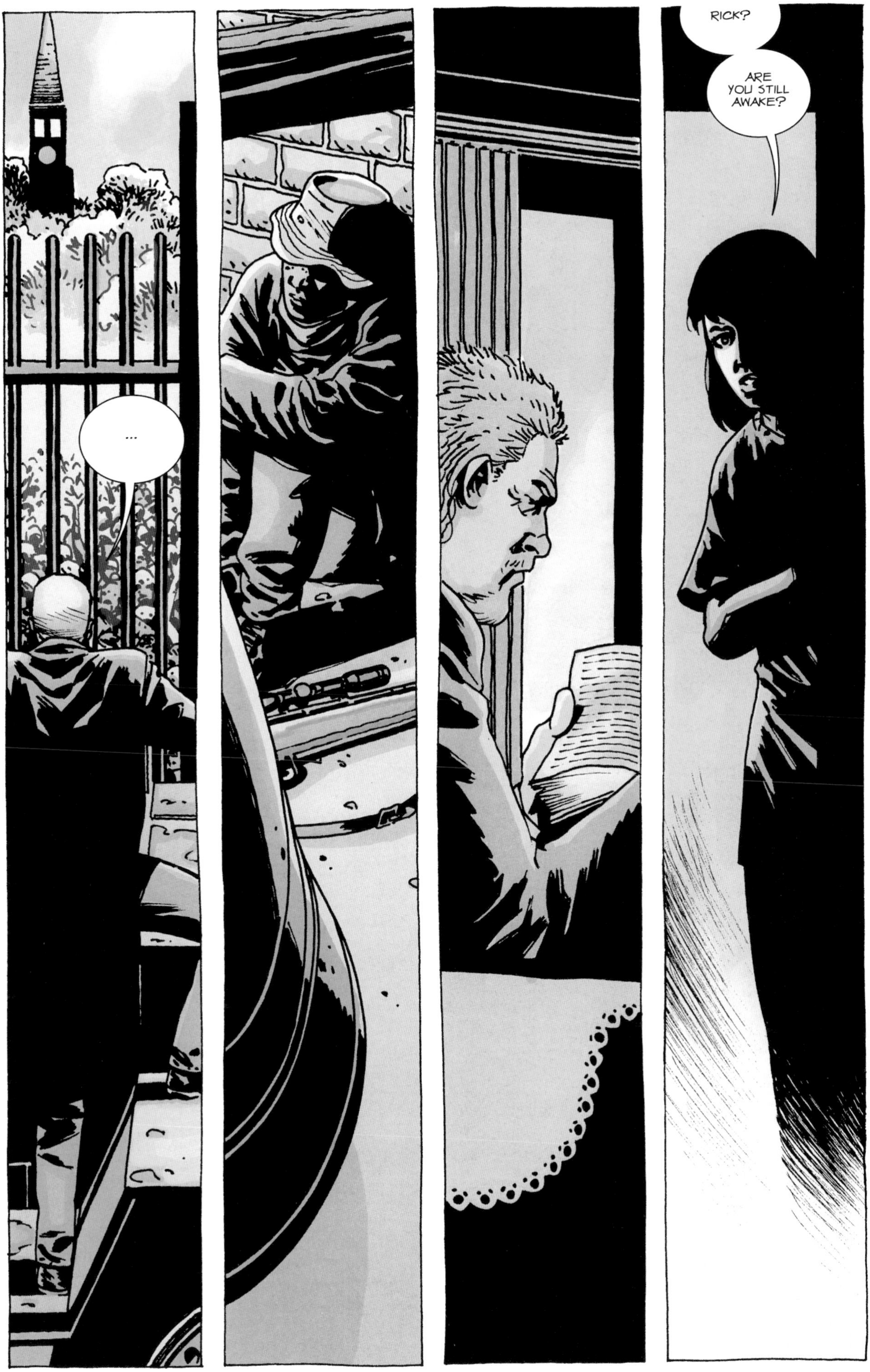
...
RICK?
ARE YOU STILL AWAKE?

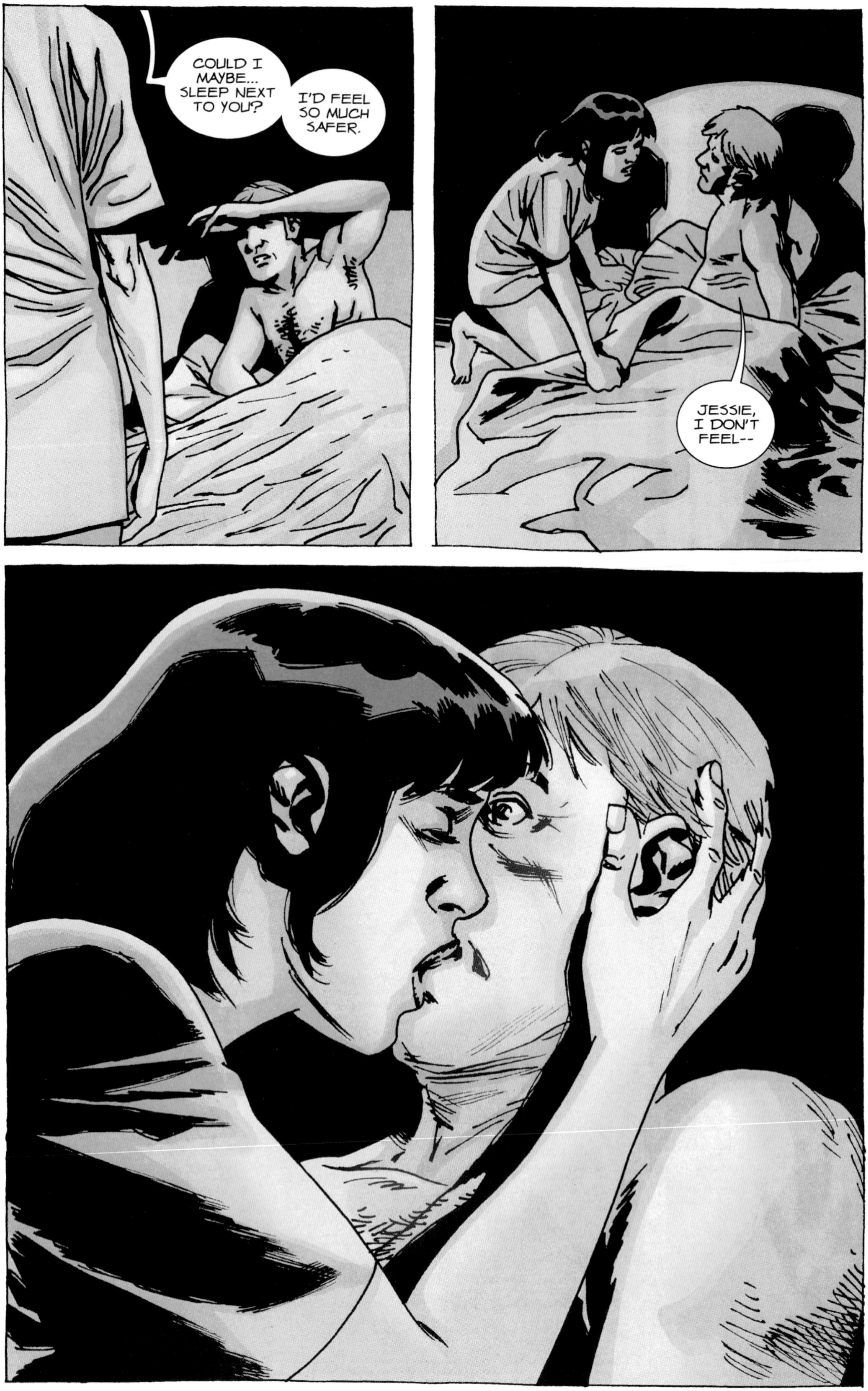

COULD I MAYBE... SLEEP NEXT TO YOU?
I'D FEEL SO MUCH SAFER.
JESSIE, I DON'T FEEL--

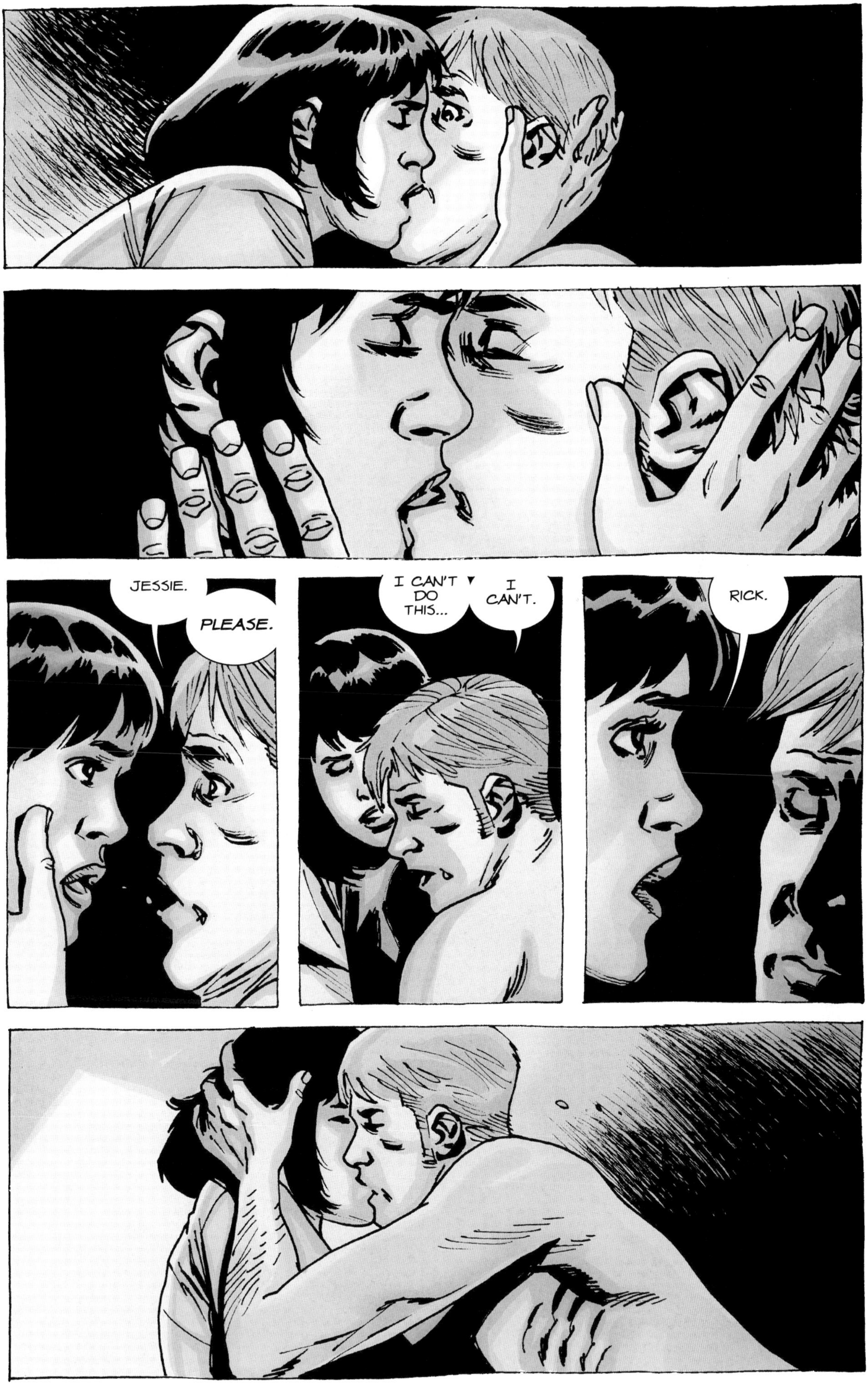
JESSIE.
PLEASE.
I CAN'T DO THIS...
I CAN'T.
RICK.

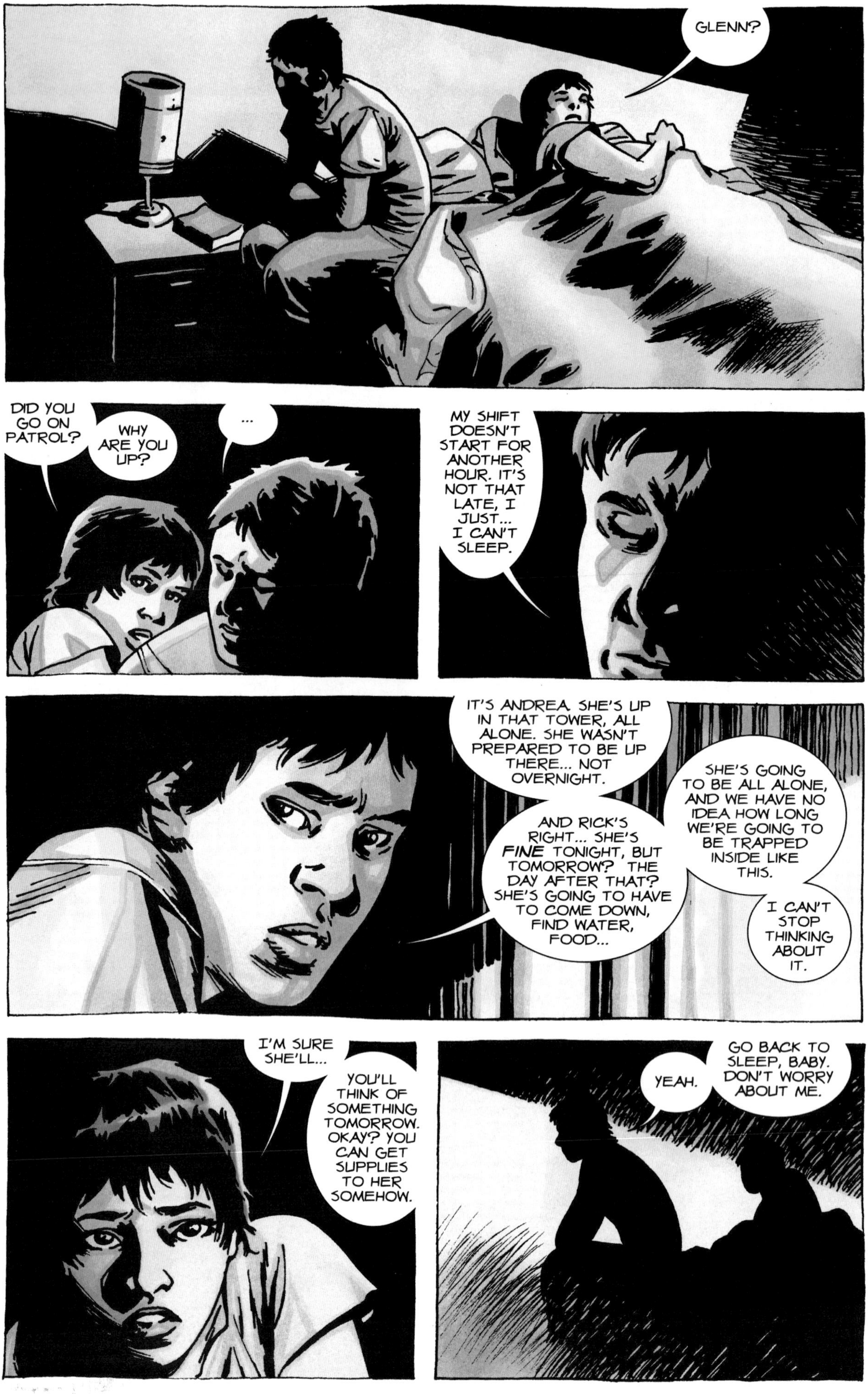
GLENN?
DID YOU GO ON PATROL?
WHY ARE YOU UP?
...
MY SHIFT DOESN'T START FOR ANOTHER HOUR. IT'S NOT THAT LATE, I JUST... I CAN'T SLEEP.
IT'S ANDREA. SHE'S UP IN THAT TOWER, ALL ALONE. SHE WASN'T PREPARED TO BE UP THERE... NOT OVERNIGHT.
AND RICK'S RIGHT... SHE'S FINE TONIGHT, BUT TOMORROW? THE DAY AFTER THAT? SHE'S GOING TO HAVE TO COME DOWN, FIND WATER, FOOD...
SHE'S GOING TO BE ALL ALONE, AND WE HAVE NO IDEA HOW LONG WE'RE GOING TO BE TRAPPED INSIDE LIKE THIS.
I CAN'T STOP THINKING ABOUT IT.
I'M SURE SHE'LL...
YOU'LL THINK OF SOMETHING TOMORROW. OKAY? YOU CAN GET SUPPLIES TO HER SOMEHOW.
YEAH.
GO BACK TO SLEEP, BABY. DON'T WORRY ABOUT ME.

I DON'T FEEL GUILTY.

I DON'T FEEL LIKE I **DESERVE** TO FEEL GUILTY. I'VE LIVED THROUGH HELL, MAYBE I'VE **EARNED** THIS.

I DESERVE TO BE HAPPY.

WHAT THE FUCK IS **WRONG** WITH YOU?

WHAT?

YOU ACT LIKE YOU'RE THE ONLY PERSON WHO'S LOST SOMEONE.

IT'S INSULTING.

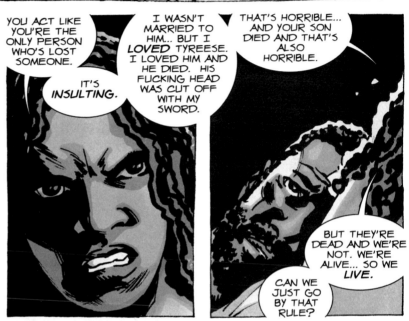

I WASN'T MARRIED TO HIM... BUT I **LOVED** TYREESE. I LOVED HIM AND HE DIED. HIS FUCKING HEAD WAS CUT OFF WITH MY SWORD.

THAT'S HORRIBLE... AND YOUR SON DIED AND THAT'S ALSO HORRIBLE.

BUT THEY'RE DEAD AND WE'RE NOT. WE'RE ALIVE... SO WE **LIVE**.

CAN WE JUST GO BY THAT RULE?

AT A CERTAIN POINT YOU JUST HAVE TO **MOVE ON**.

I'M GOING TO GET A GLASS OF WATER.

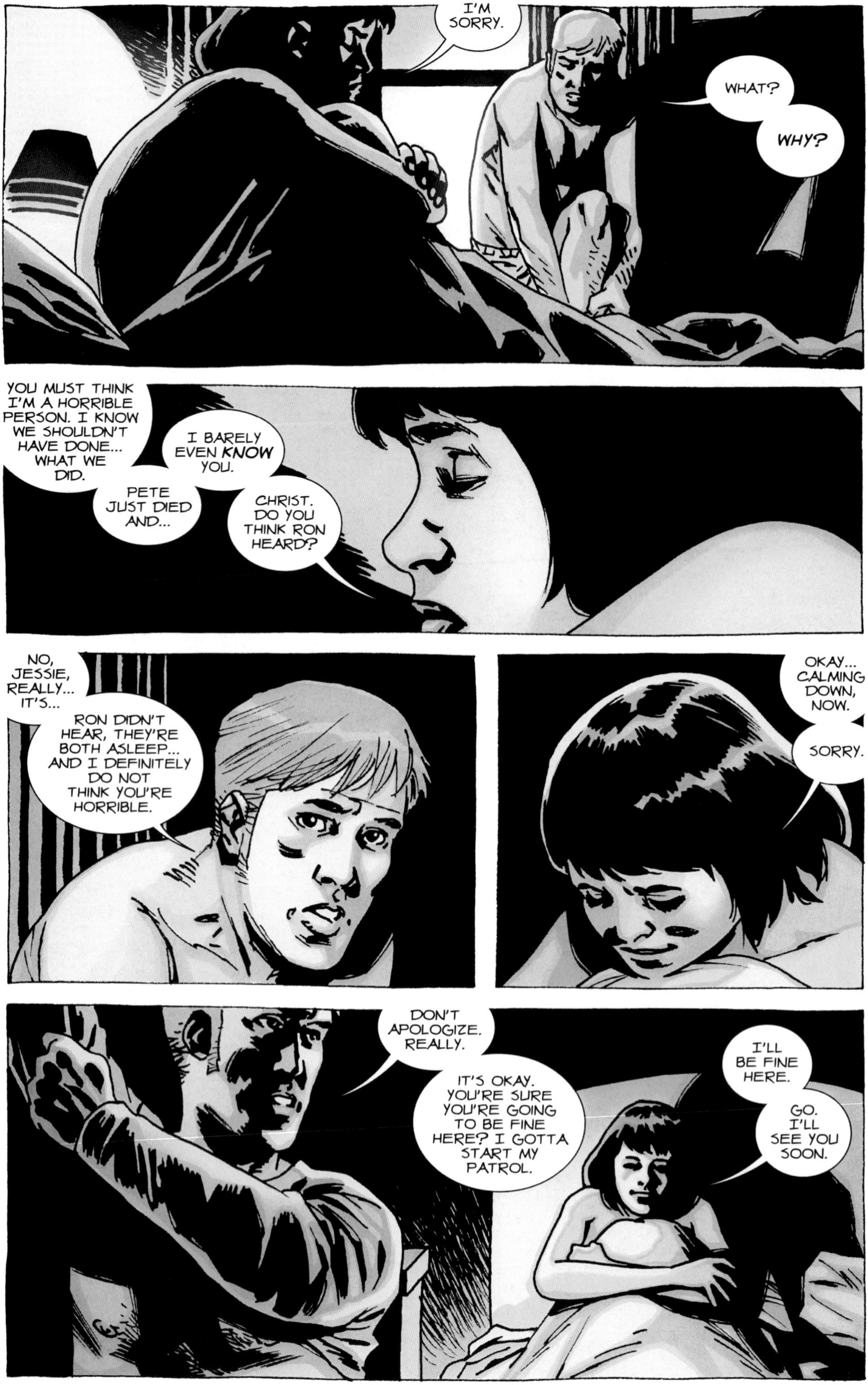
I'M SORRY.
WHAT?
WHY?
YOU MUST THINK I'M A HORRIBLE PERSON. I KNOW WE SHOULDN'T HAVE DONE... WHAT WE DID.
PETE JUST DIED AND...
I BARELY EVEN KNOW YOU.
CHRIST. DO YOU THINK RON HEARD?
NO, JESSIE, REALLY... IT'S...
RON DIDN'T HEAR, THEY'RE BOTH ASLEEP... AND I DEFINITELY DO NOT THINK YOU'RE HORRIBLE.
OKAY... CALMING DOWN, NOW.
SORRY.
DON'T APOLOGIZE. REALLY.
IT'S OKAY. YOU'RE SURE YOU'RE GOING TO BE FINE HERE? I GOTTA START MY PATROL.
I'LL BE FINE HERE.
GO. I'LL SEE YOU SOON.

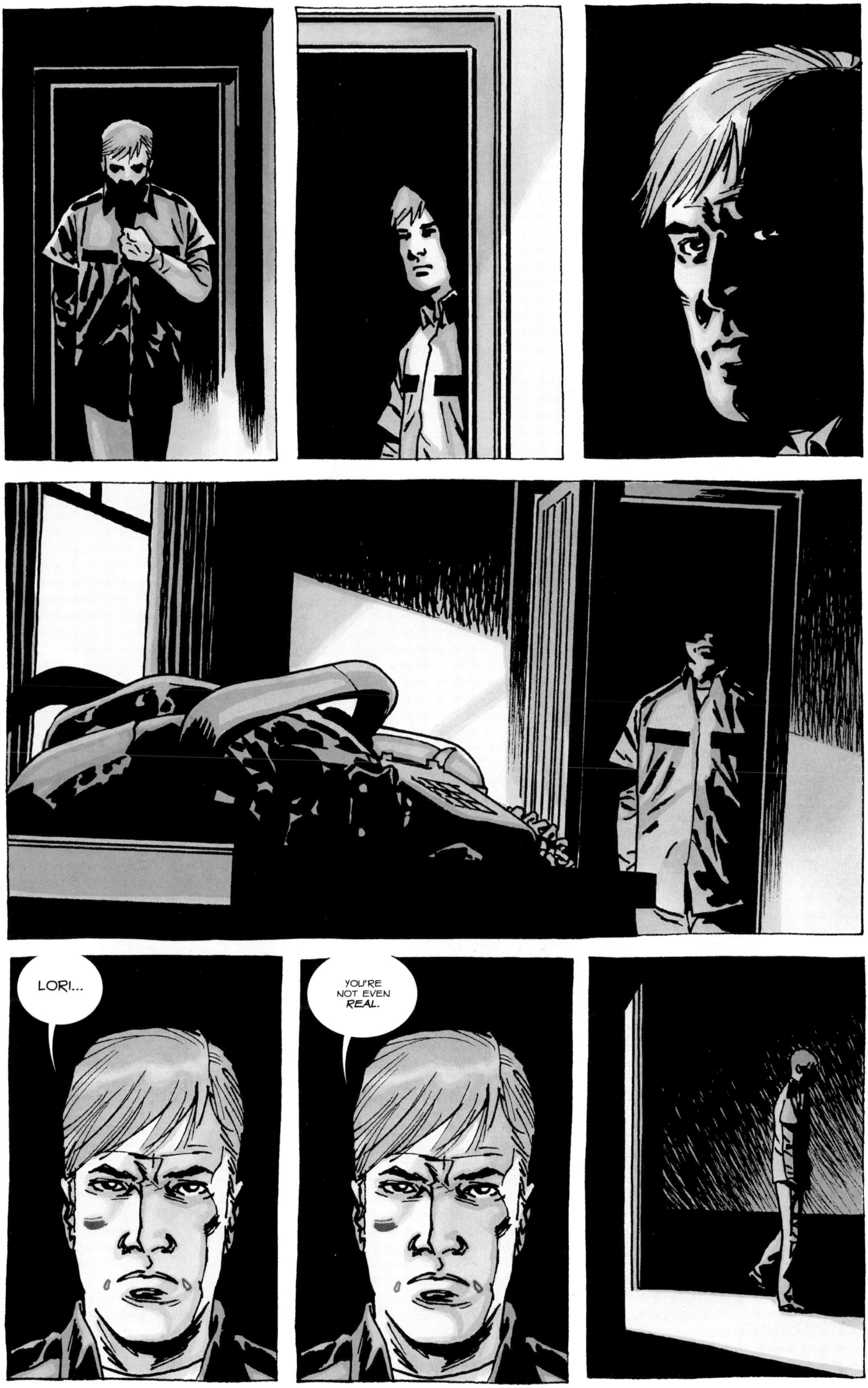
LORI...
YOU'RE NOT EVEN REAL.

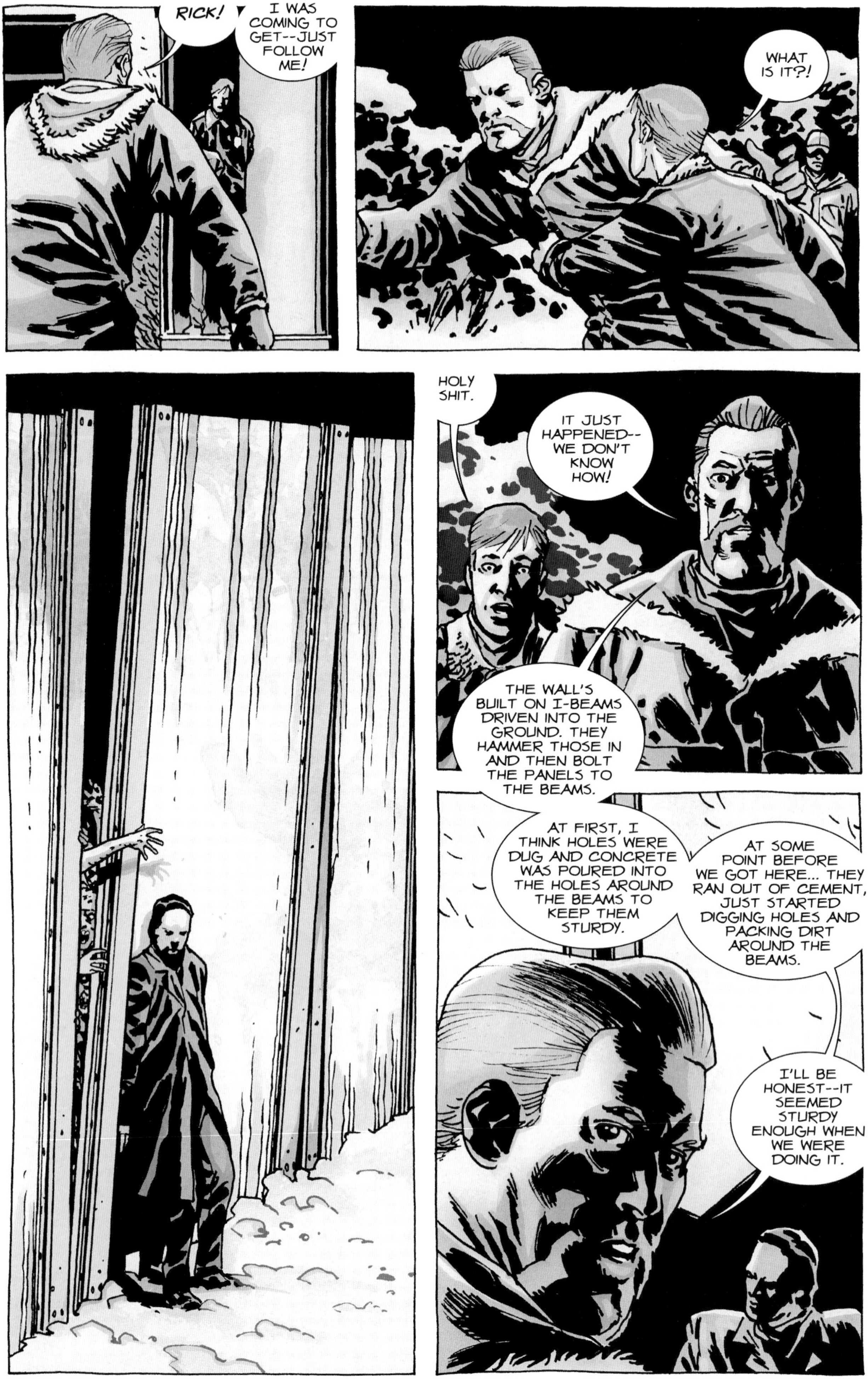
RICK!
I WAS COMING TO GET--JUST FOLLOW ME!
WHAT IS IT?!
HOLY SHIT.
IT JUST HAPPENED-- WE DON'T KNOW HOW!
THE WALL'S BUILT ON I-BEAMS DRIVEN INTO THE GROUND. THEY HAMMER THOSE IN AND THEN BOLT THE PANELS TO THE BEAMS.
AT FIRST, I THINK HOLES WERE DUG AND CONCRETE WAS POURED INTO THE HOLES AROUND THE BEAMS TO KEEP THEM STURDY.
AT SOME POINT BEFORE WE GOT HERE... THEY RAN OUT OF CEMENT, JUST STARTED DIGGING HOLES AND PACKING DIRT AROUND THE BEAMS.
I'LL BE HONEST--IT SEEMED STURDY ENOUGH WHEN WE WERE DOING IT.

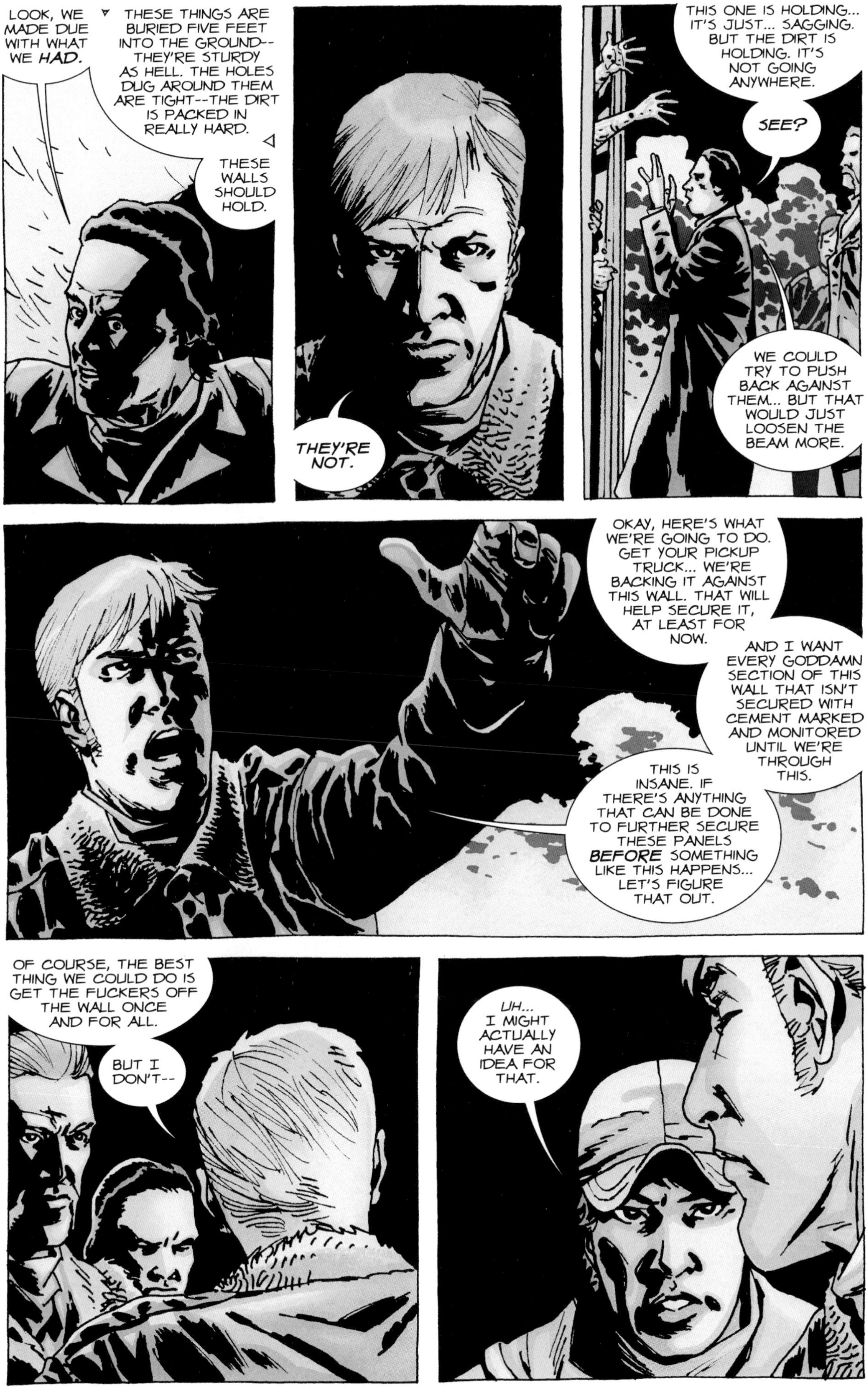
LOOK, WE MADE DUE WITH WHAT WE *HAD.*
THESE THINGS ARE BURIED FIVE FEET INTO THE GROUND-- THEY'RE STURDY AS HELL. THE HOLES DUG AROUND THEM ARE TIGHT--THE DIRT IS PACKED IN REALLY HARD.
THESE WALLS SHOULD HOLD.
THEY'RE NOT.
THIS ONE IS HOLDING... IT'S JUST... SAGGING. BUT THE DIRT IS HOLDING. IT'S NOT GOING ANYWHERE.
SEE?
WE COULD TRY TO PUSH BACK AGAINST THEM... BUT THAT WOULD JUST LOOSEN THE BEAM MORE.
OKAY, HERE'S WHAT WE'RE GOING TO DO. GET YOUR PICKUP TRUCK... WE'RE BACKING IT AGAINST THIS WALL. THAT WILL HELP SECURE IT, AT LEAST FOR NOW.
AND I WANT EVERY GODDAMN SECTION OF THIS WALL THAT ISN'T SECURED WITH CEMENT MARKED AND MONITORED UNTIL WE'RE THROUGH THIS.
THIS IS INSANE. IF THERE'S ANYTHING THAT CAN BE DONE TO FURTHER SECURE THESE PANELS *BEFORE* SOMETHING LIKE THIS HAPPENS... LET'S FIGURE THAT OUT.
OF COURSE, THE BEST THING WE COULD DO IS GET THE FUCKERS OFF THE WALL ONCE AND FOR ALL.
BUT I DON'T--
UH... I MIGHT ACTUALLY HAVE AN IDEA FOR THAT.

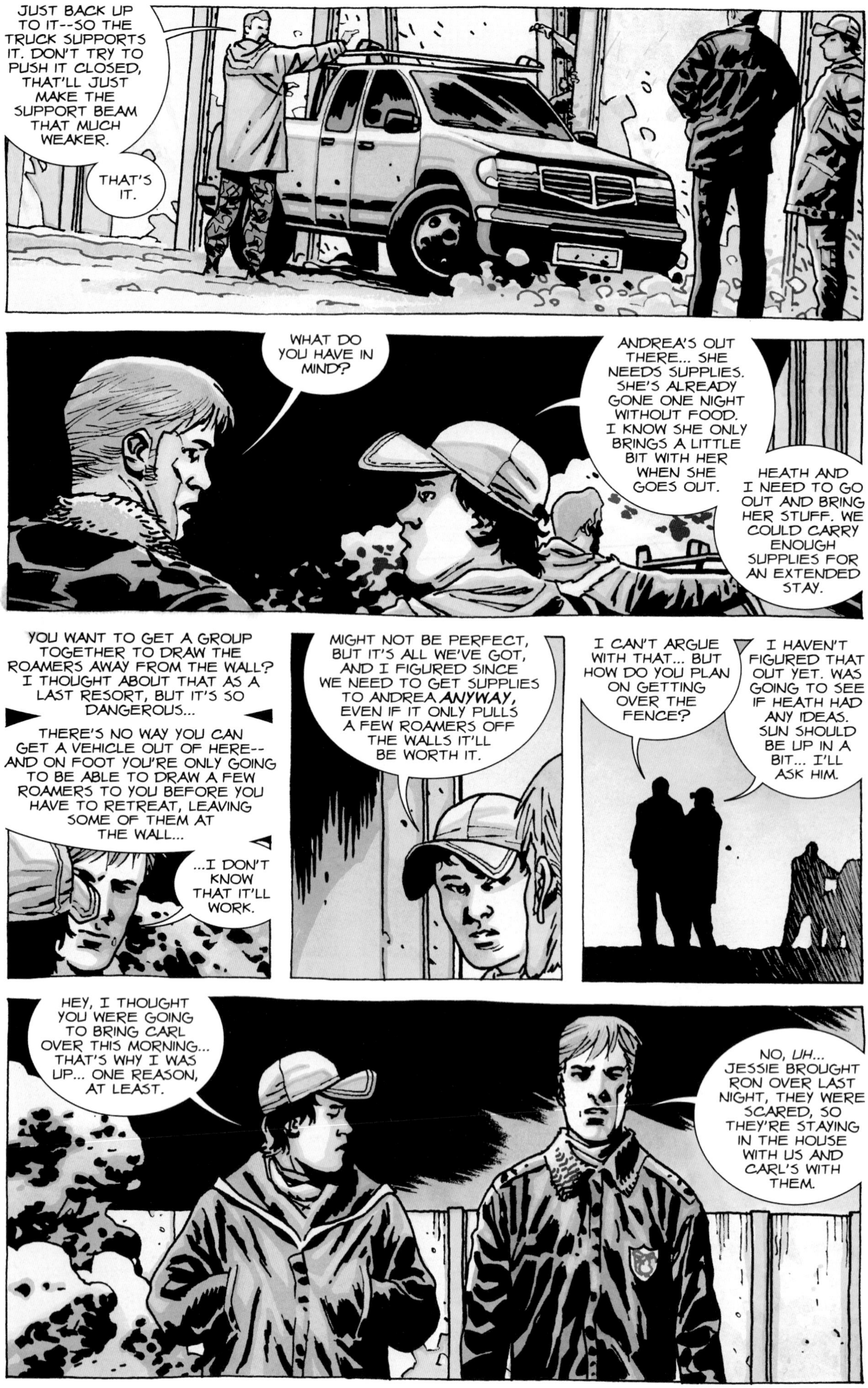
JUST BACK UP TO IT--SO THE TRUCK SUPPORTS IT. DON'T TRY TO PUSH IT CLOSED, THAT'LL JUST MAKE THE SUPPORT BEAM THAT MUCH WEAKER.
THAT'S IT.
WHAT DO YOU HAVE IN MIND?
ANDREA'S OUT THERE... SHE NEEDS SUPPLIES. SHE'S ALREADY GONE ONE NIGHT WITHOUT FOOD. I KNOW SHE ONLY BRINGS A LITTLE BIT WITH HER WHEN SHE GOES OUT.
HEATH AND I NEED TO GO OUT AND BRING HER STUFF. WE COULD CARRY ENOUGH SUPPLIES FOR AN EXTENDED STAY.
YOU WANT TO GET A GROUP TOGETHER TO DRAW THE ROAMERS AWAY FROM THE WALL? I THOUGHT ABOUT THAT AS A LAST RESORT, BUT IT'S SO DANGEROUS...
THERE'S NO WAY YOU CAN GET A VEHICLE OUT OF HERE--AND ON FOOT YOU'RE ONLY GOING TO BE ABLE TO DRAW A FEW ROAMERS TO YOU BEFORE YOU HAVE TO RETREAT, LEAVING SOME OF THEM AT THE WALL...
...I DON'T KNOW THAT IT'LL WORK.
MIGHT NOT BE PERFECT, BUT IT'S ALL WE'VE GOT, AND I FIGURED SINCE WE NEED TO GET SUPPLIES TO ANDREA *ANYWAY,* EVEN IF IT ONLY PULLS A FEW ROAMERS OFF THE WALLS IT'LL BE WORTH IT.
I CAN'T ARGUE WITH THAT... BUT HOW DO YOU PLAN ON GETTING OVER THE FENCE?
I HAVEN'T FIGURED THAT OUT YET. WAS GOING TO SEE IF HEATH HAD ANY IDEAS. SUN SHOULD BE UP IN A BIT... I'LL ASK HIM.
HEY, I THOUGHT YOU WERE GOING TO BRING CARL OVER THIS MORNING... THAT'S WHY I WAS UP... ONE REASON, AT LEAST.
NO, *UH*... JESSIE BROUGHT RON OVER LAST NIGHT, THEY WERE SCARED, SO THEY'RE STAYING IN THE HOUSE WITH US AND CARL'S WITH THEM.

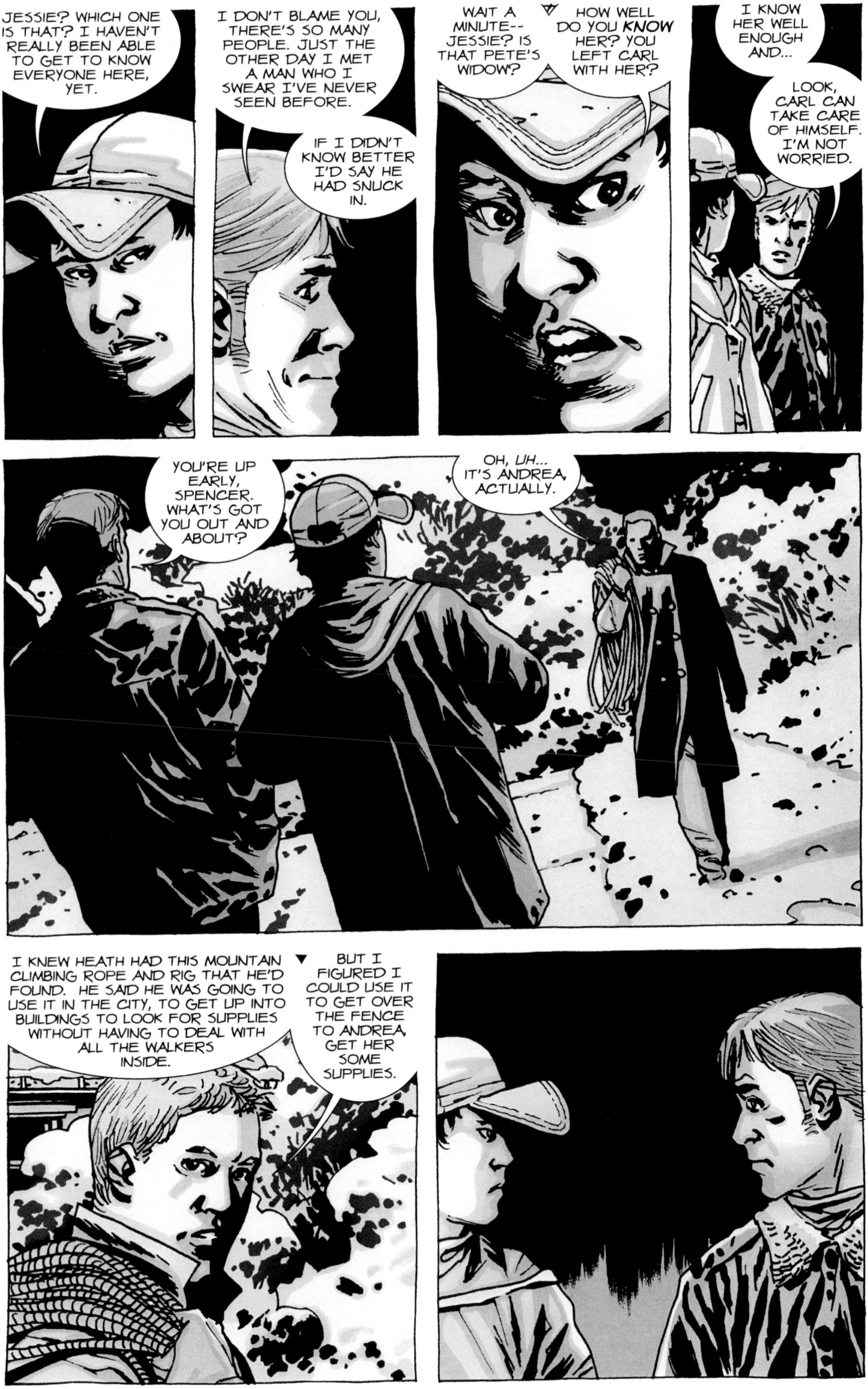
JESSIE? WHICH ONE IS THAT? I HAVEN'T REALLY BEEN ABLE TO GET TO KNOW EVERYONE HERE, YET.
I DON'T BLAME YOU, THERE'S SO MANY PEOPLE. JUST THE OTHER DAY I MET A MAN WHO I SWEAR I'VE NEVER SEEN BEFORE.
IF I DIDN'T KNOW BETTER I'D SAY HE HAD SNUCK IN.
WAIT A MINUTE-- JESSIE? IS THAT PETE'S WIDOW?
HOW WELL DO YOU KNOW HER? YOU LEFT CARL WITH HER?
I KNOW HER WELL ENOUGH AND...
LOOK, CARL CAN TAKE CARE OF HIMSELF. I'M NOT WORRIED.
YOU'RE UP EARLY, SPENCER. WHAT'S GOT YOU OUT AND ABOUT?
OH, UH... IT'S ANDREA, ACTUALLY.
I KNEW HEATH HAD THIS MOUNTAIN CLIMBING ROPE AND RIG THAT HE'D FOUND. HE SAID HE WAS GOING TO USE IT IN THE CITY, TO GET UP INTO BUILDINGS TO LOOK FOR SUPPLIES WITHOUT HAVING TO DEAL WITH ALL THE WALKERS INSIDE.
BUT I FIGURED I COULD USE IT TO GET OVER THE FENCE TO ANDREA, GET HER SOME SUPPLIES.

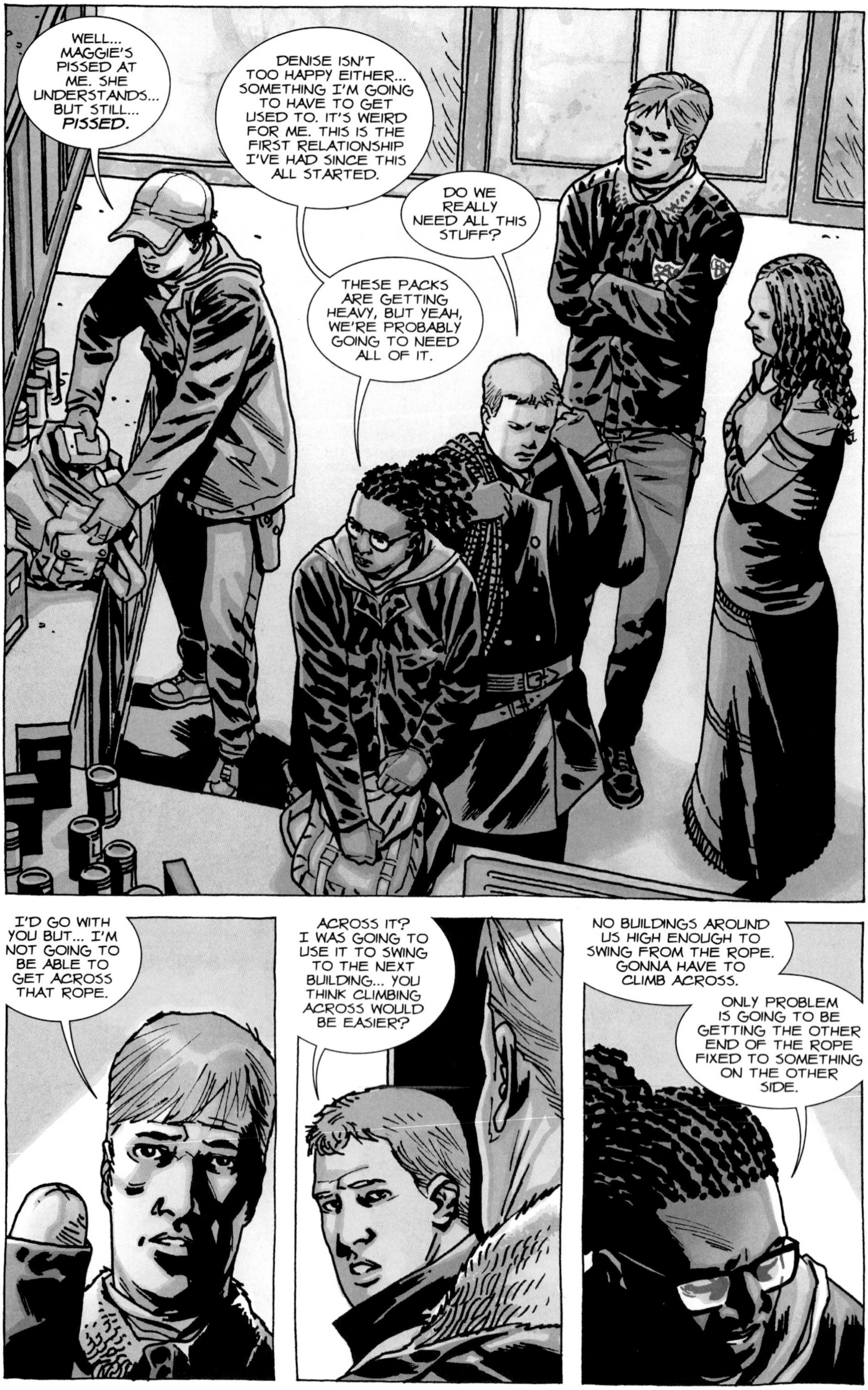
WELL... MAGGIE'S PISSED AT ME. SHE UNDERSTANDS... BUT STILL... PISSED.
DENISE ISN'T TOO HAPPY EITHER... SOMETHING I'M GOING TO HAVE TO GET USED TO. IT'S WEIRD FOR ME. THIS IS THE FIRST RELATIONSHIP I'VE HAD SINCE THIS ALL STARTED.
DO WE REALLY NEED ALL THIS STUFF?
THESE PACKS ARE GETTING HEAVY, BUT YEAH, WE'RE PROBABLY GOING TO NEED ALL OF IT.
I'D GO WITH YOU BUT... I'M NOT GOING TO BE ABLE TO GET ACROSS THAT ROPE.
ACROSS IT? I WAS GOING TO USE IT TO SWING TO THE NEXT BUILDING... YOU THINK CLIMBING ACROSS WOULD BE EASIER?
NO BUILDINGS AROUND US HIGH ENOUGH TO SWING FROM THE ROPE. GONNA HAVE TO CLIMB ACROSS.
ONLY PROBLEM IS GOING TO BE GETTING THE OTHER END OF THE ROPE FIXED TO SOMETHING ON THE OTHER SIDE.

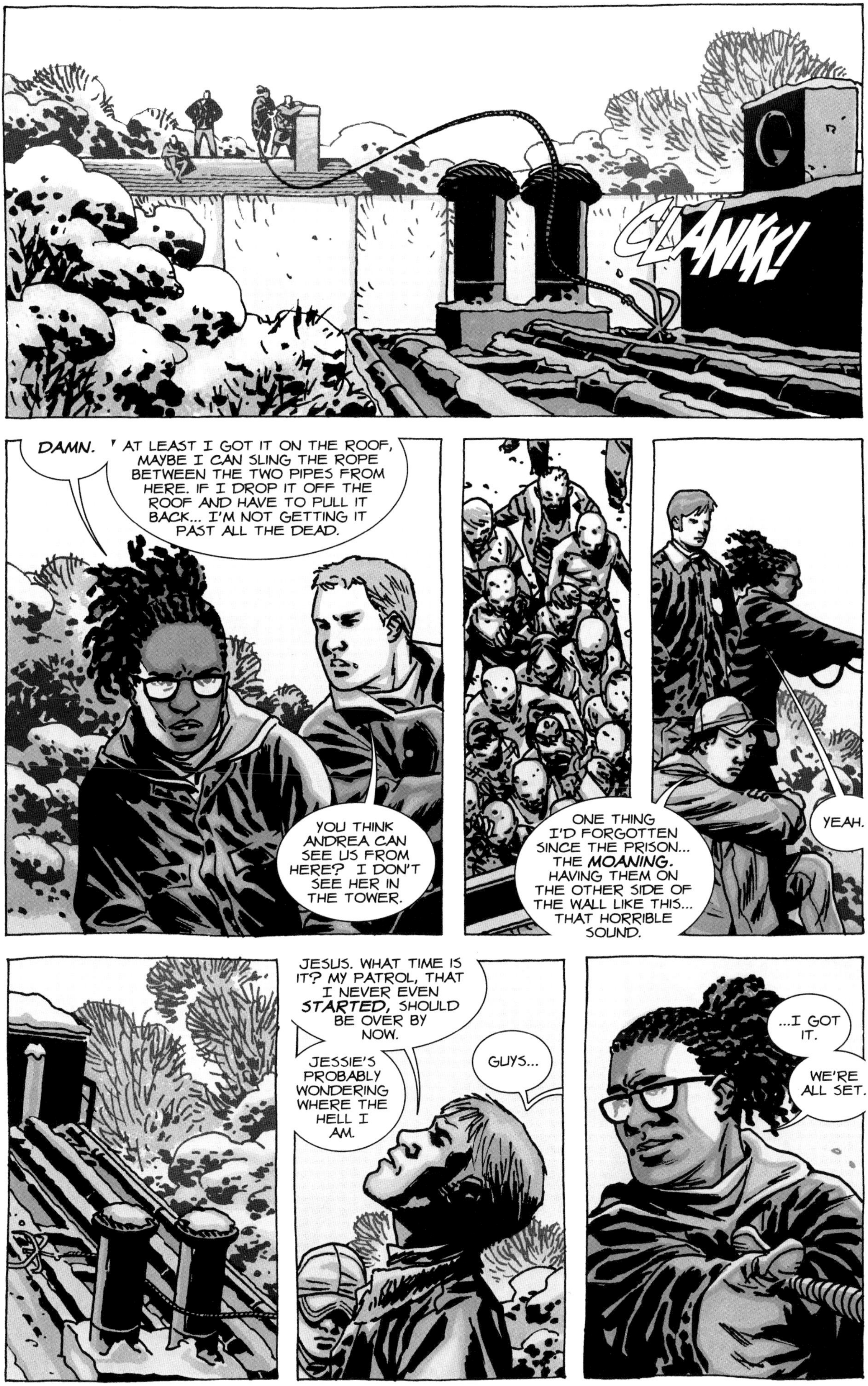

CLANKK!
DAMN.
AT LEAST I GOT IT ON THE ROOF, MAYBE I CAN SLING THE ROPE BETWEEN THE TWO PIPES FROM HERE. IF I DROP IT OFF THE ROOF AND HAVE TO PULL IT BACK... I'M NOT GETTING IT PAST ALL THE DEAD.
YOU THINK ANDREA CAN SEE US FROM HERE? I DON'T SEE HER IN THE TOWER.
ONE THING I'D FORGOTTEN SINCE THE PRISON... THE MOANING. HAVING THEM ON THE OTHER SIDE OF THE WALL LIKE THIS... THAT HORRIBLE SOUND.
YEAH.
JESUS. WHAT TIME IS IT? MY PATROL, THAT I NEVER EVEN STARTED, SHOULD BE OVER BY NOW.
JESSIE'S PROBABLY WONDERING WHERE THE HELL I AM.
GUYS...
...I GOT IT.
WE'RE ALL SET.

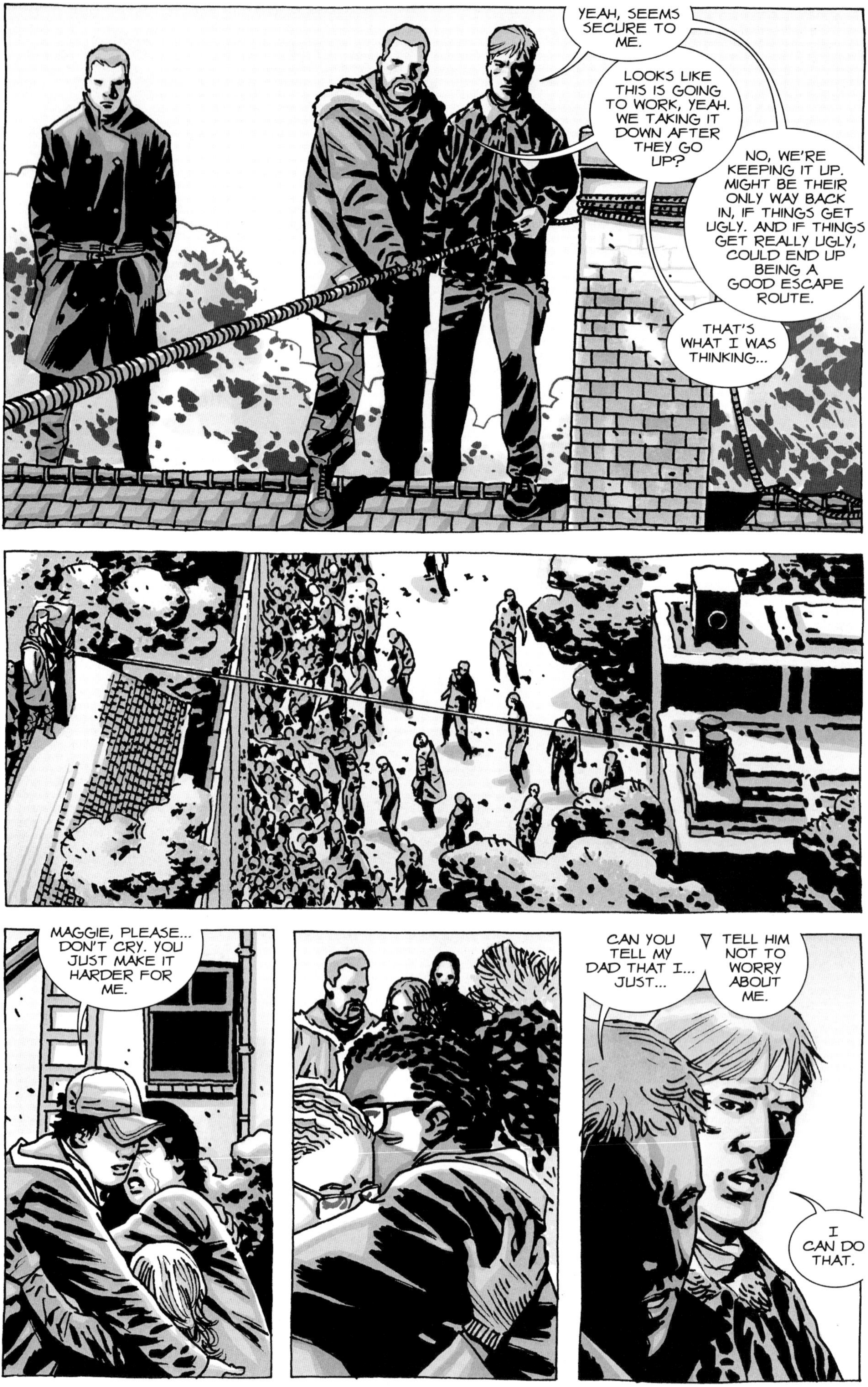
YEAH, SEEMS SECURE TO ME.
LOOKS LIKE THIS IS GOING TO WORK, YEAH. WE TAKING IT DOWN AFTER THEY GO UP?
NO, WE'RE KEEPING IT UP. MIGHT BE THEIR ONLY WAY BACK IN, IF THINGS GET UGLY. AND IF THINGS GET REALLY UGLY, COULD END UP BEING A GOOD ESCAPE ROUTE.
THAT'S WHAT I WAS THINKING...
MAGGIE, PLEASE... DON'T CRY. YOU JUST MAKE IT HARDER FOR ME.
CAN YOU TELL MY DAD THAT I... JUST...
TELL HIM NOT TO WORRY ABOUT ME.
I CAN DO THAT.

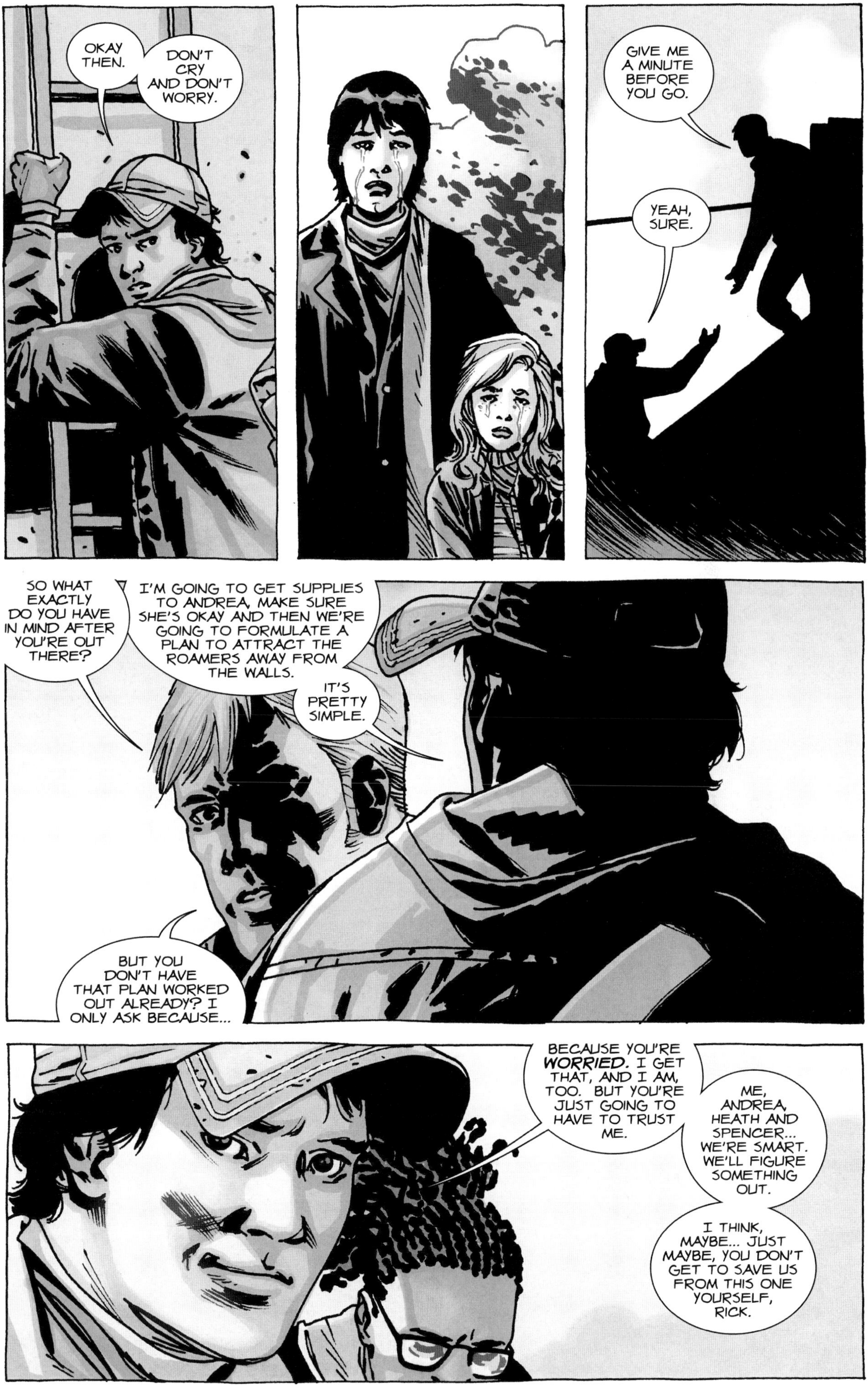
OKAY THEN.
DON'T CRY AND DON'T WORRY.
GIVE ME A MINUTE BEFORE YOU GO.
YEAH, SURE.
SO WHAT EXACTLY DO YOU HAVE IN MIND AFTER YOU'RE OUT THERE?
I'M GOING TO GET SUPPLIES TO ANDREA, MAKE SURE SHE'S OKAY AND THEN WE'RE GOING TO FORMULATE A PLAN TO ATTRACT THE ROAMERS AWAY FROM THE WALLS.
IT'S PRETTY SIMPLE.
BUT YOU DON'T HAVE THAT PLAN WORKED OUT ALREADY? I ONLY ASK BECAUSE...
BECAUSE YOU'RE *WORRIED.* I GET THAT, AND I AM, TOO. BUT YOU'RE JUST GOING TO HAVE TO TRUST ME.
ME, ANDREA, HEATH AND SPENCER... WE'RE SMART. WE'LL FIGURE SOMETHING OUT.
I THINK, MAYBE... JUST MAYBE, YOU DON'T GET TO SAVE US FROM THIS ONE YOURSELF, RICK.

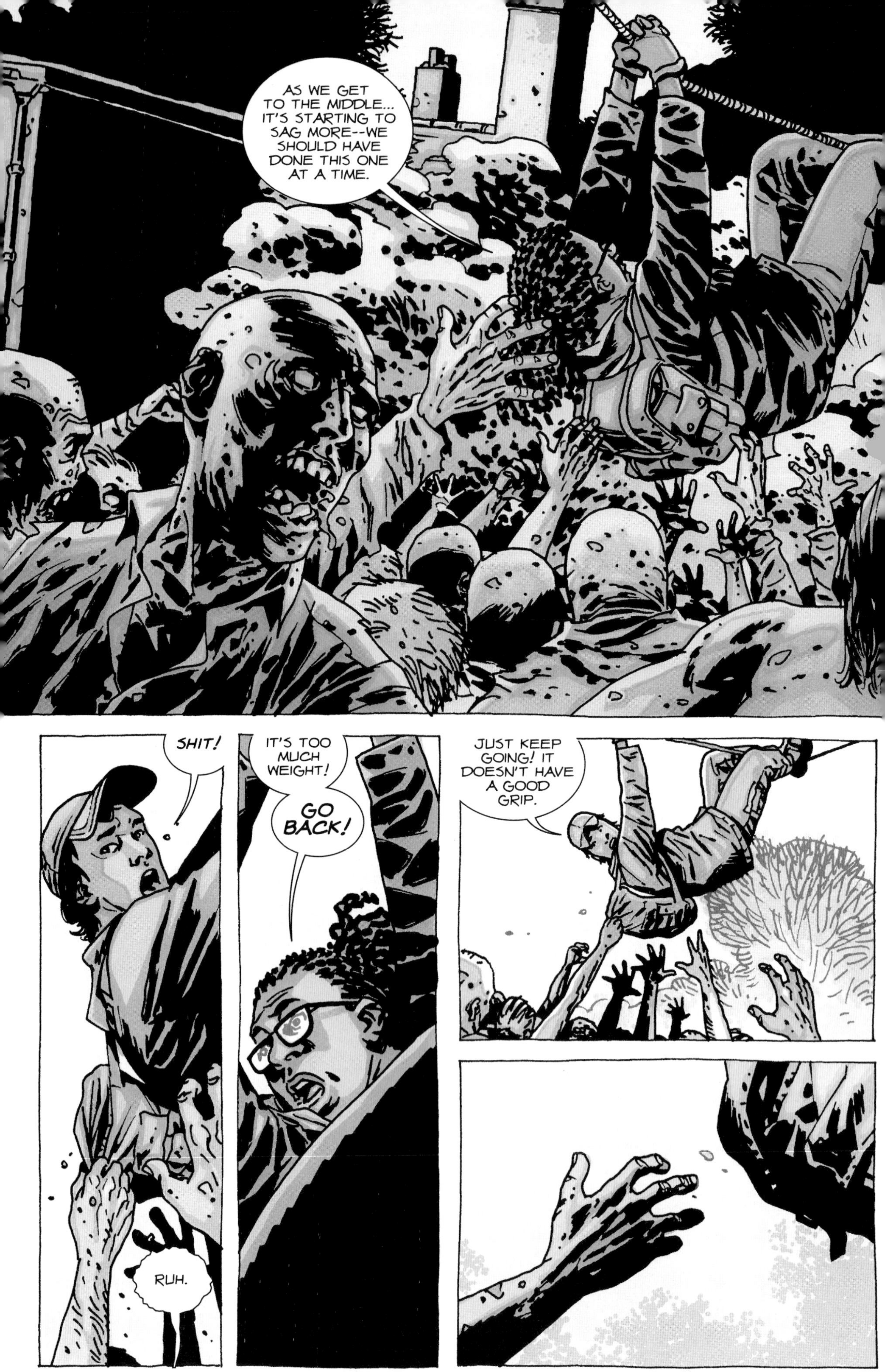
AS WE GET TO THE MIDDLE... IT'S STARTING TO SAG MORE--WE SHOULD HAVE DONE THIS ONE AT A TIME.
SHIT!
RUH.
IT'S TOO MUCH WEIGHT!
GO BACK!
JUST KEEP GOING! IT DOESN'T HAVE A GOOD GRIP.

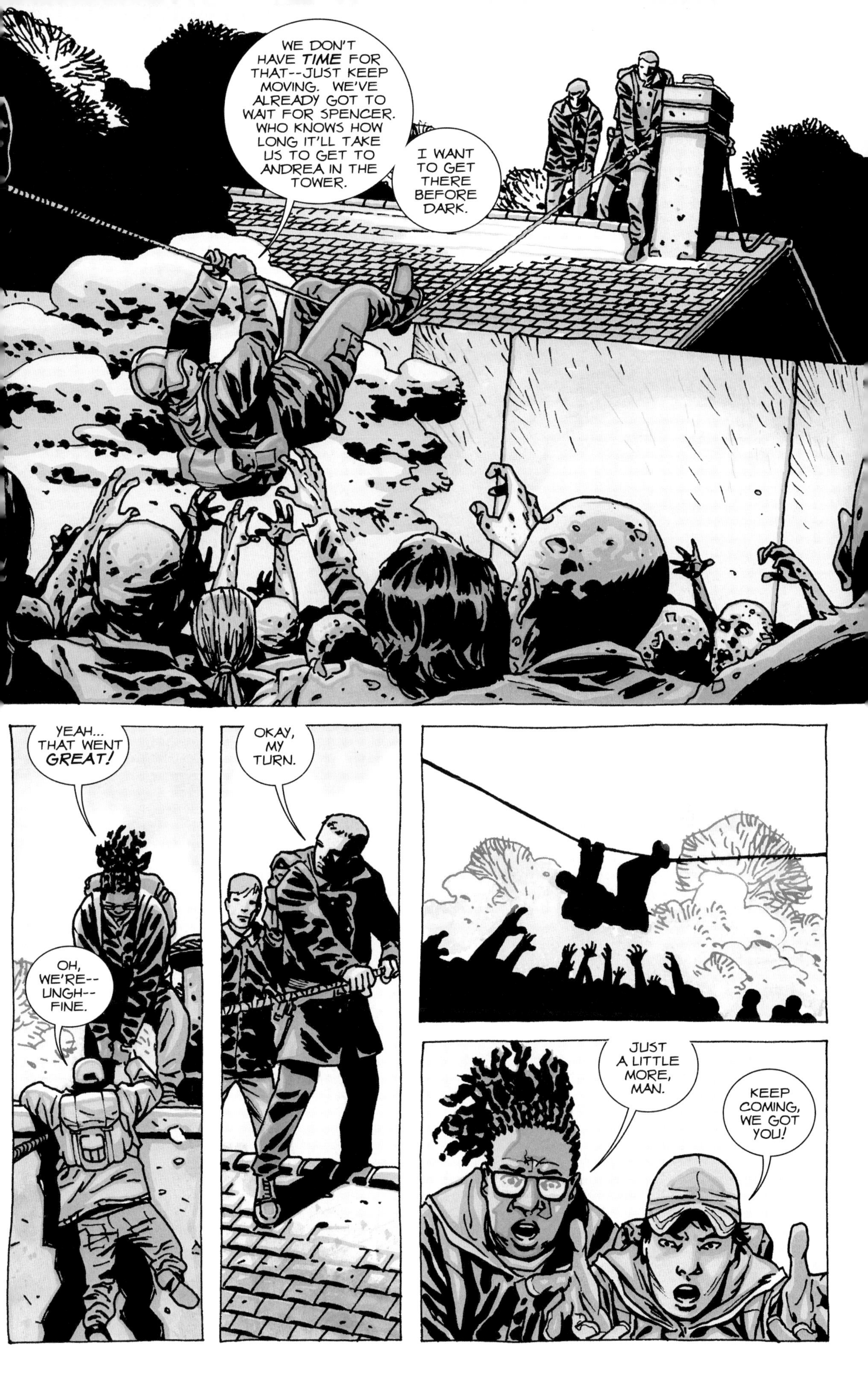
WE DON'T HAVE TIME FOR THAT--JUST KEEP MOVING. WE'VE ALREADY GOT TO WAIT FOR SPENCER. WHO KNOWS HOW LONG IT'LL TAKE US TO GET TO ANDREA IN THE TOWER.
I WANT TO GET THERE BEFORE DARK.
YEAH... THAT WENT GREAT!
OH, WE'RE-- UNGH-- FINE.
OKAY, MY TURN.
JUST A LITTLE MORE, MAN.
KEEP COMING, WE GOT YOU!

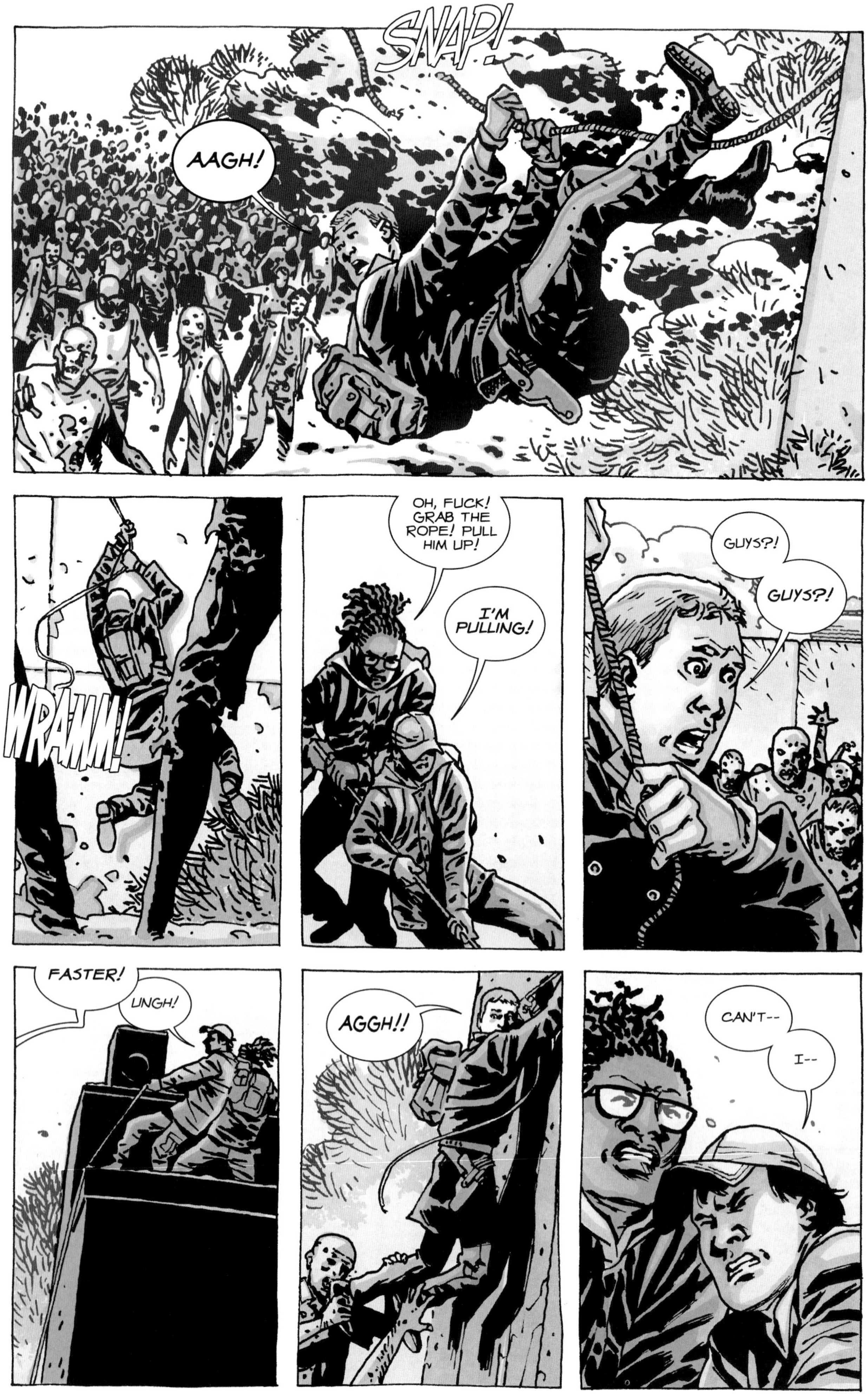
SNAP!
AAGH!
WRAMM!
OH, FUCK! GRAB THE ROPE! PULL HIM UP!
I'M PULLING!
GUYS?!
GUYS?!
FASTER!
UNGH!
AGGH!!
CAN'T--
I--

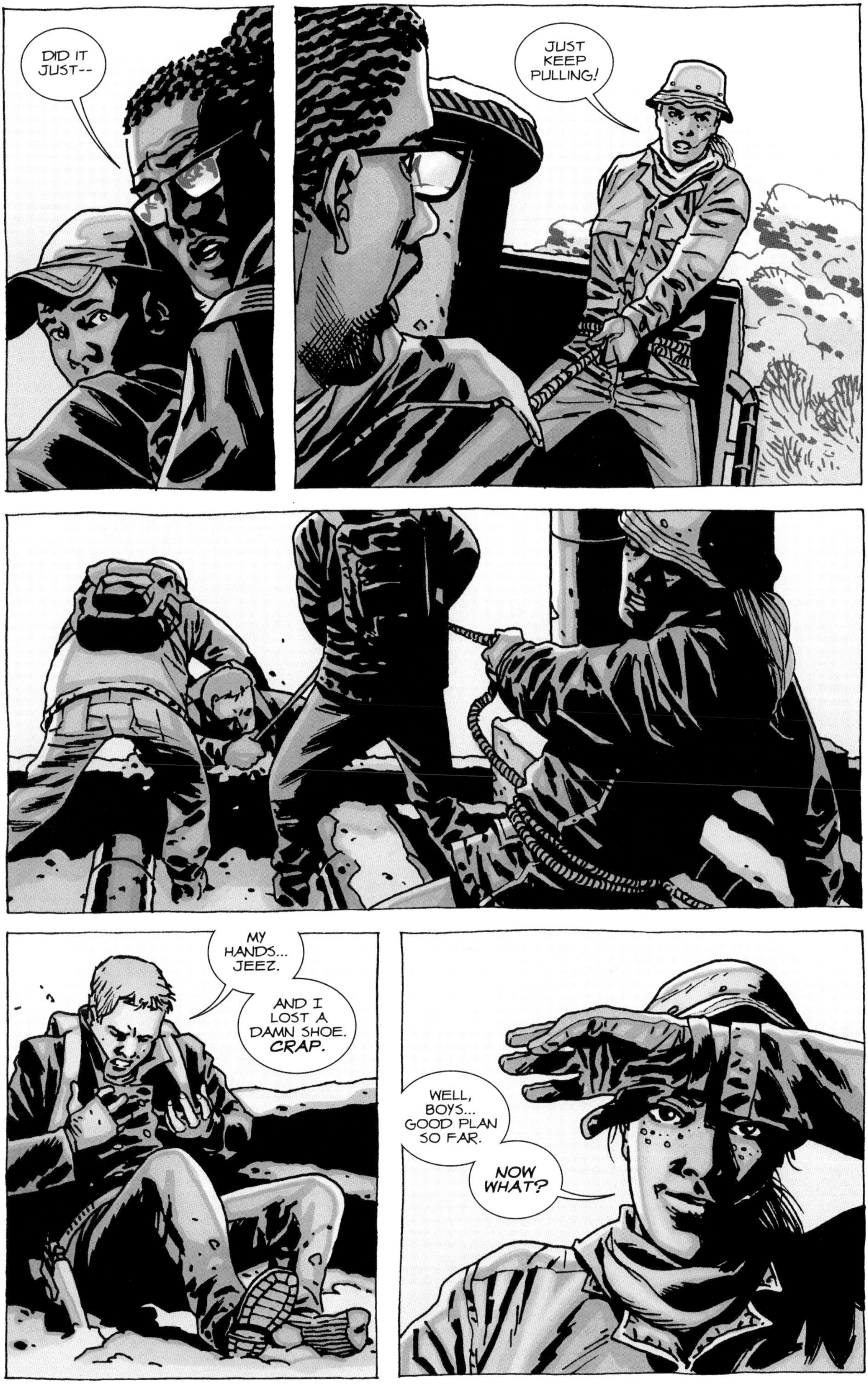
DID IT JUST--
JUST KEEP PULLING!
MY HANDS... JEEZ.
AND I LOST A DAMN SHOE. CRAP.
WELL, BOYS... GOOD PLAN SO FAR.
NOW WHAT?

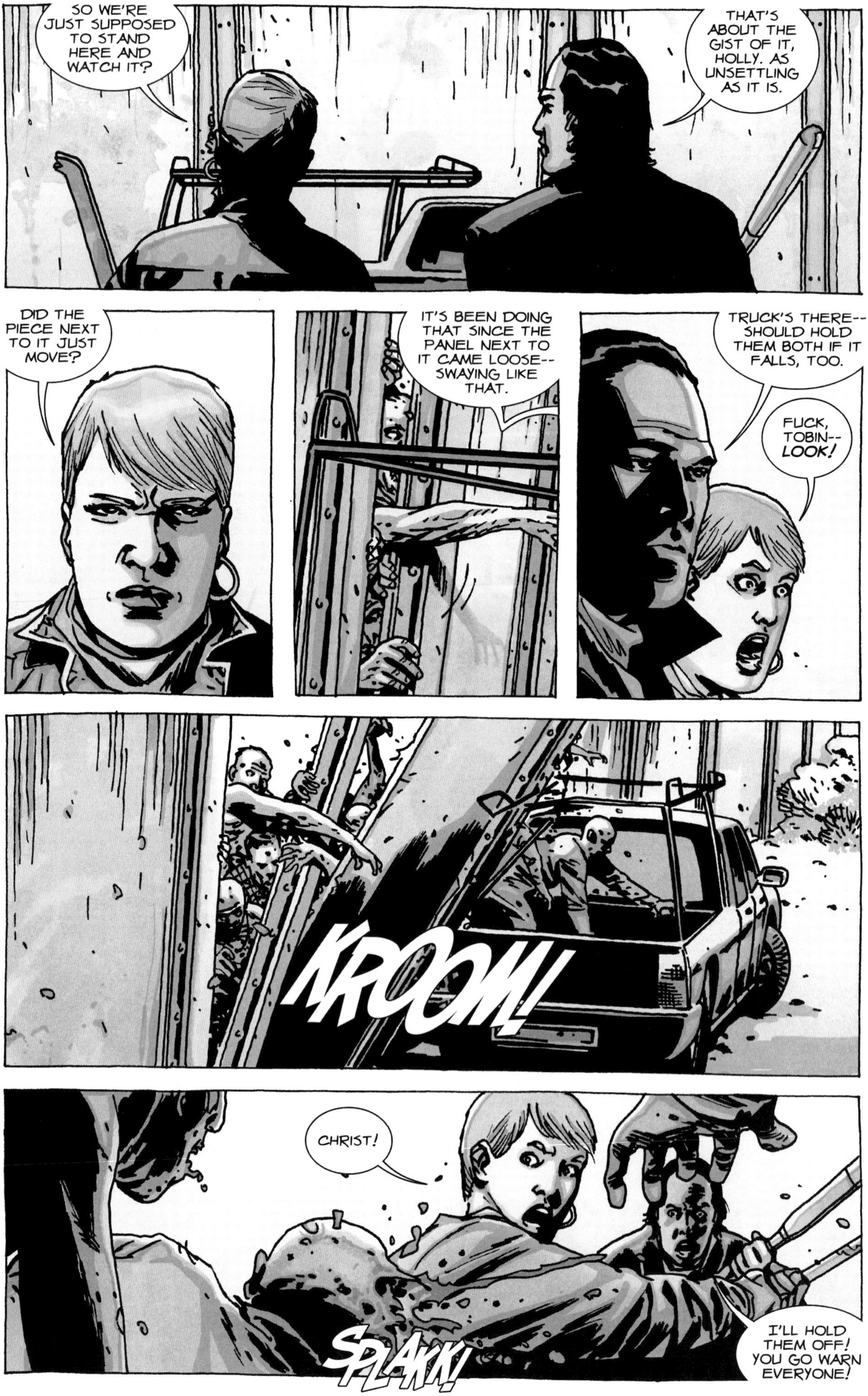
SO WE'RE JUST SUPPOSED TO STAND HERE AND WATCH IT?
THAT'S ABOUT THE GIST OF IT, HOLLY. AS UNSETTLING AS IT IS.
DID THE PIECE NEXT TO IT JUST MOVE?
IT'S BEEN DOING THAT SINCE THE PANEL NEXT TO IT CAME LOOSE-- SWAYING LIKE THAT.
TRUCK'S THERE-- SHOULD HOLD THEM BOTH IF IT FALLS, TOO.
FUCK, TOBIN-- LOOK!
KROOM!
CHRIST!
SPLAKK!
I'LL HOLD THEM OFF! YOU GO WARN EVERYONE!

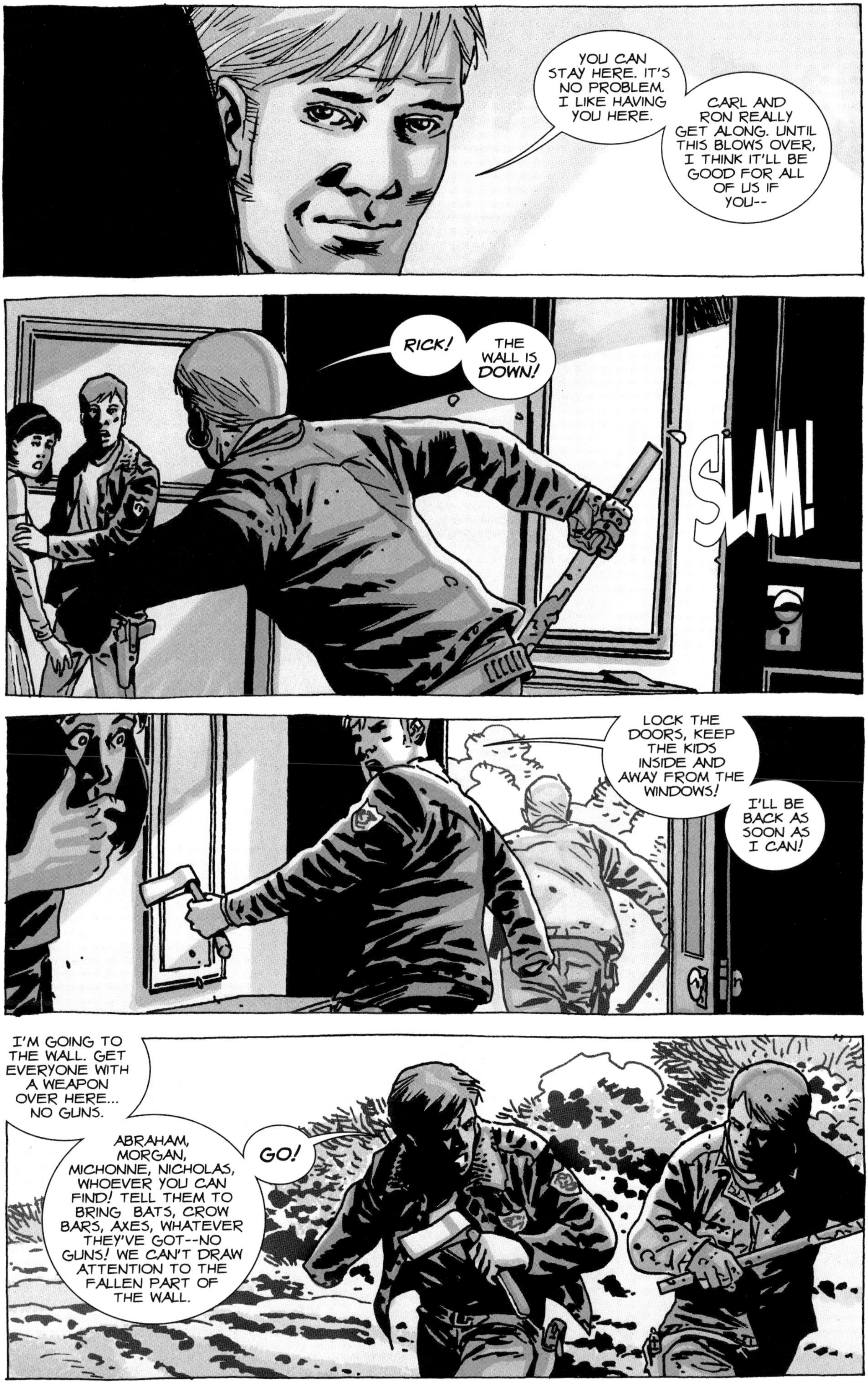
YOU CAN STAY HERE. IT'S NO PROBLEM. I LIKE HAVING YOU HERE.
CARL AND RON REALLY GET ALONG. UNTIL THIS BLOWS OVER, I THINK IT'LL BE GOOD FOR ALL OF US IF YOU--
RICK!
THE WALL IS DOWN!
SLAM!
LOCK THE DOORS, KEEP THE KIDS INSIDE AND AWAY FROM THE WINDOWS!
I'LL BE BACK AS SOON AS I CAN!
I'M GOING TO THE WALL. GET EVERYONE WITH A WEAPON OVER HERE... NO GUNS.
ABRAHAM, MORGAN, MICHONNE, NICHOLAS, WHOEVER YOU CAN FIND! TELL THEM TO BRING BATS, CROW BARS, AXES, WHATEVER THEY'VE GOT--NO GUNS! WE CAN'T DRAW ATTENTION TO THE FALLEN PART OF THE WALL.
GO!

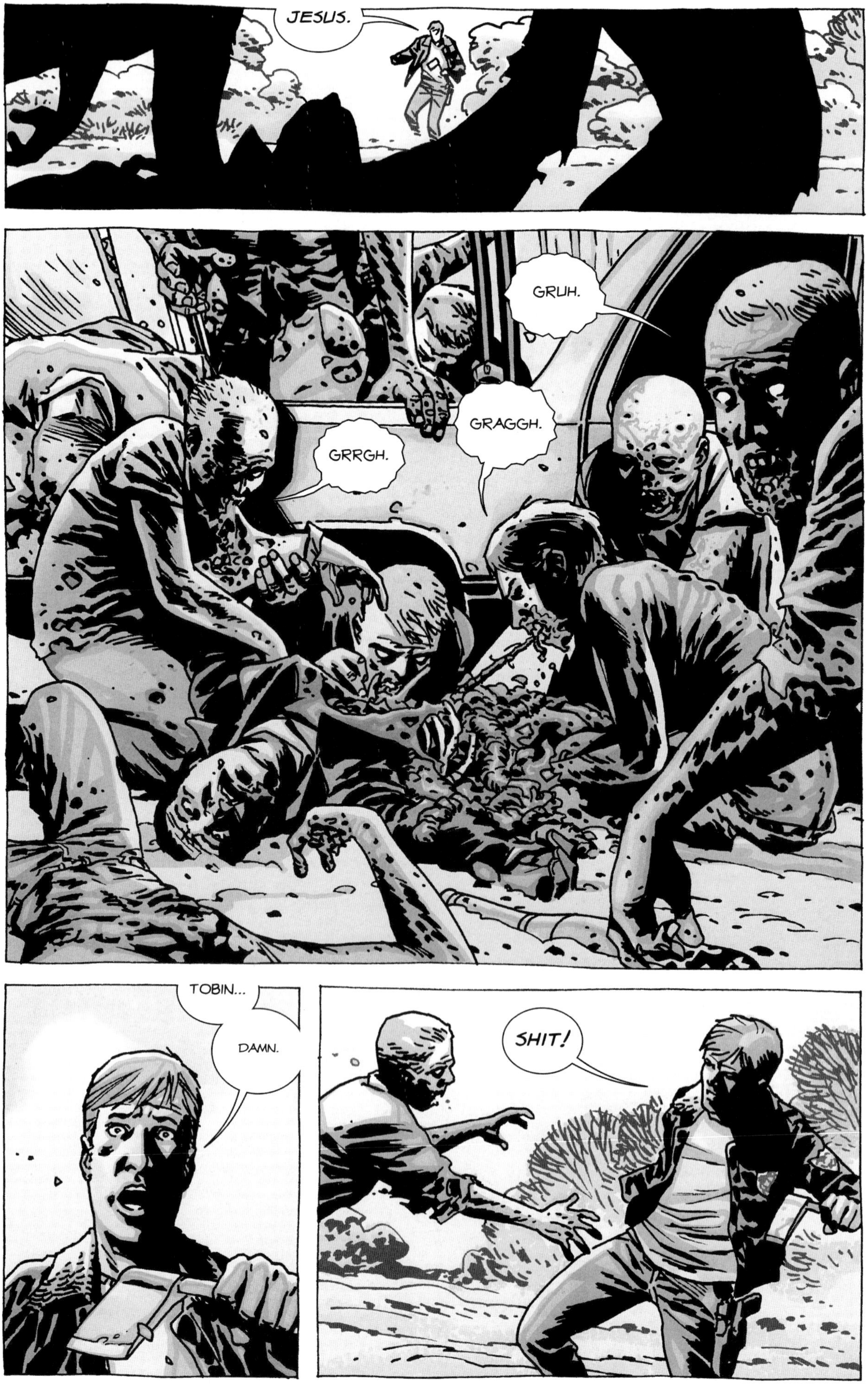
JESUS.
GRUH.
GRAGGH.
GRRGH.
TOBIN...
DAMN.
SHIT!

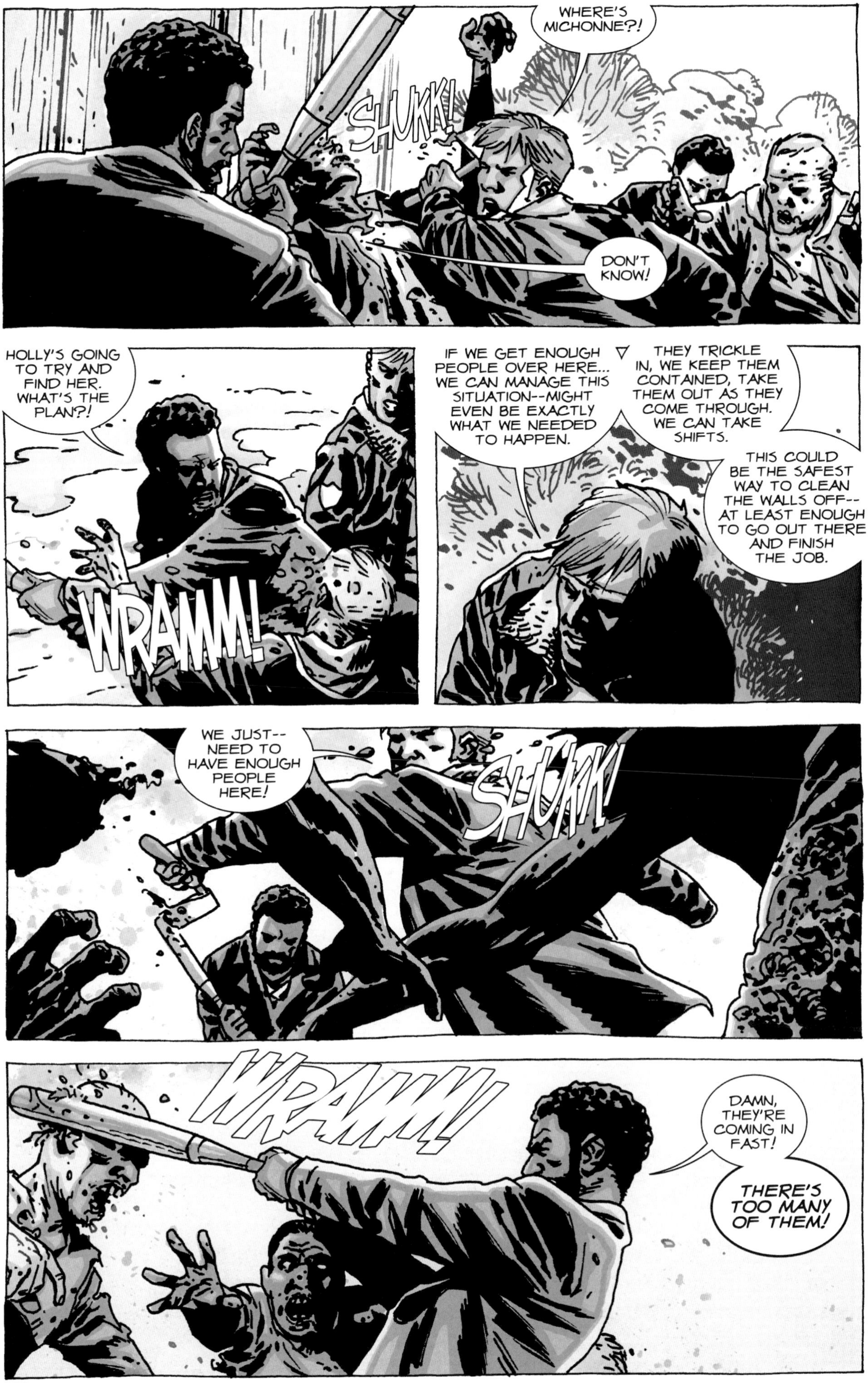
WHERE'S MICHONNE?!
SHUKK!
DON'T KNOW!
HOLLY'S GOING TO TRY AND FIND HER. WHAT'S THE PLAN?!
WRAMM!
IF WE GET ENOUGH PEOPLE OVER HERE... WE CAN MANAGE THIS SITUATION--MIGHT EVEN BE EXACTLY WHAT WE NEEDED TO HAPPEN.
THEY TRICKLE IN, WE KEEP THEM CONTAINED, TAKE THEM OUT AS THEY COME THROUGH. WE CAN TAKE SHIFTS.
THIS COULD BE THE SAFEST WAY TO CLEAN THE WALLS OFF--AT LEAST ENOUGH TO GO OUT THERE AND FINISH THE JOB.
WE JUST--NEED TO HAVE ENOUGH PEOPLE HERE!
SHUKK!
WRAMM!
DAMN, THEY'RE COMING IN FAST!
THERE'S TOO MANY OF THEM!

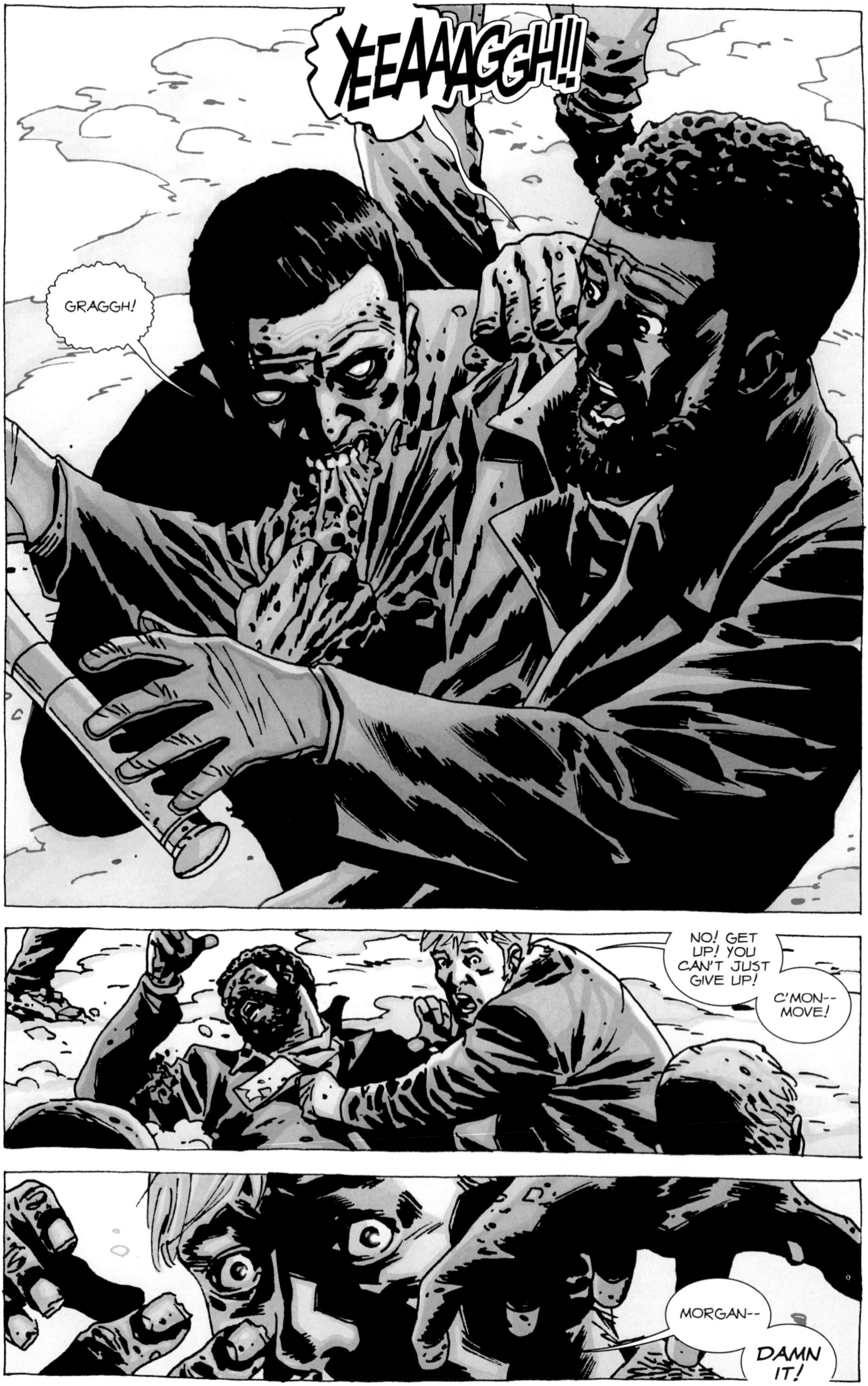

YEEAAAAGGH!!
GRAGGH!
NO! GET UP! YOU CAN'T JUST GIVE UP!
C'MON-- MOVE!
MORGAN--
DAMN IT!

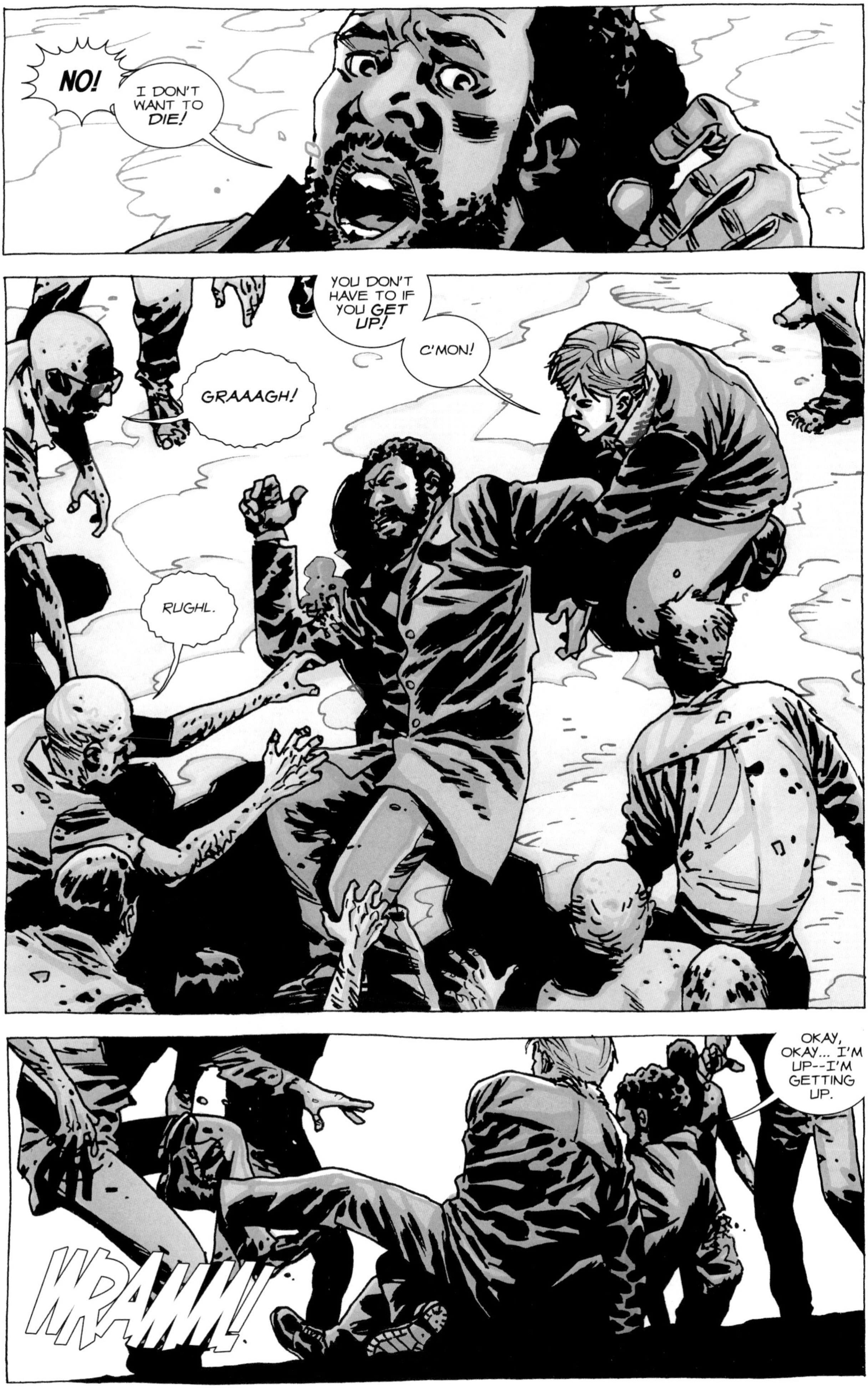
NO!
I DON'T WANT TO DIE!
YOU DON'T HAVE TO IF YOU GET UP!
C'MON!
GRAAAGH!
RUGHL.
OKAY, OKAY... I'M UP--I'M GETTING UP.
WRAMM!

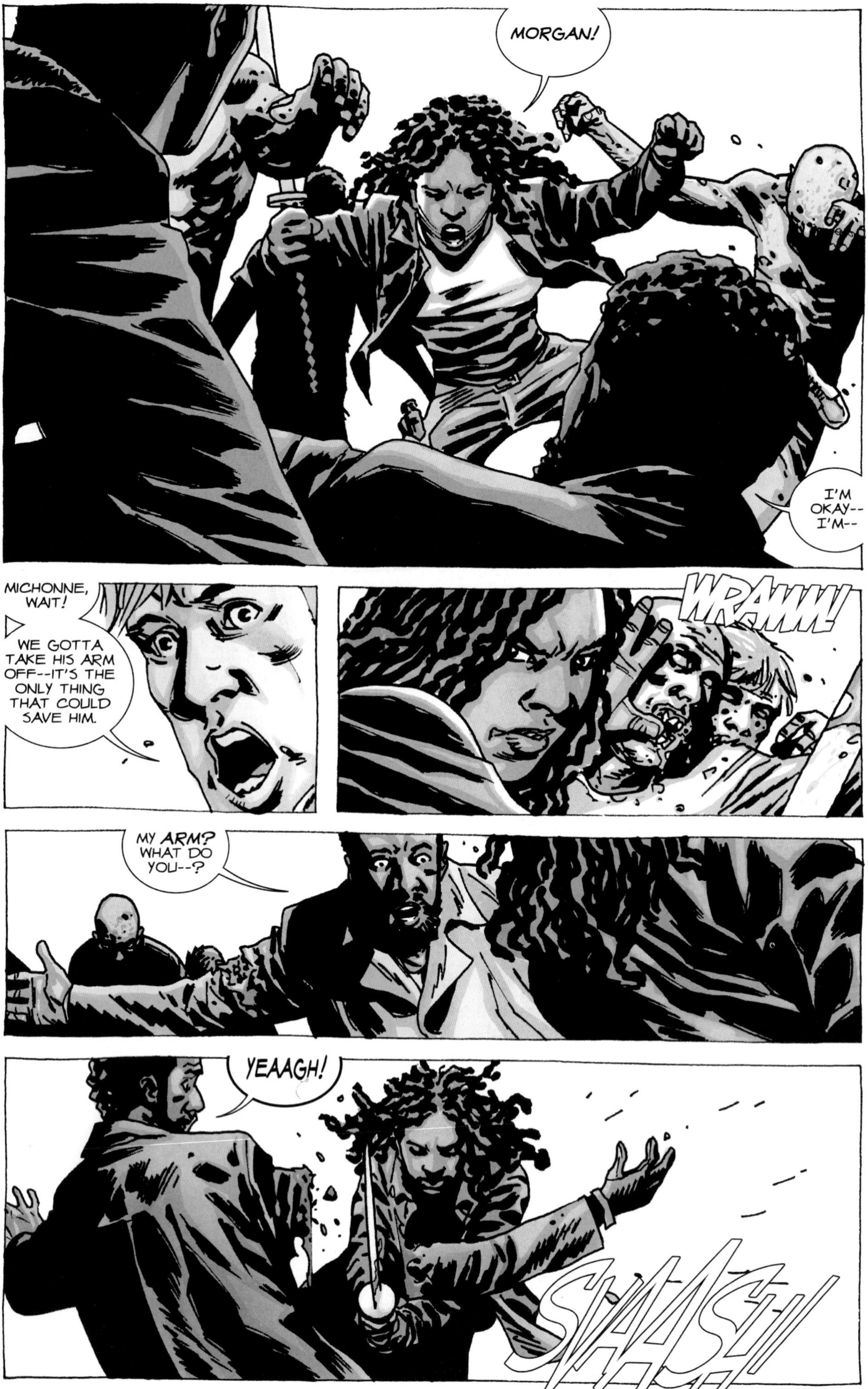

MORGAN!
I'M OKAY-- I'M--
MICHONNE, WAIT!
WE GOTTA TAKE HIS ARM OFF--IT'S THE ONLY THING THAT COULD SAVE HIM.
WRAAAAA!
MY ARM? WHAT DO YOU--?
YEAAGH!
SHAASH!

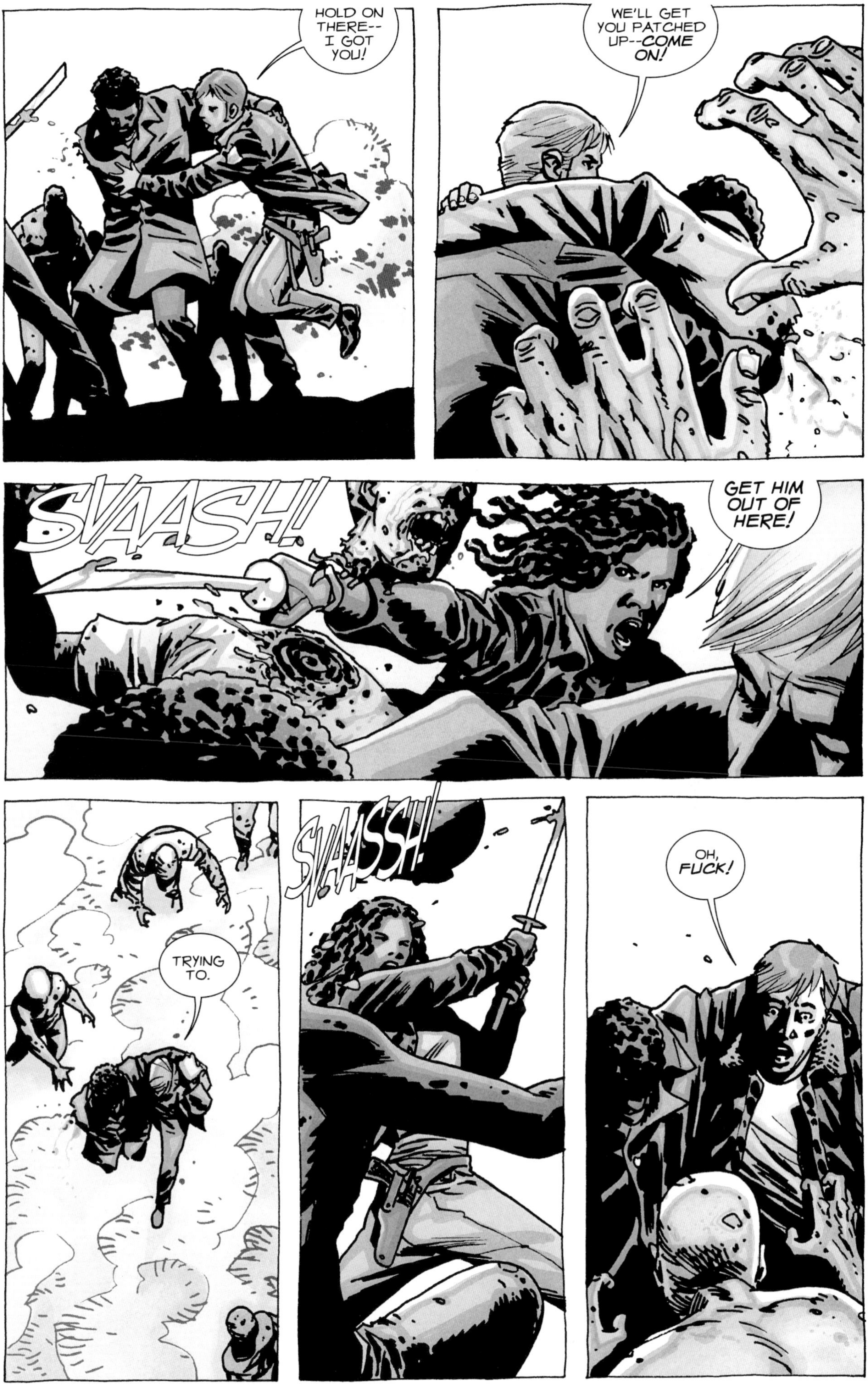
HOLD ON THERE-- I GOT YOU!
WE'LL GET YOU PATCHED UP--COME ON!
SVAASH!
GET HIM OUT OF HERE!
TRYING TO.
SVAASSH!
OH, FUCK!

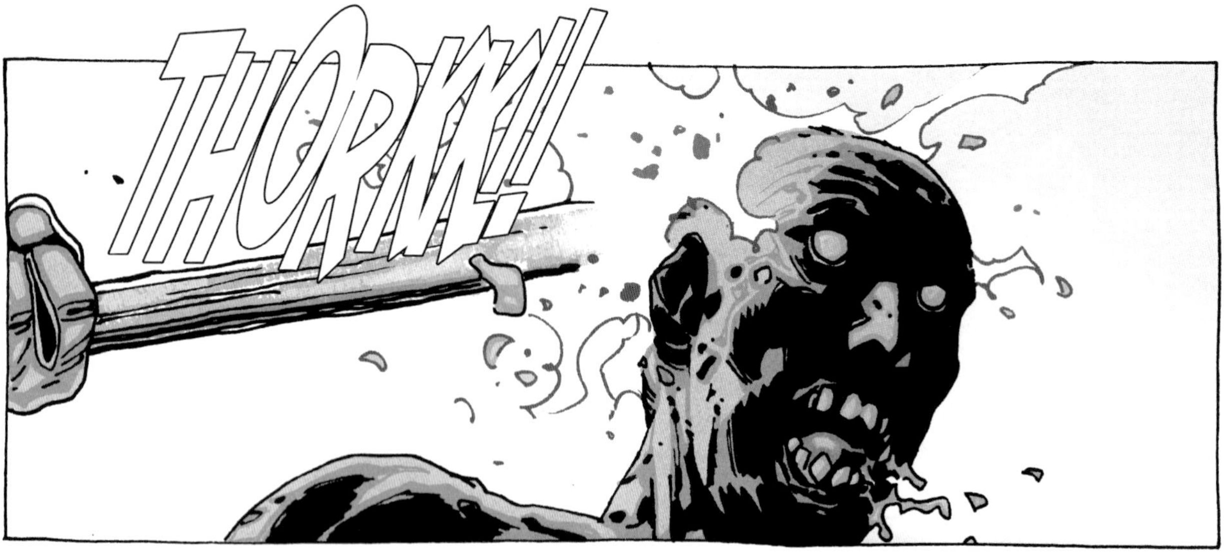
THORKK!!

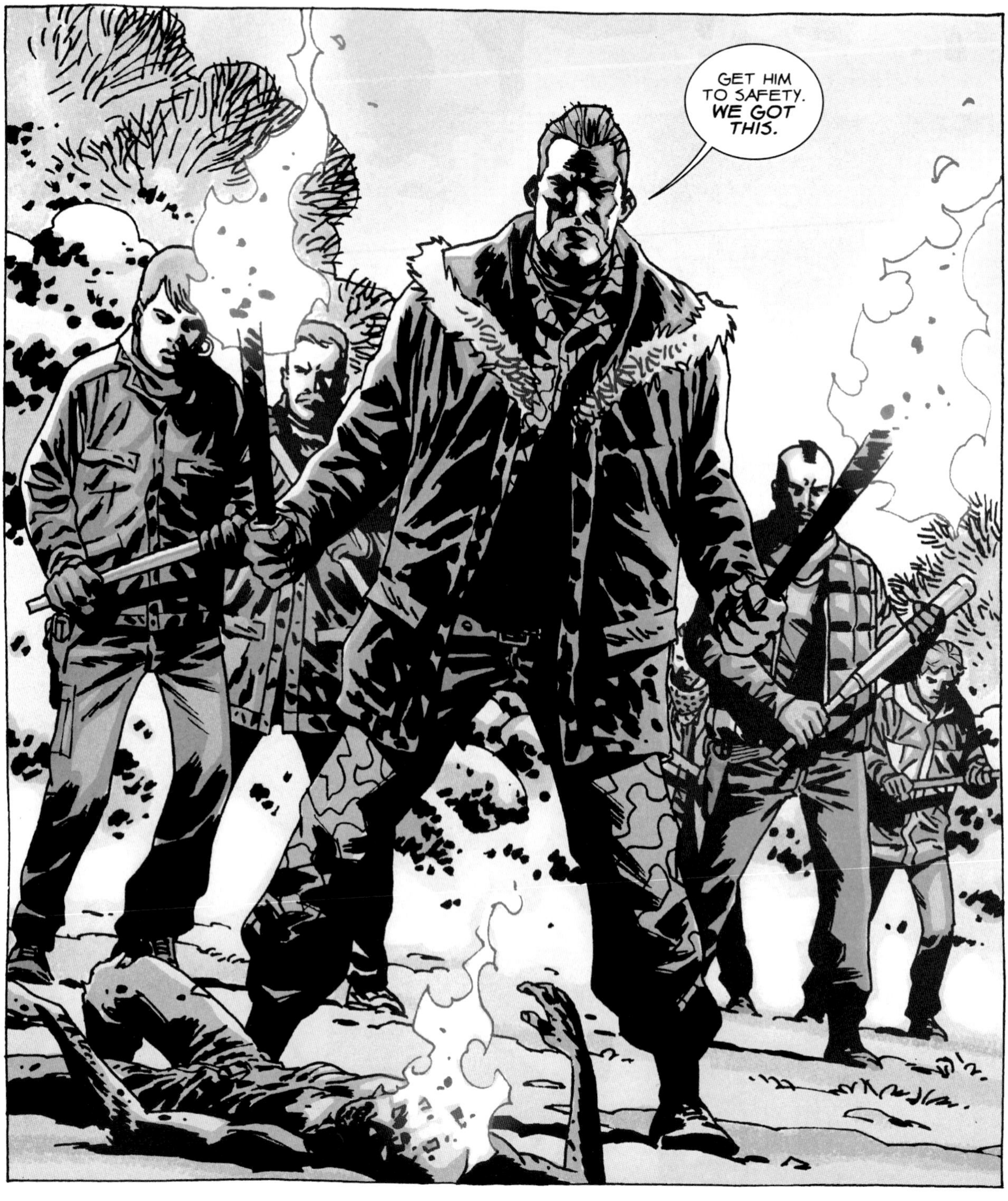
GET HIM TO SAFETY. WE GOT THIS.

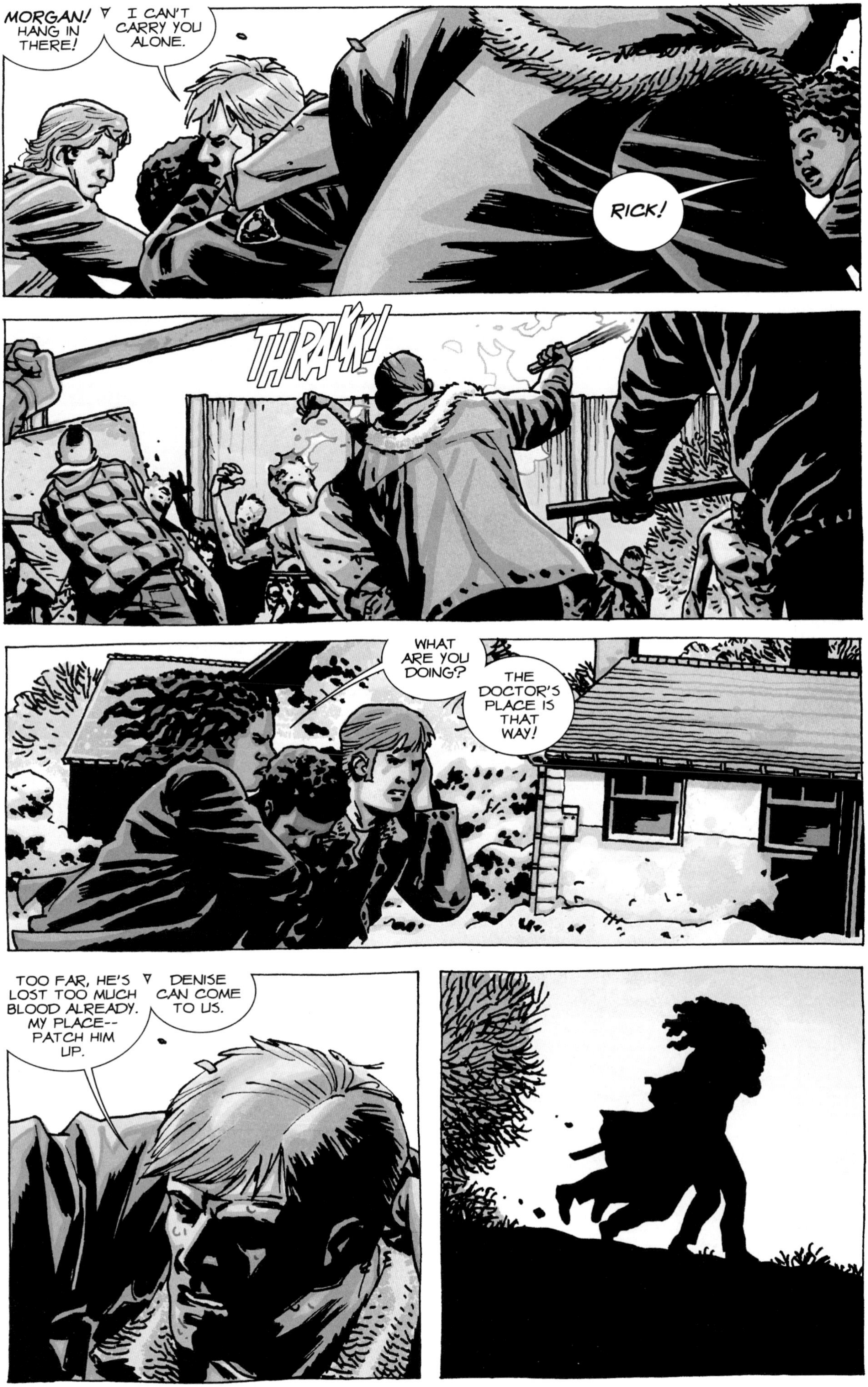
MORGAN! HANG IN THERE!
I CAN'T CARRY YOU ALONE.
RICK!
THRAKK!
WHAT ARE YOU DOING?
THE DOCTOR'S PLACE IS THAT WAY!
TOO FAR, HE'S LOST TOO MUCH BLOOD ALREADY. MY PLACE-- PATCH HIM UP.
DENISE CAN COME TO US.

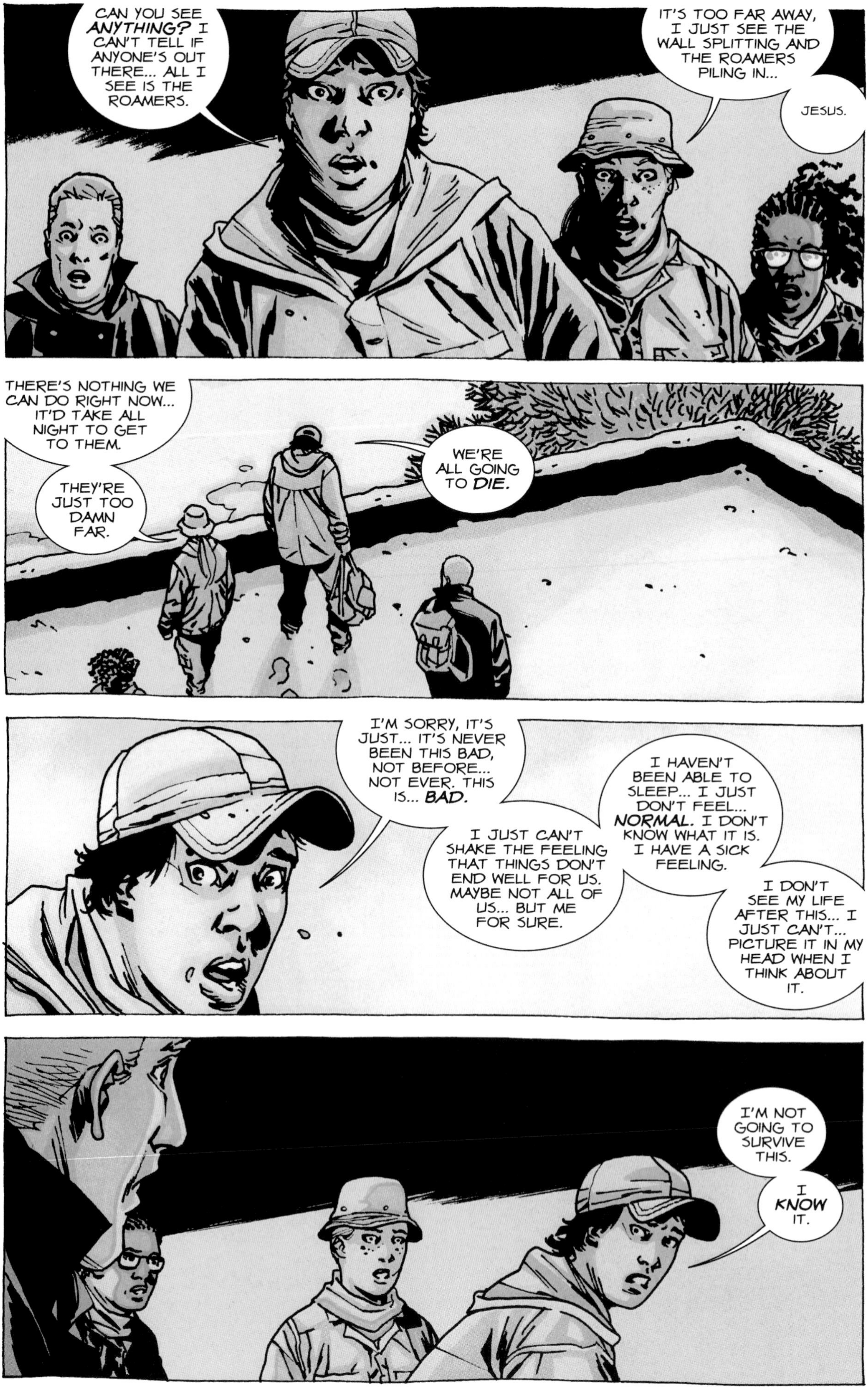
CAN YOU SEE ANYTHING? I CAN'T TELL IF ANYONE'S OUT THERE... ALL I SEE IS THE ROAMERS.
IT'S TOO FAR AWAY, I JUST SEE THE WALL SPLITTING AND THE ROAMERS PILING IN...
JESUS.
THERE'S NOTHING WE CAN DO RIGHT NOW... IT'D TAKE ALL NIGHT TO GET TO THEM.
THEY'RE JUST TOO DAMN FAR.
WE'RE ALL GOING TO DIE.
I'M SORRY, IT'S JUST... IT'S NEVER BEEN THIS BAD, NOT BEFORE... NOT EVER. THIS IS... BAD.
I JUST CAN'T SHAKE THE FEELING THAT THINGS DON'T END WELL FOR US. MAYBE NOT ALL OF US... BUT ME FOR SURE.
I HAVEN'T BEEN ABLE TO SLEEP... I JUST DON'T FEEL... NORMAL. I DON'T KNOW WHAT IT IS. I HAVE A SICK FEELING.
I DON'T SEE MY LIFE AFTER THIS... I JUST CAN'T... PICTURE IT IN MY HEAD WHEN I THINK ABOUT IT.
I'M NOT GOING TO SURVIVE THIS.
I KNOW IT.

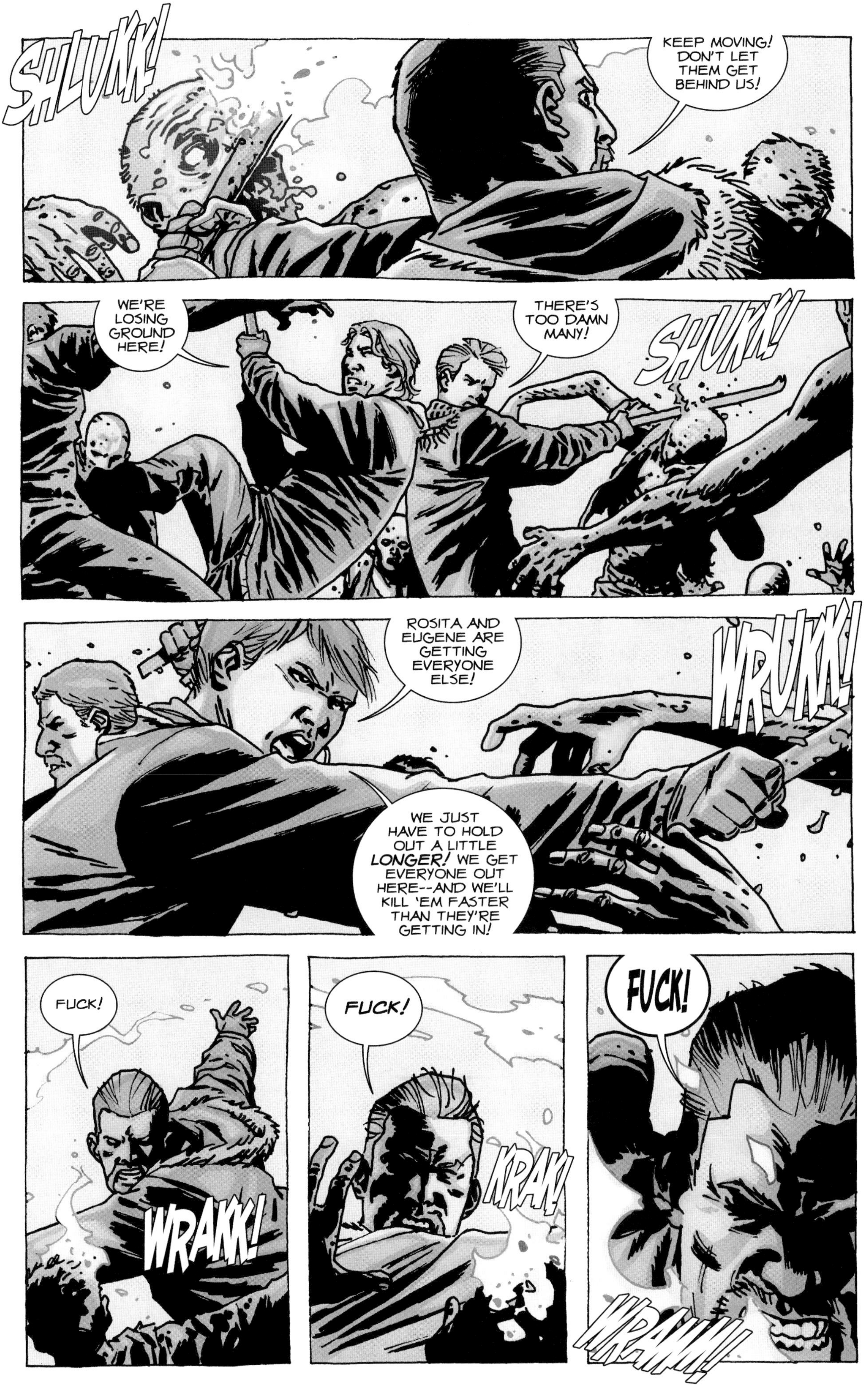
SHLUKK!
KEEP MOVING! DON'T LET THEM GET BEHIND US!
WE'RE LOSING GROUND HERE!
THERE'S TOO DAMN MANY!
SHUKK!
ROSITA AND EUGENE ARE GETTING EVERYONE ELSE!
WRUKK!
WE JUST HAVE TO HOLD OUT A LITTLE LONGER! WE GET EVERYONE OUT HERE--AND WE'LL KILL 'EM FASTER THAN THEY'RE GETTING IN!
FUCK!
WRAKK!
FUCK!
KRAK!
FUCK!
WRAMM!

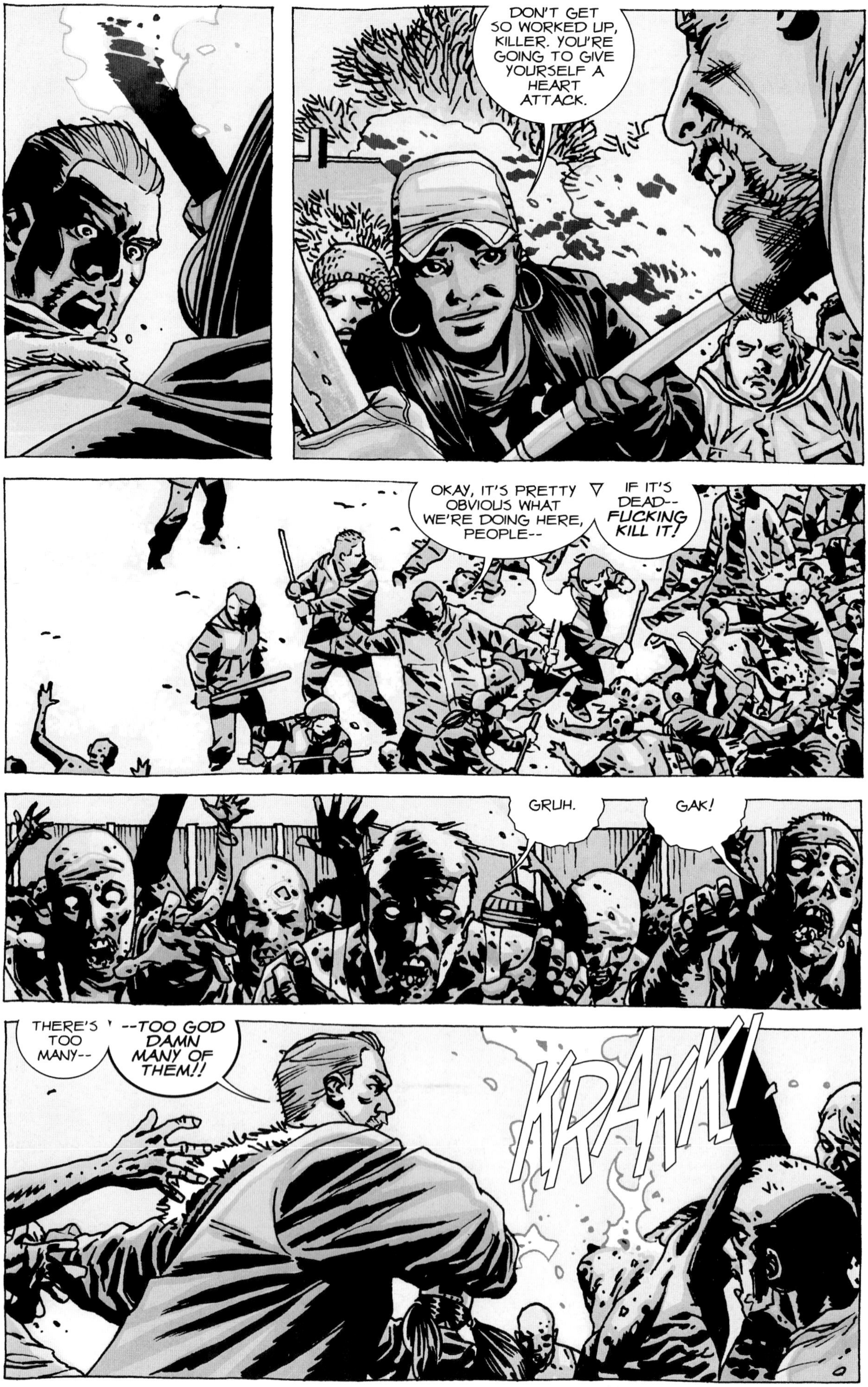
DON'T GET SO WORKED UP, KILLER. YOU'RE GOING TO GIVE YOURSELF A HEART ATTACK.
OKAY, IT'S PRETTY OBVIOUS WHAT WE'RE DOING HERE, PEOPLE--
IF IT'S DEAD-- FUCKING KILL IT!
GRUH.
GAK!
THERE'S TOO MANY--
--TOO GOD DAMN MANY OF THEM!!
KRAKK!

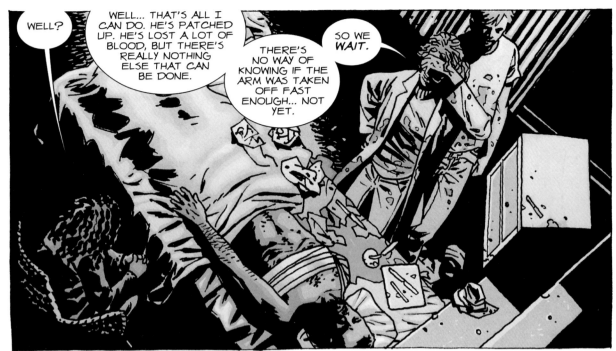

WELL?

WELL... THAT'S ALL I CAN DO. HE'S PATCHED UP. HE'S LOST A LOT OF BLOOD, BUT THERE'S REALLY NOTHING ELSE THAT CAN BE DONE.

THERE'S NO WAY OF KNOWING IF THE ARM WAS TAKEN OFF FAST ENOUGH... NOT YET.

SO WE WAIT.

HE SHOULD BE AWAKE SOON. HE'LL BE WEAK, BUT AS LONG AS THE BITE DIDN'T INFECT HIM, HE'LL BE OKAY.

YOU PRAY?

NOT REALLY. NO.

NOTHING YOU CAN DO EITHER, THEN. SORRY.

HE OKAY?

DON'T KNOW YET.

MORGAN... YOU'RE A DAMN FOOL.

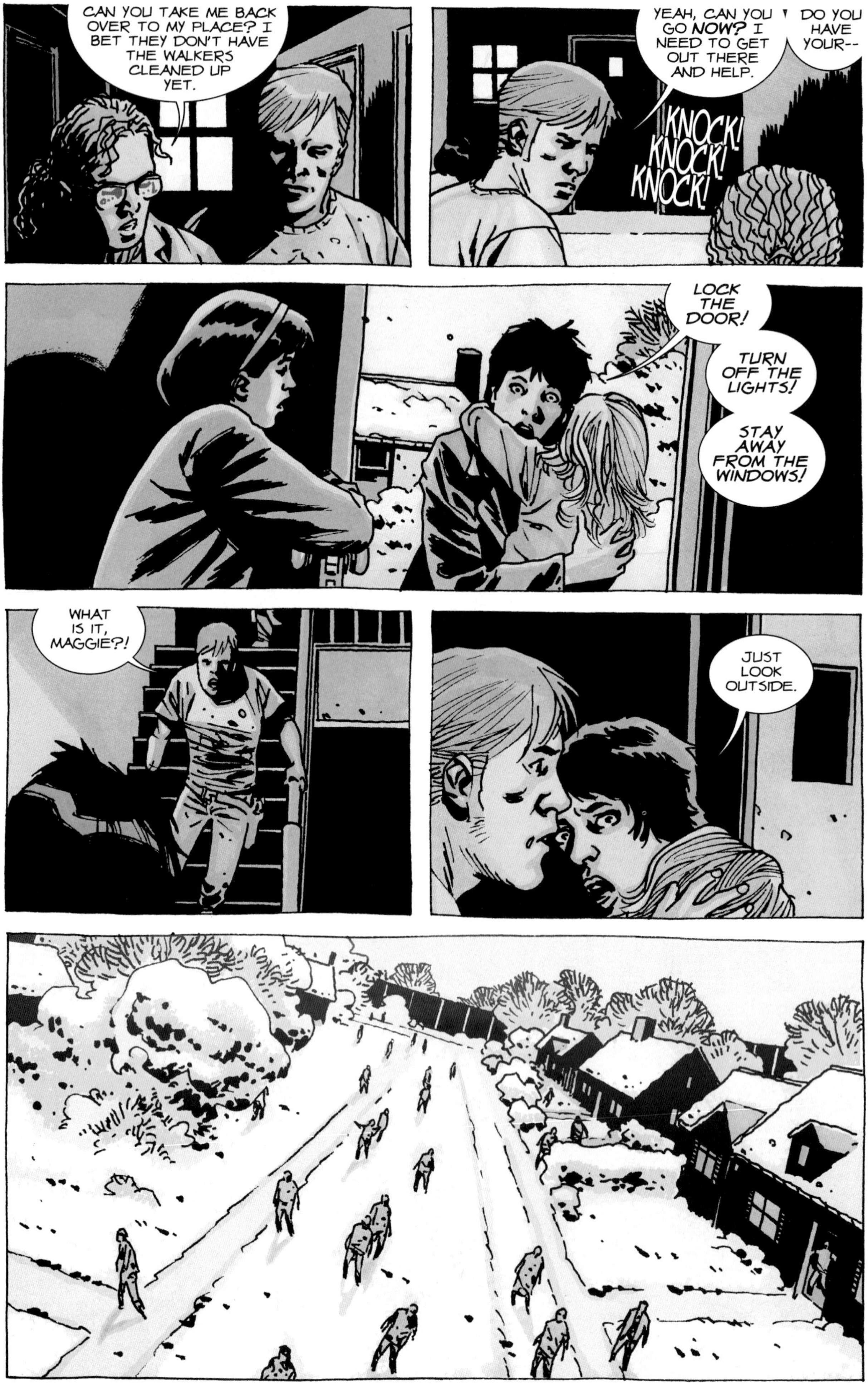
CAN YOU TAKE ME BACK OVER TO MY PLACE? I BET THEY DON'T HAVE THE WALKERS CLEANED UP YET.
YEAH, CAN YOU GO NOW? I NEED TO GET OUT THERE AND HELP.
DO YOU HAVE YOUR--
KNOCK! KNOCK! KNOCK!
LOCK THE DOOR!
TURN OFF THE LIGHTS!
STAY AWAY FROM THE WINDOWS!
WHAT IS IT, MAGGIE?!
JUST LOOK OUTSIDE.

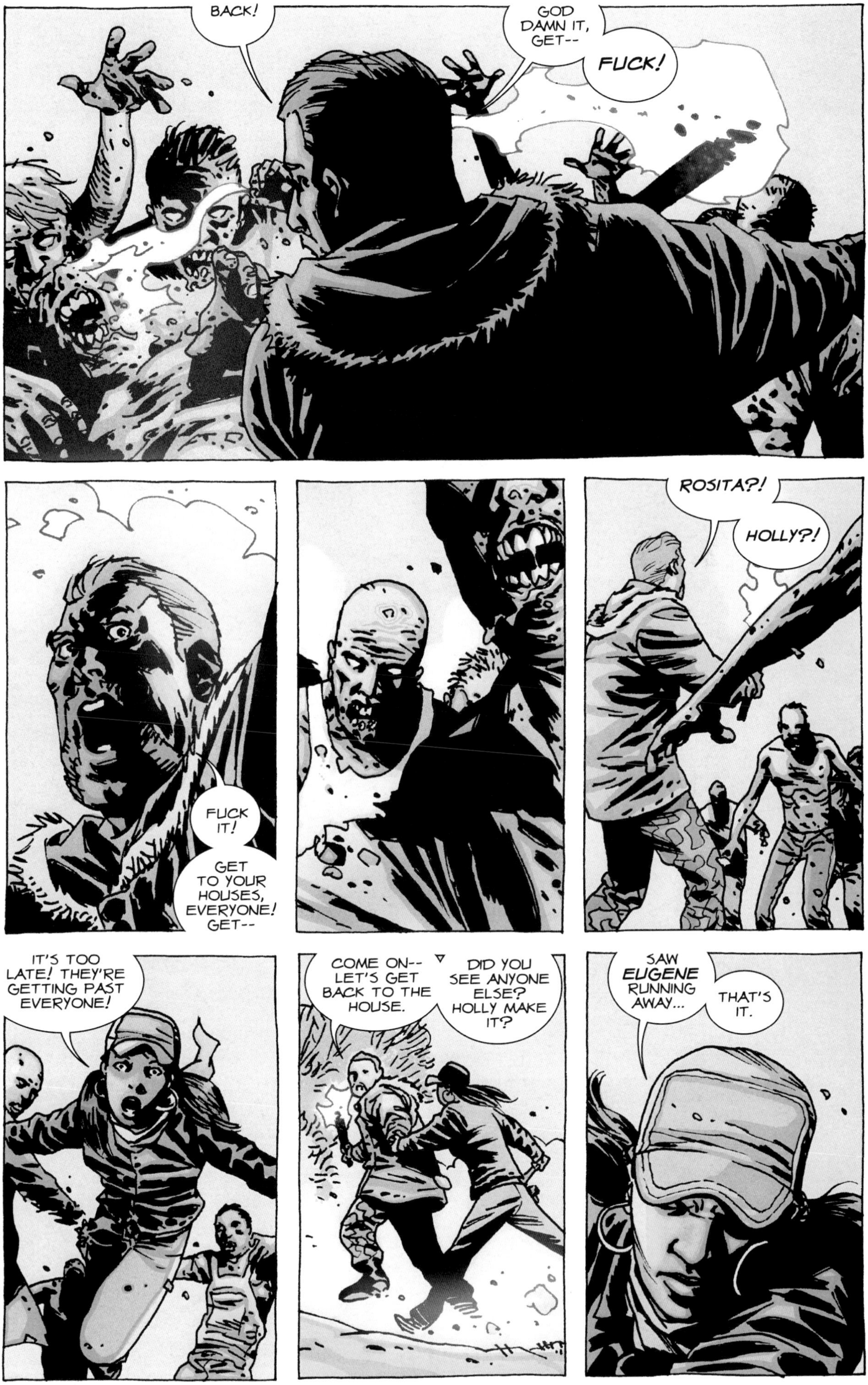
BACK!
GOD DAMN IT, GET--
FUCK!
FUCK IT!
GET TO YOUR HOUSES, EVERYONE! GET--
ROSITA?!
HOLLY?!
IT'S TOO LATE! THEY'RE GETTING PAST EVERYONE!
COME ON-- LET'S GET BACK TO THE HOUSE.
DID YOU SEE ANYONE ELSE? HOLLY MAKE IT?
SAW EUGENE RUNNING AWAY...
THAT'S IT.

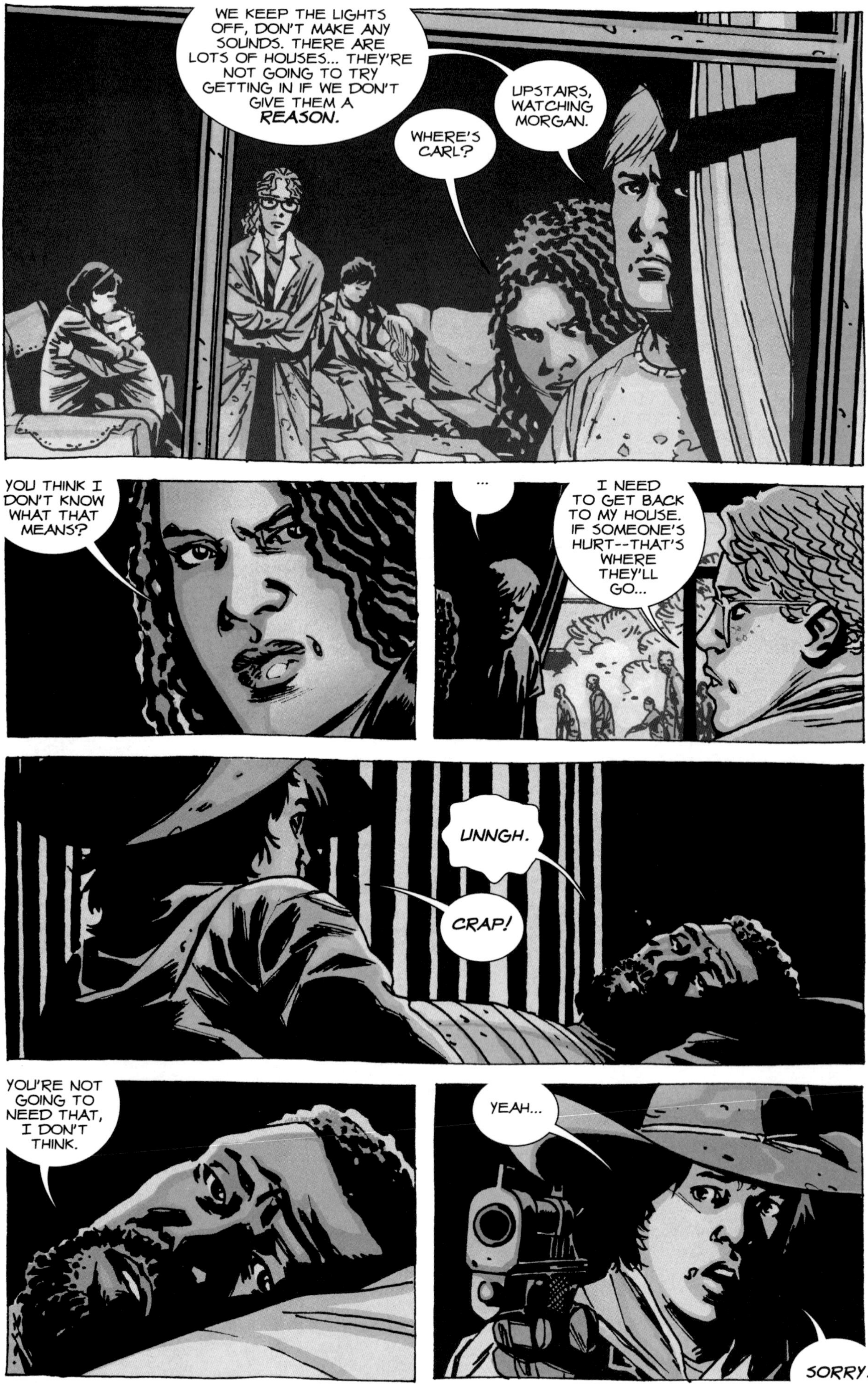
WE KEEP THE LIGHTS OFF, DON'T MAKE ANY SOUNDS. THERE ARE LOTS OF HOUSES... THEY'RE NOT GOING TO TRY GETTING IN IF WE DON'T GIVE THEM A *REASON.*
WHERE'S CARL?
UPSTAIRS, WATCHING MORGAN.
YOU THINK I DON'T KNOW WHAT THAT MEANS?
...
I NEED TO GET BACK TO MY HOUSE. IF SOMEONE'S HURT--THAT'S WHERE THEY'LL GO...
UNNGH.
CRAP!
YOU'RE NOT GOING TO NEED THAT, I DON'T THINK.
YEAH...
SORRY.

SO THEY GOT YOU... WATCHING ME, MAKING SURE I DON'T TURN?

YEAH.

I CAN DO IT... I'M OLD ENOUGH.

I KNOW... I KNOW...

HOW OLD **ARE** YOU, CARL?

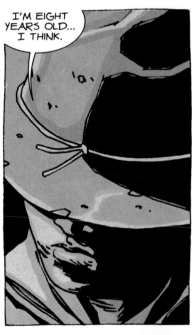

I'M EIGHT YEARS OLD... I THINK.

YOU THINK?

THEY SKIPPED MY BIRTHDAY, I'M PRETTY SURE. IT'S WINTER AGAIN... BUT I NEVER HAD ONE.

IT'S IN **APRIL.**

I'M SORRY... TO HEAR THAT...

HAD A BIRTHDAY PARTY FOR MY SON DUANE... SHORTLY AFTER CHRISTMAS... BEFORE HE...

...

CARL... I **SAW** YOU SHOOT BEN.

I KNOW YOU DID.

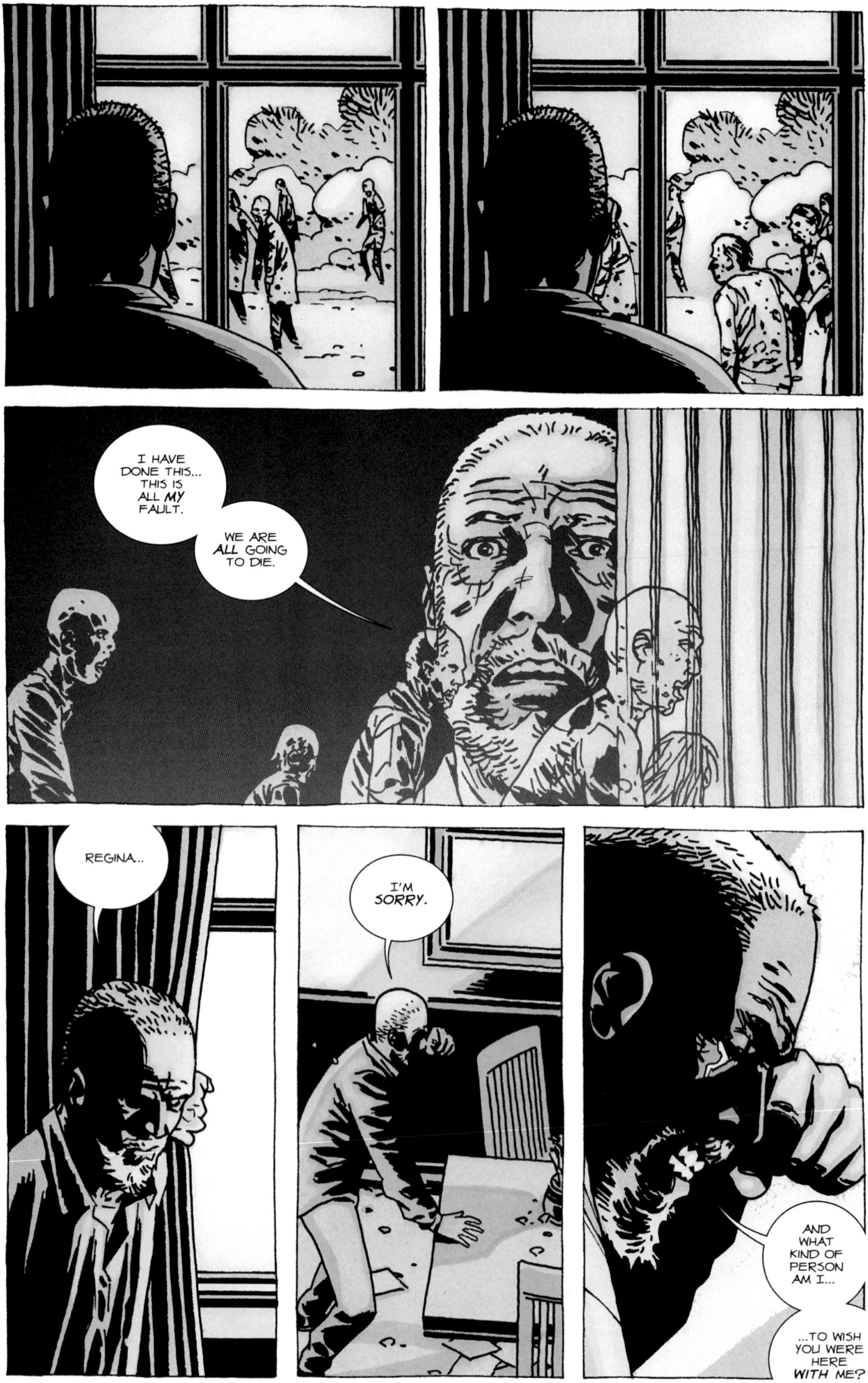
I HAVE DONE THIS... THIS IS ALL MY FAULT.
WE ARE ALL GOING TO DIE.
REGINA..
I'M SORRY.
AND WHAT KIND OF PERSON AM I...
...TO WISH YOU WERE HERE WITH ME?

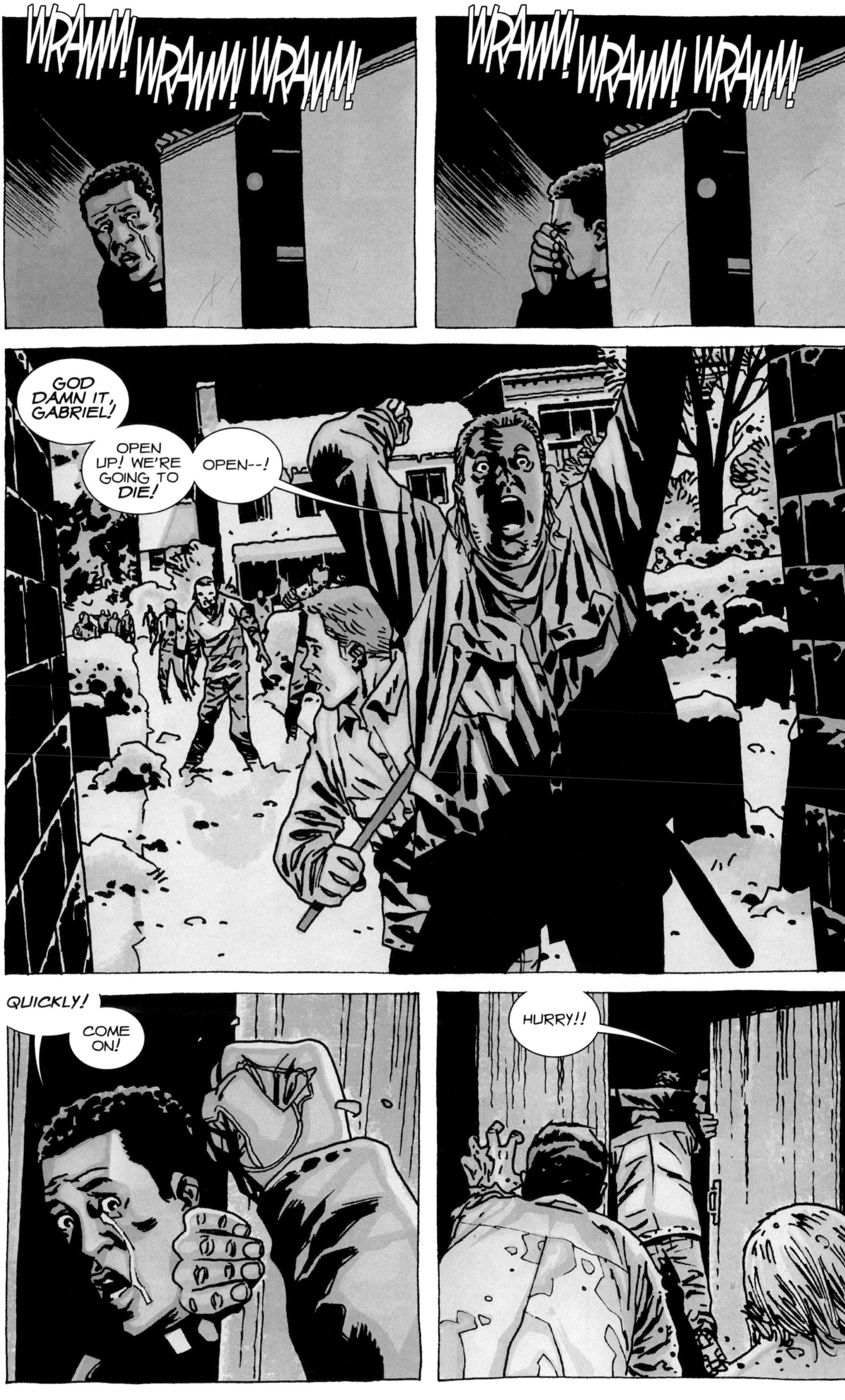
WRAMM! WRAMM! WRAMM!
WRAMM! WRAMM! WRAMM!
GOD DAMN IT, GABRIEL!
OPEN UP! WE'RE GOING TO DIE!
OPEN--!
QUICKLY!
COME ON!
HURRY!!

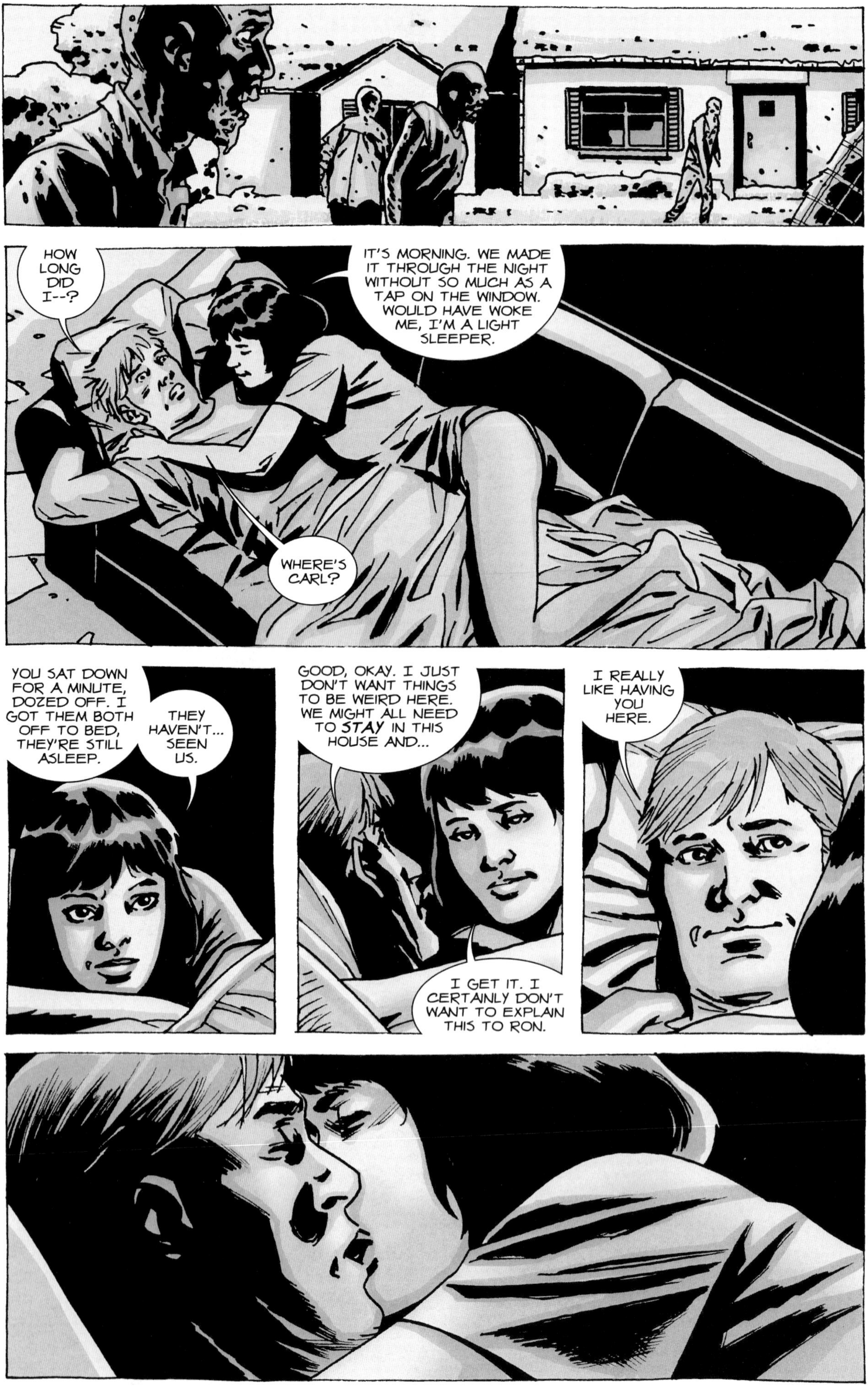
HOW LONG DID I--?
IT'S MORNING. WE MADE IT THROUGH THE NIGHT WITHOUT SO MUCH AS A TAP ON THE WINDOW. WOULD HAVE WOKE ME, I'M A LIGHT SLEEPER.
WHERE'S CARL?
YOU SAT DOWN FOR A MINUTE, DOZED OFF. I GOT THEM BOTH OFF TO BED, THEY'RE STILL ASLEEP.
THEY HAVEN'T... SEEN US.
GOOD, OKAY. I JUST DON'T WANT THINGS TO BE WEIRD HERE. WE MIGHT ALL NEED TO STAY IN THIS HOUSE AND...
I GET IT. I CERTAINLY DON'T WANT TO EXPLAIN THIS TO RON.
I REALLY LIKE HAVING YOU HERE.

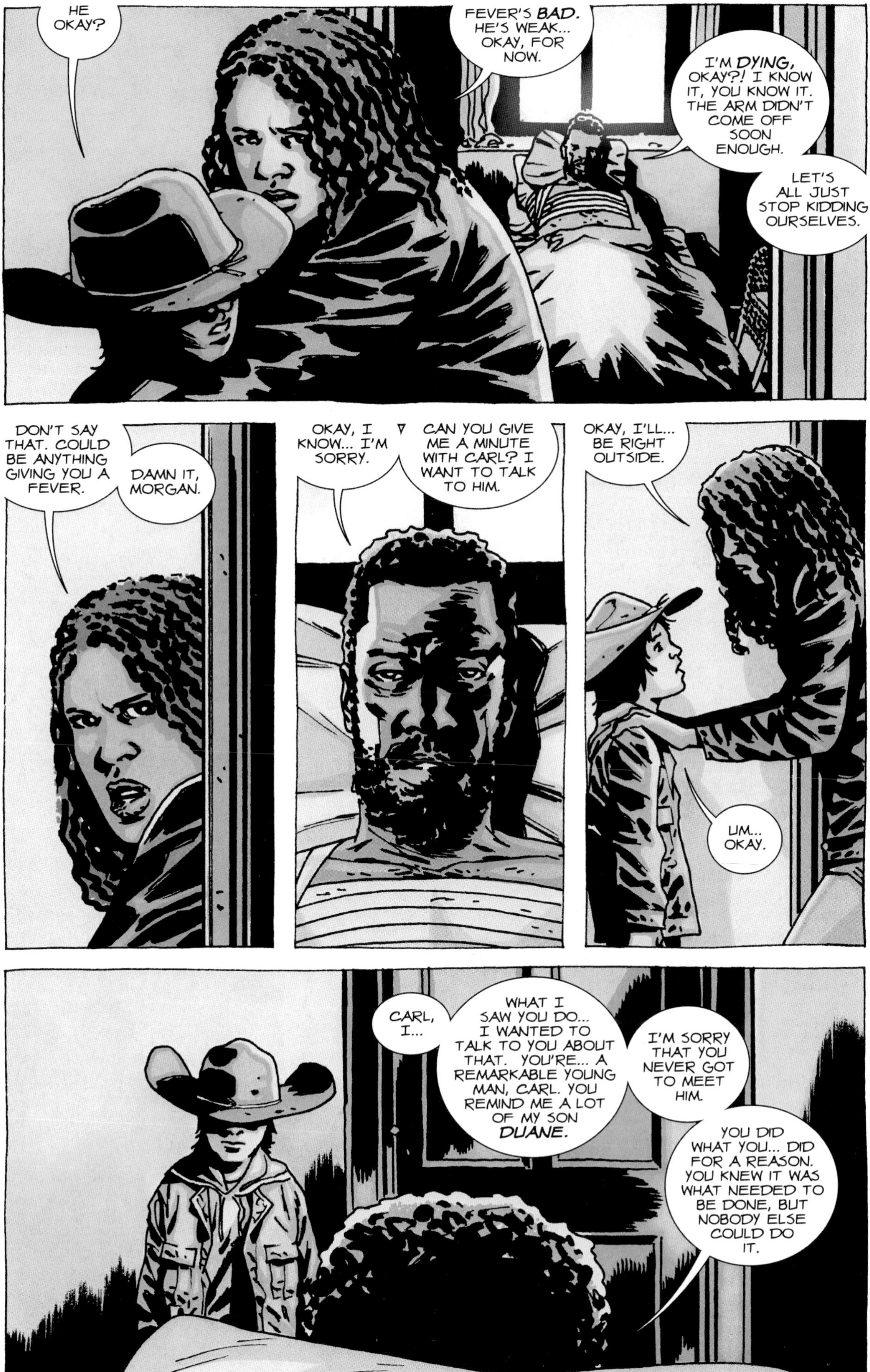
HE OKAY?
FEVER'S BAD. HE'S WEAK... OKAY, FOR NOW.
I'M DYING, OKAY?! I KNOW IT, YOU KNOW IT. THE ARM DIDN'T COME OFF SOON ENOUGH.
LET'S ALL JUST STOP KIDDING OURSELVES.
DON'T SAY THAT. COULD BE ANYTHING GIVING YOU A FEVER.
DAMN IT, MORGAN.
OKAY, I KNOW... I'M SORRY.
CAN YOU GIVE ME A MINUTE WITH CARL? I WANT TO TALK TO HIM.
OKAY, I'LL... BE RIGHT OUTSIDE.
UM... OKAY.
CARL, I...
WHAT I SAW YOU DO... I WANTED TO TALK TO YOU ABOUT THAT. YOU'RE... A REMARKABLE YOUNG MAN, CARL. YOU REMIND ME A LOT OF MY SON DUANE.
I'M SORRY THAT YOU NEVER GOT TO MEET HIM.
YOU DID WHAT YOU... DID FOR A REASON. YOU KNEW IT WAS WHAT NEEDED TO BE DONE, BUT NOBODY ELSE COULD DO IT.

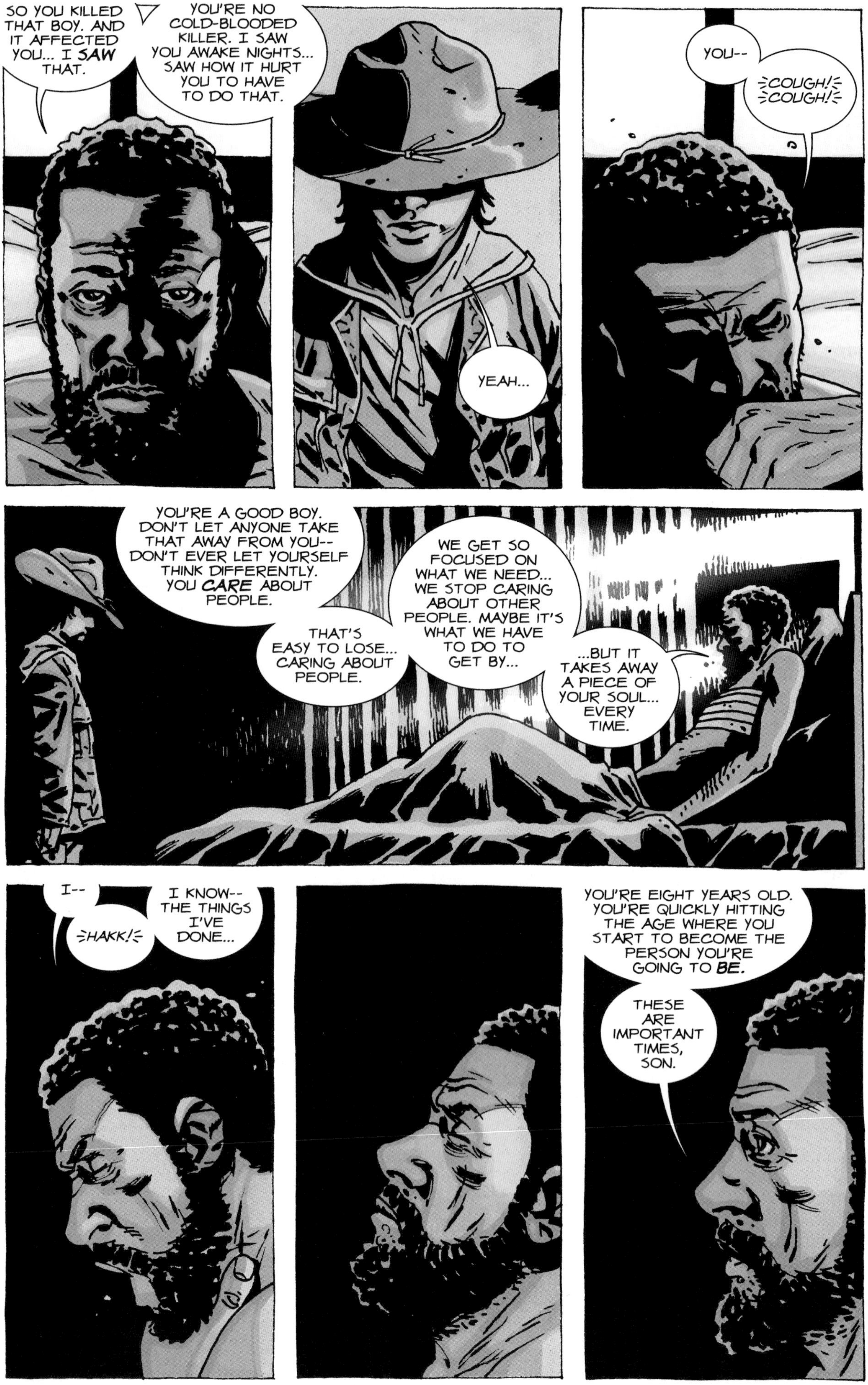
SO YOU KILLED THAT BOY. AND IT AFFECTED YOU... I SAW THAT.
YOU'RE NO COLD-BLOODED KILLER. I SAW YOU AWAKE NIGHTS... SAW HOW IT HURT YOU TO HAVE TO DO THAT.
YEAH...
YOU--
COUGH! COUGH!
YOU'RE A GOOD BOY. DON'T LET ANYONE TAKE THAT AWAY FROM YOU-- DON'T EVER LET YOURSELF THINK DIFFERENTLY. YOU CARE ABOUT PEOPLE.
THAT'S EASY TO LOSE... CARING ABOUT PEOPLE.
WE GET SO FOCUSED ON WHAT WE NEED... WE STOP CARING ABOUT OTHER PEOPLE. MAYBE IT'S WHAT WE HAVE TO DO TO GET BY...
...BUT IT TAKES AWAY A PIECE OF YOUR SOUL... EVERY TIME.
I--
HAKK!
I KNOW-- THE THINGS I'VE DONE...
YOU'RE EIGHT YEARS OLD. YOU'RE QUICKLY HITTING THE AGE WHERE YOU START TO BECOME THE PERSON YOU'RE GOING TO BE.
THESE ARE IMPORTANT TIMES, SON.

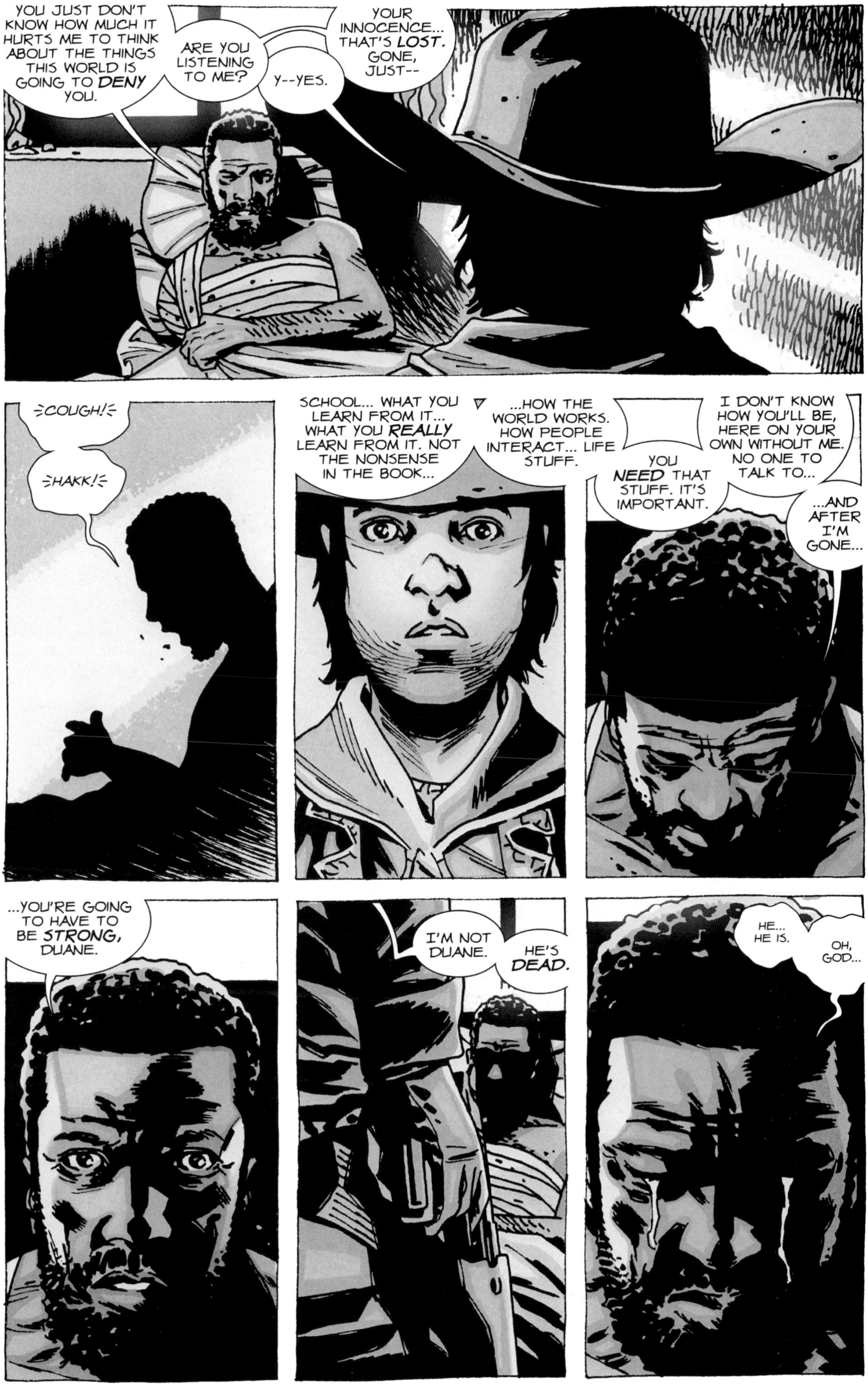
YOU JUST DON'T KNOW HOW MUCH IT HURTS ME TO THINK ABOUT THE THINGS THIS WORLD IS GOING TO DENY YOU.
ARE YOU LISTENING TO ME?
Y--YES.
YOUR INNOCENCE... THAT'S LOST. GONE, JUST--
COUGH!
HAKK!
SCHOOL... WHAT YOU LEARN FROM IT... WHAT YOU REALLY LEARN FROM IT. NOT THE NONSENSE IN THE BOOK...
...HOW THE WORLD WORKS. HOW PEOPLE INTERACT... LIFE STUFF.
YOU NEED THAT STUFF. IT'S IMPORTANT.
I DON'T KNOW HOW YOU'LL BE, HERE ON YOUR OWN WITHOUT ME. NO ONE TO TALK TO...
...AND AFTER I'M GONE...
...YOU'RE GOING TO HAVE TO BE STRONG, DUANE.
I'M NOT DUANE.
HE'S DEAD.
HE... HE IS.
OH, GOD...

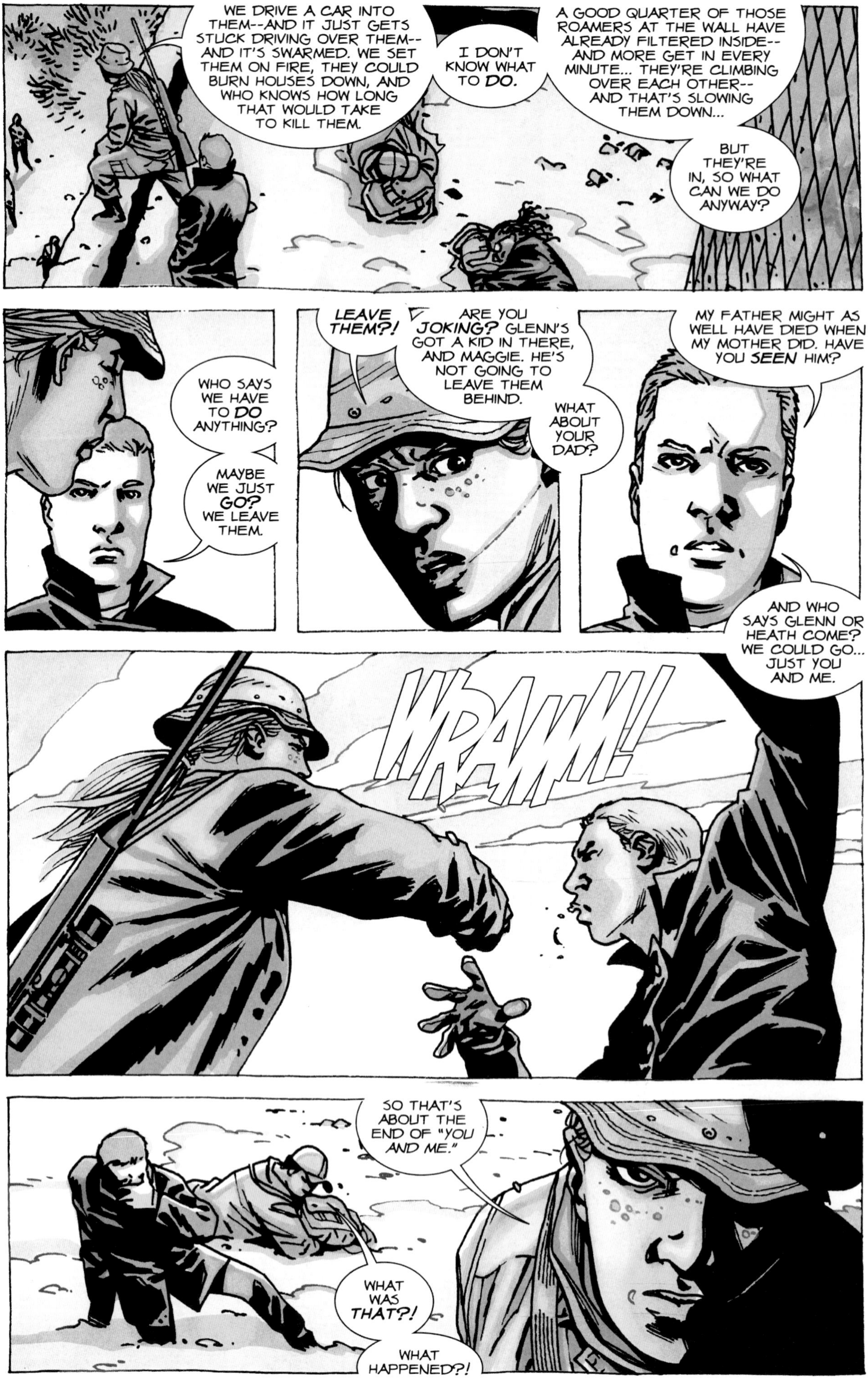
WE DRIVE A CAR INTO THEM--AND IT JUST GETS STUCK DRIVING OVER THEM--AND IT'S SWARMED. WE SET THEM ON FIRE, THEY COULD BURN HOUSES DOWN, AND WHO KNOWS HOW LONG THAT WOULD TAKE TO KILL THEM.
I DON'T KNOW WHAT TO DO.
A GOOD QUARTER OF THOSE ROAMERS AT THE WALL HAVE ALREADY FILTERED INSIDE--AND MORE GET IN EVERY MINUTE... THEY'RE CLIMBING OVER EACH OTHER--AND THAT'S SLOWING THEM DOWN...
BUT THEY'RE IN, SO WHAT CAN WE DO ANYWAY?
WHO SAYS WE HAVE TO DO ANYTHING?
MAYBE WE JUST GO? WE LEAVE THEM.
LEAVE THEM?!
ARE YOU JOKING? GLENN'S GOT A KID IN THERE, AND MAGGIE. HE'S NOT GOING TO LEAVE THEM BEHIND.
WHAT ABOUT YOUR DAD?
MY FATHER MIGHT AS WELL HAVE DIED WHEN MY MOTHER DID. HAVE YOU SEEN HIM?
AND WHO SAYS GLENN OR HEATH COME? WE COULD GO... JUST YOU AND ME.
WRAMM!
SO THAT'S ABOUT THE END OF "YOU AND ME."
WHAT WAS THAT?!
WHAT HAPPENED?!

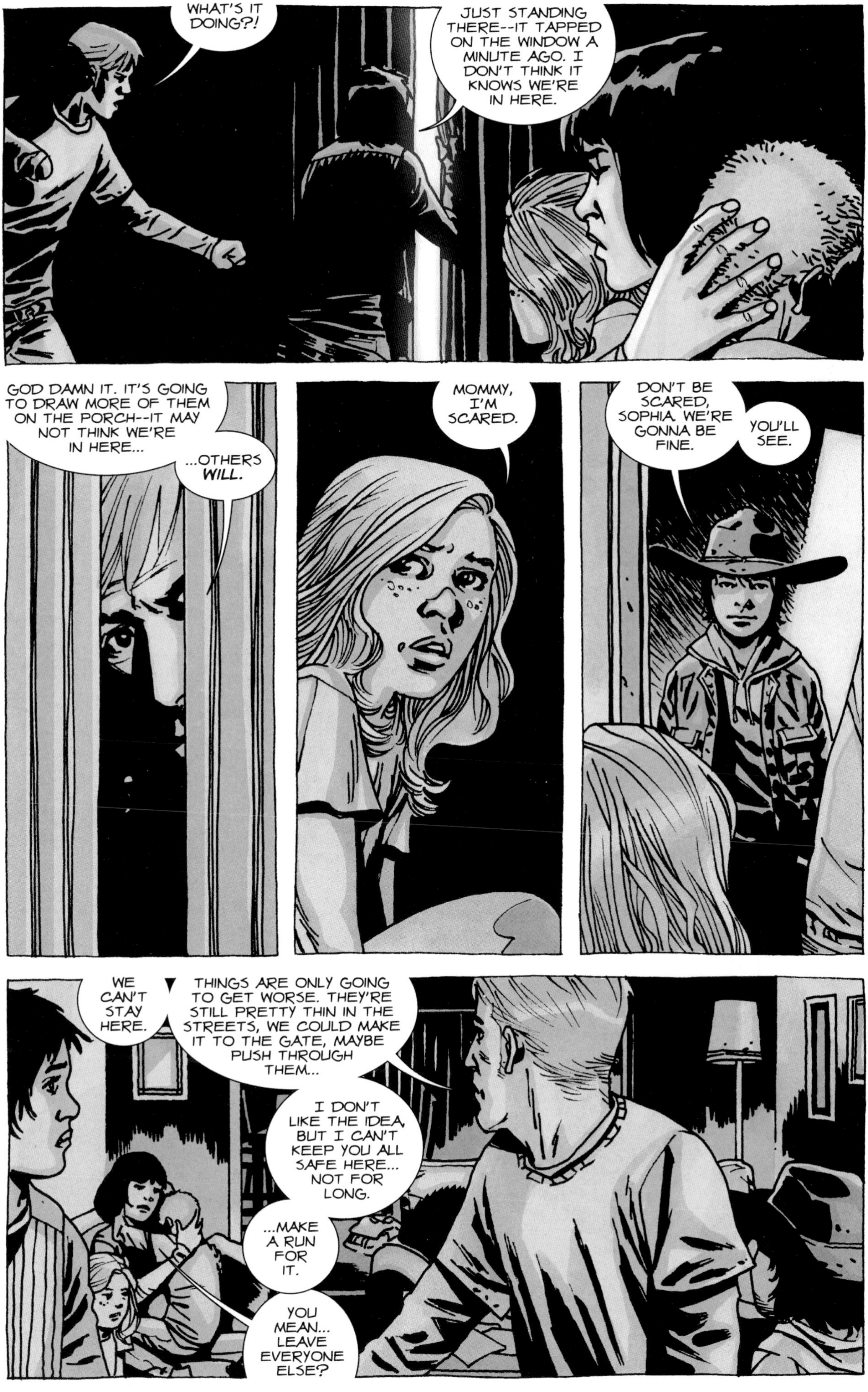
WHAT'S IT DOING?!
JUST STANDING THERE--IT TAPPED ON THE WINDOW A MINUTE AGO. I DON'T THINK IT KNOWS WE'RE IN HERE.
GOD DAMN IT. IT'S GOING TO DRAW MORE OF THEM ON THE PORCH--IT MAY NOT THINK WE'RE IN HERE...
...OTHERS *WILL.*
MOMMY, I'M SCARED.
DON'T BE SCARED, SOPHIA. WE'RE GONNA BE FINE.
YOU'LL SEE.
WE CAN'T STAY HERE.
THINGS ARE ONLY GOING TO GET WORSE. THEY'RE STILL PRETTY THIN IN THE STREETS, WE COULD MAKE IT TO THE GATE, MAYBE PUSH THROUGH THEM...
I DON'T LIKE THE IDEA, BUT I CAN'T KEEP YOU ALL SAFE HERE... NOT FOR LONG.
...MAKE A RUN FOR IT.
YOU MEAN... LEAVE EVERYONE ELSE?

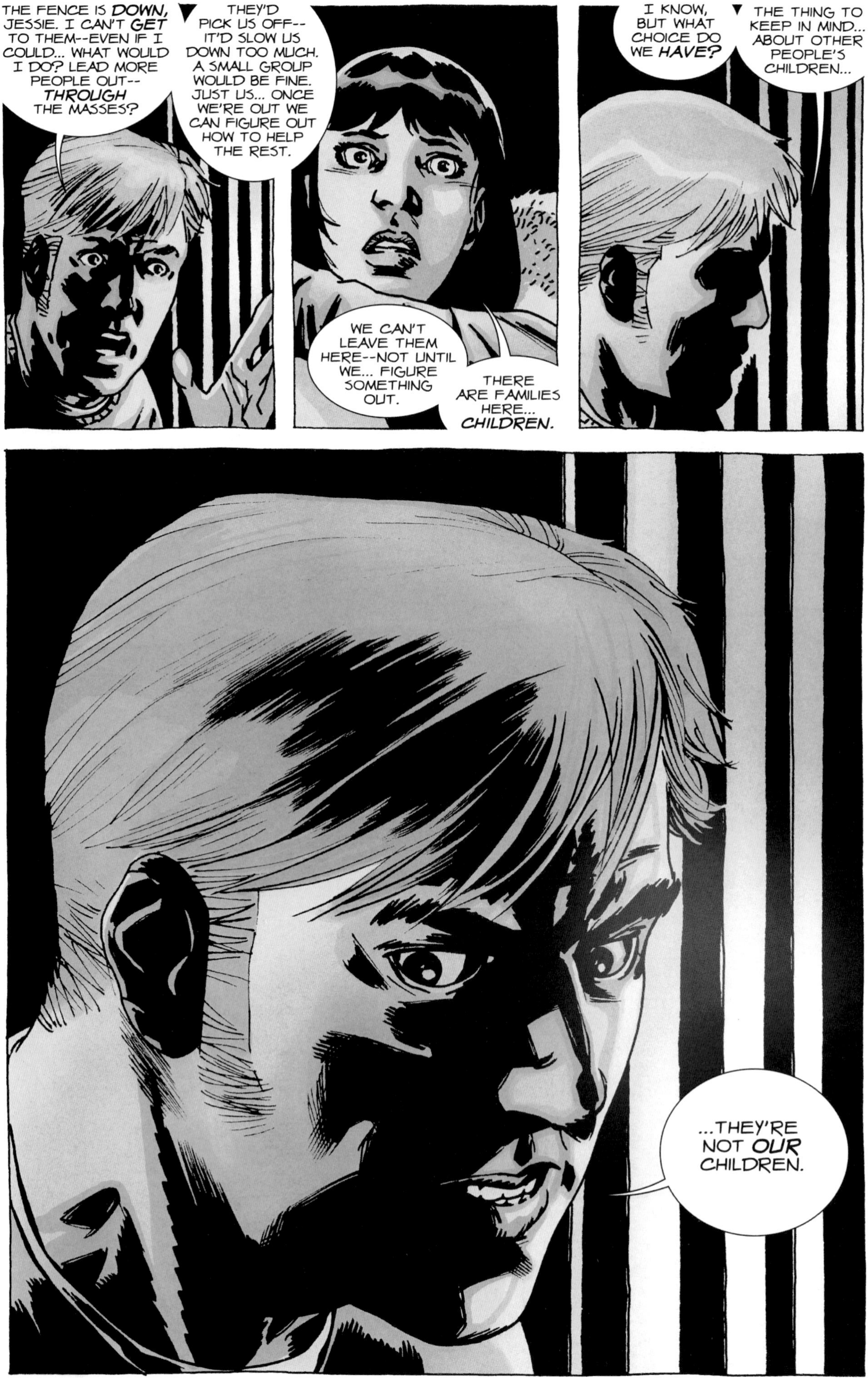
THE FENCE IS DOWN, JESSIE. I CAN'T GET TO THEM--EVEN IF I COULD... WHAT WOULD I DO? LEAD MORE PEOPLE OUT-- THROUGH THE MASSES?
THEY'D PICK US OFF-- IT'D SLOW US DOWN TOO MUCH. A SMALL GROUP WOULD BE FINE. JUST US... ONCE WE'RE OUT WE CAN FIGURE OUT HOW TO HELP THE REST.
WE CAN'T LEAVE THEM HERE--NOT UNTIL WE... FIGURE SOMETHING OUT.
THERE ARE FAMILIES HERE... CHILDREN.
I KNOW, BUT WHAT CHOICE DO WE HAVE?
THE THING TO KEEP IN MIND... ABOUT OTHER PEOPLE'S CHILDREN...
...THEY'RE NOT OUR CHILDREN.

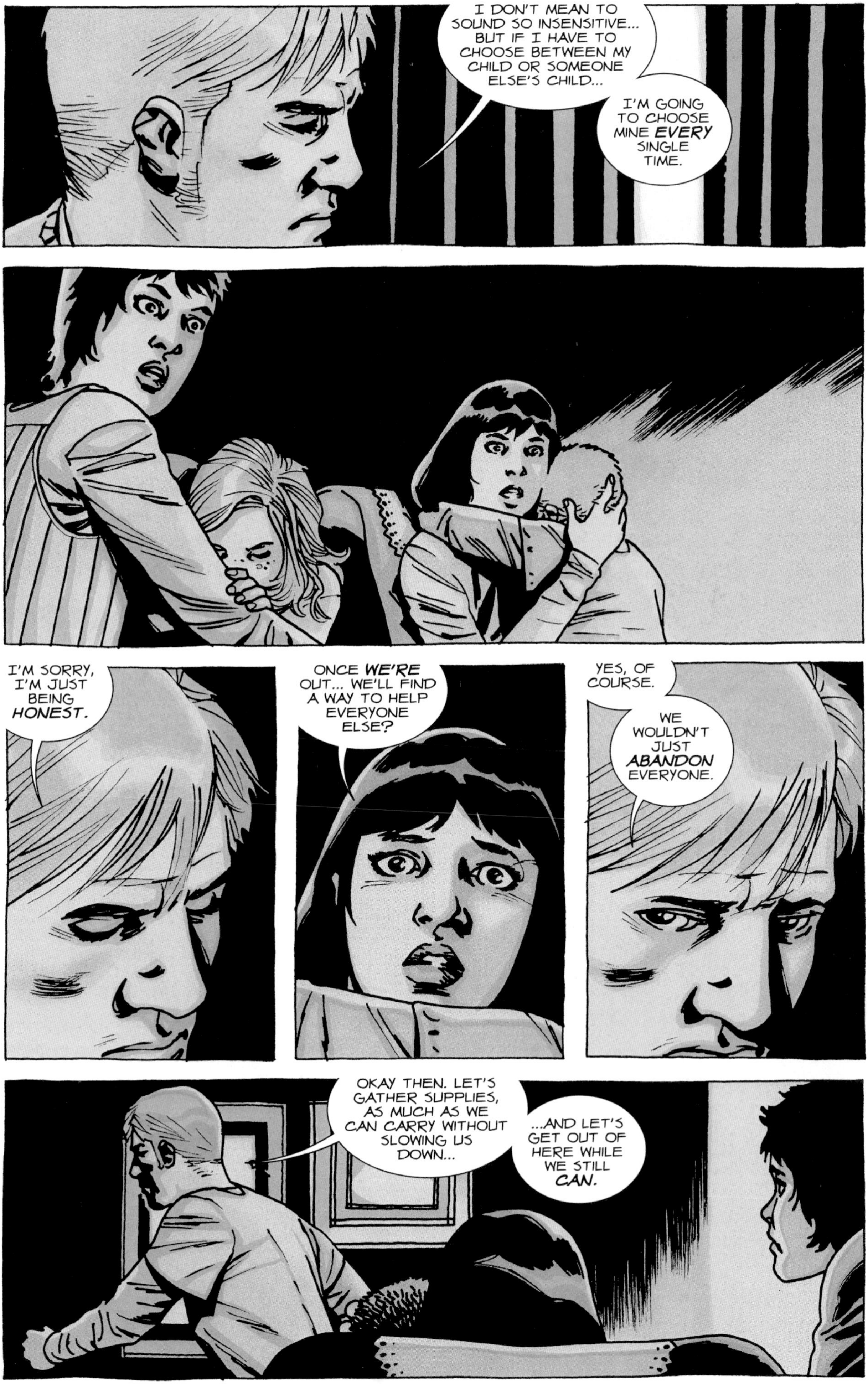
I DON'T MEAN TO SOUND SO INSENSITIVE... BUT IF I HAVE TO CHOOSE BETWEEN MY CHILD OR SOMEONE ELSE'S CHILD...
I'M GOING TO CHOOSE MINE EVERY SINGLE TIME.
I'M SORRY, I'M JUST BEING HONEST.
ONCE WE'RE OUT... WE'LL FIND A WAY TO HELP EVERYONE ELSE?
YES, OF COURSE.
WE WOULDN'T JUST ABANDON EVERYONE.
OKAY THEN. LET'S GATHER SUPPLIES, AS MUCH AS WE CAN CARRY WITHOUT SLOWING US DOWN...
...AND LET'S GET OUT OF HERE WHILE WE STILL CAN.

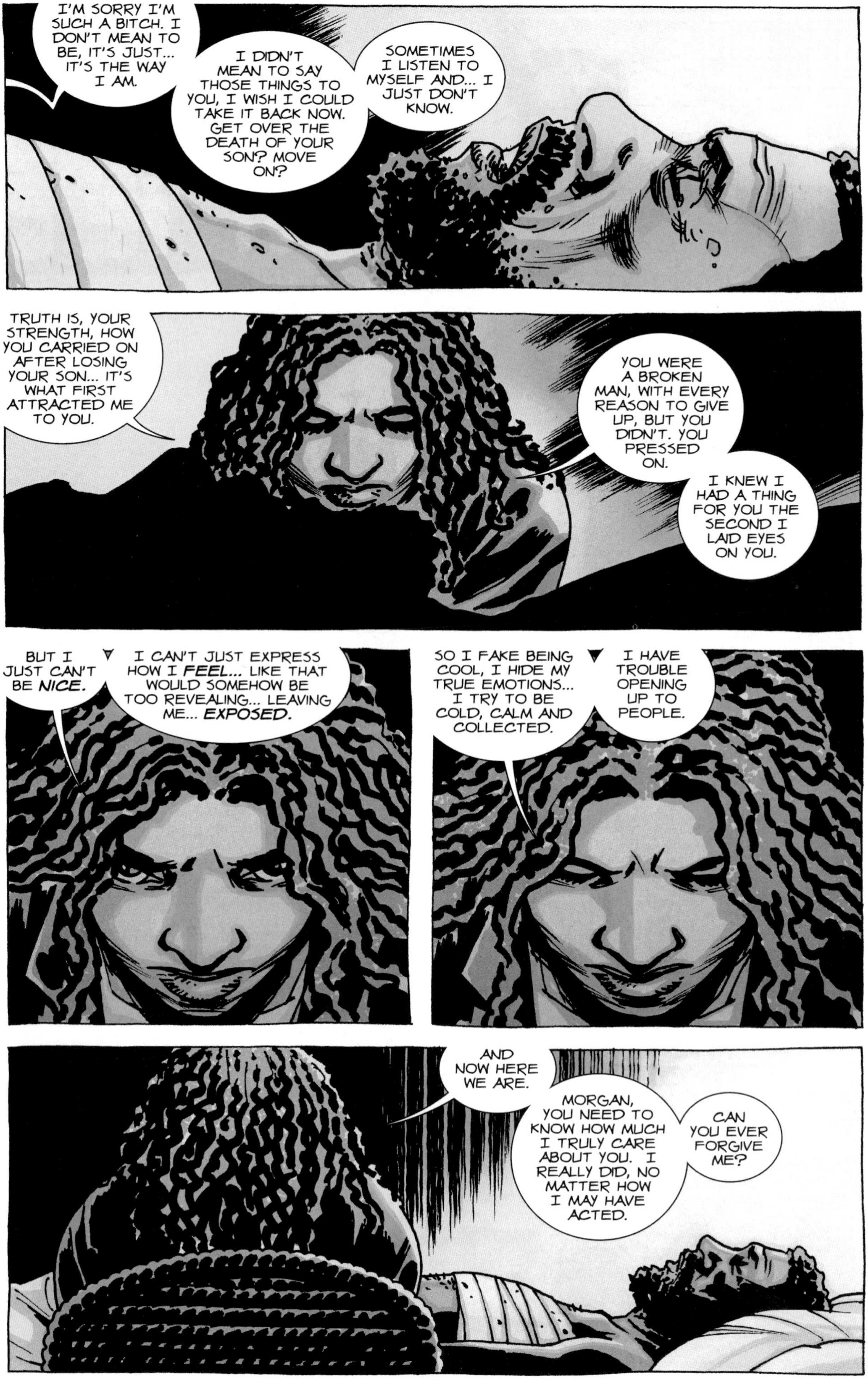
I'M SORRY I'M SUCH A BITCH. I DON'T MEAN TO BE, IT'S JUST... IT'S THE WAY I AM.
I DIDN'T MEAN TO SAY THOSE THINGS TO YOU, I WISH I COULD TAKE IT BACK NOW. GET OVER THE DEATH OF YOUR SON? MOVE ON?
SOMETIMES I LISTEN TO MYSELF AND... I JUST DON'T KNOW.
TRUTH IS, YOUR STRENGTH, HOW YOU CARRIED ON AFTER LOSING YOUR SON... IT'S WHAT FIRST ATTRACTED ME TO YOU.
YOU WERE A BROKEN MAN, WITH EVERY REASON TO GIVE UP, BUT YOU DIDN'T. YOU PRESSED ON.
I KNEW I HAD A THING FOR YOU THE SECOND I LAID EYES ON YOU.
BUT I JUST CAN'T BE *NICE.*
I CAN'T JUST EXPRESS HOW I ***FEEL...*** LIKE THAT WOULD SOMEHOW BE TOO REVEALING... LEAVING ME... ***EXPOSED.***
SO I FAKE BEING COOL, I HIDE MY TRUE EMOTIONS... I TRY TO BE COLD, CALM AND COLLECTED.
I HAVE TROUBLE OPENING UP TO PEOPLE.
AND NOW HERE WE ARE.
MORGAN, YOU NEED TO KNOW HOW MUCH I TRULY CARE ABOUT YOU. I REALLY DID, NO MATTER HOW I MAY HAVE ACTED.
CAN YOU EVER FORGIVE ME?

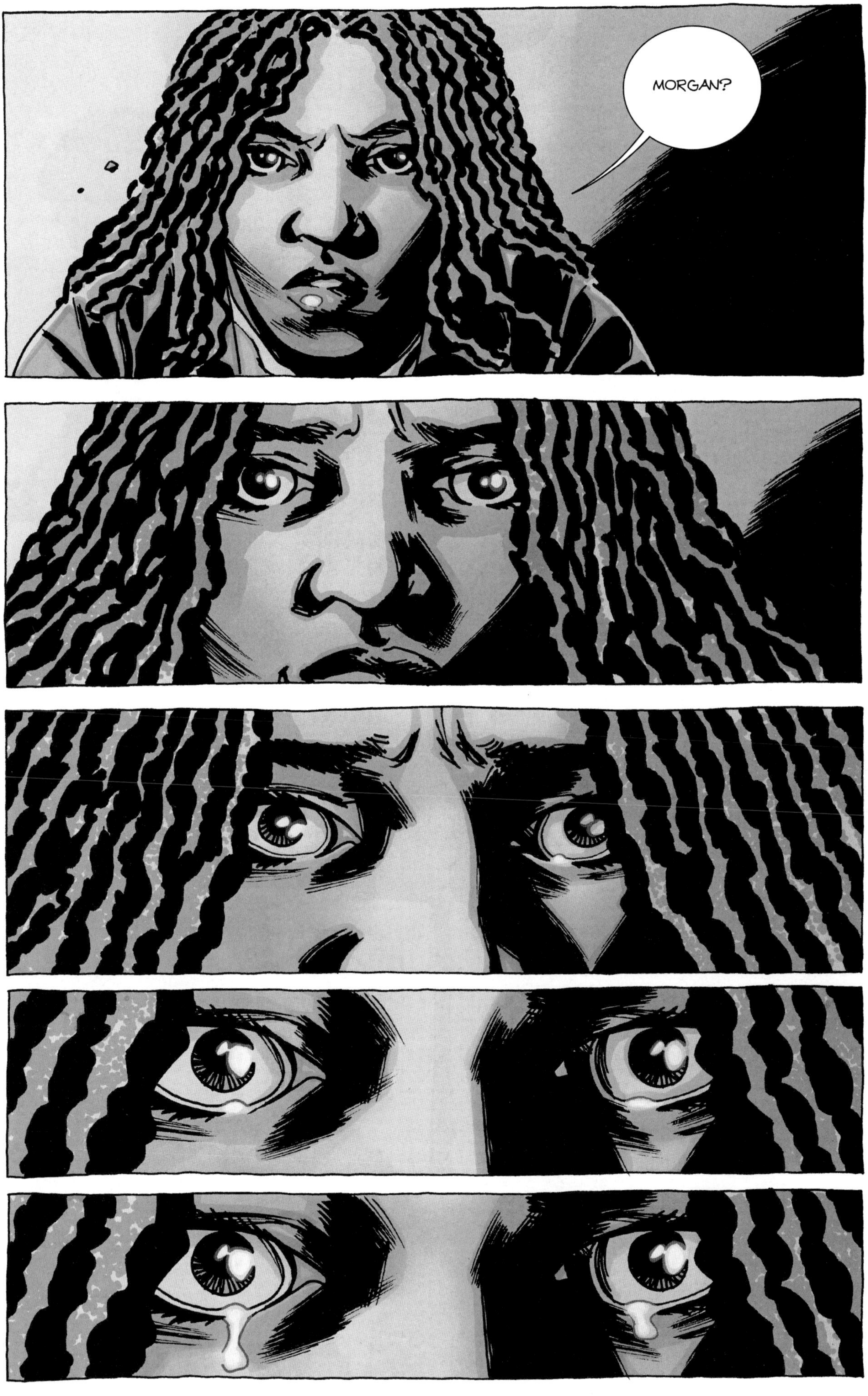
MORGAN?

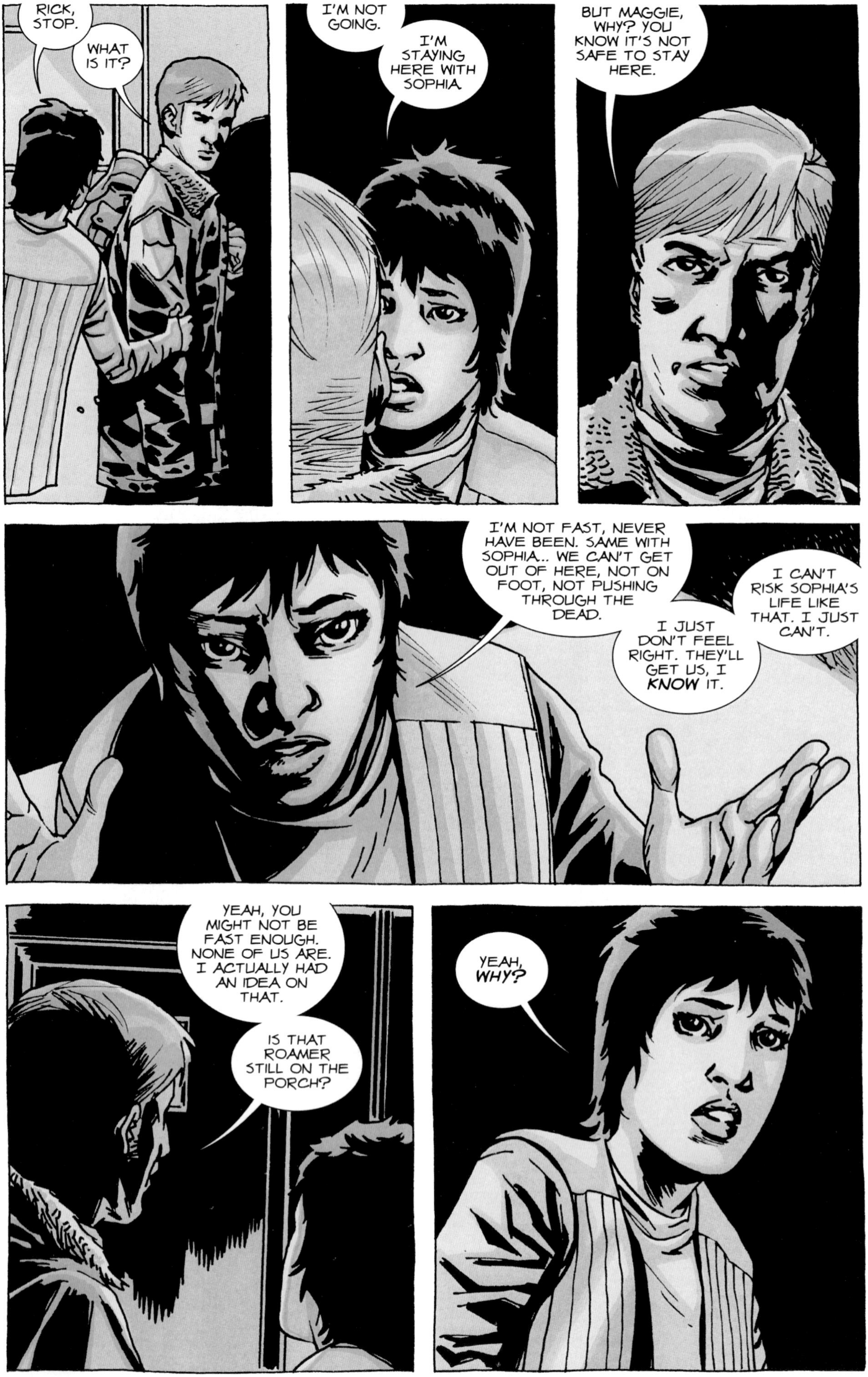
RICK, STOP.
WHAT IS IT?
I'M NOT GOING.
I'M STAYING HERE WITH SOPHIA
BUT MAGGIE, WHY? YOU KNOW IT'S NOT SAFE TO STAY HERE.
I'M NOT FAST, NEVER HAVE BEEN. SAME WITH SOPHIA.. WE CAN'T GET OUT OF HERE, NOT ON FOOT, NOT PUSHING THROUGH THE DEAD.
I JUST DON'T FEEL RIGHT. THEY'LL GET US, I KNOW IT.
I CAN'T RISK SOPHIA'S LIFE LIKE THAT. I JUST CAN'T.
YEAH, YOU MIGHT NOT BE FAST ENOUGH. NONE OF US ARE. I ACTUALLY HAD AN IDEA ON THAT.
IS THAT ROAMER STILL ON THE PORCH?
YEAH, WHY?

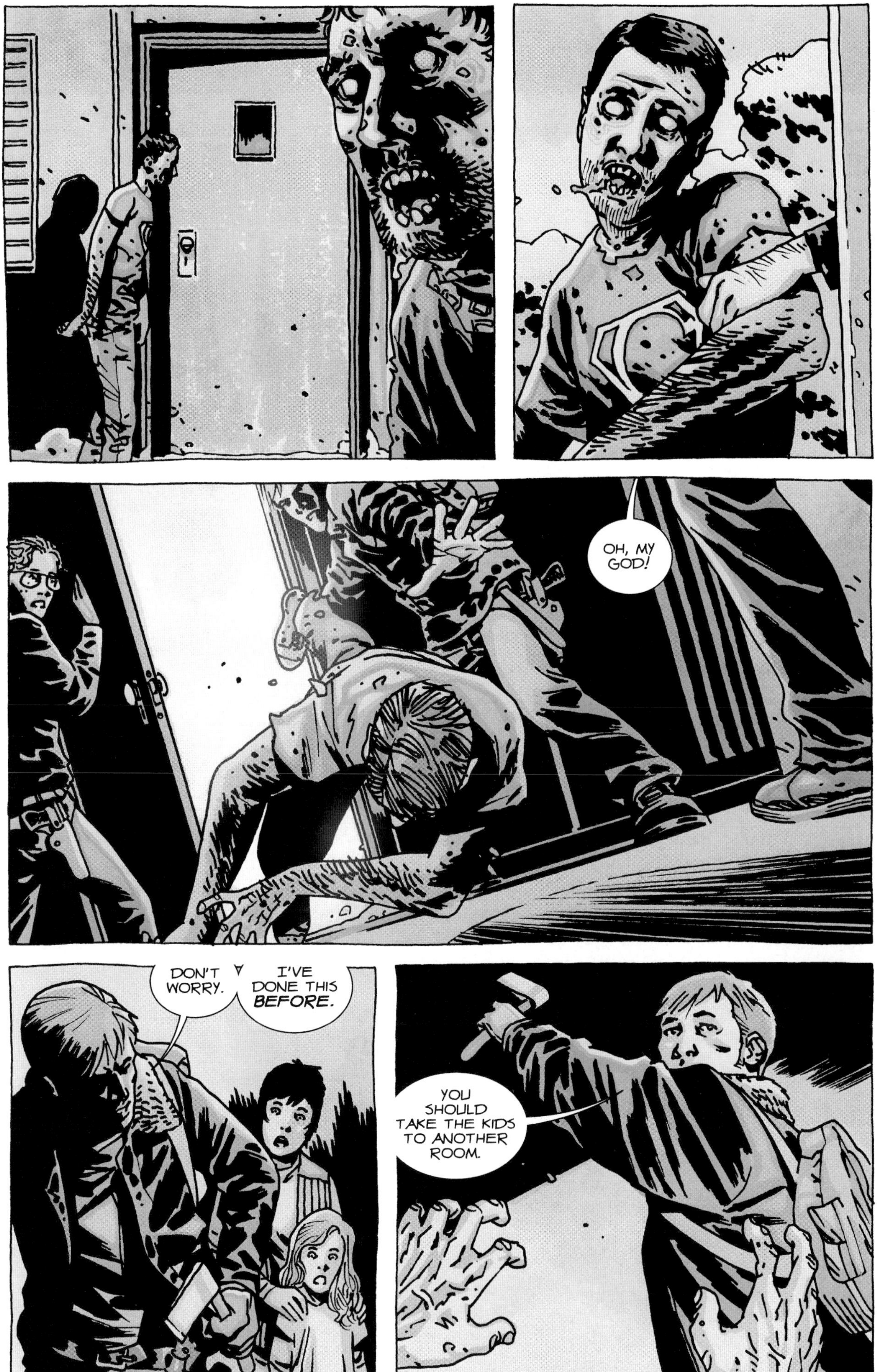

OH, MY GOD!
DON'T WORRY.
I'VE DONE THIS BEFORE.
YOU SHOULD TAKE THE KIDS TO ANOTHER ROOM.

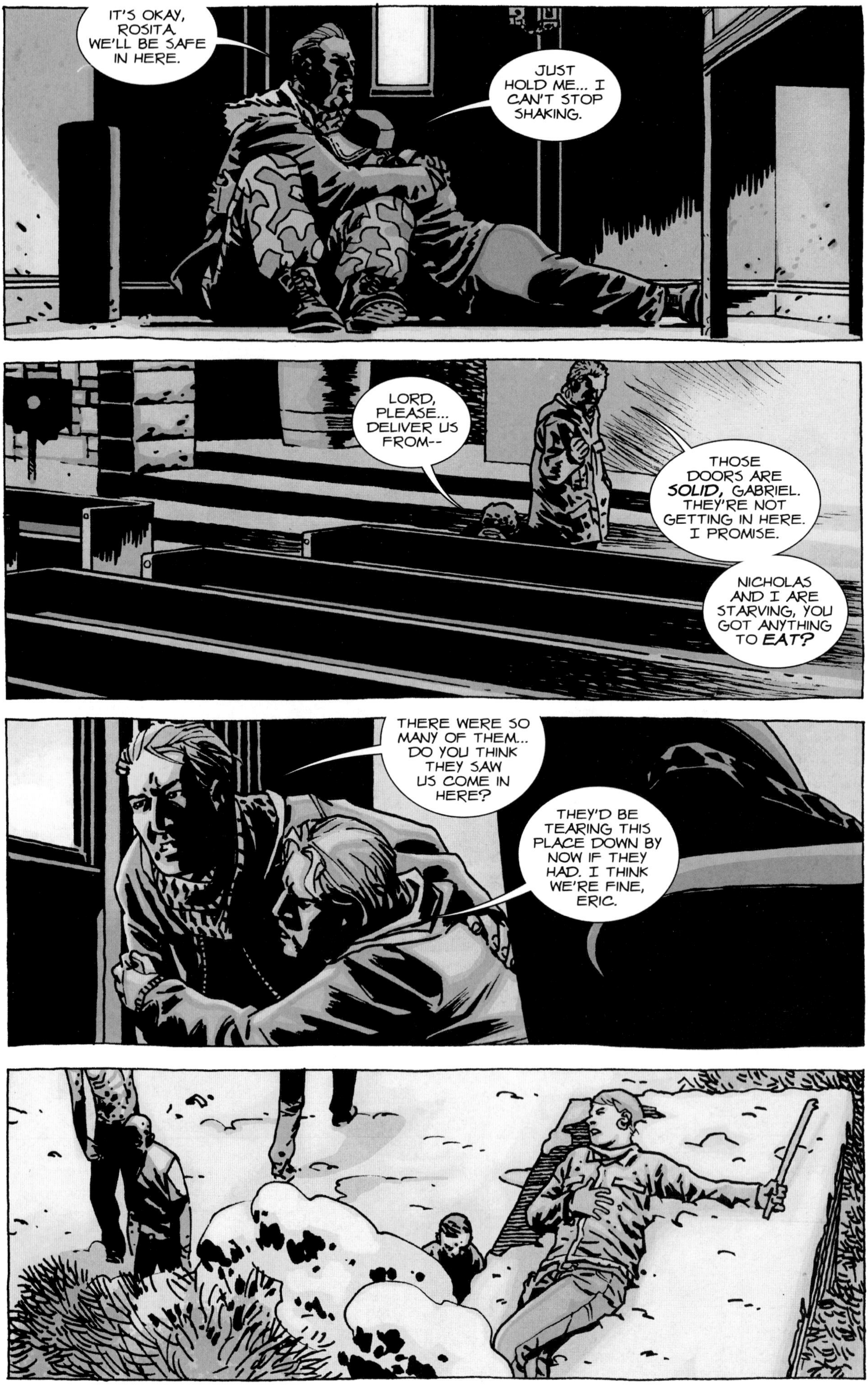
IT'S OKAY, ROSITA. WE'LL BE SAFE IN HERE.
JUST HOLD ME... I CAN'T STOP SHAKING.
LORD, PLEASE... DELIVER US FROM--
THOSE DOORS ARE SOLID, GABRIEL. THEY'RE NOT GETTING IN HERE. I PROMISE.
NICHOLAS AND I ARE STARVING, YOU GOT ANYTHING TO EAT?
THERE WERE SO MANY OF THEM... DO YOU THINK THEY SAW US COME IN HERE?
THEY'D BE TEARING THIS PLACE DOWN BY NOW IF THEY HAD. I THINK WE'RE FINE, ERIC.

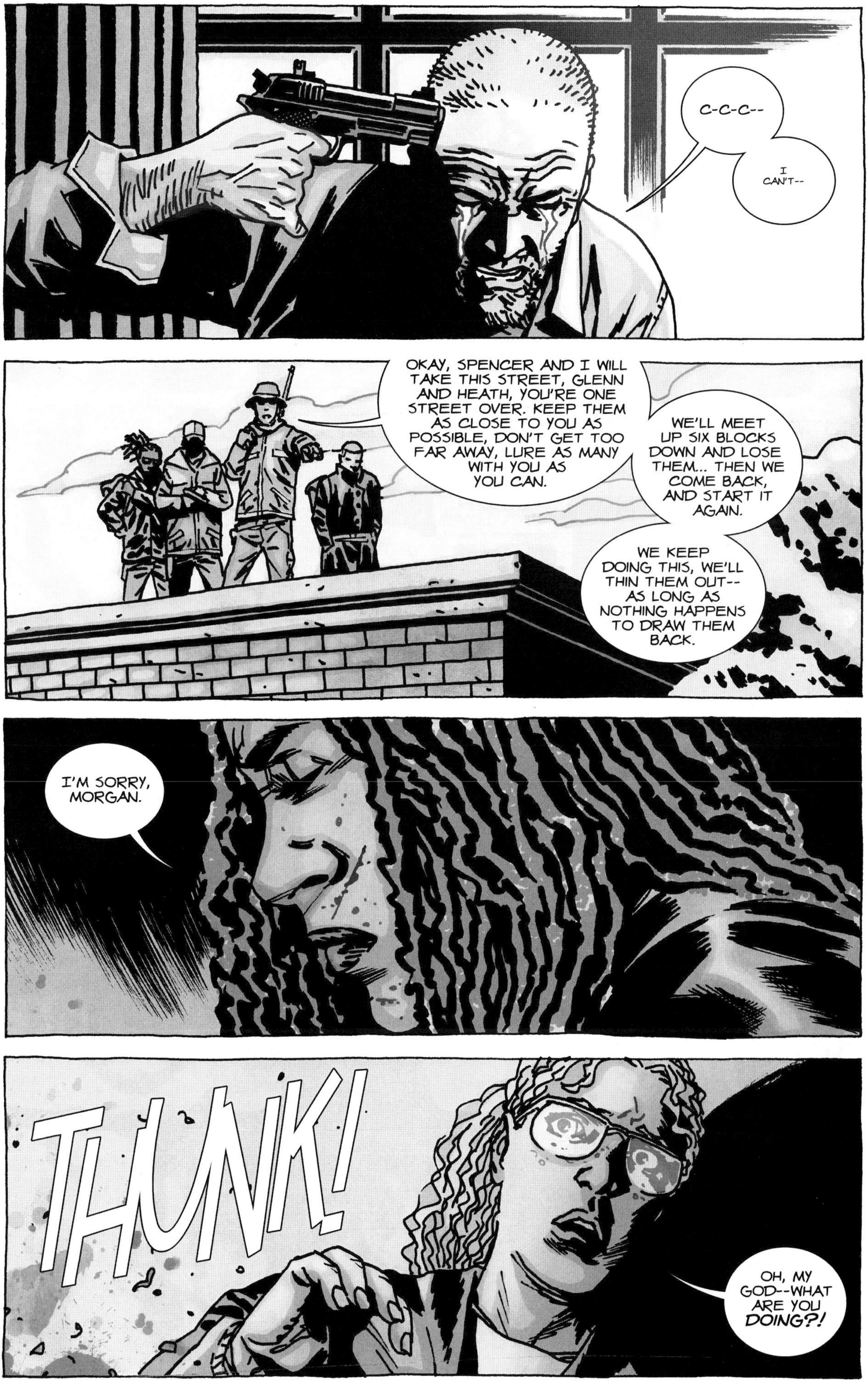
C-C-C--
I CAN'T--
OKAY, SPENCER AND I WILL TAKE THIS STREET, GLENN AND HEATH, YOU'RE ONE STREET OVER. KEEP THEM AS CLOSE TO YOU AS POSSIBLE, DON'T GET TOO FAR AWAY, LURE AS MANY WITH YOU AS YOU CAN.
WE'LL MEET UP SIX BLOCKS DOWN AND LOSE THEM... THEN WE COME BACK, AND START IT AGAIN.
WE KEEP DOING THIS, WE'LL THIN THEM OUT-- AS LONG AS NOTHING HAPPENS TO DRAW THEM BACK.
I'M SORRY, MORGAN.
THUNK!
OH, MY GOD--WHAT ARE YOU *DOING?!*

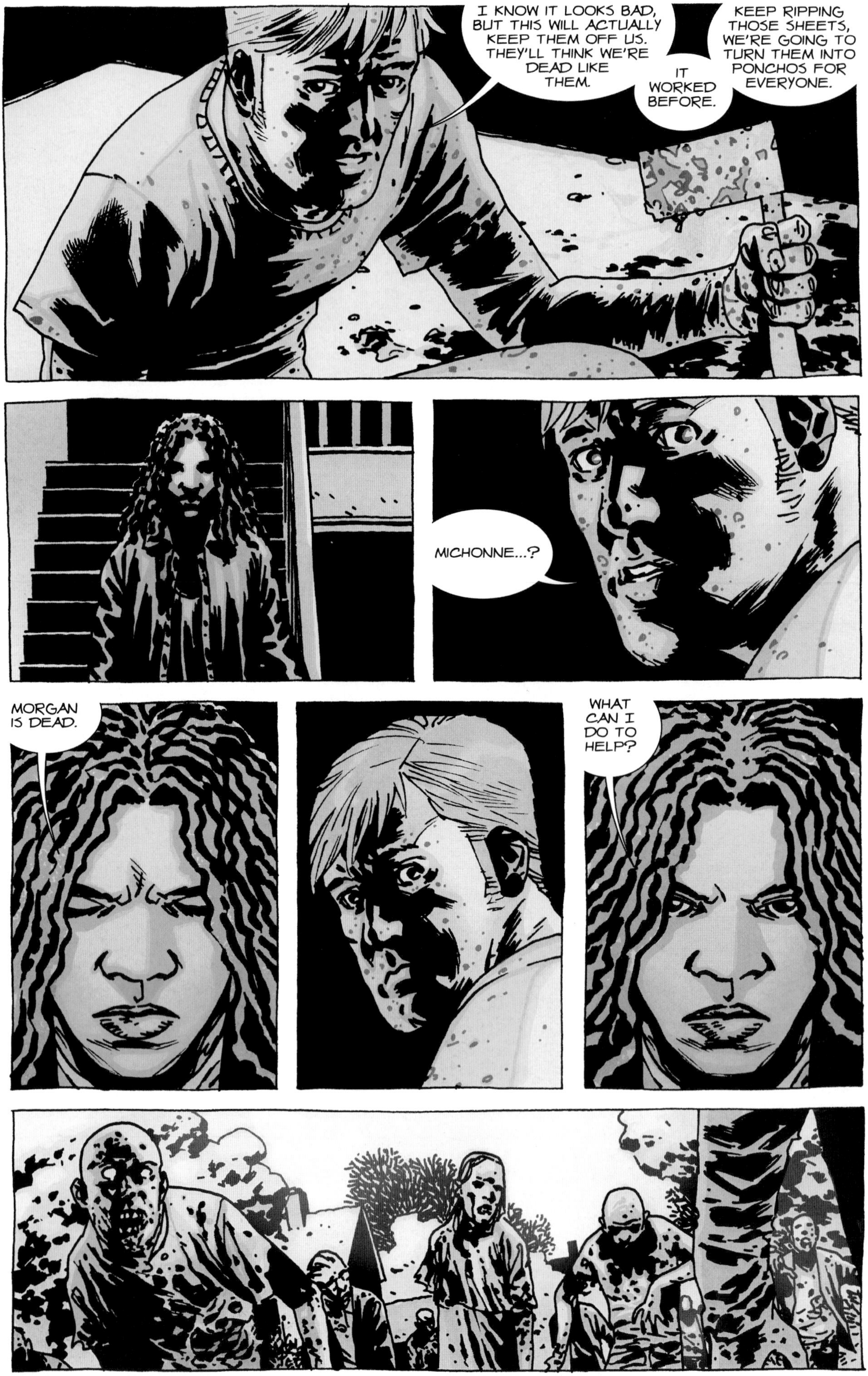
I KNOW IT LOOKS BAD, BUT THIS WILL ACTUALLY KEEP THEM OFF US. THEY'LL THINK WE'RE DEAD LIKE THEM.
IT WORKED BEFORE.
KEEP RIPPING THOSE SHEETS, WE'RE GOING TO TURN THEM INTO PONCHOS FOR EVERYONE.
MICHONNE...?
MORGAN IS DEAD.
WHAT CAN I DO TO HELP?

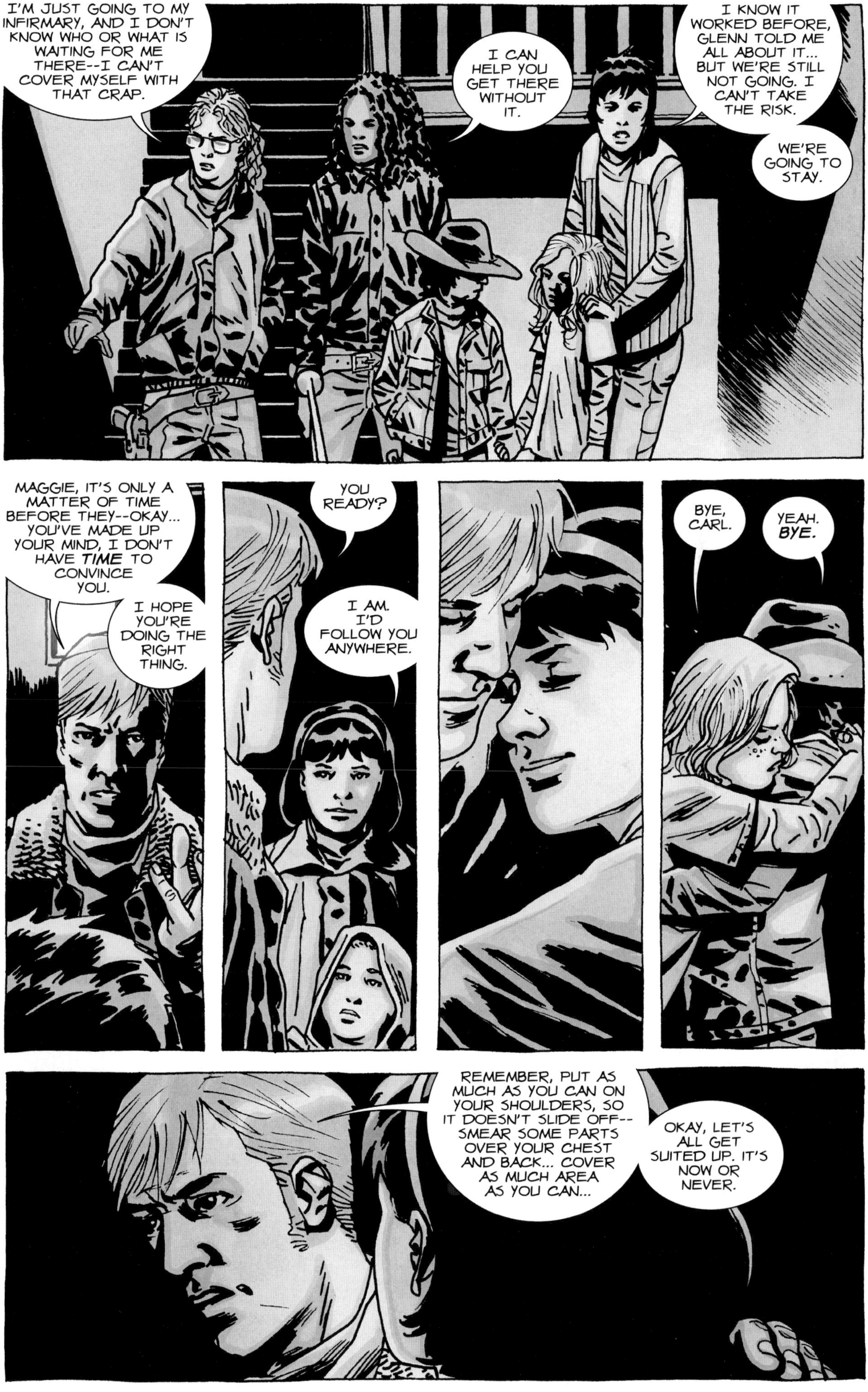
I'M JUST GOING TO MY INFIRMARY, AND I DON'T KNOW WHO OR WHAT IS WAITING FOR ME THERE--I CAN'T COVER MYSELF WITH THAT CRAP.
I CAN HELP YOU GET THERE WITHOUT IT.
I KNOW IT WORKED BEFORE, GLENN TOLD ME ALL ABOUT IT... BUT WE'RE STILL NOT GOING. I CAN'T TAKE THE RISK.
WE'RE GOING TO STAY.
MAGGIE, IT'S ONLY A MATTER OF TIME BEFORE THEY--OKAY... YOU'VE MADE UP YOUR MIND, I DON'T HAVE *TIME* TO CONVINCE YOU.
I HOPE YOU'RE DOING THE RIGHT THING.
YOU READY?
I AM. I'D FOLLOW YOU ANYWHERE.
BYE, CARL.
YEAH. ***BYE.***
REMEMBER, PUT AS MUCH AS YOU CAN ON YOUR SHOULDERS, SO IT DOESN'T SLIDE OFF-- SMEAR SOME PARTS OVER YOUR CHEST AND BACK... COVER AS MUCH AREA AS YOU CAN...
OKAY, LET'S ALL GET SUITED UP. IT'S NOW OR NEVER.

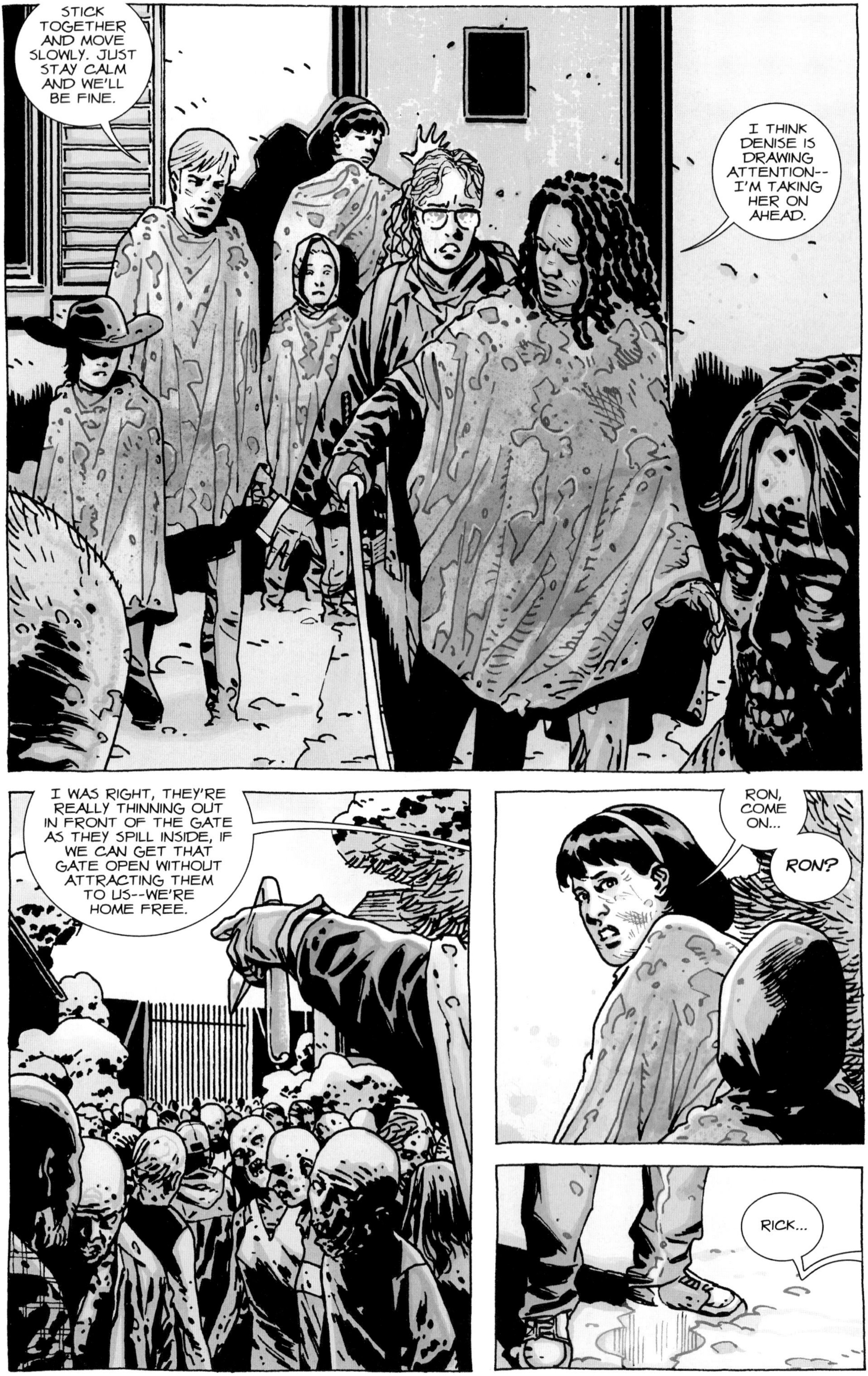
STICK TOGETHER AND MOVE SLOWLY. JUST STAY CALM AND WE'LL BE FINE.
I THINK DENISE IS DRAWING ATTENTION-- I'M TAKING HER ON AHEAD.
I WAS RIGHT, THEY'RE REALLY THINNING OUT IN FRONT OF THE GATE AS THEY SPILL INSIDE, IF WE CAN GET THAT GATE OPEN WITHOUT ATTRACTING THEM TO US--WE'RE HOME FREE.
RON, COME ON...
RON?
RICK...

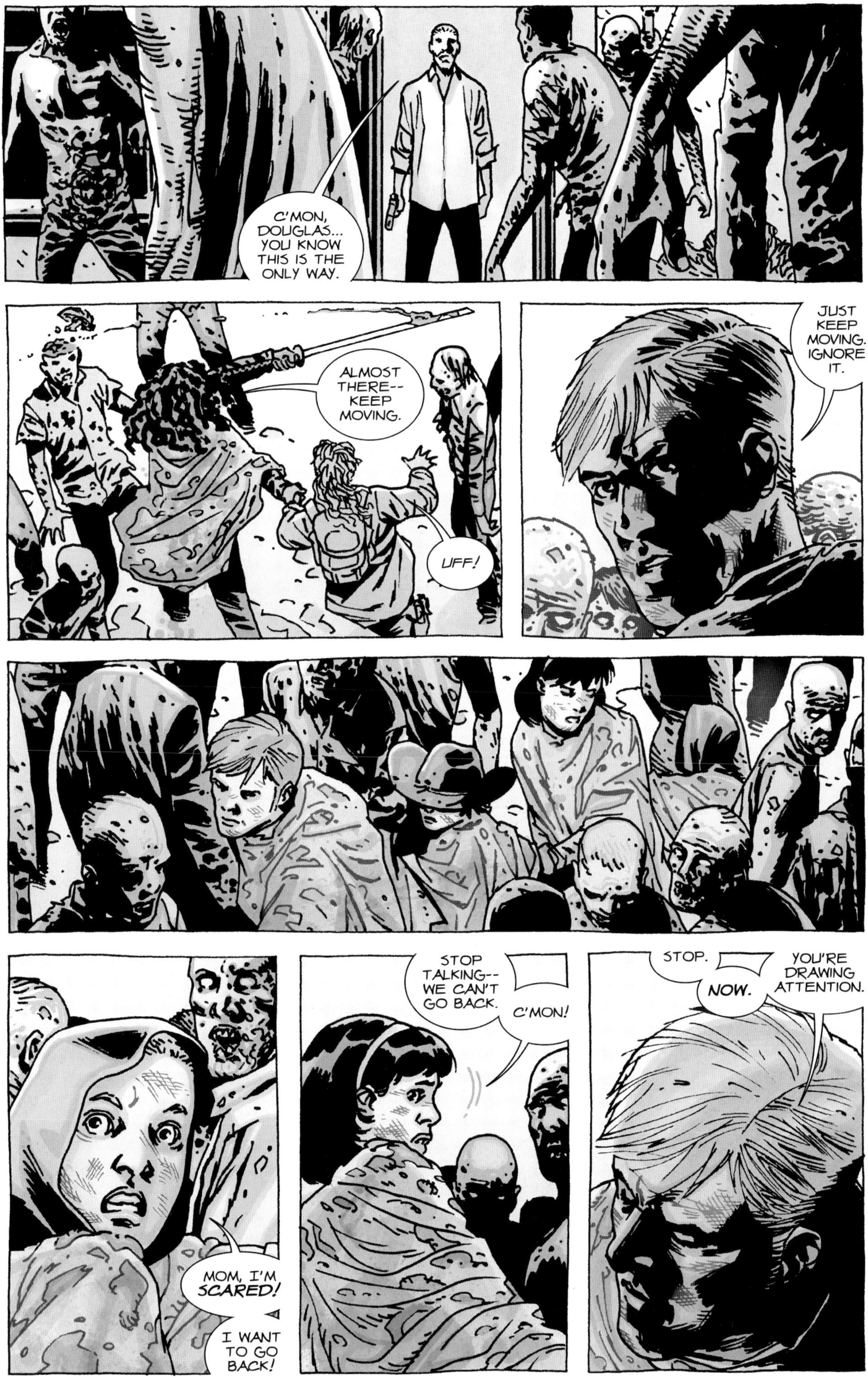

C'MON, DOUGLAS... YOU KNOW THIS IS THE ONLY WAY.
ALMOST THERE-- KEEP MOVING.
UFF!
JUST KEEP MOVING. IGNORE IT.
MOM, I'M SCARED!
I WANT TO GO BACK!
STOP TALKING-- WE CAN'T GO BACK.
C'MON!
STOP.
NOW.
YOU'RE DRAWING ATTENTION.

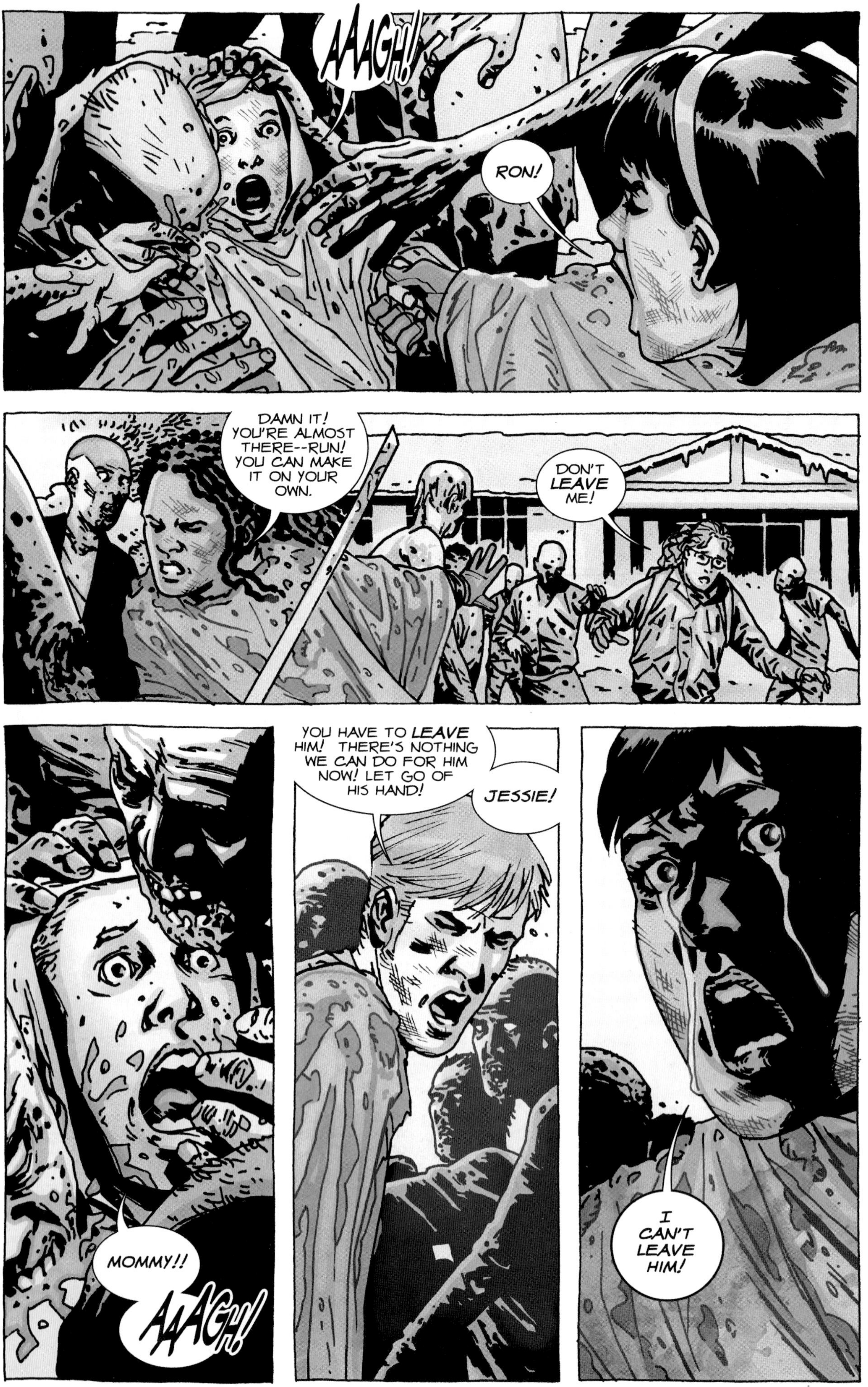
AAAGH!
RON!
DAMN IT! YOU'RE ALMOST THERE--RUN! YOU CAN MAKE IT ON YOUR OWN.
DON'T LEAVE ME!
MOMMY!!
AAAGH!
YOU HAVE TO LEAVE HIM! THERE'S NOTHING WE CAN DO FOR HIM NOW! LET GO OF HIS HAND!
JESSIE!
I CAN'T LEAVE HIM!

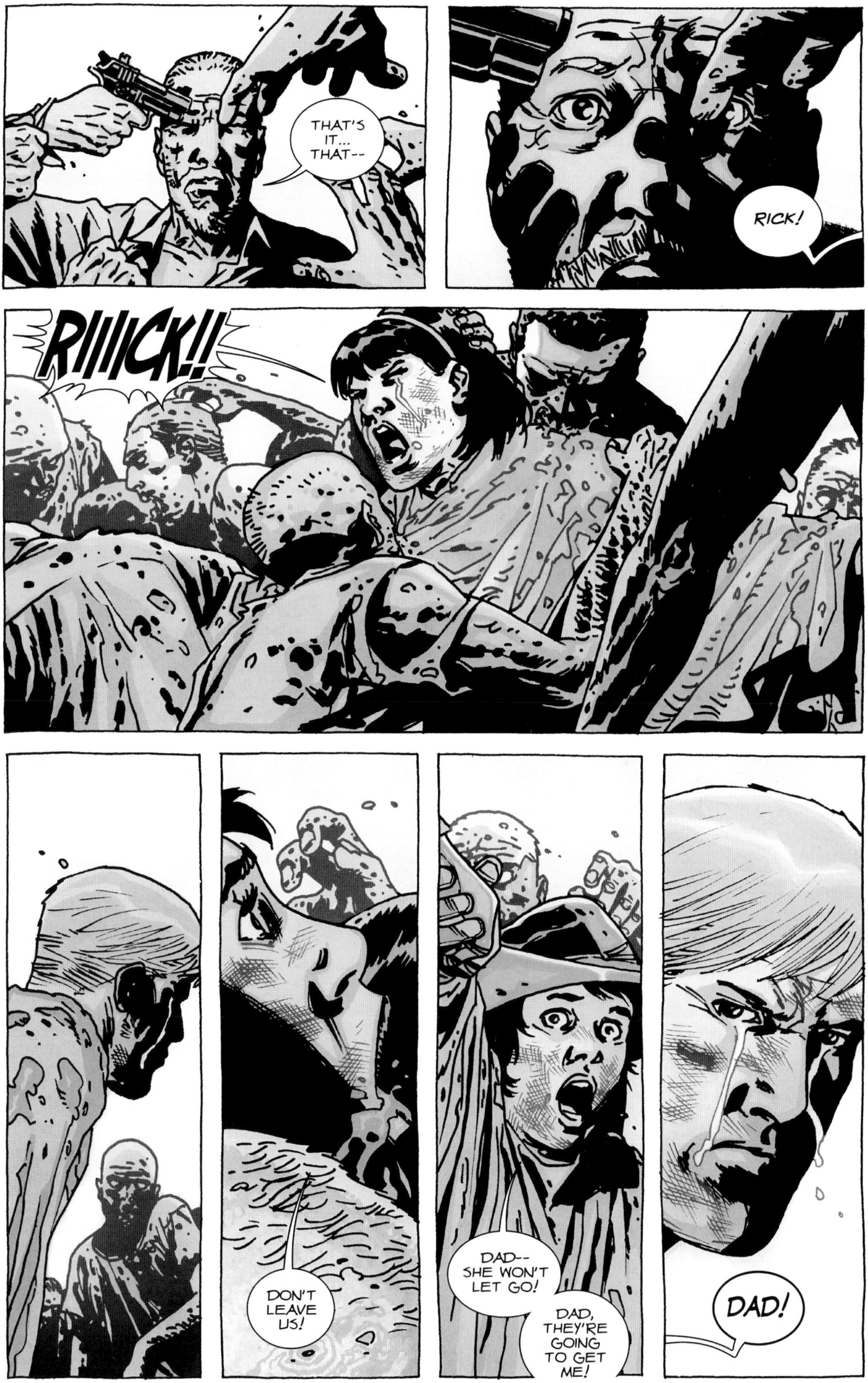
THAT'S IT... THAT--
RICK!
RIIICK!!
DON'T LEAVE US!
DAD-- SHE WON'T LET GO!
DAD, THEY'RE GOING TO GET ME!
DAD!

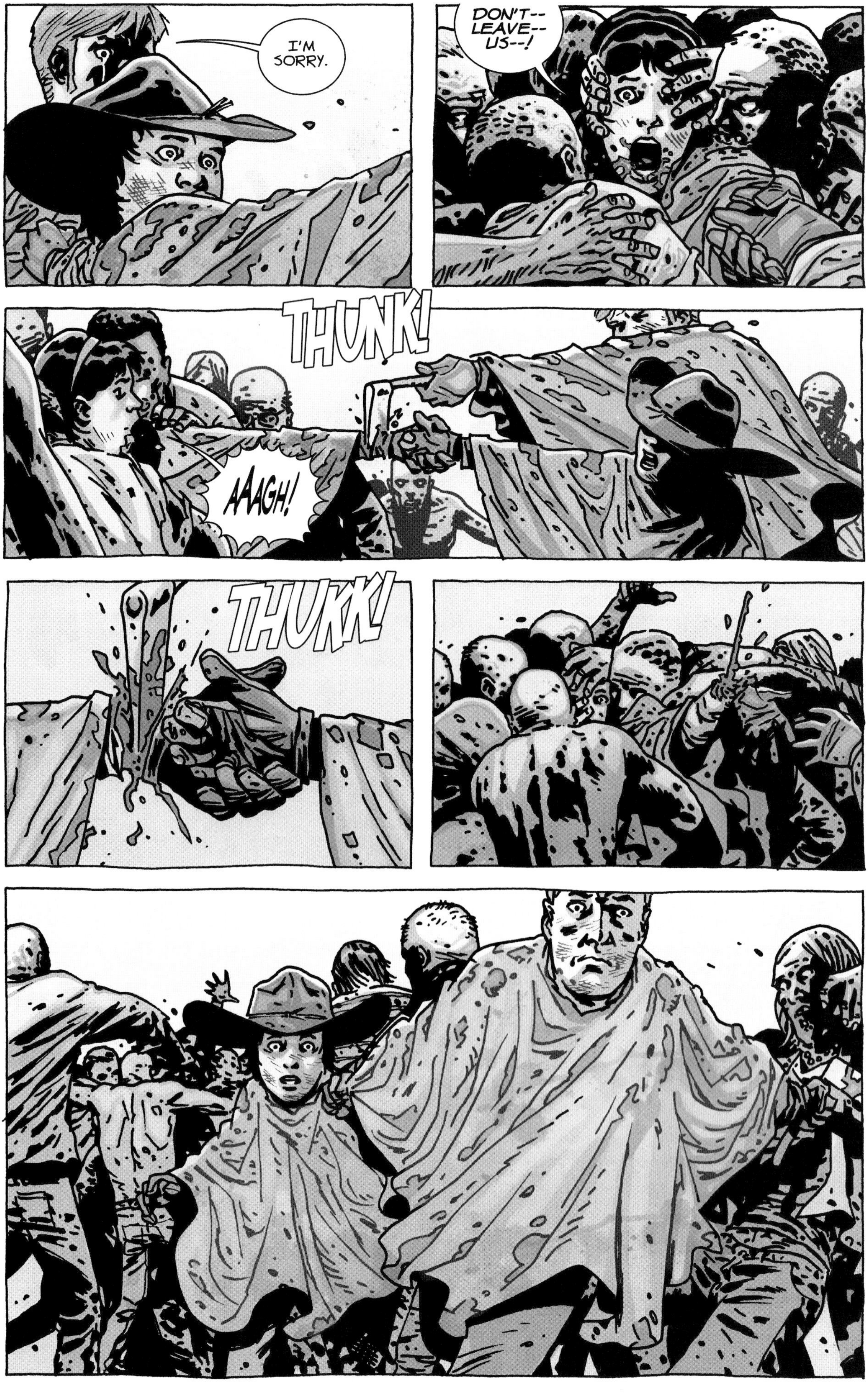
I'M SORRY.
DON'T-- LEAVE-- US--!
THUNK!
AAAGH!
THUKK!

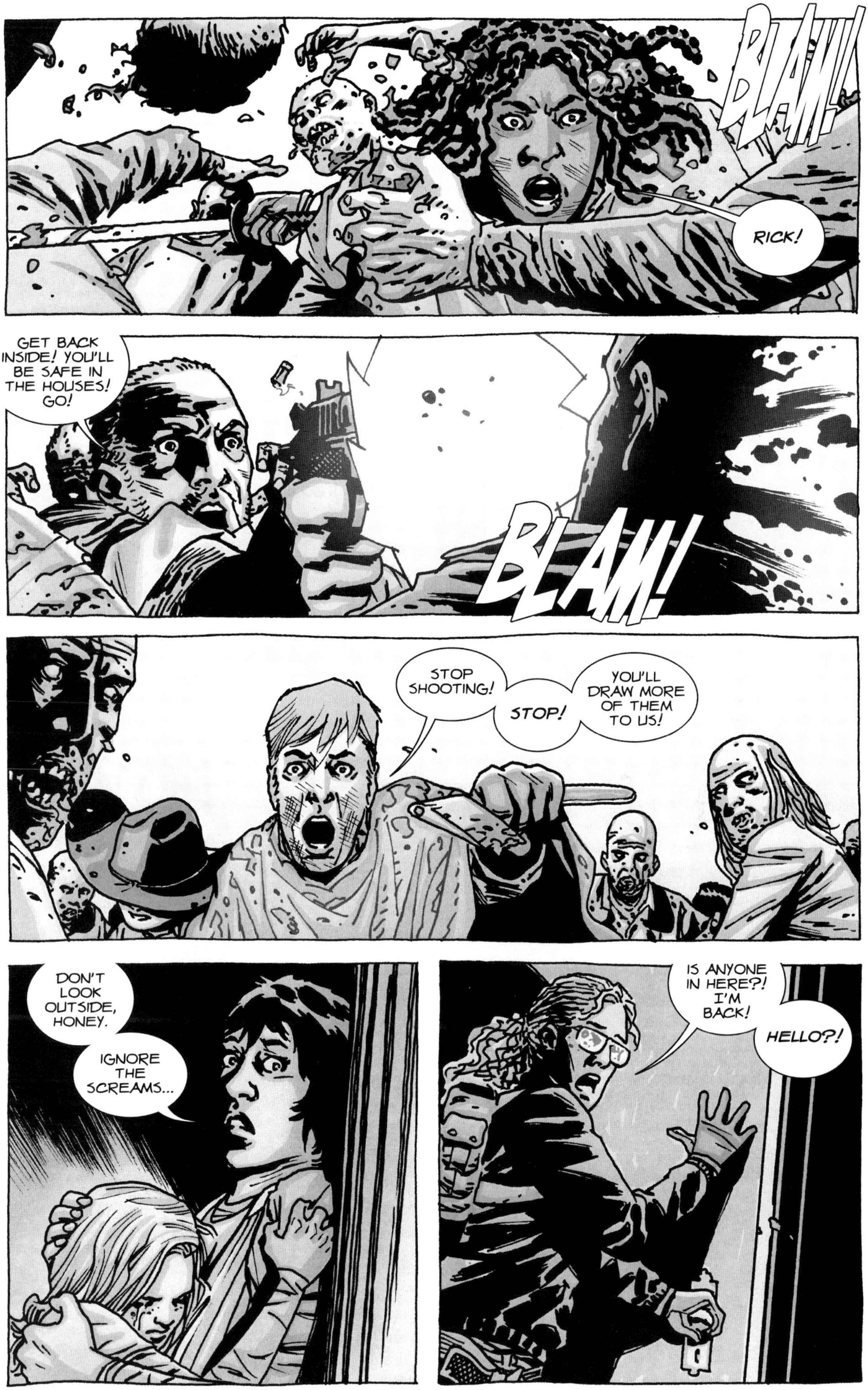
BLAM!!
RICK!
GET BACK INSIDE! YOU'LL BE SAFE IN THE HOUSES! GO!
BLAM!
STOP SHOOTING!
STOP!
YOU'LL DRAW MORE OF THEM TO US!
DON'T LOOK OUTSIDE, HONEY.
IGNORE THE SCREAMS...
IS ANYONE IN HERE?! I'M BACK!
HELLO?!

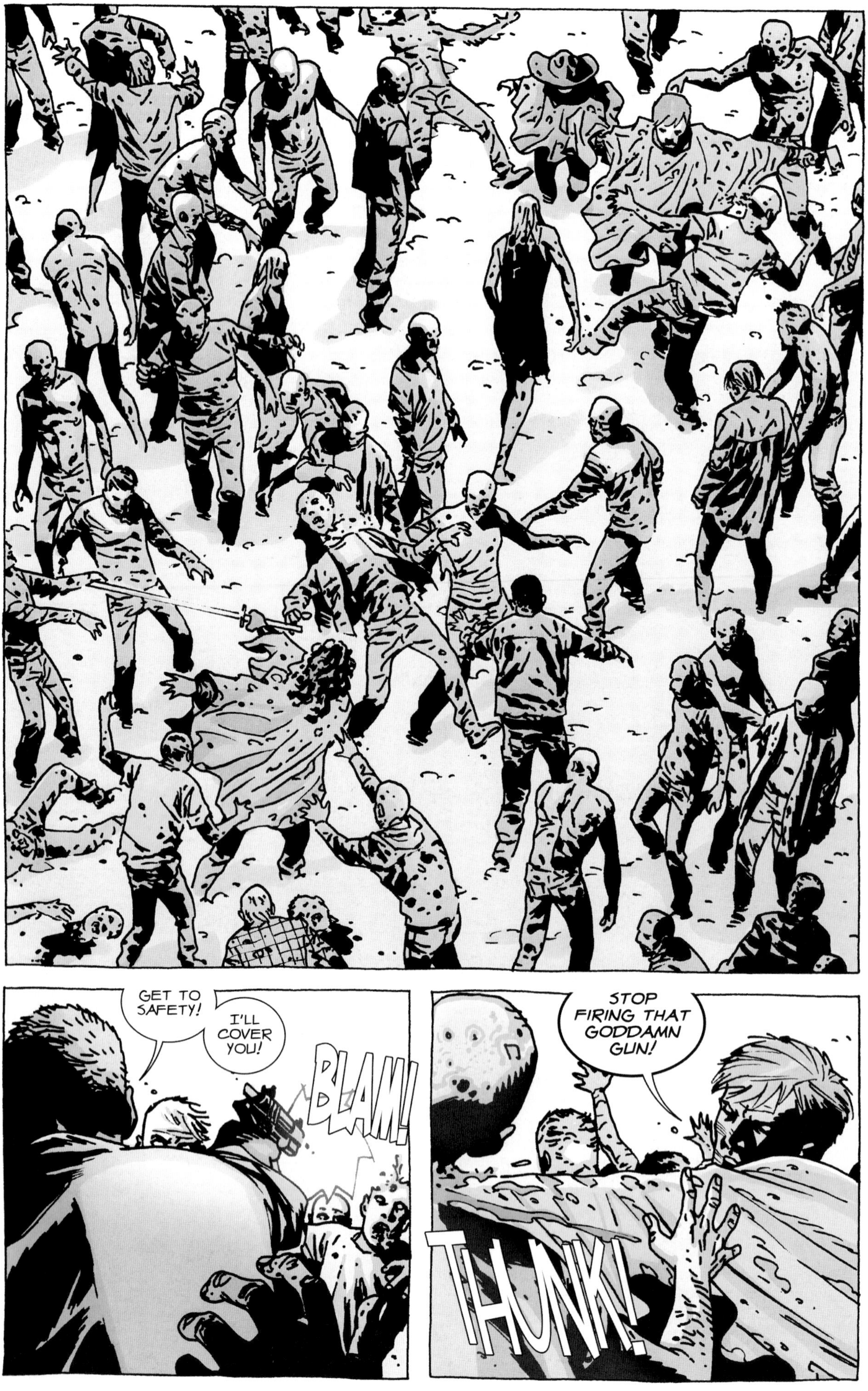
GET TO SAFETY!
I'LL COVER YOU!
BLAM!
STOP FIRING THAT GODDAMN GUN!
THUNK!

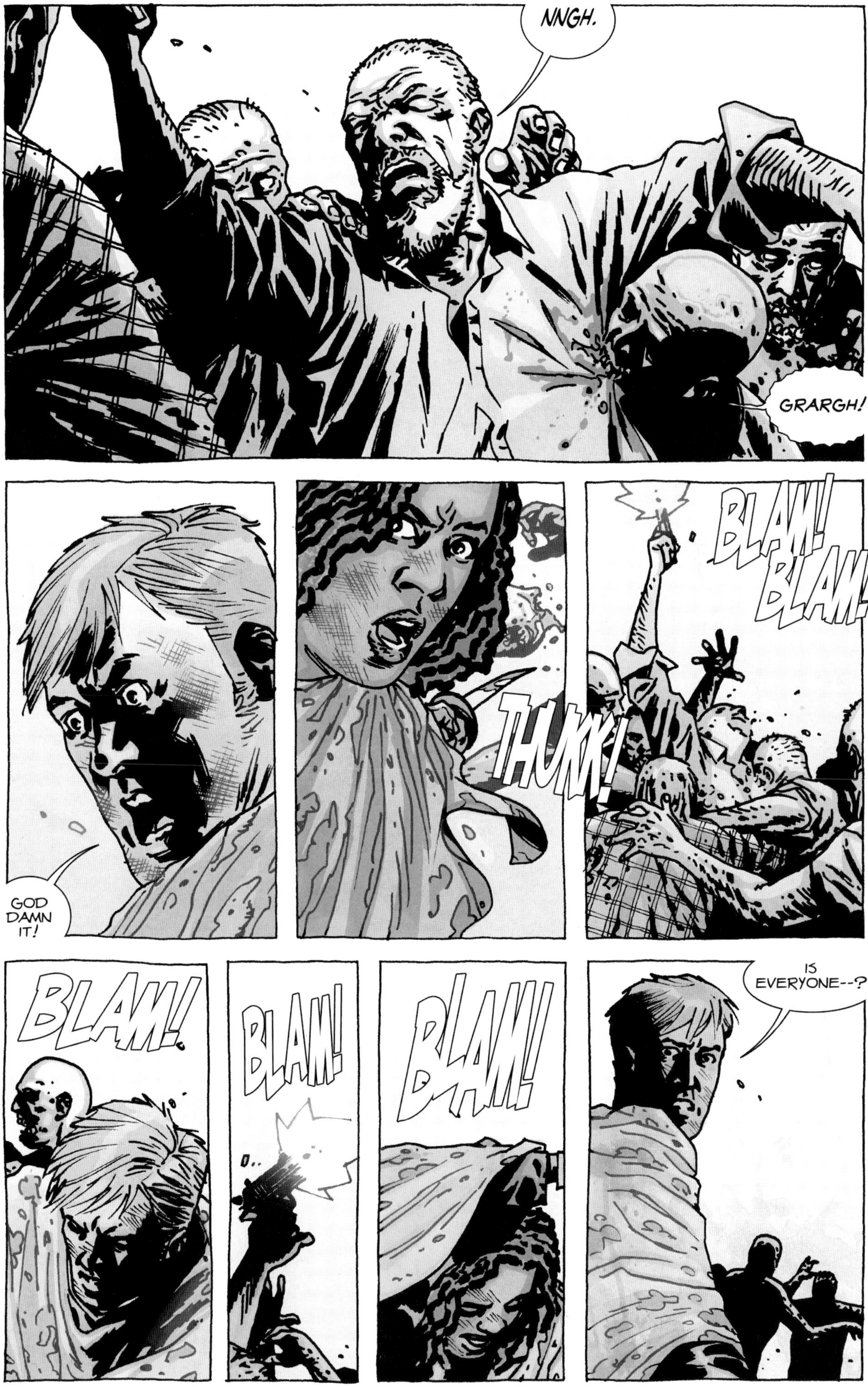
NNGH.
GRARGH!
GOD DAMN IT!
THUKK!
BLAM! BLAM!
BLAM!
BLAM!
BLAM!
IS EVERYONE--?

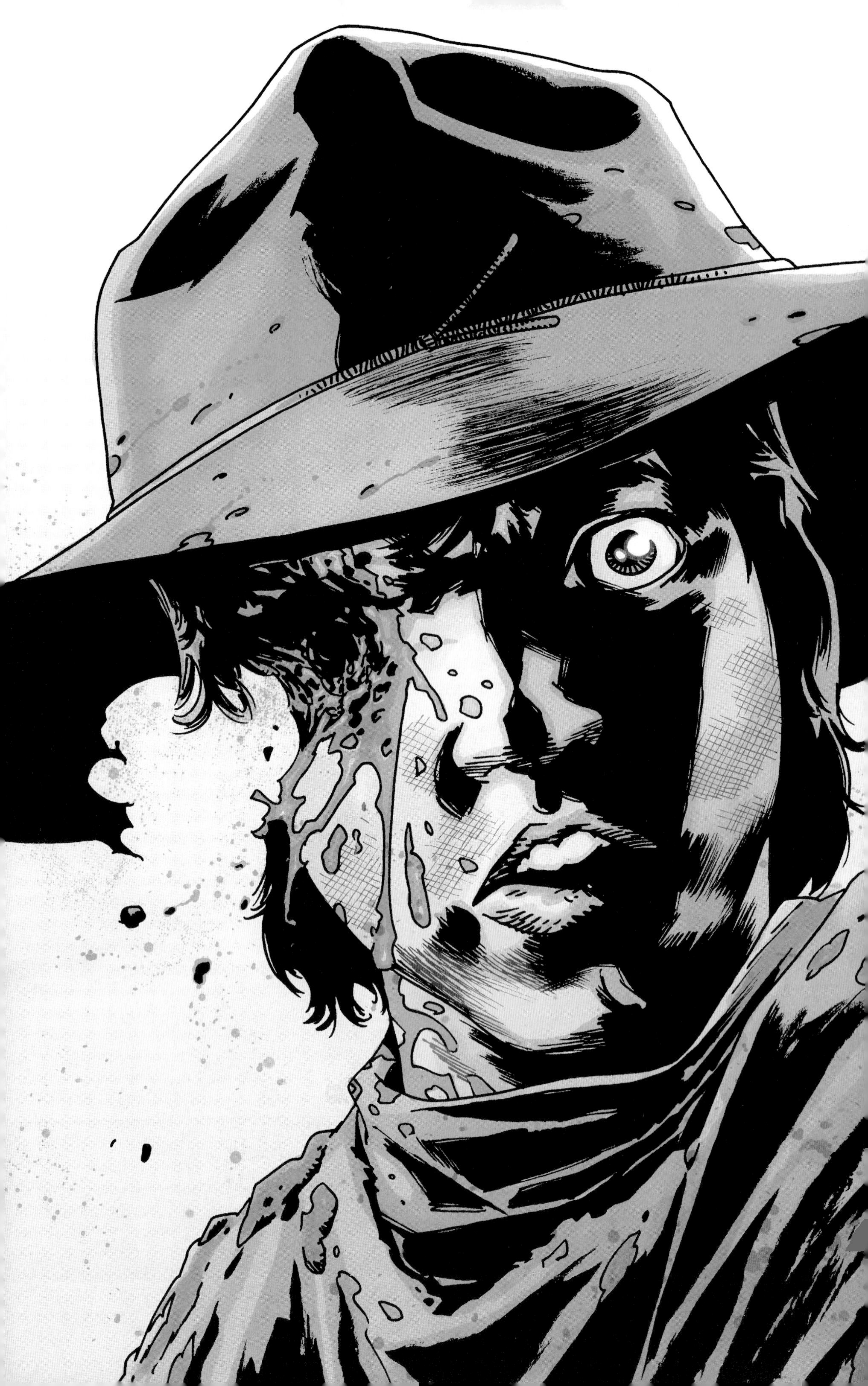

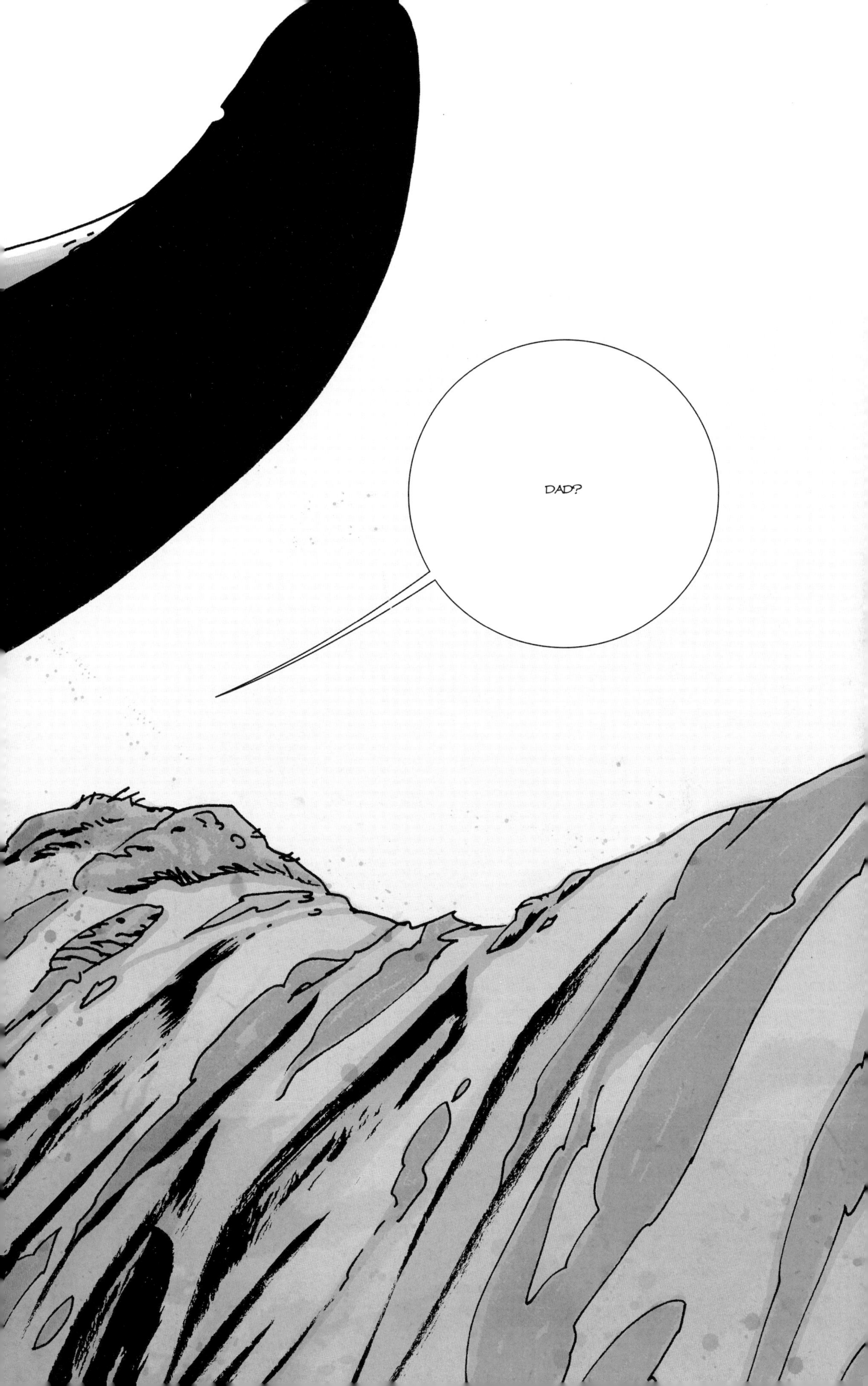
DAD?

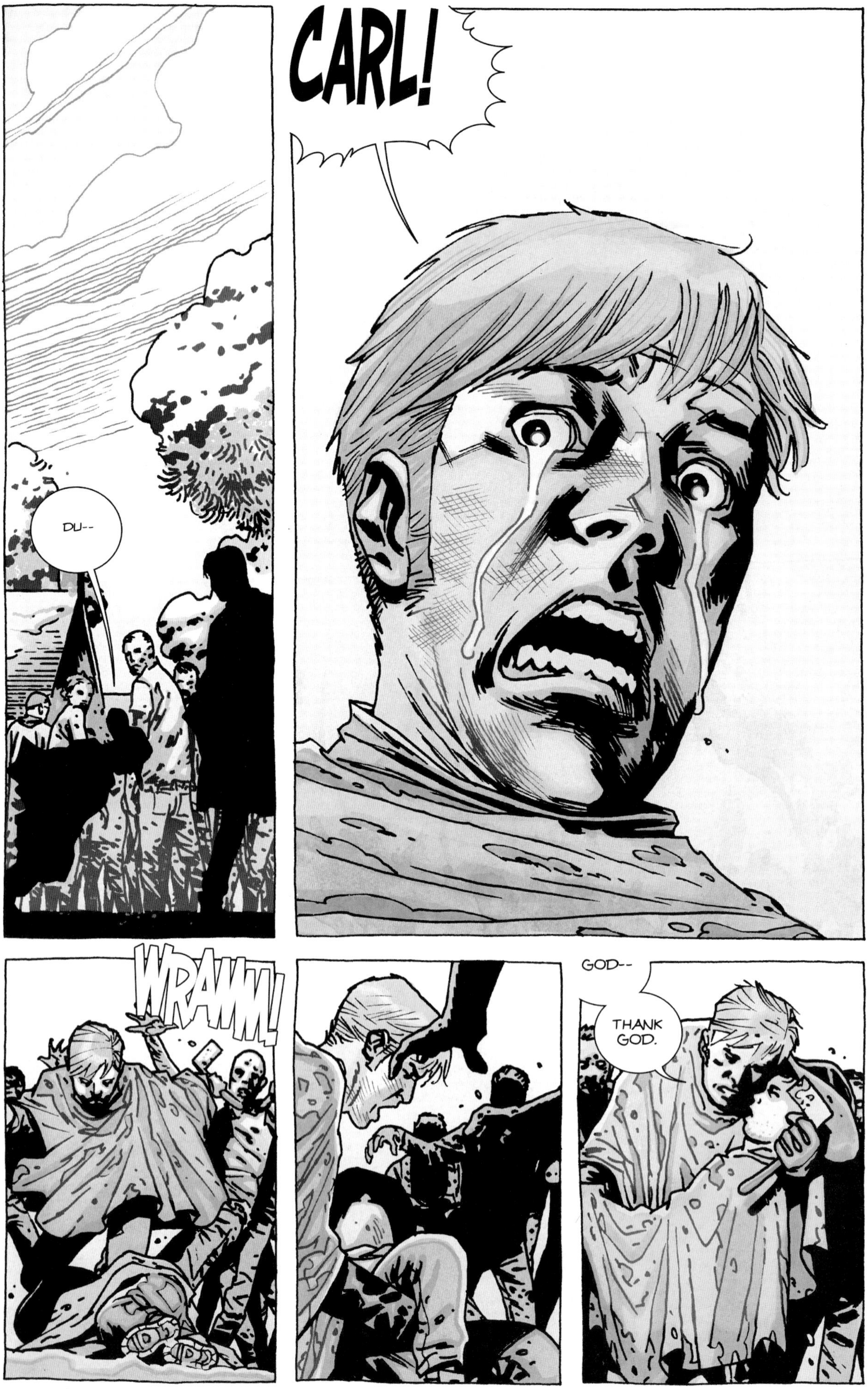
DU--
CARL!
WRAMM!
GOD--
THANK GOD.

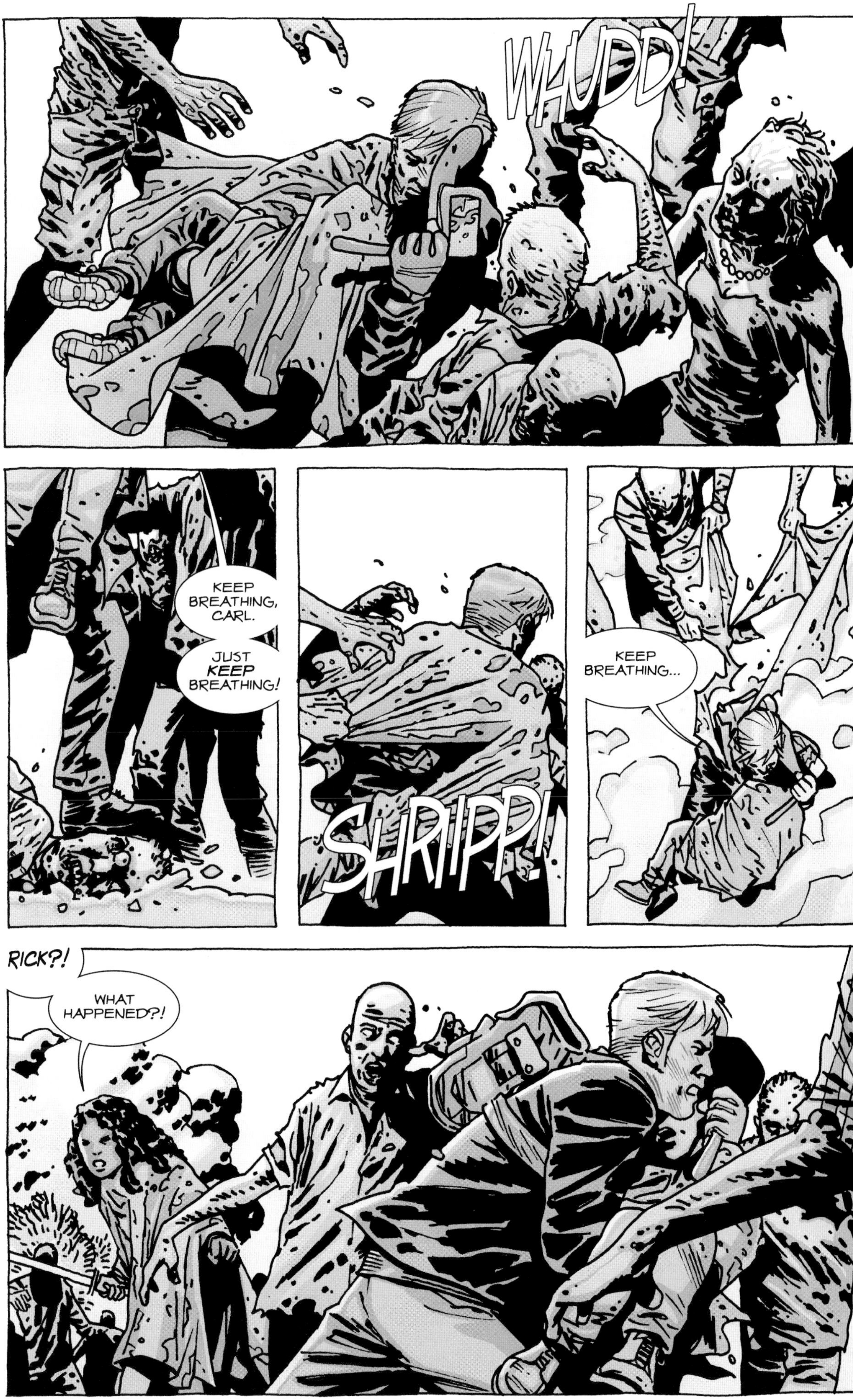
WHUDD!
KEEP BREATHING, CARL.
JUST KEEP BREATHING!
SHRIPP!
KEEP BREATHING...
RICK?!
WHAT HAPPENED?!

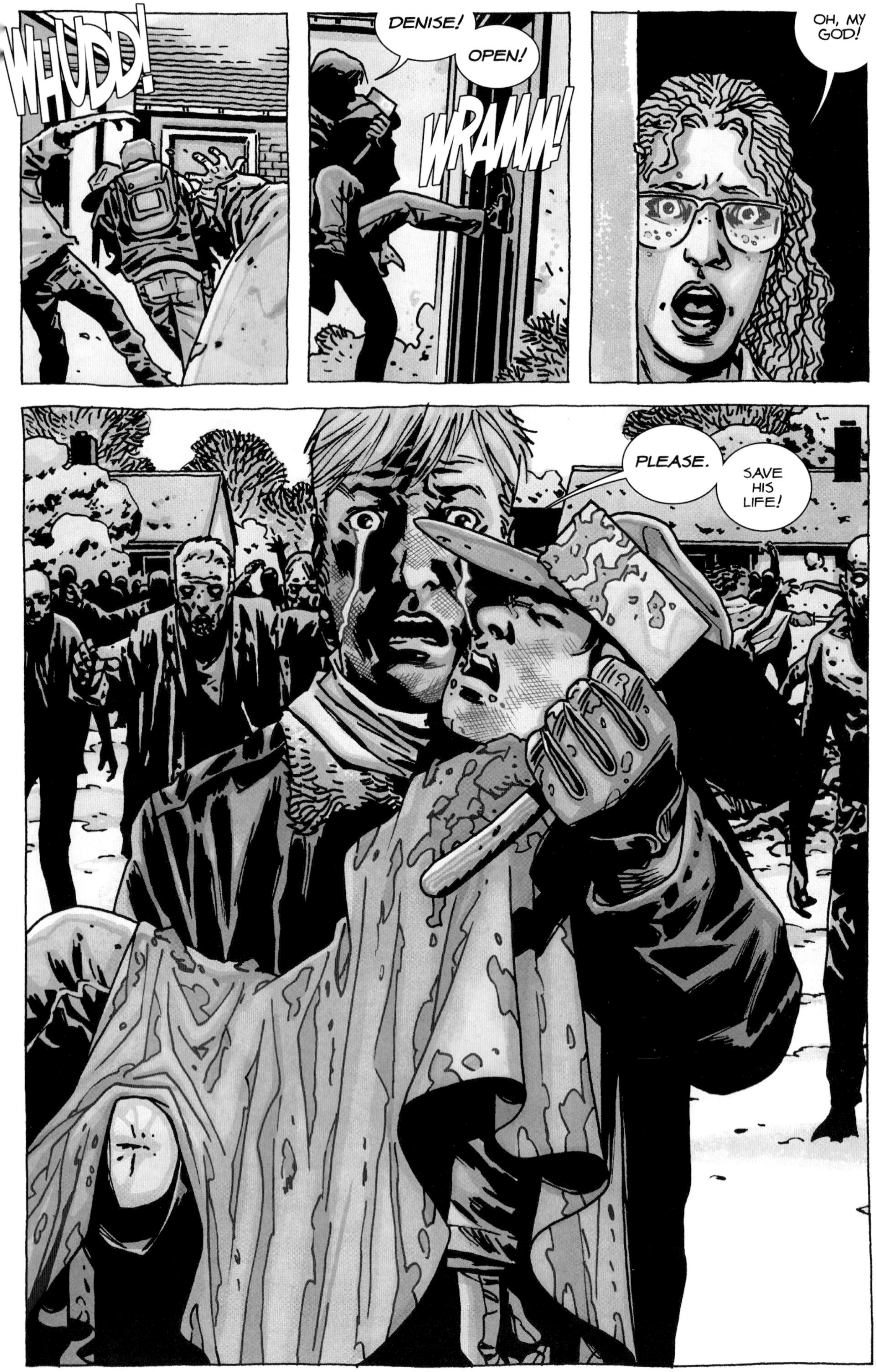
WHUDD!
DENISE!
OPEN!
WRAMM!
OH, MY GOD!
PLEASE.
SAVE HIS LIFE!

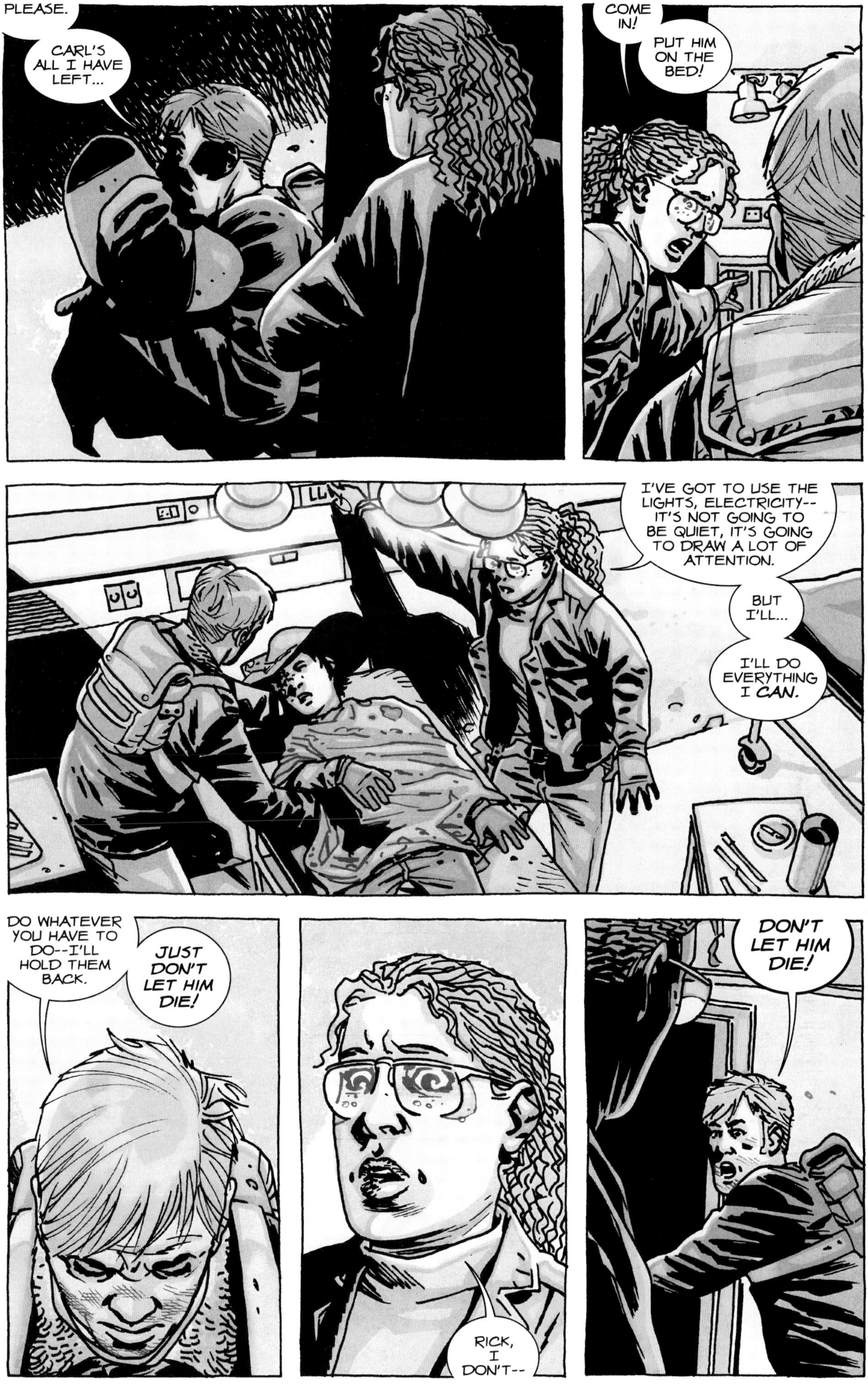
PLEASE.
CARL'S ALL I HAVE LEFT...
COME IN!
PUT HIM ON THE BED!
I'VE GOT TO USE THE LIGHTS, ELECTRICITY-- IT'S NOT GOING TO BE QUIET, IT'S GOING TO DRAW A LOT OF ATTENTION.
BUT I'LL...
I'LL DO EVERYTHING I *CAN*.
DO WHATEVER YOU HAVE TO DO--I'LL HOLD THEM BACK.
JUST DON'T LET HIM DIE!
RICK, I DON'T--
DON'T LET HIM DIE!

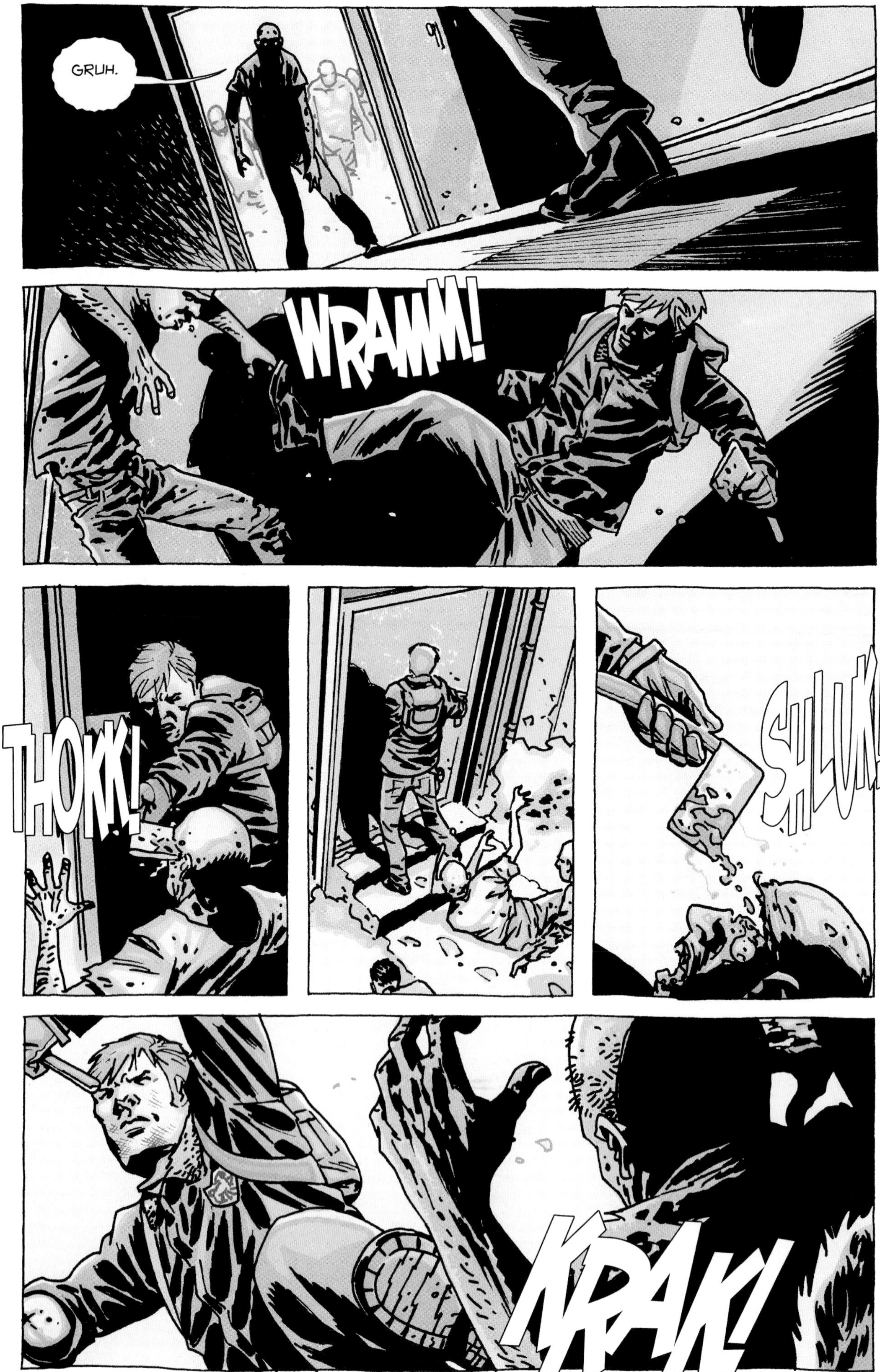
GRUH.
WRAMM!
THOKK!
SHLUK!
KRAK!

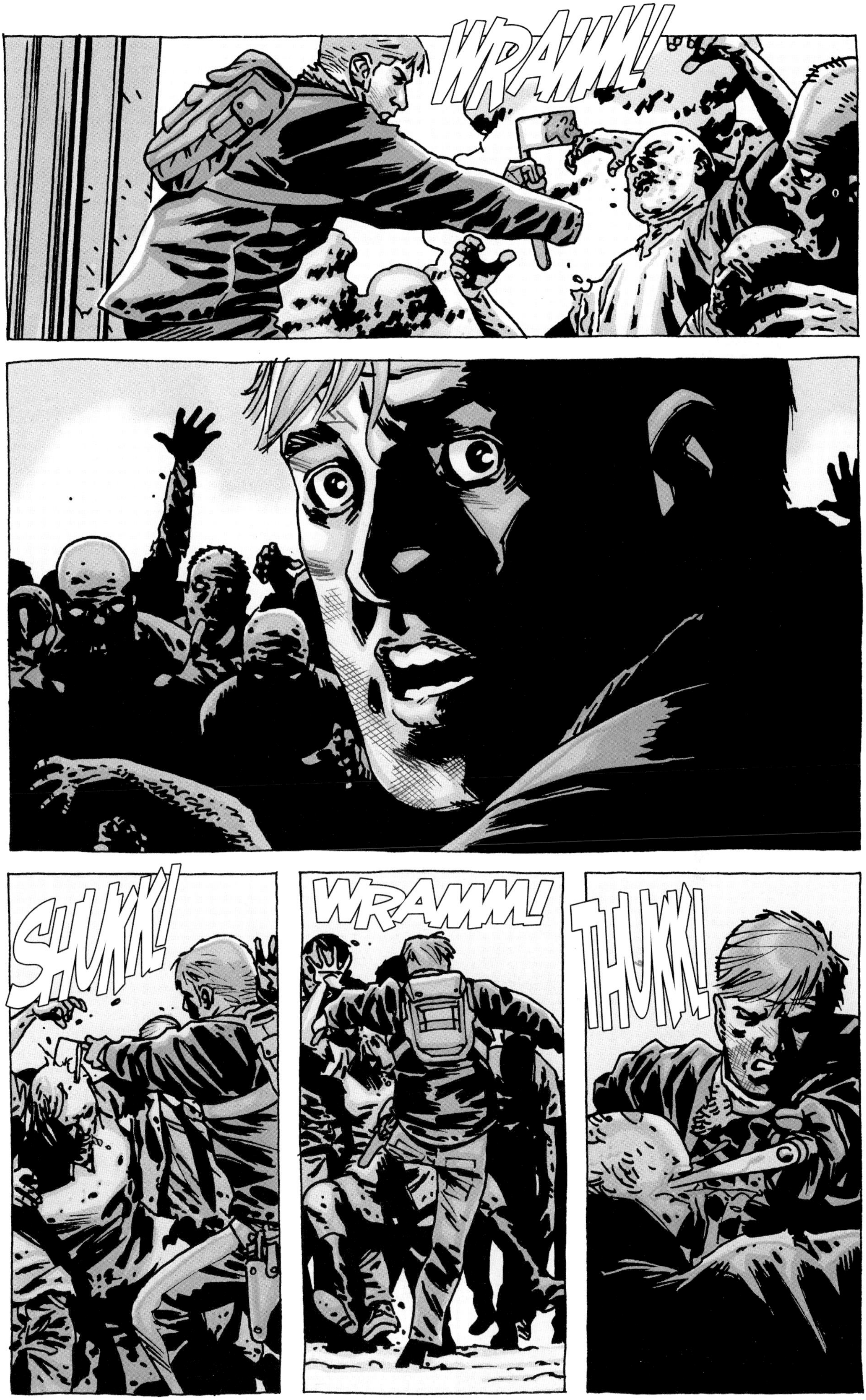
WRAMM!
SHUKK!
WRAMM!
THUKK!

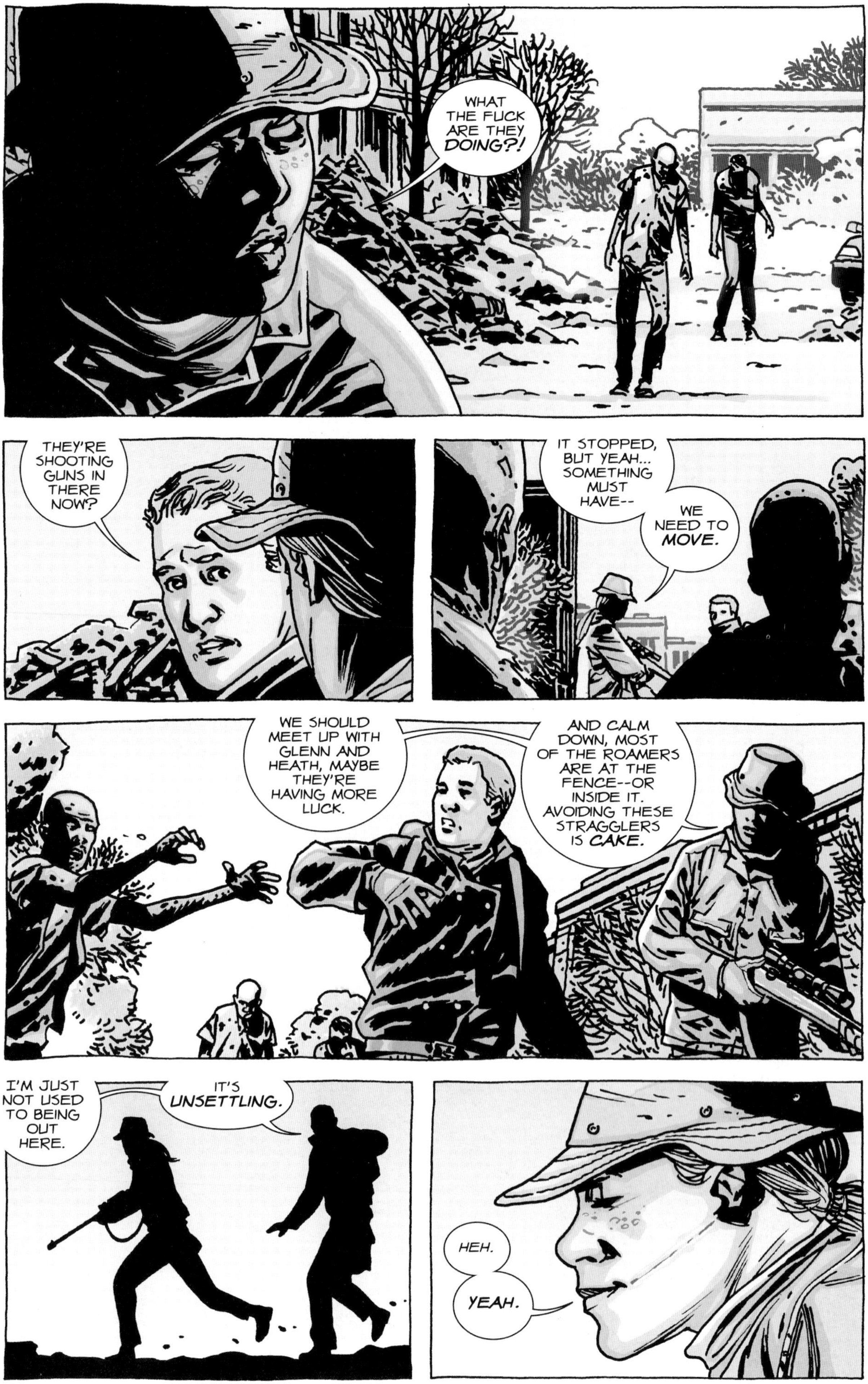
WHAT THE FUCK ARE THEY DOING?!
THEY'RE SHOOTING GUNS IN THERE NOW?
IT STOPPED, BUT YEAH... SOMETHING MUST HAVE--
WE NEED TO MOVE.
WE SHOULD MEET UP WITH GLENN AND HEATH, MAYBE THEY'RE HAVING MORE LUCK.
AND CALM DOWN, MOST OF THE ROAMERS ARE AT THE FENCE--OR INSIDE IT. AVOIDING THESE STRAGGLERS IS CAKE.
I'M JUST NOT USED TO BEING OUT HERE.
IT'S UNSETTLING.
HEH.
YEAH.

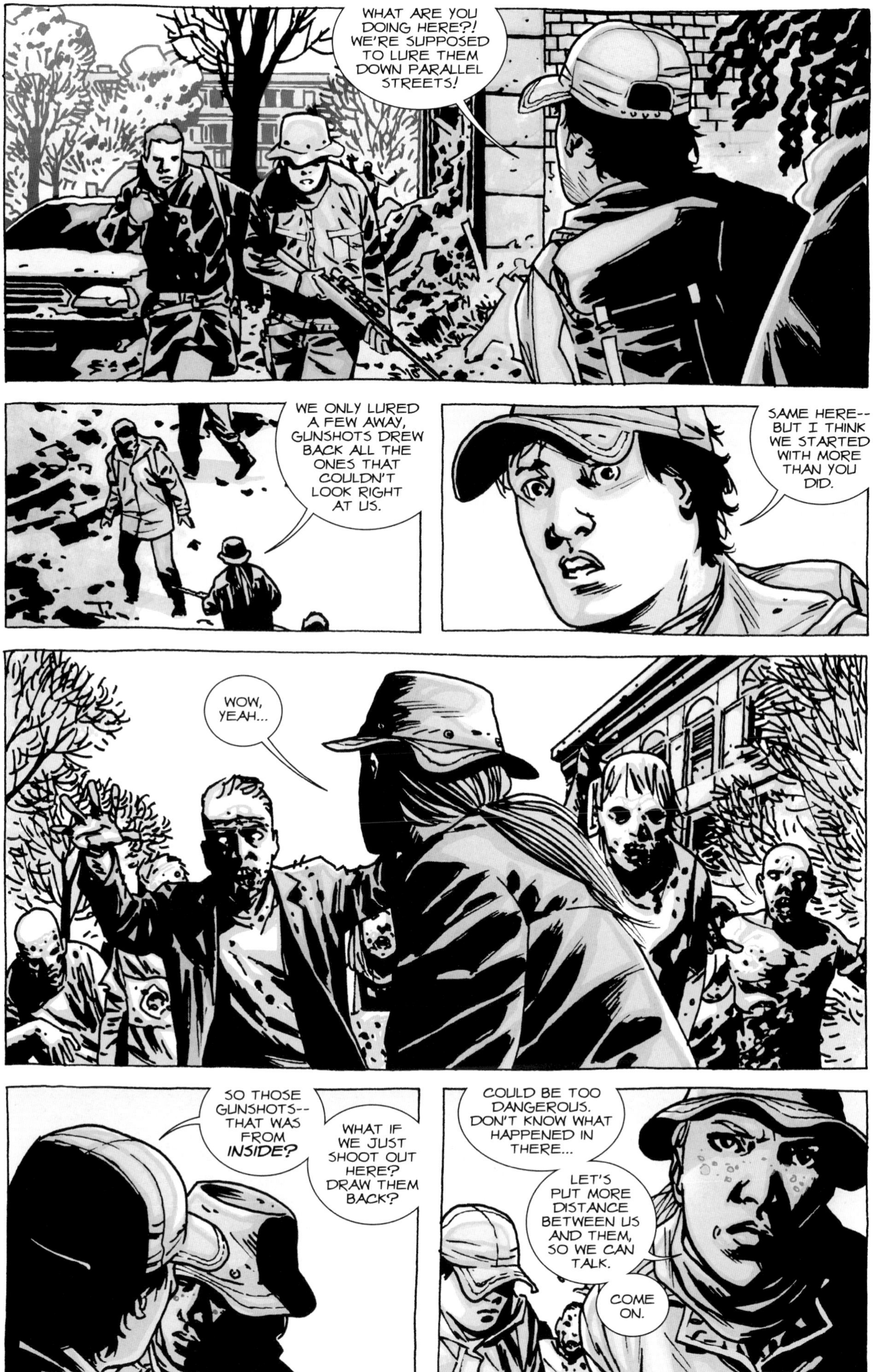
WHAT ARE YOU DOING HERE?! WE'RE SUPPOSED TO LURE THEM DOWN PARALLEL STREETS!
WE ONLY LURED A FEW AWAY, GUNSHOTS DREW BACK ALL THE ONES THAT COULDN'T LOOK RIGHT AT US.
SAME HERE-- BUT I THINK WE STARTED WITH MORE THAN YOU DID.
WOW, YEAH...
SO THOSE GUNSHOTS-- THAT WAS FROM *INSIDE?*
WHAT IF WE JUST SHOOT OUT HERE? DRAW THEM BACK?
COULD BE TOO DANGEROUS. DON'T KNOW WHAT HAPPENED IN THERE...
LET'S PUT MORE DISTANCE BETWEEN US AND THEM, SO WE CAN TALK.
COME ON.

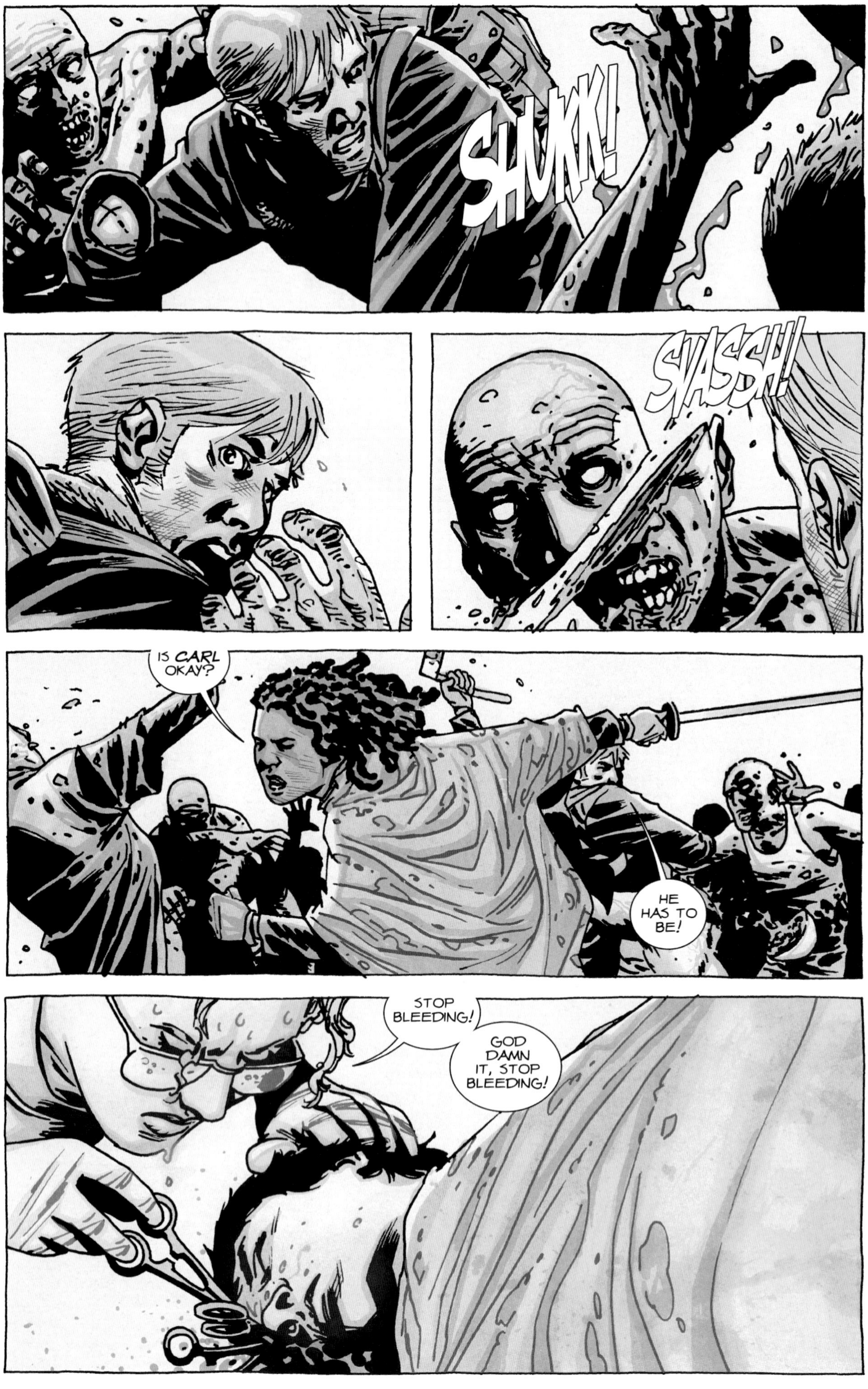
SHUKK!
SWASSH!
IS CARL OKAY?
HE HAS TO BE!
STOP BLEEDING!
GOD DAMN IT, STOP BLEEDING!

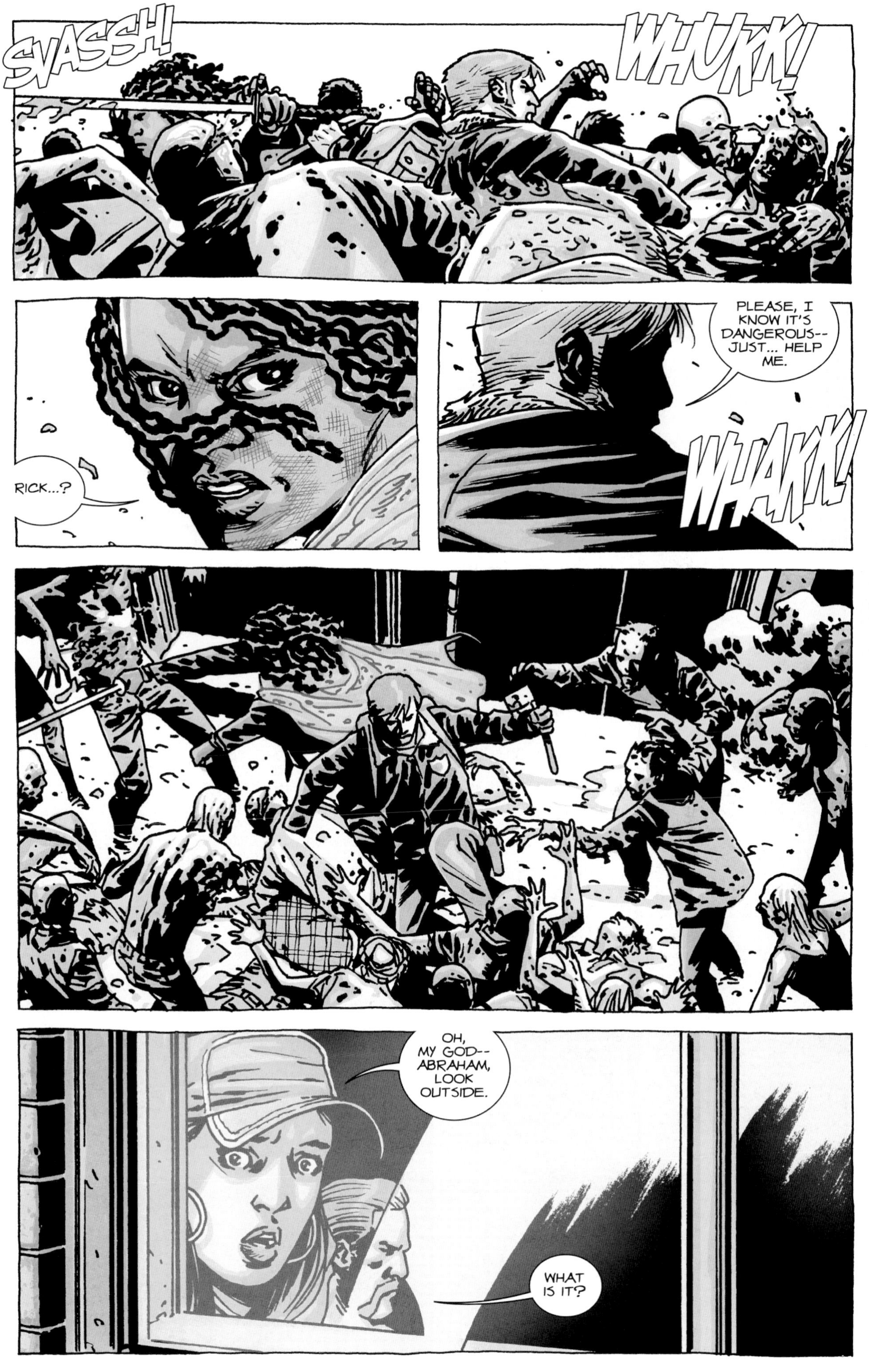
SVASSH!
WHUKK!
RICK...?
PLEASE, I KNOW IT'S DANGEROUS-- JUST... HELP ME.
WHAKK!
OH, MY GOD-- ABRAHAM, LOOK OUTSIDE.
WHAT IS IT?

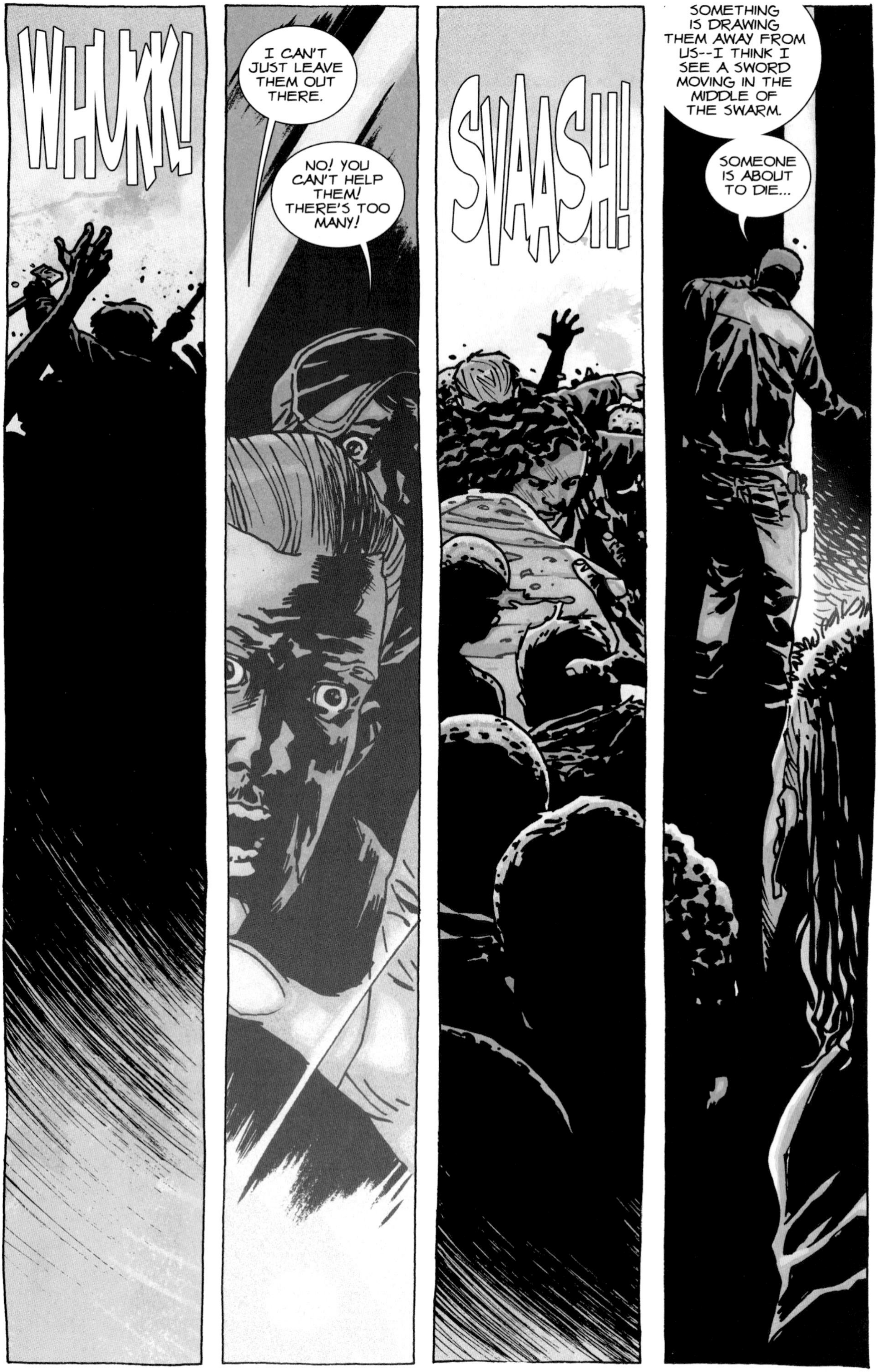

WHUKK!
I CAN'T JUST LEAVE THEM OUT THERE.
NO! YOU CAN'T HELP THEM! THERE'S TOO MANY!
SVAASH!
SOMETHING IS DRAWING THEM AWAY FROM US--I THINK I SEE A SWORD MOVING IN THE MIDDLE OF THE SWARM.
SOMEONE IS ABOUT TO DIE...

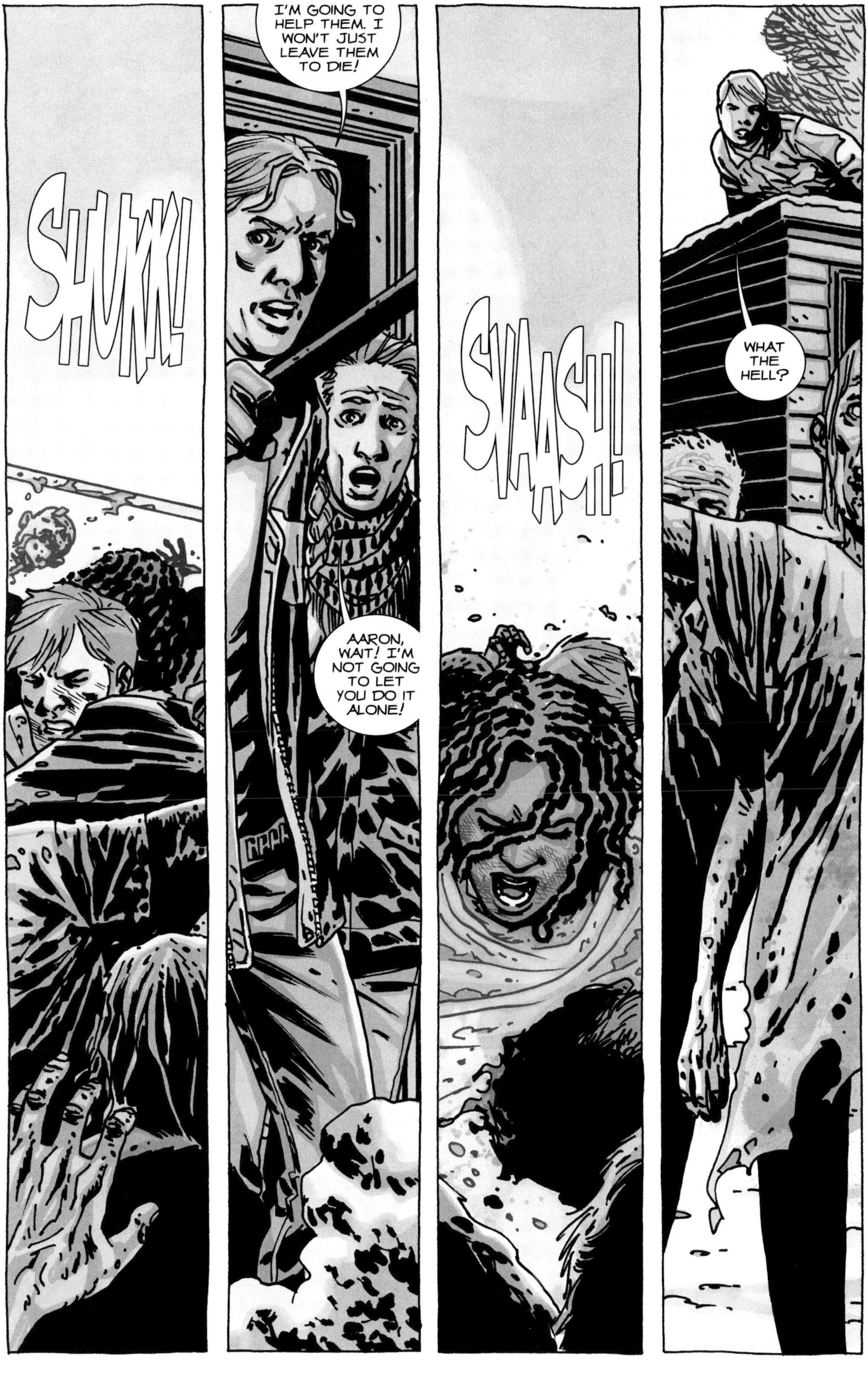

SHUNK!
I'M GOING TO HELP THEM. I WON'T JUST LEAVE THEM TO DIE!
AARON, WAIT! I'M NOT GOING TO LET YOU DO IT ALONE!
SHAASH!
WHAT THE HELL?

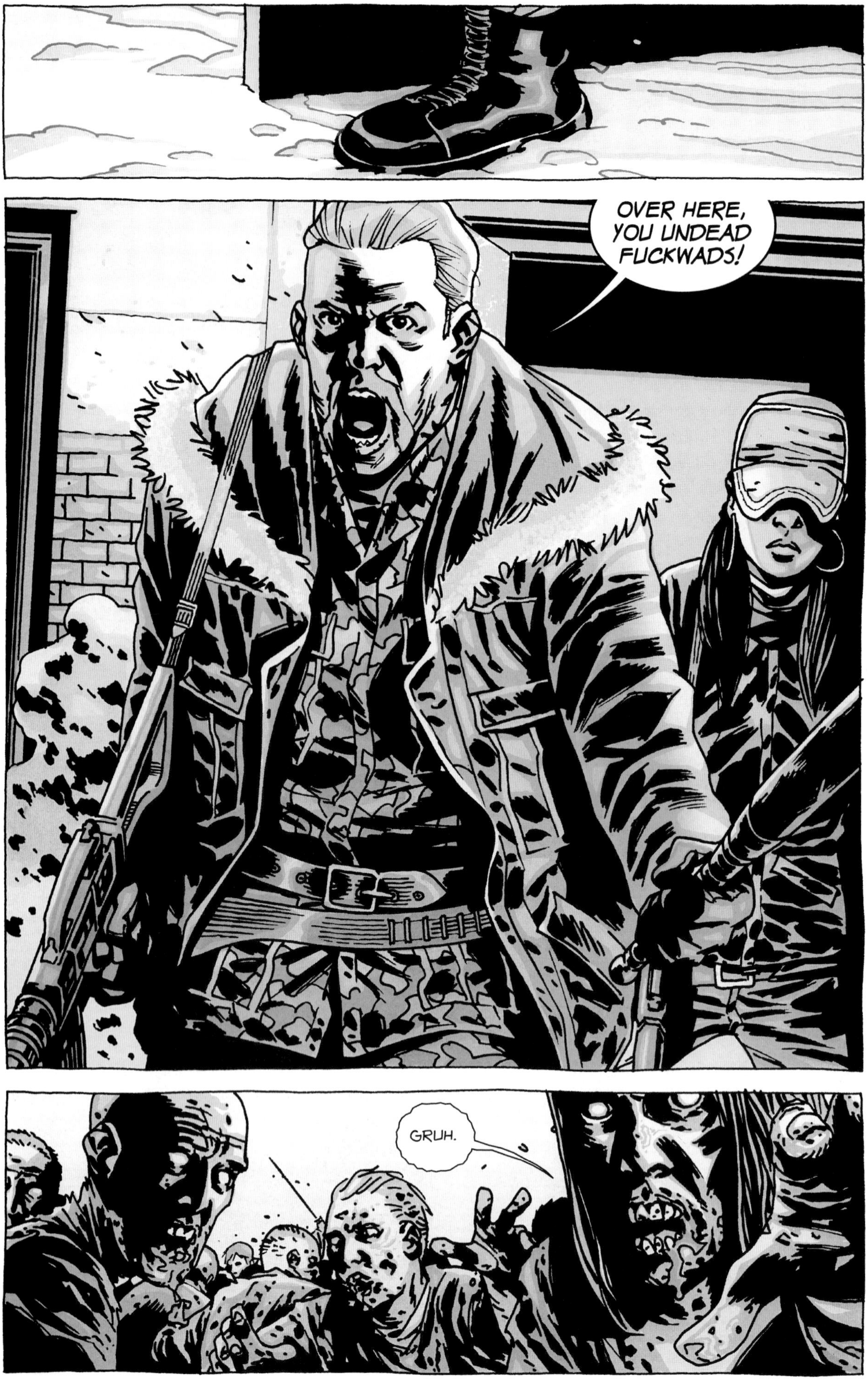
OVER HERE, YOU UNDEAD FUCKWADS!
GRUH.

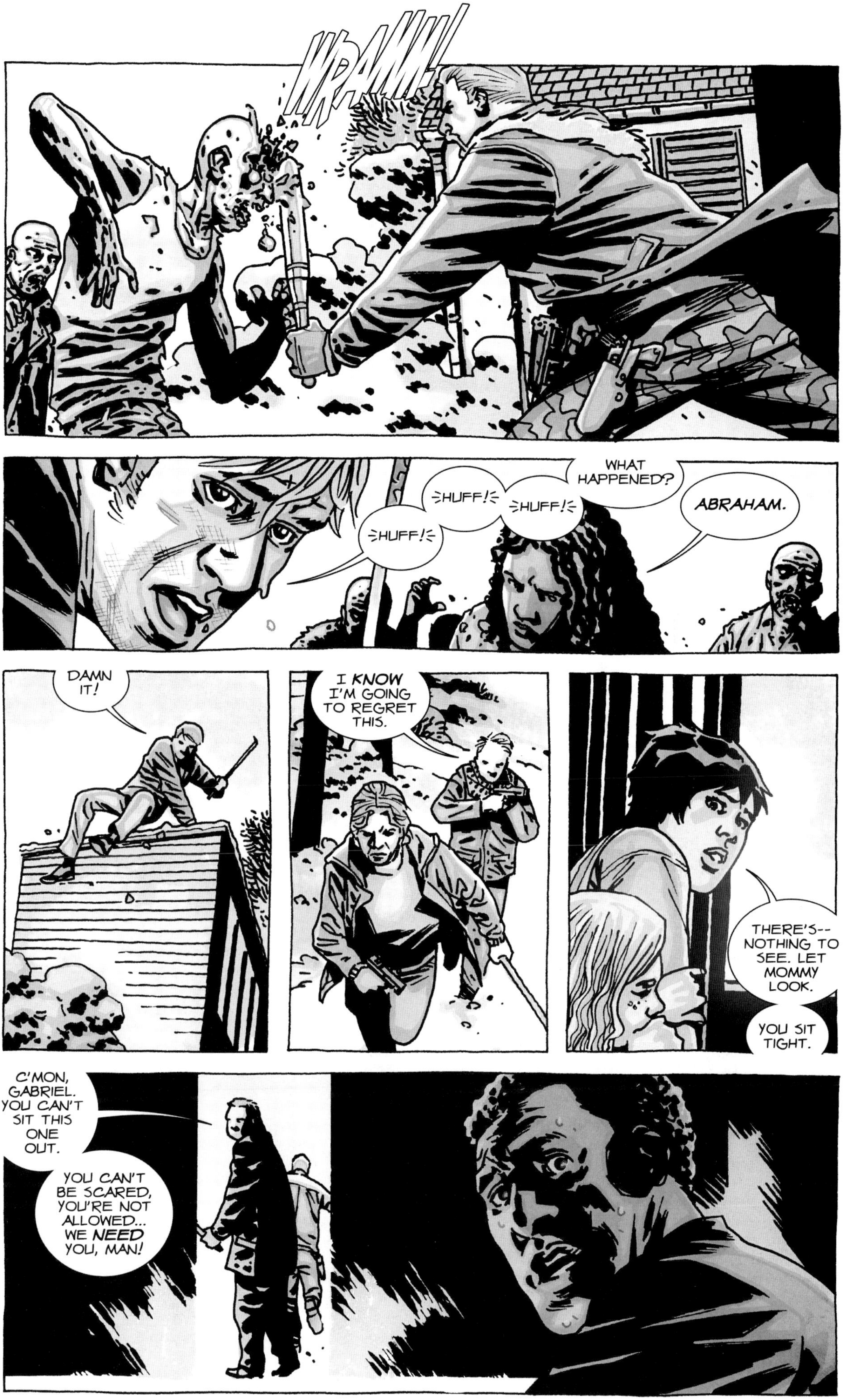
WHAMM!
HUFF!
HUFF!
HUFF!
WHAT HAPPENED?
ABRAHAM.
DAMN IT!
I KNOW I'M GOING TO REGRET THIS.
THERE'S-- NOTHING TO SEE. LET MOMMY LOOK.
YOU SIT TIGHT.
C'MON, GABRIEL. YOU CAN'T SIT THIS ONE OUT.
YOU CAN'T BE SCARED, YOU'RE NOT ALLOWED... WE NEED YOU, MAN!

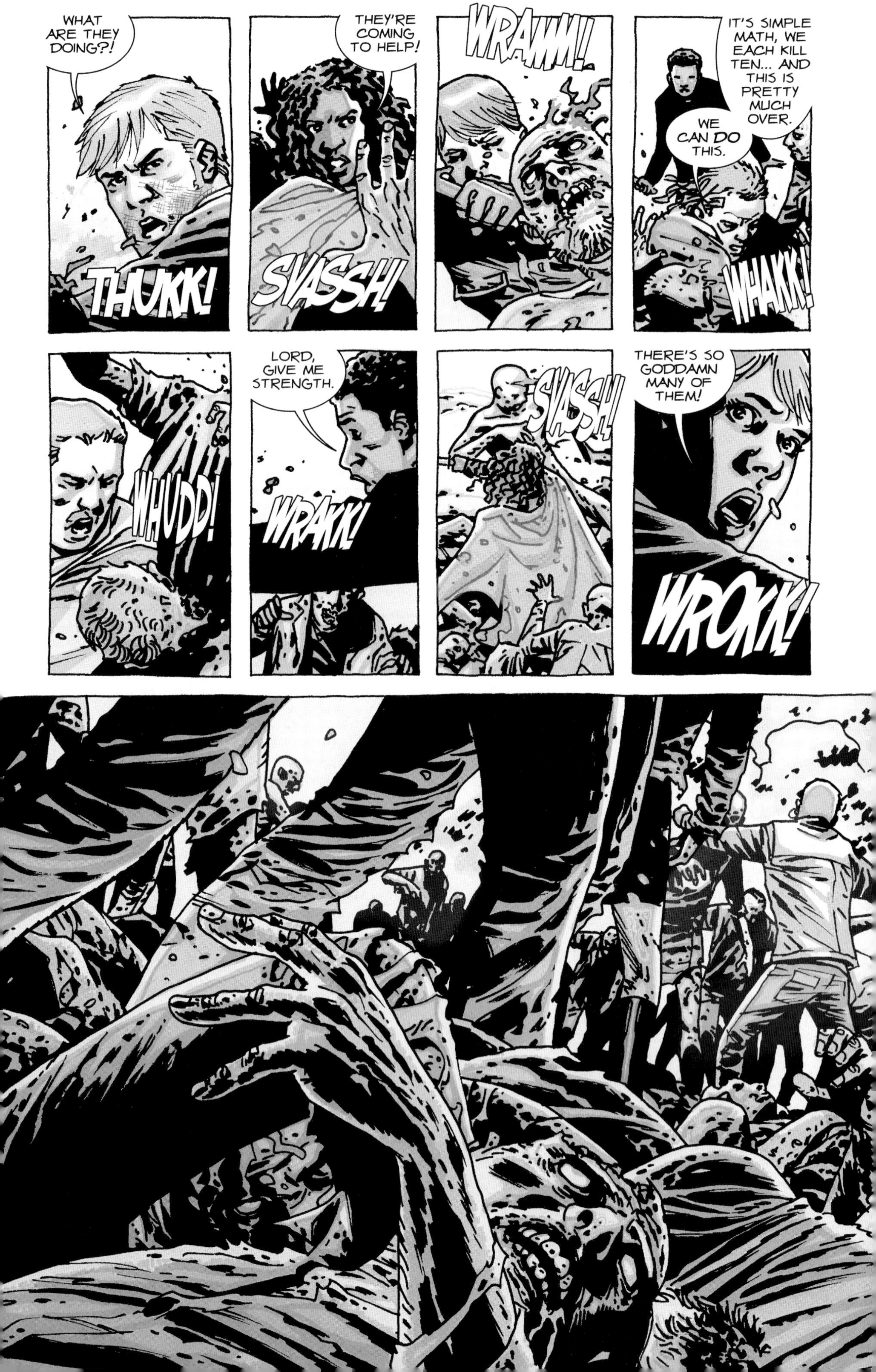
WHAT ARE THEY DOING?!
THUKK!
THEY'RE COMING TO HELP!
SVASSH!
WRAMM!!
IT'S SIMPLE MATH, WE EACH KILL TEN... AND THIS IS PRETTY MUCH OVER.
WE CAN DO THIS.
WHAKK!
WHUDD!
LORD, GIVE ME STRENGTH.
WRAKK!
SVASSH!
THERE'S SO GODDAMN MANY OF THEM!
WROKK!

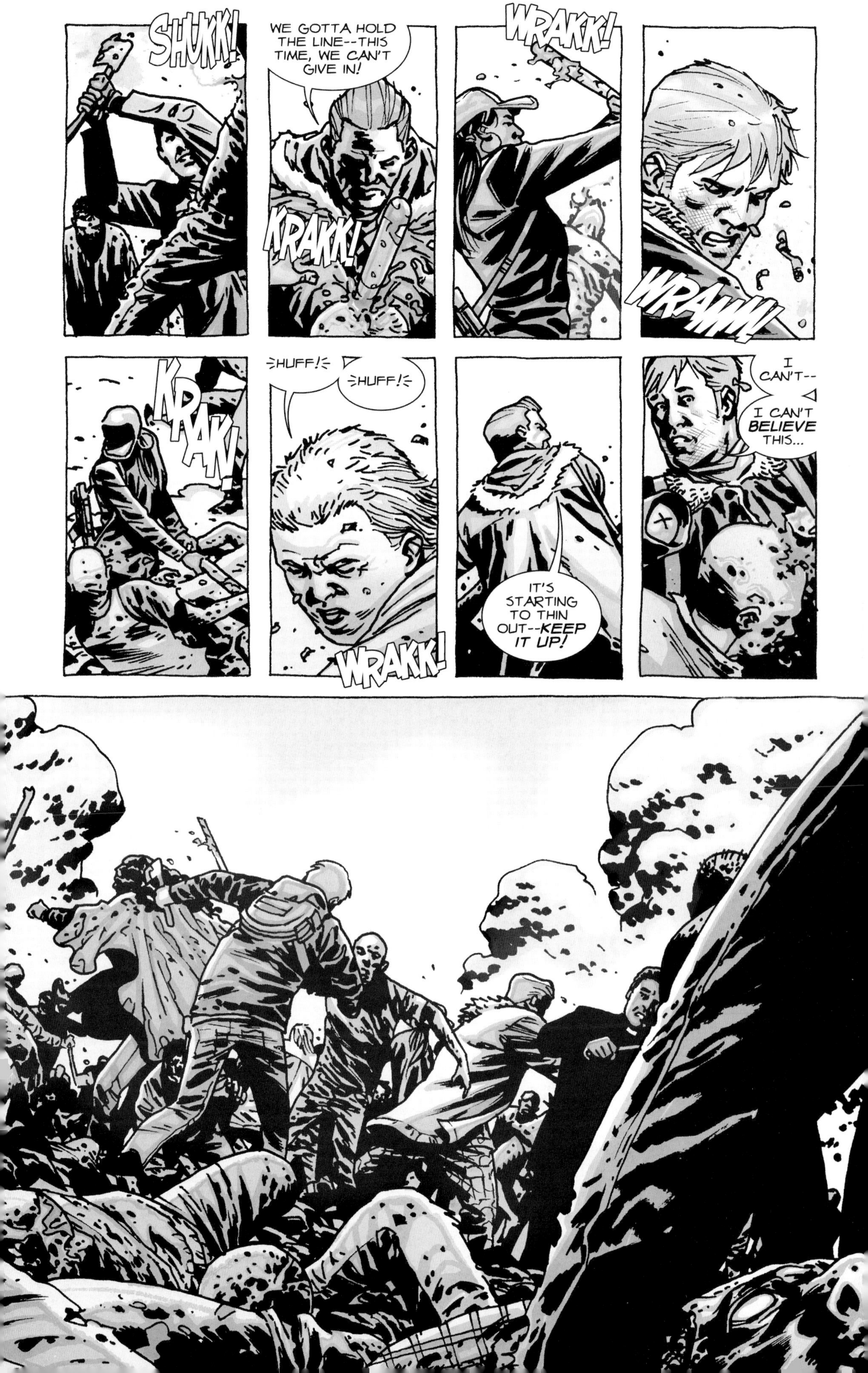
SHUKK!
WE GOTTA HOLD THE LINE--THIS TIME, WE CAN'T GIVE IN!
KRAKK!
WRAKK!
WRAMM!
KRAK!
HUFF!
HUFF!
WRAKK!
IT'S STARTING TO THIN OUT--KEEP IT UP!
I CAN'T--
I CAN'T BELIEVE THIS...

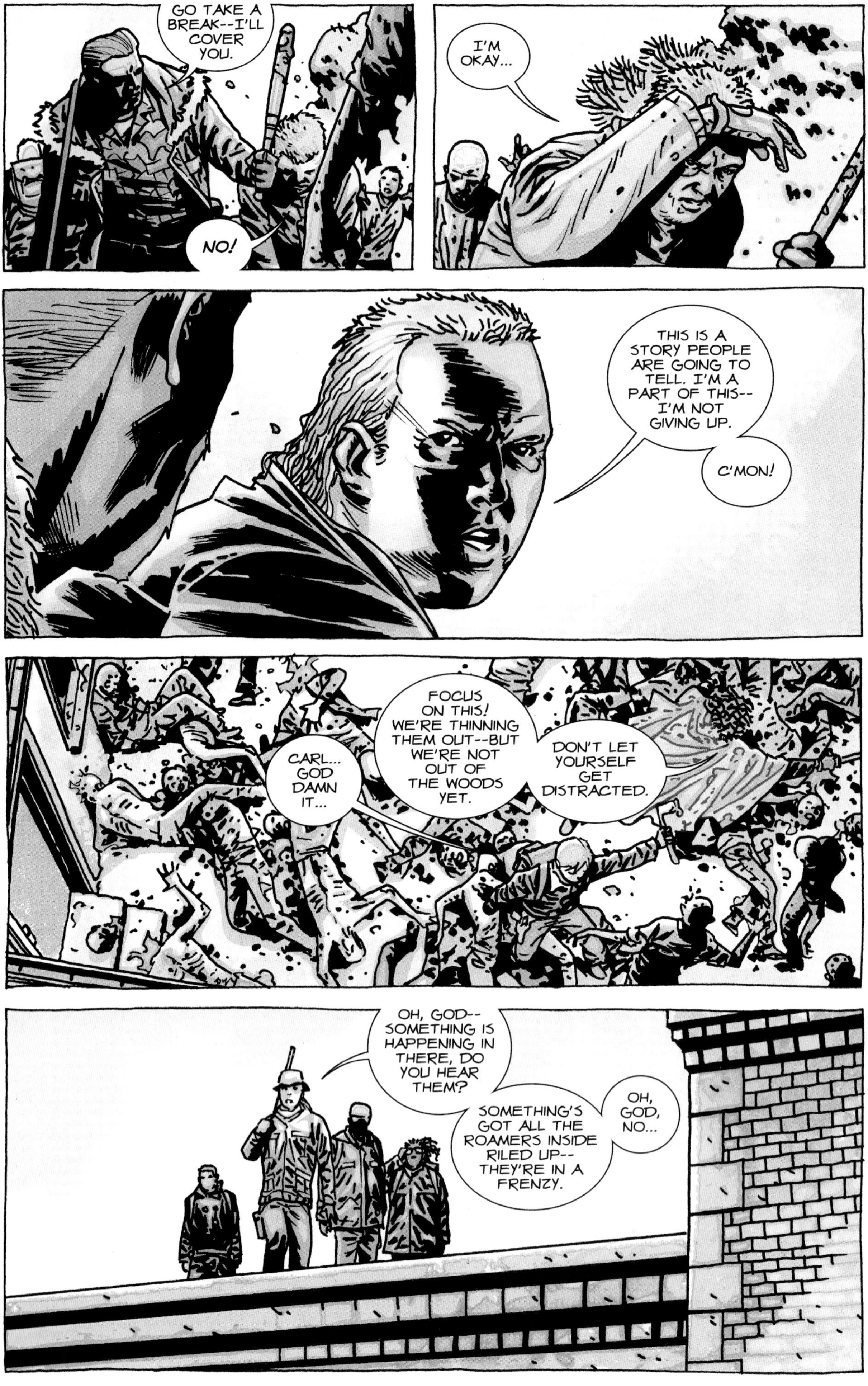
GO TAKE A BREAK--I'LL COVER YOU.
NO!
I'M OKAY...
THIS IS A STORY PEOPLE ARE GOING TO TELL. I'M A PART OF THIS-- I'M NOT GIVING UP.
C'MON!
CARL... GOD DAMN IT...
FOCUS ON THIS! WE'RE THINNING THEM OUT--BUT WE'RE NOT OUT OF THE WOODS YET.
DON'T LET YOURSELF GET DISTRACTED.
OH, GOD-- SOMETHING IS HAPPENING IN THERE, DO YOU HEAR THEM?
SOMETHING'S GOT ALL THE ROAMERS INSIDE RILED UP-- THEY'RE IN A FRENZY.
OH, GOD, NO...

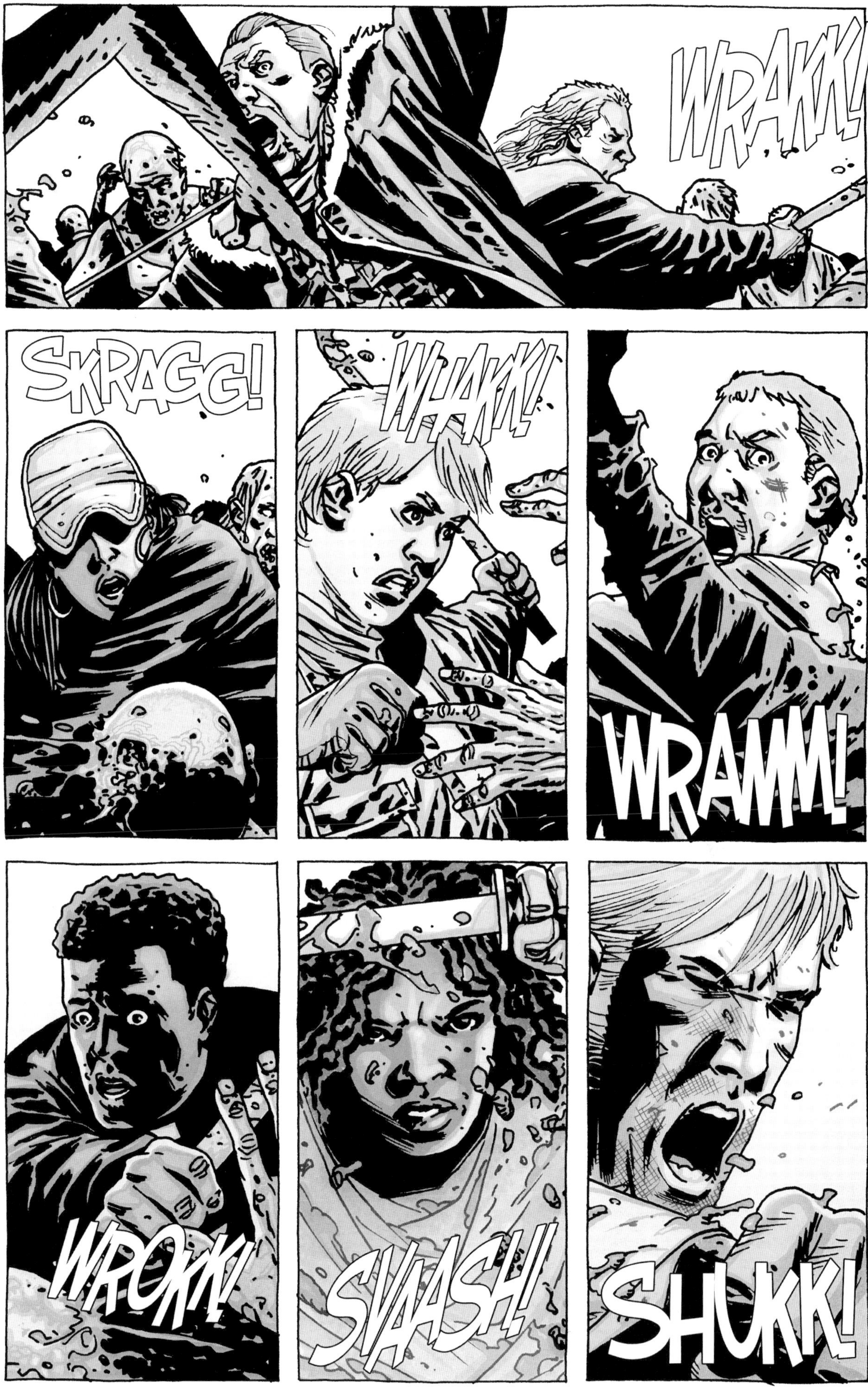
WRAKK!
SKRAGG!
WHAKK!
WRAMM!
WROKK!
SVAASH!
SHUKK!

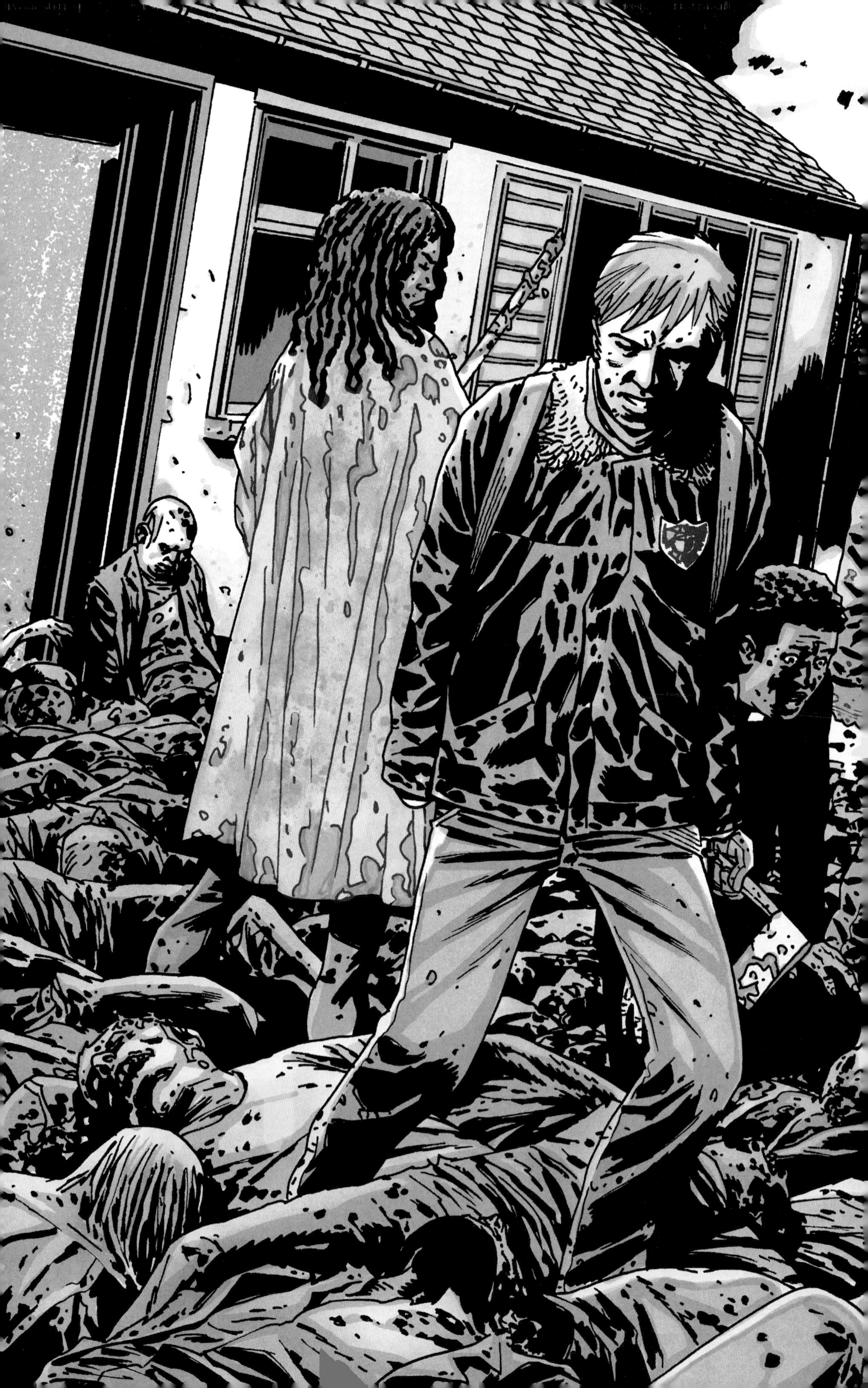

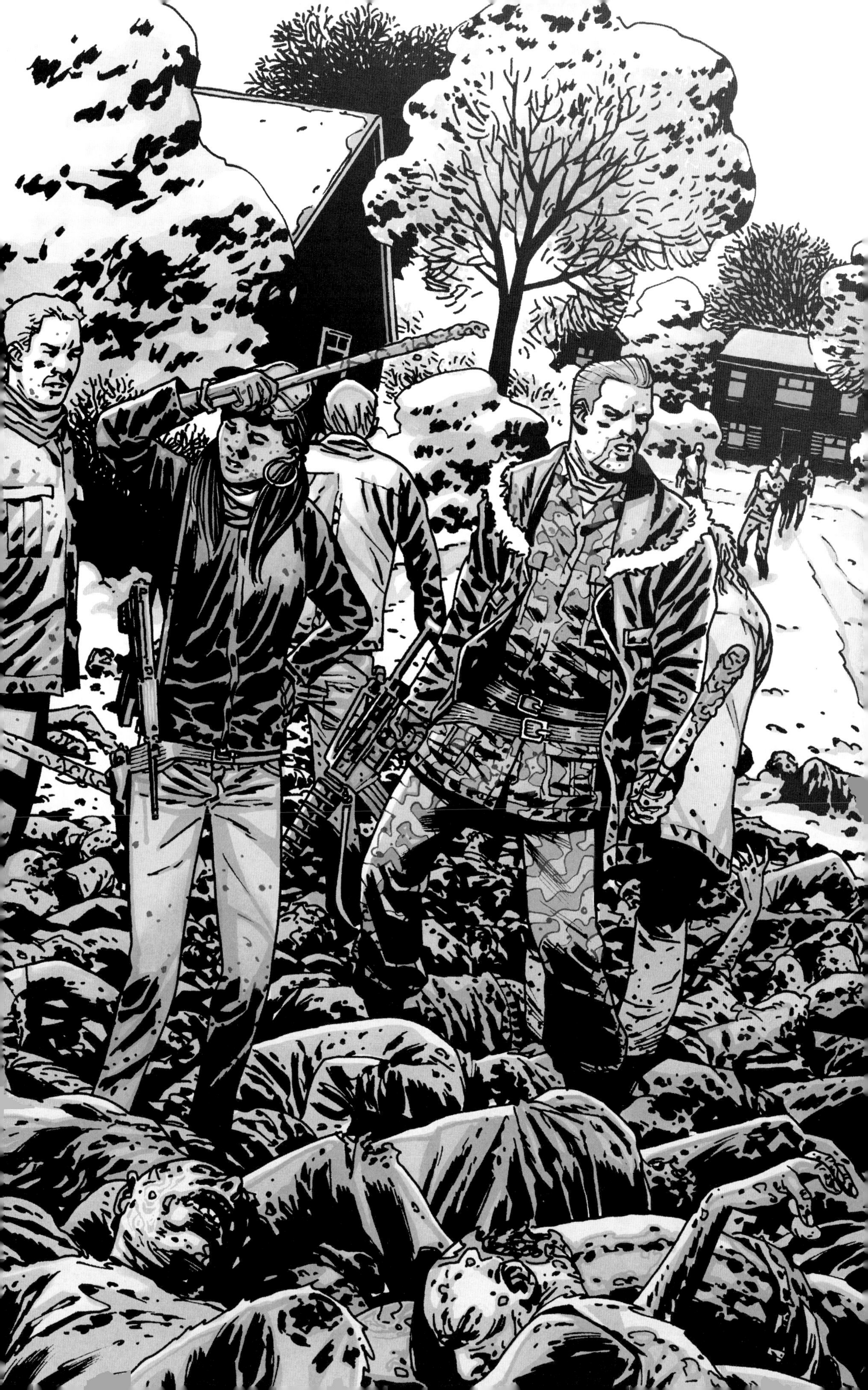

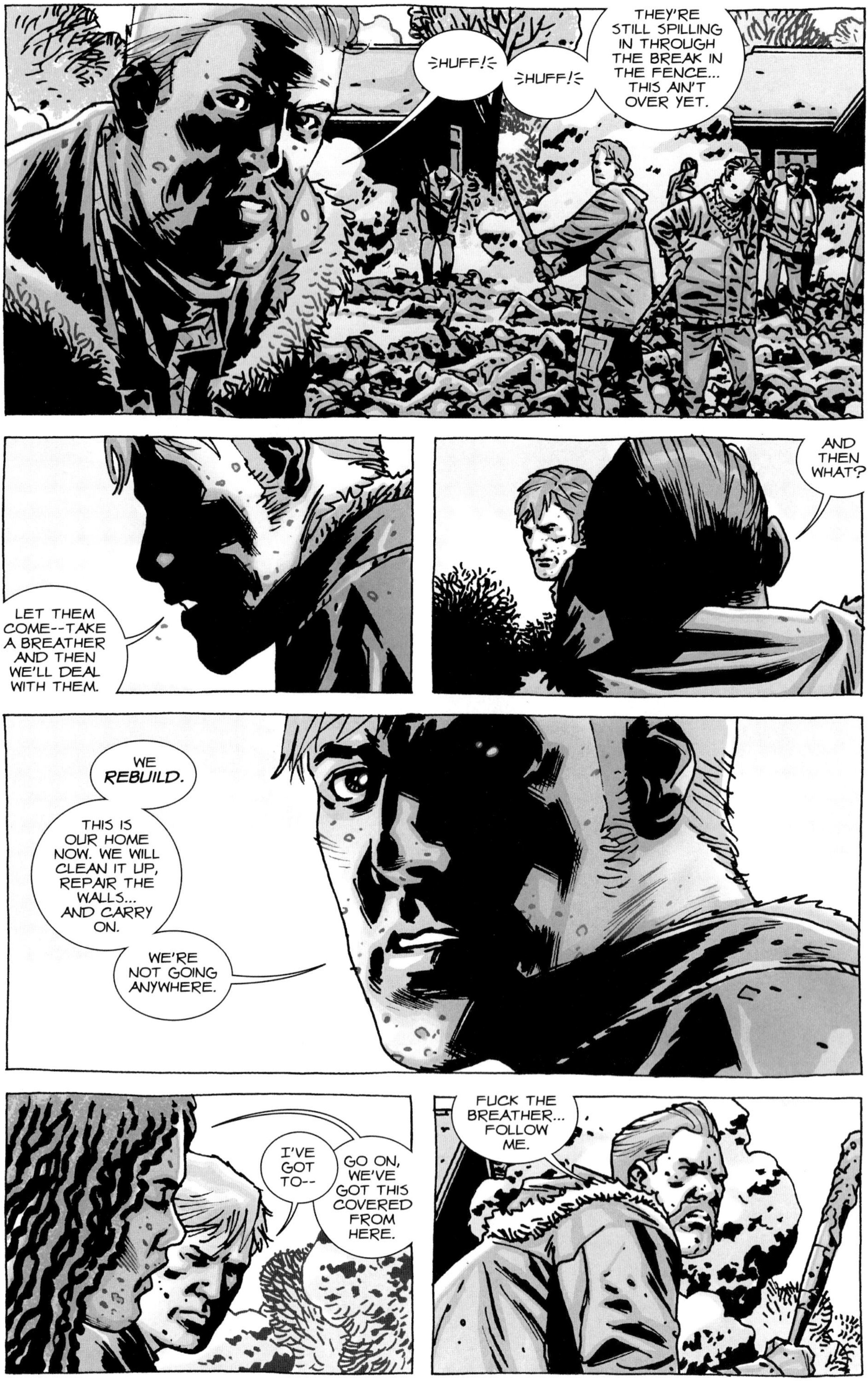

=HUFF!=
=HUFF!=
THEY'RE STILL SPILLING IN THROUGH THE BREAK IN THE FENCE... THIS AIN'T OVER YET.
LET THEM COME--TAKE A BREATHER AND THEN WE'LL DEAL WITH THEM.
AND THEN WHAT?
WE *REBUILD.*
THIS IS OUR HOME NOW. WE WILL CLEAN IT UP, REPAIR THE WALLS... AND CARRY ON.
WE'RE NOT GOING ANYWHERE.
I'VE GOT TO--
GO ON, WE'VE GOT THIS COVERED FROM HERE.
FUCK THE BREATHER... FOLLOW ME.

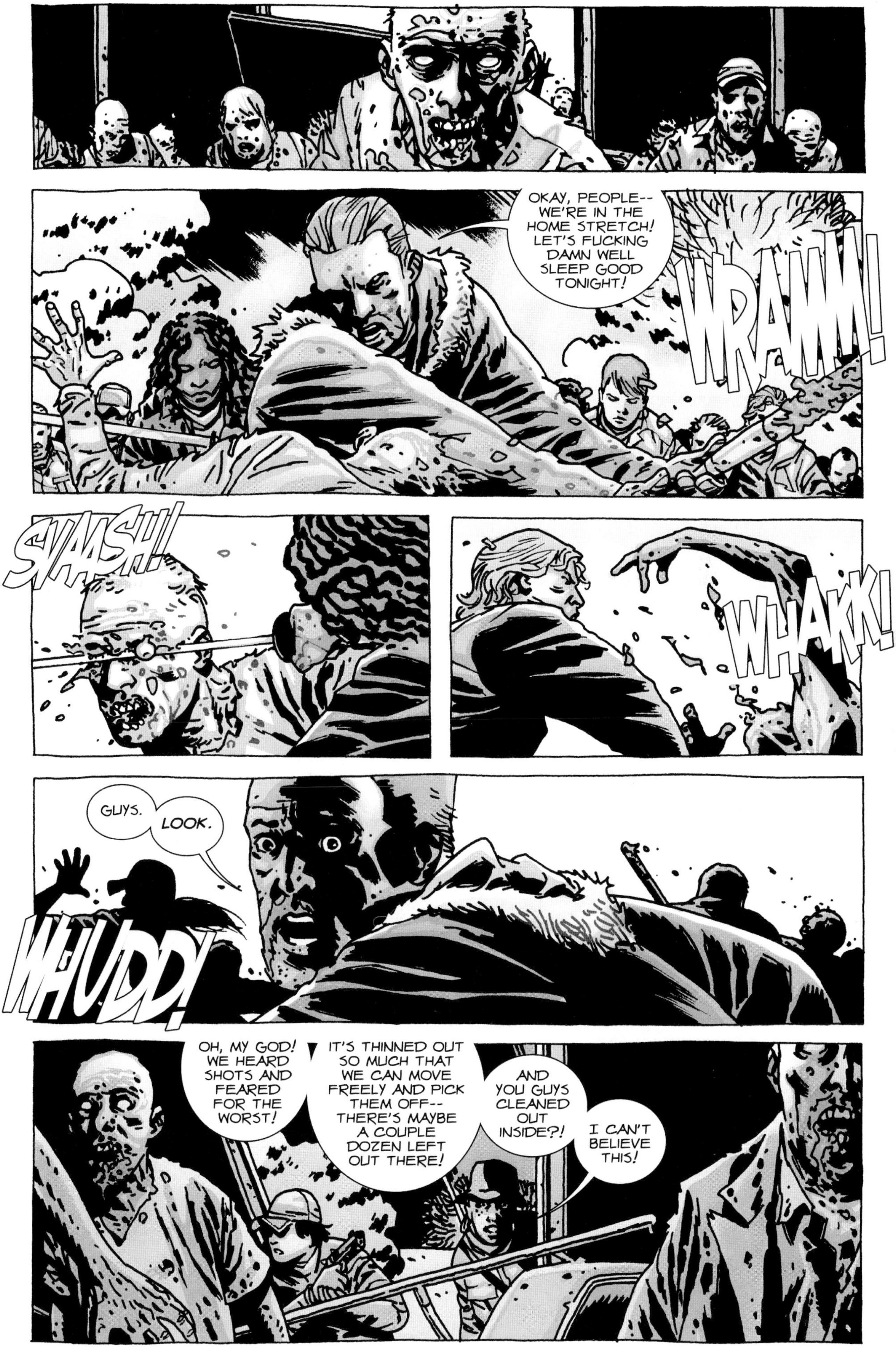
OKAY, PEOPLE-- WE'RE IN THE HOME STRETCH! LET'S FUCKING DAMN WELL SLEEP GOOD TONIGHT!
WRAMM!
SHAASH!
WHAKK!
GUYS.
LOOK.
WHUDD!
OH, MY GOD! WE HEARD SHOTS AND FEARED FOR THE WORST!
IT'S THINNED OUT SO MUCH THAT WE CAN MOVE FREELY AND PICK THEM OFF-- THERE'S MAYBE A COUPLE DOZEN LEFT OUT THERE!
AND YOU GUYS CLEANED OUT INSIDE?!
I CAN'T BELIEVE THIS!

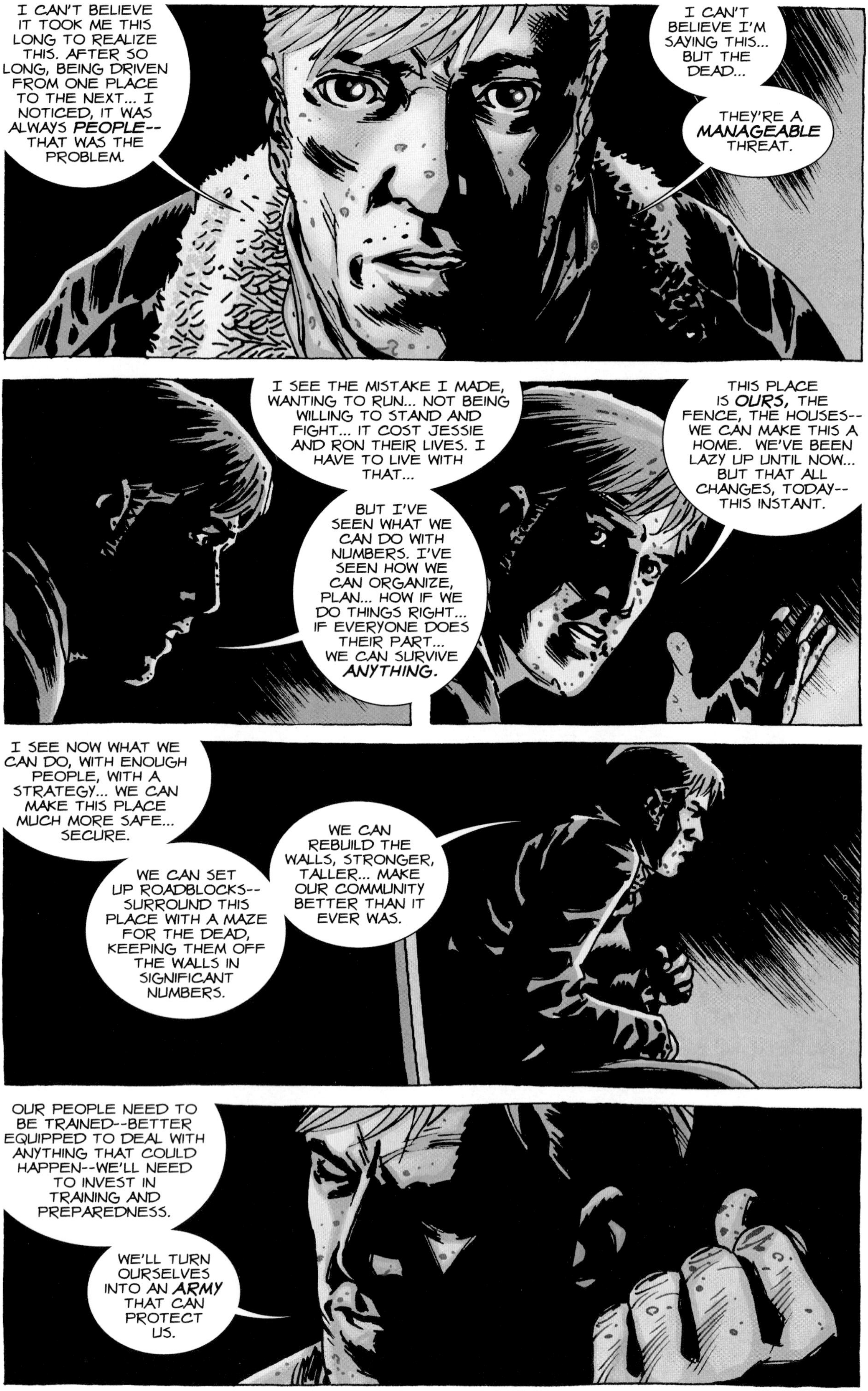
I CAN'T BELIEVE IT TOOK ME THIS LONG TO REALIZE THIS. AFTER SO LONG, BEING DRIVEN FROM ONE PLACE TO THE NEXT... I NOTICED, IT WAS ALWAYS *PEOPLE*-- THAT WAS THE PROBLEM.
I CAN'T BELIEVE I'M SAYING THIS... BUT THE DEAD...
THEY'RE A *MANAGEABLE* THREAT.
I SEE THE MISTAKE I MADE, WANTING TO RUN... NOT BEING WILLING TO STAND AND FIGHT... IT COST JESSIE AND RON THEIR LIVES. I HAVE TO LIVE WITH THAT...
BUT I'VE SEEN WHAT WE CAN DO WITH NUMBERS. I'VE SEEN HOW WE CAN ORGANIZE, PLAN... HOW IF WE DO THINGS RIGHT... IF EVERYONE DOES THEIR PART... WE CAN SURVIVE *ANYTHING.*
THIS PLACE IS *OURS,* THE FENCE, THE HOUSES-- WE CAN MAKE THIS A HOME. WE'VE BEEN LAZY UP UNTIL NOW... BUT THAT ALL CHANGES, TODAY-- THIS INSTANT.
I SEE NOW WHAT WE CAN DO, WITH ENOUGH PEOPLE, WITH A STRATEGY... WE CAN MAKE THIS PLACE MUCH MORE SAFE... SECURE.
WE CAN SET UP ROADBLOCKS-- SURROUND THIS PLACE WITH A MAZE FOR THE DEAD, KEEPING THEM OFF THE WALLS IN SIGNIFICANT NUMBERS.
WE CAN REBUILD THE WALLS, STRONGER, TALLER... MAKE OUR COMMUNITY BETTER THAN IT EVER WAS.
OUR PEOPLE NEED TO BE TRAINED--BETTER EQUIPPED TO DEAL WITH ANYTHING THAT COULD HAPPEN--WE'LL NEED TO INVEST IN TRAINING AND PREPAREDNESS.
WE'LL TURN OURSELVES INTO AN *ARMY* THAT CAN PROTECT US.

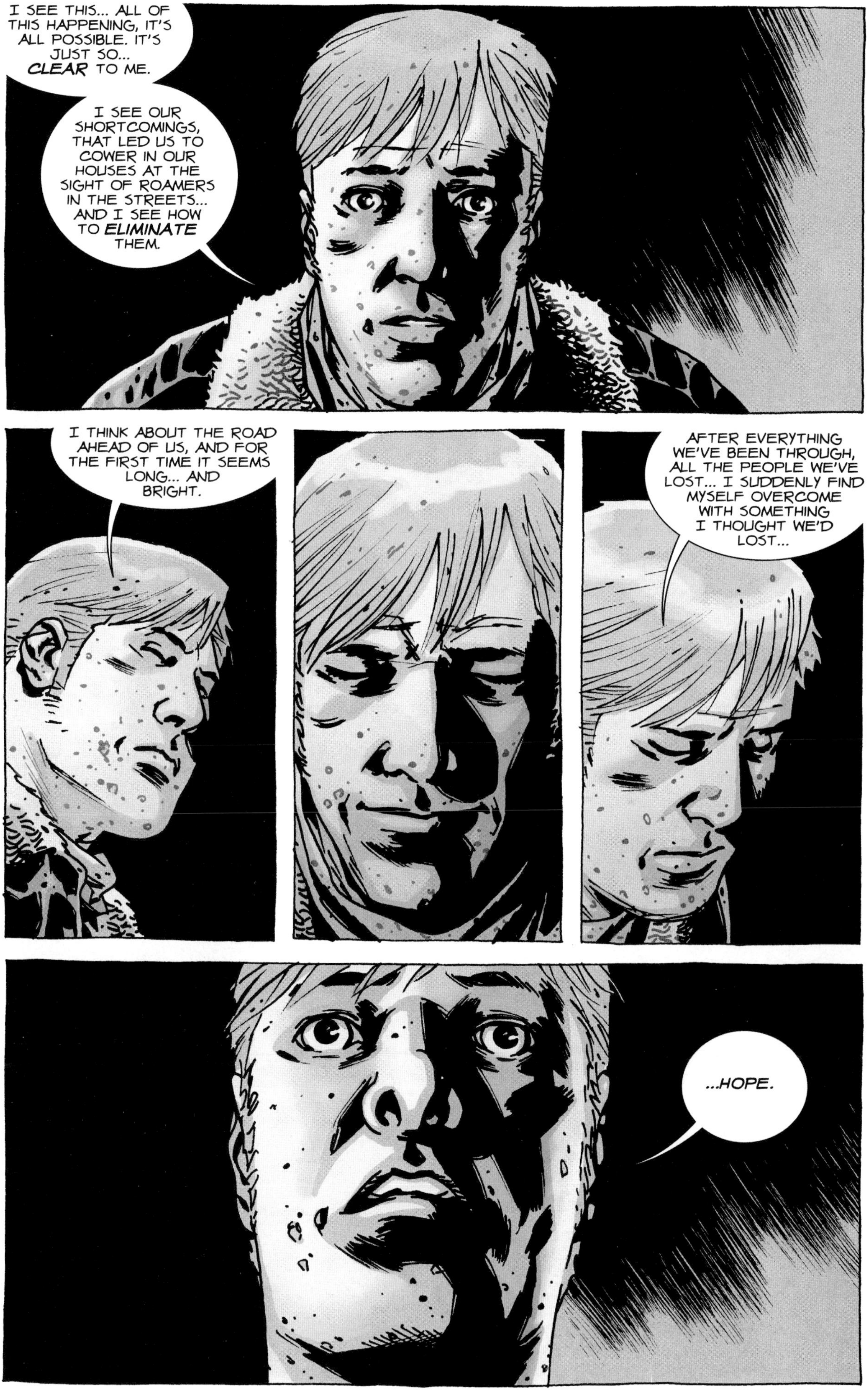
I SEE THIS... ALL OF THIS HAPPENING, IT'S ALL POSSIBLE. IT'S JUST SO... **CLEAR** TO ME.
I SEE OUR SHORTCOMINGS, THAT LED US TO COWER IN OUR HOUSES AT THE SIGHT OF ROAMERS IN THE STREETS... AND I SEE HOW TO **ELIMINATE** THEM.
I THINK ABOUT THE ROAD AHEAD OF US, AND FOR THE FIRST TIME IT SEEMS LONG... AND BRIGHT.
AFTER EVERYTHING WE'VE BEEN THROUGH, ALL THE PEOPLE WE'VE LOST... I SUDDENLY FIND MYSELF OVERCOME WITH SOMETHING I THOUGHT WE'D LOST...
...HOPE.

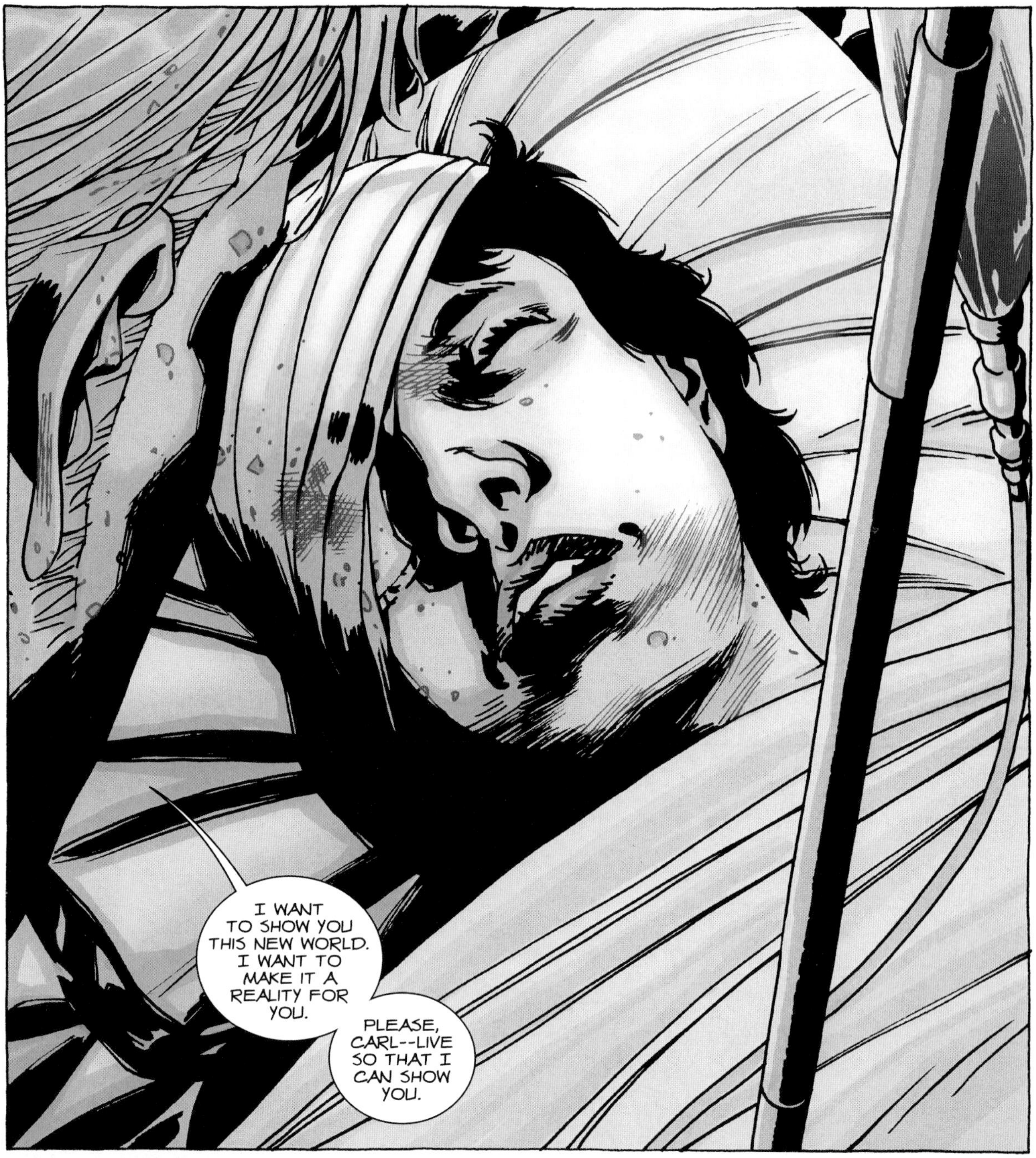
I WANT TO SHOW YOU THIS NEW WORLD. I WANT TO MAKE IT A REALITY FOR YOU.
PLEASE, CARL--LIVE SO THAT I CAN SHOW YOU.

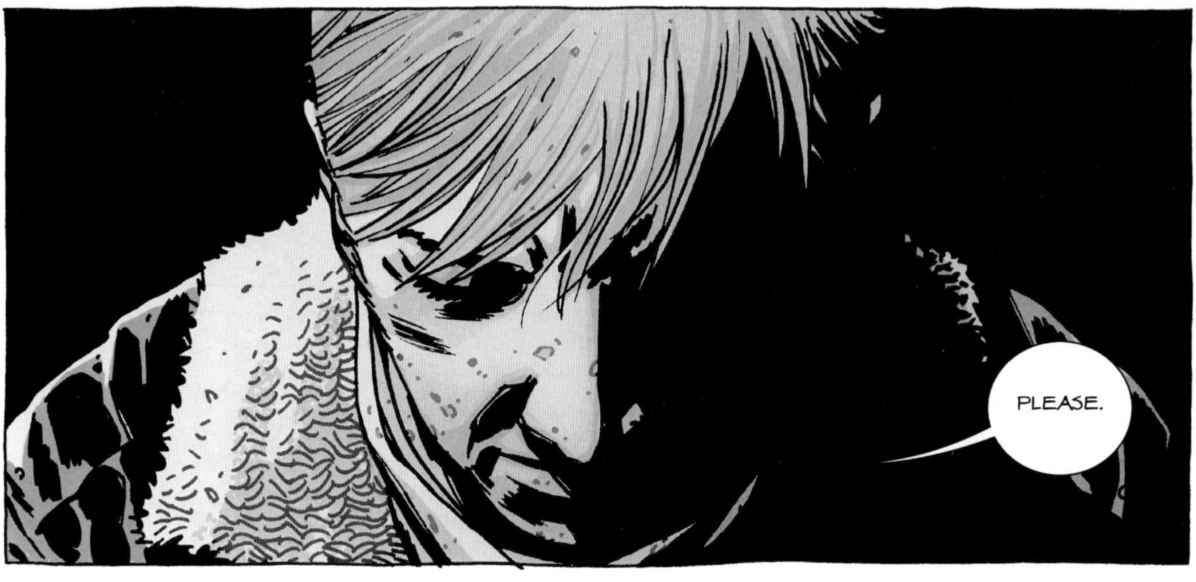
PLEASE.

to be continued...

Sketchbook

For the Walking Dead board game by Z-Man Games (go buy it) we wanted to keep the art consistent throughout. Since there were key scenes in the comic series that Charlie Adlard simply hadn't drawn, the esteemed Mr. Adlard had to put pencil to paper and delve back into the very beginnings of this series and put his spin on things. Pretty cool.

On this page you'll see the iconic "Rick arrives in Atlanta" shot from issue 2... and y'know popularized by the AMC television show we all know and love.

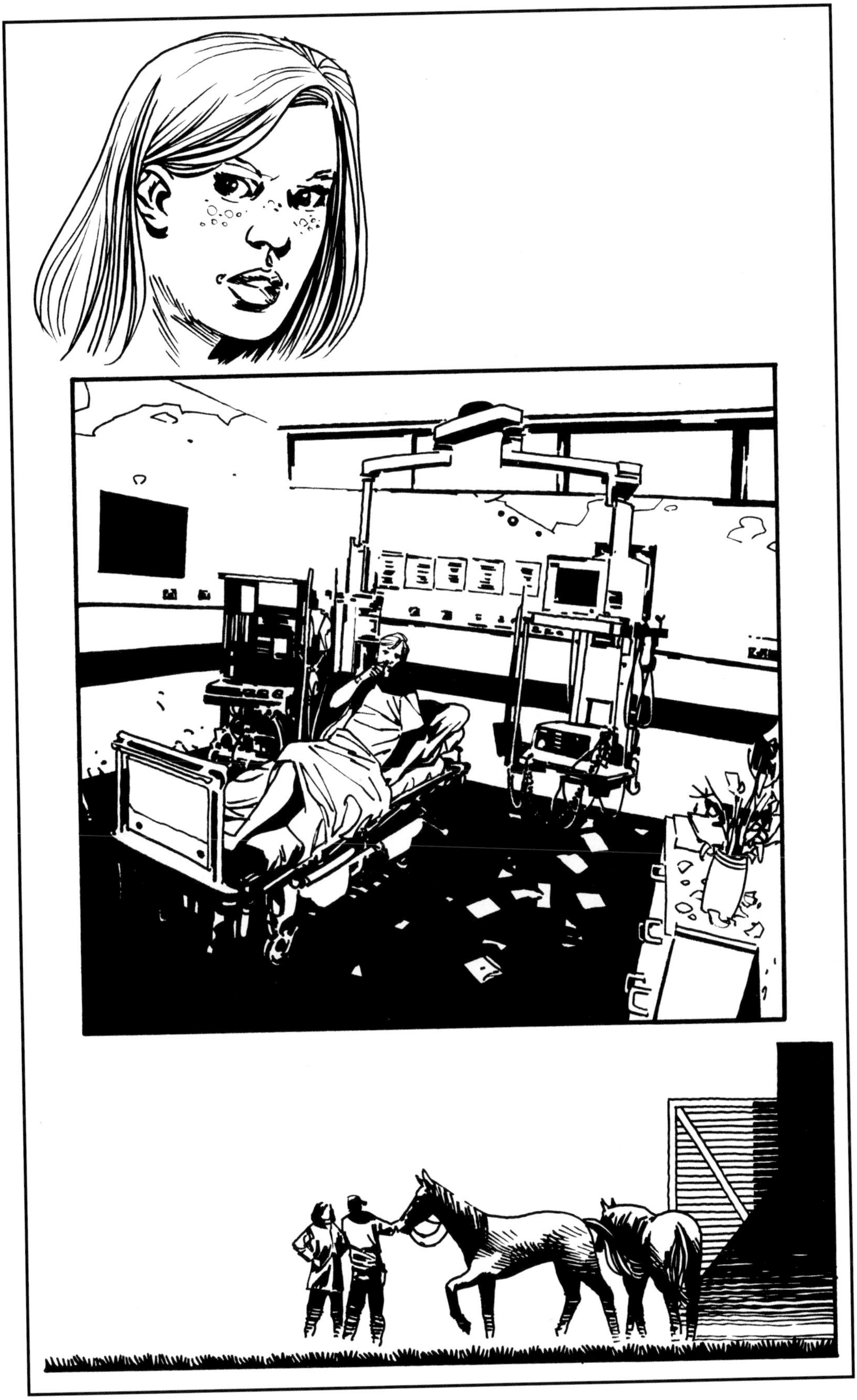

Here we see Rick waking up in his hospital bed from issue 1 and a few other key scenes.

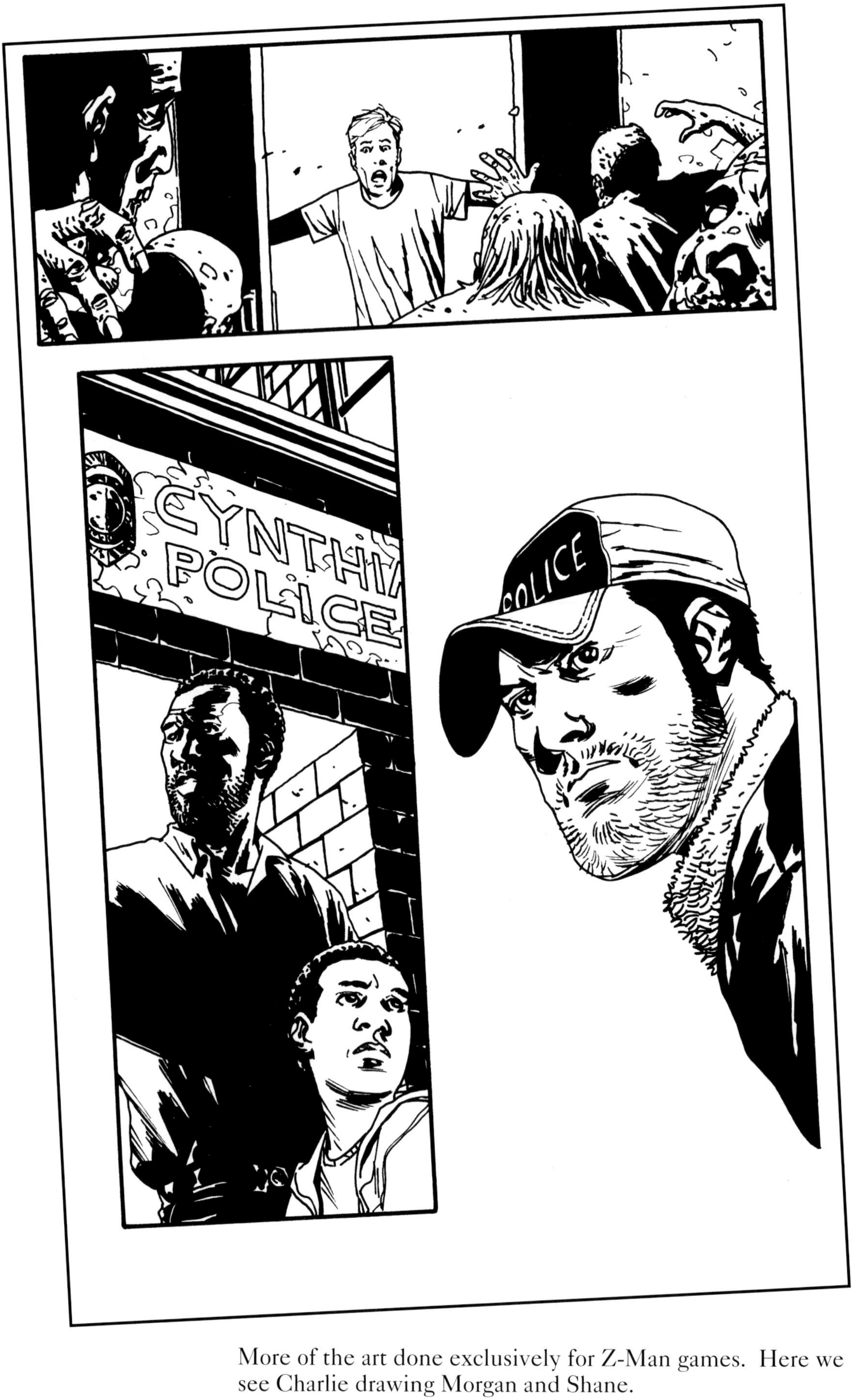
CYNTHIA
POLICE
POLICE

More of the art done exclusively for Z-Man games. Here we see Charlie drawing Morgan and Shane.

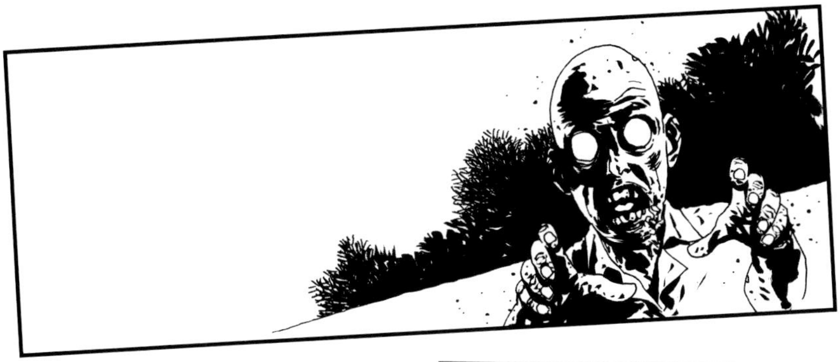

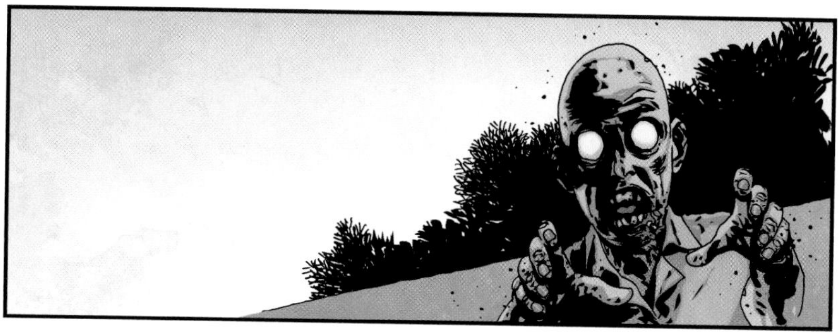

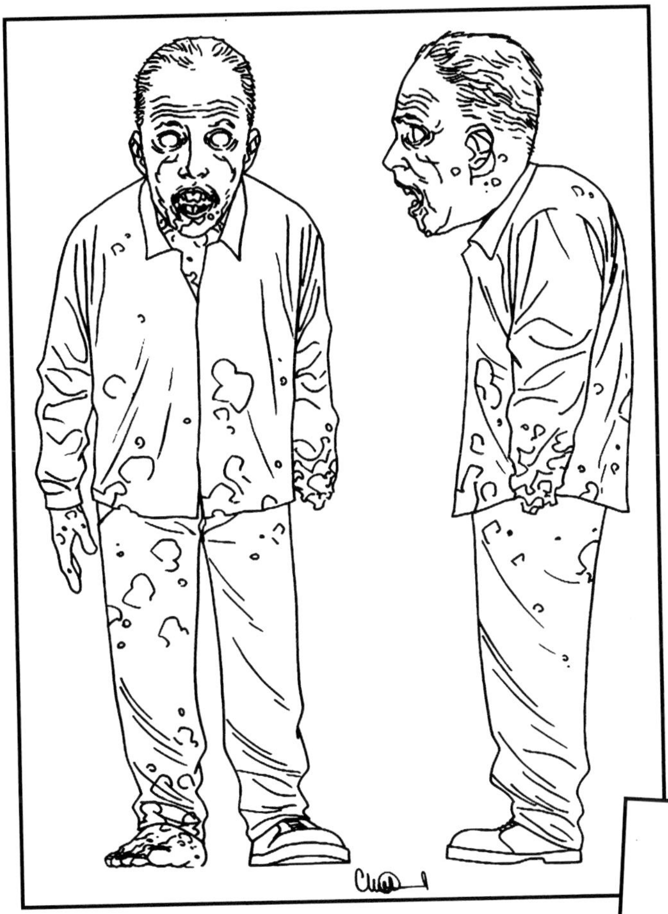

On this page we find Charlie Adlard's designs for the adorable plush zombie that Skybound made and y'know... is available in the Skybound store at www.skybound.com if you were so inclined to want to purchase such things... wink... wink.

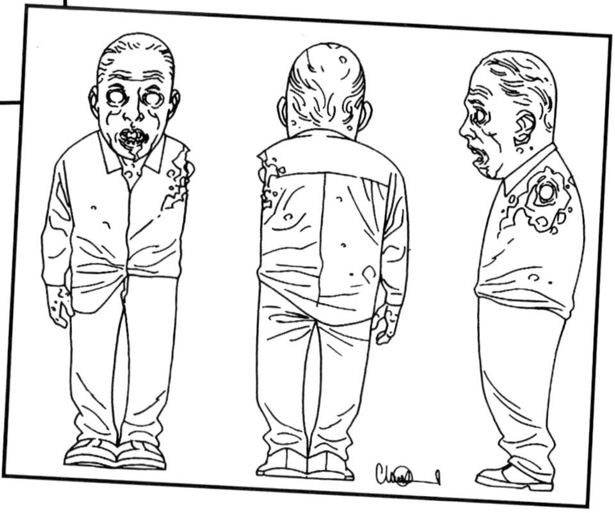

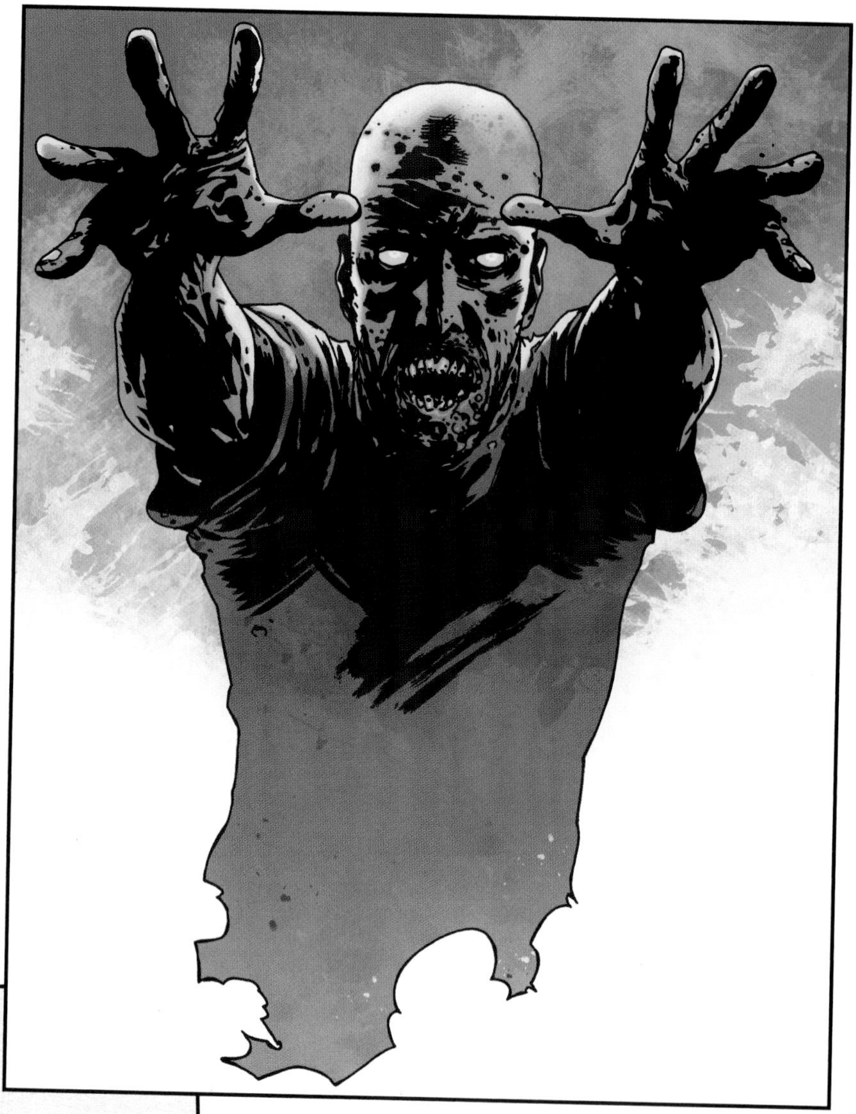

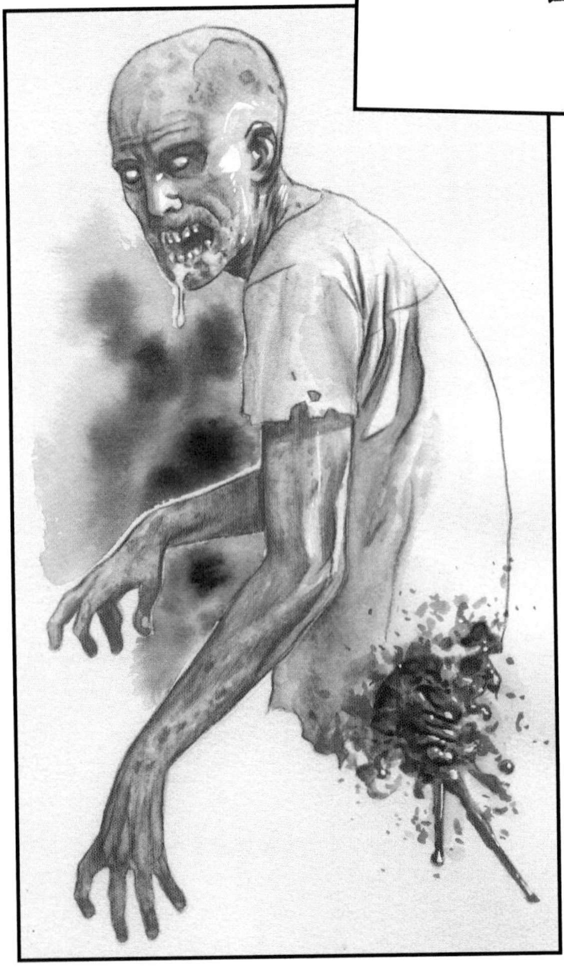

A couple of cool zombies by Charlie. The colored one above (colors by Cliff Rathburn) was used as the cover of a Comic Book Legal Defense Fund charity comic. Charlie loves doing things for charity... I don't get it.

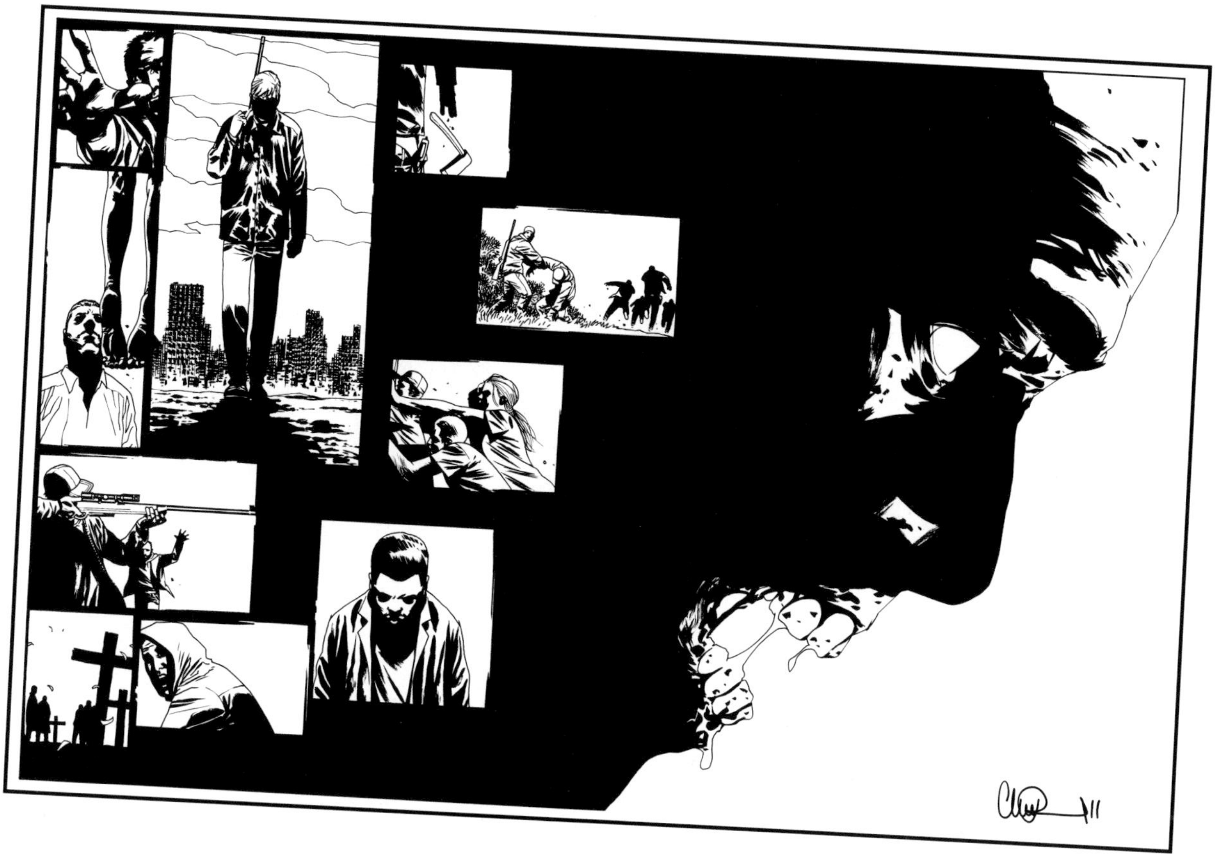

Here you'll see an illustration done for the Telltale games video game that Charlie drew--pretty sweet. And also, another zombie drawing that has appeared in a lot of places.

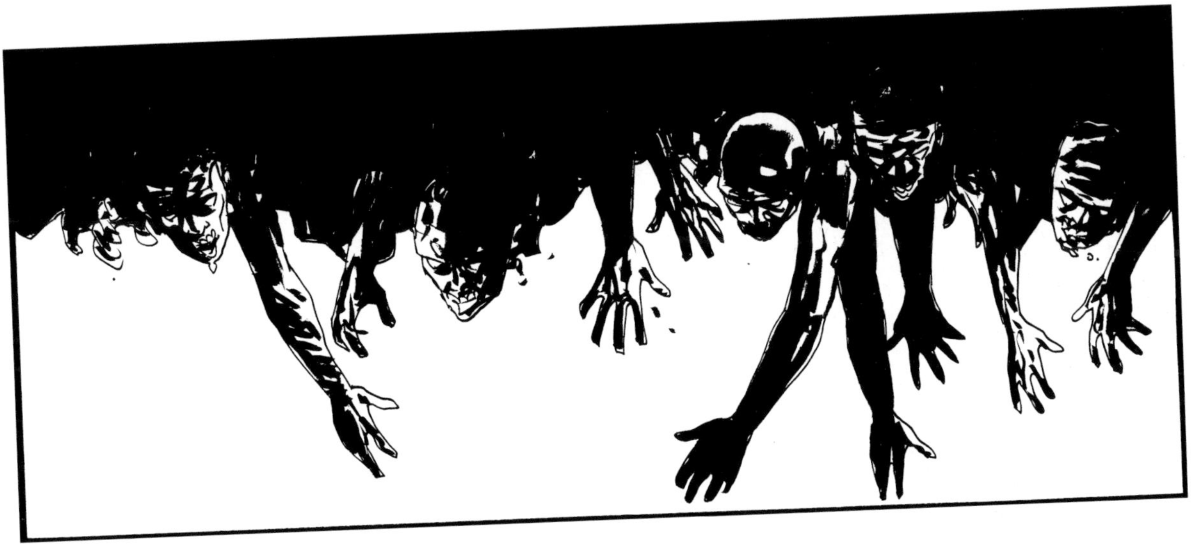

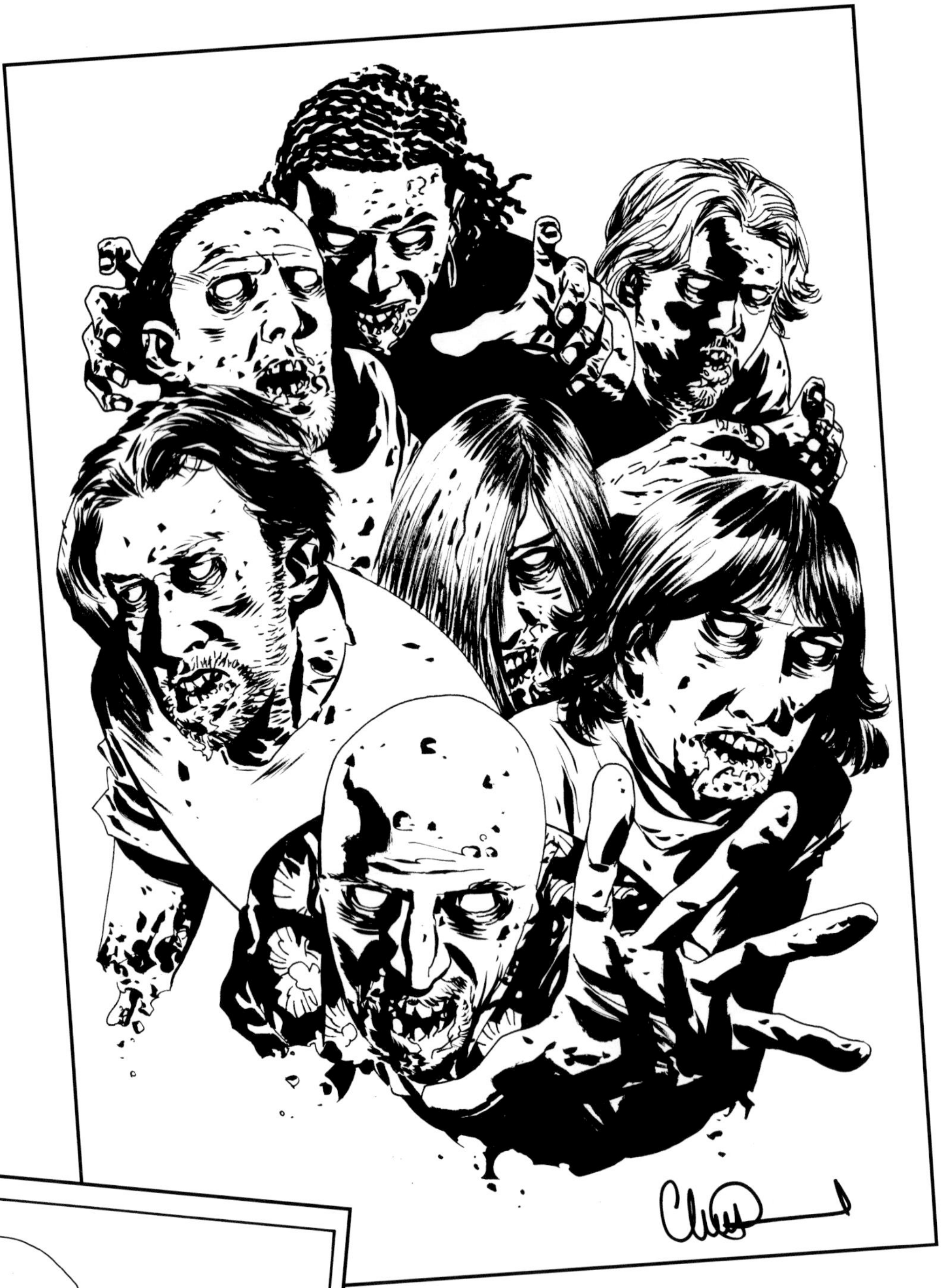

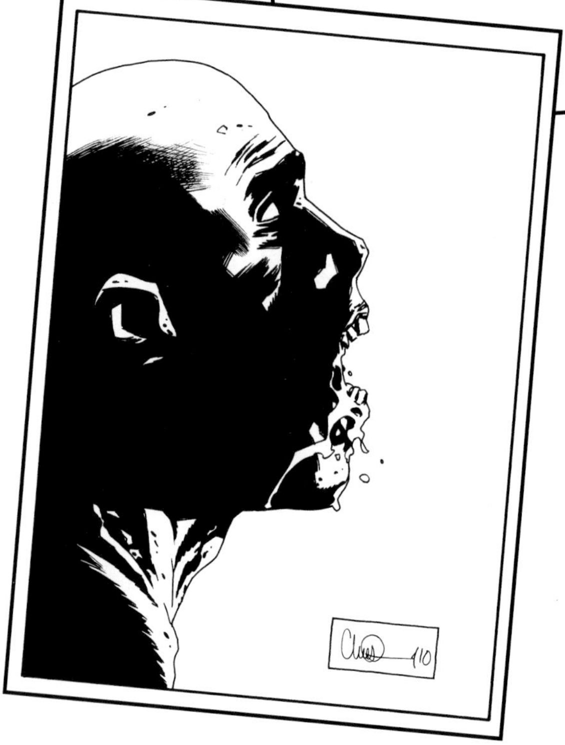

This is a drawing commissioned by Greg Nicotero, make-up effects guru on the TV show, that was turned into a crew shirt and given out as a gift at the end of shooting on season one. Out front there is Nicotero himself along with Frank Darabont and Gale Anne Hurd. Also on this page, an unusused cover for the Deluxe HC volume 3.

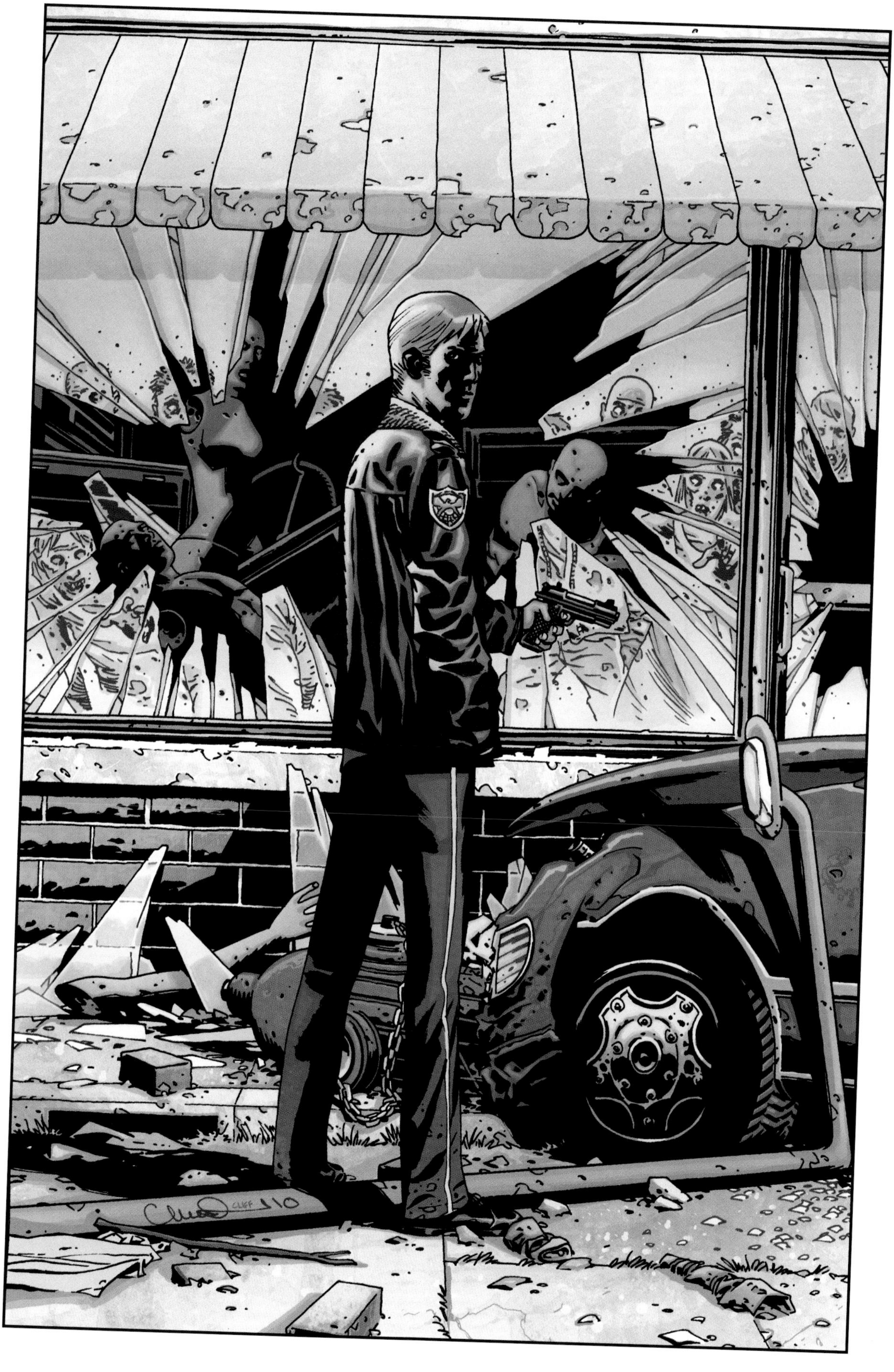

To celebrate issue 75 being released I thought it would be cool to do a new version of the issue 1 cover with the current Rick Grimes. Charlie really killed on this one!

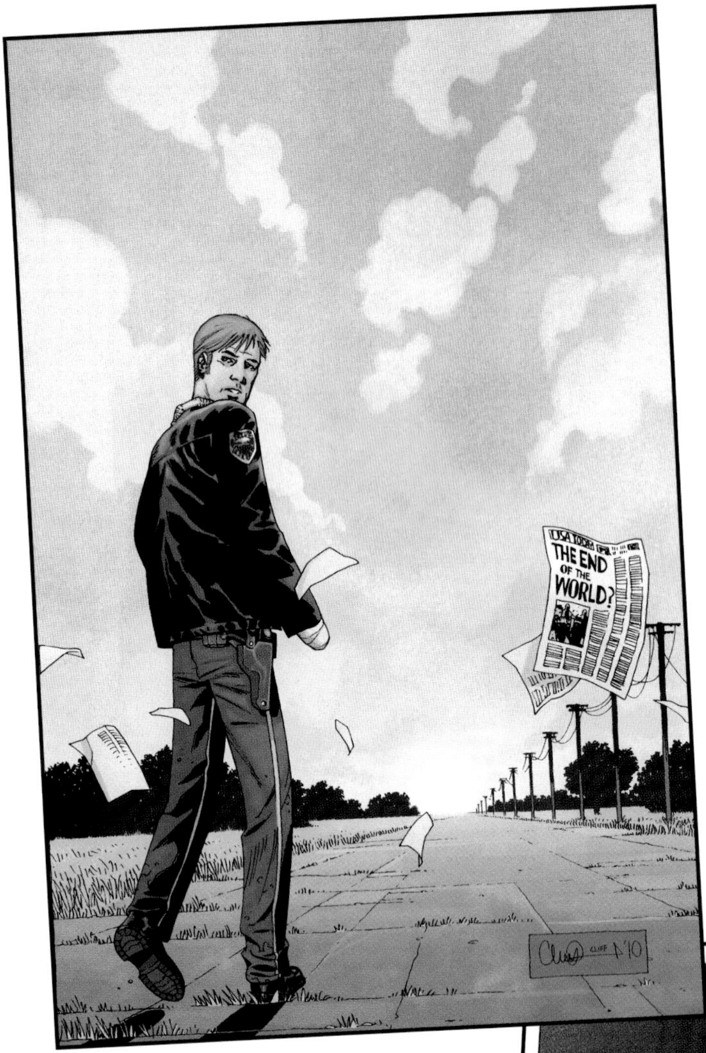
USA TODAY
THE END OF THE WORLD?

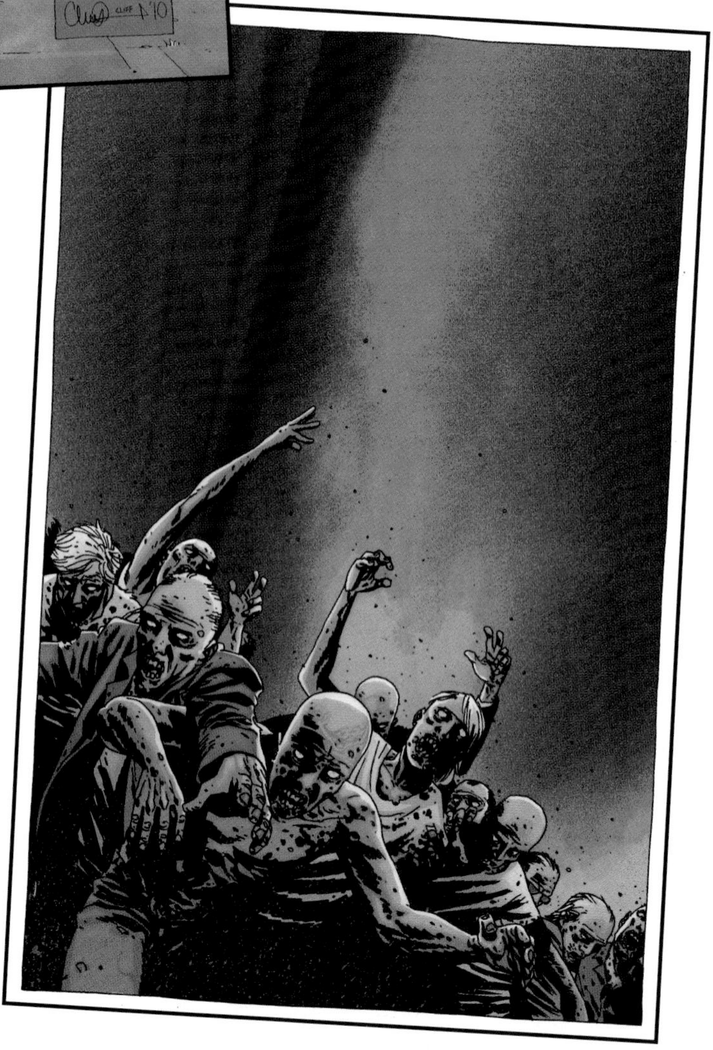

Another couple of variant covers. I'll be honest, one of these covers is just an old unused cover that was drawn, with some new elements put in. Still looks cool, though!

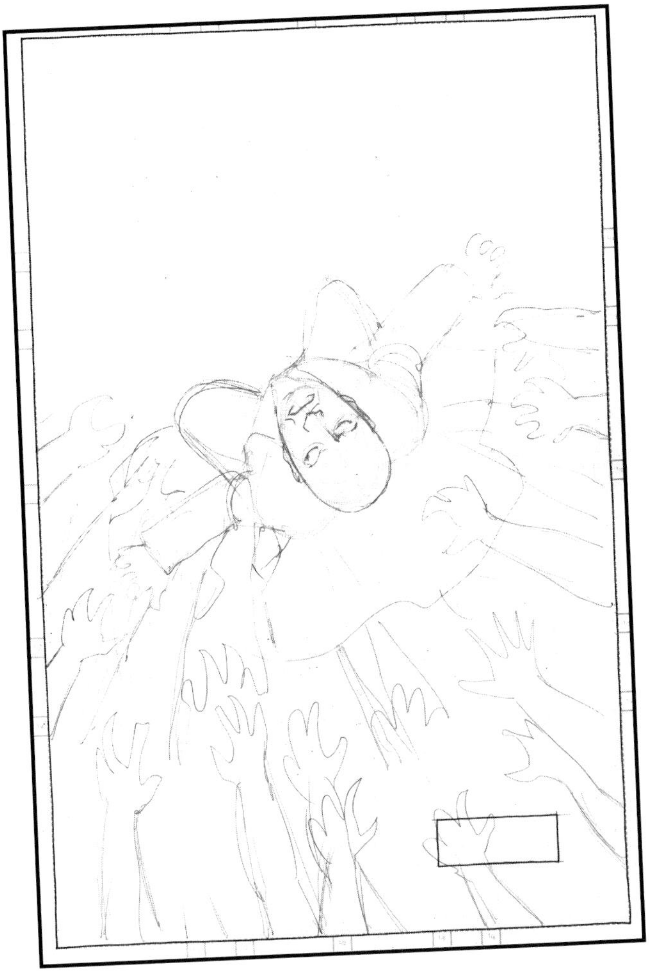

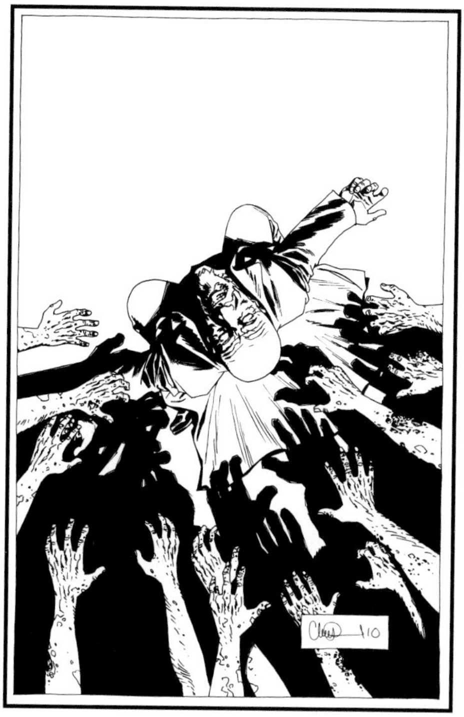

Here's a rare look at Charlie Adlard's pencils for some memorable covers. Note that the cover for 84 was altered a little bit before it was completed. I figured you couldn't actually carry someone that way if you were missing a hand. Charlie agreed.

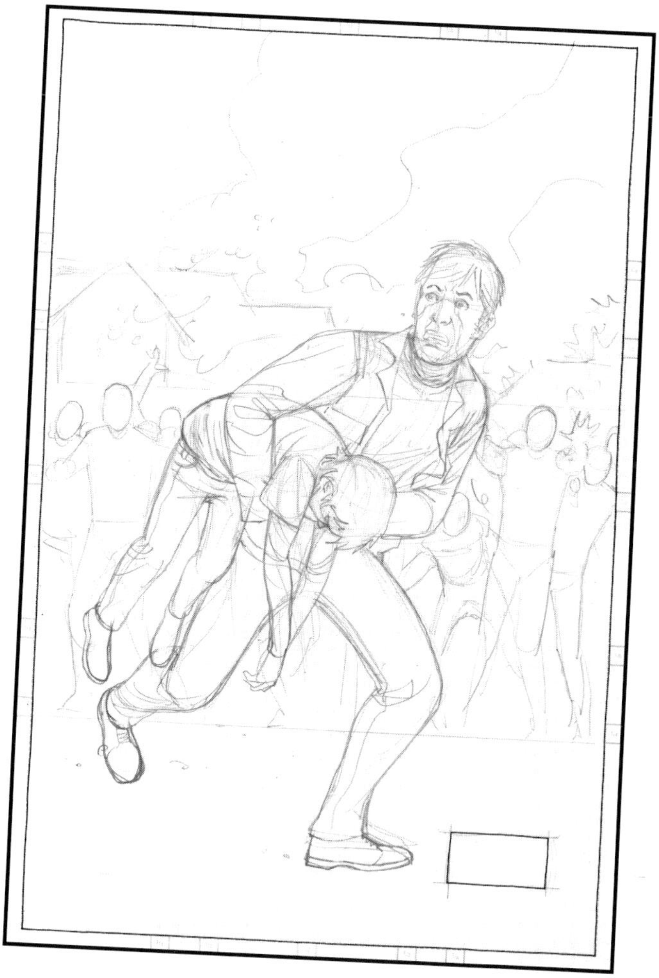

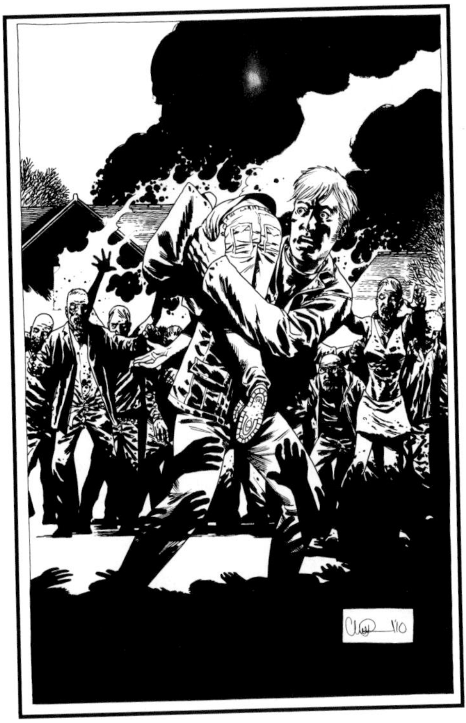

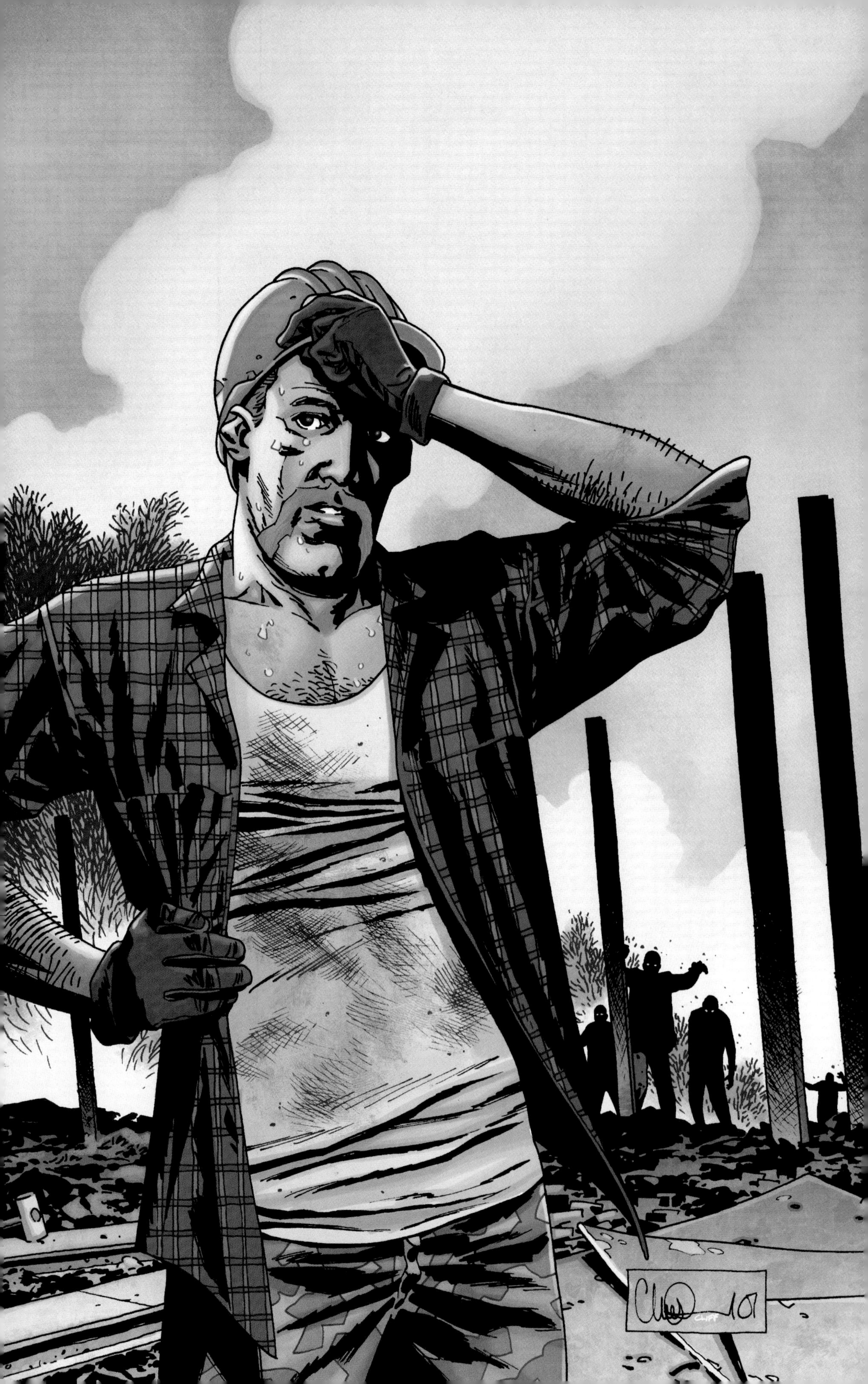

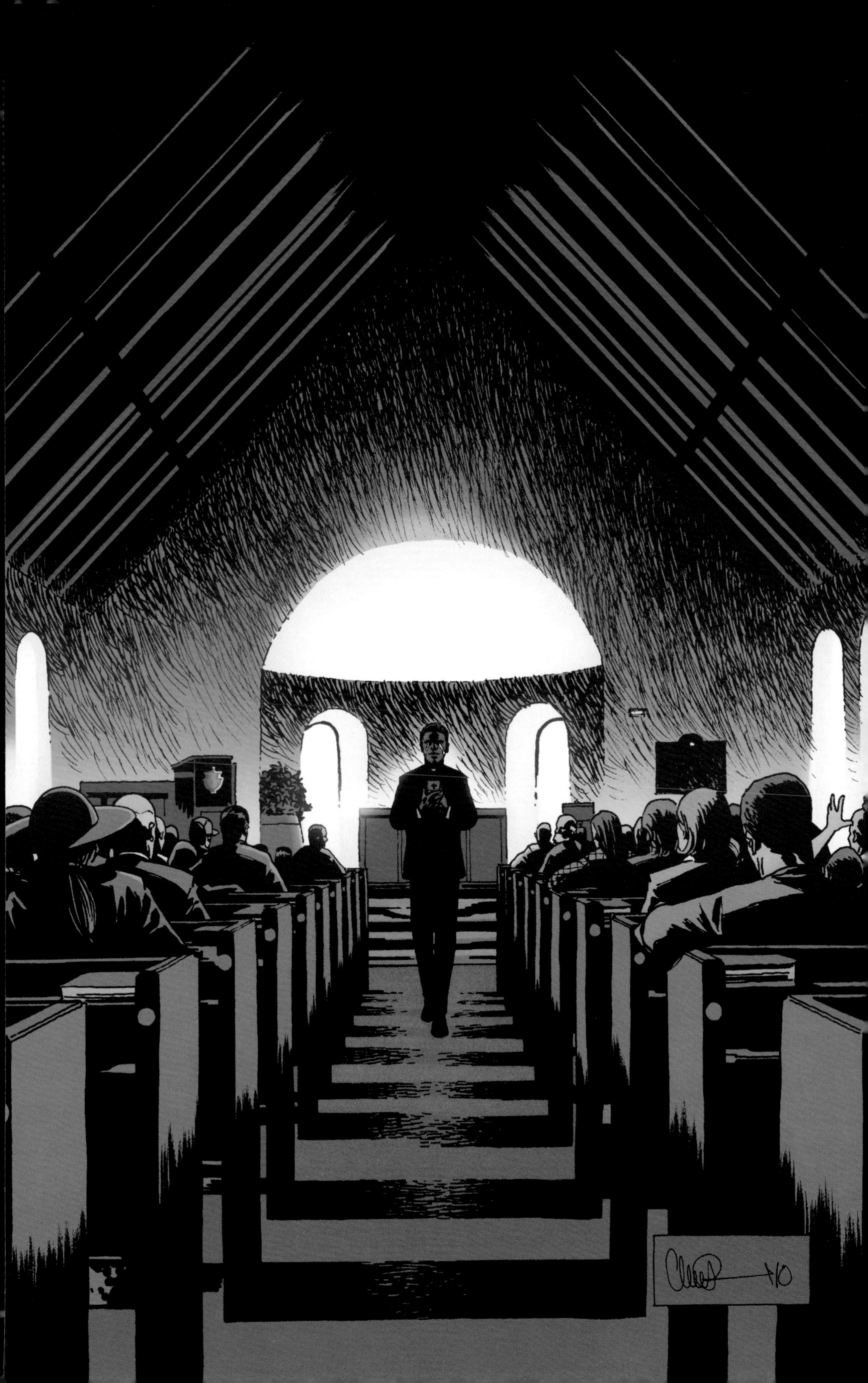

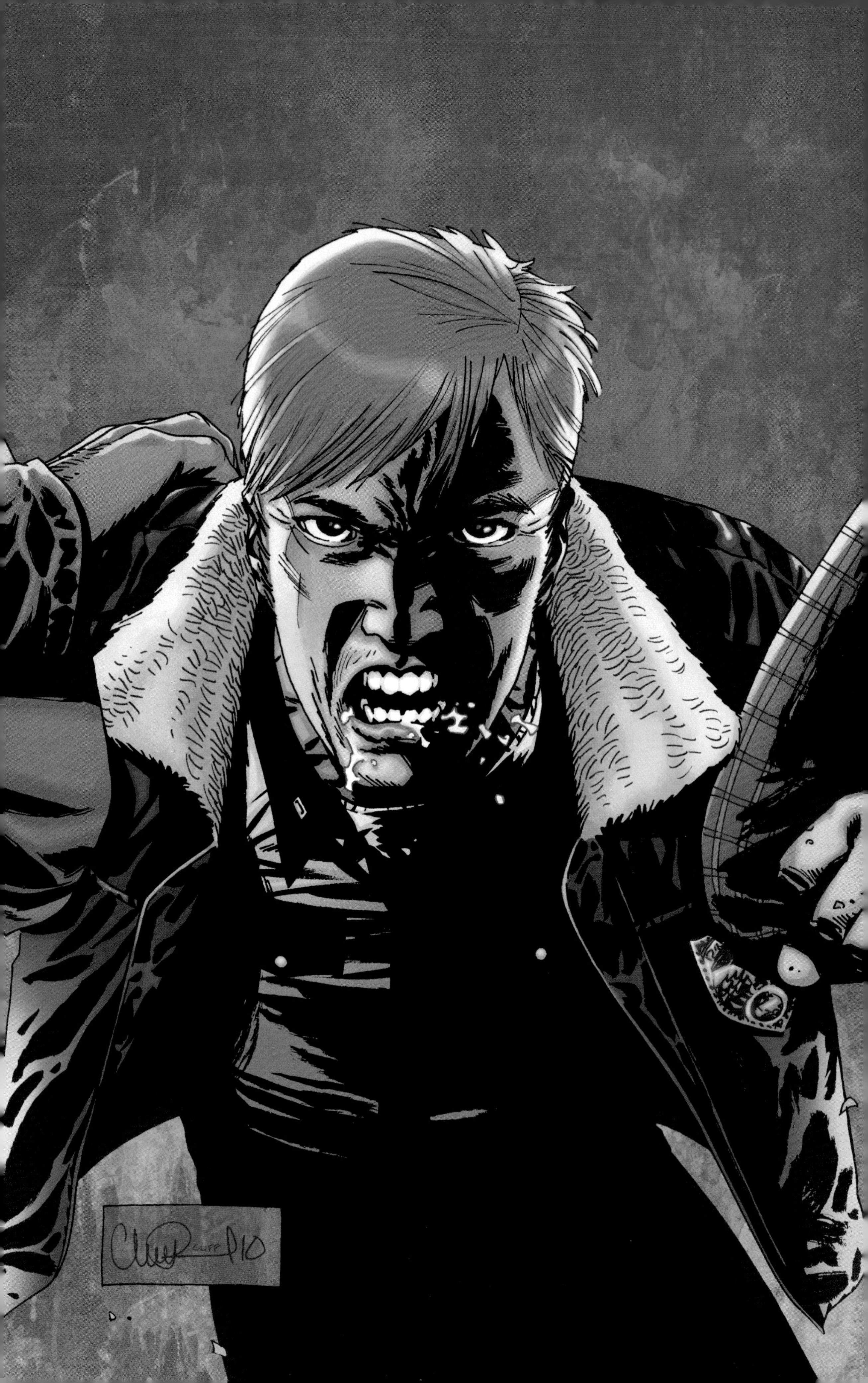

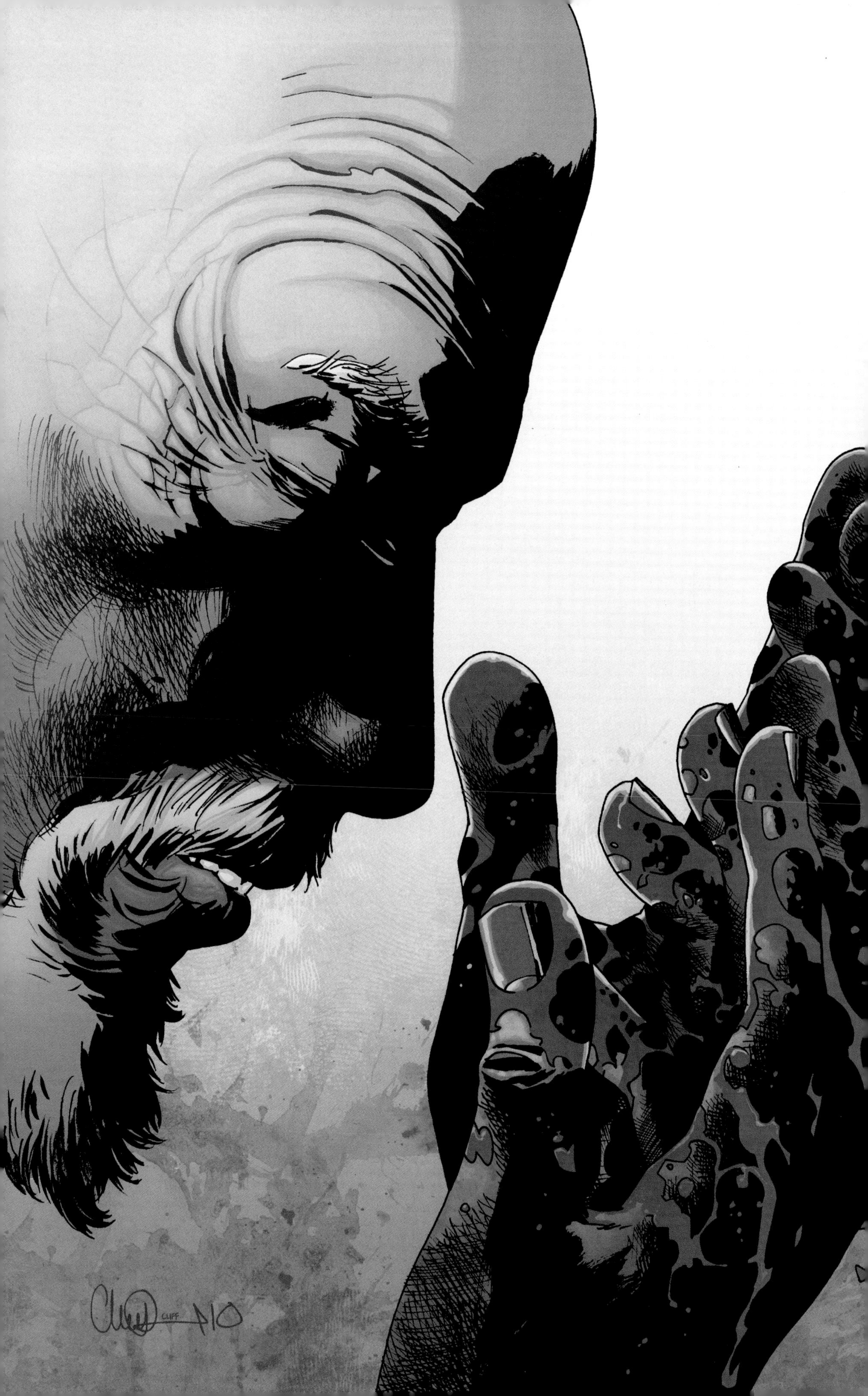

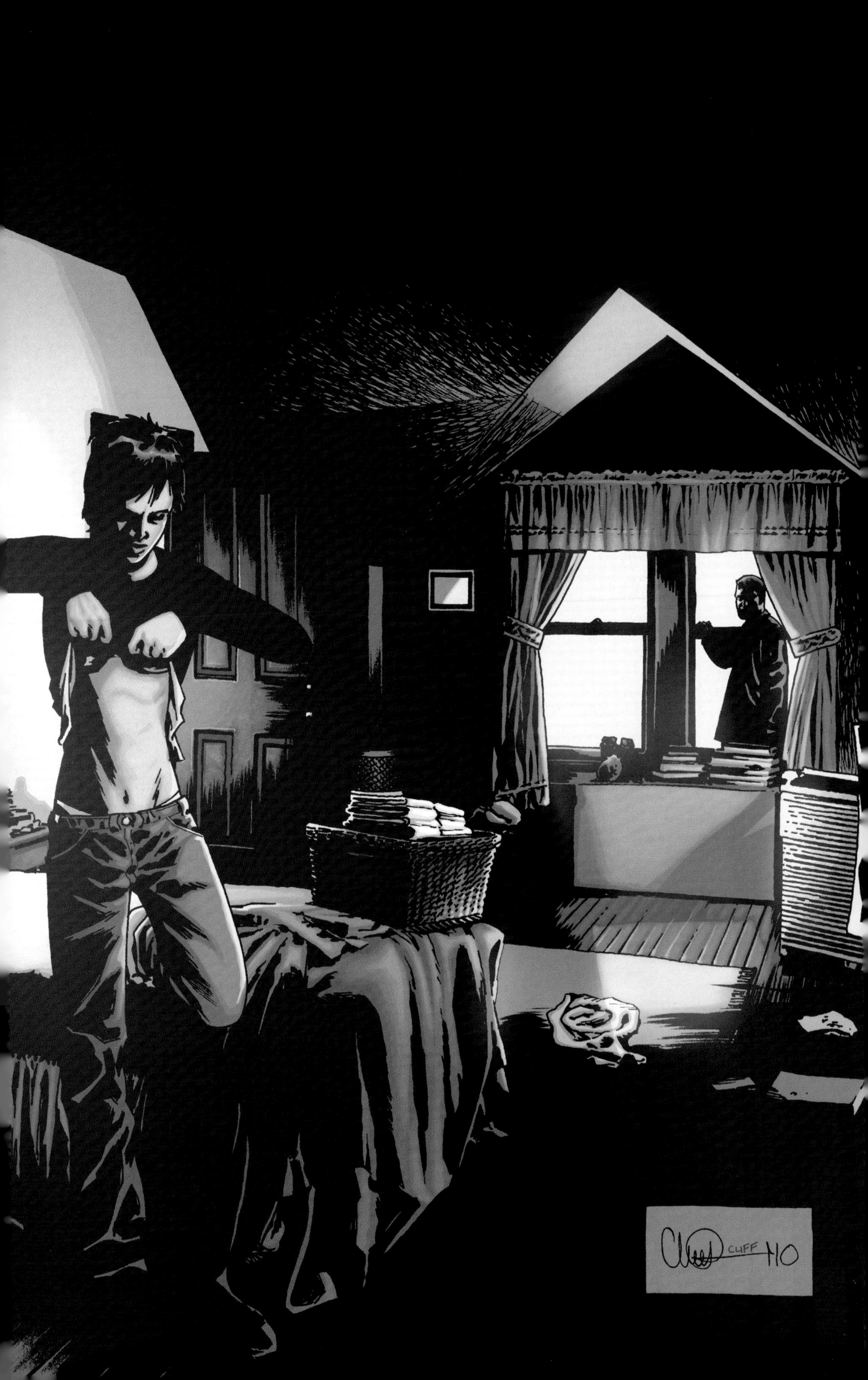

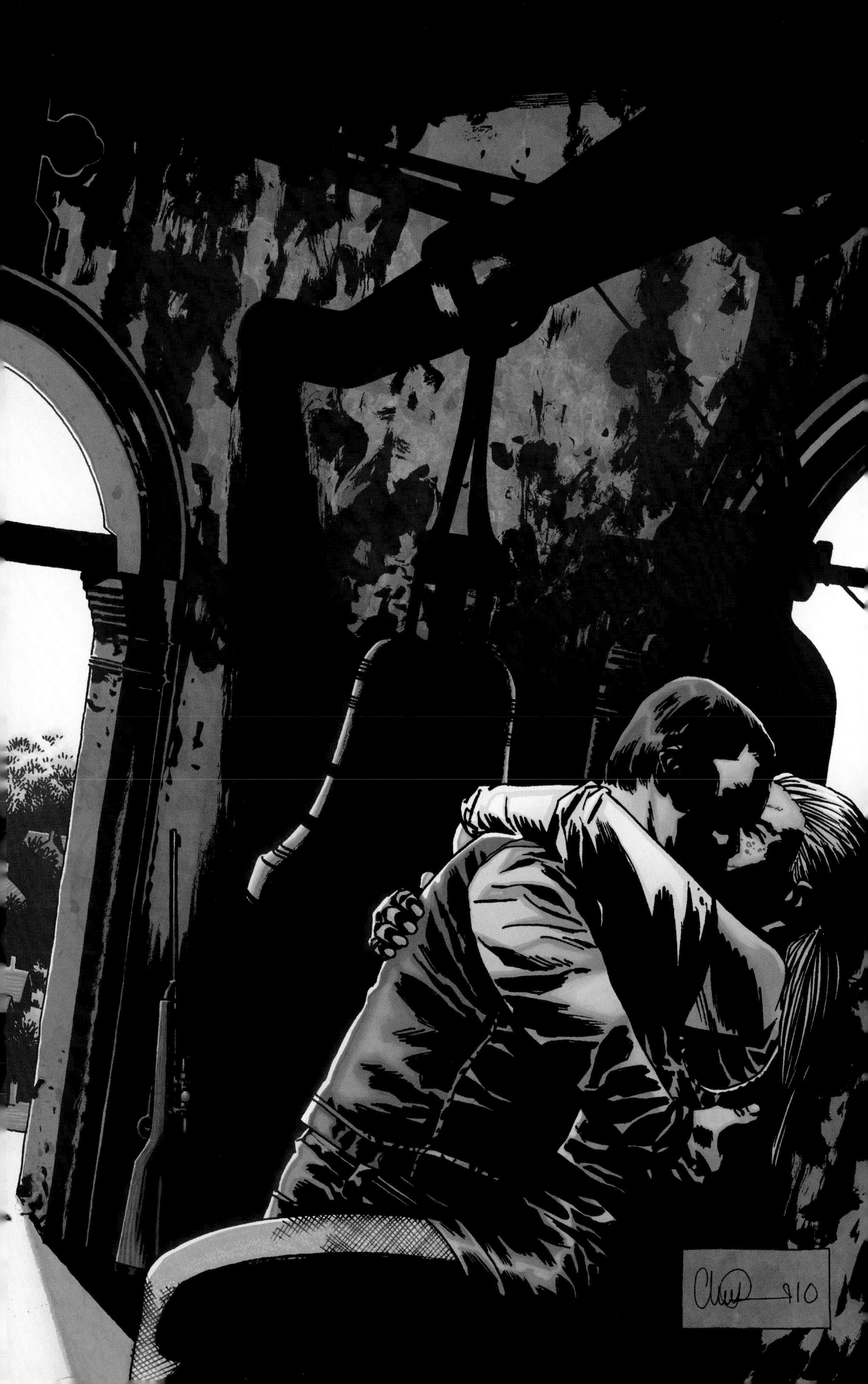

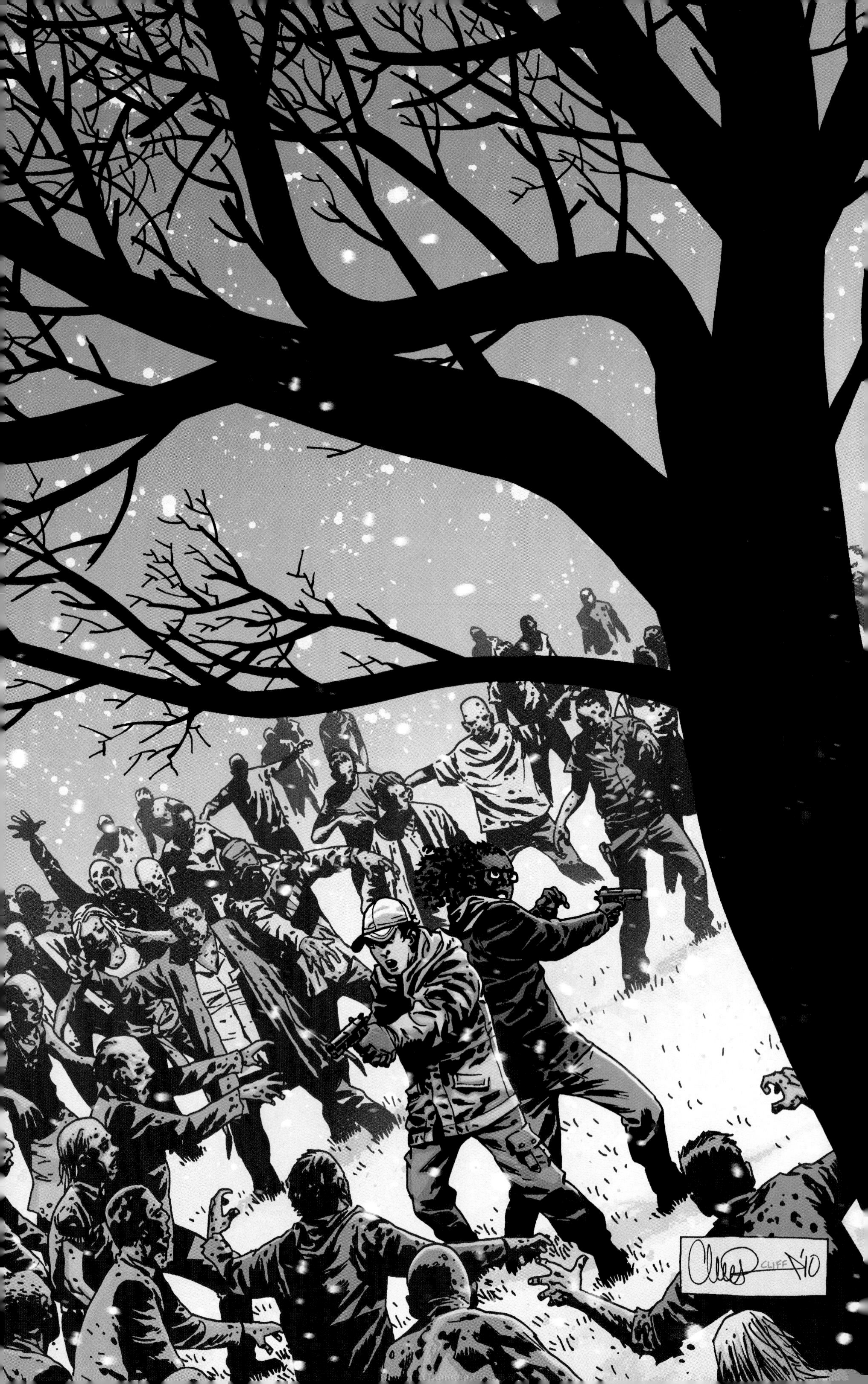

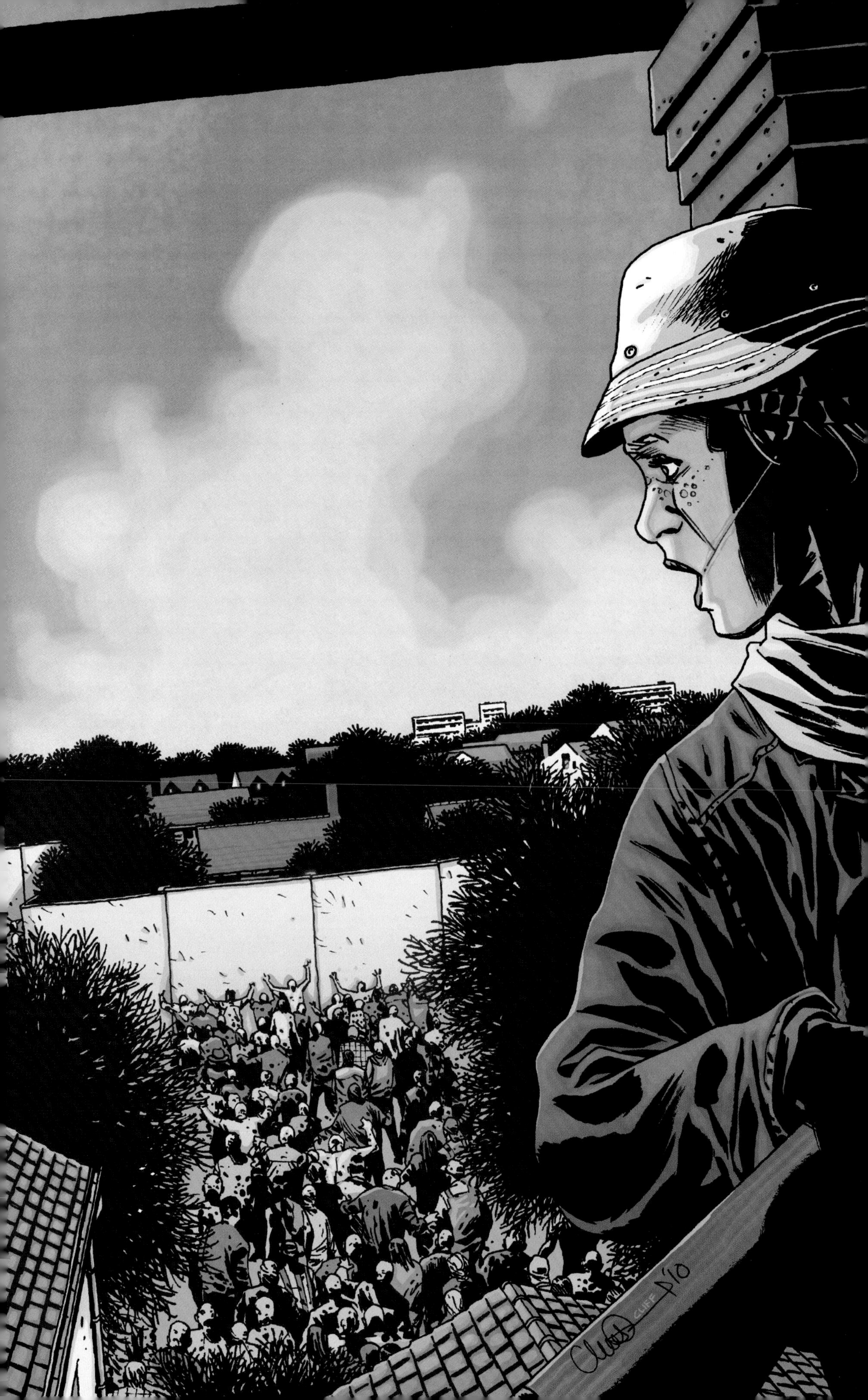

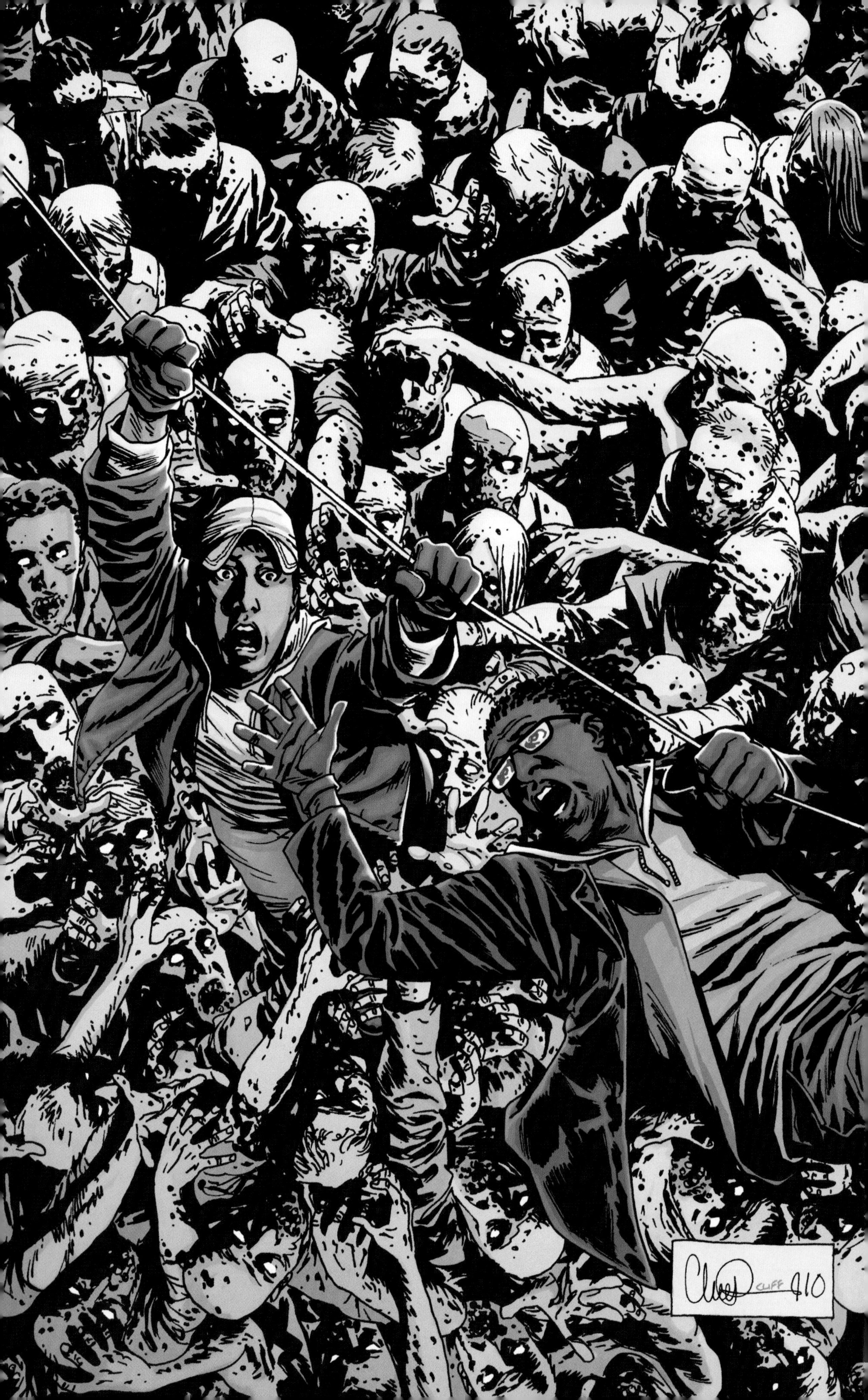

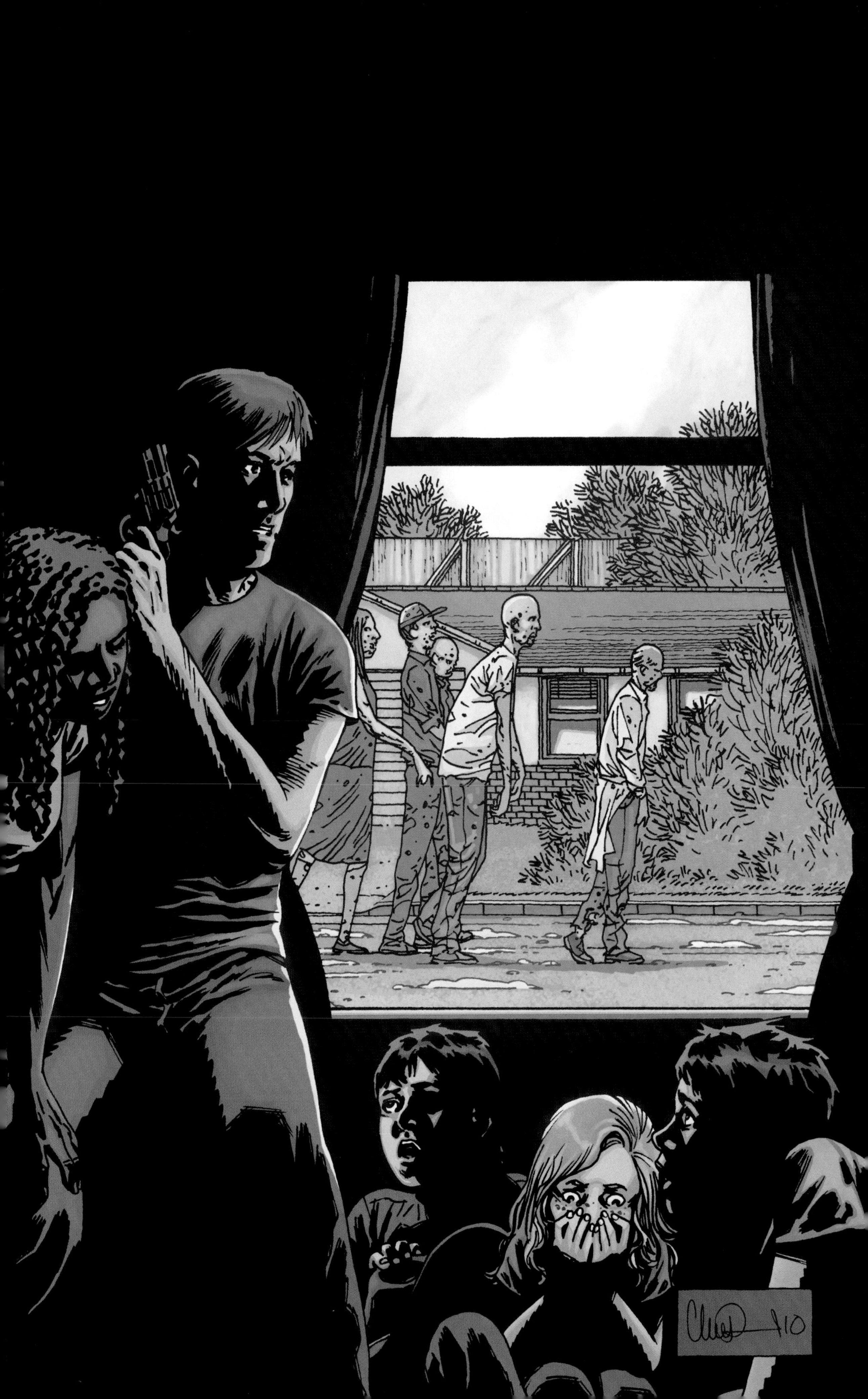

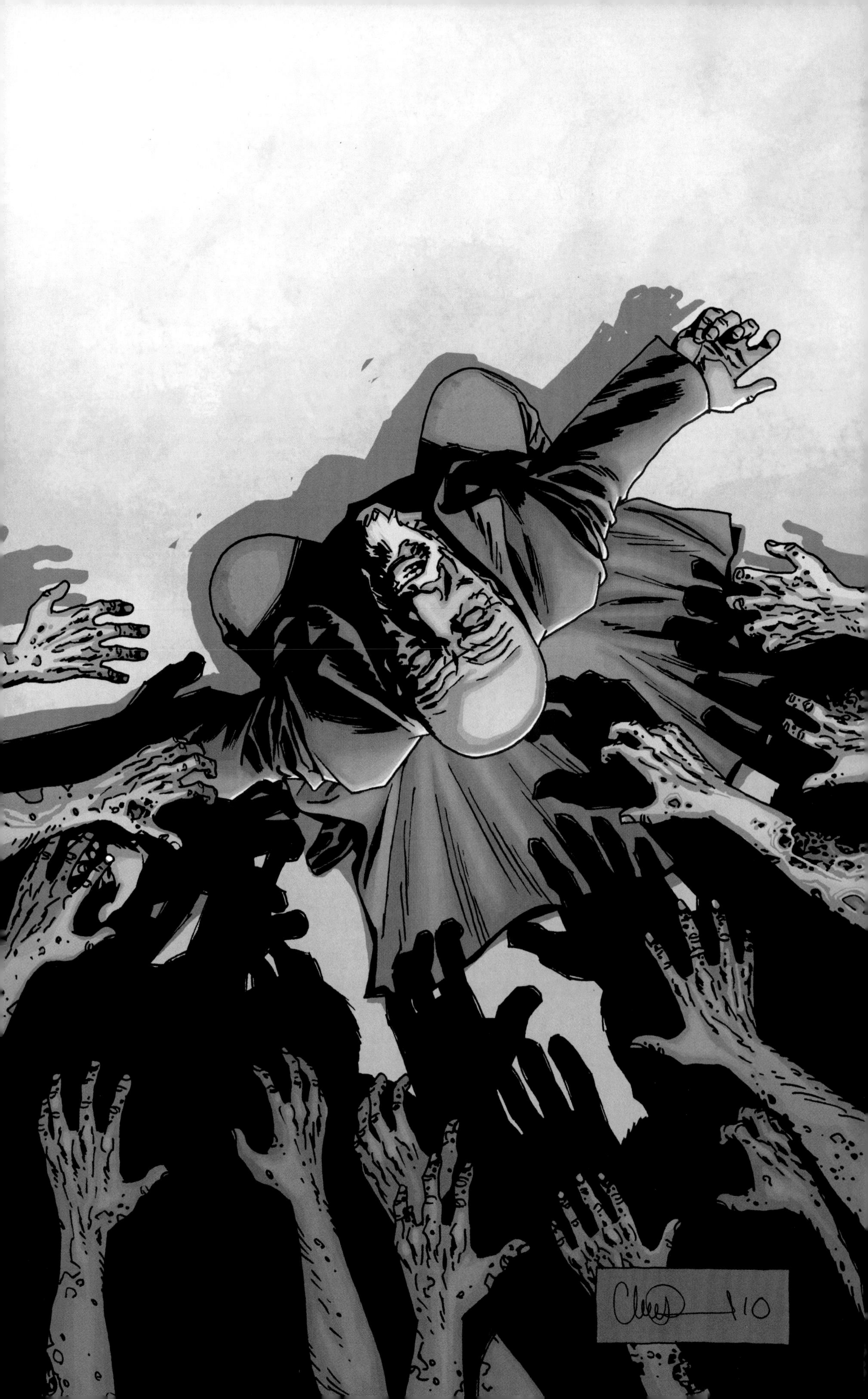

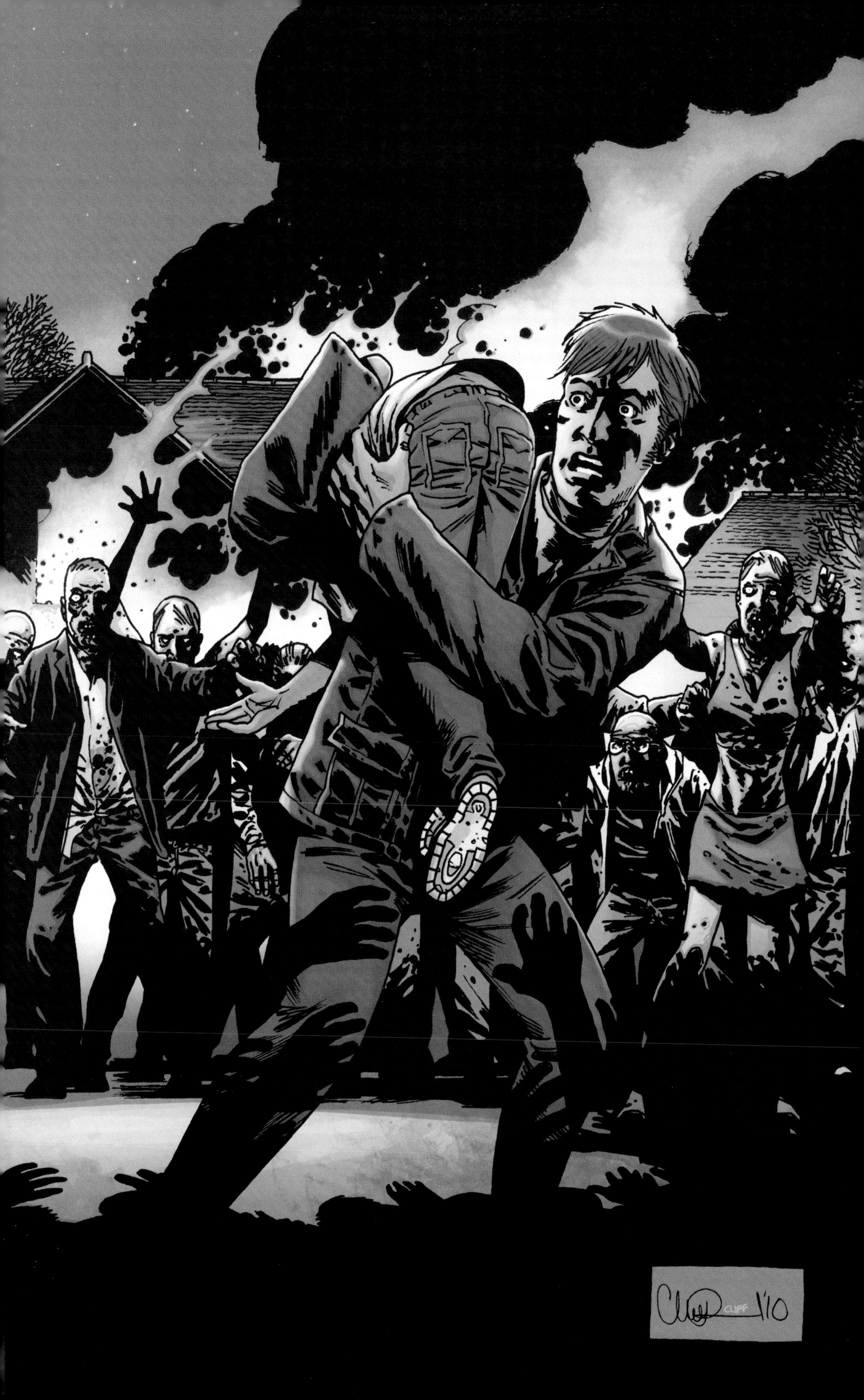

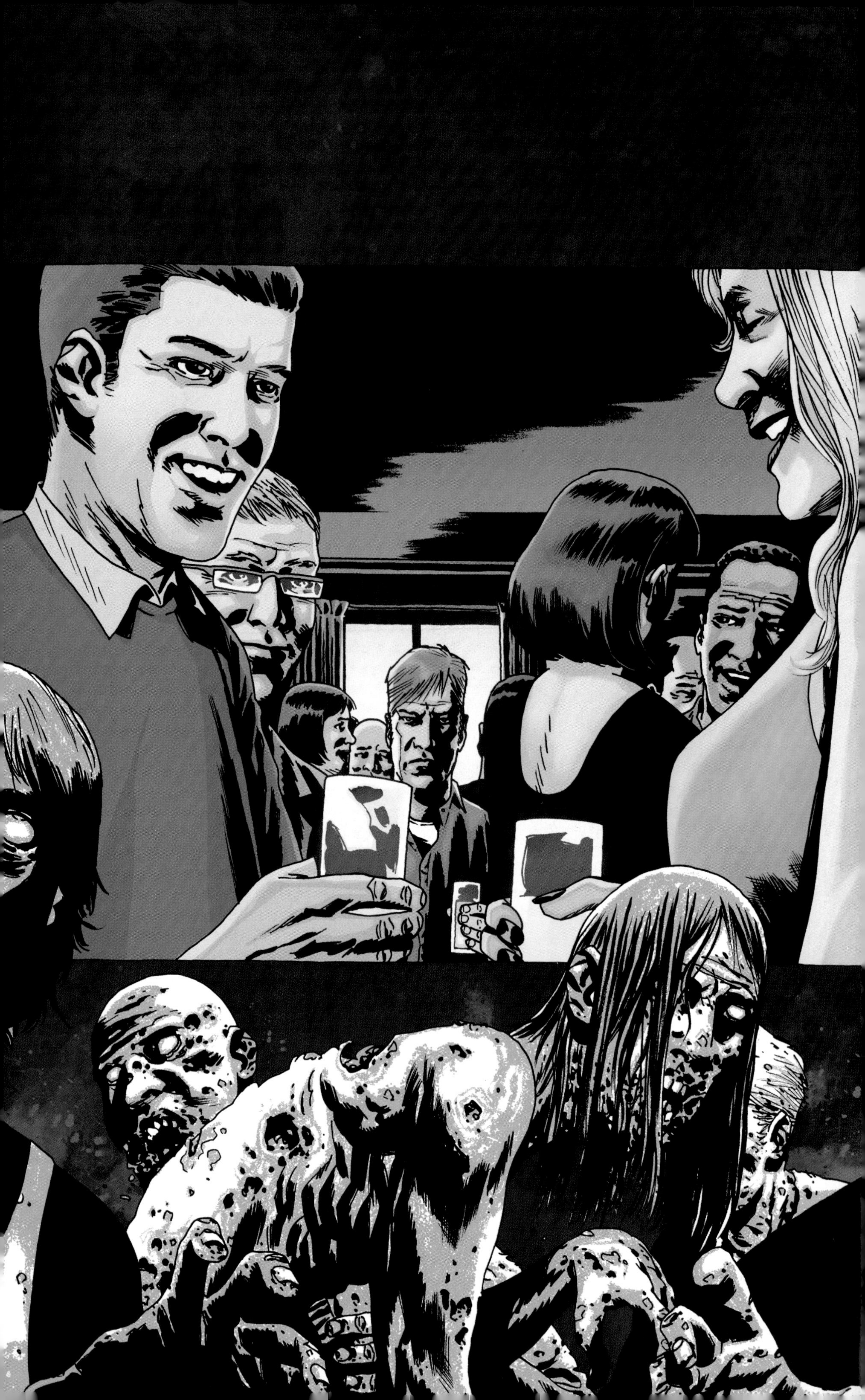